JERUSALEM COMMANDS

Michael Moorcock's fiction includes *The Cornelius Quartet*, *Gloriana*, *Mother London* and the legendary *Pyat Quartet*: *Byzantium Endures*, *The Laughter of Carthage*, *Jerusalem Commands* and, most recently, *The Vengeance of Rome*. He lives in France and Texas.

Michael Moorcock

JERUSALEM COMMANDS

VINTAGE

Published by Vintage 2006

2 4 6 8 10 9 7 5 3 1

First published in Great Britain in 1992 by
Jonathan Cape

Vintage
Random House, 20 Vauxhall Bridge Road,
London SW1V 2SA

Random House Australia (Pty) Limited
20 Alfred Street, Milsons Point, Sydney
New South Wales 2061, Australia

Random House New Zealand Limited
18 Poland Road, Glenfield,
Auckland 10, New Zealand

Random House (Pty) Limited
Isle of Houghton, Corner of Boundary Road & Carse O'Gowrie,
Houghton 2198, South Africa

The Random House Group Limited Reg. No. 954009
www.randomhouse.co.uk/vintage

A CIP catalogue record for this book
is available from the British Library

ISBN 0 099 48512 5

Papers used by Random House are natural, recyclable products made from wood grown in sustainable forests. The manufacturing processes conform to the environ-mental regulations of the country of origin

Printed and bound in Great Britain by
Cox & Wyman Limited, Reading, Berkshire

To the memory of Arnold Schoenberg who, on July 30th 1933, ten days after the formal signing of the Concordat between Hitler and Pope Pius XI, reconverted to the Jewish faith

---

FOR ANDREA DWORKIN

INTRODUCTION

I MUST APOLOGISE to readers who did not expect to wait some eight years between the second and third volumes of Colonel Pyat's memoirs and I hope they will forgive me when they understand the difficulties involved in preparing his papers for publication, in transcribing tape-recordings and fitting those into some sort of chronology. Meanwhile my own work had to be done, so it was not until February of 1986 that I found time to travel to Morocco and then to Egypt, taking part of Pyat's own journey by sea and by land (being lucky enough to rediscover the now dry Zazara Oasis), ultimately to Marrakech. Here the Colonel's account of the fabulous court of El Glaoui, Pasha of Marrakech, differs somewhat from Gavin Young's sketch in *Lords of the Atlas*.

Once again, in Marrakech and the settlements of the Sub-Sahara, I was fortunate, meeting many people willing to help in my research. Several of these remembered the Colonel as 'Max Peters'. Many older people, I discovered, revered him. They said he was the greatest Hollywood star of all. They were disgusted, they said, by the jealous rumours suggesting he was Jewish. Yet in Egypt scarcely anyone knew of him. I was lucky enough to talk to a retired English policeman in Majorca. He had been in the Egyptian Service under Russell Pasha (whose memoirs also confirm much of Pyat's account) during the time Colonel Pyat was in that country and remembered many of the facts almost identically, especially in relation to the drug- and slave-trades. Apart from their variant points of view, the facts and names agree in important detail and further research, in *The Egyptian Times* and other papers of the day, make it clear that 'al-Habashiya' was a well-known character, controlling Cairo's red-light district and with interests in every wicked business from Timbuktoo to Baghdad. Sir Ranalf Steeton and the other Englishmen Pyat mentions are more elusive, although Steeton undoubtedly ran some kind of film-distribution business, and, of course, we have all heard of Quelch's brother.

My retired policeman vaguely remembered a Max Peters. When I mentioned Jacob Mix, however, he became enthusiastic. 'The embassy chap. CIA, wasn't it?' He had known Mr Mix well, he said, not in Egypt but in Casablanca just at the beginning of the war, and they had kept in touch. The colonel's old friend was now retired and living in Mexico. I was astonished at this revelation and excited, for here was someone who could, if they had wished, have told Maxim Arturovitch Pyatnitski's story from a very different perspective.

As soon as I was back in England I wrote to Mr Mix and we corresponded. That correspondence was extremely helpful in assembling the present volume, but it was not until May 1991 that I was able to get to his part of Mexico, and make the journey to the village where Mr Mix lived 'in heavenly exile', just outside Chapala, on the shores of the beautiful polluted lake.

Mr Mix had retained the so-called 'Ashanti' good looks Pyat had described, though his beard and hair were pure white so that I was unwittingly reminded of the benign Uncle Remus in Disney's *Song of the South*. Until he spoke, it was hard to believe he had been an American spy. He was courteous in a delicate, old-fashioned way, typical of Southerners of his generation, and his quiet irony was also familiar. In spite of his advanced years, he was relatively fit. Certainly he was happy to talk as much as he could about his time with Colonel Pyatnitski, of whom, he said, he had fond memories.

Mr Mix admitted that Pyatnitski often made Adolf Hitler seem like Mother Theresa but said he had remained fascinated by him partly because of the contradictions, but the main reason for his staying with the Colonel was, he said, entirely self-interested. 'The man was plain lucky,' said Jacob Mix, laughing. 'I held tight to him the way you hold on to a rabbit's foot.' He confirmed that the Colonel had, indeed, won fame as a film-star in B-Westerns and serial 'programmers' for several shoe-string independent producers of 'Gower Gulch' (the Hollywood location of most such operations) and showed me a box-office placard in full colour, with vivid reds and yellows, solid blacks. It was for a film called *Buckaroo's Code* and showed a mounted cowboy, a bandanna veiling the lower half of his face, waving out at the audience. The film starred Ace Peters and was from a studio called DeLuxe. It was clearly from the period of the mid-1920s. Sol Lessor, whom I knew in the late 50s, mentioned his involvement with a fly-by-night outfit making dozens of cheap Westerns and adventure movies for theatres that needed to show at least two features, a serial, a cartoon and a newsreel to remain competitive. Mr Mix also let me see a cigarette card issued in England by Wills and Co. – a cowboy in a tall white Stetson, with a dark bandanna hiding his nose, mouth and chin, with the caption *Ace Peters as THE FLYIN' BUCKAROO (DeLuxe)*. There had been other memorabilia, said Mr Mix, but most of it had been lost when, shortly after his retirement, his flat in Rome was set on fire.

I had never thought I would associate Colonel Pyat with one of my childhood heroes. Many boys who grew up in postwar Britain read the exploits of *The Masked Buckaroo* in the weekly and monthly 'penny dreadfuls' of the day. Although he originated in America, he survived longer in Britain. Like Buck Jones, The Masked Buckaroo was a potent folk-hero. Jones had been forgotten in America after his death in the famous Coconut Grove fire in 1944, but survived in the UK with his own magazine until about 1960. *The Masked Buckaroo* magazine itself folded in 1940 due to a shortage of newsprint. Colonel Pyat had a few tattered copies from the 20s and 30s and they are seen rarely, even in specialist catalogues. My own collection was inherited from my uncle, a great Western enthusiast.

I mentioned to Jacob Mix that in his fashion Colonel Pyat

had spoken highly of him. This made the old Intelligence agent laugh heartily. He remembered Max's praise, he said. He was as helpful as he could be and some of his detailed information was invaluable in making sense of parts of Pyat's manuscript. Sadly, Mr Mix died very soon after we had enjoyed his company and hospitality and is now buried in the 'Protestant Cemetery' near Chapala.

With no experience of formal religion I found the colonel's views often baffling and frequently primitive. He argued that any social stability we had was due to our efforts to make the best of God's gifts. We were duty bound to maintain and extend that stability. For me Pyat's argument, that entropy is the natural condition of the firmament and that the physical universe, being in a perpetual state of flux, was not an environment friendly to sentient life, though couched in modern scientific terms, had a somewhat mediaeval ring. 'Constant change is the paramount rule of the universe,' he claimed. 'To reduce the rate of entropy, we must make enormous efforts, using skill, intelligence and morality to create a little justice, a little harmony, from the stuff of Chaos.' His flying cities represented a kind of clearing in the universal turmoil. He valued the ideals and institutions of democracy, he said, 'as embodied in the pre-war United States'. The only cause to which he subscribed at his death was, I discovered, Greenpeace. 'I shared my love of nature with all the real Nazi leaders,' he told me. 'We were great conservationists long before it became fashionable.' He claimed he himself had played an important part in a successful recycling scheme in Germany but when I asked him for details he became oddly elusive and changed the subject entirely, asking me if I knew the German rhyme from *The Juniper Tree* by Grimm.

This was a typical strategy of his, veering off into an exotic literary byway or contentious political track so that anyone who had come too close to some truth he was in danger of recognising in himself would be carried into fascinating excursions or bound from conscience to respond to some of his more reactionary outbursts. It could also have been that I was not always sensitive to every associative leap he made – from recycling to Grimm, for instance – and it is when I have doubts

4

of this kind that I wonder if I am perhaps the best editor for these memoirs. At such times I am seriously tempted to abandon the whole thing – lock, stock, barrel, papers, tapes, notes, scrapbooks and all the half-festering, crumbling, encrusted bits and pieces of that old man's extraordinary life, most of which dates from before he was forty. After he settled in England he had few very dramatic adventures.

I cannot claim that Pyat's ravings make any great sense to me – it was hard enough to follow him in interview when I could ask him for dates or clarifications – but the family claims he makes perfect sense and if so I suppose it's fair to say I lack their imaginative gifts or, indeed, their considerable experience. I really had no idea what Pyat's memoirs would reveal nor can I guess why the family spend so much needless time and money on useless lawsuits. My rights were not merely moral but legal. I have the colonel's own letters giving me his papers in trust until such time as I have edited them into what he called 'our Mrs Cornelius book'. His story will go up to 1940, when he arrived in England, whereupon I am to offer the papers to the Bodleian Library, Oxford, where they will be available to any *bona fide* researcher. The tapes, however, remain my property. This has now at last been established through a long process of law and I hope we can all return to our normal lives without rancour. I for one am distressed at the enmity I have earned from a family whose interests I believed I faithfully served, much as I have served Colonel Pyat's. It does not seem to me either respectful of the dead or of the truth to obscure the 'negative' side of a biographical subject. I say once more and for the last time – I never wished to show the slightest ill will towards any member of the family, especially Mrs Cornelius, for whose memory I continue to hold the greatest affection and admiration.

But spades, as Colonel Pyat often insisted, must be called spades and if *A Notting Hill Family* was not completely flattering to Frank or Jerry, neither did it trivialise them. This study was my first non-fiction and I do not deny that as a thesis it perhaps deserved its success but as a popular book it gave something of a false impression of the family and I did everything I could to make amends in the many books which followed that first one's wholly unexpected success.

5

Part of Colonel Pyat's fascination for a person like myself, with almost wholly contradictory views, was his larger than life manner and concerns. Everything was always marvellous, grandiose, romantic, and perhaps in some ways I remain the best medium for a man possessed of such a vivid and singular imagination.

I cannot, however, explain his lapses into foreign languages (he was not wholly fluent in any and I have reproduced parts of his manuscripts exactly as he wrote them) and there is no consistent reason for his using them, except where he describes some of his sexual adventures (almost always in French). As for his racialism, my own views and actions on the subject are a matter of record, but I was duty bound to keep some of his to me quite disgusting opinions. Sadly, his is a voice which did not die in 1945 and seems to have more echoes now than at any time since the end of the War.

More than once, in the past eight years, my wife has mentioned how like my subject I have grown and I must admit the thought was distasteful, since I have so little in common with him, but I have observed in mental hospitals how the traits of one patient can be passed on to another until the imitated symptoms become as established as the real, so it is indeed possible that frequent exposure both to Colonel Pyat and everything he left behind did have some effect, although I was insulted by one critic's suggestion that I had failed to distinguish between myself and my subject.

Lastly I should mention the considerable debt I owe to my wife, who helped especially with the additional research, to John Blackwell, whose steady eye and sound judgement got me through some of the worst times, and to Langdon Jones, who so successfully reconstructed Mervyn Peake's *Titus Alone* and whose remarkable skills were invaluable in putting this book together. I would like to thank those already mentioned in previous volumes, together with friends in Egypt – especially 'Black-and-White Josef', Mustafa el-Bayoumi, Colonel 'Johnny' Said and the El Fawzi family, all of whom helped keep me on Pyat's trail, to 'Rabia and her sisters, her mother, grandmother and brothers, for their wonderful hospitality and help as I followed the colonel to Marrakech; to Jean-Marie

Fromental, who was able to verify much of what Pyat reported of 1920s Marrakech. Thanks also to 'Mad Jack' Parker, The Ephemera King of Crawley, who was able to supply me, from his own stock, several pictures of Ace Peters as The Masked Buckaroo. I must also recognise the special help of Sir Alan and Lady Taylor for invaluable information about Egypt, of the Manchester Savoyards, Francesca V. ('El Enaño') Luce-Maria and Jesus of Ajijic, Old Doc Gibson of Delaware, Captain Robert Harding, Lord Shapiro and Waterbury Pasha, whom I visited at his home near Reading to look through his remarkable collection, much of which, he claimed, came from the famous al-Habashiya house after it was opened up by the Nasser authorities in 1957. It is not something I would wish to do again. All I shall say here is that I feel able to vouch for the substance of Pyat's story but must leave it to readers to make what they wish of his interpretations.

Michael Moorcock
December 1991

ONE

I AM THE VOICE and the conscience of civilised Europe. I am all that remains. But for me, and a few like me, Christendom and everything she stands for would today be no more than a forbidden memory!

This at least Mrs Cornelius understands. 'Yore a bloody miracle, Ivan,' she says. 'A bleedin' monument ter a bygone bloody age.' But her children are lost to her. Their naive scepticism will not shield them against the coming night. They challenge my 'racialism'. They say that I generalise and that there are many exceptions to every rule. I agree! I have known noble camels and extraordinary horses whom I have respected and admired as my superiors in character and soul. But this did not change the camel into a horse or the horse into a camel and it turns neither into a human being. Equally, I tell them, it is both foolish and unscientific to pretend there are no differences between peoples. This logic defeats them. Few were ever a fair match for my intellect, even during my childhood. I have devoted a lifetime to mental training. But the consequent self-knowledge can, you will understand, be a curse as well as a blessing.

Already, at the age of twenty-four, on August 24, 1924, I had some intimation of my vocation. In the glory of refreshed success, having earned acknowledgement at last of my engineering genius, I was soaring towards New York to reclaim my soulmate. I had begun to sense how I might become a positive force for good in a war-weary world where humiliated enemy and exhausted victor alike were preyed upon by every form of human carrion. (I refer, of course, to those amoral and ubiquitous descendants of Oriental Africa, the minions of a Carthage which has for centuries coveted our dignified wealth.) I rarely thought of God in those days. I attributed everything to myself. It was not until later that God provided me with a salutary lesson in humility and I came to find the wonderful rewards of Faith. In 1924 I was, in almost every sense, 'flying high'. What happiness I anticipated when Esmé and I were at last reunited!

> *Oh! Wehe! Wehe!*
> *Erwachte ich darum?*
> *Muß ich? – Muß?*

Eybic eyberhar? This will not do. They say there is a question of my being mistaken! But I did not become a *Musselman*! An ethereal *Parsifal* drifts across the desert. The aeroplane banks and glides over wooded Pennsylvanian hills as wide as the gentle Steppe. I am flying towards my past and my future, towards my Esmé and the East. I will claim my bride and take her back to live forever in *der Heim*, in Hollywood. We shall build a twelve-bedroomed Beach House and redis-cover our passion. I recall and anticipate the delicacy and variety of our love-making! In Constantinople we were Adam and Eve in Eden, the innocent children of Fate. Brother and sister, father and daughter, husband and wife: all these rôles and many variations extended and refined our spirits. I am no stranger to Rasputin's theories. I have personally guided many a young woman to the profoundest realms of sensual fulfilment. But Esmé was more; she was my feminine self, a further dimension. *Incubus* and *succubus* as the old Norwegian had it. In Paris a random trick of fate had almost destroyed the being that was our single united soul. Oh, how I longed to know that unity again; that delicious, breathtaking blending of spirituality and sexuality which both threatened and enhanced my reason, taking me to new emotional and intellectual heights beyond those achieved even with the finest cocaine. As the plane, a confident *Walkyrie*, drew us closer, I could feel her, smell her, touch her, taste her. She rode on the great Atlantic breakers, plunging towards an as yet invisible shore. She was music. She was ecstasy!

Faygeleh? This is nonsense. I was always above such definitions. *Es tut vay daw*. Besides, these practices are natural in Egypt.

Deliver me from that god that is both male and female. May I not fall under their knives. Shuft, effendi, shuft, shuft, effendi. Aiwa! Murhuuba! Aiwa? Let them tug at me. Let them insult me and rub their hands and *sholom-al-aichem* me as much as they like, those mocking wretches. They have no self-respect. That bastard nation will ever remain a warning symbol to us all. O, Egypt, thou art fallen to Carthage and cruel Arabia lounges in the ruins of thy glory! But Spain, ever our bastion against the Moor, again triumphs! In Spain the sons of Hannibal Barca are destroyed or fled. There is one lamp still burning in the camp of Christ –

Her engine uttering a discreet grunt, the DH4 began a downward curve. I was surprised. I looked at my watch and saw that it had stopped. We were not due to land until New York and we were banking over the chimneys of a small industrial town built at the convergence of three rivers, one of them almost certainly the Delaware. (Like most Cossacks, I have a memory for rivers.)

The late August sunshine, thrusting through clouds of black, yellow and grey smoke, glittered on the lacquered white canvas of the plane as we flew low over a suburban settlement so elegant it rivalled, in its new colonialism, its Tudor dignity, the better parts of Beverly Hills. Levelling out, we headed for the twelve-storey brick towers of a prosperous and familiar-looking business district. We reached the meeting of the rivers and I smelled machine oil in the smoke and the sharp sweetness of summer pines. I at once remembered coming here to Wilmington; my first, startled meeting with that accusing angel, Justice Department Agent Callahan. Wilmington was not a place I associated with tranquillity of mind. Yet, even as behind me Roy Belgrade, a startled sloth in his flying goggles and fur-trimmed helmet, threw out a reassuring gesture and guided the plane towards a green area, probably a public park, I was not excessively nervous. We had already made two routine stops in Colorado and Ohio. I had come to understand that Belgrade was a cautious pilot, obsessed with checking every change in the engine note. Once the young man had satisfied himself that his machine was in perfect order, we should be in the air again within minutes. I still had the best part of the day to reach Esmé in New York. At worst, she was only a few hours away by train. Good engineers that we both were, I assured myself, Belgrade and I had left a considerable margin for error. The story would just be part of another adventure to laugh about when Esmé and I were reunited.

Fairly suddenly, the DH4 banked again, over a stand of oaks, and straightened into a climb, as if Belgrade had missed his mark and was determining another approach. The field, some quarter of a mile from a river bend, backed on to a large building whose windows were suddenly filled with excited faces. I was tempted to wave. The field was full of flowers, a profuse geometry, a kaleidoscope of colours and scents, rich and ordered. It was a glimpse of a perfect world. The plane lifted and I saw the faces again – so many undernourished plants pressed to the glass and gasping for the sun. As we wheeled and were levelling down towards a space between the trees and flowerbeds only a cretin would consider big enough for landing, I had my first doubts about Roy Belgrade. Then the hot smell of resin was mixed with the scent of roses and lavender, the stink of the Rolls Royce Eagle as it wailed with sudden life and as suddenly cut dead before we struck a bank of red, white and blue poppies (no doubt some patriotic memory of Flanders). I yelled out to my pilot but he was too far away to hear me. We cleared the flowerbeds in a burst of earth and petals, bounced, and were taxiing over the grassy area watched by two old men (one excessively fat, the other excessively slender) who remained seated on a bench at the far end of the garden. They were clearly enjoying the whole display. I looked about me in disgust. Save for the poppies we had done very little damage, but the surrounding walls, trees and power-lines would make it impossible for us to take off. We needed immediate help to get the plane to a more suitable field.

Controlling my temper, I climbed out of the plane, stepping from wing to lawn while Roy Belgrade remained in his cockpit studying his map with the familiar air of one who is completely lost. At my signal he loosened his helmet.

'We're in Wilmington, Delaware.' I spoke a little abruptly.

'I know that much, sir.' Belgrade returned to his map. 'But I don't reckon this here is a baseball diamond, do you?'

'Did you think it was?' The man was half-blind! 'It's clearly a public garden.' I advanced towards the grinning oldsters. 'Excuse me, gentlemen. Can you help? To take off again we need to wheel our plane into open space.'

'Why in heck did you fellers want to land here at all?' The skinny man had the narrow features of the typical New England peasant, the flat, grudging accent of a people for whom stinginess had been elevated to a moral virtue and generosity made a cardinal sin.

'We had engine trouble. I suppose I should find a telephone!' At least the park had only low fences and we should have few problems once we got the plane into the open street.

'If you want to call the police, don't worry about it. Look there, Mr Meng, I told you so.' His plump companion indicated the gate where four or five uniformed officers had appeared, clearly confounded by the sight of our flying machine and the havoc it had done to the municipal blooms. I approached them at once. 'Thank heaven you're here, gentlemen! Naturally, I apologise for the damage and will ensure all concerned are generously reimbursed. I regret we were forced down here but a few sturdy lads like yourselves will soon get us back into the air again.'

The policemen were of the good, old school. 'Don't worry, mister. We'll have you up there faster than a pigeon out of a trap.' The leader was a grey giant, probably an ex-prizefighter.

Our surroundings were those of a lower-middle-class suburb. The gables and turrets of an earlier prosperity mingled with the present's tract houses while the only high wall was the far one separating park from office building.

Roy Belgrade remained in the plane, fiddling with some instruments. As we approached, he switched off the ignition, folded his arms and grinned at us. 'Well, gentlemen. This is

12

a pretty rare situation, eh?' He got to his feet and sprang from cockpit to wing and from wing to ground. 'Sorry about the mess. Naturally, we'll pay the city back. We're from the movies.'

'Then it's the Du Ponts you'll be wanting to see.' From the rear a portly youth, sweating in his unseasonable serge, offered this with a certain pride. 'This park belongs to them.'

'Well, I guess we haven't put them too much out of pocket!' Belgrade responded almost with hostility. 'Okay boys. Can you lend us a hand? Where are we, by the way? This can't be Brandywine Park.'

'It would be a little small for that, mister.'

Strolling round the plane the sergeant ran his hand over the canvas and admired the lines. 'I never saw one of these close up, you know. Even in the War. I sure admire you fellows. We'd better get some kind of truck or maybe we can give you a tow with our car. There's an airfield out there, now. You might as well use her. Why the devil didn't you head for that?'

'It happened too quick.' Roy Belgrade was relaxed charm again. He slapped the youngest policeman on the shoulder. 'Why, boys, I don't know what we'd do without you!'

My anxiety was retreating but I could not help associating the city with the Justice Department's keen interest in my old Klan connections. They did not know the Klan was now also after my blood.

Yet I had probably convinced Callahan of my innocence. He had, anyway, turned a blind eye to my unorthodox papers. Surely the DH4's problems could not be very serious? Within two hours, I guessed, we would be on our way again. As his men debated the problem, I confided to Sergeant Finch that I would be especially grateful for anything he could do. 'I'm currently engaged on top-secret work,' I told him. 'If I am not back in California within two days, the consequences for the country could be alarming.'

He greeted this information with considerable gravity. 'Sir, it's no more than a couple of hours to Washington, on the train. We can get you back and on your way again in no time.'

While there was nothing to be gained by telling him we

had not come from Washington, Roy Belgrade seized on this misunderstanding and compounded it.

'It's urgent that we return to Washington by tonight.' He made a serious mouth. 'The Professor's an inventor, see. National security's involved.'

I wondered why he bothered to say this, since he had now contradicted himself and involved me in his bungling and pointless lies. But it was of little consequence to me. Mr Belgrade and I would have no further business once he had delivered me, safe and sound, to New York. I began to enjoy the touch of the sunshine on my face. A quality of light in the American North-East recalls my childhood in Kiev, the steppe and my Cossack ancestors, and I am so easily overcome by it that I can frequently do nothing but weep. There is no sweeter agony. Every Russian understands this.

Sergeant Finch expressed some concern for my health, but I reassured him. 'A little airsickness, I suppose. Or hay fever.'

Roy Belgrade was chuckling to himself and shaking his head. It occurred to me that he had taken a strong pull from a bottle before joining us. There was a faint smell of whiskey. I would not allow him to indulge in another drink until we reached our destination. At my urging, he accepted the police offer. They would tow us to the airfield. By now a small crowd had grown around the entrance to the park. They were mostly youths, children and old people, calling out questions in support of their own particular theories as to how and why wé had landed in such a tiny space. We were followed by the two old men, who had assumed something of a proprietorial air and were now explaining how Belgrade and I were government agents, testing special equipment. I was becoming alarmed at these claims and had almost made up my mind to squash them when from around the corner of the wide, tree-lined street, a large touring Ford braked to a dramatic stop beside the squad car before uttering, through every door, a gang of civilians, each flourishing a large pistol in our direction. Had Chicago come to Wilmington?

A long crowbar in his hand, their leader, a black-browed ape, swung from the front passenger seat and unbuttoned his jacket. From the top pocket of his waistcoat he drew a card and displayed it to an impressed Sergeant Finch.

'What do you want us to do, Mr Nielsen?'

'Keep an eye on these fellows while we check out the plane.'

Nielsen nodded to his men. Holstering their weapons they moved expertly about the DH4.

'We were expecting you in Brandywine Park, Roy.' Nielsen grinned at my pilot. 'Your partner blew the whistle on you. Now, let's see where you've stashed the booze.' With that he moved deliberately up to the plane and drove his crowbar through the fuselage. It was wanton damage.

'Stop this at once!' I cried. 'You have no evidence at all. I am a *bona fide* traveller on my way to New York!' But even as I spoke I remembered seeing the lockers crammed with Belgrade's branded bottles. 'I am a paying passenger, sir!' I was insistent. Mr Nielsen ignored me and the sergeant put a firm hand on my chest. 'I don't understand this, mister, but we'll sort it all out at headquarters. Why don't you two gents settle down in the car while these gentlemen do their work.'

'My luggage is in the plane.'

'Then it will be returned to you.'

'Someone must have put it there,' Roy Belgrade lamely told the officers.

Even I was briefly amused by this.

Of course, they had come upon the alcohol in the storage lockers. It was not exactly a major haul for the police and I suspected they had been tipped off by people resentful of Belgrade and his partner's inroads into their business. Now I realised what the other stops had been. In both cases I had been mildly surprised at how rapidly Belgrade had found assistance and how quickly we had returned to the air. This passenger service was a disguise for his bootlegging! I became furious with him. His criminal activities threatened everything! There was still plenty of time to meet the ship but I would be forced to continue the journey by train. Meanwhile I could not tell how long it would take the police to realise I was no common bootlegger. As we sat together in the back seat of the police automobile I could do nothing but glare at Belgrade as he lit a cigarette and, whistling to himself, awaited the next turn of fate.

15

At a signal from the plain-clothes man, the police squeezed into the car with us and headed down the wide leafy road, over a river reflecting dreamy skies and deep green trees. The tranquil afternoon streets of residential Wilmington soon gave way to shop and office buildings enlivened by busy trams, buses, trucks and cars, a smell of grease and human sweat, all the reassuring realities of a booming manufacturing town.

As soon as I could I would contact my acquaintances the Van der Kleers. Those powerful mine-owners had been my hosts some eighteen months earlier. They would not fail to remember me, if only because of the Federal Agent who had called at their house to interview me in connection with my missing partner Roffy. It was not a particularly happy association, but I recalled the Van der Kleers had remained perfectly friendly throughout the incident. They would at least be prepared to vouch for me to the authorities. After all, I was mixed up in nothing more than a seedy minor stratagem of some bootleggers' territorial war. They would surely soon realise that someone of my standing would not volunteer for such a rôle.

At the rather graceful-looking precinct house, Belgrade and I were taken to separate rooms. Captain Nielsen himself decided to question me. This suggested that he already believed in my innocence. The room was not uncomfortable, with a high, barred window, a cot, two chairs and a table with a desk lamp on it. The lamp's bulb was a little too powerful for my eyes, but otherwise there was nothing sinister about the place. Mr Nielsen sat down on one of the chairs and I remained where I had settled myself on the bed. He asked me if I minded his smoking and when I made an acquiescent gesture he took a cigar from his case and lit it. 'How well do you know Roy Belgrade, Mr Petersen?' He looked at the sheet which had been filled out by the duty sergeant when we had arrived. 'How often have you used him as a pilot?'

'I had never seen him until yesterday,' I said. 'I am on my way to meet a ship. I work for an engineering company on the West Coast – it also has movie interests – and it's important I return quickly. The company was prepared to pay for me to take a plane. I did not even speak to Belgrade personally. I suggest you get in touch with his employers, Western Aviation Services.'

'As far as we can tell, Mr Petersen, Western Aviation is Roy Belgrade, one airplane and a local contact. We just nabbed the entire outfit.' With the air of a man who had personally supervised the arrest of Legs Diamond and his gang, he blew satisfied smoke towards the ceiling.

'Congratulations, captain.' I got up from my bench. 'Now I would suggest you contact Mr George Van der Kleer, who is a friend of mine, and ask him to vouch for me. He will tell you that I am a scientist.'

'And you know nothing of Belgrade's rum-running activities?'

'How could I?'

'You saw the liquor in his lockers?'

'After I was airborne, yes. I intended to inform the authorities as soon as we reached New York. But you can imagine, I didn't think it sensible to alert him. These people reach for the gun and the blackjack as casually as I reach for a slide-rule!'

Nielsen was close to being convinced. I extended a placatory hand. 'If you could see your way to speeding things up, Captain Nielsen, I would be deeply grateful to you.'

'You're prepared to make a statement for us?'

'I have nothing but loathing for people who abuse their responsibilities in this way. My moral views are well known. I have spoken publicly on the subject. I saw Belgrade make two stops, I saw him transfer cases to a waiting truck in Colorado and in Ohio. The man is a common criminal. Give me half-an-hour and I shall write down a clear description of the whole business. Meanwhile, if you could contact the Van der Kleers . . .'

'It's a deal,' said Nielsen. Taking his cigar from his mouth he rose. 'I'll have some paper sent in and you can write out your statement. If this Van der Kleer speaks for you, you're on your way again.'

'But the plane?'

'Impounded. You'll have to get the train to New York, Mr Petersen.'

My fury against Belgrade intensified. When the moment

came for my statement I ensured that my erstwhile Icarus would not again spread his wings for some time. Then I grew agitated when there was trouble contacting Mr Van der Kleer. 'He doesn't seem to want to know you,' Nielsen informed me. I told him to mention the name of Mrs Mawgan. By now it was growing dark and my little girl disembarked from the S.S. *Icosium* next morning. I was assured by Mr Nielsen that the last train did not leave until around midnight. He went to the telephone and returned after a while with something of a frown on his face. 'You're okay. Van der Kleer says he'll stand guarantee. He also told me to say that while in other circumstances he would be delighted to see you again he regrets,' and Nielsen smiled at me, 'that he can't see you personally and wishes you a speedy journey to New York.'

'He was always a gentleman.' I sighed with relief. I had over an hour to get to the station. My bag was brought to me and I confirmed that its contents were all intact. I was relieved that I had taken the precaution of keeping my usual supply of 'sneg' on my person. 'I wonder if you'd be good enough to find me a taxi.'

'We'll do better than that. We'll personally make sure you get on the train.'

Their attitude had changed now they realised my powerful connections in the State, but I was too well-bred to take advantage of our reversed positions. As we waited for the car, I chatted about the city and its problems and assured them that I was working on plans which would one day revolutionise the manufacturing industries and rid the world of smoke and filth. 'Sanitary working conditions ennoble the worker and advertise the humanity of the employer,' I said. 'A clean worker is a happier worker.'

'I'll buy a bottle.' Nielsen seemed laconically enthusiastic. 'Keep that pitch up and I'm liable to buy two.'

It was 11.30 before a car was ready. 'It's five minutes to the station,' Nielsen reassured me as he handed me my bag. Together we walked into the silent street. One trolley disappeared with an introspective clank around a corner, its lights blinking out even as it moved. A uniformed man was driving the car. Nielsen opened the door for me and helped

18

me in. 'Make sure he gets on that eleven fifty-one,' he told the driver. This was the first time I realised he was not coming with me. 'I'm very grateful to you, captain.'

'Sure.' He touched the brim of his hat. 'Have fun in New York, professor.'

With that, the car took off at top speed, its siren a caged gull, forcing me back into the seat. 'What's the hurry?' I asked. 'The captain said it was only five minutes to the station.'

'That's right.' The driver took a corner at a terrifying angle. 'But he's forgotten there ain't a eleven fifty-one no more. Last summer train leaves for New York eleven forty.'

'And what's the time now?'

'Eleven forty.' We moved downhill through the density of office buildings and hotels, passed through two traffic lights, crossed the tracks, heard the long, authoritative note of the great locomotive, and pulled up at the station in time to see the train lurching steadily into a blackness where its smoke resembled those mocking spirits who from time to time insinuate themselves into my dreams.

I was in despair. I sat, unable to speak, and watched as a uniformed man ran from the station to the car. For a moment I thought my driver was going to ask him to telegraph up the line to stop the train, but it was only some message about a burglary near the marine terminal. 'There's a hotel across the street.' The policeman opened the door for me. 'You can get the first train in the morning.' Then he left me to struggle from his car to stand with my bag on the steps of the Union Station while a railway employee informed me that the first morning train did not leave until eight that particular day and that the hotel was a good, clean 'commercial' place where I could get a decent night's rest. By now I was almost gibbering with anxiety. I told him the urgency of my situation. I had to be on the quay when the ship docked. Esmé was innocent of New York and its dangers. He could not help me, he said. He did not really care if I met the ship or not. Several terrifying possibilities went through my head. I pointed to the yards, down the line, where a number of massive shadows showed locos still making steam. 'You say there are no trains. Where are they going?' He told me they were freights and laughed.

'You could try and ride the rails with the bums. But be careful.' He sniggered. 'Between the bulls and the darkies, there might not be much left of you by morning!' Again, he indicated the hotel and advised me to send a telegram to the ship to say I would be a little late then catch a few hours sleep. I ignored the fool. I looked about for a taxi, but I was not sure even the hundred dollars in my wallet would cover the fare to New York, assuming I could find someone to take me. I became still more frantic. I followed the railroad man up the steps but he locked his door and pulled down his blind and would not respond to my rapping. I became confused for a while and simply sat on the step with my head in my hands. Then the call of the trains from the nearby yards reminded me that there was still a way of reaching New York in a few hours. I set off down the tracks towards the great confusion of steel and steam. I would bribe a driver to let me ride with him on the footplate. It was commonly done, I had heard, by travelling salesmen with urgent business.

Twice I fell full-length in my haste to reach the yards, stumbled to my feet, found my bag, lost my hat and did not stop to look for it. The third time I fell, I was only a few yards from the caboose of the nearest train and this time I was helped to my feet by a large, unkempt individual who, from his breath, might have been Roy Belgrade's biggest customer. My bag was picked up by one of his several ragged companions, all yellow-eyed wastrels and loafers. I took them for the kind of scum which collects around any wealthy centre, hoping for a few free scraps from the rich people's tables, willing to stoop to petty crime if necessary, but too cowardly to be a serious threat. 'Thank you, my good fellow.' I patted the large man on the back. 'Help me to the nearest New-York-bound train, and I'll make it worth your while. Fifty cents apiece! Hurry now! I am a plain-clothes police officer on urgent business!'

This changed their scowls to smiles. One of them even bowed to me. What happened in the next few seconds has always been hard to explain. I felt a violent blow in the kidneys and fell again to my hands and knees. A metal-shod boot struck me on the forehead and I was blinded, shouting with pain. I felt one more violent blow on my thigh and heard a guttural voice say something about a 'fucking squarehead bastard' before I passed out. Even at that moment it was clear to me that the Klan had never been far away and that it had been a mistake to use the name of Van der Kleer. Evidently he remained connected to that perverted quasi-Klan which had overthrown the old, pure-hearted band of idealists now jailed, framed for crimes they did not commit, or scattered across the continent. I had been led very cleverly into a trap.

I awoke to hear more yelling. Someone who had been tugging at my shoes suddenly stopped and cursed. Then I felt a warm hand on my jugular and for a second thought they meant to finish me off. But the hand was simply looking for a pulse. 'How bad are you hurt, do you know?' I heard the deep, lazy voice of the better type of black man, my rescuer. Nobody can ever reasonably call me a racialist. I am the first to tell the story of how a negro saved my life by single-handedly driving away the white men who would cheerfully have killed me. The cur-dog pack of the KKK, operating like cowards out of darkness, were all that remained of those hooded vigilantes who had sworn to wipe away the evils of the world but had been betrayed by cross-bred infiltrators of every foul persuasion, united only in their determination to destroy the best and noblest blood of Christendom. The black giant was lifting me to my feet. I was in almost as much pain as after the Klan's last attack. I was becoming something of an expert on their strongarm methods. Next, I checked for my wallet and found that, together with my left shoe, my overcoat, my bag and my belt, it had disappeared with my assailants. 'We'll get you to the cops,' declared the noble black. Like some friendly, large dog, he had attached himself to me for reasons best known to himself. I was not ungrateful and made it clear he would be well rewarded once we reached New York and I cabled Los Angeles for funds. *Ich furchte, die Tiere betrachten den Menschen als ein Wesen ihresgleichen, das in höchst gefährlicher Weise den gesunden Tierverstand verloren hat* . . . 'But our first priority,' I informed him, 'is to get there before dawn. I am due to meet my sweetheart's boat when it docks. My innocent knows nothing of America.'

He was clearly sympathetic. He helped me along the track towards the wailing locos, the stink of smoke, the sudden beams of tested lights, the flash of oiled metal, the gleam of polished brass, the sputtering sparks from the boiler stacks. 'She's starting for the Smoke.' The negro indicated a massive freight train some distance away on our left. 'And she's pretty well guarded, so we'll have to jump her when she gets going or the bulls'll spot us for sure.'

'You're going to New York, too?'

'Pilgrim,' said my dusky guardian angel, 'I am now.' And he lifted a great, African head and opened a red mouth to bellow his cryptic amusement. I felt as Androcles must have felt to be befriended by some jungle beast for reasons that had little to do with the motives of a more advanced species. And yet there was a certain kind of self-contained dignity about my rescuer, a quality of loyalty, which more civilised whites might envy and seek to emulate. An intelligent black, like an intelligent woman, is one who recognises his limitations as well as his natural skills and virtues and puts himself at the service of some decent citizen who appreciates and respects him for what and who he is. This is a natural symbiosis. Again I do not speak of 'superiority' and 'inferiority' but of *difference*. There are few rational people who would question the white man's natural grasp of technology and the nuts and bolts of the civilised world, or his sophistication in matters of political and religious institutions, and it is these things, of course, which have put us a rung or two above the others on the great Ladder of Civilisation. Make no mistake. I am the first to extend a hand down to my less-developed cousins, but that is not the same thing as artificially setting them on the rung *above* me. What good can that do for anybody? Many a negro has told me sincerely how he wants no part of this unnatural elevation, just as the majority of women are contemptuous of the so-called suffragists and feminists who make such fools of themselves in their ludicrous pseudo-male masquerading. Why assume the vices of an envied race and ignore the virtues of one's own? I have never understood this impulse. We Russians have an instinctive grasp of the fundamentals of life, the great forces which are always at work in nature and which dictate so much of our fate. Woman serves man but man also serves woman, each fulfilling a rôle which, when in complete harmony, can make for almost heavenly happiness. Such is the relationship between master and servant, between priest and God. Christianity tells us these facts. Why are we forever forgetting or ignoring them?

To my immense relief I discovered, in a waistcoat pocket, my packet of cocaine. Soon I would be able to banish much of the pain. Determined to put myself in the hands of this good-hearted darkie (whose name, he announced, was Mr Jacob T. Mix), I already planned to offer him in Los Angeles a permanent job as my body-servant. Through no fault of his own he had fallen on hard times, a victim of prejudice in a world which had been happy to use his services in its negro regiments but had no use for him in peace. This, of course, was the hard lesson of 'emancipation'. What use is freedom without the dignity of work?

In a daze, I was limping rapidly down the track, jumping over ties and rails, until I had reached a slow-moving box-car and was almost thrown into it by the strong arm of my new friend. I landed heavily on oily timber and banged my head again. Rolling over, I saw Mr Mix, his great tattered overcoat flying around him so that he resembled Doré's Ancient Mariner, appearing to expand and fill the entire doorway. Then he had turned and banged shut the sliding door. 'We'll sit here in the dark until we're through the town,' he said. This suited me well enough, for I could now make surreptitious use of my cocaine. I did not offer him any, nor would he have expected it. There is a great difference between what happens to a white man under the influence of cocaine and the effects produced in the typical negro 'hophead'. Besides, I heard the sound of a bottle being opened. 'You'd better take a drink until you can get those bruises fixed up,' murmured my concerned Man Friday, but I refused. I was already feeling considerably better, knowing that I was *en route* for the city and Esmé.

When Jacob T. Mix lit a tiny pocket oil-lamp the car was suddenly illuminated by a wonderful radiance which turned every blade of straw to gold, every strand of wire to silver, made the walls glow like the warm, old wood of a comfortable cabin, while everything swayed gently, a huge, reassuring cradle, with Mr Mix's enormous, scarred, kindly face peering down at me, enquiring with rough good will if I was sure I would not take a pull on his bottle and try to get some sleep.

'How long will it be before we reach New York?' I asked him.

'Five or six hours, I'd reckon. She's slow, this old train, but she's steady. Then we have to look out for the bulls. In that early light they can stay hidden until they're right up on you. But stick with me, Max. I'll get you to your boat. Your girl promised to you, is she? From the old country?'

In essence he was right so I did not correct him. While Mr Mix began to tell some story of a Nigerian sailor he had once known and the stories of Africa the Nigerian had told him, I drifted into a half-sleep where I consoled myself with a vision of Esmé and myself, a prince and princess of Hollywood, driving through the hills and valleys of California, the harbingers and personification of an inevitable and glorious Future.

How cautious they were, those fools! *Was ist Originalität?* asks Nietzsche. I can tell him. It is what the majority would instinctively destroy. And how they have tried to destroy me! Yet I survived. I still survive! They cannot bear that.

Even then, I knew that I could not perish. Mrs Cornelius told me this, only a week or two ago, when she came into my shop in search of a new jumper for her boy. 'Yore bloody indestructible, Ivan!' Perhaps that is why I have always had this particular relationship with her. We have in common the not unenviable achievement of surviving the greater part of the twentieth century.

Adjusting the wick of his miniature lamp so that it should offer only the minimum necessary light, Mr Mix opened a book, remarking with some surprise at my stoicism and my powers of recovery. 'You don't complain much for a white boy.'

'We Petersens,' I told him, 'are a hardy breed.'

TWO

THESE CATTLE CARS have always depressed me. They smell and look much the same in Russia, America, North Africa or Germany and it is demoralising, whatever the circumstance, to travel in them. Inevitably, there will always be at least one bully-boy to terrorise you, even when you are on board and moving. Jacob Mix and myself were spared the sound, that night at least, of steel-shod boots pausing with invisible menace on the roof overhead. How they loved to piss on us! And we were grateful if that was all they did. Those who mourn the passing of the Age of Steam mourn a romantic myth, not the squalid reality so many experienced.

Mr Mix proved to be a fellow of some intellectual ambition. He had educated himself in a rough and ready manner and, as such, proved a far more enjoyable companion than I had expected.

The good-hearted, self-improving negro is the best type in the world. What he lacks in the more sophisticated intellectual functions he more than makes up for with his virtues of loyalty and integrity. He has time neither for black loafers nor 'white trash'. Thus, unable to sleep and anxious to divert myself from anxieties concerning Esmé, I was more than happy to engage Jacob Mix in conversation. He had been born in Alabama, he said, but had come North, to Philadelphia, to work in the mills during the War. The War over, the white men had wanted their

25

old jobs back. He did what menial work he could to stay alive and had just today made up his mind to put all that behind him and see if he could get work on a ship out of New York. I was delighted by the coincidence. 'So all along we were heading in the same direction!'

'I guess so,' said Mr Mix and again grinned his indescribable and savage grin. I had found a friend and a guide in the urban jungle, a beast finely tuned to modern-day survival. It was only fair that I should let him know what sort of man he had befriended. As briefly as possible I told him a little of my own life and my plans. I do not remember falling asleep.

A great shudder shook the train and I awoke feeling horribly chilled. Still asleep, Jacob Mix rolled a little until his face was in line with mine, then he opened his eyes and winked at me.

'We should be in Jersey City.' He peered through the slats at the grey, pre-dawn sky then climbed to his feet, brushing straw from his aged flannels and adjusting the shirt beneath his waistcoat. When he teased the door open I saw only cloud and a few gulls but the sound of an early-morning port was unmistakable. I knew it from Odessa and from Constantinople. It made my heart beat with fresh optimism. We were at the docks! Now all we had to do was find the *Icosium*'s assigned pier. I wanted to burst through the doors and run towards the water. I could smell the salt, the motor oil, the sea-wind. *Esmé, meyn bubeleh. Es tut mir leyd.* Esmé! Esmé! I looked at my watch. If on time, the ship had already docked, but would not yet be disembarking. I had forgotten the pier number, but some official was bound to help me.

'Okay, colonel.' Suddenly Mr Mix opened the door and beckoned me through. 'Make for that stack of crates straight ahead. And go fast, man!' I jumped easily to the concrete of a busy marshalling yard, surrounded by cranes, great locomotives and goods wagons of every description, quickly reaching the crates and a small gap created by careless stacking. Mr Mix joined me almost at once. 'You can run good, too,' he said. 'You've had about as much practice as me, right?' (I remember these questions because they struck me as so mysterious. I have never fathomed them. Sometimes I believe my companion was doing nothing but parrot phrases he had heard or read, without any real sense of meaning.) He took hold of my left foot and inspected it. There were some blisters, and the sock was a ruined mass of blood and cotton. Mr Mix said something about seeing to my foot before continuing, but I was anxious to reach the *Icosium*. 'How are you going to do that, without no dough?' he asked quietly.

'I don't need money to approach a ship's pier, my dear fellow.'

'But you need three cents to get on the ferry.' Mix pointed across a stretch of dirty water in which every description of garbage floated. 'That's the Hudson, man. I guess the Cunarders dock over there, on the Manhattan side.'

I had imagined the train would take me directly to the docks, as it would have done in Odessa! Foolishly I had made a too obvious assumption. I had no money. And all my papers were in my stolen wallet. But at least I had a companion who knew where we were. 'I shall have to pawn my watch,' I said. 'We had best get out of here and seek the necessary Jew.'

'It'll take too long and it'll be too risky.' Jacob Mix dug his hand along the back of his trousers and removed something wrapped in the tail of his shirt. It proved to be a ten-dollar bill which he brandished at me as if he had discovered the Koh-i-Noor diamond. 'I'll take the watch as a pledge.'

I argued that I would get far more in a pawn shop. 'Maybe, but you ain't in a pawn shop and you ain't got time to find one.' Mr Mix added, 'Besides, I'm sticking with you for a while. I'll get my ten bucks back, I know.'

'Within hours,' I promised. 'You are wise to trust me, Jacob Mix.' And with that I accepted the exchange.

'First, we get the ferry.' He led me in a zig-zag course between stacks of cargo. 'And then we find a pharmacy. We've got to clean you up, man, if you're going to make a good impression on that girl.'

Suddenly I realised how I must look. 'I shall get another pair of shoes,' I said. 'And some flowers. And perhaps another suit and a shirt.'

'You got my only ten dollars,' said Jacob Mix. 'How you spend it, mister, is up to you. But there ain't no more.' By

27

now we were creeping along the side of a dock, with the river, sluggish and filthy, directly below us. 'Pick up that plank. The other end.' Mix took hold of the nearest part of the plank which we shouldered as he led the way across a wide, unprotected stretch of dock, towards green iron railings, behind which a small, sturdy steamboat rode at her moorings in a choppy sea while her passengers filed aboard. As we approached the end of the queue we dropped the plank and joined the line of working people paying their three cents at the turnstile before boarding the ferry. I was a little nervous of producing my newly acquired ten-dollar bill and Mr Mix seemed to anticipate this, because he pushed ahead of me when our turn came and gave the man six cents. 'Make sure you stick to the back of the boat,' commanded the ticket seller as we moved towards the gangplank. He thought we were bums and did not want his respectable passengers bothered by us. It was no use arguing with him, said Jacob Mix quietly to me. It was easier to let him think what he liked. At least that way he wasn't alarmed and wouldn't become aggressive. I saw sense in this advice. After all, it was only what I had already learned during the Bolshevik War.

There was a clammy mist on the leaden water and the far bank was not clearly visible. I glimpsed a few bulky shapes rising from the fog like the Ice Giants of the Slavic epics. The sounds from the invisible ships were melancholy voices bewailing the defeat of their supernatural power. The high-pitched little ferry answered tremulously, baffled and a trifle afraid. Then, detail by detail, the buildings began to form familiar outlines, the elegant towers of Woolworth and International Telephone, legendary hotels like the slender Sherry-Netherlands or the exquisitely classical Savoy-Plaza! Living monuments to American enterprise, to Hecksher and Flatiron, the Straus, the Paramount and the Union Trust! That splendid blend of Gothic and Egyptianate styles which is so characteristically New York! That soaring, almost delicate beauty of her famous 'sky-scrapers' was revealed to me again as the sun burned away the last of the fog to display the city's million blazing windows! The glinting granite and marble of her towers were soaring optimistic tributes to the very latest futuristic architectural ideas. Here was the consummate city in those wonderful days before the forces of Carthage flowed out of their sewers and occupied her streets, before she became the capital of polyglottal mongrelism. A melting-pot indeed! I call it a witches' cauldron which the world allows to bubble and brew until it creates a poison strong enough to threaten the extermination of everything fine and noble and human. But this morning, blazing with the purity of silver, it was a New York which, I believed, could only grow more marvellous and more beautiful. Of course I was optimistic. The little steamer was bearing me steadily towards my darling. My adventures had indeed only served to give extra piquancy to our reunion. I felt, as it were, that I had earned the happiness I now anticipated.

With the morning sun warming my skin, I looked with admiration at the great liners alongside the piers to our right – so many self-contained cities, built to survive the enormous forces of nature which ruled the Atlantic, built to ensure that their passengers would hardly notice that they had left the parlours of Kensington and Fifth Avenue. They rose above us now, those monuments to civilisation and the engineers' art. I said as much to Jacob Mix, but the darkie was in a dream of his own. 'I always wanted to visit Africa.' He was as oblivious of the monsters as they were of us. 'Just to see what it was like, you know?'

'You'll have to go to Europe first,' it was my duty to inform him of the realities, 'and then perhaps in Marseilles you'll find a ship for Tangier.'

'Marseilles seems the best bet,' he agreed. He had read a good many travel books and memoirs and was almost as familiar as I with places I had actually visited. In his profoundly alien mind he held ambitions as important to him as mine were to me. I recognised this, and the mutual recognition bound us together in a peculiar way. I think he had begun to see me as something of a spiritual guide, an intellectual mentor who could help him achieve the vague goals he so desperately desired. He knew, I suspect, that he did not have yet either the higher mental functions nor the social standing to fulfil himself on his own; thus by attaching himself to me he might see something of that world and of society which until now had been denied him. In turn I knew the stirrings of a powerful emotion I am forced to describe as paternal. Although probably a year or two younger than the negro I was dominated by an impulse to take care of him. Perhaps again it was recognition, this time of our common humanity, that made him attach himself to me. I shall never exactly know. As the ferry docked below the streamlined buildings and gleaming machinery of the Chelsea Piers I stared almost idly at the medium-sized twin-funnelled boat which lay, hissing and sighing from recent exertion, at anchor a couple of hundred yards below. It was only as the ferry turned a point or two to come alongside the wharf that I realised I was reading the name of the vessel in bold, black letters against the white paint – S.S. *Icosium*, Genoa. It was Esmé's boat! I had only to descend the gangplank and walk along the dock to where the ship waited. But then the irony struck me. I could not present myself to my darling looking as I did. Beyond the ferry buildings was an elevated stretch of roadway and through the pillars I made out a series of grubby storefronts where I was bound to find some shoes and, if not flowers, at least some candy. Again I was in luck. As Jacob Mix and I reached the busy street, we saw a quilt of colour, a flower-seller's stall. She had set up, of course, to take advantage of the likes of myself. To Mr Mix's wonderment, I spent five dollars on a large bunch of mixed blooms and handed them to him to hold for me while I cast my eye across the street then led him towards a store advertising Quality Apparel, where black suits were hung up like so many punished felons. I was limping rather painfully, now that the cocaine had worn off, and it was not expedient to be seen taking more. Mr Mix followed behind me, clutching the flowers and telling me he was beginning to suspect that my vicissitudes had turned my brain. I would have been irritated by his presumption had I not realised that this was his way of displaying his solicitousness. My jacket and trousers were badly torn, but my shirt and waistcoat would serve until I could get to a telegraph office and have funds cabled to me. Esmé, I was sure, would be so delighted to see me that she would scarcely notice the condition of those garments. However, I could not bear to greet her smelling of a cattle-truck and the filth of the railroad. I entered the clothing store while Mr Mix waited for me outside, studying the boots and shoes on the racks which the overly suspicious old Jew who ran the shop had ensured were not in pairs.

The Jew asked, in curt Yiddish, what he could do for me. I refused to speak that decadent patois and demanded, in English, to see one of his best suits in my size.

'They are nine ninety-nine, any one you like,' he told me, looking me up and down to gauge my measurements. Then, with a long, hooked pole, he wandered down a great cavern of cloth to find the appropriate suit.

'Presumably,' I said, 'you are interested in part exchange.'

'These suits are all bran-new, my friend.' He scratched himself under his *yarmulke* as he stared up at the ranks of trousers and jackets. 'You want second-hand, you go down the street. Here it's cash, strictly. What have you got to exchange?' And he hooked down a suit with a swift flick of his hand and arm. 'That's you, mister. Do you want to try it on?'

'My jacket and trousers are of finer quality,' I said. 'It must be obvious to any judge of cloth.'

'Once,' he agreed, 'that was a good suit. Whoever had it made was a man of taste. But now – look at it! It would have to be repaired. It can't be saved.'

'Take it and five dollars,' I offered. Whereupon the man's mood changed and he reverted to type, shouting at me and telling me to get out of his shop and not to waste his time. Furious, I left with dignity, calling to Mr Mix to follow.

I made my way towards a sign advertising Pledges. Here, I thought, I might get what I needed. But before I went in, Mr Mix grasped my arm.

'Put this on,' he said softly. 'It'll help balance you up at any rate.'

He had taken a brogue from the rack. It was a near-match to my own and, astonishingly, an exact fit. 'I thought it looked about right,' he said. He steadied me on the kerb while I tied the laces. 'You'd hardly know it weren't a pair. Now that was lucky, wasn't it?'

I murmured that it was more a tribute to his skill as a thief than to the intercession of any Guardian Angel and this made him chuckle. Somewhat heartened, I entered an even darker cavern than the last. This one reeked of mouldy leather and damp paper, of mildew and old dust. The clothes hung on racks on one side of the shop while the other was crowded with a miscellany of household goods, of bicycles and washtubs, of mechanical kitchen utensils, and all the gadgets bought to appease wives who had waited with growing fury while their housekeeping was poured down the throats of the feckless immigrants crowding these disease-ridden slums. Such shops were set up to exploit the likes of myself and, I supposed, sailors needing to enter the civilian world. My five dollars, I was told, was good for a jacket but 'pants is another two-fifty'. Time was running out. I could not waste it in bargaining. At length I settled for a jacket which, although a little small for me, was a reasonable match to my trousers and at least, though stinking of camphor, was clean. I jammed the money into the Jew's hand and ran from his premises. It would not be more than half-an-hour before I was reunited with my soulmate!

The great liner in all the glory of her scintillating brass and chrome, her white, jet and scarlet livery, still quivering from her journey, now dwarfed even the three-storey embarkation sheds to which her gangplanks stood ready to carry the first flood of passengers. There was a general rattle and clatter, great thumps and clangs. Sailors and dockhands shouted to one another, hawsers and chains were flung in expert loops, the securing blocks slammed into place: the stink of oil and smoke mingled with the sharp ozone from the sea, and I knew that I was not too late. The passengers were only now coming off the ship. A line of customs and naval officers strolled down the main gangplank casually giving the signal for the ropes to be clipped back. The first passengers, hastily refreshed, peering down into the sheds for sight of their friends, began to emerge. With Jacob Mix in pursuit I ran to a door in the fence facing the main street and banged on it for some while until it was opened by a uniformed guard whose angry questions were couched as unpleasant rhetorical oaths. 'What motherfucking son of a bitch bastard of a camel's whore is making all that noise?' I told him I was late and needed to go straight through to the ship. He laughed in my face. 'Even the VIPs can't do that without my say-so.' He seemed to have spent the worst of his rage already. With some dignity I informed him that I was a man of considerable substance; my appearance was entirely due to unfortunate circumstances. He laughed again and asked in that case who Jacob Mix was.

I put a defensive arm around the negro and told the arrogant official that Mr Mix was my valet. At which point, no doubt shamed by his misreading of my status, the fool slammed the door rather than apologise. I accepted a pull from the bottle the negro handed me. 'I ain't your valet, Max,' Mr Mix pointed out as I ran alongside the fence, turning the corner to the main entrance of the sheds where a large sign proclaimed ARRIVING PASSENGERS. But this entrance was also guarded by another corpulent individual in the company uniform who, below a purple nose, sported a moustache like a hunter's trophy. He stepped forward as we made to enter. 'And what would the likes of you gentlemen be wanting with the First-Class passengers?'

'One of those passengers, my good man,' I told the beefy mick, 'is my future bride. It was my money which paid for her ticket. Do not be deceived by my appearance.'

'It ain't so much your appearance as your smell.' Theatrically the cretin waved his hand in front of his nose. 'On your way, boys. You won't pick up a hand-out here. And there's regular porters to carry people's bags as wants them carried.'

'My fiancée is on the ship,' I said levelly.

'And his, too?' The guard indicated Jacob Mix. 'This ship sailed out of Italy, not Cape Town. Go on away now, boys, and don't give me a hard time, or I'll have to get tough with you.'

'You are uttering nonsense.' I controlled my mounting hysteria. So little sleep and food, so much pain, so much ill fortune, had begun to affect my mind. 'I warn you again – you'll lose your job if you don't let me through.'

'More likely lose it if I do.' He dismissed us. 'I'll take my chances.'

I could see the women in their brilliant silks and furs, the men in their beautifully cut Continental suits, laughing and calling as they descended to where the customs people gave respectful attention to the occasional valise. I sought my

Esmé, but she was doubtless shyly hanging back, hoping to catch sight of me from the rail. My mind was filled with the image of a frightened, bewildered little girl, so desperate for one reassuring glimpse of her beloved. I pushed through the gate, towards the barrier where others awaited their arriving friends. Suddenly I was grabbed by my hair and coat, hauled backwards while Jacob Mix pleaded with the man to release me. 'You can see the poor bastard's had a hard time.'

But there was no pity in that officious oaf's unChristian heart. By now the first passengers were coming through, stepping into waiting private limousines. Others hailed eager taxis. My Esmé must certainly come through to the street. We should eventually at least be together, but until then I could imagine the anxiety, the uncertainty she might already be feeling.

I shall never cease to curse that fat *commissar* and his appalling arrogance. Had I known how his actions would change the whole course of my life, I think I might have risked arrest and murdered him. *Ferbissener?* Can I blame myself? Surely not. I was no *schnorrer*. I was a mere *pisher*. Come with me now, Esmé, there is still time.

I tried once more. 'Please, sir, will you listen! I am a man of substance. Do not be deceived by outside appearances. I can explain how I came to this. The story begins in Hollywood, California – '

'You said it, Jerusalem!' sneered the swaggering *kocheleffel*. And produced a monstrously phallic club from within his costume.

Then I saw her! *O, Esmé, meyn naches.* I am coming! The vision in my heart was suddenly a reality. She glowed with an unreal radiance like some ambassadress from the Land of Dreams. Her hair, short against her head in the latest fashion, shone like black fire. And she moved naturally with exquisite lively grace.

I had not deceived myself. She was everything I had imagined, everything I remembered. 'Esmé!' She was passing through the barrier to where the cars were drawn up. 'Esmé. My darling. Here!' She was going the wrong way. Jacob Mix made some ridiculous suggestion – that perhaps this was not the goddess I had described! I ignored him. *'Esmé! I am here!'*

She turned at last and I was sure she recognised me. Then her attention was taken by the crowd and I was shouting once more. 'Here, my beloved!'

A shadow passed between myself and my wife-to-be (a great camel-hair overcoat, a wide panama, a cigar and a cane) and she was gone, spirited into a massive yellow and black Rolls Royce.

'Esmé!'

'I guess she's found herself a new beau.' Mr Mix tugged at my coat. I informed him coolly that white girls were not so promiscuous with their favours. In a sudden change of mood he left me. I saw him speak in a placatory tone to the guard. I was not interested in what he was saying. As the Rolls Royce turned into the main street, I began to run after it. My weariness caught up with me. I stumbled, fell forward, and lay soaking in an oily puddle as I watched the car bear my darling up towards the elevated road.

She must think herself deserted! She had turned to a stranger for help. What kind of stranger? A whoremaster? A gangster? Some unscrupulous Levantine 'theatrical agent'? There were a thousand possibilities. My stomach churned and bile rose in my throat as I got to my feet to discover that Mr Mix, at any rate, had not deserted me. I apologised for my remarks. It is bad form for a white man to use his superior social position to insult a negro. I have always held to this. Yet that Cornelius girl still laughs at me and calls me a bigot. What must I do to convince her? Put on the boot polish and sing 'Mammy'?

Mr Mix told me that my behaviour was understandable in the circumstances. Once he, too, had had a sweetheart whom he had last seen 'loungin' with her legs wide apart in the back seat of Paul the Pimp's Doozie.'

I said, with mild astonishment, that my fiancée was scarcely the sort of girl to be found in such circumstances. Believing herself abandoned, Esmé had clearly turned to someone else for help.

The man owned a car. He was obviously rich. Somehow I would find out who he was and track him down. Suitable explanations would be made, I would be reunited with Esmé and all would return to normal.

'His name's Graham Meulemkaumpf the Third and that car was taking him across town to Grand Central.'

'The station?' I was aghast.

'That's her. This guy's based in Chicago. He's in cattle.'

'A cowboy! My angel with a cowboy?' What other horrors were in store for me? Even when Jacob Mix explained how the guard had told him that Meulemkaumpf owned the Rolls Royce and was one of the richest men in the Midwest, I could not rid myself of that terrible image.

Not two seconds upon the American shore and my sweetheart had been abducted by a buckaroo! It was everything a European most fears when he sees his relatives take ship for the United States. How could such a thing happen to me, who had worked so hard for his new country, who had identified himself entirely with its most idealistic causes? (God was testing me, but then in the arrogance of my youth, I did not understand that.) *Me he perdido*.

Unable to pursue the car, I determined to discover the address of its owner. First, however, I would need funds. I told Mr Mix to accompany me to the Western Union office at Pennsylvania Station. 'What are you going to pay with, colonel?' he asked me. 'Red gold?' Anxious to save breath to make the run over to Seventh Avenue as rapid as possible, I did not answer, but I had already determined that I would cable collect asking Mucker Hever to wire me a couple of hundred dollars. The busy traffic of downtown New York City was meat and drink to me, I breathed it as another might inhale the wild movements of the pine forest, but that morning, dazed by all my disasters, I was helplessly gripped by a nightmare. I do not recall how we reached the Western Union office and pushed through the smart glass doors to join the waiting line.

No doubt again I have Mr Mix to thank. Did ever a man deserve such noble loyalty?

As my turn arrived I produced a business card which had not received too much of a soaking and handed it to a Neanderthal clerk who eyed us with considerable distaste and asked us to wait at one side. Ah, how easily we fall when we lack access to a simple suit of well-cut clothes!

When he returned, his first question, almost inevitably, was 'How do I know this is you?' Patiently I explained that my servant and myself were set upon in the railroad yards of Wilmington, Delaware and robbed of everything. By use of our wits we had arrived at our destination, only to be thwarted by an officious know-nothing who had managed successfully to separate me from my betrothed. 'Even now she is disappearing into the clouds of the upper elevated in some outlaw's coupé!' I was an inventor employed by Hever of Los Angeles. The card proved that much. I searched through the pockets of my waistcoat and trousers for proof of identity but could find only a half-ticket issued by Western Aviation Services. 'Call the police in Wilmington. They know me. They arrested the pilot of this plane. I was travelling on it. There was some question of bootleg liquor.'

'Nothing to do with Mr Petersen,' said Jacob Mix from behind me.

'I was innocent, of course.' I realised as I spoke that if Mr Mix had been with me, he would have had to have ridden on the top wing. I tried to play down this unnecessary piece of confusion. 'Had it not been for the fortunate arrival of my valet here, I should be dead in the freight yards by now. Simply cable to Mr Hever and ask him a question. He knows me.'

'And who'll pay for the cable?' the anthropoid wished to know. Meanwhile others behind us, all with urgent business, were calling out for us to move on. At this, quite justifiably, I lost my temper. I raised my voice, I must admit. I began to curse the clerk and the company and all its customers. I always find myself speaking a mixture of Russian and Yiddish on such occasions, perhaps because I learned bad language first in Odessa, amongst the polygenetic young criminals of the Slobodka drinking dens where I had enjoyed my salad days. I had not learned then what I later learned of the perfidy and cunning of the Jew. I knew only his charming side in those days. I have always said that I was born without prejudice. What people choose to call prejudice is simply the very opposite. It is common experience. I mean no harm to any individual of any race. I am a man of infinite tolerance and sensitivity to the feelings of others. How could I not be? I have been in their position. I know what it is to have a mind and a heart yet to be treated as a beast. I am lucky enough to have brains and talent and good looks. These things have saved me from at least a permanent life of despair and poverty. Not all are so fortunate and it is our duty to care for them. But this does not mean setting them on pedestals or promoting them over better-qualified people! Society is a compact between millions of individuals. Lines have to be drawn somewhere. This is what they understand in South Africa.

At some point in my argument with those jacks-in-office Jacob Mix had disappeared. I could not have blamed him for making himself scarce. If they were prepared to humiliate a white man as badly as they humiliated me, there is no telling where he might not have finished; perhaps at the end of a rope. My faith in the decency of human nature was badly threatened by that terrible experience. I found myself outside the Western Union office in the company of two policemen warning me that if I made a further nuisance of myself I would be thrown into jail as a vagrant. I set off back towards the docks with the vague idea of picking up Esmé's trail at the ships' offices. A few moments later I was joined by Jacob Mix who grinned at me and, as casually as if we were passing acquaintances on the street, enquired where I was going. When I told him, he shook his head. 'Why waste time? Her train's just about to leave for Chicago.' He had telephoned Meulemkaumpf's New York number and learned that the millionaire had already boarded the 20th Century Limited. The Pullman was due to leave within minutes. I remember my dash up the Avenue of the Americas as a blur. Mr Mix followed, panting. The cops, he said, were still on our tail. At last I ran into the sunbeams and shadows of the station, was sighted by the two policemen, sprinted towards the 20th Century's wrought-iron boarding gates to be caught between this barrier and the cops in time to hear the confident gasps of the mighty silver locomotive as she began her journey West. *He perdido mi rosa! He perdido mi hija.*

'Esmé!' I was sure she would hear me somehow through the voices of the departing travellers, the squeal of the pistons and the clatter of the metal. 'Esmé!'

A loud commotion from the other side of the station, a sudden yell from a stall-holder, made the policemen hesitate. I saw Mr Mix signalling to me from the far exit and I dashed towards him. How ironical, I reflected, that I, Colonel Maxim Arturovitch Pyatnitski, late of the Don Cossacks, perhaps the last scion of an old and aristocratic Russian line, should find as his only friend in New York a humble darkie. I knew a little humility myself at that moment. God speaks to us in strange ways, sometimes, and sends us help in even stranger guises. If nothing else, this is what I have learned over the years.

'How are we to get to Chicago, Mr Mix?'

'There's only one way I know,' ironically responded my dusky comrade.

So, in Jacob Mix's company, I plunged again into that seedy wilderness, that unmapped land of despair and hope-lessness which is home to the railroad bum. Three nights later, as we neared Chicago, with my beard and my chills, a nose that would not stop running and no means of finding a little cocaine to take away the worst of the symptoms, I was not to be recognised as the gifted teenage genius whose final dissertation in Petersburg had brought an entire college to its feet applauding my precocious and sophisticated vision of an Earthly Paradise which, with a little sense and good will, could so easily have been made a reality. Instead, what is this? I have become a *gendzl* again. *Gey vays . . . ? Es dir oys s'harts. Es dir oys s'harts, Esmé.* That *meshuggeneh hint!*

I am back in the cattle car!

THREE

HOW RICHLY IS CONFORMITY and mediocrity rewarded! I am reconciled now, but as a youth I was constantly shocked by examples of that truism. Reduced to nothing, I was again forced to rely on my wits. I am not ashamed of this. I have nothing to hide. This does not mean I never valued my privacy. Dame Gossip makes such capital of a few sensational speculations! Who can afford to offer her so much as a thimbleful more material? Only once, after we had reached Chicago and learned from a newspaper that, irony of ironies, Meulemkaumpf, and doubtless my darling, had already left for Los Angeles, did Jacob Mix ask what I considered to be an impertinent question about my fiancée. I was forced to silence him immediately. I was in no doubt that Esmé had prevailed upon Mr Meulemkaumpf to escort her to California, trying to find me at the address I had given her before she took ship. This irony did not outweigh the urgency of the situation. I had to get to her as soon as possible. What would they tell her? That they had last heard of me being arrested for bootlegging and that my bits and pieces had been discovered amongst the effects of a few vagrants? She might think me dead, run over by a freight train as I desperately sought to reach New York. What would she do in her grief? The thought was horrifying. I was reminded of what my other Esmé had done. Lost, believing herself betrayed, she had become the whore of anarchists too depraved to dignify by the noble name of Cossack. She had been fucked so many times, she said, she had calluses on her cunt. She had become the plaything of my worst enemies. I could not force from my mind the picture of my sweet child innocently seduced by the evil words of some neo-Klansman, the kind who had already sworn to be revenged on me. What sweeter revenge is there than to rape the victim's most treasured possession? I already knew much of human evil. I had seen virtually every aspect of it, especially during the war against the Bolsheviks. I did not think my sanity would stand another experience of that kind.

Some of this I confided to Mr Mix, who seemed to suggest that the chances of a situation recurring so exactly were remote. 'Because a brick once dropped on your head don't mean you're the kind of man who has bricks drop on his head.' I must admit I found his simple wisdom calming, and perhaps my liking for the negro was based on the man's peculiar ability to help me regain my reason when, as many highly-strung creative people find, I temporarily lost control of myself.

Further attempts to telephone Mucker Hever collect or else to borrow the fare for Los Angeles failed miserably and we were arrested. Those few days in jail are not the worst I have spent. At least there was adequate food and no beatings. But of course I was hard put to quell my panic. I spent a day in the infirmary but the doctors there were unsympathetic. They determined I was merely suffering drug-withdrawal symptoms. At this foul lie, I did not help my own case by shouting my outrage and trying to strike the orderly who conveyed the quacks' ridiculous diagnosis. They would not accept that my release might well be a matter of life and death. Of all places, California was where Esmé most needed protecting. Like any city which has attained the status of a myth, Hollywood was full of predators ready to pick up all unconsidered trifles, human or financial. Thousands of young girls were sacrificed each day to a dream of Fame.

With Mr Mix's help I began to make some sort of fresh plan. On the morning of our release, we headed directly for the highway. Eventually, in the company of three lambs' carcasses and a somewhat introspective ewe, we got all the way to Valparaiso, Indiana and the railroad yards. After sunset we climbed into a west-bound box-car, closing the doors with all the emotion of returning home. Our long journey begun, there was little to do but talk. Jacob Mix was fascinated by all I had to tell him and frequently exclaimed that I was the best education he had ever had, but all was not one-sided. Mr Mix was a skilful modern dancer – foxtrot, Charleston, even *tango* were all familiar to him, picked up either from an earlier mentor, a down-and-out music-hall performer who had learned his trade with Cohan, or books and films. He had seen *The Four Horsemen of the Apocalypse* twelve times. Many a night we would step carefully to the rhythm of the swaying freight car while he instructed me in the steps of the waltz, the polka and the cakewalk. Then somewhere in Kansas one evening we found an empty grain truck. Sweet-smelling as it was, and with enough grain still remaining to make us both comfortable, the truck carried us eventually to Hannibal, Missouri, where an attempt to kill us by pouring new grain onto our sleeping bodies barely failed. We found ourselves promptly jailed, this time in separate 'tanks' while we served our profitless time and were released. After we had begged unsuccessfully for food at the back door of Huck Finn's Original Catfish House we fled and were separated. I became familiar with the Mississippi river in Memphis, Tennessee, where I worked as a slave-labourer for a month on a 'chain-gang' building up the levee after the flood. By that time I had lost all my ambition and a good deal of my identity and was merely grateful that none of my old acquaintances passed by and recognised me. I had left Memphis under something of a cloud, in Major Sinclair's airship, and was now especially glad I had given the name of Paxton to the arresting policeman. My guess was that Boss Crump, undisputed ruler of Memphis, would think nothing of ordering the death of a man he regarded as his arch-enemy. I prayed daily that he would never know I was at that moment working on the river wall not half a mile from Mud Island, but my time passed without event and, released, I had lost all contact with Mr Mix. I heard from another bum that he had headed for New Orleans, but my own destination remained Los Angeles.

Occasionally I raised enough money to visit a movie. They

were all that remained of my lost reality. I watched that other Gish, Dorothy, in *The Beautiful City*, a wonderful tale of racial misunderstanding and reconciliation with William Powell and Richard Barthelmass as the Italian, and it reminded me of my ideals, my own faith in humanity. Mostly however I could not afford the first-run, full-orchestra, theatres and went to houses where Ken Maynard or Hoot Gibson were the biggest attractions and Colonel Tim Holt's adventures were considered too 'up-market'. This was where I saw Tom Mix and observed how he represented all that was noblest in the Anglo-Saxon race. He truly was a Knight of the Prairies! Now at last I understood the value and influence of the modern kinema. Griffith remained my ideal – I watched, borne away from all my misery for two hours, while Lillian and Dorothy Gish performed the harrowing story of *Orphans of the Storm*, and *Broken Blossoms* had me in tears in an old Kansas City mission hall lined with painful pews, where I saw it three times, my own hardships seeming as nothing to the tragedy of 'The Chink and the Child' so marvellously played by Richard Barthelmass and Lillian Gish. I went to see her the other day in a horror film by the fat actor, Laughton. She was the only redeeming feature in the whole thing. We all have to compromise occasionally. I did not blame her. My own compromises were many through the summer of 1924.

I got a lift as far as Silverado. By now the September nights grew chill and my yearning for Esmé had become a constant familiar ache. Like the hunger, thirst and sleeplessness it was familiar enough so that I was no longer always conscious of it. I am used to hardship. I have survived many kinds. It has helped me to encourage in myself a kind of mental hibernation. I put my brain to sleep, save for those functions absolutely necessary for day-to-day living. Anyone who met me in those days would have considered me merely another young bum. I was superficially no more nor less coherent and wretched than any of the other derelicts in the 20s who spread in increasing numbers across the North American continent. But there too I did not become a *Musselman*. Unacknowledged, I kept that little secret spark alive. My spirit remained my own.

What was the point of making a *tararum* about it? Some things are best forgotten or, if not forgotten, not spoken of.

Some things only bring back trouble. A person must survive as best they can. Nobody blames them. Certainly one has a duty to others, but how can one help others if one has not helped oneself? You see, this is what they refuse to make allowances for. It is the socialists who force me to silence on the matter.

Red tsu der vant. I am not ashamed. Are we to rely upon the word of some worthless *hasidim*? Some stemwinder? What happened in Sonora was never proved. It was a beautiful town. I was against the idea but the others were committed. The fence was black iron and the shrubs were cedar. That is what I remembered. That is what I told them. Neat little lawns rolled where once forty-niners had brawled in their own vomit. Northern California was never a lucky place for me. Even my bargain with William Randolph Hearst's agents in the matter of the Thomas Ince affair emanated from the Southern half of the State although I am sworn to remain discreet on all matters involving the Hearst family so in honour say no more. I would only add that I had become desperate to have my old life restored and was no more than a tool in the matter having no moral involvement. That was on November 20, 1924. I had a full pardon and an assurance of work, should I ever require 'an honest job', at Cosmopolitan Studios.

I do not think it worth describing the degradation of my journey across the sub-continent. Sometimes one cannot afford a conscience. Sometimes one must sell whatever is valuable. I am not ashamed of this. I retain my Cossack soul. I survive so that my people, those Slavic heroes who wait to be awakened in all our menfolk, shall also remember how to survive. And the day is not too far off when our final battle is to be fought. That is the important battle. Nothing else is worth dying for. Love – mutual love – what else have we to comfort us against the cold terror of Entropy? Only human love increases, constitutes itself, intensifies – it is our only antidote to Entropy. We do not value enough our capacity to love. For love alone will save us, in the end – not ideologies, not even religion – but love, decent, honest, human love of one for another, all for one and one for all! *Pah sah?*

If one cannot change society one can at least hope from time to time to remind it of its virtues. The Moslem does not do this. Under the Tsar, under Christ, the Moslem came to see the virtues of conversion. Not so, of course, under the godless Bolsheviks who offered him no alternative. Thus he remains barbaric, backward, unenlightened. Civil War is the only future for him, when Mahomet's servants decide the time is right to support their co-religionist! God has spoken to me and I to Him but I told Him I could do His work without His comfort. When I am old and weak, God, I said, then I shall come to deserve and ask for Your comfort. Now I am old. I am weak. And God is gone, a drooling dotard, with only His son and His prophets and saints to help us. They are not strong enough. Sometimes, in those grey, despairing hours, I wonder if the Devil is indeed our rightful master and I am half-tempted towards the Synagogue, to the House of Loss itself. Hopelessness, powerlessness and death lie there. You do not know whose side I am on. It is probably yours.

Willst du ruhig sein, du Judenschwein? Ci ken myn arof gain in himl araan, ju freign bas got, ci sy darf azoi zaan? But is this not how Sexton Blake addressed the Jews?

In a horse-box shared with a stallion of uncertain disposition I invented, in the early winter of 1924, the jet engine. Jet reaction and gas turbine propulsion was always theoretically possible. I was remembering an article I had read as a boy in one of my English periodicals about Hero's Alexandrian steam engine, which, some 250 years BC, he called an *Aerophile*, and which is thought to be the first machine to convert steam pressure into jet force. My mind wandered on to Newton's third law of motion, his never-built steam carriage. The power/weight ratio was of course the chief problem for aeroplanes in those days, since a bigger plane always required a more powerful, and therefore bigger, engine. A jet turbine could deliver considerably more power for its size and therefore lift much larger machines at greater speeds. It occurred to me that some sort of high-velocity fan could be operated to draw in air which could be compressed and used in the powering of a turbine. For a few minutes I longed for my instruments and blueprints, still waiting, with my steam car, in Long Beach, California. Years later, when I heard about Whittle's work in England, I realised I had hit upon his solution some ten years earlier.

But of course this is not an unusual experience for me. In other circumstances I should probably today be the richest man in the world. If my vision of the jet engine had come to me while seated in some plush study lined with old brass instruments, like Sir Francis, then indeed, I might today be strutting the corridors of Buckingham Palace with a garter on my knee and a knighthood in my pocket, destined to rest in Westminster Abbey, to lie through the centuries and hear the blessed mutter of the mass. And this is the man who gave the world the sub-machine-gun! Blessed mutterings indeed!

They push at you from all sides, these young barbarians, these worshippers of pagan images, in the costumes of comic-opera gypsies. But the gypsies have an old knowledge, a knowledge of God, which made them a people apart. I have always found a fellow-feeling with them. They too were doomed to wander, to be reviled and humiliated, to be refused the comforts and rewards of the securely privileged.

But these are not gypsies who come to Portobello to sell their coloured candles and their beads where once an honest cabbage could be bought for less than a beggar now demands for tea. They have set up ranks of Indian silks, rows of perfumed oils and spices, in frank acknowledgement of their nation's conquest by the Orient. The sons and daughters of Surrey stockbrokers importune you like carpet-sellers in some Marrakshi souk. They jeer at me. I know the names. I speak all languages. But I refuse to be silenced by their mockery. We are on the brink of what the Chinese call *Luan*. I have seen the famous ruins of the world. I have seen the end of the Enlightenment. I have earned the right to speak. They use words whose meaning is lost to them. The true fascisti, the self-disciplined heroes of modern Italy, had no part in taking this world to war. They were against it. Is Christ a villain because some self-proclaimed Christian kills a child? My feelings are of the noblest kind. My emotions are profound. I have nothing but love in my heart, yet they take my actions and distort them and pervert them and call me that creature who personifies what they most fear and despise in themselves! They put me in jail. They try to shoot me. They shudder at the idea of sharing their land with such a creature as myself. One look is enough to show that I am a criminal. And yet what are these crimes? In Japan, in India – even in parts of America – they are ordinary practices. They know this really. What they hate is the cunning and malice in their own souls. I am an innocent mirror – this, of course, is typical. But it is not pleasant to be Billy Budd. I have fought prejudice all my life. The young Cornelius girl says I have an overdeveloped sense of sin. She says I am blaming myself too much. Though I appreciate her interest I laugh at this. I am not blaming myself at all, I tell her! And I doubt very much if God is blaming me, either! After all, even in His dotage He knows how much I have suffered and for what end. Even when I did not realise it, I was doing His work. Even in Egypt.

It is neither here nor there, at any rate, how on November 21, 1924, circumstances brought me, in a good-quality three-piece suit of the latest 'jazz' fashion, with matching Derby hat and spats and smoking a Havana cigar almost a foot long, once more to Hollywood, my 'home town'. Only, I need hardly say, to be denied my triumph.

I had no intention of accepting Miss Davies's offer of work and was confident that I would soon be back in harness, married to Esmé and my vocation in an exhilarating harmony. I had no doubt, just then, that Science was my true master. From a rather substandard room at the Hollywood Hotel still commanded by Mrs Hershing combining the styles of the Madam of a high-class bordello and a somewhat puritanical Mother Superior, I telephoned my erstwhile backer only to be told that 'Mucker' Hever was out of town. I called Information, but could locate neither Meulemkaumpf nor Esmé's surname, Bolascu. Even Mrs Cornelius was unlisted. Finally, on visiting my bank, I discovered that my retainer had not been paid for months and I had little more than four hundred dollars in my account. But at least I was soon to discover what had happened to Mrs Cornelius. I left the hotel restaurant that night and idly wandered down towards Grauman's Chinese Theater to take my mind off my obsessions and spend an hour or two comparing the feet, hands and hooves of the famous. Instead, after a couple of blocks, I was confronted by an enormous floodlit billboard in vivid, almost Oriental colour. I at once recognised my guardian angel, my greatest friend, my conscience and my confidant. It was Mrs Cornelius. Of course, she was not billed as Mrs Cornelius. Instead, here she was at last as she had always longed to be (though she also was no longer *Charlene Chaplin*). As Gloria Cornish she had shed about a stone in weight, but her warm beauty was unmistakable. It began to seem that whenever I was lost, whenever I was in despair and did not know where to turn, I received just a vision of my old *amie-du-chemin*, as they say in France.

I made a note of the film company, Sunset Motion Pictures. I would write to her.

The movie itself was one of those jazz-baby pictures got up to look as if it possessed a social conscience. I hate such hypocrisy. It was called *Was It A Sin?* and I went to see it purely so that I could have something to say when we met. Actually, the film was not without merit in its tragic story of a woman who commits adultery and is ultimately forced into prostitution, drugs and worse by cynical young opportunists who buy and sell women like meat at a cattle market. Mrs Cornelius played the fallen woman with a mixture of pathos and 'It' which comprised some of the finest acting I had ever seen upon the screen. And yet, at the same time, *heimisheh*. But that was Mrs Cornelius *au naturel*. It was how she always was. Unspoiled by any of life's vicissitudes. She was purity personified and I would fight a duel to the death to that effect. A lady, through and through, and a great artiste in every sense of the word.

She alone has stood by me through all my ups and downs. She is the only one who really knows me. In Kiev when I flew so high above the Babi gorge my mother and Esmé loved me. Since then, only Mrs Cornelius has acknowledged my achievements and understood my soul. If I go out now there is always some smirking embryonic gangster leaning on the corner of the bed-shop at Colville Terrace, across from the Midland Bank. 'Hello, professor,' he says. I ignore his mocking challenge and march straight to Stout's, the grocers. They at least have some old-world courtesy. They all wear white coats and put on gloves to serve the biscuits, even the women. It is a tradition of service long since lost, even as a notion, to that jeering lout. As I

48

return up Portobello Road Mrs Cornelius waves to me from the ironmonger's. She lives in the basement of Number Eight and, like me, is plagued by the unsympathetic young. But she continues to resist, to challenge anyone who seeks to reduce her, either by virtue of her age, her sex, her class or her appearance. This is her quality of resilient courage. She has always had it. At once she dismisses the youth with a rude gesture. 'Come in for a minute and 'ave a cup o' tea, kernel.' When feeling sympathetic she always addresses me by my title.

I enter the warmth of her moist abode, down below the level of the road, and there she comforts me with conversation almost wordless, a kind of croon. She is all there is and all I need now, my good old *compadre*. The world was ours once. We enjoyed it freely, that Olympus. I cannot regret those days. They are what they will never take away. Better to have such memories and no future than to have a future with no memories.

These children reject history. To them the past is merely *passé*. How can they learn not to make the same mistakes if they fail to accept the nature of time? Now they even insist the nature of time has changed. If so, surely we must still develop a morality so that we may not descend again to feral brutes? Mrs Cornelius tells me I worry too much about such things. She reminds me I can do nothing. But a man must try, I say, if his conscience demands it. In Inglewood I gave a note to the studio concierge at his little kiosk by the main gate. Sunset Moving Picture Company seemed a thriving concern, not one of the fly-by-night little movie businesses which so proliferated in those days, frequently under high-sounding titles hiding the real names of familiar shysters. My fears that Mrs Cornelius had become entangled in some shady operation dispelled, I boarded the No. 5 Yellow Car back from Manchester to downtown Los Angeles where I changed for Hollywood. The journey through the suburbs accounted for the best part of the day but it was pleasant enough and my time was well rewarded, for when I returned to the Hollywood Hotel Mrs Cornelius had already telephoned to say that her car would arrive at seven to take me to dinner with her. At last I had some sense of my burden's lifting a little. I knew fresh confidence. If I was being tested by

God, clearly I had done enough for the moment to merit His mercy, for by that evening I was in Beverly Hills dining *tête-à-tête* with my old friend, in a room overlooking a pool and palms which might have been anywhere in the romantic East. Had I not known better, I should have assumed a determination on her part to seduce me.

She was now a gorgeous white blonde, with huge eyelashes and a delicious cupid's bow, even more beautiful in all her pink English flesh than she was upon the screen. She wore pale blue silk and pearls. She was drenched in Mitsouko. I was again entirely intoxicated, hypnotised by her exquisite beauty, her aura of glamour. She listened with few comments, eating as I told her my story, every so often urging me to elaborate or continue. She was horrified at what had happened. 'I just thort you an' yore bint 'ad decided America wasn't good enough fer yer and orf yer went, back to wherever it was. Cor, you poor littel bugger! I can let yer 'ave a few dollars, if yer like.'

I told her that I was provided for at the moment, though I did ask discreetly for the name of a reliable cocaine supplier. I felt it was high time I refuelled my brain. She put me in touch with a well-known actor who, down on his luck, was supplementing his income working as an agent for a big-time dealer and meanwhile told me her own story, which explained much of what had been mysterious. The very day she had left me at the airfield she had met a handsome young man who, like Hever, was a partner in a film company. 'The only difference is, Ivan, that this feller was also bloody good-lookin', in a sleazy sort of way. Like old Trotsky used to be before 'e started takin' 'isself so fuckin' seriously. I 'ear 'e's in France now, by the way. Them blokes was orlways squabblin' amongst themselves. Gord, it got borin' towards the end!' And then she smiled, remembering some comic incident of those terrible Civil War years when she had helped me out of more than one difficulty. She did not know what had happened to Hever or my steam car. 'It only larsted a fortnight an' then I met me Swede, Wolfgang. 'E sounds like a kraut, but 'e ain't. Well, 'Ever *was* bitter, I'll say that much. Very bitter reelly. Took against me an', I suppose, you. 'E wrote this stuffy note, talking abart breach o' promise an' rubbish like that. Said 'e wasn't bloody surprised we'd skipped and we was bofe a pair o' blackmailin' scoundrels and he didn't give a damn 'oo said wot abart ther fuckin' KKK, 'e was buggering off ter Europe and after that he was goin' 'untin' in Africa. Innit amazin' 'ow many poor bleedin' animals get killed jes' 'cause some bloke don't get the rumpo 'e's after!'

'He said nothing of my car?'

'Not in as many words, Ivan. But I'd guess yer can forget abart that one.'

'It would have made him millions,' I said. 'And me, too, of course.' I would go to Long Beach tomorrow, gain access to my invention, and perhaps drive it away. Technically, according to our contract, the car was our joint property, but with Hever abroad I must quickly find a new backer. I explained this to Mrs Cornelius, who said I should do what I liked. She'd mentioned, she said, my name as a script-writer and actor to her friend Wolfgang Sjöström, the famous Swedish 'Sex Director' who had arrived in Hollywood just as Hays came into office and had, ever since, been gloomily frustrated by what he called 'the bourgeois kinema'.

He was interested in employing me. I was grateful for her kindness but explained my destiny lay with the conquest and harnessing of the forces of nature for the greater benefit of mankind. Only necessity had made me a play-actor.

She seemed a little disappointed, even sceptical, but she said the chance was always there if I wished to take it. Sjöström had a contract with Goldwyn Studios to make two pictures a year, but he also was a partner in DeLuxe. He could put plenty of small parts my way. I could earn some money while I worked on my inventions. I promised her I would consider this idea.

An hour or two after we had finished the meal and the black servants had cleared it away, 'Wolfy' Sjöström came in. I was surprised at his weight. I had visualised someone altogether slimmer and more romantic. Yet clearly Mrs Cornelius saw in this bulky Norseman a hero! I must say I did not care for him much myself. His features had fallen into the deep lines of anxiety neurosis and even when he smiled one had the impression of a man in the throes of indigestion. He seemed condescending and over-eager to me and I suspected that Mrs Cornelius had exaggerated my artistic achievements, especially when he made reference to my books and expressed the breathless piety that some day the American public would be ready for the Philosophical Novel. Of course, my natural frankness made me want to tell him that I was no writer but a practical engineer who merely needed a little financial backing to astonish the world, but, not to embarrass Mrs Cornelius, I remained silent, and soon he had left for another room with my friend. She came back alone about ten minutes later and slipped a few screws of paper into my hand. She had found me the cocaine. Now I understood everything and was grateful. The chauffeur would take me back to the Hollywood Hotel. She would telephone me in a day or so, to see how I was settling, she said, but she evidently did not understand how baffled and unhappy I was concerning Esmé. Unenthusiastically she promised to ask around and find out where Meulemkaumpf, at least, might be discovered.

In greatly improved humour I returned through dreaming groves and gardens to my hotel and spent the night drawing up fresh plans. In the morning I would visit my old landlord to reclaim the belongings Mrs Cornelius told me he was retaining in lieu of rent. Then I would take a Red Car down to Long Beach and gain access to my steam auto. In all justice the Pallenberg Flyer was mine. Let Hever raise what devils he dared, I would take possession of her come what may!

Next morning I arrived at the Long Beach docks where our machine sheds were. Stretching almost to infinity along the concrete quays and bays, the pumps, cranes and oil-derricks were like skeletal dinosaurs, the salt air was crazy with the screech and growl of labouring machines, thick with the stink of a blue industrial haze mingling with the harbour's cool December air, drifting over water as blue and flat as new-forged steel beneath the winter California sun. Our own sheds had scarcely changed save for a board now advertising something other than Golden State Engineering Developments. Inside the main shed a few mechanics were repairing a little seaplane whose floats had evidently struck the water at the wrong angle. One of the young men, whose overalls bore a profound stratum of stains, had a familiar look to him. Politely I hailed him from just inside the doors. It was Willy Ross, the bright-eyed foreman who had done so much to help get the PXI ready for the road. He looked up, squinting in the light, and then grinned as he recognised me. He came forward, wiping his fingers on a rag, and put out an almost clean hand for me to shake. 'We all thought you were dead or gone back to Europe, Mr Pallenberg. It's good to see you. What's the story?'

I told him briefly what had befallen me and he listened with some sympathy. 'But I came here to collect my car. The PXI. Where is it now, Willy?'

He put awkward fingers to the back of his neck. 'There's not too much of her left, Mr P. I don't know what you did to him or what he thought you did, but he came down here only a day or so after you'd gone to New York and told us to wheel that steamer out. Just there, on the quay. So we did. We wheeled her out. Then he went to his own car and got this forty-pound sledgehammer from the trunk and just started whanging away at her. Well, you know, he was the boss . . .'

It would not take a half-crazed Viennese Jew to know what had set John Hever off. It appeared that his only reason for funding the project was to ingratiate himself with Mrs Cornelius. What contempt I suddenly felt for the man! It was clear that he had no vision – even clearer, he had not even sense to respect mine! I let Willy lead me to a metal dump, used by all the machine shops, and there amongst the discarded boilers and engine parts, amongst the ruined elements of every land, sea or air vessel ever made, the pathetic remnants of more than my own dream, I saw the great PXI, its Buick body dented and smashed, every piece of glass destroyed. The hood had fallen open to reveal a ruined mass of tubes, wires and boilers. My steam car was unsalvageable!

At this point horror gave way to anger. What childish folly! *Gevalt!* What a fool I had been to trust such a *chozzer! Mah nishtana! Me duele aquí.* They put a piece of metal in my soul. *¡Estoy el corazon! Tak sie raz osiel dasaù!* I could not stand any more. I left in some disorder shivering with anger and disappointment. 'He went to Europe,' Willy told me. 'We were fired. But it's not hard to get a job around here. I liked your car, Mr P. We all figured she'd do okay.' He was wistful. 'I told Bob we were on to something.'

An understatement indeed! Imagine my despair! This was not the first time, even at such an age, I had been bitterly disappointed in my hopes. Is it the fate of all men of vision to be treated thus? I think so. One has good years and bad years. 1924 was, perhaps, not to be one of my better years.

Taking a taxi back to Venice I located the landlord of my old San Juan house and, when he had extorted a vicious $50.00 from me, recovered my bags and bore them back to the hotel. Thankfully the Georgian pistols, all that I had left of my homeland, were still there, along with my plan cases, my clothes, some money and about four ounces of cocaine which I had placed in an air-tight tobacco tin and which was as fresh as when first distilled! The quality was much better than the version familiar to the lower classes, which I had grown used to, and so, save for dashing off a quick letter to Mucker Hever, which would not make his homecoming any more pleasant, I did nothing that evening but clean my goods and get them into order, luxuriating in newly-discovered ecstasy. I was glad to have my wardrobe restored to me and, determined not to brood on Hever's appalling perfidy, dressed in formal elegance. Leaving the hotel, I was delivered by cab to the beachfront at Venice where fashionable bohemians mingled with actors and tycoons. I determined to order myself a magnificent meal at my favourite restaurant, The Doge's Palace, and then enjoy a cigar and some brandy while I considered how best to approach a new backer for my inventions. The steam car had never been the only card up my sleeve. Afterwards I planned to patronise Madame France's famous 'maison'. Soon I would begin to build up another list of telephone numbers from the 'baby stars' who were always up for a good time and charged you nothing, save that you promised to help them in their careers if you ever got the chance. The Doge's Palace remained undimmed in its fanciful glory, framed by tall palms, its forecourt lit by hidden yellow and orange lanterns and I was about to enter when an apparition in the livery of a 15th-century *condottiere*, its black face grinning like the sudden winner of some mighty sweepstake, bellowed from where it was frozen in motion, about to enter a local mogul's massive Duesenberg: 'By God! If it ain't the Flying Dutchman himself!'

Irritated by this insolence I had almost complained to an unsettled doorman when I recognised with dawning pleasure the features of the 'parking valet'. It was my old railroad companion, my amanuensis, who had shared so many adventures, so much hardship, so many nights talking of books, philosophy and politics when, I like to think, I contributed to his education, encouraging his eagerness to learn and to make something of himself.

'Jacob Mix!' I exclaimed in delight. 'You are in California? How? Why?'

'Looking for you.' His grin was self-mocking. Then he became serious. 'I figured you'd surely make it back here sooner or later. With your luck, it was only a question of waiting till you just naturally came by.' He spoke without irony, with absolute certainty. For him this meeting had been inevitable.

Laughing happily, I clapped him on the shoulder and reassured the doorman. 'This gentleman and I are old friends!' I told Mr Mix I would see him again as soon as I had dined. He continued to offer me his delighted beam. 'Oh, things are going to get a whole lot better now!' He spoke almost to himself.

Just as the restaurant door was opened for me by the flunkey, Mr Mix added, 'I guess I've seen that fiancée of yours around town. But maybe you've caught up with her by now. Or wised up.' All thoughts of food driven from my mind, I whirled round. But Jacob Mix had started the Duesenberg and was driving it to the rear of the restaurant. I heard the doorman's startled shout as I ran in frantic pursuit of that black Cassandra, the scent of a fresh spoor suddenly in my nostrils. Esmé.

Meyn shwester. Meyn trail buddy.

FOUR

YOU THINK YOU ARE without blame? Well, as we used to say in Kiev, there is always room on the tram for one more saint. We were fair judges of people, Jew or Gentile, in the old days before that pseudonymous Red trio saturated the map of Russia in blood and called the result 'Progress'.

I am not here however to plough up old graves. I myself was once a great believer in the future. You could argue that my convictions were my weakness as well as my strength. Also I trusted others too much, for in that I was always my own worst enemy. I admit it. I continue as best I can to lift high the Torch of Christian Civilisation against the Darkness of the Beast. What better torch indeed! Yet I too have known the burden of guilt and moral ambivalence, the most painfully, the most unbearably, when I have betrayed a fellow human soul! By giving a machine priority over a person and by not arriving in New York earlier to make all appropriate arrangements for transport and hotels, I had betrayed the trust Esmé had placed in me. I had come to understand how it was entirely my fault and no surprise that, in her grief and terror at my presumed betrayal, she had blotted me, her rescuer, her passionate, loving husband, almost entirely from her consciousness.

I was soon to become well aware of her state of mind when I telephoned her at the number Carmelita Geraghty, a well-known 'baby-star', gave me.

56

The hotel agreed she was registered but, every time I called, said she was not available. It was a small but very sophisticated palm-shaded private hotel on Sunset Boulevard, West Hollywood, in its own grounds. When I presented myself the concierge was polite, accepted my messages, but was otherwise extremely close-mouthed and rather haughty. I understood that this was his habit. I explained some of the tragic events leading to the misunderstanding between us, but nothing I tried would get him to tell me when Esmé was expected back.

My pain was admittedly no more than a dull persistent ache now and I was able to go about my ordinary business without too much effort of will while Carmelita Geraghty, Hazel Keener, Lucille Rickson and Blanche McHaffey helped me forget my heartache. My attempts to contact Esmé became a matter of routine. Every day I left a message. I was a great optimist then. The future seemed infinite and could only improve. It is different now. There are no rules, no boundaries to Time. I grew to maturity and old age in a world that sought to give new shape, even a new meaning, to the universe. What was I to do? Like some ancient mariner cast adrift in an open boat, I made my best effort to chart a safe course for myself across an alien sea beneath an alien sky. The *schwartzes* swagger into my shop. They say this is their territory now. I am sure it is, I say. It is what things have come to.

Do they delude themselves that I have any time for their zoot and jives, that I envy them their acid society held together by soporifics? I was born into a world of work and pain, where pleasure was earned and paid for, where Nature was not to be Nurtured and Sentimentalised but Tamed, and where crime was punished. There is a piece of metal in my womb. They placed a white-hot iron upon my spirit and my agony filled the galaxy, destroying stars, but I survived even that. I was strengthened by it. I died and came alive. I survived a holocaust. I survived the humiliation and the despair. And even now, living this life of a tradesman, buying and selling the discarded costumes and uniforms of the 20th century, I at least have my voice, my memory, our history; and I have survived to tell the truth of it. To these children the powerful personalities who created their world have become mythic ogres and demigods. I have seen the realities of an entire planet undergoing profound and unprecedented agonies, the most momentous changes she has ever experienced in this Age of Man. I have seen the reality of individuals dying in abject terror and spiritual agony, one by one, to make – death by death – first one million, then two million, then ten million: million by million they died, and one by one, in ditches and in woods, in trains and in camps, in churches and barns, flats and huts, in snow and rain or perfect sunshine. Shot, buried or drowned, tormented, dehumanised, corrupted, robbed of self-respect, they died one by one, children and old people; people of every age. Million upon million they watched their loved ones killed. In the name of progress they died for a future that turned to ash even as they themselves perished. That ashen future still clings here and there in those parts of the world most susceptible to temporal cancers. Once those cancers take hold they are almost impossible to eradicate, even with the subtlest, most radical surgery. Not that anyone will listen to those of us who are capable of performing such an operation. This is scarcely an era of bold and unselfish decisions. Greed is now a respectable Virtue and Envy a fine spur to 'ambition', or the lust for power. The Lie is commonplace. The old Virtues are mocked and reviled. They roar with laughter at the noblest sentiments and aspirations. It is why I stopped going to watch for glimpses of myself and Mrs Cornelius at the National Film Theatre. *The Roads to Yesterday* and other great moral fables of our time were the subject of scarcely suppressed mirth. Now occasionally on TV I get to see a 20s movie not entirely murdered by the introduction of a mocking soundtrack. In those days the cinema was worth visiting. It had moral responsibility; it recognised its influence on the public – it offered a new morality, sometimes, too – to lift them above the level of the greedy herd – a level of aspiration. *The Roads to Yesterday* with Hopalong Cassidy and Vera Reynolds (whom I met years later in the flesh and was able to congratulate on her performance) showed us the world of the past and illuminated the world of today. On the same day I saw a last lyrical tribute to an older West by William S. Hart who had been superseded by the glamorous daredevil Tom Mix in Zane Grey's *Riders of the Purple Range* with

Charlie Chan. I enjoyed Ricardo Cortez and Betty Carney in *The Pony Express*. I was astounded by *The Lost World*, which I had read as a *Strand* serial, with Wallace Beery and Bessie Love – it captured my imagination that year until I saw *We Moderns*, that great moral fable for our time with its powerful climax as the jazz-babies dance obliviously on the deck of the great airship unaware of the plane about to crash into the hull! Certainly, it was based on Zangwill's book. I have never said that all Jews were immoral! I also saw *She* with Betty Blythe, *Lord Jim* and *The Wizard of Oz*, but *We Moderns* made the lasting impression and I would have gone to see it more times if I had not begun to realise I was running short of money.

By now I also had the company of some of those 'jazz-babies' I watched on the screen. Joan Crawford, Clara Bow and Alberta Vaughan were all ladies who found me attractive enough to spend a little time with and through them, of course, I could obtain good-quality cocaine. The excellent cocaine helped me get a better grip on the truth of my situation. The remaining money in my bank account, together with the assets I had brought with me, would keep me for little more than a month (especially with regular visits to Madame France's) and I had no wish to borrow money from Mrs Cornelius. She had of course made her generous purse available to me. I was anxious to avoid association with Hearst for a while. I recalled my meeting with Mucker Hever's erstwhile partner, Goldfish. He had suggested I send him my synopsis of *White Knight and Red Queen*. As always, rather than mourn a ruined opportunity, I concentrated on reviewing my immediate resources. I had no intention of becoming a full-time script-writer, but I had to earn some money quickly and this was the only way in which I might do that. I would, of course, continue to seek for my inventions a backer with more vision than Hever, an 'angel' whose interest in my work was moved by something more substantial than an 'inflatable conscience'. Equally, I was determined not to take advantage of Mrs Cornelius's offers to have her boyfriend employ me: I had learned my lesson in that area, at least for the moment!

Thus, from the plethora of pretty, talented and sexually experienced young girls who in those days flooded the market,

I found a competent typist and had her write out the plot of the play Mrs Cornelius and I had given up and down the State. In essence I performed the whole thing for her, scene by scene, while she took notes. She was able to help a little with my English spelling, which was not perfect in those days, and before long we had produced some dozen pages ready to send to the famous maverick producer, hero and victim of two great film companies, who by this time had changed his name to Goldwyn and was again starting up as a patron of quality films. 'Rubbish,' he often argued, 'has no long-term shelflife. With your quality you have an investment, a high profit margin which will last you for years.' It was this belief in quality as a matter of commercial good sense which was to win me to him and offer us both a somewhat radically different place in cinema history. My one regret is that Mrs Cornelius and I were cut from von Stroheim's *Greed*. The pirate Meyer took it over and cut forty-two reels to ten! It was a travesty of what all who saw the first version agreed was the greatest movie ever made. It was a masterpiece of epic realism. I would even be prepared to say it eclipsed *Birth of a Nation*, but von Stroheim was never the professional Griffith was.

Madge Puddephet, my secretary, a pretty girl from Missouri, was impressed by my casual familiarity with the personalities of the screen world. She herself was a great admirer of Mrs Cornelius and, soft-hearted as I was, I promised to get her my friend's autograph. (Madge later became famous as Vivienne Prentiss, with a particularly large following in France. Drink ruined her but when I knew her she was a smart little jazz-baby who was amazed I should even have heard of Hannibal, let alone spent time there. I did not see any point in explaining the circumstances.) She came to my hotel twice a day and of course it was not long before our natural attraction took us, almost without realising it, to bed. Those were the years before Hollywood succumbed completely to the bourgeois ideal, the notion of the 'normal', and Madge provided the consolation I needed. She had been trained, like so many of these girls, by her father.

Poor, martyred Arbuckle, whom I came to know quite well, and Hays between them sent the American movie down a road which ultimately put middle-class slacks on Mickey Mouse and replaced Pearl White and Theda Bara with *Blondie* and *Kiss Me, Hardy*. When this happened, they said America had 'grown up'. But we had a code and a wisdom of our own and might have looked after our own had not Big Business and International Zion conspired to attack that love of liberty and tolerance which made the film community what it was in those early, innocent years when sexual liberation was something less reverent and more pleasurable than it seems nowadays. The final victory over Art came when we at last had a chance to speak, to give our own interpretations to our rôles – whereupon every artist of integrity and individuality was systematically replaced by the Nice American Guy and the All-American Girl. Clara Bow, with whom I last corresponded in 1953, knew all about the conspiracy, as did Mrs Cornelius and Norma Talmadge. Louise Brooks wrote about it. John Gilbert was destroyed by it, as was John Barrymore. Clara married. She tried to be a good girl. But it drove her mad. Her nature was free as mine. Freedom is a threat to easy profits. It is the first thing the Corporations eradicate. They substitute a range of choices and call that Freedom. But we knew what real freedom was in 1924.

Madge herself took my manuscript to Goldfish's office but she was only able to hand it in to a flunkey, so we were both thoroughly surprised when a telephone call the next day ordered me to visit Goldfish at four o'clock that afternoon. These were the days when he had already severed his partnership with Metropolitan and with Meyer (whose fortune, ironically, was founded on Ham). He was again an approachable eccentric aristocrat rather than one of the Hollywood kings. Samuel Goldwyn Productions had already made some highly successful and critically acclaimed films like *Tarnish*, *In Hollywood With Potash and Perlmutter* and many others. He was a typically flamboyant Warsaw Jew. Out of politeness I addressed him in Yiddish, but he insisted on English until he grew more relaxed, and returned to Yiddish in which he was more fluent. He was impressed by my story. He had been looking for something like it.

'We need,' he said gravely, 'to show people how it is over

there.' He liked my basic plot and he thought he had just the man to direct it. 'He's Swedish as a matter of fact, but who's counting?' He chuckled at me and winked. 'What does anybody know anyway?' I found him a warming and engaging type, not unlike some of those who had inhabited *Esau the Hairy*'s, my old Odessa friends of the Slobodka. We were both nostalgic for pre-war Russia.

Goldfish said my story had that ring of authority, had clearly come from personal experience. He asked a little about my part in the Civil War. I told him how I had actually ridden with the White Cossack Host, how I had been captured by Anarchists, how I had escaped to Istanbul. He seemed sympathetic but not greatly impressed. 'With a lie like that you should be Roman Novaccio,' he said. Doubtless he had heard many tall tales from newly-discovered relatives and countrymen who wanted a job. I was determined not to trade on my military career, although naturally I was anxious to demonstrate to him my thorough lack of anti-Semitism. This, too, he accepted naturally, as if there were no other civilised position. Indeed he seemed a trifle discomfited by my references to Benya the Accountant and all my other Hebrew pals in Odessa. No embarrassment resulted, however, for soon we gave our whole attention to the realisation of my tale which, though changing in detail as Goldfish suggested ways in which it might be better presented on the screen, remained essentially true to my original conception. More than once he remarked how my story gripped him to his soul. He asked me how I would visualise the scene where the commander of the Women's Battalion of Death, Tatania (a Countess before the Revolution), sentences Prince Dimitri, the White leader, to the firing squad.

I explained that I was by training a civil engineer and that it might be better if I drew the scene for him. He handed me a block of paper and I quickly sketched out the scene – the accusation, the verdict, the sentence. Goldfish was approving. 'Not many of us have the right talent for pictures.' Then, abruptly, the interview was terminated. A secretary who introduced herself as Sadie escorted me to the front gates. Goldfish would let me know if the studio could use the story. Meanwhile Sadie had an envelope for me which I should sign a receipt for. I walked a block or two until I was sure of not being seen by anyone from his office, and opened the envelope. It contained a cheque for $250.00 and a letter from Goldfish himself telling me that I was now officially retained by Samuel Goldwyn Productions to write a script based on my story. He would contact me as soon as he returned from Berlin.

To celebrate this further upturn in my fortunes, I took Madge to Christmas dinner at the *Café Alphonse* and from there we went on to a nightclub for cocktails. It was not possible to get her into the Hollywood Hotel without inviting disapproving attention so instead we booked a room for the night at Madame France's, where we spent a memorable Yule. Everywhere soon began to go to seed, however. Even in those days, downtown Los Angeles showed evidence of social decline and the hotels were almost all what we used to call 'commercials'. Every one of them is that now, of course. Possibly inspired by her surroundings, Madge proved to be a woman of imagination and spirit. I had, I discovered, only sampled a soupçon of her outstanding sexual menu. It was impossible to believe that she had developed certain of her appetites and proclivities in rural Missouri. I concluded, discreetly, that she was no stranger to the cheap hotel and a *nom-de-guerre* in the register and possibly had worked at establishments like Madame France's; yet I came to feel a strong attachment for her and soon decided to employ her regularly as my secretary as soon as I was in work again. Even after a night's extravagance I was still in pocket to the tune of some $150 and might reasonably expect considerably more if Goldfish were as good as his word. The money in hand would take care of my bills for a month and give me time to find employment more suitable to my talents. I had already considered approaching William Randolf Hearst in his capacity as chief of a great engineering concern rather than a studio boss, and drafted letters to various other eminent tycoons, including Hughes and Dupont, offering them the opportunity to develop some of the inventions I had begun to see realised in Russia, Turkey and France before circumstances brought me to America. Madge would type them for me as soon as she had time.

I took her with me to enjoy the rest of the season with Mrs Cornelius, her beau and their friends, who were mostly established movie people. Mrs Cornelius displayed considerably less jealousy towards Madge than she did towards Esmé. She confided to me that she thought Madge a 'decent sort' and advised me to stick with her. I pointed out that I remained betrothed to another. I was in no position to give Madge more than a temporary commitment. Moreover there were other young ladies available. I am, I hope, a gentleman, and would not take advantage of a young girl from Missouri. Although, as I pointed out, she was no shrinking virgin when we met.

'*An*' she's not th' only one!' Mrs C. was emphatic, but whether in reference to herself or someone else was not clear.

Since we were alone together in the drawing-room I used the chance to ask if she had managed to discover anything more about Esmé. All she knew was that Meulemkaumpf, a notorious avoider of publicity, was at present unusually assiduous in pursuing privacy. 'That could 'ave somefink ter do wiv 'is wife, I shouldn't wonder, Ivan.'

I took her meaning. The Press would be bound to read the worst into Meulemkaumpf's offer of protection to my darling. Now, knowing more about the man, I no longer suspected him of bearing her away to have his will with her at some lonely ranch. I realised that Esmé, believing herself deserted, had appealed instinctively to a native American gentleman. I longed for the chance, I told Mrs Cornelius, to explain what had happened. She offered the opinion that it was possible we both had some explaining to do, but before she could elaborate we were joined by Buck Buchmeister and a couple of his louder technician friends who were discussing a set they had just constructed for J.M. Schenk's *Graustark*.

Buchmeister had had some hand in directing the picture, I gathered, under a pseudonym. It was not particularly uncommon in those days for people to 'moonlight' for rival studios sometimes for the extra money, sometimes to help out a friend, or to fly, as it were, under flags of convenience. It is safe to say that in Hollywood not more than one person in three retained anything like their original name. This fashion was started by the Jews who, of course, had every possible motive for encouraging the habit, since it helped so many of them to assimilate into American society. Not that these particular Jews were illiterate or uneducated. I have nothing against the better type of Jew. They contribute a good deal to our society and are frequently very charitable. My only reservation is the common one, that it is not healthy or sane to have one minority race, with all its inherited traditions, many of which are at odds with our own, dominating our culture. It is not surprising that certain alien ideas crept into the cinema in those years. I need only mention *The Enemy*, *Name the Man*, *He Who Gets Slapped*, *The Case of Lena Smith*, or *Man, Woman and Sin*, most of which were set abroad and dealt with subjects in ways that scarcely married with the ideals of the American people. Not that I had anything against Jeanne Eagels, whom I admired in all her films, but it was no surprise to me when I learned of her tragic death. There is a certain strain accompanying the kind of rôle she had to play in, say, *Jealousy* and *The Letter*. And, inevitably, Communism had eaten into Hollywood's great heart by the 40s when it became necessary to cauterise the wound by methods some found crude and brutal, even cruel, but which many of us knew to be all too kind. The proof of this was that the communists did go to other countries to continue to propagate their messages while others, as in the case of the infamous 'Kubrick', simply changed their names and did not stop for a second! And we now see the results, day after day, on BBC and ITV which are nothing but a catalogue of every disease ever carried by word of mouth. Tolerant and easy-going as I am, sometimes I think my 'live and let live' attitude was inappropriate, especially during my Hollywood glory days.

For all that my thoughts were constantly turning to Esmé and speculation as to how she was spending her first holiday in America, that Christmas at Buchmeister's was happy enough. I got to talk to several of the set-technicians and to discuss solutions to their problems. It seemed they thought I had a natural talent for their discipline and one of them, Van Nest Poldark (a Cornish buccaneer, as he styled himself, descended from a long line of novelists, smugglers and wreckers), told me I should be working in the technical department of a major studio. I laughed and pointed out that I was an engineer by profession and vocation. He argued that this was all the more reason I should try my hand at film designing. 'It requires the knowledge of an Isaac Newton coupled with the aesthetic eye of a Michelangelo,' he said. I thought he, in the manner of so many members of the kinema fraternity, was exaggerating somewhat, but then he gave me his card and suggested I come to see him at Paramount, which he had just himself joined. I did not throw the card away. As I told Madge later, if I could not see my inventions come to life in the real world, at least I might have the pleasure of seeing them realised on the movie screen. Thus, too, I might acclimatise the public to, as it were, my cerebral vision. I have never disdained nor, I hope, abandoned the popular arts. Fired by this vision of how I might popularise some of my ideas, I began to consider Poldark's offer.

My enthusiasm for this was quickly replaced, however, by an altogether different diversion. Madge and I, availing ourselves of the festive confusion, were actually able to slip back into my bedroom where, to help her sustain her pleasure, I introduced her to the benefits of that much-maligned substance its original discoverers called *el nevada* and which has proved such a peculiarly apt servant to 20th-century Man. By the following afternoon we were both exhausted, having attempted almost every sexual variation possible for two athletic young people to enjoy in the confines of a small hotel room on a bed four feet by six. I loved the musty stink of a creamy dark skin which suggested that long ago there had been a lick of the tar brush in Madge's family. It has been my experience that women of the octoroon or mulatto persuasion make the most passionate lovers, particularly if there is also Jewish blood in the mixture. One need hardly speculate as to why Moorish women are still very highly prized in the harems of North Africa and the Middle East, but I will come to that later. (It was Madge, needless to say, who first raised the notion of extending our number to three.)

I told Madge to report for work the next day. I would rest and prepare further notes for the proposed script. She said that she would have to come in the late morning rather than the afternoon as she had an appointment at four, an audition for a movie at last. I wished her luck but warned her not to get too involved with the idea. For every hundred girls in Hollywood perhaps one or two ever got legitimate movie work.

Informing me that she, better than anyone, knew how to keep her head screwed on, my spirited little floozy kissed me on the nose and left. Half-an-hour later the telephone rang. The concierge told me a young lady had arrived and was asking for me. Conscious of the exaggerated morality of the place, I told him I would come down to the lobby. Doubtless Madge had forgotten to clarify something and since she had no easy access to a telephone she had simply turned in her tracks and come back. I dressed quickly, aware that while I did not look at my best, neither did Madge, and descended yielding Turkey and red plush to the lobby where, all in white, like the angel I knew her to be, her hair in a fashionable bob so that anyone might easily have mistaken her for Ruth Taylor, my darling had come to me at last! With joy I advanced towards her and then, conscious of my lack of sleep, I paused. 'Esmé?'

If I needed confirmation her wonderful, trilling laugh filled the great lobby. 'Maxim! Now it is Emily Dane. Like you, I am at last an American.' She opened her arms to embrace me. Though this was what I had longed for, again I hesitated. I could smell the stink of the past sixteen hours on my body. Madge's perfume was still in my moustache. 'I am filthy,' I said. 'I have been working all night. Sit here and let me get clean. I can be back in fifteen minutes.'

'But Maxim, I only *have* fifteen minutes! The car is waiting.' She made a gesture of desperate, apologetic impatience.

'The car?' Stupefied, I gaped at this vision of my bride-to-be. Here at last in the flesh was the child I had rescued from the most vicious slums of Istanbul. My boyhood sweetheart, she had been fucked so much there were calluses on her cunt but this reincarnated Esmé was Esmé purified, my own sweet little angel, my little sister, my restored betrothed! And she said she was leaving? 'Where are you going?'

'I have to meet Willie. It's so awful. He's, you know, moody. I've been *longing* to see you. This is the first chance

I've had, my darling!' She writhed with helpless desires. I began to reach towards her, then halted the gesture.

'You forgive me?' Tears were starting in my eyes. I held them back.

'For what?' she said. 'Kolya explained you had to do what you did. And when you weren't at the ship, I simply assumed you were still in hiding and would contact me in Los Angeles. Willie was so kind. He had a train of his own which was going to the Coast from Chicago and offered me a lift. Now he's putting me up. Well, you know how it is, darling. I have to be diplomatic. But here we are, together at last anyway, no harm done. There's a strong chance I'll have a part in a picture soon! Won't you be proud of me?'

'I'm already proud of you, my angel. I have so much to tell you, to explain. I am probably going to be working for the movies myself.'

'Oh, darling! You're already a film-star!'

'Not exactly. I shall probably be directing the film I am currently writing. As to an acting rôle, well I have certainly had the experience. We shall see.'

'I have read all your letters and your little notes and everything, Maxim.' She was a distant bloom, a dream of heaven in white flowered silk and fur, her little heart-shaped face framed by a sculpted helmet of newly blonde hair, her blue eyes glowing dark against all that fairness. I had never seen her so beautiful, even on that first occasion when I had suddenly noticed her, my resurrected muse, at *La Rotonde*. *Ma soeur! Meyn shvester! Moja rozy! Dans la Grande Rue, lallah . . . Hiya maride. Ma anish råyih . . . Qul bi'l'haqq, ma tikdibsh! Awhashtena! Awhashtena! Samotny, Esmé. Samotny!* So lonely, Esmé. So lonely. Oh, I have longed for you down all those empty ages. They took you, my muse, my ideal, my reason for living, and they made a whore of you. Was it not a sign, I now wonder, of God's eternal grace, that you should come back to me, time after time, as if in confirmation that real beauty, real love, real altruism, is imperishable, no matter to what depths we think the world has sunk and that these imperishable values should never be rejected or forgotten? And here you were, speaking rapidly of Meulemkaumpf's kindness, and your situation in which you were now somewhat compromised, not having told Meulemkaumpf every exact detail of your story. 'He thinks my brother was to meet me and was probably killed in the gangster-fights.'

How could I blame her for a white lie or two? I had told them myself, in exactly similar circumstances, and while they rarely do any harm, they can sometimes prove a shade embarrassing or produce unexpected complications, which is why I long since gave them up. 'When can you get away to see me?' I asked.

'Very soon. We're going north for a couple of days, to visit Hearst at his ranch, and should be back by the end of the week. Maybe you could speak to someone about a part for me?' This last was begged with that disarming, humorous sweetness I could never forget. 'Of course. But we must talk more soon.' Even though her innocent mention of Hearst had produced an unwelcome *frisson*, I was far more terrified that she should leave me again and we should be parted for another eternity! I drank in her beauty. She had hardly changed. Rather more sophisticated than when I had last seen her, of course, because in Paris she had begun to learn the manners and demeanour of a well-bred lady and doubtless Kolya and his wife had helped her. Her marvellous poise could rival Theda Bara's. I mentioned that Mrs Cornelius was now making a great success of her movie career and Esmé murmured a remark in Turkish which I did not catch. Nor was there time for her to repeat it. She dropped her voice and asked in French if I had some '*neige*' I might spare her. She had run out and Willie Meulemkaumpf was disapproving of both drugs and alcohol, so was no help. 'It's what he and Hearst have in common apart from their millions.' I was glad merely to be of service to my sweetheart.

The drug had already become a bond, a way of remaining in touch until such time as she was able to save Meulemkaumpf's feelings and return to me. I had heard it was possible to get married in Nevada without producing too much in the way of identity papers and tried to communicate all this to her as I returned with the little paper packet and pressed it into her warm, childish hand. How extraordinarily beautiful she was!

Louise Brooks was to model herself on my Esmé and make a fortune in Germany. But that, as I know too well, is the price one pays for being ahead of one's time. Not only do you receive no credit, but you rarely receive the kind of money made by your imitators. And then I moved to kiss her, but thought better of it. In an explosion of silver, she had sped to the waiting Mercedes, flung herself into the cavernous upholstery and waved her negro chauffeur on, for all the world as if instructing a coachman to whip up his horses.

Only when she had disappeared did it come to me that her uniformed driver was also familiar. It had been none other than Jacob Mix himself. Perhaps I had him to thank for Esmé's change of mood?

Me duele. Tengo hambre. Me duele. Me duele.

FIVE

I AM NOT ESPECIALLY PROUD of the ways in which I earned my living in 1925. There was little honour in it. Yet I do not think I knew a time since my childhood when I felt more light-hearted or thoroughly fulfilled. Spending so much of the year in a state of near-perfect euphoria, I almost forgot I was born to suffer for science and humanity, destined to build my great flying cities, not create the baroque palaces and Gothick villages, mediaeval castles and Futurist ballrooms that Fantasy demanded. Yet, during that year in Hollywood it seemed possible to realise every single dream I had ever entertained and to do so easily. I could have been happy there and lived out my life there, with Esmé, my wife, my children; an honoured illusionist as famous as Walt Disney or von Stroheim and probably richer. With his wealth 'Uncle Dizzy' created a Land populated by his petit-bourgeois dreams of a prosaic future. I should have built Pyatnitskiland! Each part of my world would have demonstrated an invention of my own – the solid-hulled, turbo-powered aerial cruiser, the Atlantic aeroplane refuelling platforms, the radio oven, the space-rocket, the radio satellite relay, the desert liner, the television, the dynamite engine and the super-rapid ocean-clipper – and would have realised my greatest vision. Uncle Dizzy and Uncle Joe had that dream in common: they longed for a world populated entirely by programmable robots. Ultimate predictability as a guard against death. However, I dreamed of ultimate freedom. My great cities of the skies would at last release humanity forever from its chains, from the sucking hampering mud of its origins. Almost single-handedly I could have built a glorious future, transforming the planet in a thousand ways, harnessing all the bountiful resources of the American continent. There would have been no Second World War, no triumph of Bolshevism. Indeed, Bolshevism would have crumbled under the weight of its own delusions. Russia and America would have formed a noble alliance, a united Christian nation. I should have been content to have been recognised merely as the architect of all this. I have never desired political power, certainly not for its own sake. But circumstances would alter my life radically. Another future would be built: its proudest achievements a man-sized, incoherent duck and a monstrous mechanical ape.

This god is Set, who is also Sekhet, the goddess. Sekhet is called 'the Eye of Ra' and is the instrument of mankind's destruction.

Sometimes I go to the Polish Club in Exhibition Road, just up from the Science Museum. It is still possible to get a good, cheap meal there and meet a few like-minded souls. They know I am not really Polish, but are prepared to turn a blind eye. They recognise suffering. All Slavs are welcome. The rooms of the club are tall and cool, even in summer, and there is a garden. I once took Mrs Cornelius with me as my guest. Nobody was rude to her. That cannot be said for everywhere one goes in London today. She found the atmosphere a little depressing, I think.

She still lives for the present. Though she is proud of her past and enjoys her memories she does not dwell on them. I became too morbid at the club, she said. I explained the difference between the spiritual contemplation of history and mere self-pity but she did not really listen. She, too, has had excessive pain in her life. Perhaps she, like me, cannot afford to dwell overmuch on certain aspects of the past. But she enjoys our reminiscences. Sometimes we sit together in her flat in Colville Terrace and talk. If the sound of the steel bands rehearsing and the prostitutes quarrelling with their pimps is not too loud we often continue well into the night. Mrs Cornelius recalls her successes, the times when she was a great star of the stage as well as the screen, but she has kept relatively little personal memorabilia. She reminds me of my own fame. Indeed, I have more recorded about her in my scrapbooks than I have of myself. She enjoys leafing through these glue-crusted heavy pages, screaming with laughter at her make-up, her dresses, her more outrageous stage-names. I suppose it is healthy, this response, but I find it a little disconcerting. My friend puts too little value on her talents. Always, she has done this. That is why I want to tell the world what she was. My own future was stolen from me but she, careless goddess that she was, threw hers away as casually as she tossed a cigarette over a ship's rail. Yet she has never said she regretted it. Her regrets are of a different order, usually concerning some gentleman she failed to attract for a night's passing pleasure. She has been loved by some of the greatest men in modern history, been the mistress of the most influential financiers and politicians, and if she were not discreet, she could fill the tabloids daily with her memories. Yet she seems to have little respect or nostalgia for them. 'Blokes're fer yer 'olidays, like icecream and drinkin' yerself silly. Too much of 'em and it makes yer sick.' She has as much and as little to say about the Persian playboy who first took her out of Whitechapel and abandoned her in Odessa as she does about Trotsky, whose paramour she became. 'They corl it I-ran now, an' well named it is, too. 'Oo fuckin' wouldn't run if they 'ad the chance? But 'e 'ad some fuckin' gelt, the bastard. An' 'e never whinged on like Leo, 'oo couldn't bloody stop. Especially after 'e got ter France. Remember Cassis, Ivan?'

E partito il treno? C'é tempo per scendere? Attraversiamo la frontiera? She was no *yachna*. And I live because of her. She is, I say, the actual keeper of my life. She laughs when I try to explain. She slaps my shoulder and calls me her sentimental little Russki. She has always been my friend.

We travelled towards Fastov through avenues of lime trees with a red flag flying from the mast of our Mercedes. She smelled of summer, of the roses, though she was wrapped in the finest fur. Later, you could inhale the bloody stink of dead horses piled into ditches by the side of the road and sometimes

73

there were festering human corpses among them, those poor ignorant followers of Petlyura. He said he would give them land, but he was a friend of the rich. He gave them snow. His promises were insubstantial and melted away with the spring sunshine. If he had listened, if he had genuinely loved our Ukraine, as I loved her, I would have saved him so easily! He abandoned my Violet Ray. They were all greedy for our wheat and steel, those Moscow Jews. They are greedy still. But she says I am morbid and lets me talk only of the good times, the best of which were in Hollywood when I became a prince, a star, a man of substance and influence to rival all the other great aristocrats of Hollywood whom I admired, especially Griffith. Once I was his peer I invited the great director to my home, but even then he had become reclusive and suspicious. I should have taken a lesson from him. You are a king in Hollywood only while your work is popular, while you obey the studio's power. Take some action in the name of art, idealism or even social conscience and make money and you are still celebrated for your virtues. But follow your conscience and *fail to make money* and you are destroyed overnight. You become a villain. This was the bitter truth Griffith had learned. But I was happy, perhaps because the future faded and the past became less painful, no more than a record of my triumphs. I learned from the great myth-makers of Hollywood how to present my *curriculum vitae* in the best and most dramatic light. Tom Mix was from Peoria and Greta Garbo from Detroit, but the world was told otherwise, not because they were liars but because they knew this was the only means by which they could maintain their authority with the public and, ultimately, the studio. But the studio, of course, could create other, less beneficial myths if it felt so disposed, so one always had to be a myth or two ahead of them. I had accounts in stores. I had my car. I had my little house in Venice. I had admirers. My social standing rose so high that I was sought after at dinner-parties. Frequently I attended these with Mrs Cornelius, also a star, and occasionally I saw my Esmé!

My success had come about largely through good fortune, through my natural gregariousness and through a certain talent for acting, part of which had been developed during my periods of hardship and captivity and which was, since one was so frequently in the power of those who did not speak your language, highly dependent on mime. By early 1925, while on the set assisting Poldark, I had been 'roped in' for *Ben Hur* both as a galley slave and as a Christian. This led to me serving for a while as a stand-in. There are parts of *The Dark Angel*, *Beau Geste*, *The Master Singer* and *Tricks* which owe their special vibrancy to the fact that my back and half-face were used in place of a star too drunk, drugged or hung-over to perform as his public expected. I was already appearing in small parts by April 1925 when Goldfish had returned and commissioned a draft script of *White King, Red Queen* with a view to putting me on the strength. I visited him at the new offices which he shared with Cecil B. De Mille – a great white marble 'colonial' mansion which stood on Washington Boulevard not far from MGM and was, by coincidence, the old Thomas Ince Studio, sold to settle the dead director's debts. He was in a fatherly mood. 'Pleasure is pleasure and business is business.' He spoke the idiomatic Yiddish of the Warsaw gutter. 'You've got to divide up professional and amateur. I used to be taught the rule – the amateur you screw, the professional you hire. Me, I preferred to screw the professionals and let the others waste their time with amateurs. Two birds in one bath. You are not, I believe, whatever else, an amateur, Max, I hope.'

I assured him I was a pro's pro of the old school.

'Anyway I thought that was a better use of the time and time was money. Now, I've learned moderation. I *married* an amateur and now I don't have to screw the professionals!'

I found Goldfish's confidences both baffling and irresistible.

'As a man of the world, Max, you know what I mean?'

I assured him I understood him most profoundly. His sentiments, I said, were an exact version, almost word for word, of my own. Only he had phrased it better. I congratulated him on his extraordinary literary turn of phrase. He said in all modesty that he was, by and large, a self-made man. 'Reading is the answer. Travel, like I did, in gloves, and you get to reading a lot. And seeing movies, of course. Bit by bit you understand how ignorant you are. Bit by bit you start to remedy it. That's me now, Max – remedied. Though they stole every idea, every

75

property, every star and every hour of every hard-working day I put in for them – Art for Art's sake remedied me. Quality, now, is what we do here. Small but prodigious, like in gloves. That way you make more profit for less work, believe me.'

I not only believed him, I said, I applauded him. We parted very cordially.

Mrs C. was Gloria Cornish now, of course, and in some ways the instrument of my success (or diversion, if you like). While Goldfish had been impressed by my writing and had commissioned a draft script with a view to 'putting me on the strength', it was Lon Chaney, the great character actor, who saw my drawings one evening and suggested immediately that I should be designing whole storyboards. I had until then been working as a part-time apprentice to Poldark. Chaney introduced me to a pleasant Scot called Menzies, a student of the great Grot, who was primarily known for his delicate children's illustrations. Menzies was at that time trying to work with Valentino's wife, who claimed to be some sort of Russian aristocrat, a painter, stage-decorator and *haute couturière* whose ideas were so extravagant that even when the sets were built they could hardly be filmed. The colour of the sets was important, since they tended to show up in certain pronounced ways. In her designs for *Monsieur Beaucaire* she had ignored all considerations of cost or technical capability and produced Valentino's first failure. The sophisticated comedy was scarcely appropriate material for that elevated lounge-lizard, who looked exactly like the Italian gigolo he had been in real life and whose taste and manners continued to reflect his origins. Later Bob Hope far eclipsed him in the rôle. Some of us Hollywooders were able to rise above our humble beginnings. Valentino sank beneath the weight of his own unfounded self-esteem. *Mayn schvitz der spic gonif trenken!*

My natural skill as a draughtsman, the basics of which I had come by, of course, at the St Petersburg Polytechnic Institute, impressed Menzies. He said I had the kind of imagination that was best suited for movie work. I thought big, he said, but more importantly I produced designs which could be built and used. He was a great believer in the fluid camera and while he admired his master, Grot, he felt that Grot's particular talent produced a beautifully static set. It was from Menzies that I learned most about designing for the films.

When I heard he was out at Korda's studios during the War I tried to contact him. He was not very far from where I was living in Hammersmith at the time but even though I explained I was calling from a pay box at enormous cost I could not get anyone to bring him to the telephone. He was a fellow spirit. In the late thirties he would be the guiding hand behind a picture that came closer to the spirit of Griffith's *Birth of a Nation* than anything I have ever seen.

The title was not to my taste and the thing was spoiled a little by the inclusion of that insipid *halbjuden* 'Howard' with his dyed blond hair, but *Gone With the Wind* was a wonder to me when I saw it at the Kilburn State soon after arriving in England in 1940. In its silent predecessor Gloria Cornish played the part of Nellie and now another Englishwoman, Vivien Leigh, reminded me so much of my Esmé, and yet she also had the determination of Mrs Cornelius. Of course, Clark Gable was magnificent. A flyer, in real life, like myself. With Fairbanks (and myself) he represented the American virtues of manly courage and rugged good-humoured honesty. Now save for John Wayne such virtues have all but disappeared from the screen. I remember Goering, also a flying man, in that jocular but at the same time deeply serious way of his, saying, 'What *are* we going to do about America?' This, I need hardly say, was at a time when Hitler had not been goaded into war by those interests most resistant to his ideals. *Wohin gehen wir jetzt?* I could have told him then.

At first Menzies gave me a few individual scenes to develop for Schenk's comedy *Her Sister From Paris* with Constance Talmadge and Ronald Colman. This did not require any great imaginative efforts, especially for the scenes Menzies entrusted to me, but it got me work on *The Eagle*, Valentino's next film, in which we could indulge our lavish fantasies. We designed and built some of the screen's most gorgeous sets.

They were romantic, extravagant (though not especially costly) and were the very spirit of everything I had ever demanded from the moving picture play. Unfortunately, although our designs were made and used, the script was lightweight and the film was not a particular success. I can, incidentally, be identified in several scenes as Valentino's stand-in. Valentino chose to blame me for his failure, since the studio had refused to let his ludicrous spouse work on another picture. Not wishing to make an overt enemy of the more powerful Menzies, she took against me. Menzies however proved a good friend and by then every studio in Hollywood knew what Valentino and the pseudo-aristocrat were like. I did not, in the end, work with Menzies on the remaining Valentino picture, but he did give me scenes for *Graustark* and *What Price Beauty?* in which Mrs Cornelius had an important rôle but in which my only featured scene was cut. Gradually I grew to love my new medium. I became familiar with every creative and practical function. I built palaces, monuments, whole cities, I even populated them – sometimes as hero, sometimes as villain – and, for a while at least, my genius was satisfied. Lon Chaney became my patron – possibly because I did not condescend to him as some of the parvenu star-lings did. He had been a professional most of his life, which had not been an easy one, and like me had begun his career as a travelling player. Perhaps he recognised in me some version of his younger self. Whatever it was, he took me in hand and for a while was my guiding light through the hazardous maze of Hollywood. Though he himself nursed an abiding love for a legless married woman and was frequently in despair, he yet found time to advise me on matters of etiquette, on brothels and their inmates, on drinks and their various properties. While he did not introduce me to the pleasures of opium and hashish, then undergoing a small vogue with the fad for things Oriental freshly stimulated by the discovery of the treasures of Tutenkhamun, he had excellent advice about the properties of the drugs and the character of those who dealt in them. Together we toured Chinatown. Menzies enjoyed such drugs. With their help he created two of the most memorable Arabian Nights fantasies ever seen by an awed public. One was for Fairbanks, the other for Korda. Both were called *The Thief of Baghdad*. (The nickname was enjoyed by Samuel Goldfish for a while, though he was not of Mesopotamian Jewish origin. Neither Goldwyn nor Goldfish is an Iraqi name!) Though

Chaney advised me to stay away from such people, to sign a contract with one of the smaller studios and got me a screen-test with DeLuxe, there was hardly time to think. I was being given design and acting jobs as fast as I could say 'yes'. It would have been foolish to say 'no' since there was no telling when it might not suddenly end. As a freelance I was frequently paid in cash. But a studio contract, as an actor and director, would bring me all kinds of security and that was, after all, what Esmé so keenly desired. It offered decent security and steady weekly money. I would accept it. Meanwhile I was saving my dollars. I had them in the Bank of Southern California earning 11 per cent interest. I was becoming for the first time in my life a citizen of material substance and responsibility. Increasingly I had the company of Esmé whenever she could get away from G. W. Meulemkaumpf, who had become her official sponsor in the US, and could withdraw his patronage if he discovered she was already engaged. While I understood the difficulties of her position the situation remained painful, even with the resourceful Jacob Mix as a reliable intermediary. In my worst moments I remembered that she was after all virtually my own creation. Had she not been Esmé Loukianoff's half-sister, she would still be in Galata contracting diseases and earning pennies from a hundred nations' sailors.

Sometimes, when she proved particularly whimsical or took Meulemkaumpf's part too enthusiastically, I was tempted to remind her that if I had not found her she would bear a close resemblance by now to her hideous witch of a mother. But that would have been unfair. I loved her, after all, with a love above self, nation or even, sometimes (I will admit), duty. And my love translated itself into intense passion during our brief times together. Sometimes my love was so overwhelming I made her laugh.

My capacity to love impressed the usually cynical Mrs Cornelius. She doubted in all her life she'd seen a man make more of a fool of himself over a woman, particularly a bloke who was doing so well. It was not in my nature, I explained, to hurt my little girl. She would have no reminders of her origins from me. To raise such questions would be to threaten that delicate and most precious illusion of all: of my

Esmé (who gave satisfaction to anarchist Cossacks) reborn (virgin once more) in the slums of Constantinople. I am not an idiot. *¿Cuanto se tarda?* I can tell truth from fiction. I'll be seeing you in every lovely summer's day in everything that's light and shade. I'll be looking at the sun but I'll be seeing you. *¿Es viu? No, és mort. ¡Era blanca com la neu! Si hi ha errores els corregiré. Elmelikeh betahti! Elmelikeh betahti!* Oh, how I loved them. I lived to make them immortal. I did not become a *Musselman*. That wire, those pits, were not for me. Mistakes, however, are rarely rectified under such conditions. The Germans worshipped bureaucracy as if it were the ultimate reality. Did Nietzsche teach them nothing? I kept my identity. I am not ashamed of anything. Let them call me *golem*. At least I am a self-made *golem*. *Ayn ferbissener goylem*. And what does it mean in the end? Must every town in Germany called Büchenwald bear the burden of one such place?

Paid as a freelance by Menzies to fill in jobs for him or to design specific sets, I was like some apprentice to Raphael except that I suspect I was better rewarded for my unacknowledged labours. Menzies was scrupulously fair. I was able to move a little more freely than most Hollywood employees. The so-called 'Studio System' had not yet taken complete hold of the industry and designers at least could still work for different producers, though there was a tendency to stay with one company. I enjoyed producing the sets for Browning's *The Show*, which I got not through Menzies but through Chaney, who was a friend of Browning. Even Goldfish did not know I was working for him. The producing studio was the recently formed MGM, now Goldfish's most hated rival. By a rare coincidence this was also one of the few films starring Mrs Cornelius that I was closely involved in; she appeared under another name with John Gilbert and Lionel Barrymore. 'Renée Adorée' remains to this day a mysterious and under-rated actress.

As Gloria Cornish Mrs Cornelius played second lead to Clive Brook and Greta Nissen in a Paramount picture called *The Popular Sin* and then her Swedish director took her back to Universal. In a very short time they made a series of sophisticated modern dramas. While she was not always top of the bill, Gloria Cornish became identified with the stylish, highly refined school of acting then being promoted on the London stage in the persons of Noël Coward and Gertrude Lawrence. She was a WAMPUS Baby Star with Joan Crawford. She received considerable critical acclaim for *Fifth Avenue Models*, *Peacock Feathers*, *Woman Chasin'*, *Watch Your Wife*, *The Woman Who Did*, *The Blonde Saint*, *Carmen Valdéz*, *She Who Stoops* and *Into Her Kingdom*, while I too began at last to have some small successes in my own right, at first under the name of Max Peters. This change was Chaney's doing, while he insisted I appear in *The Phantom of the Opera*, which I also helped design, working with the great Ben Carré and a good-natured man called Danny Hall, who would one day be famous for his work on *City Lights* and *All-American Co-Ed*. Chaney had made friends with him on *The Hunchback of Notre Dame* and the three of us became bosom buddies for a while, visiting restaurants and nightclubs together and enjoying the pleasures of the town as best hard-working people could. I had begun to work at night with my designs while performing on screen during the days. I have always been granted plenty of energy and the wonderdrug which Freud and Trotsky succumbed to, through inherent weakness of character, has always been a friend to me. Thus I was able to satisfy my darling whenever the opportunity arose and continue to fulfil my duties. Madge, unfortunately, had to be dispensed with. She became unreasonably jealous, more and more dependent on drugs and given to outbursts of pointless rage, perhaps because she was threatened by my association with DeLuxe, perhaps because my fortunes steadily improved and I was obviously destined to be one of Hollywood's favoured. For a time I managed to see something of my former secretary to sustain her interest with increasingly outré sexual encounters, and attempted to keep her working for me, but she demanded too much. I regret that one night, after I had exhausted myself at Fox all day on a particularly unpleasant horse as Dirk Collingham in Buck Jones's *Lone Star Breed*, I told her I no longer wished to use her services. I had been offered $95.00 a week contract with DeLuxe, to star in a new serial idea they had, but saw no point in rubbing salt in her various wounds. Lon Chaney's friend Sol Lessor had liked what he had seen and was, he said, 'ready to work'. No older than me, Lessor was one of those ambitious young producers involving himself in a dozen ideas at once. DeLuxe was not his only company. We became friendly in the fifties again when he was over here with RKO making Tarzan movies. He was always generous with his expenses. Madge might not have gone at all but for Chaney and Hall dropping round to suggest a visit to a particularly good cabaret. She threw the hundred dollars I had given her onto the Axminster and stepped through the front door as if she had accidentally walked into a trench of dog-droppings. This caused some hilarity from my friends who enjoyed speculating on why she was so furious. I took this fun in good part, but I was sorry our relationship ended on such an unpleasant note. Madge had been a great comfort and distraction in the times when Esmé was indisposed. Her anger was, as I said, simply jealousy, but then ironically she was beginning to do somewhat better in the acting profession than Esmé. My darling had yet to find a director or a photographer who could capture what was essentially a subtle and sometimes transient beauty. Mrs Cornelius, far from ethereal in real life, was one of those lucky women who could convey enormous presence on the screen while appearing completely casual and insouciant, perfect for the parts her 'Seaman' (as Sjöström now styled himself) had in mind for her.

This failure to inspire enthusiasm in directors was Esmé's constant disappointment and I still had nothing like the influence needed to force some studio boss to acknowledge her talent. In all honesty I did not think screen-acting was the right occupation for my darling, who was far too sensitive for such a life. Much as I loved her I found her thirst for the limelight a trifle disconcerting since I knew she had no way of controlling that fame once she had it and her real inclinations were those of a homeloving little girl who wanted nothing more than to look after her adored husband, her 'dadda' as she sometimes called me, and to iron my shirts. For a while she even tried to make me jealous by hinting that the Jew 'Chaplin', well known for definitively paedophiliac inclinations, was interested in her. But every girl Chaplin favoured appeared in his films and Esmé was never offered a contract. Arbuckle died a dishonoured martyr while his ambitious rivals went on to greater and greater triumphs. I personally had no liking for the little communist. He never made me laugh. I told him so to his face one night, at a party of Norma Talmadge's. He remarked that he didn't mind a bit. 'As a matter of fact I don't find you very funny, either,' was his nonsensical retort. I am not, after all, the comedian! Some *mensch*! Such *mishegass*! What can one make of such people?

With my DeLuxe contract signed and sealed I lived a life of gorgeous variety, surrounded by every kind of beauty, enjoying every type of pleasure. At MGM and Paramount marvellous cities were created in a matter of days; whole countries were born out of my brain and my hands, as if I, myself, had been blessed with the gifts of the great Thief, merely to rub a brass bottle and unleash limitless power, to have a thousand slaves at my disposal, a million warriors to command! The most beautiful women in the world, wearing exotically elegant clothing, the costumes of a score of centuries, graced my invented universe and more than one of them found me attractive. In my first featured screen rôles with Fox it had been my destiny forever to threaten and never to be fulfilled in my designs upon the female sex, but off-screen it was a rather different story. Those Hollywood girls were perverse. For a night or two at least they found my screen rôle attractive; they wanted me to be the heartless creature whom Buck Jones or Hoot Gibson gunned down in the last reel and, since they desired it, I was sometimes willing to please them. This 'Valentino-craze' was a welcome relief, I'll readily admit, from a somewhat paternal rôle with my little fiancée. Now I see how my life was beginning to resemble Faust's after Mephistopheles became his servant. More than one of my parties might have been the original for the Walpurgisnacht revels. So many stimulants and narcotics were involved that I have only the haziest memories of soft flesh, of wild hair, of sweat, of jewellery and a confusion of discarded silk. I was being given everything I had ever desired and more. I was only twenty-five years old. How could I know that I was so close to falling into the Devil's power? Satan was even then gaining the ascendancy which, by the 30s, was to make Hollywood little more than a propaganda tool of socialist Jewry. Ah, Goethe, what a message you still have for all of us!

On May 5, 1925, I began my first starring rôle with DeLuxe in the serial *White Aces* which ostensibly featured Buddy Brown as the daring young English Ace but it was Max Peters as his friend Count Topolski, the daring Russian flyer, who stole the first episode so that by the fifth reel, 'Spies from the Skies', 'Ace' Peters was sharing equal billing. In those days the one-reel serial was often used to fill ten or fifteen minutes' space while the other projector was set up for the main feature, so a serial star was as well known to the public as Valentino or Swanson. Very soon my salary came to one hundred and ten a week and I was again a flyer for ten episodes of *The Air Knights*, leading my squadron of gentlemen volunteers against the German hordes and then, in *Send for the Air Knights*, fifteen chapters of equally hazardous derring-do against the new enemies of America, foreign business interests and their criminal stooges. This was followed by some three-reelers, *Ace of the Aces*, *Aces Up*, *Aces and Kings* and others, in which I played a flyer with all the authority of an expert. Because of my value to the studio, it was left to others to do the flying (much of which was borrowed footage, to save money) though I, of course, appeared in the cockpit while the dogfights and so on were projected onto a screen behind me, giving a wonderful illusion of reality. But it was my first starring Western part, where I took to the saddle as *The Masked Buckaroo* in a hugely successful ten-chapter programmer, which had the public calling for more *Masked Buckaroo*s, that made my half-hidden face more famous than La Roque's or Cooper's! Lessor seemed to be having trouble with colleagues at MGM suspecting him of 'moonlighting' and wanted to make, he said, the most of our roll. We began to shoot two or three reels a day – completing a serial in less than a working week! These were heady times! What was more, Goldfish sent word that he liked my script but felt someone a little more conversant with English should, as it were, polish it up. He offered me a further $1000, which I decided to accept, which is how *Red Queen and White Knight* came to appear some while later as *Mockery* with Ricardo Cortez, Barbara Bedford and, at my suggestion, Lon

Chaney in the starring parts. I still have the cuttings about it from a magazine I found a few years ago when I was dealing in general second-hand goods. *The Picturegoer* described my film as an important story for our times and thought Chaney gave one of his most touching performances as Sergei the Harelip, a peasant with intelligence and spirit, who loves the heroine from afar and eventually dies defending her honour from the Red Army. *Photoplay Magazine* found the suspense 'marvellously sustained'. I always felt a little betrayed that in the end 'Walter Seaman' claimed most of the story. But by that time I suppose he had learned from Goldfish the art of crediting himself with the work of others! I have never seen the film, in spite of writing many times to the BBC and the National Film Theatre. They went so far as to claim that the picture never existed, though I sent them copies of the cuttings. They told me that there was only a limited audience for the silent films. This, at least, I could believe. The taste of the public has been thoroughly corrupted since the Levant established its home-away-from-home in Hollywood. I am grateful for having experienced a little of the Golden Age before Mephistopheles captured the city as the Turks captured Constantinople in 1493. Then the Jews had flooded in from Spain, having been banished by a triumphant Christian king and a Church determined to cauterise their country's diseased wounds and rid it forever of the corrupting influences of Hebrew and Moslem alike.

I saw a new Byzantium. I saw her rising from the seas where the nations of the world all meet. I saw her feasted upon by carrion, her stink carried on a foul wind from the East, her glories despised, her achievements forgotten, her meaning distorted. She was to have been the capital of Christendom, the seat of her wisdom. Her works would have brought light to the entire planet. Hollywood's power could have transformed the globe. I should have been one of her most influential architects. But I do not think I was destined for much happiness. Soon my life became full once more of unwelcome complications. What disgustingly small minds, what small ambitions, what miserable goals most people have! How they hate those who are prepared to risk a little more, to seek both the dangers and the rewards of life! How disappointed I have been to discover that even those I cared for and trusted were not only incapable of sharing my vision and my humanity, but actually feared it! By October 1925 I had become an established and respected figure in Hollywood. I was everything that city most admired. I had looks, success, brains, imagination and my own starring part in feature films. My success as *The Masked Buckaroo* was followed by four more serial stories, *The Masked Buckaroo's Return*, *Buckaroo's Code*, *Buckaroo Justice* and *The Masked Buckaroo at Devil's Jump*. These were snapped up by the distributor so that I was next given by DeLuxe the rôle of Captain Jack Cassidy – the Ace of Aces – in their 15-part *Ace Among Aces* (with Gloria Cornish!), then *The Sky Hawks*, and *Heaven's Hell-riders*. By now the showcards displayed the name with which I would become most famous. To Hollywood and the world I was 'Ace' Peters, The Sky Hawk. The studio made a great deal of my wartime flying career and my pioneering flights, but did not feel it was sensible to mention that most of this had occurred in my native Russia. Popular as I was in the rôle of flying ace, it was The Mysterious Vigilante – the young cowboy-turned-law-bringer Tex Reardon, in mask and chaps – whom the public most demanded. Within a few weeks I was back in *Lone Star Buckaroo*, *The Fighting Buckaroo* and *Buckaroo's Buddy*. Even when, one Monday morning, I turned up at 'Gower Gulch' with others to begin *Song of the Buckaroo* to find most of the studio dismantled, the office furniture gone and no sign of an executive anywhere, I was undismayed. We were, it seemed, only minutes ahead of the bailiff. With the director's help I was able to gather up and hide a good many canisters of film – in most of which I starred. These were smuggled to my car and from there to my home. I was not at that time especially upset. I had already planned to leave DeLuxe and find a better studio. As young Tex Reardon, sworn to bring justice to the West, I had attained great moral and artistic success – in spite of the fact that most of the time my lower face was covered by a bandanna. The enormous popularity of *The Masked Buckaroo* (based on the adventures by Earl G. Stafford in *All-Star Weekly* and *Munsey's*) made me a hero, frequently invited to open rodeos, which I was obliged to decline because the studio thought my accent was not Western enough. Now I had three careers: to MGM I was a set designer, to Goldfish a writer and to the public a major star! Yet so little interest did Hollywood's moguls take in one another, let alone the rest of us, that not one of them realised the truth! Many women found my features romantic, they said I was a more refined Valentino. Some were prepared to fight for my favours.

As usual women were to cause a downturn in my fortunes but in retrospect perhaps I should thank them, even 'Vivienne Prentiss', who was perhaps the initiator of my discomfort. Looking back in the light of reason I know I would not have survived the advent of the Talkers, an idea which, ironically, I had myself suggested to an uninterested Goldfish earlier that year. To those peasants any foreigner was a Jew and I had already been insulted as *The Masked Bucka-Jew* and, *The Heebe Who-Flew*, not to mention more obscene concoctions, so I need explain to no one how my natural voice would be received and perhaps for this reason, too, Goldfish – happiest in Yiddish – took to me. But I would not have volunteered for my future. Towards the end of 1925 a number of events combined to decide my destiny. The discoveries of Tutenkhamun had led to a wave of story projects set in ancient Egypt, most of which were merely the vehicle for a sex-object and which were of doubtful authenticity. I remember seeing *The Queen of Sheba* with Fritz Leiber and Betty Blythe, who was supposed to be the new Theda Bara, and thinking how ludicrously bad it was. Leiber's Solomon was clean-shaven and the costumes the invention of an incompetent design department. Columns bore pictograms which were not even vaguely Egyptianate but derived from Norse and Irish myths! Yet the thing was a great success. There was a plethora of what were called in the trade 'Sheikh movies' following the popularity of Valentino's paean to miscegenation (which must have done untold harm). We had *East of Suez*, *Desert Dust*, *Her Favourite Camel*, *Queen of the Pyramids*, *When the Desert Calls*, *Feisal*, *Silk and Sand*, *Carstairs of the Camel Corps*, *Burning Gold*, *Passion's Oasis*, and hundreds more. They were not merely Hollywood productions but from every other country where films were made. Yet there had not been a good picture set in the time of the

Pharaohs, unless one counted certain of De Mille's Biblical subjects. I mentioned this casually to Seaman one day and he became unusually enthusiastic. It seemed he was bored with the flood of sophisticated comedies he had directed and wanted to do something more substantial, an epic. In those days the successful epic was what a director's reputation finally rested upon. Though no Griffith, he had already seen some of the exhibits brought back from Egypt by Carter and Carnarvon and testified to their beauty. He was gloomily fascinated, too, by a curse which had taken the lives of several members of the expedition and their associates. Carnarvon had been struck down almost as soon as the Tomb was opened and his dog, who had also been there, fell dead mysteriously. Bethell, his secretary, died in peculiar circumstances. Westbury killed himself. Carter's partner, Mace, died just as he was about to X-ray a mummy. Then Carnarvon's wife and his two brothers died and Arthur Weigall died of fever. That same night we sketched out an idea for an ambitious story set partly in Ancient Egypt and partly in the present, concerning a love-story between a Queen and her High Priest and a passion so powerful it would last two thousand years. We would work in the idea of the cursed tomb, the consequences of disturbing the dead, and we would call it *Tutenkhamun's Queen*. I was already visualising the magnificent sets I could build, the lavish costumes and the gorgeous interiors we could make. I do not remember now whether it was Seaman or myself who conceived the notion of setting our story against the authentic landscapes of Luxor, the Valley of the Kings and the Pyramids. I could see no reason against the idea. It made artistic sense. The light was, if anything, better than California's and, with the British in charge, there should be no working difficulties. Seaman grew enthusiastically determined to show the story to Goldfish, who was specialising only in epics. I thought no more of it except to hope that 'Walt' himself might be struck down by the Curse of Tutenkhamun. I resented his proprietorial attitudes towards 'his' star, my friend, who would always see her film career as a 'bit of a larf'. Mrs Cornelius took her luck, she said, as it came. She saw no point in trying to hang on to it. It should be enjoyed to the full while it was available. This is the simple philosophy which kept her sane and by which she survived.

Esmé continued to beg me to get her a part in one of my pictures and I promised I would try, not having the heart to tell her how I had been turned down by Colony, Monogram and Universal so far. These were lean times for actors. She said that Meulemkaumpf was growing 'moody' and suspicious and Mix confided that the sausage king had offered him a handsome bonus to spy on her and report her movements in detail. I did my best to find work for her through my continuing rôle as designer and writer, but was informed by everyone that pretty foreign girls were a dime a dozen in Hollywood. To get work they must have exceptional talent of some kind. I knew that this was not the whole truth of it, even if the footage of Esmé's several tests did not reveal my girl to be a natural actress. Things came to a head one afternoon, however. Esmé, dressed in her special frock, was squatting on the carpet and I had my trousers ready when we were interrupted by an urgent Jacob Mix rapping on the bedroom door and whispering as loudly as he dared that we were discovered. Then the flat vulgar tones of a Mid-Western industrialist all but drowned him. 'You're fired, Mix. And that floozy in there had better not trouble to come back either. I've cancelled her contract.'

I was never to meet Meulemkaumpf. By the time I pulled up my trousers and stormed into the living-room the tycoon had gone, driving one car and with the detective he had hired following in the other. Mix, still in his smart chauffeur's uniform, stood there grinning at me. 'Well, now, boss,' he said, 'it looks like you have yourself a couple of new dependants.'

'My clothes!' Esmé was in despair. 'How will I get my clothes?'

'Missy,' said Mr Mix with an expression of humorous sympathy on his broad, honest face, 'you've *got* your clothes. You're standing in them.'

With a deep sigh of resignation, my darling returned to our bed and did not rise for almost two days. The emotional shock had proven too much for her. The following morning I read in the *Los Angeles Times* that Mucker Hever was back from

Europe where he had married an Austrian aristocrat and had bought himself a house near Versailles. By the Wednesday of the next week I received a call at MGM, where I was working on the *Beverly of Graustark* sets, designed as a Marion Davies vehicle, and Hever's familiar, faltering voice, no longer friendly, asked me to meet him at his office the following morning. I told him that I would be busy until the afternoon (when I had a further screen-test with First National). He said that three o'clock would suit him. Believing that he had seen the stupidity of cutting off his nose to hurt his face and that he wanted to resurrect our steam car, and in spite of being told by First that nobody needed 'a Russian cowboy', I was in good spirits when I called on Hever.

He had lost weight but he wore the same suits. They made him look like an elephant with a wasting disease. His lugubrious eyes regarded me across the familiar desk with what I mistook for a knowing amiability. He told me that he had been in Paris, that he had met some acquaintances of mine. Grinning, he opened a folder and showed me a series of press cuttings concerning my ill-fated airship venture. I was viciously and untruthfully characterised by the French newspapers as a rogue, a confidence man, a cheat. I dismissed the reports. 'My friend Esmé Loukianoff will tell you that they are lies. And Count Nikolai Petroff can also vouch for me.'

'Petroff? He's as crooked as you are.'

Then my friend's name, too, was now blackened! 'The allegations were part of a plot. They were always nonsense.'

'As nonsensical as my involvement with the Ku Klux Klan?' He planned to blackmail me! But what did he want? 'You and your fancy woman suckered me good, Max, I'll say that. But I won't let you do it to anyone else in this town.'

I was astonished by the man's pettiness, and said so. It was not I, after all, who had taken up with a Swede.

'I'm giving you a month,' he said. 'And if you and your damned accomplice aren't out of LA by Thanksgiving Day, this stuff, and a whole lot of other stuff too, goes to Callahan at the Justice Department. Remember Callahan, Mr Pallenberg?' He gloated like a von Stroheim travesty, almost drooling with the taste of his triumph.

'Who offered you all this rubbish?' I was beside myself. Scarcely able to think, somehow I saw Brodmann's hand in this chain of events. He, clearly, was hampering my progress. The Chekist had dogged me all the way from Ukraine. I could still see his knowing eyes, the only witness to my humiliation. My buttocks burned with painful reminiscence.

'You've made more enemies than friends out there, Max.' He shrugged. 'Does it matter now?'

'Brodmann is here! You are being deceived by a Bolshevik, I promise you. You have been misinformed. It is their way. They will go to any lengths. Look at the Zinoviev letter if you want proof such things are done!'

He stared at me for a moment as if he was going to answer, then he shook his head and shrugged. 'Get out of my office, Max.'

I demanded he hand over all my papers, especially my designs. He claimed he had burned them. 'A pile of ash is all that's left of that whole damned stupid scam.' His voice was a disgusted whisper.

I was helpless. I was furious. Yet I attempted to reason with him, not for my own skin but for my friend's. 'For pity's sake, Hever, save your spite for me if you will – but spare that honourable lady. Try to rise above your petty jealousy. Is it her fault she found another fellow more attractive? Besides,' I added, 'we are both men of the world, both gentlemen. We can neither of us afford a scandal.' I hoped he would take my meaning.

But he merely laughed in my face and brandished the file. 'I'm giving you a break, Max. I have the goods on you now. When I show this to the papers, who the hell is going to believe anything you say? Sure I don't want a scandal. Not a whole heap, anyway. That's why I'm giving you time to move on. But if this blows to the papers and Hays gets hold of it – as he inevitably will – believe me, you'll never work in this town again. And if you want a taste of what I mean, check back with FBO and Universal to see if they'll give you a contract.' His voice had become a threatening bleat.

It was my turn to smile. I admitted that he had me by the *boules d'amour*, as they say in France. 'Hollywood, Hever and

Hays might turn against me, my elephantine friend, but History will remember you only as a foolish hulk; nothing more than a hazard on the highway of Genius!'

(I should have demanded those plans. Of course he had not burned them! He and his companies have been living off my inventions ever since. But I was still confused when I walked proudly from his office, my future in ruins.)

My first act was to call Cosmopolitan and make an appointment for the promised job; my second was to call Miss Davies, but in spite of our professional closeness she said she had never heard of me. Mr Hearst similarly had never heard of me. His secretary added that Mr Hearst was used to fantastic attempts to blackmail him, especially since Mr Ince's heart attack had created so many baseless rumours, and that such people were dealt with by due processes of law. Even I, innocent of guile as I was, understood the threat. Thus I was betrayed and abandoned in the same day!

SIX

I AGREE THERE ARE more demeaning fates than exile
into Egypt, even through the agency of a *feigling* like Hever;
but that Turk-sick nation could never be my first choice of
destinations. I gladly acknowledge Egypt's history, her ancient
glories, her inventions and her other somewhat less practical
achievements. I doubt however that Rameses II, returning to
modern Luxor, would find much to please him. I had to go. I
was no longer welcome in Gower Gulch and Seaman's enthusiasm had sold Goldfish on the notion of an Egyptian picture
'shot where it actually happened, in the tomb of Tutenkhamun
and his ancestors!' The publicity would be considerable, especially if we were to claim, for instance, that members of our
party had died under mysterious circumstances. What was
more, I could be certain, from his attitude, that Goldfish
knew nothing of the threatened scandal. He had only recently
married. What was also an advantage was that Ronald Wilson,
Goldfish's famous publicity chief, saw the idea's potential. Mrs
Cornelius assured me that she too was prepared to face down
Hever, but on the other hand the Egyptian picture would
be her most important rôle – as Queen Tiy, widow of the
boy king (we would open with his death scene) and lover
of the High Priest. Goldfish had bought her contract from
FBO and was calling her a second Madge Norman. Rumour
had it that this displeased Frances Farmer (Mrs Goldfish)

who knew her husband's famous passion for the drug-ruined star and was giving him trouble about it. For my part I had sketched so much of this story, almost frame by frame, that I could already visualise Gloria Cornish astonishing the audience as she moved like a freed lioness towards the great window, hung with barbaric drapery, and reached a lovely hand towards the risen sun as if to take it for her diadem. We had all become extraordinarily keen on the photoplay, even Esmé and Mr Mix. I think they both saw work for themselves. I was supporting all three of us now. Jacob Mix in particular was of an independent disposition, often a rather unnecessary or unsuitable one, but I put it down to the chip on the shoulder exhibited by even the best of his kind. Generally speaking he remained good-humoured and his clear-sighted observations might have fallen from the lips of the most well-educated white man. I regarded him in many ways as an equal. In our spare moments we continued with my dance lessons.

Esmé became especially seductive around the subject of the Egyptian film. 'Let me be the beautiful slave girl, Max! Imagine me in those wonderful costumes!'

I admitted that while this did indeed excite me, I had emotional difficulties about sharing that excitement with several million other men.

She made a face and hugged me and told me that in her heart I would always be her only real audience, no matter how she appeared on screen. I often attracted this kind of loyalty in women – in men, too, less frequently – but it is a great burden. I felt powerful responsibilities for my strange little family and was naturally honour-bound to fulfil them. They were my chief considerations when I left Hever's office. I was not impoverished, of course, and as far as the moving-picture world was concerned I remained a man of creative energy and genius to rival the greater actor-painters of the Renaissance, a man of wealth, reputation and substance, but I was in no doubt how swiftly I could lose my power and reputation if Hever began to publish his distortions in the Los Angeles press. There was a lesson in the rapid fall of Fatty Arbuckle. The comedian had been completely exonerated by a jury which demanded it be made clear that Arbuckle was not guilty of the death of the girl and that he was the victim of a particularly vicious blackmail plot to rival the worst ever committed in a country where the arts of blackmail and kidnapping were brought to unprecedented heights, thanks to the expertise of certain Sicilians whom a tolerant nation allowed to prosper in the New York, San Francisco and Chicago slums. Expose a Catholic or a Jew to the liberties of a Protestant community and you can always be sure he will abuse, then threaten, the very institutions designed to benefit the abused and threatened. It is the same with Islam. There would be no chance for me in this new Hollywood determined to present herself as the very quintessence of middle-class respectability. Arbuckle had been a world star with a massive income and tremendous personal power. He had been destroyed in a matter of hours. If Hever did as he threatened there would be precious little chance for me. Mrs Cornelius and I would have plenty of time later to clear ourselves of any charges, especially if we meanwhile arranged visas and fresh passports abroad. Reconciled to a temporary strategic exile, I closed up my house and put dust-sheets on the furniture, explaining to my bank that I would be in Europe and the Middle East for a while. Fees due to me would be paid directly into my account. I certainly had no sense of committing myself to any permanent change, but I was grateful for the time I would gain. When Hever and I next came face to face it would be Major Maxim Arturovitch Pyatnitski of the Don Cossacks who would confront him. In my triumphant hand would be a sheaf of documents, all proving my innocence and the truth of everything I claimed. Hever would scowl, chew his lip, shrink away, defeated, and I would leave his office, opening a door into sunlight where my Esmé and my Mrs Cornelius awaited me, to embrace me as their hero and their saviour. I would be completely vindicated! Redeemed!

So thoroughly could I now create realities from my imagination that I was supremely confident of the situation's ultimate outcome. While away from the country I would contact various friends, have them make testaments as to my character. I would find Kolya Petroff. We would vouch for each other. I had my diplomas, my Georgian pistols, my blueprints. I had funds and family in England. England ruled Egypt. Perhaps I could at last visit the country I most admired after my own. I began to see the many advantages. Fate had not dealt me an unfriendly blow. She had decided to rouse me from my pointless euphoria so that I might continue my mission. I thanked gratefully those Gods whom I substituted then for direct acknowledgement of God Himself. I know better now, but that cannot change the errors and follies of youth. Δέν ἔχω κατρό. IR TUT MIR VEY! *Ir tut mir vey! Ma yelzim an te'mal da Uskut! Uskut! Ighsilu ayadikum* . . . Still, it is generally bearable.

This was no cowardly flight away from my Promised Land, *der Heim*, but an expedition into new territory, to expand and deepen my wisdom. When we returned in triumph with enormous publicity, we should all be world-famous. We would be lauded as the makers of the first Egyptian picture actually filmed in Egypt. The enormity of such a venture, considering the equipment and people needing transport alone, was considerable, but Goldfish had a ready answer to that problem. He owned a steamship. The ship had been part of a bad debt, I gathered, incurred by Goldfish during an earlier period of independence. It represented security on a large number of movies taken to South America by some now-deposed president who had planned to grow rich as Goldfish's main distributor in Latin America. Goldfish had owned the ship for some time and I had heard that his new gentile wife was embarrassed by the amount of scandal still attached to the vessel. Even I knew of the *Hope Dempsey* and her legendary rum-running exploits. Celebrated in rhyme and story, she was always barely a length ahead of the customs men, loaded to capacity with bootleg whiskey, Bacardi and gin from Panama, Cuba and Bermuda. I had heard famous film-stars apologising for the paucity of their bars and cellars because 'The *Hope Dempsey*'s a day late in docking.' Reputedly, Goldfish had been visited more than once by federal agents and his wife, knowing the cash-value of presenting a clean, Anglo-Saxon, Protestant image to an attentive world, was helping him to catch on at last to the real nature of their beast, the world's most profitable industry. So while the old guard quarrelled over the reparations and disposition of battleships, the new immigrants, schooled in the subtle methods of the East, took hold of the real means to power. I have never failed to credit them with cunning and far-sightedness. They also knew, as Goldfish did, when to abandon a venture. My opinion would be confirmed by the ship's skipper, Captain Quelch, who had commanded ironclads in the Great War, had taken part in the Battle of Jutland, came from a very well-known English family, and still bore the stamp of a gentleman.

I met him first at Wolfy Seaman's where the lugubrious Swede had invited him for professional reasons. Seaman had to assure himself of our captain's familiarity with the East. And it was important to him, he said, that we had a captain sensitive to our specific artistic needs. Delayed by Esmé, too ill to come but not wishing to say anything until the last minute, I arrived in time to hear the weathered tar talking with some nostalgia of Tangier and Port Said. He had captained vessels in the Mediterranean and Persian Gulf before trying his luck in Rio de Janeiro, where he had cousins. In Rio he had found himself in command of the *Hope Dempsey*, ostensibly the property of a Panamian company but actually owned by Presidenti Bertorelli, whose brief rule of, I think, Paraguay, had earned him enough to retire to the South of France and take a villa next door to a number of his fellow advocates. 'His mistake was going into the movie business,' Quelch was saying, 'it isn't a traditional line of work for a South American dictator. But he was so enamoured of the screen he saw it, I think, as the new *ultium ratio regum*. But we were his only loss. *Ultra vires*, you know.' He gave a slight insouciant shrug.

Quelch was a tall, Anglo-Saxon type, very thin, with the lantern jaw and heavy eyebrows that distinguished his class, his long nose veined and lined from exposure to the elements, his cheeks ruddy from the winds and waters of the Seven Seas. He dressed with casual good taste and spoke that languid, almost sluggish, English I had learned to recognise as the best. Again I heard the pure literary accents of my *Pearson's*, *Londons* and *Strands*! How I loved to listen to it. Even his Latin sounded exotic, authoritative. When he offered me a glass of claret from the bottle he had brought with him, it was, of course, first-class. I had not enjoyed such good wine,

I said, since leaving Paris. I began to remember what it was to be an educated, cosmopolitan European; it was as if half my being were coming alive again.

'Paris?' Quelch was dismissive. 'Is she not completely *vieux jeu*, these days? With all those Americans!'

We sat in the candlelit semi-darkness Seaman favoured, a trademark of his pictures, which had to be underlit to pass any code of decency. Mrs Cornelius tuned in to the radio, the headphones almost perfect decoration on the twin rolls of hair she had arranged in Oriental style. With her loose silk gown, she acknowledged the occasion. We smoked cigars and enjoyed a cognac from another bottle Quelch had brought. I told the elegant old seadog that I recognised one with the true undemonstrative taste of an English gentleman and he smiled modestly. 'The taste but not the pocket, unfortunately, old chum. A taste for champagne and *foie gras* was always my downfall in the end. Never women.'

Wolfy asked about his background and he revealed a twin brother in England. 'Not an identical twin, I fear. There are three of us in all. Our mother was blessed with my younger brother exactly a year after we were born, Horace is now a very successful academic. He's my twin. Our family motto, you see, *Aut non tentaris aut perfice!* It's Malcolm who'd interest you, sir, I'd guess.'

'The Egyptologist?' Seaman's voice was somewhat thickened by the cognac. He was not entirely sure if he had pronounced the word correctly, and repeated himself less successfully, but Quelch understood.

'That's the chap. Brainiest fellow in the family. *Avito vivet honore!* For some reason he prefers it out East. It's his temperament, like mine, really. As soon as I know our plans I'll write him in Alexandria and tell him when we're arriving. He's a stalwart sort, Malcolm, and just the lad to give you all the gen on Egypt "A" as well as "M". *Primus inter pares*, they will tell you at the British Museum. There's nobody with Malcolm's contacts West or East of Suez.'

All this served to further fuel Wolf Seaman's enthusiasm. Clearly comforted by Quelch's sophistication and education, he had, in his awkward way, begun to relax. This meant he slapped

Quelch and myself on our shoulders quite a bit. When Mrs Cornelius removed the headphones with a grumbled complaint that it didn't sound so much like a band as a bunch of flatulent krauts after a heavy night on the beer and sausages, Captain Quelch suggested they must therefore be playing Mostfart and we all collapsed with laughter. Then Mrs Cornelius told me to bring out my cocaine since we were all friends. After sampling it the experienced old salt told me that my 'snow' was on the same level as his '*sangue de vie*' and congratulated me, in my turn, on my taste. There was a bond very quickly established between Quelch and myself, though I remained instinctively wary of Seaman. Since he had identified his siblings, I asked Quelch what his Christian name was. After some hesitation he admitted it was Maurice and this set Mrs Cornelius to giggling. Eventually she asked, between gasps, 'Yore Maurice, yore twin's 'Orace and yore ovver brovver's Malcolm! Yer'd fink yore ma an' pa would ave corled 'im Boris, at least!'

Over his glass Captain Quelch's expression was both mournful and serious. He was only a little more sober than Wolf Seaman or myself. 'It's my belief that they lost heart,' the seadog told her sadly. 'You see, Miss Cornish, I rather think they'd set their hearts on a Doris . . .'

We were to learn no more for at that point Mrs Cornelius began to choke and was forced to speed in unstable panic for the bathroom.

And so, in an atmosphere of jolly expectation, looking forward to good company and with a marvellous artistic edifice to create, as it were, out of the sands of the desert, I prepared for my brief leave from the United States. Captain Quelch had a poor opinion of the Egyptians and a worse one of the generality of races and religions in that part of the world. He pointed out that there is really no longer an Egyptian race as such. Instead it is a mongrel mixture of all races, a living example of the disaster that occurs when white, brown, yellow, black and olive intermarry, especially where Negro and Semitic strains predominate. 'Omar Sharif Bradley' is no advertisement, I think, for the future! My estimate of Julie Christie certainly went a very long way down after I saw her embrace first an American Jew pretending to be a Russian and then an Egyptian Copt posing, of all things, as a Slav! I would say that Slavic blood was the only blood not spilled during that particular piece of cinematographic nonsense. It was the work of Lean, the communist, who made his reputation with the novels of Charles Dickens and Graham Greene before he accepted millions to produce a distorting and ignoble version of the Lawrence story. I met Lawrence more than once. He was a quiet man, a visionary like myself whose warnings had been ignored. He told me that if it had not been for the jealousy of the British High Command he would neither have been forced back to work in the pits as a common miner, nor had to produce pornography for a living. Of course he picked up those particular habits in Port Said, that sink of filth.

In spite of all these considerations I will admit that some of the romantic expectations which filled the others also touched me. I found myself succumbing to the Lure of the East, at least in my imagination. In one's imagination, of course, there is no harm in the Lure of the East. But the dusty realities are another matter. *Hadol el-'arab haramiye.*

I was spending more time than I wished in Seaman's company, chiefly because I hoped to convince him that Esmé would be an ideal supporting actress and that Mr Mix, my servant and assistant, was absolutely essential to me wherever I went. Of course no one understood the desperate urgency of our situation, so on one hand I had to pretend to casualness and on the other to professional pride. Once or twice I came in danger of parting company either with Seaman or, more importantly, with Goldfish or with MGM, for whom I had just completed the gigantic mechanical revolve so remarked on when *The Show* was eventually released. My revolve was to help make Browning's reputation long before he offered his obscene *Freaks* to a thrill-greedy public. As 'Tom Peters', I also had a small part in the picture, in the famous Salome's Dance sequence where I was the clown who plays Herod. My other large parts at that time were as Rasputin in *Last Days of the Romanofs*, Cardinal Richelieu in Seaman's *The Queen of Sin* and John Oakhurst in Ingrams's *The Outcasts of Poker Flat*, from which Ford stole his ideas for *Stagecoach*. I was never to see most of my Hollywood films in the city of their origin. Instead, I saw them in the most disgusting conditions, in the worst possible prints, in various run-down cinemas which continued to show silent films before the talkers completely drove them to ruin. So many fine films are now gone forever, including many of my own, the brown, brittle celluloid cracking and crumbling to dust within their canisters. It is as if certain seminal books in the history of literature had been tossed on a bonfire, never to be read again. I sometimes wonder if there is some heaven where these films still live, where their stars and their crews murmur of the trials and triumphs of their glory days. Stalin, in his war upon the word, was never as successful as Time, who let the old, volatile film stock powder into nothing. I read only reviews of *The Show*, for instance, for not a single print still exists. Someone came to me from the National Film Theatre after I had written about my involvement with Hollywood in *The Kensington Times*. As usual they milked my brains for information and gave me nothing in return, hardly a mention in the programme. Why should I have trusted a man called Brownshirt? But I got to see some of the pictures Mrs Cornelius and myself had worked in. We went together to watch *Ben Hur*. Like our Egyptian pictures it had been filmed partly on original location, until politics forced them to complete it in America. Some of the sketches credited to Mastrocinque are in fact mine. And Mrs Cornelius appeared only briefly as a priestess in the final cut.

I am always astonished by the assumptions of these young experts who explain to me how such-and-such a scene was shot by so-and-so, designed by so-and-so, featuring so-and-so! When I tell them who was who and what was what they say I am wrong! It is the same with ethics. It seems experience is good for nothing! They view me as an old *boltun*, making some sort of personal case, when all I am describing is what I actually saw. Equally with Egypt and Nasser. Those same children who took his part in 1956 are the ones who call me a Nazi! Yet Nasser was not merely a good friend to Hitler, he looked up to him as an admired rôle model! This is also true of Sadat, whose support of the National Socialists is a matter of record and whose talk of peace with Israel is a very different line to the one he took in the forties and fifties! But that is how it is, these days. I must say nothing in favour of the Third Reich but I am supposed to think of the pro-Nazi Third World as brothers. I remind them that 'socialism' is not a synonym for 'humanism'. Just because some swarthy power-seeker chooses to call himself a socialist makes him no more or less credible than a dictator who claims that God has called him to office, or Hugh Hefner declaring himself a feminist. I point this out in relation to Vietnam, but I am always shouted down. I have never quite been able to see why a 'Left' dictatorship is morally superior to any other kind. But simplicity is what these children demand and they are determined to make the world simple, even if the facts refuse to accord with their theories. Why does youth so often reject the delights of complexity and variety? Only the wilder Cornelius boy seems to take after his mother in that respect, and I would guess his mind is now permanently influenced by drugs. Today's children do not even know how to use drugs properly. For that I do not entirely blame them. The quality is so poor. As with air-travel, once you make something available to the masses, you immediately observe the decline of quality. The cocaine I occasionally buy these days is so adulterated I might as well be putting Vim and Lemsip up my nose! This is one criticism I would never make of Egypt, at least in 1926.

Goldfish's interest in our film was given extra fire by his desire to see the *Hope Dempsey* and her captain swiftly gone from US waters, while Mrs Goldfish, for her part, was hoping to see the back of Gloria Cornish.

The ship, its cargo, crew and passengers, were well insured. If we all went to the bottom everyone who survived ashore would actually benefit. In spite of the experience of *Ben Hur* Goldfish felt our picture could be a considerable success. Interest in Tutenkhamun had awakened again with more stories and curses and treasure and he saw considerable public interest, so he gave us his blessing but still on condition that the film be shot so Valentino could be substituted for me if he thought the footage we brought back merited it. When I demurred, he took me aside, man to man, speaking quietly in Yiddish. 'Listen, Max. This could be your biggest chance yet to get everything you want. Do you follow me?'

Perhaps, I said, but I saw no reason for Valentino substituting for me.

'Max. You're a professional. Must I say more?'

I admitted I had let the problem get out of perspective and we shook hands. Goldfish could always charm me. At the end of the meeting he announced that he was allowing us a budget large enough to finance the whole venture which was adequate but not generous. It would be extended if we needed to build interiors on our return. I would get to play some important scenes with Mrs Cornelius and, even if that Italian sweetboy were to replace me, my time with her would make the experience worthwhile. There was also some talk of taking Valentino to Egypt once we had sufficient material 'in the can' and he'd completed *The Son of the Sheik*. Needless to say, Mrs Cornelius was more excited by this prospect than I. We had a brief meeting with the off-handed little *gonsel*, in which he smoked a great many perfumed cigarettes and constantly referred to himself in the third person. He seemed sickly, even then, still a posturing braggart, full of boasts and false claims. We had nothing in common and hated one another on sight! I was not flattered by Goldfish's assertion that I was a good substitute for Valentino, who looked twice my age. He had already ruined himself with over-indulgence. But the producer's brief enthusiasm enabled me to get the papers I needed for Esmé and Jacob Mix. It was not everything I hoped for but it was the best Goldfish could offer me. Officially Esmé would be Mrs Cornelius's dresser until we reached Alexandria, then, if Seaman so desired, she would be used in an acting rôle. Mr Mix, at present my valet, was on the manifest as the second projectionist, for which he had had some occasional training. I would entrust him with the cans of film I had removed from the abandoned DeLuxe Studio. He would show them on board. I had not yet had a proper chance to see any of them and planned to watch them to while away my leisure time at sea. I returned to our little house full of my success and was disappointed by their responses. Neither Esmé nor Mr Mix seemed as pleased with their positions as I expected and eventually the negro admitted he, too, had more professional ambitions in the direction of acting. I found this amusing and patted him on his broad shoulder. 'Well, well, old fellow, I'm sure there'll be an opening for a Nubian or two once we begin shooting!'

The rest of our crew – cameraman, technicians and an elderly male make-up artist known as 'Grace' – was to be a relatively small one. In those days the Unions had not imposed their ridiculous quotas, so we would be able to recruit local labour when we needed it. Seaman preferred to work with a small unit. The chief cameraman, a small, saturnine Serbian with a huge nose, known as 'O.K.' Radonic because for years that was the only English he had ever been known to speak, had worked on many prestigious pictures and was recognised in Yugoslavia as a pioneer of documentary film. Radonic and Seaman had already made *A Princess Confesses* and *Siege* together but were unhappy with their Hollywood work. 'The camera,' said Radonic to me, 'is an instrument of sensuality and subtle narrative. These dogs make of it no more than a showman's toy. They are unfair to their own people.' To which he added in English, 'OK?' I could not entirely agree with him but sympathised, for they too sought something which would stretch their creative talents. I knew what it was to grow bored with easy success. *Queen of the Nile*, as it was now called, would be my chance to emulate my hero Griffith. The story was still mine and the choice of backgrounds would largely be my responsibility. I felt that if I never made another picture, this one must stand as my masterpiece! I would be designer and writer, carving a milestone in my own career and in the history of motion pictures themselves. With that ambition accomplished, I could turn my attention to directing and from there to my true vocation again, dedicating myself to the engineering achievements necessary to ensure the New Millennium.

Was it any wonder I knew a surge of optimism, like wonderful fire through my system? While I took Hever's threats seriously, I knew in the end I should be vindicated. I had no need to be gone long from my new home. My affairs were in order. They would run themselves until I returned. I had never known such a solid sense of security. But History was never much of a friend to me. Over the ensuing months all I had won would vanish. Only now, in the tranquillity and wisdom of age, do I understand how God had certain plans for me. *Die Fledermausen in der Turm? Der Dampf in der Darm? Das Haupt is Hauen! Sie brechen ihr Wort.* Is that my fault?

¡Tengo fiebre! ¡Estoy mareado! ¡De'jeme tranquila!

SEVEN

HISTORY RARELY REPEATS ITSELF and usually offers us no more than an occasional metaphor; but events will, I think, somehow find an echoed chord. Such echoes help us reach a better understanding of the world. Gradually a significance sometimes emerges. I saw the Goat. I saw Him in Odessa. I saw Him again in Oregon where the dead live in caves hidden amongst the crags. I saw Him in Death Valley where I pursued the badmen. I saw the Goat and He tempted me. He put a piece of metal in my stomach. He showed me His sister Esmé. He told me she was my daughter. He said He would make her my wife. He promised me power over them all. He assured me that He welcomed and celebrated the rise of Science. Why should He fear Science? Why should He care if we disputed His existence?

By indulging in such disputes, He said, we always gave Him additional strength. Where He was not recognised was where He was strongest. He spoke in a hollow, weary voice and each breath was a torment to Him. Once I saw the entire Triumvirate: the Goat, the Cow and the Ram. I saw them in the shadows of that terrible temple. Rosie! Rosie! There is metal in my womb. He reached out with that cold claw and seized my heart.

I met a brother in Odessa. He was a good Jew; he is probably dead now. The wideboys sprawl in the alleys; the little birds sing untruthful songs. The synagogues are burning. And in Orange County the ashes of executed Japanese are stirred by the feet of tourists to rise on a wind that blows from Nagasaki where the steel hulls of great battleships are tormented into the ikons of our victories, rising and falling as the water turns to steam around them and their crews die unquiet deaths. And the air is like mother-of-pearl and your skin turns scarlet, stretches upon volatile flesh, then bursts and your blood blends with the sun and you and your city die in a single violent convulsion. But this was not the fault of America. It was the fault of those who, without understanding its institutions, would take advantage of our Enlightenment, our old Law, and grab at the trappings, the obvious wealth which it had gained for us. The Goat whispered to them in Odessa. It whispered to them in Memphis and Carthage and in Los Angeles. They bled me. They drank my blood. I follow no flags. I am myself. I waited for him to touch me but he never touched me. He went with me to the tram-stop. I never saw him again. Fanatic man denies the universe and apes a cruelty which is no cruelty at all but sublime equilibrium. The cities breathe and are themselves. Identity and the city fuse together. They will fly. They will fly, my cities. I am a child of my century and as old as my century. I am one of the great inventors of my age. I am the voice and the conscience of civilised Europe. My achievements are a matter of history. A record.

Thoth, disguised as a bird, was our guide through that House of Death; and Nekhbet, the vulture-crowned, was our protectress. At night we waited in the sands by the oasis and there were some who argued that the palms themselves were weeping or that the water whispered alien names, yet I saw only the face of God, benign but unapproving, looking down on me through the stars. Those stars were like little pricks of truth, like so many epitomous points which I could gather in my hands and bring together as a blinding, illuminating whole, truth in singularity, truth in simplification. My truth. My reconciliation. And my death. I was never afraid of that. Only they would not let me die with dignity. A hawk which flings himself on sudden currents and, embracing random Nature, hurtles into mystery, cares not what crushed his body while his spirit's free. And I was to be called the *Hawk*. I was to be loved and called the *Hawk*. By the one they'd named *Al War'd*.

Kull al-medina, al-medina kulliha. Fi 'l-medina di buyut ketire: Al-lela di hiya tawila tawila. Safirt min America ila hena we-ma'i sahibi we-sayisna. Bashayrt? Maybe. Suddenly I knew the release and the escape of sea travel. I was leaving all our anxieties behind me, I became my old ebullient self in no time!

'Are we not halves of one dissevered world, whom this strange chance unites once more?' Captain Quelch asked me as we sat together in his comfortable cabin celebrating, at his suggestion, the fact that, with Panama behind us and Haiti dead ahead, we had left American waters once and for all. He was given to such fanciful language when relaxed, and admitted that it was a habit of all his family to quote poetry. The others tended to prefer Greek, Latin or old French. He was really the only modern. He got on with me, he confided, because I preferred the present to the past and, like himself, seemed inclined towards contemporary or near-contemporary artists. I was quick to protest that I was no Futurist or faddist of any kind. I enjoyed the good, solid poetry and tales to be found in the higher type of English magazine. He agreed with enthusiasm and added, a little mysteriously, that Browning was actually his limit in that direction. 'Although, to tell the truth, Peters, the lines seemed rather apt, you know. It does appear to me that we have a certain bond. As if we'd been pals in former lives, sort of thing. Actually, I'm a great believer in reincarnation.'

I was not surprised by this. Frequently I have found the most practical of men – soldiers, sailors, engineers – to reveal a spiritual side not out of place in a cleric and which is often noticeably absent in a man of the cloth. Captain Quelch's education had been impeccable – Haileybury, Cambridge and, for a term or two before he decided on the Navy as his career, Doncaster – 'Where I developed a greater interest in the racing than the ritual' – and he was fully conversant with the classics. But his thirst for knowledge had not stopped at Cambridge. His library, testifying to a broad range of interests, showed that he lacked the prudish streak common to most Englishmen. Baudelaire and Laforgue kept company with Wilde, Swinburne and Dowson, while Meredith and Hardy rubbed shoulders with Balzac and Zola. I was especially pleased to find a small volume of Wheldrake's *Posthumous Poems* which Captain Quelch said, in some delight, was amongst his favourites. He felt that, while Wilde and Wheldrake had both suffered terribly for their sexuality, only Wilde had ever fully been reinstated in the public taste. I could not agree with him more. Homophobia, I assured him, was never one of my vices.

As the lair of a notorious rum-runner, the captain's cabin was something of a disappointment to anyone expecting a scene from *The Iron Pirate* or some other stirring tale of seaborne skulduggery by Pemberton or Mayne Reid. Instead, the captain's quarters had almost a fussy air to them, and might have belonged to some college-bound don. Everything was very tidily stowed. There were Liberty-print curtains at the portholes, a deep, adjustable armchair in some dark brocade, its wood and brass polished to perfection, fixed lamps in the modern Italian style, mahogany and brass shelves or cabinets containing the mementos of six continents, all carefully fitted so that only the heaviest seas might dislodge them. I was especially impressed by his neatly-secured collection of Meissen harlequinade characters and Tang figurines, all of the highest quality and condition.

'I got the Chinese stuff mostly from the same old merchant. He brought them with him to Shanghai after his province was snaffled up by some local saviour.' Quelch ran his long fingers over the mane of an ethereal horse. 'It was in May, almost three years ago, just before I decided to try my luck in America. Since he was willing to finance the trip I agreed with more than ordinary alacrity. But there was a nasty run-in with some pirates off Taiwan and the poor old devil had a heart-attack. Since he wasn't on board officially we slipped him into the drink while I read a few words over him, thanked him for his help, and set course for the Philippines. I'll tell you, old boy, China's being eaten alive by those bandits. Another few years, what with them and the Japs, there'll be nothing left of her. Life's cheap enough almost anywhere these days but it was never cheaper than in China. The whole country's up for grabs and if the Yanks don't take it, the Japs surely will. That year in South America was like a rest-cure.' While, like many well-informed people, he foresaw a war between America and Japan over their imperial ambitions in the Far East, he did not foresee the gigantic scale of the conflict. Few of us did. Events in Europe were beginning to change the fundamental ways in which we viewed world politics, but in those days we were still highly optimistic, in spite of the continuing volatility of the Balkan states and France's punitive attitude towards the exhausted and beaten Germans (an attitude which was, of course, to lead to a war almost everyone thought could have been avoided). Europe rejected America's last great effort at peace-making and, disheartened, Uncle Sam gave herself up to pleasure-seeking, with a determination worthy of the Byzantine court.

Calm seas and warm weather meant that we spent a great deal of our days on deck. For November it was unusually mild, even when to Mr Mix's considerable relief Port-au-Prince was behind us and we moved out into the wider waters of the Atlantic. Captain Quelch planned to head either for Tenerife or Casablanca, depending on our available time and the duration of our supplies. He called the Mediterranean his 'old stamping-ground' and was, he said, looking forward to getting back. He was feeling nostalgic. At least he had a better ship now than the last one.

'We had to scuttle the *Nancy Dee* off the coast of Albania and wade ashore with whatever we could salvage,' he said. 'But we lost the guns. Not that they were worth much. Even Arabs won't buy Martinis these days. Everyone wants Lee-Enfields and Winchesters.' He sat back and sucked a reminiscent pipe. 'Lost a wonderful wardrobe, too.'

I was content to glance through his Wheldrake while the old sea-wolf reflected no doubt on the nature of a present where the sophisticated repeating rifle was available to even the most barbaric peoples. He had told me that, long after the Armistice, it had been possible to buy a good German weapon, with a hundred rounds of ammunition, for as little as a hundred piastres, Egyptian. 'They bring them in from the Western Desert and sell them in Palestine, mostly. But the *fellahin* get quite a few, too. British weapons are worth a lot more. A Lee-Enfield will set you back a fiver. And they're still out there, hardly rusting, in the Cyrenaican and Libyan battlefields. I suppose we should be thankful they use the majority of the guns in blood feuds amongst themselves. Heaven help us if they decide to go political like those ridiculous johnnies in Cairo.' This in reference to a newspaper report about the demands of the Egyptian Wafd 'nationalists'. 'Arms make a profitable cargo, by and large, but I'd never sell someone a gun that was going to kill a white man.'

Esmé was not proving a good sailor. Now I recalled her discomfort on the boat from Constantinople. Although the *Hope Dempsey* was a considerable improvement on that leaking pleasure-launch we took to Italy, she confessed she had not been entirely well on the *Icosium*. In fact, she revealed, she had met Mr Meulemkaumpf when taken faint on her first day out. The poor child rarely appeared for meals and ingested what little sustenance she could hold down in the privacy of her cabin. For propriety's sake we had separate accommodation, although there was a connecting door between our rooms. Very little unseemly was going on, however, given my little one's condition! I tended to spend rather more of my evenings with Quelch, Esmé being content to take the laudanum our captain supplied from his own medicine chest, so spending most of her hours in uncomplicated and relatively comfortable slumber. *Das Mädchen sieht schön aus. Er hat ihr den zucker gern gegeben. Mir ist kalt. Was heisst das? Ich bin nicht ein feygeleh!*

Mrs Cornelius spent most evenings in a saloon a good deal better furnished than the one we had known on the old *Rio Cruz*. We had sailed on her together from Odessa some five years earlier. Mrs Cornelius enjoyed the company of simple-hearted men and found the ship's crew as compatible as the film crew, who generally spent their free time singing songs or playing cards, both of which were favourite pastimes of my life-loving friend. Wolf Seaman, after a night or two in which he awkwardly tried to be 'one of the boys', took Ahab-like to walking the decks alone or in the company of Mr Mix who, though accepted in the saloon, had said something about not being sure he wanted to be a cheap source of entertainment for others. This chip on his shoulders denied him the chance to improve himself, but I had long since ceased attempting to reason with him.

With women on board, there was always the danger of racial tension flaring. Meanwhile my darling had a devotee. Grace, our make-up artist, was full of sympathy for Esmé. He made it his business, whenever I took my break with Captain Quelch, to ensure she was provided for and looked after. Grace could not do enough for his 'little treasure'. These effeminate homosexuals balance their tendency towards small-mindedness by being marvellous carers for the sick. They are at once the best and worst exemplars of their kind. It has often seemed unjust to me that the honourable love of the Greeks, of man for man, has to be tainted by this overly-visible image of degeneracy. It is not something, however, that I have ever discussed in detail and never had the opportunity of raising with intimates such as Kolya or Maurice Quelch. *I'tarim Nafsak*, as the Moroccans say. It is the most important thing. *Maalesh. Mush Mush'kil'ah.* One learns patience, a little self-knowledge, if nothing else in the Arab's world. But patience has always been one of my virtues. It was this quality which enabled me to enjoy our voyage, even when the seas grew very rough, and make the most of the company of a man whom I grew increasingly to admire and, indeed, to love. His knowledge of music, literature, history and science was far superior to my own. He passed on to me the benefits of the finest education in the world. As a Russian refugee whose own learning had been cut short by the follies of October 1917, it might be said I was privileged to enjoy, on an intimate basis, exposure to the English public-school system, to Cambridge and to the Royal Navy.

Soon it was Mrs Cornelius's turn to resort to Captain Quelch's medicine chest. One by one the passengers fell to the terrors and miseries of a heaving Atlantic. One by one they accepted the cures of the generous old salt's Red Cross cabinet. It supplied them with a variety of soporifics. Wolf Seaman found the morphine to his taste while Mr Mix, who, like myself and Quelch, was not hugely affected, chose to avail himself of what in those days was called 'Tunisian tobacco'. This was actually Mexican in origin. He shared a taste for it with Harold Kramp, the ship's mutton-chopped, half-caste Chief Engineer, son of a Dutch mechanic and a Javanese girl, with whom he had formed a friendship. They would talk together for hours while passing the brass pipe back and forth. With the exception of myself, Captain Quelch and the somewhat abstemious O.K. Radonic, it would be fair to say that almost the entire company and crew crossed the raging Atlantic in a state of complete and cheerful euphoria. Captain Quelch and I preferred to keep our minds sharp and happily his 'refuelling stop' in Haiti had provided us with a good supply of best-quality Colombian '*Frost*'. I have to thank that god-given miracle-drug for bringing us so close together and making the trip, for me at least, both an education and a pleasure. Such male friendship is of the highest quality, as the great Oxford philosopher Lewis tells us, though he himself, of course, was chiefly interested in the prepubescent, at least as subjects of literature and photography. We are not discussing here those European grotesques who inhabit the squalid bars and *bals exotiques* of Tangier and Tripoli, or who seek out the wretched freaks for which Beirut is famous, but the best type of *homme de bien*: physically and mentally healthy, of whom Röhm's poor, murdered young men were so frequently the exemplars. Another crime laid at the door of the German leader, another accusation which led him, in his final years, to take the disastrous steps towards defeat which, had he been supported rather than attacked at such crucial times, might never have occurred. I am no apologist for Hitler's excesses, or Röhm's either, but most will agree there is a balance which has been lost. Those were not holiday camps, I am the first to admit. Nobody claimed that they were. Sacrifices had to be made or, as Goering said to me in a moment of intimacy, '*wir werden keine die Zukunfte haben.*' What was Hitler expected to do when faced with such a *fait accompli*? Betray his own people? It was a terrible dilemma. *No puedo esperar*. Could any of us have handled it better? This is the stuff of noble tragedy, of Wagner and May. *Alle Knaben. Alle seine Blumen.*

113

Ayn solcher mann! Und alle guten Knaben. Viele guten Knaben. Vor langer Zeit. Sie hat sich verändert. Captain Quelch would have understood this better than anyone. Sadly, by 1933 he was a ruined victim of French colonial politics and, I suspect, Spanish perfidy. He had, if anything, an excess of courage. He trusted his fellow-creatures far too much. That was why the older man so quickly became my mentor, a veritable Charon, kindly and full of practical wisdom, to ferry me across an especially agitated Styx, which after more than a week of gales, in which our little steamer behaved with wonderful precision and steadiness, made even me somewhat squeamish. All I needed to restore myself was a glass or two of Captain Quelch's special laudanum, after which I was happy to join Esmé in the land of dreams whose beauty and strangeness was hardly a match for the tremendous realities of Nature which, night and day, continued to hurl our steamer about as casually as a mayfly in a mill-race. But even those forces could not distract her by more than a few miles from her chosen course. With all his other qualities, Captain Quelch was also an instinctive navigator who frequently took over the wheel himself. It was this, I think, which made his laskars so loyal to him. Together with Chief Kramp (to whom our Hindoo sailors referred sardonically as 'Sri Harold', in reference to his visionary leanings) they had sailed with him from the South China Seas, through the Malay Straits, the Indian Ocean, the Pacific and the Atlantic and now they sailed with him into the Mediterranean. Christopher Columbus or Francis Drake never had a better nor more loyal crew than was commanded by that unsung hero of a hundred daredevil ventures, truly a reborn Elizabethan navigator, his blood that blood of the gentlemen of England who sailed to defeat the mighty Spanish galleons which would make Romans of them once more. That mixed bunch of heathen Chinese, Malays, Dacoits, Muslim and Hindoos from the sinkholes of the Far Orient would have followed no one else save Satan Himself. They and 'Sri' Harold would have sailed with Captain Maurice Quelch across the fiery oceans of Hades if that was where he took a cargo.

A glass of brandy in one hand, a book of verse in the other, he would stride sure-footed up to his bridge and there drawl out his orders. Only his Second Officer, a feeble, pasty-faced individual by the name of Samuel Bolsover, seemed in any way critical of him. But Bolsover was of that typical British petite bourgeoisie which agonises so frequently about status and righteousness, and spends so much of its time squatting on a toilet straining for a bowel movement, that it has all but forgotten the unavoidable actualities of life. For him any mild sensation was like a spiritual experience. Also, as I pointed out to him one morning when only the two of us were left at breakfast, if he set so much store by the mores of the *Boy's Own Paper*, he should have remained in the Merchant Navy. This remark was perhaps a little unfair, since I happened to know he was a morphine addict wanted for the murder of a whore in Maracaibo. (Yet all the more reason, I should have thought, to keep his moralistic *BOP* hypocrisies to himself.) His reply, given at length, amounted to telling me that my opinion was worthless since I was foreign.

When Captain Quelch took his 'private time', I would have Mix set up the projector and show me my escapades in plane and on horseback, a daring transplanted son of the Steppe. I told Esmé she should join me to watch *Buckaroo's Code*, my finest. She would be proud of me. Instead she became agitated.

Between her periods of sickness and her laudanum-slumber, I had little chance to know from Esmé what upset her most. By now, my darling was despairing of everything. From a spider-web of ruined mascara she wailed about her unhappy fate, convinced she would never get back to Hollywood, would never become a motion-picture star and was doomed to die in some nameless ocean. Her little fists pounded on the walls of her cabin like Lillian Gish in *Broken Blossoms*. I reassured her that the Atlantic had a name and that the ship was wonderfully seaworthy.

We should return home in triumph. The critics would celebrate her presence in *The Bride of Tutenkhamun* (Goldfish's final suggestion for a title, wired to the ship in the Gulf of Mexico).

'Celebrate what?' she asked, lifting her pale, pouting, delicate head from the pillows. 'My employment as a lady's maid?

115

I could have got that job, Maxim, without going further than fucking Pera.'

'A flag of convenience. Once in Egypt, you'll have your chance. I am altering the script even now to give you a larger part. You will be Cleopatra.'

At this she revived a little. 'The Queen of Egypt?'

'Perhaps,' I said, 'eventually.' Actually the part was for a Greek slave-girl who becomes Tiy's rival. The plot would pivot on this triangle. The suggestion was not mine but a man named Thalberg's. He was a friend of Seaman's and Mrs Cornelius and had some experience with scenarios. A German of the best sort, he later went on to direct *Gone With the Wind* with my own mentor Menzies. I think Mrs C. met him through one of her actress friends. I was not sure Esmé would be objective enough, at that time, to appreciate the irony of her final fate (although it did offer the chance of a sequel). I contented her with some elaborate sketches of herself on top of one of the smaller pyramids, framed by a huge rising sun, flanked by palm trees. She would be clad in gold and jade and lapis lazuli and in one hand she would hold the rose of life, in the other, the rose of death.

'You will be a vision!'

But she was not to be calmed. 'I'm bored with being a vision, Maxim. I would like to be an actress. Show me my lines.' At that stage I could offer her no further consolation.

In the saloon, much later that same night, with the sea relatively smooth, I encountered Jacob Mix. He was smoking one of his Haitian cigars, his feet stretched out before him in the ship's only comfortable lounge chair, a look of considerable satisfaction on a noble face which could have graced a Benin relief. Somehow I felt I had intruded on a moment of history. All the lazy, beautiful barbaric pride of Africa was present in his muscular frame and I again reflected on the injustice of that wholesale and unselective stealing by slavers of every tribe and type. The nobler breed of negro, the dignified warriors of the Ashanti, the Zulu or the Masai, were treated exactly the same as the more degenerate natives. Even the Dutch admit to the difference between King Chaka and some ignorant Bantu houseboy. The Zulus and the Masai will tell you so themselves. Africa is, after all, a large continent. Civilisation was born there and there, some believe, it will meet its final decline. But it was the old African dignity, an ancient dignity that had existed long before Arab or white man discovered the wealth the negroes themselves despised. This is to blame neither white nor black. It was the forces of history that moved Livingstone and Rhodes into the Dark Continent in obsessive pursuit of knowledge. It was not their fault they also found gold, diamonds and timber and millions of acres where food could be grown. The black man did not want these things. The white man had to feed his people. One only has to see what the blacks do with their resources once they are given back to them – Burundi, for instance, or so much of the old Congo, and we need not discuss here the obscenity of Uganda – to see how little they value the gifts of nature which the whites cherish for their scarcity. The Bantu or Biafrans have no will to tame and control, as we have. They are merely content to pass their time in tribal squabbles and watch their women do whatever work is immediately necessary for their well-being. Machismo is the undoing of the Third World as it is of our inner cities. The infusion of negro blood into the Arab race produced an entire philosophy and religion based on this attitude. They call it Islam. A dignification, in my view, of the notions of a singularly lazy half-bred Arab, a complicated justification for an attitude summed up by a Jamaican sailor in a Soho drinking-club one evening in 1953 when I was dancing with Mrs Cornelius. 'You're working too hard, man.' He barely moved his own body and occasionally snapped his fingers. 'See? You got to let the *woman* do the work.'

Jacob Mix had benefited from an unusual intelligence as well as Christian values. He was neither particularly lazy nor immoral. He lay in his deck lounger with the satisfied air of a man relaxing after a hard day's work. Having volunteered to help Mrs Cornelius with her lines, he had taken the part of Tutenkhamun as well as the High Priest. Few actresses were as conscientious as she. Most simply learned what they needed as they went along. No prompter could be heard on the silent screen. Besides, so much more depended on pantomime. But Mrs Cornelius had been trained in a tougher school and Mr

Mix understood that. He, too, had known real hardship, real despair. Seaman meanwhile, having grown somewhat sulky for reasons I could not be bothered to comprehend, confined himself to his cabin and was no great comfort to his 'protégée', even when he was well enough to visit her. Since so much of my own time was spent tending Esmé, it was fortunate that Mrs Cornelius had Mr Mix's help. Such a good-hearted fellow. Naturally, I did not require any special 'valet' duties from Mr Mix and only used him as a projectionist when the seas were calm enough to let us watch further episodes of *The Masked Buckaroo*. In all other matters I neither needed nor missed his assistance.

I was glad to come across him in the saloon. Captain Quelch aside, Mr Mix was the only man on board with whom I had any real rapport.

After giving him another moment or two of privacy, I pushed open the door. I was jovial. 'Well, now, Mr Mix! What's this? Planning to purchase your own plantation?'

He started, seemed to scowl, then realising it was me, turned his expression into a grin. He knew I meant no harm. 'You got it, Max.' He shifted a little in the chair and took another cigar from his pocket. 'Care to join me?'

I accepted an Havana and lowered myself into the nearest basketwork armchair.

'Think the storm's over?' he asked me.

I was no mariner but I admitted the weather seemed to be settling. 'Not before time. We should be able to see the conclusion of *The Fighting Buckaroo* tomorrow, with luck.'

'Has the captain told you yet where he plans to put in? Tenerife is it?' Mr Mix seemed hardly awake.

'Probably Casablanca.'

He smiled. Fingering the corners of his mouth he peeled a piece of tobacco from his heavy lip. 'It'll be good to get my feet on that continent.'

I heartily agreed with him. I told him how Esmé was growing increasingly depressed. 'The fact is, Mr Mix, she has no talent for pictures. Perhaps she'd be better if she had some stage experience.'

'Maybe she don't need no more experiences for a while,' he suggested. 'She's only a kid, Max.'

I knew that better than anyone, and it was my duty to protect her. I had failed at least once in that duty and I did not intend to fail again. But was it also my duty, I asked Mr Mix, to help her persist at something for which she had not the slightest vocation? All the big nigger could say was that I had to do what I thought best. 'I guess you got her hooked on this glamour shit, Max, and everything else you promised her, and you got to deal with the consequences as best you can.'

I had not meant her to become addicted to Hollywood. I had wanted only a soul-mate. A comrade. A wife. It was still what I wanted.

'Then you'd better look for someone your own age.' Mr Mix spoke softly so that I knew he was not criticising me. But his gesture with his cigar was clear. He had no more to say on the subject. He rose and went to stand at the window. The sea was unstable ebony. 'What language do they speak mostly in Casablanca, Max? French, Spanish?'

'I would guess it was chiefly French and Arabic. But I think English, Spanish and German are used a great deal, too. Don't worry, Mr Mix. I'll see us through. I have something of a gift for languages.'

'I picked up a little bit of the Spanish during the time I was in Mexico,' he said. 'I guess they'll understand me.'

I reminded him we would only be in Casablanca for a few days at the most, refuelling and taking on supplies before we completed the journey to Alexandria. While I did not expect to find much in Casablanca not found in any similar international port, it was clear that he thought it would be magically different.

'It's Africa.' He was reverential.

From something in his movements I assumed him to be thinking of women. He hoped, perhaps, to find a wife amongst the Nubians, or probably only a whorehouse where the colour of his skin would not be particularly remarkable. I was sympathetic and about to ask him more when Captain Quelch, returning from his sojourn on the bridge, went by with a wave, then came back through the door which led to the boat deck. 'I supposed myself the only one still awake,' he said. He walked towards the small bar. He always carried a key to the liquor cabinet and he took it out now. '*Gaudeamus igitur!* Would you two gentlemen care to join me in a night-cap?'

Diplomatically Mr Mix declined and left us together, saying he had to get a few hours sleep.

'We've picked up some speed.' With a nod to the nigger, Captain Quelch settled himself in the vacated lounge chair. 'We might even spot the Canaries by morning. *Conjunctis vivibus,* our ordeal is over! Does that lift your gloom at all, Mr Peters?' I was surprised. I had not realised he had so sensitively read my mind.

He raised his glass and broke out with a few lines of *Jerusalem*, which he was always inclined to sing when in good spirits. He saluted me. '*De profundis, accentibus laetis, cantate!* That's my motto, Max, old boy. It's the sailor's anthem!'

'You're pleased to be close to home again, eh, captain? Glad to visit some of your old haunts?' I found myself responding in kind to his high spirits.

'Oh, I suppose so, Max. But you know what they say: *Plus ne suis ce que j'ai été, Et ne le saurois jamais être.*'

Long after the captain had retired to his bunk, I stood reflecting on the sad truth of this last remark.

EIGHT

'O, THE WILD ROSE BLOSSOMS on the little green place,' sang Captain Quelch a trifle obscurely as he supervised his laskars running with the ship's lines back and forth upon the slimy cobbles.

He had planned to lay off the port a small distance and send people ashore from the lighter, but the French authorities had ordered us to dock. Grumbling, our captain had anchored at the far end of a long stone mole, curved like a hockey-stick, which extended out of the old harbour and was thick with yellow weed. The new harbour lay on our starboard side and was still in the process of being built. From it French engineers and local Arab labourers watched us heave to. Casablanca crouched beyond, a scruffy, unremarkable medina surrounded by half-ruined mud-brick walls, and suburbs which were the usual miscellany of any boomtown from the Klondike to Siberia. There were a few nondescript mosques, lean-to shanties, traditional Arab tiled houses built next to elaborate Gothic mansions whose internal timbers were warping so rapidly they took on an oddly organic look, reminiscent of my more fanciful sets, something von Sternberg was to imitate for *The Scarlet Empress*. An Arab two-storey house with a flat roof steadied itself against a fretwork fantasy from which paint had already flaked in Casablanca's famous foul weather. Here and there stood solid-looking customs sheds and official buildings, in the usual nondescript French 19th-century style which makes Paris a beautiful unity and everything else a piece of unsightly *haute bourgeoisie*. Here and there attempts had been made at the 'Moorish' manner, but these miniature palaces already had the air of follies erected in some South American interior. Elsewhere were commercial premises which could have been transported from the 'Gower Gulch' back-lot.

Indeed, some were so flimsy that any carpenter building them for MGM would have been fired for his sloppiness. And upon this sorry sprawl of pseudo-European and pseudo-Berber a grey rain was falling with that unique steadiness that only comes from the Atlantic, as one damp billowing cloud, occasionally a little darker or a little lighter, followed another with such remorselessness that you immediately believed it had always rained like that and would rain like that forever.

'Shoot!' said Mr Mix, joining us at the rail. 'I hadn't expected Africa to be so damned wet.' Yet there was a gleam in his eye as he inspected the city, cloaked with steam and mist, and its damp miserable droves of bodies making muddy chaos of the narrow streets, sending up a noise and a smell to make Constantinople's seem as sweet as Kensington's. Apart from a miasma of coalsmoke, oilsmoke, woodsmoke, garbage-smoke and dungsmoke characteristic of many such ports, there was the cloying stink of phosphates from the holds of the tramp steamers trading in minerals, the fumes of charcoal and a thousand boiling pots of semolina, of new paint, of mint and coffee, of rain-soaked filthy clothes and panting donkeys, camels, horses and mules, of carbon monoxide from the buses and military vehicles, of half-rotted fish and slaughtered ruminants, of filthy seaweed flung upon the rocks to port where half-naked little boys scampered in and out of the grey breakers and called to us to throw them coins (yet even they fell silent when they caught sight of our laskars). And everything so sodden with the rain, so dulled by the cold and the cloud, that Captain Quelch could only grin and quote poetry in response. 'Doesn't it remind you, Peters, a bit of mournful, ever-weeping Paddington?'

'Or Summers Town,' I said, not wishing to disabuse him of his impression that I was directly familiar with England. Moreover, my reading and my listening to Mrs Cornelius's early life were enough to give me a knowledge of London a native might have envied.

'Well, it sure isn't Babylon.' Now Mr Mix bore the almost comical air of a man who knew he had somehow been cheated at chuckaluck but could not easily prove it. Wide-eyed, he enquired, 'Is it all like this, cap'n sir?'

'Africa has a way of making her coast seem her least attractive aspect.' Captain Quelch was avuncular. 'That's how they hung on to everything for so long. Nobody suspected the wealth and the beauty of the interior.' Kind as he was to Mr Mix, I fancied he was like myself a little nervous. Neither he nor I had parted from the French authorities on the best of terms and while I relied on my American passport, my change of name and my new career to afford a fairly reliable smokescreen, Captain Quelch had only time on his side. He had not, he said, been in this particular port as an independent master since 1913 when he had commanded a Tripoli-registered freighter the French had attempted to seize as he took on a cargo of opium for Marseilles and the European market. 'I can still smell the cases of dried fish we were carrying it in,' he had said. They had outrun the French customs launches but had been forced to sink the cargo in international waters. 'The damned Moroccan Hebrew went witness against me and a notice was issued. I doubt if they could make anything stick now, but there's always a chance some bureaucrat will remember my name and they use the bloody *Code Napoléon* here! You could be locked up for bloody ever! Still, *L'univers est à l'envers*, as they like to declare these days. A large-scale war is a great obscurer of small sins, old boy. A fact which many of us have learned to our profit.' He was rarely anything other than cheerfully optimistic.

It emerged that the French officials, noting we were American and carrying a film crew, assumed we were all natives of the USA, hardly looked at a passport, and wanted only to enquire after Charlie Chaplin and Constance Talmadge. When they learned that our lady stars were still feeling the effects of the wintry Atlantic they made all kinds of offers of accommodation and medical help. We refused the accommodation, but accepted the services of a doctor. There was no way, however, that we could refuse an invitation to dine with Major Fromental, who was in temporary command of the garrison. At seven a procession of broughams, each driven by a uniformed native, conveyed us to the Official Residence, which stood in its own grounds above the town, aloof – half-Moorish, half-French, protected by palms imported from Australia. A thickset giant with dark Breton good looks, Fromental spoke excellent English, though we were happy enough to converse with him in French. He told us how there was rebel trouble in the interior, under the notorious Abd el-Krim. They were a little short-staffed as a result. I had a high opinion, I said, of Marshal Lyautey, whose drive to modernise Morocco without losing her essential qualities was admired by many who usually thought poorly of French colonial policies. Lyautey, I added, would soon have the Rif in order again. At this, Fromental, his eyes hiding some fiercer emotion, murmured that the Quai d'Orsay, in her wisdom, had recently recalled Lyautey and replaced him with Pétain, the hero of Verdun. 'They argue that since today el-Krim employs the tactics and rhetoric of Europe, he should be fought by someone with European experience. Pah! It will break Lyautey's heart. He loves Morocco more than wife or God. What's more, he already had the Rif on the run. El-Krim flew too high. He's finished. Pétain will get Lyautey's glory and Lyautey will die of homesickness! The old *africain* still has his vital roots in the Maghrib.'

A personable and impressive young officer, Fromental had gained his promotion, like so many, in the trenches of Flanders, but he had an enormous admiration for his ex-commander and, inspired by what Lyautey was trying to do for these people, had volunteered for the colonial service. 'He was a realist. When he came here every little sheikh and caïd claimed to be in charge and everyone was corrupt, everyone was poor. Now we have only a few big chiefs in charge. They are corrupt, of course, but we know who we're dealing with and the people are richer. It is a further step on the long road to constitutional democracy. In a few generations, no doubt, they will be making laws about minimum wages and maximum hours. Every so often the Italians or the Germans or someone else slips a local pasha a few cases of repeating rifles or a Gatling gun so he can set himself up as an "anti-imperialist" or "nationalist", or in other words some such try for a traditional power-grab! But Lyautey always saw to it that the bigwigs stayed in power so that it was always in their whole interest to support the French. The Sultan is a cipher. El Glaoui, of course, holds the real reins of power amongst native Moroccans. It makes him our best friend.'

At dinner that night, conversation returned to the Pasha of Marrakech, El Glaoui (whose family title was similar to 'the MacTavish' in Scotland). 'Indeed,' said Captain Quelch, 'the whole system seems thoroughly Scottish to me. One day they'll make a great race of engineers and music-hall comedians!' We sat beneath chandeliers, eating off a vast mahogany table furnished with that excessively heavy silverware the French feel is necessary to set off their normally exquisite food. I must admit the food in this case was not entirely worthy of the knives and forks, as I had hoped, but it was served very elegantly by native servants in a livery of white, dark red and royal blue. Esmé, Mrs Cornelius, Wolf Seaman, Captain Quelch and myself were the guests, while Mr Mix had gone ashore with O. K. Radonic, Harold Kramp and some of the film crew to explore the pleasures of the medina. Bolsover was the duty officer.

'I heard El Glaoui was the original of Valentino's Sheikh,' said Seaman, 'and was told that the Pasha spends more time beside the *Oued Seine* than he does beside the *Oued Dra*.' He offered the company his least constipated smile.

'He is a charmer.' Madame Fromental was one of those very plain French women whose features assume a kind of frosty beauty when animated. She put pretty fingers to her hirsute chin. 'But scarcely a Valentino. A little darker, perhaps?' At which everyone laughed. It seemed to me that Madame Fromental had spoken with a less than impersonal warmth of the Pasha whose reputation as a lady's man had already been mentioned.

The French officers and their wives found my Esmé delightful and enjoyed her strangely-accented French, learned from her Roumanian mother. Mrs Cornelius was also a considerable success. She made no attempt to rid herself of her Cockney lilt while her frequent shrieks of laughter and '*oo la la*'s made her a hit as usual, at least with the younger officers. Esmé's girlishness appealed more to the older men, who made great play with their whiskers (much as a woman unconsciously fingers her hair before a man who attracts her), yet the wives were tolerant and were happy to talk to my innocent, if only to annoy their entranced husbands.

'*Elle est un bijou*,' confided one of the matrons to me just as Mrs Cornelius came by on return from the powder room.

'She bloody well should be!' – my friend was a little the worse for the local claret – 'She fuckin' corst enuff!' Before I could admonish her she had returned to her party, but Esmé had caught something of the exchange and directed a glare down the table which, had the child really been Mrs Cornelius's dresser, would have put the terror of Satan into my friend.

After more toasts and all kinds of assurances of their co-operation if we ever wished to film in Morocco, we returned very late to the *Hope Dempsey*. With our gossip of Hollywood's famous we had more than sung for our supper and everyone was thoroughly satisfied with the evening. From that moment we were assured of impeccable consideration from the local Arabs and might have been visiting Royalty to the military and police. Of course, Captain Quelch found the whole thing hugely amusing. 'It would be almost worth telling them, Max, that we're a couple of wanted outlaws!' In one of our close moments I had decided to reveal the circumstances of my sudden departure from the USA and my problems in France. The confidence had only served to deepen our sense of common experience.

'*Volvitur vota*,' he remarked the next day on the bridge as he oversaw our ship's move to a more respectable part of the quayside. He was delighted by the irony of our situation. 'The wheel turns, eh, old boy?' The entire episode was affording him considerable pleasure.

It was all he could do, he said, not to go into the *mellah* and strike some deal with one of the Hebrews. 'Could we ever have a finer cover? We'd make a certain fortune overnight! Especially with the Rif in the Spanish territories.'

'Guns, captain?' I reminded him that he said it was against

126

his principles to sell a gun that might kill a white man.

'Good God, old boy,' he said in some astonishment. 'You don't regard those dagos as white men, do you?'

I was rather discomfited by this racialist display from a man I respected for both his learning and his experience. While I was bound to admit that the Pope's greedy hand had squeezed proud Spain's wealth from her every pore, she was still a noble land who had single-handedly cleansed herself of the curse of Jewry and of Islam. Yet I would learn there are two kinds of Spaniard, one largely untainted by the blood of Carthage, while the other, true to form, was soon to attempt what the even more polyphyletic Castro succeeded in accomplishing some years later: to create the first Latin Bolshevik state. Unfortunately there are many Castros and only a few General Riveras. In retrospect I came to understand what Captain Quelch meant. From Phoenician to Barbary pirate, Oriental Africa left much of itself behind before the brave Iberians drove it back to its own desert domains. That part of Europe is still rich with their ancient sorceries, however, their barbarous creeds.

I reminded the adventurous old sea-dog that it would not do to upset Mr Goldfish, who was still technically the owner of the ship, even though we were supposed to be independent 'Seaman Pictures', and that there would be plenty of perfectly legal opportunities for him once we arrived in Alexandria. 'So long as they don't look too closely at my passport,' he said. It had cost him a two-guinea bribe in Belize and had been obtained to replace one still held by the Cape Town police. He promised he would take no illicit cargo on board the *Hope Dempsey*. However, later that day he disappeared into the *mellah* and returned some hours later sporting an oily stogey of anonymous origin and the air of a man completing or predicting an excellent piece of good fortune. All I could do was turn the discreet eye of a friend but I would have speculated more on this had not Mrs Cornelius appeared in my cabin asking, with some concern, if Mr Mix had said anything to me about 'jumpin' ship'. I admitted that he had not. 'Why should he?' Whereupon she became even more alarmed. 'Eiver 'e's done a bunk or that scamp of a captain's sold 'im,' she declared.

Naturally I defended Captain Quelch. That she was attached

to our 'Sancho Panza' was understandable, but this was no excuse for idle mud-slinging!

'If he has been sold,' I told her, 'all we have to do is inform the French police. They'll have him back for us in no time. Slavery is illegal in French Morocco. In fact, if you are worried, why not ask Major Fromental to look into it?' My view then was that Mr Mix was enjoying himself mightily amongst his own kind and I did not think it fair to disturb him. It was not like Mrs Cornelius to panic or make silly accusations.

' 'E wos due back larst night,' she said. ' 'E swore 'e'd be on board before midnight.' She had clearly become used to Mr Mix's help, even though she no longer needed it, and seemed singularly grieved.

'I would guess he has been temporarily diverted by feminine charms,' I suggested delicately.

' 'E'd bloody better not've bin,' she declared in some heat. I hastened to reassure her that the ladies Mr Mix would be visiting would be of a suitably dusky persuasion.

We were due to leave on the evening tide. I told her that I was sure Mr Mix would be back well before then. Unconvinced and still in poor temper, my friend flung herself from the cabin.

I found her later on deck, staring out towards the medina and looking at her wrist-watch. I had rarely known her so worried.

Though the rain had eased there was an unpleasant chill in the air, and the grimy smoke, drifting from factories and ships alike, hung close to grubby buildings and filthy streets as if reluctant to join the general greyness above. Donkey-carts and overloaded camels slipped and lumbered through the befouled mud to the screams and curses of their owners. Mix was nowhere to be seen. I wondered if he had taken passage on another ship. The port was half full, but there were vessels of many flags anchored there, steamers from Hull, Hamburg and Le Havre, from Genoa, Surabaya, Marseilles, Casablanca, from Athens and from Amsterdam, some of them phosphate carriers, all of them tramps, save for the white-painted warships of the French navy, gathered together some distance away, as if in disgust at the company they were forced to keep. I could tell that Casablanca was not the favourite station of France's services.

Captain Quelch, in fine spirits despite the weather, climbed up the companionway to our left, pausing beside the ventilator pipe to glance towards the shore. 'Lost somebody?'

Mrs Cornelius offered him a look of profound suspicion. 'Only Mr Mix,' she said.

'He went ashore with that chap Radonic and the Chief, didn't he?'

I had seen Radonic earlier. 'Is everyone else back on board, captain?'

'As far as I know. Your Mr Seaman is keeping a check on his people and mine are AP and C, including a somewhat hungover Chief Kramp who remembered seeing Mr Mix hailing a cab outside the *Penguin Verte* in the Rue de Londres. I've put him to work cleaning his engines. Can't afford to let my chaps have a lot of time off. Your Mr Mix can't get into much trouble out there unless he profanes a mosque or something, though they're not fond of blacks much. Still, they'll assume he's an off-duty Zouave and leave him alone. And if they mistake him for a Senegalese, they will certainly leave him alone. Those chaps make our Ghurkas look like maiden aunts.' He sniffed the cold wind. 'I can tell you, this place hasn't improved since I was last here. It's even more of a cesspit. Crawling with every kind of riffraff. I'll be glad when we're underway. Not my kind of progress, I'm afraid. *Past flowed forward and future backward fled, While ever-turning Tellus wove new fabric of the present.*'

I loved to hear those rich, educated tones quoting Wheldrake and was not looking forward to reaching Alexandria where I would be deprived of the enormous luxury of the captain reading from his favourite books while we enjoyed a drink and some good cocaine in the wonderfully civilised surroundings of his cabin. Captain Quelch's quarters were an intellectual, artistic and sensual oasis in a desert of vulgarity and pretension. I refer in particular to our self-important Swede, who had grown even surlier since arriving in Casablanca.

A certain distance had grown between him and Mrs Cornelius, possibly on account of my friend's determination to have a good time with whatever company available. It was in her nature. Those who were attracted to this *Erdgeist* must accept her, as I had, for the free spirit she was. Attempting to control my friend was as fruitless an occupation as attempting to control a South Easterly.

Mrs Cornelius scowled after the departing sea-dog. 'I bet 'e effin' knows more'n 'e's effin' lettin' on, bloody old booze-artist.'

It pained me that she should hold such a low opinion of our master. I still believed that jealousy, as displayed in her manner towards Esmé, was at least part of what motivated her, though I never have been able to get her to admit it, even during our evenings, when we sit and look through scrapbooks and relive our happier times. She maintains that she always had my self-interest at heart. 'You wos a sucker, Ivan, orl yer bloody life. You wos so effin' *much* of a sucker, you even let *you* sucker yerself!'

It is true. I can now see that often, in mistaken kindness or generosity, perhaps, I was my own worst enemy. And yet, ironically, I have found myself accused, even today by Mrs Cornelius's children and their friends, of the most outrageous and grandiose crimes! Some of them admire me for it. I am a kind of Captain Macheath to them. They expect me to quote the degenerate ditties of Brecht and Weill, as if that pair ever knew anything about the underworld or, indeed, the ordinary world! It is always the same with these Communists. They have either seen too little of real life or too much of it. The average European is, in the main, happy to have his necessities, a few luxuries, an opportunity to vote for a representative to look after his interests in the community. He is an honest, good-hearted fellow, willing to help any neighbour, be he German, Dutch, French or Slav, but perhaps he is also a little lazy-minded. It is here that he comes to find himself exploited. The Jew, whom in kindness he welcomes to his town after he hears how badly Jews are treated elsewhere, becomes a money-lender, a pawnbroker, a landlord, a factory-owner, a shopkeeper, and soon, Lo and Behold!, all the wealth is suddenly in the possession of that one, poor, put-upon Hebrew who is now building a synagogue in the middle of town and turning the honest burgher out of his house to make way for those of his co-religionists who can pay more! Karl Marx saw the problems of our world solved through the abolition of Capital, but the problems of the world will be instantly helped if we see to the abolition of Karl Marx and all he bred. *Böyle bir yemek ismarlamadik!* as the Turks say. *Die Menge hält alles für tief, dessen Grund sie nicht sehen kann.* But I suppose we are all subject to such self-deceptions from time to time. Karl Marx offered us a simplified Future. Martin Luther only offered the simplicity of God. Yet both have done damage in their time. God and Communism grew senile together and we can look only to their offspring. *Kyrie eleison! Kyrie eleison!* The little girls sing so sweetly in the cathedral. The blue and white mosaics reflect the light which cuts through that comforting gleam like the voice of Christ Himself. *Ecce stolec!* Behold the Fundament! We are granted a vision of Holy Russia resurrected. The glorious Russia into which I was born and where for many years I had hoped to die. But she is gone and I am doomed to perish in an English slum.

Yet, as Captain Quelch was fond of quoting from Wheldrake, *One sweet moment is worth the suffering of the century.* I have no regrets. Soon I shall be dead and I shall die knowing I have done all I could to pass on the wisdom of my experience, to show the world something of what went wrong since 1900. And if they do not wish to listen, I cannot feel guilty. The Holocaust, if you care to call it that, was not my fault, after all, any more than it was Adolf Hitler's! I think we would do better to ask ourselves 'Who was betraying whom in those days?' Then perhaps we might see who continues to betray us and all we dream of. We are the people of the New Testament, not of the Book. *El-kitab huwa sa'ab 'ala 'l'walad essaghir. Das ist meyn hertz. Rosi! Ayn chalutz, ich bin. Ayn gonif,* never! *Teqdir tefham el-Kitab da? El-'udr aqbah min ed-denb.*

'The excuse is more shameful than the offence,' Captain Quelch frequently declared. Which was one reason, he said, he did not make excuses for himself. 'If I step outside the law, well it's for my own profit and I take a high risk. But I can't honestly say, old boy, that I feel I'm doing anything wrong.

131

And most people agree with me, certainly my customers.'

At Mrs Cornelius's insistence the three of us were in the lobby of the French Line Hotel, about the only civilised place in the city, to meet Major Fromental's Chief of Police, a soft-faced little man in an unnaturally smart white uniform and a képi which was drawn down almost to his thick, black eyebrows. He introduced himself as Captain Hourel and spoke in smooth, rather affected Parisian tones, assuring us that the slave trade had been completely wiped out under the French. He admitted the local moonshine might have KO'd Mr Mix. It was even possible he had been wounded in a quarrel. 'But that we shall soon know, gentlemen.' With the air of a man called from more important business he escorted us from the hotel to his waiting Daimler. The native chauffeur was driving curious youths away with an old-fashioned camel crop, clearly kept for this purpose alone.

In the large, closed limousine we steered through a chaos of trucks and beasts of burden into the old town. Surrounded by the awnings of shops and stalls, busy with donkeys, women and boys, with squatting oldsters, wobbling handcarts, impossible burdens, squalid bargains, Bab Marrakech Square sold the discarded junk of three continents. Tin cans, broken toys, yellowed magazines were offered by ill-fed urchins who threw back the frayed pieces of oil-cloth or old linoleum with which they protected their pathetic wares from the elements and sang their virtues in shrill voices while elsewhere a variety of grubby entertainers performed their frequently puzzling and sometimes grotesque tricks like toddlers in a school yard.

All the news in Casablanca was to be heard here, said Captain Hourel. He sent his Berber sergeant to investigate.

There was nothing to do but take a table outside the café and watch the snake-charmers and tumblers go through their rather limited paces while Captain Quelch quietly thanked God for the invention of the printed book and the moving picture. Even these performers had a bedraggled hopeless mood not designed to improve the spirits of their audience. Captain Hourel drove away a group of boys who approached us pointing at their bottoms and their open mouths. 'They are hungry and they have dysentery,' Captain Quelch observed with an amiable wave to the departing troupe, whose only response was to scowl and spit. On the far side of the square, under sodden awnings, in heavy woollen *djellabah*s which even from here stank like wet sheep, men of all ages sat sipping mint tea and discussed the gossip of the day or whatever international news affected the fate of this wretched monument to unchecked commercial greed. 'It is where the detritus of Africa, Europe and the Middle East finally discovers it can flow no further and it silts up here in a great heap. The population grows greater every week. It's hard to believe that this was not much more than a village whose people were massacring Frenchmen in this very square less than twenty years ago. After that, of course, Paris had to take control of the damned country. And they're thanking us now.'

'All but a few ingrates.' Presumably Captain Quelch referred to Abd el-Krim.

The sergeant returned with the news that a tall negro had been seen with a party of nomad tinkers buying provisions in the souk only a short distance from the west side of the Bab Marrakech itself. He had visited the shop but the owner had been able to tell him very little. He thought the tinkers had a camp out near the new airfield. 'Well, let's get off to the bloody airfield!' demanded Quelch as if determined to suffer every possible discomfort and inconvenience on this, in his view, pointless quest. '*Fiat justitia, ruat caelum!,* etc.' And so there was nothing for it but to drive out through the sleeting rain on the freshly-laid wide black road, past a succession of modern concrete and steel factories, to a broad, glittering strip on a horizon as flat as Kansas with one very small white control- and customs-station and a spanking new single-engined mail-carrier, a Villiers biplane of the latest type, bearing the blazons of both France and her Postal Service, on the far side of the field. Near some ruined dirt-walled farm-buildings, cleared in the progress of modernisation, we came upon the tinkers' abandoned camp. They had left the usual collection of litter and dung, but there was no sign of Mr Mix ever being with them. 'We shall have to get a Berber tracker,' Captain Hourel decided. 'If those people have your friend or have harmed him, don't worry – we shall soon know.' But it was clear to me, at least, that he thought the expedition had been a waste of time. He kicked suspiciously at a black and red paper sugar-sack bearing the cheerful features of a French provincial pierrot, and revealed the half-burned corpse of a day-old child. 'A girl.' He shook his head. 'But we'll have to get after them for that.'

He sighed and spoke in Arabic to his sergeant. The man saluted and took his rifle to stand guard. We drove back to Casablanca in moody silence. 'We are overworked,' said Captain Hourel out of the blue. 'Ever since Lyautey went.'

Captain Hourel assured us that he would send a telegram to the *Hope Dempsey* just as soon as he knew what had become of Mr Mix. We had to be content with this. We returned to the ship to tell Mrs Cornelius that the entire Casablanca garrison had been put to work to locate our friend and the tinkers who might have captured him. We had also informed the American consul. Privately I wondered if Jacob Mix were fulfilling some strange ambition to journey to the heart of the Dark Continent in search of something he might recognise as his homeland. I could certainly understand this yearning for a place to call home. Scarcely an hour of my own life goes by when I do not remember Kiev and those happy years before War and Revolution robbed me of my past, my mother and my sister.

So furious was Mrs Cornelius at this unexpected but hardly tragic event – I, too, held Mr Mix in considerable affection, but did not fear for a man so evidently resourceful – that she turned almost scarlet and all but accused us both of having sold the negro for Arab silver. ' 'E never said *nuffink* abart leavin',' she said. 'I'd 'a sensed it. I've *orlways* bin able ter sense fings like that.'

'Well, madam.' Captain Quelch was understandably sharp, having spent a great deal of his valuable time trying to track down our errant Mix. 'It appears your darkie has been abducted by the gypsies. Either that or he has run off with them to join a circus. Or he has become a cannibal. Or they killed him, sold him or worshipped him as a devil. We shall know soon enough. *Pastor est teu Dominos*. Meanwhile you'll forgive me if I return to the running of my ship. We have just discovered a serious theft – no doubt conducted during the hue and cry for Mister Jacob Mix. I would be particularly grateful, Colonel Peters, if you would join me this evening after supper.'

And with the curtest of salutes, he went back to his bridge.

Mrs Cornelius remained dissatisfied. She accused me of not trying hard enough to find the man. She reminded me that he had saved my life. Was this, she demanded, how I repaid him? I pointed out that everything had been done. I felt sure Mr Mix would find a means of rejoining us in Alexandria or possibly even Tangier, if he did not return or radio before we sailed. Personally, I still felt he would be back, perhaps shame-faced, perhaps somewhat hung-over, perhaps with an elaborate excuse, before we sailed. But I was to be proven wrong. When the *Hope Dempsey* upped anchor that evening to plough on through adumbrate air and gloomy breakers, Mr Mix was no longer of our company.

It was only when I joined Captain Quelch in his cabin that night that he broke the news which shattered me. One of our film projectors had been stolen, doubtless during the hue and cry for Mr Mix while we pursued him in the bazaar, but what was worse was that almost every can of film was gone – every adventure of Ace Peters, virtually the only surviving proof of my starring career in the cinema, had been taken! The thieves had stolen the only things they could find that looked valuable. 'God knows what they'll make of them.' He had reported the theft to the police. They assured him that they would locate the culprits and seize the films and equipment on our behalf. They would telegraph as soon as they had news.

'Don't worry, old chap. They'll turn up in the Bab Marrakech tomorrow and some copper'll spot them.' I was reassured by his hearty confidence.

Having settled the complaining Esmé down with her night-lantern and her laudanum and escaped Mrs Cornelius, who remained unreconciled to Mr Mix's disappearance, I was exhausted. I, too, was sorry to lose such a loyal companion, but perhaps loss is more familiar to me than to others. Thus I have learned to bear loss mostly in silence, even to denying it entirely and driving it from my mind. I bore the loss of my movie plays with a stoicism Quelch himself might have envied.

We had both had enough of speculation. We agreed not to discuss Mr Mix's fate or the fate of my films, until we had further intelligence. Instead I listened while Captain Quelch told of his adventures on the Gold Coast before the Great War which had eventually made him the owner of a white girl not more than thirteen. 'She was German and had been bought and sold several times since her abduction, at about the age of seven, somewhere in the Congo. Her father had been in charge of a Belgian mining concern. Happily I spoke a little German and she seemed pathetically grateful for that. She was a lovely little thing and with a wealth of experience, as you can imagine. I was soon in two minds whether to keep her for myself or inform her relatives and claim whatever reward was going. It turned out there wasn't one. Everybody she knew was dead so she was content to stay with me. I had the pleasure of her company for almost a year.' He poured us some more cognac as I untwisted the paper containing our cocaine. 'Easy come easy go, eh, Max? Bad luck, really, my deciding to sail for Java. She caught something pretty odd and incurable up-country while I was doing a river job near Puwarkarta. I had to leave her with some nuns in Bandung. I often wonder what became of her.'

We agreed that *les femmes* were a glorious weakness which, sensibly or not, both of us would always indulge. I had to admit that Esmé, though my joy and delight, sometimes seemed in certain moods more of a burden than a comfort. Yet what could I do? I had always been a slave to women. Captain Quelch recognised this side of me and shared his own romantic intimacies. He had that same Spartan nobility of temperament, the Greek's demand for excellence, moderation and balance in all things, a tolerance for every road a man takes in quest of a spiritual and sensual education, his mind always curious and explorative, forever probing in fresh directions, which I remember in Kolya, especially during our Petersburg days. Like Kolya, perhaps, my new friend represented a Byzantine rather than a Roman ideal. *'Dux femina facti!'* The remarkable old sea-dog was philosophical as he bent a nostril towards his *sneg*. 'Mother warned me women would be my ruin. But I'll always be an incurable romantic, old boy.' Again I remarked how, in so many ways, Captain Quelch was my perfect soulmate.

NINE

LITERACY IS OUR most valuable gift, the source of memory and enduring myth; the wellspring of all we now call civilised and the means by which we pool our commonwise. Communicating thus from Past to Present we improve our understanding of the world and our universe. Here in the Mediterranean (where a few years earlier I had been reborn) on December 18, 1925, barely a month before I began my second quarter-century, I came to understand the true value of literacy when I tried to imagine the emotions of the first man realising one day the potential of a written language!

Rising early, a little impatient with Esmé's groans from the other side of a door she insisted on locking ('in case you see me puking. I should hate that'), I begin to feel a certain pleasant excitement as I grasp the sparkling brass rails and ascend the companionway. Everyone has assembled on the boat deck. The sea is an uneasy blue and the clouds are turning to white and from white to wisps of vanishing mist while the black hull of the *Hope Dempsey* breaks up yellow spray. We are not yet in Paradise but we are passing at last through the gateway between Gibraltar to port and Morocco to starboard, with a great golden sun rising like a fortunate omen on our forward bow to release, it seems to me, an army of golden beings so brilliant as to be intolerable to the naked human eye, to drive the cold Atlantic back and lift up all our spirits so even the laskars wail what is clearly some native triumph as they go about their work. From his cabin, shaving, Captain Quelch stands up to chant a dirge, antique and monkish, in time to his open door's creaking.

> *'Ad conflingendum venietibus undique Paenis,*
> *Omnia cum belli trepido concussa tumultu*
> *Horrida contremuere sub altis etheris auris;*
> *In dubioque fuit sub utrorum regna cadendum*
> *Omnibus humanis esset, terraque marique.'*

That was a subject dear to my own heart, and singularly apt as we sailed not three miles from the ghost of old Carthage. Hindsight says Carthage's ghost was grinning at my back even as we glimpsed the white and green terraces of the great port which, three thousand years earlier and before their pagan empire was crushed by vengeful Rome, the Phoenicians named Tingis. Now it seemed to me to symbolise the very best of the ancient world combined with the finest of the new. At this distance Tangier was the perfect image of the modern, civilised city. Now you will say Tangier was an illusion, but I would prefer to call what I saw a vision. That the reality would prove both sordid and terrifying I was not to know for some time. Just then I relaxed in the presence of a silvery perfection, a city framed in the foliage of cypresses, poplars and palms, her terraces occasionally broken by the golden dome of a mosque or the vivid blue of some caïd's summer home, the dignified green of Royalty, and this all festooned with natural draperies of violet, scarlet and deep ultramarine, of vivid ferns and vines, shrubs, grasses and brilliant pines, all ranked above us on seven hills, a Roman's dream of tranquillity, a Christian's dream of heaven, the promise of a new world order.

As the province of France, England and Spain, Tangier could well have become one day the thing I first imagined. The *Hope Dempsey* steams through the glowing mist of the morning to drop anchor in the offing where the dirty brown and orange motor launches rush back and forth between the steamers and the wharf.

A pleasure ship disembarks her white froth of passengers into more of these boats (the only means of reaching the

139

shore) while a boat which follows is loaded with nothing but cabin-trunks and suitcases, and is rapidly followed by a further wave of white cotton and peach lace as a party of German ladies, each with her pink-trimmed parasol and crocheted gloves, flies in on the foam to flirt for a week or two with the exotic. Through Captain Quelch's glasses I watch other tourists disembark on the quay to entrain directly for Fez and Rabat while soldiers, primarily of the Spanish Foreign Legion, ensure their safety, though not, I imagined, their complete peace of mind. Nothing protects them from the hordes of little boys, the trinket-sellers, the carpet-merchants, the grinning purveyors of moist and mysterious sweets protected from the sun by a solid covering of black bugs I mistake at first for raisins, until they move.

'*Odi profanum vulgus et arceo.*' Captain Quelch joins me, taking the glasses to scan the port. 'Still, it's our last chance to restock our supplies.' We have rather overindulged in *le poudre* during the last several nights.

'I've 'ad four 'arf-pints at the *Magpie an' Stump*, an' two goes o' rum jes ter keep up me sperits, me mince pies are waterin' jes like a pump, and they're red as a ferrit's. 'Cos why? 'Tain't the missis nor kids wot I've lost. But one wot I care-ful-lie doctored and fed, the nussin' an' watching' 'as turned art a frost, the *Jeerusalem*'s dead!' Considerably more cheerful, Mrs Cornelius comes strolling along the deck, singing with sturdy professionalism the song she always uses to get herself on top, as she puts it, of her blue devils, and jerks a thumb towards the donkeys on the dock.

'Albert Chevalier's one of my favourites!' Captain Quelch lifts his cap in salute. He is wearing an old-fashioned bow-cravat, a smart 'bum-freezer' white jacket and tight blue trousers. He is every inch a gentleman of the sea. 'Funny without being vulgar, eh, dear lady?' He fingers some slight cut on his jowl.

Mrs Cornelius is always unrelenting and will not be drawn. 'Actcherly,' she says in her best accents, 'I'm more partial to Gus Elen meself.'

Up comes the Swede, disconcerted to find such a party already here, for he is usually the only one of us to exercise before breakfast, and turns a surly colour when he sees his paramour, the star of his movie play, staring eagerly towards the shore as if trying to catch a glimpse of a friend. He tries to turn, to go back, but Captain Quelch takes him by the arm. 'Tell me, old boy, wouldn't this do for Babylon?'

'We are not doing Babylon, Captain Quelch. Nor are we doing Sodom, nor, indeed, Gomorrah. There are no records, I'm afraid, of *Egyptian* orgies.'

'I thought one of Mr G's wires specifically mentioned an orgy. And my brother says they couldn't stop themselves, though it was religious, I gather.' Captain Quelch has a habit of goading the Swede, whose lack of humour is notorious.

'And the next wire completely contradicted that,' says Seaman, shrugging free of the captain's hand. 'I intend to make my original picture, my friend, come hell, high water or Samuel Goldfish! That will fulfil my contract. Then I shall return to Sweden.'

'I can't say I blame you, old boy. They'll be missing you, I should think. *Absens haeres non erit*, don't you know.'

To which the Swede replies, with unnecessary venom: '*Magna est veritas et praevalebit!*' But, refusing to expand, he wrenches his awkward limbs through our company, and descends.

' 'E's bin orf-colour fer days,' says Mrs Cornelius by way of vague apology. ' 'E ain't wot y'd corl a natchral Vikin'.' And she roars with her old good humour, though her manner still grants no special intimacy to me and I understand I am not entirely forgiven for my non-existent crime.

There comes a half-subdued shout or two from below, as if lovers quarrel, but it is only Esmé passing Wolf Seaman who, for some reason, has tried to hamper her, and here she comes up in ruddy disarray, to join in the viewing of 'the white city of the seven hills' as Pierre Loti called it in one of those pieces of erotic trash he wrote in later years in order to maintain his exotic lifestyle. (There indeed was a man thoroughly infected by the poison of what the British used to call 'Arabitis', who did more to distort and romanticise the Oriental East than Ned Buntline the American West. Yet posterity will doubtless prefer his lies to mine, for the myths of Saladin, El Cid or

Buffalo Bill endure beyond any commonplace reality, while the *beau monde*, of course, changes only its clothes, never its character.)

'*O, elle est très jolie,*' exclaims my little lady in her prettiest French. And she claps her hands, a noise which brings a frown from Mrs C., a smile from Quelch and me, a sudden excessive wailing from the town as the dawn muezzim begin noisy admonitions to their grim old God. At which Captain Quelch turns from the rail with the news that he intends to order from the galley a decent English breakfast. 'Sometimes it's the only reminder of who and where you are.' 'That,' says Mrs Cornelius in full approval, 'an' a reelly 'earty cup o' tea.' With this she links her delicious pink arm in his, the other in mine, and we are forgiven. Only Esmé elects to remain. To let the air, she says, dispel the last traces of her *mal-de-mer*. We bump into Seaman coming towards us as we make for the dining-saloon. Pressing back to let us pass, he glares at us but will not say a word. 'Wot's the matter, Wolfy?' calls Mrs Cornelius over her shoulder, 'orl the free luv gettin' too much fer yer?' This is a somewhat cruel reference to the Swede's joyless pantheism, a creed which has replaced religion for so many socialist Scandinavians. Some of them must surely long for the days when Thor could coax at least an occasional lusty laugh from even the Lord of Gloom, the brooding Odin? Months of sunlessness have made that people suspicious of spontaneity, I think. Even Scandinavian hearths are designed to discourage any random flame.

Much as I find their English ritual reassuring, so self-confident is it, I am forced to decline the pans of greasy bacon, eggs, tomatoes and fried bread with which the co-nationalists celebrate their arrival in the Mediterranean. Contenting myself with some bread and a little marmalade, I watch through the portholes the scheduled tourists, many of them day-trippers from France, Spain and Gibraltar. I doubt if tourism has changed much. A quick rush around the main points of interest – sometimes infrequent or pathetic – thirty minutes to see the *souk*, to savour the squalor and filth of foreign parts and shudder with pleasure at a fleeting whiff of Africa before being steered back to the security and comfort of their P&O or French

Line cabins. Whereupon another parlour in Toulouse acquires a camel saddle or a brass hookah and some Guildford sitting-room shall soon sport a set of shoddy Bedouin flintlocks. They brought them in to me in bushels when I still dealt in general goods, before this present interest in old clothes enabled me to become an antiquarian costumier and exploit, I will admit, that *folie de nostalgie* which reflects youth's unadmitted yearning for the spiritual values of their forefathers. They think that by wearing those clothes they will somehow restore the Golden Age. I say I would like to see this Golden Age of theirs. I point out into Portobello Road where the chip papers and the Wimpy boxes lie trapped in rotten fruit and animal droppings. Is it here? Or where? *Firt mick tsu ahin, ikh bet aykh!* I tell them clearly both who and what is to blame – and they laugh at me or swear or even threaten now I am too old to fight. There is nothing wrong with the Old Testament. I know what it is to be a Jeremiah. It is not an insult. They call me 'anti-Semite'. I tell them they are ignorant fools. Our whole civilisation is Semitic. What is civilised about us is Semitic. Are these the statements of an anti-Semite? You will never hear me say anything against those great Semitic founders of our civilisation who brought about the Golden Ages, the real Golden Ages, of Sumeria, Babylon and, yes, Ancient Israel. But, at some point in the life of their race, noble Semites fell to internal warring and from there, exhausted, slipped into despondent slavery whereupon, for the price of their immortal souls, they bought from Satan a kind of freedom. And still today they fight, this Jew-and-Arab, Arab-and-Jew. As a united people they were great and noble, producers of monumental architecture, sculpture, painting, decoration, literature, philosophy and science. It is as if God punishes them. As if God keeps them perpetually on the very edge of Heaven and is forever devising new means by which to divert them and thwart them from building and keeping for themselves the earthly Paradise He placed around the Middle Sea so that they learned to treasure, not destroy, His gifts to us.

It is not the Semite I fear. It is the 'Jew' and the 'Arab'. All that is barbaric, decadent, immoral, everything which engulfed and drowned that great civilisation as surely as it were Atlantis, can be explained in those two words. They are the creeds of the barbarians who overran Semitic Africa and Mesopotamia, challenging the sublime justice of those Greeks who were themselves the inheritors of the ancient world's best. And I do not say this Semitic decline was consistent. Until idolatry and war finally divided it, there were times when it seemed halted, when the sanity of the Phoenicians still mediated the lust for conquest best symbolised by haughty Carthage. There were periods when the ages of Solomon and David and Haroun al-Raschid seemed to have come again, before that bizarre will for self-destruction overtook them in quarrels and warfare, even to this very day, where Egypt sides with Syria and Libya sides with Algeria and Algeria sides with Syria against Egypt and Libya or Iraq or Jordan and even the time-bomb that is Israel cannot unite them or, the thought is impossible, persuade them to consider uniting with their fellow Semites to found a common state where religion becomes a matter of spiritual choice, not of politics or of life, or of death. This is the 'principle' they would export to the West, to match Voltaire's or Tom Paine's? But they have won, anyway. It is no longer even permitted to voice such warnings any more, let alone represent them in Parliament. More and more we descend to imitating them, our old principles and virtues forgotten. Certainly allow these people to bring back blood-war and the feudal system! They have that ambition in common, at least, with Comrade Stalin. (Nobody in Russia was surprised by this. They know their Georgians. Those people are themselves scarcely a foot-step away from Allah.) I am not, you must realise, saying we should do away with those hopeless millions, but at least we might encourage some form of sterilisation? Or, at the minimum, maintain the system which worked so well for everybody in Ukraine, before the Bolsheviks, before the Babi Gorge was anything more than the background of my first great triumph as I ascended into the purity and freedom of the skies. Now infamous smoke obscures that vision, that wonderful memory; yet no single one of us, I think, is to blame for that. If we conspired, we conspired in ignorance. If we all colluded, it was in our determination to believe that there were simple political answers to our ills, in our clinging to old simple virtues, to old securities, as a falling man will innocently cling to a rotten limb, believing himself saved.

Captain Quelch has some business ashore but none of the rest of us wish to go through the complications of passports and bargaining involved in landing so, after we both receive the captain's assurance that he will enquire for news at the local police station, Mrs Cornelius and I return to our former closeness around the phonograph, singing snatches from the latest records. *'I'm tellin' the birds, tellin' the trees . . .'* murmurs Whispering Jack Smith to Mrs Cornelius's rudimentary soft-shoe shuffle, while I pretend that my plate is a ukelele. *'You can bring Pearl, she's a darned nice girl . . .'*

'I miss my Swiss . . .'

'I'm the Sheikh of Araby, as all the world can see!'

As we try out the Charleston to the music of the Savoy Orpheans, Esmé enters the saloon and stands at a critical distance until we stop. Mrs Cornelius has the giggles.

I gasp, 'What is it, my dearest?'

'I was hoping to go ashore,' Esmé says. 'To do some shopping. I need proper clothes. And other things. For women.'

'No need ter worry there, dear,' says Mrs C. 'I've a bloody suitcase full o' stuff. Yer carn't be too bloody careful in these parts. I know to me corst.'

'I wish my own.' Esmé mutters this last in English, staring at the floor.

'Suit yerself.' Mrs Cornelius shakes her head and collapses into a cane armchair. My girl receives from me a glance of admonition for rejecting a friendly gesture. I remain mysteriously awkward when both women are present. Perhaps I make them jealous.

'We shall be disembarking in a few days now.' I hope to placate her. 'In Alexandria. Where they have English shops. They have a Whiteley's, so I've heard.'

'There are French shops in Tangier,' she declares. 'There is a Samaritain and a Bazar Nürnberg.'

'Wot yer want wiv Kraut knickers?' Mrs Cornelius has risen to change the record. It is noon, now, and seems warmer than the barometer's guide.

'I fear that one pair will not last *me* an entire journey.'
Esmé is sharp but no match for my old friend.

'I wouldn've thort you've 'ad 'em on for more'n a minnit.'

This bickering was not confined to the women. Virtually everyone aboard not from the South China Seas was suddenly at odds with everyone else. I would be relieved to reach Alexandria where the confines of the ship would no longer force so many temperamental human beings into over-frequent contact. O.K. Radonic, of such usually placid temper, was refusing to take his meals with the rest of the film crew, Chief Kramp had become gloomily reclusive, while Grace had fallen in love with a laskar and was no longer as attentive to Esmé as he had been. Only myself and Captain Quelch, perhaps because we still discovered so much in common, were content. I wished, indeed, that I could please my girl, but most of the time she had little need of what I could offer. The friction between me and Mrs C. at least was over, though she made one or two jibes, demanding to know how much Quelch and I had got for 'the big buck'. I longed for a telegram from Captain Fromental to say that Mr Mix was safe and sound. I longed still more to hear that my reels were recovered! Recently the Second Officer, Bolsover, had begun to make notes, in an extremely small hand, on a pocket-sized pad of the kind carried by a police constable. He seemed to be starting some sort of account. I had watched him in the evenings when the rest of us were entertaining ourselves. Seated in a corner he wrote down the number of gins the captain had taken with the passengers, how many whiskies the barman had donated to his favoured customers. I think he had some idea of reporting Quelch and the rest of us to the owner, but I was not sure even Goldfish would concern himself with such pettiness. After all, our little picture was not costing a fraction of what had been spent on *Ben Hur* before the whole thing was recalled to Hollywood and built again in Burbank. Since we were most of us under contract, very little money was being wasted at all, and if the movie play were a success it might compensate for some of the more costly failures at that time alarming the cinema world. *Temptress of the Pyramids*, as we currently called it, would not merely be a popular success, it would positively impress the jaded critics. Wolf Seaman was, I guessed, staking his future reputation on it. His brand of 'jazz-baby satire' had worn a little thin and historical spectacle, especially associated with the Orient, was the taste of the day. In this, at least, we were secure. Goldfish wanted his ship as far from American waters as possible and I think he felt much the same about Seaman, just one more foreign embarrassment like Maurice Maeterlinck. Indeed, it was almost impossible for anyone to like the Swede. He combined Scandinavian high-mindedness with a Teutonic aggressiveness, a blend which no doubt made Catherine the Great the woman she was. Unfortunately he had neither that lady's looks nor her charm.

I had no trouble in stealing Bolsover's notebook for a few hours and sharing its contents with Captain Quelch. That astonishing list of crimes even suggested unnatural acts amongst the laskars and members of the film crew – something which I knew Quelch had carefully discouraged. ('A buggered laskar is a lazy laskar,' was his familiar motto.)

There came a sudden scent of roses as Esmé flung herself from the saloon while Seaman stared gloomily out towards the bow. I thought to follow her to comfort her, for I knew my refusal to let her go ashore had upset her, but in such moods she preferred to be alone. Mrs Cornelius was singing a duet of *Rose Marie* with the wonderful Oscar Lavern record as she peered again through the porthole towards the tiered orderliness of distant Tangier and speculated if Captain Quelch had yet heard something about Mr Mix. Although reluctant to touch upon the subject at all, I was forced to disabuse her (for I knew the actual nature of Captain Quelch's expedition, which was to replenish our supplies of *shney*). 'He will not go immediately to police headquarters,' I said.

'Buyin' 'isself a bum-boy 'is 'e? Thass gonna send yer ter ther five-fingered squeezebox ain't it, Ivan?'

To this day she refuses to tell me what she meant, but she shakes with laughter whenever I bring it up. It confuses me to find her so frank in so many ways, and so ambiguous in others. I think she believes she is saving my feelings, but she must know that I have always preferred the harsh facts to obfuscation, no matter how comforting. If it sometimes makes me less happy than many people, I am also more realistic.

In answer to my question at that moment, she pointed out of the window to a local launch, its varnish flaking like leprosy, which pushed through the busy water traffic towards the *Hope Dempsey*. At the tiller was the obvious owner, a native in filthy golfing pullover and battered fez, while Captain Quelch was seated amidships side by side with a younger man who wore the latest in exaggerated suit fashions, including a wide-brimmed cream-coloured hat, and had something odd about his left sleeve. Their backs were towards me. I was intrigued. Captain Quelch had said nothing of returning with a visitor.

I went on deck to greet them as they clambered up the side. The young man's hat continued to obscure his face until he was actually standing beside me. He wore smoked glasses, which he removed and slipped into his pocket as he grinned at me, holding out a sun-tanned hand. He was as handsome and as full of himself as he had ever been, as large as life! I scarcely believed it. I burst into tears.

'But your arm!' I could not avoid noticing the empty sleeve. 'What's wrong?'

He knew a few seconds' sadness. 'There was shelling in Odessa. I was hit. Then I was shot trying to get to a ship. I'll never know who got my arm – Reds or Whites! Maybe both.' And he shrugged in that old insouciant style of his, bringing a flood of wonderful memories.

It was Shura, who they told me was dead, killed by the Red Cossacks. It was my cousin, my old mentor and playmate from Odessa with whom I had quarrelled over nothing more important than the affections of a common little Moldavenka whore. All that bitterness was long since vanished and my soul sang out with joy! I embraced him! Kissed him! Held his strong, arrogant body close to me and wept again! Shura restored to me! It was all I needed to bring my normal optimism flooding back. Shura, my childhood friend! I had such a story to tell him and such a story to hear! 'How long can you stay?'

'Until Tripoli!' Shura was as moved as I. Tears ran down his cheeks and he dashed them from the corners of his full lips with his remaining arm while he laughed at my own tears.

'Little Max the Hetman. You're a film star now, I hear. Doing all kinds of wonderful things. You told us you'd be famous. We should have listened, eh? *Le plus fameux des chics types!* Wanda was your best friend, you know. She predicted a great future for you. You look well, *mon joli bagage.*'

Realising Captain Quelch had only a little Russian we both slipped into French, to inform him of our gratitude at this extraordinary reunion. 'What a marvellous, unwitting catalyst you are, captain,' I said.

'I'm happy you approve, old boy. Actually Shura's boss is an old business associate from the Marseilles days. I was hoping to do him a favour. Sure you don't mind?'

Only Bolsover or Seaman would object to an unauthorised passenger, but Captain Quelch and I were already in the process of concocting a plan which would get Bolsover arrested as soon as we had berthed in Alexandria. Captain Quelch had purchased the necessary morphine when he picked up our *sneg*. Seaman would grumble. His film was paramount. In the saloon Mrs Cornelius was immediately charmed by Shura, who kissed her hand and introduced himself as my cousin and an old university comrade.

She was not deceived. 'Yore one o' them Slobodka mobsmen, ain't yer? Ya 'ad style, you fellers. It's orl that French yer tork, innit?' Shura was baffled by her English and delighted by her Russian, which he understood scarcely any better but he loved, he said, the melody of it. I was pleased that they got on so well at first meeting. Even Captain Quelch seemed charmed by Shura's company. With two arms he was a winning rogue. With one he was irresistible.

The only cabin available for Shura was Mr Mix's vacant cubby hole. It took no time to fill the negro's suitcase with the few books, toilet articles and clothes he had left behind. I was not greatly pleased to see *The Martyrdom of Man* among those effects and joked to Shura that at this rate we should soon find a copy of *Das Kapital* under every camel blanket! (I was innocent enough in those days not to believe my own fantasy.) My cousin was swiftly supplied with bed-linen and toiletries, then we spent a few minutes in the cabin sampling the cocaine he had brought with him. I reminded him that it was he who had first introduced me to this natural stimulant. 'There's scarcely a sniff goes by that I do not think of you, darling Shura!'

My cousin laughed. I was, he said, the same old Max. He suggested we stroll back up to the saloon. He told me that these days he was in partnership with an Odessa acquaintance, the man who had inadvertently been the cause of my first meeting with Mrs Cornelius. S.A. Stavisky was now in Marseilles and chiefly involved in the importation of cocaine which could be processed cheaply and more or less legally in Tangier where it was not against the law to import South American paste. 'But he's branching out, these days, into politics, so I handle most of that drug business. Political stuff and the stock market was never my style. But you know what opportunities there are, now! Millions are being made. One of the people helping Stavisky is an old friend of yours, I gather. Another émigré. Remember a Count Nikolai Feodorovitch Petroff?'

By now I was breathless with the shock. But Kolya surely was in Paris, married to an aristocrat?

'He still travels to Paris, I think. He's definitely based with the boss in Marseilles now, though.'

'You are sure it is the same man?' Pretending to be dizzy from the drug, I rested for a moment against the bulkhead. Only a few steps lay ahead before we ascended to the saloon.

'Very tall, rather pale. Good-looking in a sort of effeminate way. Excellent tailor. Knew you in Peter? Was in business with you in France?'

It could be no one but Kolya. 'You say he travels?' Somewhat falteringly I continued towards the companionway and paused again before I climbed.

'Yes. He was in Tangier, for instance, only a couple of weeks ago. That was probably politics, too, but he didn't say. He stayed at the *Villa de France*.'

'His wife was with him?' Almost supernaturally, Esmé had appeared overhead on the deck above, her dress and mood thoroughly changed. Now she was a little Mary Pickford, a Victorian angel – everything I knew her to be deep within herself. 'No, miss.' Shura looked up with friendly candour. 'At least, I wouldn't have thought so.'

I was delighted to introduce two of my most beloved friends. As we brought ourselves up to stand in formal attention before her at the stairs, she stood there like a queen while I made the proper courtesies. 'Alexander Semyonovitch Neeva, may I introduce Esmé Bolascovna Loukianoff, my betrothed. Esmé, my cousin Shura.'

Shura kissed Esmé's tiny hand and murmured some courtesy. Esmé excused herself. She had been on her way to her cabin, she said, and looked forward to joining us later, perhaps at dinner. Our ship was already drawing up her anchor and turning to the open sea. I took Shura into the saloon and found my own bottle beneath the bar. It was Old Beaumont Plantation, the best bourbon in New Orleans. Captain Quelch had a case of it and had presented me with three quarts for myself. Shura was highly appreciative. 'You get sick of cognac and whisky and the wine here's dreadful. One longs for the aged golden vodka we used to drink in Esau's in the Slobodka.'

To be honest, I remembered nothing so wonderful on sale at Esau's, but I would not have disagreed with my cousin and spoil this reconciliation if he had remembered that the Tsar was a Jew! I drank the bourbon for that very reason, I told him. I described some of my adventures since I had left Odessa on the *Rio Cruz*, my time in Constantinople, my meeting with Esmé there, our flight to Italy and France, my engineering achievements in Paris and Los Angeles, my film career, which he had already heard about from Captain Quelch. I saw no point in describing the negative parts of my story.

Shura was highly impressed by my success, but for his own part was self-deprecating. Even with one arm, he had been conscripted into various armies before he managed to get first to Varna and from there to Sofiya, where he had, he said, fallen in love for a while. He had gone on to Fiume until D'Annunzio's antics turned the place into an uninhabitable slum, whereupon he made his way slowly to Marseilles where he had fallen in with our old acquaintance, the dentist's son Stavisky, now a French citizen. 'We're a sort of Old Odessan network,' said Shura. 'He even found a job for Boris and Little Grania. She's in Tangier at this very moment, buying and selling.'

'And Boris is doing the accounts?'

'Exactly! Of course, Marseilles isn't Odessa, though it has certain similarities. I've learned to need the heat. I'm not sure I could easily live in Ukraine again.'

I had not thought of that aspect. I, too, had grown used to California and the way that good weather brought out the best in people, as, of course, it had done in Odessa, compared to the rest of the Empire. True to form, Shura was somewhat mocking of my three-piece suit. He said that his own costume was absolutely the latest Paris rage. Americans were so unstylish! I reminded him that I had always found his taste a little flashy. I had been raised in a more old-fashioned tradition. I did not remind him that our branch of the family had always been somewhat more intellectually sophisticated than his own, who were, after all, shopkeepers. I told him instead that I would find myself a good English tailor the moment we docked in Alexandria. I wanted to know what he planned to do in Tripoli. He was looking over, he said, a group of oil-fields being developed there. The 'firm' was considering some sort of flotation. Then I understood immediately why Kolya was involved. A wizard who had taken naturally to the mysteries of High Finance, Prince N.F. Petroff had become an eminent member of the Bourse. He would be called to assess the value of the fields and suggest the best way of launching the shares. It was through no fault of his that our *Rose of Kiev* had rotted in her shed, a victim of Levantine Big Business which wanted our Transatlantic Aerial Navigation Company to fail, which plotted our destruction. I shall never learn the whole of that wretched story. Certainly it was not Kolya's fault that the burden of the blame for our defeat fell on me and I had been branded a swindler, forced to flee. He, after all, had courageously volunteered to remain behind and fight on. I could only thank heaven that in the end the powers opposing us had chosen not to pursue him. No doubt it was fortunate his wife's father had been one of the other directors and, anxious to avoid an inter-family scandal, sent him into some sort of exile, but I was rather surprised to hear of Kolya's sudden change of occupation. Maybe, after all, he had merely grown bored with the routines of the Parisian *haut monde*. Like me,

Prince Nicholai was fundamentally an adventurer, a risk-taker, a restless seeker after fresh experience. This latest news suggested that I might meet him again sooner than I had dared hope. Our paths were sure to cross. I began to nurse the idea of returning to Europe. With my American passport and my credentials as Tom Peters, the moving-picture actor, I was sure I would have little trouble there. After all, the screen confirmed my honest American identity! But I would still avoid France for a while. It would be wonderful, I thought, to see Rome again. I had good friends there. The events of 1922 had heralded the beginning of a great social experiment just being realised to its full potential. Mussolini had brought a wonderful new stability to Italy.

When we had completed our Egyptian picture, I told Shura, I would probably take Esmé on a honeymoon in Europe. My friends da Bazzano, Laura Fischetti and Annibale Santucci must surely still be there, eating fried artichoke and arguing over the future of nations. I would love to see them again. And people told me that Berlin was far more interesting than Paris, these days. We would go over to London, where I still had money awaiting me. I laughed about this. It had seemed such a fortune before I began to earn my own living. But it would be a good excuse to look up Mr Green and Mr Parrot. 'I heard those two old crooks were doing well for themselves with my dad's money,' said Shura cheerfully. We had gone out on deck to enjoy the sunset over the distant city. 'I doubt if you'll get what you're owed, Simka darling. And we'll never know how much they had. Dad was shot early on. By the Reds, I think. Anyway the *pogromchiks* changed their name and went out looking for "profiteers"! The results were much the same. You can't make a Cossack change his hobbies overnight. The female profiteers were mostly raped, the males were butchered along with the children. All in Slobodka. They said Wanda got away.'

I had a soft spot for his sister. 'I hope so.' There was no mercy in telling him that she was probably dead.

By the time Esmé rejoined us, and Captain Quelch, Mrs Cornelius and the rest were ready for dinner, Shura and I were sadly the worse for drink. I remember very little of the evening, save for the warmth and security of our nostalgia, and remained in this euphoric state, with the help of Shura's cocaine and my bourbon, until the ditty-boat took him towards Tripoli. We were on our way to Alexandria almost before I could be sure that I could read the drunkenly traced letters of the hotel, his permanent home in Tangier.

My reunion with my cousin had begun a healing process. Until then I had carried a bloody wound with me for some five years; a wound made when I wrenched myself away from my native land, the land of the Steppe and wide rivers where my Cossack ancestors established their *sechs*. I had never planned to leave Odessa or my motherland. I had been forced to go as the Bolsheviks stamped their terrible will on the nation. I was part of an exodus making the Jewish exodus a weekend holiday. All the best that was Russia belonged to that exodus. All the best that survived. Scientists, writers and scholars, engineers and soldiers, so many of us fought to pretend we had no throbbing wounds, no aching longing for our Slavonic home. Since leaving Russia I had lost my way. I had forgotten that necessary pain. With Shura's stories of old friends and old times, I knew something of the past must survive. The past can never be recreated but on the other hand it need not be lost to us. My scapegrace, charming cousin, before he left the *Hope Dempsey*, had restored to me a few vital scraps of my past. Like healing tissue, those scraps would knit to form at last a protective scar upon my wounded spirit.

Shura would never know how, almost in the nick of time, he had brought me the healing gift of tranquil recollection.

TEN

THEY TELL US THAT WITCHCRAFT is banished to Africa. They assure you it is dead and forgotten in Surrey and all the civilised counties of England. They tell you this on the wireless, when it is the BBC that broadcasts the worst heresies and blasphemies, night and day, while herbalists and homeopaths are forever recommending their rubbish to the listening millions! What else is this but witchcraft? *Jimmy Young* and *Woman's Hour* are nothing but a medium through which the Satanic creeds of Alchemy and Black Magic are transmitted to eager converts. What if the TV people offer us *Stars on Sunday* or a *Final Programme* or that we hear a priest, or more often than not these days a rabbi, for a few minutes a day on the Home Service – it scarcely matters, when twenty-three of every twenty-four hours broadcasting is given up to the propagation of Communism, Occultism, Judaism and rampant Buggery, where the 'pagan spirit' is the informing genius of the BBC Plays and Talks departments, and not improved, I would add, by replacing a godless Presbyterian with a crypto-Catholic. 'But this is England,' you will tell me, with your usual smug condescension. 'There is no changing it. We have always been a pagan nation. It is the secret of our success. What do you think the Reformation was all about? Not to mention Cromwell. We made a God of our own sublime vices and set about proving to the world that He was the superior of all others.' Yes! You are surprised that I know these arguments? Young people are fools. They think we have always been old and powerless. Why will they not observe and learn? Yes, I have seen witchcraft and feudalism in the flesh, under my nose, and if that does not make you value our rationalist and enlightened universe, very little will. They say those who come back from the colonies have the ideas of a hundred years ago. That is because they come from a world still having the *experience* of a hundred years ago or, in some cases, a thousand or a million. We should not despise the experience of people less civilised than ourselves. We should help them gently along the path of progress, teach them to write and read in their own language, but we should also listen to what *they* can teach us. Sometimes this method has excellent results, as in the case of Hawaii, but the case of Egypt, for instance, is the saddest of all. It is not the first time she has refused the helping hand of a nobler power and slipped instead into yet another pit of corrupt barbarism, an easy prey to Turk and Bedouin alike, those jackals who will feast on any civilisation but only when it is thoroughly rotten, when the stink of its carcass permeates the planet. And the British wonder why today the mongrels of the world are suddenly attracted to their little island! Sugar is sweet, but putrefaction is sweeter, as we used to say in Odessa. There was witchcraft there, too, but we knew it for what it was.

Mrs Cornelius tells me I am an alarmist. 'There's nuffink wrong wiv a few ol' biddies putting a bit o' comfrey in their tea, Ivan.'

'It is not the comfrey, my dear friend. It is the implication of the comfrey. The comfrey is a symbol of what has gone wrong.'

'Usually indigestion'd be my guess.' Sometimes Mrs Cornelius can be overly down-to-earth. Perhaps this is why we are attracted to one another, for I have the sensitive, romantic kind of imagination while she, eternal female, has the less intellectual, earthier, instinctive qualities men value in women. These feminists who want to turn Titania into Oberon have no conception of the true, deep meaning of equality, that union of opposites which can be the most beautiful and transporting experience of all.

In that Mrs Cornelius would concur, and she is, after all, very much a woman, even now, when time has faded her beauty and stolen her health but nonetheless left her great heart beating stronger.

She remains too generous, my friend; incapable of detecting sin, for the most part, or of judging her fellow creatures too harshly. She was the first to drink with the Bishop, for instance, upon his release (though grave-robbery, even in London, is still frowned upon by some). For some years she earned a small living as a child-minder. It never mattered to her, she said, if they were little micks or little piccaninnies; they all shit their pants just before their mums came to pick them up.

'It's just a fad, orl this black magic stuff,' she tells me. 'The kids was inter it a few years back. Voodoo dolls an' pentawotsits an' 'exes an' orl that. It's them 'orror pictures, Ivan. On ther telly. *Rosemary's Baby* an' *Frankenstein Meets the Wolfman*.'

'There is a difference between the two.' I grow tired of this perpetual round. 'When you and I were in Hollywood we knew who was Evil and who was Good. That was the difference. Our pictures pointed a firm moral – and not always the conventional sentiment. Now it is all up in the air. Is it surprising the children are confused?'

What is the point of turning on that television? The Cornelius children inform me I should buy a colour set. Why should I bother, I say, I know where I am with black and white. The wireless gets worse and worse, full of childish smut and self-congratulatory panel games featuring the same people responsible for the smut. If Tony Hancock is a comedian, then so is Harold Wilson. Both seem to blame the rest of the world for their misfortunes. They should face it. The public does not want what they offer. It is the same with the plays and books these young men produce. Is it art? If self-pity has become an art, then it is no surprise, I say, that all Jews are now artists. If self-congratulation is an art, then every Briton is an artist!

I try to recollect the beauty of the world. Before my legs grew so numb I used to go for walks to Kensington Gardens and then, as the whole of Hyde Park gradually became a playground for a disgusting cosmopolitan lower class, to Holland Park, where the foreign trees and shrubs grow in profusion but the hybrid is a short-lived rarity. How I love this London in spring-time, still, with the scent of early lilac and daffodils, the carpets of wallflowers, tulips, forget-me-nots, those fields of lemon and scarlet, the great chestnuts coming to leaf, the blossoming cherries. I would walk up to the top of Ladbroke Grove, where all the substantial gardens were, and then stroll slowly down to Holland Park Avenue, smelling the shrubs and the flowers, the honeysuckle, the sweet plane trees, remembering my boyhood in Kiev. Then I would wander to the Kreshchatik on one of those days we know so well in Russia, when suddenly, in the blink of an eye, winter is gone and spring has arrived. Kiev's warm yellow brick would begin to absorb the sun again and all the parks and avenues and cleared spaces, all the little suburbs like our own Kurenvskaya, explode with varied colour, while the bright shopfronts fling open winter shutters to reveal their new treasures and even the trams become glittering carriages of light floating on sunbeams, bearing us through the hills and valleys of paradise. A city built on hills always has a singular spirit. London, built where the river was shallow and fordable, has all the additional fortification necessary to a valley city. A hill is a natural defence and those who live upon hills naturally feel more secure. Londoners are always sounding the reassuring trumpet of their own superiority, as if they know how vulnerable they are. It is the same with Berlin. Yet there remains nothing like a London spring, fresh with rain and silvery sunshine, with as many shades of green as a forest of jade and alive with tulips, with violets and daffodils. The British, unable to express affection for each other, lavish their love on flowers and animals. They flourish pictures of roses where others display crucifixes. Even their weeds and vegetables are national symbols. There is no city on earth more full of contented dogs, cats and herbaceous borders. It is, if not Blake's Paradise, at least a Jerusalem for the Jack Russell, the Oriental shorthair, the African Grey, the British Queen or the Rhode Island Red. Even their polecats are domesticated!

What would otherwise seem deplorable, this lust to give affection to animals or plants, is more understandable when you consider the average representative of the English *hoi polloi*. He is as fatuously self-inflated, as belligerently stupid, as ill-mannered, ill-smelling and ill-contented as any creature upon the whole round world. One grudgingly admires those who still try to save him, when the only use for him, the only use the tribe ever produced him for, is to serve in some horrible overseas army. Without the colonies, the British have nowhere to send him. Their posturing becomes an empty charade, bereft of substance, plot or meaning. Is it any wonder that the annual entertainment for these people, the only living show they are ever prepared to attend in a theatre, is the Christmas Harlequinade in which down-and-out comedians regale a fresh crop of proto-louts with the full weight of their inheritance of prejudice and filth? These cattle have learned to praise themselves for their own vulgarity. What better *Lumpenproletariat* than one which makes virtues of the very things which keep it from aspiring to some better state? *The Sun* is their Bible. It is a Bible of Pride bereft of dignity or spirit. If this is the salt of the earth, this chanting army, then I will take my food with a little less flavouring. They are the same louts who brought disrepute to the Nazi party and who seized control of the Duma in 1917.

Mrs Cornelius can forgive these people everything. She says she is proud to be working-class. I can only mourn the collapse of good taste and public morals. I have offered my experiences to the BBC more than once but, of course, I am not of that Bum-Boy Clique as the Bishop calls it and refuse to prostitute myself. On my one visit to the World Service, I kept my trousers firmly buttoned and any attempt to lay hands on me were met with polite but firm disapproval. I am too old, I said, for that sort of thing.

'Yore too proud, Ivan. It's bin yer tragedy,' she says. Mrs Cornelius has always suggested that my integrity was the worst obstacle to my success in any course I chose. Like von Stroheim, I would neither corrupt my talent nor sell myself to the highest bidder merely to make a profit or win some politician's approval. So many émigrés found it necessary to do that and I cannot say I blame most of them; but neither do I blame myself. It is not my fault if I am the victim of an unfashionable sense of honour. We are created as individuals. We should respect this. The modern move towards making us all one standard, thinking the same, acting the same, wanting the same things, all in the name of 'mental health', is not to my taste. We are becoming the slaves of dull-minded computer programmers. I was the first to condemn Bolshevik and Fascist alike for such fallacious mechanistic understandings. In this, Freud and Marx have much to answer for, of course. They were put on pedestals while Nietzsche, ignored or reviled, who stood, like Max Stirner, for the individual, for the potential super-being in all of us, who provided the philosophical stimulus for my flying cities, my vision of a spiritual samurai caste extending a helping hand to every race and class, each according to its level of maturity, was silenced. Nietzsche became associated with Nazis, certainly, but that is no more his fault than Saint Joan's becoming identified with the House of Tudor because she was politically useful to Henry the Eighth. We do not ask what Henry's general attitude towards women was! I have always been willing to give credit where it is due and to place blame where it belongs irrespective of Party or Religion. But now, as Goethe discovered, it is against the law to offer the opinions of experience. These days one must toe the computer's line, and woe betide the fool attempting to set a lifetime's experience against some youth's imaginary notions of reality! In that respect, at least, the other brother, Frank, is not so bad but one need not bother to try to talk to Jerry or Catherine. Whether she agrees with them or not, Mrs Cornelius defends her children. She is a she-tiger, in this respect. Only she is allowed to criticise. I telephoned Jerry that day and he went to see her. He was with her when she died. I was looking in all the time, but I had to protect the shop, there are so many vandals. He came at once and for that, believe me, I grant him a great deal of leeway. But he is jealous. And nowadays I think he avoids me. She told me things she would not tell her children.

Even to me she would never reveal her exact age. It was one of her rules. Also I was only allowed, in company, to bring up our more recent experiences, in England. Apart from between ourselves, she refused to discuss the early days.

160

I sometimes suspected it was because she had discovered the secret of eternal life! Only in her last decade did she begin to show her years. But then she used her age as she had used her beauty, as a finely-adjusted weapon to get what she needed. I always admired her that ability to recognise her best interests.

In private, the past returned with a vengeance! She kept a great number of scrapbooks and boxes under her bed, many of them held together by nothing but greasy dust. They contained cigarette cards, magazine cuttings, letters, ration books, birth certificates, dirt-veined official documents and worthless currency – her entire lifetime's collection. There were clippings of her from *The Picturegoer* and *Movie Magazine*, stills featuring her in scenes with John Gilbert, Ramon Navarro, Lon Chaney and myself, from the only shocker we appeared in together, *The Weasel Strikes Again*, in which I played the mysterious Weasel himself. I asked about it shortly after the funeral, but her boy kept all his mother's papers and is reluctant to let me go through them. He promises he will find the picture for me. I do not hold out much hope. He fobs me off. And the other brother is completely crazy now. My only hope is Catherine, but she is away.

Vos hot ir gezogt? Well, this is my story. It is the only one I have. Mrs Cornelius was the best kind of mother. She did not believe in interfering. They never listened to me, anyway, even when they were young. She believed they took after her father, especially the one who is now an actor. He was given to 'passin' enfusiasms', she said.

' 'Is gran'dad wos barmy, reelly. Orlways wanted a teashop in Kent. 'E joined the Masons and abart ev'ry bloody religion yer c'n imagine. As a matter o' fact thass 'ow I got me names – Honoria Catherine – 'cause me dad converted ter Rome fer abart free weeks one September. It wos annuver of 'is crazes. Well, ter be fair, everybody wos doin' it in Notting 'Ill that year, blankets and ther bully beef bein' better at the Irish church. It wos orl Irish rahn' 'ere, then. That wos before we moved back ter Whitechapel. Then 'e wos off on some ovver wicket. Anarchism or somefink. We 'ardly ever sor 'im. Well, mum'd kicked 'im art, anyway, an' 'e wos livin' rahnd the corner, but I wos orlways 'is favourite, even if 'e wasn't too sure I *wos* 'is,

161

yer know. Well, they wos orl anarchists in Whitechapel just then. Yer could say 'e flowed a bit wiv ther tide, but I don't blame 'im, I'm ther same meself. You an' me, Ivan. We got frough it an' we're not nuts. An' thass ther main fing, innit?'

I was never fully able to concur with this. I remember how one day we had pursued a monstrous black fly which had flown into her basement flat. It was early springtime and I could not credit that the creature had grown so fat and sleek in a brief day or two. He seemed possessed of supernatural senses and to anticipate every move we made with swatters and rolled-up magazines. The fellow was the big game of the fly world. He was cunning and resourceful, scarcely sentient and therefore incapable of morality, neither good nor evil. He had no purpose beyond maintaining the existence of himself and his kind. His every instinct and physical component was designed for that single purpose – to survive; *merely* to survive. He was part of no natural cycle, he fulfilled no function in the Eternal Scheme. He did no good and only incidental harm. He was without value. And yet his eggs were surely laid so that if he were killed he could be replaced again, almost infinitely, and become a legion of fat, black flies whose only reason for existence was to survive. I could not accept this as a truism. The notion, I told her, was far too French for me. It was not an accurate symbol. I have the instincts of that fly but I am not that fly. There was far more to my decisions than a simple desire to survive. I wanted to do good for the whole of mankind. Now all I can offer mankind is experience.

I had a vocation. I survived in order to fulfil that vocation. But we need not speak of this *tragish kharpe* any further.

I leave her basement and walk past the new blocks of flats for whose erection the nuns of the Poor Clare Convent were evicted. Once there was tranquil mystery on the other side of a wall. Now the mysteries are altogether more prosaic. The police are frequent visitors. I reach the corner of Kensington Park Road and pass the Blenheim Arms, where the Bishop and Miss Brunner, from the school, still drink. In this area once everyone knew everybody else, but soon, because it was cheap and not far from Paddington, it began to attract the Jamaicans, then the bohemians started to arrive with Colin

Wilson and his Black Monks, his pop groups, and soon the pubs and cafés were full of dwarfish writers seeking to revive some dream of reality by rubbing shoulders with degenerates whom they insist on addressing as 'locals' and who are as much interlopers as the intellectuals! I don't know which attracts which! Do the writers follow the rabble or does the rabble look for the writers, knowing those middle-class misfits are the only people on earth willing to give it the time of day? This area was once a little rough, certainly, but one knew who one's friends and enemies were. Now it is impossible to tell. Who writes these articles in the American press? I suppose I should not complain. Those few of us not squeezed out by hippies, perverts and Rotarians are at least able to make a living. You can sell almost anything to an American so long as you offer him a history, a provenance. An old coat becomes 'Mick Jagger's old coat'. They force you to tell them these things, otherwise they are disappointed. The entire antique trade seems devoted to inventing ludicrous covenants for the most unlikely and useless articles. I have Roy Wood's motoring jacket, Lord Curzon's dress uniform and Winston Churchill's smoking-cap. Yesterday some pork-fed doughboy tells me he paid a mere £35 for Disraeli's chamber-pot. 'And what if it had had Disraeli's turd still in it?' I ask him. 'Would you have paid £350?'

'Only if it was definitely genuine,' he said. The boy was serious. History for these people is a matter of commercial evaluation and romance, not of experience or learning. Or is it a matter of points and grades? Perhaps that is better than the English children who are nowadays only inducted into the mysteries of Bolshevik politics and can tell you any minor thing you might wish to know about Chairman Mao but have never heard of Primo de Rivera! And they say the system is not biased! It was to resist the takeover of the country by communists that many patriots went to jail. I met them on the Isle of Man. Mosley, I rarely spoke to. He tended to be avoided because of his breath. To this day, I believe, his followers have been unable to broach the subject. Even his wife says nothing. Perhaps she is used to it. He came into my shop one day, with his lieutenant, Hamm, and he said that he wanted to free Poland.

163

He was standing for Parliament. It was 1958 or 9. I used to go down to Portland Road and have scones or crumpets with Mrs Leese. She was contemptuous of Mosley. He had failed, she said, to develop a firm line on the Jews. In those days she was still publishing her husband's magazines, *Black and White* and *Gothic Ripples*, although the grand old fighter himself was long gone. She supported Mosley because he was better than nothing. We put copies of her magazines through every door in Notting Hill, advising people to vote for the Union Movement, which was what the British Union of Fascists had become. As it was, Mosley received 159 votes and went back to France with a clear message from the powers-that-be. Myself, I voted for the Conservative. Now, of course, it is illegal to air any but the most conventional views on the subject of Race. Mosley conspired in this censorship even before the infamous Race Relations Act gagged Mrs Leese and all those of her people continuing to fight, as best they could, under the banner of the Phoenix. When Mrs Leese died I stopped going to Portland Road. I still have some of their records. Of course it would be madness to try to play them now, especially the famous Nuremberg speeches. The people who took over laughed at me. I told them I was there from the beginning. I knew Mrs Leese's protégés, I knew them well, those young men of fine words and noble motives. They created the National Front out of the ruins of the old movements but then through bitter in-fighting proceeded to destroy everything they valued. What if Hitler had thrown away his chances that way? I asked Mr Jordan one day, when he was speaking on the corner, as he used to, What would have happened to Germany, then? We would all now have pictures of Uncle Joe on our walls! Jordan agreed with me. He was trying to hold the party together. The trouble was, he said, that people were too contented. Eventually, when Socialism had brought the country to ruin, then perhaps we should see some progress. Well, the country is close to ruin but I do not see the emergence of a strong leader to save us, though the country cries out for one. Edward Heath is a petulant old queen. The 'voters', the public, slouch outside my shop wearing the banner of Anarchy on their chests while they pour cans of beer, purchased at state expense, into their loutish throats and wash down their 'blue beauties' and their 'bombers' and glare at me from permanently glazed eyes, the true inheritors of Makhno's drugged rabble, who lost our Ukraine to Ulianof, Bronstein and Djugashvili, that First Triumvirate who ruined old, noble Russia much as their predecessors had ruined virtuous Rome.

In Odessa the black smoke drifts and the goats sprawl sleeping in the streets, possessed of a power they hardly understand and for which they feel no responsibility, while against the riot of the hellish sky the great black He-goat rears up, frothing and glaring, his voice a victorious bray, and brings his pointed hooves of brass down upon the Cathedral of the Transfiguration, smashing the gold and white dome like an egg. I took the tram from the Greek Bazaar and was for a while in Arcadia. My life was saved but they had put some metal in me while I was trapped in their *shtetl*. The metal is still there. Much of the time I do not feel it, then comes a little stabbing, then a sharper, harder pain, then some sort of convulsion. It has poisoned my blood. The doctors will not prescribe or operate. Only the cocaine controls it and of course that is so expensive, these days, I cannot always afford it. These silly little boys. They think it is strange an old man likes a drug they believe they invented! They do not even know what the pure thing is. Cocaine was always the king of drugs. Even their progenitor Freud admitted that. The rest is rubbish. I control the pain, but there is anxiety, too, and a certain numbness. I have explained all this to Doctor Diamond and he says that it will heal in time. I have more than once suggested an exploratory X-ray or investigative surgery. He says it would be too expensive and they might not find anything. He is an idiot, a Donald Duck. Give me a magnet, I tell him, I'll find it for you. It has sharp points. Sometimes I think it is in the form of a star. It brings nausea, often at night, when I wake up suddenly. The good Jew in Arcadia was just a little too late.

He was a journalist. He worked for the newspapers in Odessa. He had a wife, but she was already in France. He knew what they had done, I think, and felt guilty on their behalf. But he was not to blame. I loved him. Should I trust my emotions so completely? He was so gentle. Sometimes I

165

wonder if it was not he in fact who did this to me, while I slept. Was I seduced by Lucifer? But I will not judge a man just because he is a Jew. It is not in my nature. I love all humanity. I should not suspect the journalist. It would spoil too much.

Oddly, these thoughts were often with me after Shura had gone. I felt depressed and lost and even the smooth, blue waters of the Sunny Med could not improve my mood.

'Alexandria is like no other Levantine port,' Captain Quelch told us as we went down to quarter-speed. He and I stood in shirt-sleeves on the main deck enjoying the evening heat. We would not see the city of Julius Caesar, Napoleon and Lord Cromer until the morning, and there would be no Colossus, as in ancient times, to signal the port's position. We had crawled all day along the Egyptian coast, occasionally meeting customs launches and bum-boats, so as to steam in early next day when, Captain Quelch said, we should not have to sit outside at anchor all evening waiting for the pilot to come aboard in the morning and we would also have the first choice of docking berths. 'And yet, she is all of them combined.' He laughed at this contradiction. Wolf Seaman and Mrs Cornelius were with us in the stern, drinking some new cocktail Shura had invented while aboard. 'At first sight you'd think you'd arrived in Yarmouth. The façade is that of a prosperous English resort disguising a particularly disgusting version of the Naples slums. We British are masters at disguising wretchedness not with grandeur and pomp, like the French or the Russians, but with respectability. The very dullness of the buildings suggests they have nothing to hide. Look at London. The most impressive building in St Pancras is a Gothic railway station. It is all the visitor remembers.'

Since the rest of us had never visited Alexandria and only Mrs Cornelius knew London, we had no means of judging the measure of Quelch's descriptions, although I was inclined to trust them. He did not hate the Middle East, but he did not idealise it either.

That evening I was feeling somewhat gloomy at the prospect of parting from my new friend when I had only recently been forced to lose an old one. Since Tripoli I had been especially

166

glad of Mrs Cornelius's company but inevitably this made Esmé jealous. Once more, she was taking her meals in her cabin, though the sea-sickness was no longer a problem. Thanks to her, however, Wolf Seaman had recovered his humour, such as it was. He had been nervous, I think, afraid his master Goldfish would learn of our unofficial passenger and decide to recall the expedition. With Shura safely in Tripoli, he became merely surly, no longer quick to start an argument. What was more, for all Mrs Cornelius's declaration that my Esmé was as useful as a roast ham at a synagogue outing, my little girl overcame her natural shyness, devoting her time to placating Seaman. I reminded Mrs Cornelius how Esmé had become a useful peacemaker. Mrs Cornelius tartly suggested the word I wanted was *pirsumchick* and I decided to hold my tongue on the subject. Women can be baffling at such times and I suppose I should be grateful they did not come to active war on board the *Hope Dempsey*. I saw nothing wrong with Esmé's wish to win the approval of a man who might be useful to her but it was hard for me to understand why Mrs Cornelius, who was not above such strategies herself, could be so critical of a child who would never be her match in the art of 'vampirism'. I am being complimentary. I have been too long in the world to judge the way anyone – man or woman – makes their living. And for women I agree it is harder, these days. Men are no longer bound by religion and conscience to protect them. Women have more to lose and they must take greater risks. That courage was what I admired in Mrs Cornelius. Why should she despise the same qualities in another woman? Is the competition so fierce? Are the losses so great? *Ikh farshtey nit.* Because I cannot bear to see two women whom I love at odds, this is somehow a sign that I am insensitive? Here, too, I have also learned to keep my mouth shut. If Catherine Cornelius asks, believe me, I am a feminist. Besides, I have never been against another person's sexual preferences. Love, I always argued, is the only really important thing. Love, even now, could save us from the pit, from the suffering God puts upon the earth to warn us what Hell is like. It was love which saved me from the camp, in the end. 'We must learn to understand one another. It is our only chance. To succeed in that will make the rest of this worthwhile.' With tears in his eyes, Herman Goering himself spoke these words to me. He could not bear to hurt a fly. He had become a vegetarian. I suppose I should think myself lucky that because I try to tell them about the whole man I have merely been accused of fascism. They hounded Goering, after all, to his death. I wept for him when I heard the news, but I was not allowed to speak. I remained silent, like Peter, and I am ashamed. For it was Herman Goering who saved my life. Yet still the world refuses to let me honour him. Society has become too simplified for me. Paradox and contradiction are now the sole province of TV futurists and pop surrealists. They were allowed to make it their own. They became a commercial monopoly. Thus the very qualities distinguishing humanity from the beasts were isolated and turned into a show, something speculators could invest in and which spectators would pay to look at. Fantasy and invention, vision and speculation, all were placed in their own ghettos during the Great Simplification. The human race warred on the very elements which made it distinct. It warred on the Twentieth Century. It devoured and destroyed its own Time. It fought complexity. It fought variety. It fought individuality. And slowly, like Stalin, it began to win. It stifled those elements to death first by putting them into special categories, then by eliminating them entirely from the consensual consciousness, making them something alien and perverse.

All the qualities separating mammal from reptile were burnt out of us. Not for nothing is Satan represented as a snake. What does it matter how they style themselves any more – Tories or Trotskyites? They offer the same thing. Authority demands conformity because it has made conformity and familiarity synonymous with security. They have made a positive virtue of similarity. They have outlawed plurality and take power by promising to eradicate all inconsistency from the world. Do we need such heroes? Alexander the Great united the world while celebrating its variety. He did what no socialist has ever done. He drove Carthage out of the Semitic lands into equatorial Africa. He gave the Semites their chance to be whole again, to continue God's work and his. Ptolemy and some of his successors tried to maintain Alexander's momentum. To some extent they succeeded, but then Carthage cunningly returned in the form of a woman. Cleopatra caused the civil war which robbed Rome of her noblest men and ensured the destruction of Egypt's capital, the greatest city of the Ancient World, famous for her learning and her art, '*sweet, dreaming Alexandria, palm-shaded city of the sun, crucible of all that reason values*,' as Wheldrake had it. Captain Quelch was the first to note how, in so many of his works, the poet influenced Eliot.

That night, as it became unpleasantly warm, I sought out Captain Quelch, anxious to enjoy the comforting ambience, for the last time, of his wonderful cabin. He, too, was in a sentimental mood, wearing his scarlet Chinese dressing-gown and the pearl-trimmed smoking-cap he had won at a fan-tan game in Shanghai. He insisted I borrow the blue gown, undress and enjoy the sensuality of the silk while I sipped a ballon of perfect cognac, relishing the clear-headed heightening of mind and senses which is conferred by the best cocaine. He talked of home a little, of his schooldays in Kent, the vicarage where he and his brothers had grown up. He revealed almost casually that he had a wife of his own in England. 'And two strapping lads, a pretty little girl. They're in Cornwall now, near Bugle. We stay in touch, you know, and I hope to retire there, eventually. Don't be mistaken, old boy, they never go short, even when I do. I think the pups are a little proud of their sailorman papa.'

'They plan to join the navy, I suppose?' I felt oddly embarrassed by a note I interpreted as regret.

'Good Lord, old boy, I hope not! There never was any money in the sea. I keep hoping they'll turn out to be lawyers. We could use some of those in the family. You must have a few in yours, eh, Max? Not to mention doctors and violinists and so on.' None of these occupations was traditional either for a Cossack or a Russian aristocrat, I said, and we shared a minute or two of relaxing laughter. He said that his brother and I would get on famously. '*More*,' he said, '*Hibernico*.' And with an air of priestly pleasure he carefully lowered the first disc of *Lohengrin* to his turntable.

ELEVEN

THE PEOPLE whom you would call heathen or ignorant or merely 'alien' have amongst them as many heroes and great men, as many possessed of the finest virtues, as any Christian society; you would recognise as many amongst them as malcontents or evil-doers (the kind who sometimes rise to power over you) as you observe amongst yourselves. So why do you therefore single out and exaggerate these minor differences between you, so that you may feel free to mock and attack them? Is this not a true sin of Pride?

What possible virtue is there in all this terrible competing and quarrelling? You are like a rabble in a maze fighting amongst yourselves rather than pooling your resources to find a way through, to make a common plan. We are *all* frightened, *all* desperate for certainty. Not one of us does not secretly yearn to be given a real reason why we should suffer so and then die, perhaps even a reason why some win all life's rewards, when the equally gifted (or equally ungifted) are allowed to exist in perpetual squalor. We refuse to accept the random qualities of God's universe, and until we accept them, we shall be forever quarrelling in a maze of our own creation. A political creed is a maze. A religion can be a maze. Even simple faith can create a maze – for we impose simple models upon that which is not simple – as Americans visiting London attempt to impose a grid system upon the tangled streets. Their logic not only fails them at this point – they become fearful. Their inability to cope with the warren of streets encourages them to curse the fools who did not have the sense to simplify and lay a rule upon their city. The simple-minded dinosaur did not survive; he could not cope with change. Only by accepting the world as it is and fulfilling our lives in an unpredictable world can we ever know the universal harmony the majority of us long for. Contrary to what these hippies believe, harmony can be achieved by political and philosophical means; so long as the means are not imposed but are presented as arguments in a natural 'pluralist' democracy where humane Reason and uncorrupted Law are commonly respected. This is not too much to hope. The means is there. The only logical means of satisfying all Man's spiritual, physical and psychological needs under a single idea which accepts plurality as its fundamental faith. I speak of the true church, the Church of Constantine, the First Christian Emperor. Ah, Tsar, remebre vus! Эта причёска не можная! The little girls scream in the cathedral. *Kyrie eleison! Kyrie eleison!* The ghost is risen and those temples were so cold one might have thought their contents cryogenically preserved and that the entire Dead of Egypt would, thanks to our warming blood, begin to rise and walk the earth again. *Die Geschichte ist niemals gleich; doch es kommt vor, das Ereignisse sich wiederholen.* Thus did Hannibal command his legions, 'Rise from the ashes, and fight again!' So Carthage sleeps; beautiful Carthage stirs; golden, heathen Carthage groans and opens up one hot and greedy eye to behold the Valley of the Nile, the fertile wonder of our world, the verdant birthplace of all we value and the fount of all we ever knew.

Mother Egypt, our universal Mother Egypt! With what great beauty were you dressed, mother; in what rich splendour! And all the vivid colours of Africa and all the subtleties of an English spring harmonise in you. You are forever beautiful, mother. Even your squalor, your vice, your danger, is beautiful. You were half-beast, still, when you began to build your nation. Your very diseases are exotic and beautiful. Mother Egypt! Mother Egypt! I had not expected you to be so beautiful. *L'histoire est un perpetuel recommencement.* The Greeks understood this. Even the gods must submit to fate.

Carthage opens up her other eye – and there lies Europe, luscious and rich. Sweet Europe, from the wheatlands of Ukraine to the apple trees of Kent, the pine forests of Lapland, the olive groves of Greece and Spain, the rich cities of the Romans. And Carthage blinks and Carthage grins and golden, mighty, wakening Carthage grinds her savage teeth and licks her scarlet lips and her burning breath stinks of roses. She prepares to feast. Soon, we shall all be silenced. Frightened and bribed into perpetual passivity we shall become no more than the domesticated cattle of Carthage. Then Carthage shall have no need of arms. She shall not need to hunt. Great Carthage becomes a financier and feeds the cows and chickens at weekends, a gentleman farmer called Collins or Carter or Green or some such reassuring English name. This is how Carthage, barbaric and devious, shall enslave us without our ever knowing it. Anyone detecting a glimmer of this truth, who attempts to broadcast the news of our imminent conquest and humiliation, is at best shunned as a lunatic, at worst killed in torment as a lesson to the rest never to utter the fact that our very souls are mortgaged to Satan.

I set this down *meo periculo*, at my own risk, but I am well aware that no public is likely to see it. Carthage has won not only our bodies but our minds. To her advantage she has learned from English insularity.

Now no one will ever let me tell the truth lest they too enjoy my punishment. They see a great man already humiliated and reduced. The Bishop said so to Mrs Cornelius. Like Abdias in the story, I learned all I know by suffering, by travel and intellectual solitude. Unlike his creator Stifter, I see no special virtue in Abdias's suffering, solitude or even his travels. I never sought them out. But neither would I let their threat deter me from my course. I once thought I was doomed to wander until Judgement Day, doomed to speak the truth and never be heard.

We should live in harmony with Nature. I am prepared to provide the means by which that is possible. The Gods learned to live with random Nature. Tieck knew that and all the great German writers. We must use our ingenuity to live in *accord* with Nature, not try to overpower her!

172

My flying cities allow Nature to exist without interference from us and yet remain there to be enjoyed whenever we wish.

Throughout all my vicissitudes this has been my dream. I have a gift for the world. Why would they accept so much dross from those frauds – from Marx and Einstein? What makes Faust a villain and Freud a saviour? There is one obvious answer but of course we are not allowed to give it any more. We have been fully conquered. Already we are refused the basic right to identify our masters. We are fully enslaved. We are even ruled by the Saxe-Coburg-Gothas, who as everyone knows bought their titles in Warsaw! I have a leaflet which proves it. It was written by one of those old churchmen from the Polish Club. The Poles of all people know the perfidy of Carthage. They prize Christian chivalry above everything. No wonder the women complain. Chivalry and good manners are a thing of the past. Once a man had to court his woman, prove his wit, his talent and his courage. Today it is all godless, joyless power-coupling – the boy to boast, the girl to feel even a taste of loving a man, her common sisterly dream, virgin or whore. For true love is all, the only dream she is allowed to call her own. Assured that this chimera is theirs to achieve through appropriate acts of obeisance and devotion to men, by appropriate speech and appropriate dress, the women become devious and spiteful. The boys are taught that to fuck and vomit are the two truest tests of status in their community. Their football chants must be a clue. *We're here because we're here.* The desperate call of nihilists down the centuries. *We want, ra-ra-ra. We want, ra-ra-ra. We'll never walk alone! I did it my way.* The dumb confidence of the herd. The women I could save. The men are hopeless. They should be sent to the Gold Coast or the Congo or the Andes. One day I shall write about my months in South America following the shipwreck of the *John Wesley*. I have ever since had a phobia of snakes and alligators which I suspect will stay with me for eternity. We went to *The Wandering Jew* at the Majestic in Lisbon. It was almost as good as the play, with Matheson Lang recreating his famous rôle. I was deeply moved by the final speech when, refusing to renounce his faith to the Inquisition, Mateus says: 'The

spirit of your Christ is nearer to my heart as I stand here –
a Jew – than it could be to those who would so thrust Him
between their lips.' A wonderful speech. I wept. They had a
full orchestra. Is this anti-Semitism? The message of the film
was clear – we are becoming so far divorced from the virtues
of our religion that it takes a noble and envying Jew to show
us that what we have is of infinite value. I have pointed this out
more than once to that *yentzer* Barnum, who runs the Festival
Novelties in Elgin Crescent, though half of it is toys now. I say
his skull is as empty as one of the giant pantomime heads in
his window. He says I am just an old *Judenhetze*. I say this is
ridiculous. How can I be? True, he says, it is a miracle to hear
such *mishegass*. Maybe Charlie Chaplin was Adolf Hitler, after
all. 'A split personality, maybe.'

'It is you who are crazy, my friend,' I tell him. 'My God,
what nonsense I have to suffer. One of my oldest friends was
a Jew. From Odessa. I owe my life to him. Does this make
me a likely anti-Semite?'

He cannot answer. They never can, these 'wise' guys.

Rabbi Davidson up the street, on the other side of the
bridge, claims so much greater an understanding of religion
and the world than I. He can never have known the temptations
and the terrors of the wilderness, the luxurious pleasures and
forbidden tortures of the Orient. I know the East. I have personally experienced the world that gave birth to our common
Testament. If I understand nothing else I understand religion.
Davidson knows I respect his position and his faith, but I always
defeat him in finding Talmudic examples or something from the
Apocrypha. He says to me, 'I believe you must have lived since
time began, Colonel Pyatnitski.'

'No,' I tell him, 'I was born when Christ was born.'

He recognises symbolism and plays on words, but only on
that rather primitive level of the English who gave the world
Browning and then refused to understand him. He is famous
today for his passing whimsies, the firearms which bear his
name and some verses done for children and old friends. And,
of course, for his long-standing feud with John Gielgud, the
cinema star. It was on the television recently. When I asked
her why she was crying, Mrs Cornelius said she felt sorry for

174

the dog. I had just come out of the toilet and didn't understand her. 'Flush,' she said. 'Flush!'

It is true I have become a little absent-minded about this. My recent memories are sometimes hazy but I can recall the smell of the vast sweet mint fields gathered up to the walls of Fez like a besieging army, and Alexandria where her mint is diffused to form a liquor that is like drinking scented air which brings springtime back to old men. Who knows what real mint is like now? Today it is debased to flavour envelopes, lavatory cleaner, toothpaste and sex-creams. We had to make do with Vaseline in my day and then the only flavour was petroleum! The pilot brought us into busy Alexandria and even from the lanes I could smell the heady breeze of the real Africa brought to us down from the Nile. On that cool Mediterranean morning when with visible breath we ascended to the deck to find the mist not completely lifted off the water, I imagined I would enjoy a view of Greek and Roman grandeur, rising above the lesser architecture of Turk and Arab, for Captain Quelch had entirely failed to impress me with his insistence on Alexandria's quintessential dullness. Instead I saw the municipal buildings of provincial England, laid out wherever possible with the kind of flower-gardens one finds assembled in Swiss cities (though a little more wilted), with a minaret here and there as a tasteful reminder of our geographical reality. Here, indeed, was the reassuring Gothic granite and Queen Anne brick of some faintly exotic Bradford. Yet she had a reassuring stateliness and I admired the efficiency of her huge harbour. Ships of the British Merchant Navy were around us on all sides, in company with equally smart ships from the major civilised nations. It was to avoid the 'miscellaneous' dock, full of unsavoury native tugs, dhows and rusty tramps from the four corners of the earth, that Captain Quelch, flying a prominent Stars and Stripes, announced himself to our pilot as 'Samuel Goldwyn's party', a fact which was quietly relayed to those on shore, and got the usual escort of honour from our culture-starved sailors who knew the secret identities of their film favourites better than they knew their mothers' Christian names. Today only Hollywood provides that universal glory once the sole privilege of Alexander the Great. And so remote were these Englishmen from the centres of civilisation that they were keenly prepared to believe us the stars of a dozen as yet unseen epics. Some of them did not even know of the Arbuckle scandal! Had we wished, we could have cheated them of everything they valued, just as itinerant relic-sellers and blessing-brokers of the Middle Ages went amongst ignorant villagers far from Rome or Paris. The sense of power was enormous. These people longed for stories, for glamour, just as their ancestors had. And we, of course, could provide it, perhaps in even larger quantities than Norma Talmadge or John Gilbert, for we had seen all aspects of Hollywood – from its lowest vices to its highest aspirations – and between us could give them far more than any film would ever provide. The pilot apologised. There were extremely tedious and meticulous customs and immigration rules for American citizens bringing special equipment, especially photographic equipment, into the country and it would take several hours to clear us. Almost immediately after we had docked a rosy lieutenant presented the Governor's compliments, together with his regrets that he was not able to welcome us personally, but that our party was invited to a special reception the following evening. Meanwhile all facilities were at our disposal.

Captain Quelch had, that morning, received a couple of wirelesses which he had told the operator to say nothing about. Eager for news of my missing reels, I had been with him in the Radio Room when he had dropped in on his way to the bridge. One wire was from Goldfish and this he showed me, but the other he folded and placed inside his white cotton jacket. He wore civilian clothes, this morning, apart from his cap and had the air of a man going courting, I said. He laughed. I was not far from the truth, he told me, tra-la-la. Was the Goldfish message of any immediate interest?

TITLE CHANGE NEEDED TRY OLD STOP   AWAIT NEW STAR
ARRIVING AIR ALEX IMMINENT STOP   DO NOT PROCEED UNTIL
YOU HAVE STARTED STOP   WE HAVE PRINCE OF INDIA STOP
WE DO ONE LOCATION REEL FOR THIS STOP   IGNORE
ALL PREVIOUS MESSAGES STOP   CONFIRM EGYPTIAN
CHARIOT TRACK STOP S.G.

The telegram is in my scrapbook. It is what is left of the

evidence of my fame. Mrs Cornelius has more things in her boxes, she says, but lately she told me that the rats had got into the paper as the maggots got into the clothes in her cellar, so I suppose my clippings are returning to the slime as maggots crawl across the frozen moments, the rotting stills of long-since-crumbled celluloid. I only have this because, absent-mindedly, I forgot to show it to the others. I was thrown out, I think, by the notion of a rival actor coming to break up our circle just as things were going well again. Was the star a Constance Bennett or a Barrymore? Goldfish was famous for his sudden decisions to introduce 'quality' – or more money – into a project. I put this unpleasant idea from my mind and, in doing so, forgot the wire until I found it again, much later. By noon, after the excitement of the British welcoming party, we were receiving yet another visitor who, by his appearance, could be none other than the captain's brother, Professor Quelch, who came aboard, swinging his way up with a sprightliness which cost him most of his breath by the time he was on deck attempting to apologise. 'Awfully sorry – dashed train – always late – should have left earlier – my fault – how do you do. Malcolm Quelch.' And I grasped a bony, weather-beaten hand extending from a body even more angular than his brother's. 'Hope you people got my wire. I replied as soon as –' A sign from Captain Quelch silenced him and he shook my hand with silent, bewildered fury while waiting for his brother to rescue him.

'How could you have known we were arriving, Malcolm? The papers, I suppose! Something from Casablanca? I say, isn't it amazing what communications have come to?' Clearly Captain Quelch had planned for our arrival to coincide with his brother's, so that a good British guide should at once be available to us. I saw nothing wrong in this. Captain Quelch's chief concern was for our safety. He knew that he could trust his brother to look after us with the same conscientious good sense as he had. I, for one, was grateful.

'Keepin' it in ther family are we, gents?' Mrs Cornelius grinned at the world in general. 'Enjoy a drink, do yer, prof?'

Only just recovering himself, the tall academic, whose sallow features resembled ancient papyrus, whose jaw was if anything more lantern, his nose more a predatory beak, than his brother's, and whose grey-blue eyes had the quality of a faded tomb-painting, turned what became a mild blink upon my friend. 'Not at all, madam. I am a strict teetotaller born. My family are all TT.'

'Totally tipsy, wot?' Laughing, she slapped him on the back. He wore a crumpled European suit which, like his skin, had turned yellow in the Egyptian sun. He had removed his panama as he came aboard. His black, greying hair was stuck thinly against his scalp by sweat which he now attempted to mop with a handkerchief so well-laundered that it was almost startling against that otherwise somewhat weathered figure. He gave up a small, uncertain smile. I shall never know the reason why she accepted one person as readily as she rejected another. For my part I was glad I had purchased, very reasonably from Captain Quelch, a long-term supply of *coca*. His brother seemed something of a prig and would probably be shocked at any suggestion of his helping me obtain an illicit drug. Egypt was famous for its drug traffic. British-run customs people were forever alert on the seas and in the deserts, where the camel trains brought hashish, opium and heroin along the old trade-routes from Asia. But I did not wish to misjudge Malcolm Quelch. Perhaps one needed such people in Egypt to remind us to maintain at all times our European standards. He was what the Greeks call *kalokagathos*, the perfect gentleman. And a scholar, as I was to discover very quickly. He asked if we had enjoyed the 'innumerable laughter of the waves' – '*kymaton anerithmon gelasma*, as Aeschylus has it?'

'Sorry, I wosn't payin' attention the first time neiver,' said Mrs Cornelius, offering him a hug around his bony shoulders and causing his mouth to pop open in surprise as she bellowed good-humouredly into his face. 'You'll do, prof. Ho! Ho!'

The ill-named Wolf Seaman came pounding around the deck in a running costume which displayed the very hairs of his body, he had grown so plump. The suit alone was tight enough to provide the agony on his face as he came to a florid stop before us and glared through sweat and tears at the newcomer. 'Good afternoon? Sir.'

'This is Perfessor Q. – Don Q's better-educated bruvver.' Her arm tightly about Quelch's waist, Mrs Cornelius steered him like a salvager with a new prize towards her would-be Svengali, her surly paramour. 'Perfessor, this is Sweden's greatest artist since 'Ans Andersen. 'E's made orl sorts o' posh pictures. An' I've bin in some of 'em meself.' This with one of her smiles at the disconcerted archaeologist who lifted his hat to Seaman and to everyone else, as if he had just stepped by accident into a play in which he was expected to perform a part. 'Well,' he said, '*viva, valeque*, I must say.'

'We'll go to the saloon, I think, for a confab, shall we?' says Captain Quelch with firm determination, for some reason wanting his brother off the deck. And we all troop down to the bar, where Captain Quelch himself acts as jerk and serves us our choices. His brother takes a soda-water and Captain Quelch does the same, in deference, no doubt, to their dead parents. And the first thing we do is toast the King of England, the King of Egypt, the President of the United States and Samuel Goldfish. The ice broken, we gather round a rather more relaxed Professor Quelch, who does not seem to mind being entirely surrounded by people with cocktails in their hands, who listen to the phonograph and try to help him join in the choruses of the songs. '*Vive la bagatelle!*' he pronounces, and proves himself less of a prude than I had at first supposed. But he will not be, I fear, the comrade that Captain Quelch has been to me.

The celebration settled down as lunch was served by our happy laskars, who were no doubt looking forward to their own shore-leave. Professor Quelch was an expert on all things Egyptian. Indeed, the Ancient World seemed more familiar to him than the Modern and it was easy to see that he felt considerably more enthusiasm for problems of hieroglyphic interpretation than for the passing heroes and heroines of the moving-picture theatre, while Romance, I suspected, found fullest expression in the mystery of an oddly-coloured ankh held by one of the less prominent Egyptian deities. He also had a rather confusing narrative style. Nonetheless Malcolm Quelch seemed the man we needed to guide us through both the shadow-realms of the distant past and the alleys and temptations of our immediate present. Certainly as shore beckoned there was much talk of temptation amongst the film-crew. Malcolm Quelch won the approval of our team and displayed his ability to respond to practical needs by recommending a *salon des poules* which, he guaranteed, was both safe and versatile. Only Esmé did not take to him and went below almost immediately to see, she said, to her packing. Seaman, too, divorced himself early from the happy table, needing solitude, he said, in which to mature his ideas. His absence displeased nobody. There was a noticeably looser atmosphere amongst us when he had gone. Goaded by Mrs Cornelius, the good-natured professor regaled us with a little of the Cairo gossip, which concerned people of whom we had never heard and mostly revolved around buggery and adultery, with a touch of incest for variety. I grew bored with this. I made an excuse to go back to my cabin where my bags were carefully packed, having passed inspection by a customs officer whose curiosity about my Georgian pistols was satisfied when I explained they were for use in the film. Tapping on the connecting door, I called out to Esmé so that she should not be startled. I heard something crash. I tried to open the door but it was locked. I asked if she had hurt herself and, after a moment, she replied that her case had fallen off her bunk. She began to murmur to herself as if embarrassed. I offered to help but she insisted shrilly that she could manage. She was a resourceful little creature, no matter what Mrs Cornelius believed. Reassured, I strolled up on deck and found Captain Quelch enjoying a pipe with the chief immigration officer, a sandy-haired man called Prestange who handed my passport back to me saying he was honoured to make the acquaintance of such a talented man. (My passport gave my occupation as engineer, but my entry card, of course, explained my current employment.) For me the stamps and visa gave the passport a substance and validity it had never previously possessed. I had the approval of His Majesty's Government. In those days, of course, such approval also meant complete security. The British Empire took that responsibility for its dominions and protectorates, to maintain the law equally for all. That was why the Empire was the admiration of the world. I have always been contemptuous of those people who drag up a few obscure incidents to indict the British, to prove they were no better than the French, say, or the Dutch, at running an empire. I disagree. While they ran their Empire on Roman lines they knew nothing but success, the spread of a common justice. They had to be stern, both in Egypt as well as India and parts of Africa, in particular, for that was all the natives would recognise as authority. They had no conception of the institutions which protected them. I have often wondered at this notion of nationalism, of freedom. All they ever seem to want, when it comes down to it, is the freedom to slaughter one another in acts of horrible sectarian violence. They were taught about the institutions. They claimed to envy them, to desire them for themselves. But they did not have the appropriate history, experience or intellect to understand them. A few Indians might well have died at Amritsar. How many more died in 1948 when the British were gone? They are greedy for 'freedom' the way our ancestors were greedy for the millennium. And, as when the millennium failed to come, they are inclined to riot if disappointed. Yet your *fellaheen*, your basic descendant of the people who built the pyramids and conquered much of Africa and Asia Minor, is without doubt the salt of the earth, a willing worker and a cheerful servant, if not unmanned by the *bilharzia* which now infects the whole Nile, thanks to the British dam, or by the *hasheesh* he smokes to forget his troubles. 'It is the same in China, with the coolies,' Professor Quelch told me. He had been on more than one archaeological expedition to the Far East. 'I was little more than a youth, then. But I can tell you, Mr Peters, that neither Alexandria nor Cairo can compete with the fleshpots of Macao or Shanghai. Such sweet little creatures. You would not think them of this planet at all! I am old-fashioned in my tastes, I'm afraid. The modern girl does nothing for me.'

'It depends what you want, dunnit,' says Mrs Cornelius, ready in Gainsborough hat and blue-trimmed lace, to face the pleasures and the pressures of Alexandria. She winked at her new 'beau'. I was almost jealous, but I knew there was a deeper bond between Mrs Cornelius and myself than any passing fancy. She was followed at a distance by sailor-suited Esmé, escorted by a somewhat more cheerful Wolf Seaman, no doubt pleased at the prospect of taking charge again. He wore a pale blue suit that looked a size too small for him. He had put on at least a stone since we had left Los Angeles. I wondered, since he had been so frequently sick, how he had managed to hold so much food. Esmé, with a smile to Seaman, whom she was clearly lobbying for a substantial part, took my offered arm. I handed her over the side in Mrs Cornelius's wake. She fluttered into the swaying launch like a paper doll. Billowing awful black smoke, the boat took us to the passenger dock where a car from the hotel took us to our lodgings. When I saw the round Nubian face behind the car's wheel I almost thought Mr Mix had come back, to reveal an elaborate trick. But I quickly realised this negro, while handsome and cheerful enough, was nothing like my friend who was an altogether more refined type.

'I fear you'll find the people here something of a *rudis indigestaque moles*,' called Professor Quelch beside the river brushing back the touts with his malacca. 'And the city itself is almost completely bereft of archaeological interest. It was torn down by various victors, you know.' He hid a titter behind his long fingers, as if he had said something rather *infra dig*.

His brother had come with me to the quay. I shook hands briefly, unsuccessfully trying to stop my tears. 'Good luck,' I said.

'And the same to you, lad. Malcolm's picked up a lot, don't you think, since I doctored his soda water with a spot of Gordons?' He winked and gave me a hearty buffet on the arm. 'Good luck to you, too, old chum. If I hear about your films and your darkie I'll find a way to let you know.'

There was a wealth of affection in those few words and gestures. Warmed by this, I saluted and climbed into the car, facing a haughty Herr Seaman and an eager Esmé who was, as always, delighted by the prospect of a new city with new shops. Mrs Cornelius sat beside me. 'I 'ope they 'ave cold beer at this place. It's not *too* English, is it?'

When I pointed out that it was only about 65° – a temperature we had come to think of as cool in Los Angeles – she replied that she had always hated warm beer, even in winter.

Before the car started, Captain Quelch leaned through the

open window and said, *sotto voce* to me, 'Oh, and by the way, old boy, it looks like the law's caught up with poor Bolsover. I hear he's to be arrested this afternoon. Drugs, apparently, poor chap.' He winked and blew me a platonic kiss. And then he was stepping back. 'Remember, dear boy,' as the car moved off, 'put your trust only in God and Anarchy.'

We turned now onto a palm-lined seafront promenade of white hotels and summer residences looking directly at the sea. With its wrought-iron balconies and its air of calm gentility, it reminded me very much of Yalta in the spring. But I could not have saved those girls if I had tried. They were thoroughly given up to the thrill of the situation. I had no intention of joining in and left them all to it. Along the promenade, a light wind stirred breakers and fronds while the traffic was chiefly horse-cabs, private motors and the occasional tram, all as spick and span and Bristol-fashion as was ever possible in that dusty nation. Even in Alexandria, between the ocean and a lake, one quickly became used to the fine, khaki-coloured dust that settled on newspapers, books, clothing and the well-polished counters of bazaars. Everything turned yellow or brown. Now, as the ochre fog cleared, a soft blue sky appeared above the stately rooftops. Pale, golden light gradually spread over blue waters, white promenade and stern granite institutions, intensifying the delicate colouring of the palms from lemon-yellow to sage-green. The oranges, browns and reds of their trunks, the variety of grasses which grew at their bases, helped the palms soften the severity of authority's brick and diplomacy's sandstone, giving a gaiety rather than a dignity to the national flags and blazons, giving the stucco flanks of native palaces the sheen of freshly-woven cotton. In those moments the city seemed to possess the patina of an old mural; it was as if her vivid colours forced themselves through layers of time before they reached us. I grew almost drowsy with the pleasure of the vision alone and, since I had slept very little that night, was dozing by the time the car pulled up outside an edifice that was a cross between a crusader castle and a Mexican bordello. Professor Quelch was amused by my surprise as I dismounted from the running-board and looked up at the hotel's five magnificent storeys. 'This is what we should have seen if the Moors had conquered Troon,' he whispered. His remark came to mean something only twenty or more years later, when I visited Scotland. The British have a habit of taking a local style and turning it into something cheerfully unalarming. The cool interior of the hotel smelled of beeswax and jasmine, her palms were washed and polished to unnatural brilliance, at one with the dark woods and Turkish inlays of the reception hall. We were welcomed by the manager, a Greek with a French name. We had been given an entire floor of the hotel for ourselves. The Christmas holidays had begun and many residents were up-country or visiting relatives in England. The wealthy Egyptians and the British all tended to summer in Alexandria but remained in Cairo during the cooler months. I never did keep the name of the hotel in my mind, but I think it was named after some English lord, perhaps the Hotel Churchill. Its airy rooms looked out to the corniche and harbour where, if you felt a little nervous of the country's interior, or her natives, you were immediately reassured to see the British flag flying from the masts of half-a-dozen modern ships of war, while from time to time came the well-disciplined riders of the Egyptian Mounted Police, in handsome blue or scarlet, with red fezzes or *képis*, riding their beautiful Syrian Arabs along the wide roadways, their assured masculinity in contrast to the soft, white ghosts who drifted in and out of the shadows, pausing to murmur to one another or address some disconcerted tourist already in difficulties with his Baedecker or *Guide Bleu*. Many of these wore the official tarboosh, cream *gelabea* and red slippers of the official guides, who displayed large bronze discs around their necks as proof of their legality, the self-styled dragomans whose daily ambition was to attach themselves to a party of well-heeled Americans greedy for a certain kind of Romance. Little groups of children, frequently in rags and bearing the signs of disease, scuttled about the beaches and gardens, avoiding the police, running after any carriage which bore a European or an Egyptian of the better class. Strolling native policemen gestured them on their way with stern good humour. Here was the daily bustle of a modern cosmopolitan port. I had returned to civilisation!

Furnished in the ubiquitous Indian colonial style, my rooms

did not adjoin Esmé's. It had not been possible to control the key allocation at the reception desk without raising suspicions. In fact Mrs Cornelius and Esmé shared a suite in the southern corner of the hotel and I was very glad that we were due to stay in Alexandria only for one further night before taking our reserved places on the Cairo Express. I was equally relieved not to be billeted with Wolf Seaman and to find that Malcolm Quelch would be my room-mate for the next thirty or so hours. I looked forward to further intimacy. His brother had not been misled, it seemed, in his enthusiasm for Malcolm's scholarship and local knowledge.

That afternoon, after a late lunch, Esmé and I went shopping. Her normally cheerful spirits had returned and she was full of interest in the world around us, the well-tended gardens and ornamental trees, the beautifully ordered avenues, the jostling *fellaheen* who filled the sidestreets, the heavily veiled women, the gaudy Jews and the sober Copts, and all the other myriad creeds of this city, which had welcomed most and persecuted few; and everywhere were casual reassurances to show how the founder of the city was still acknowledged. There were signs in Greek everywhere. There were Greek cafés and bazaars and shops of all kinds. There was a Greek cinema and a Greek theatre, Greek newspapers, Greek churches. Here the two great defenders of our Faith had come together to bring order and renewed life to that old and decadent nation, just as Ptolemy, following in Alexander's godlike footsteps, brought a refreshing and outgoing new dynasty to the country at its most corrupt moment, when it most needed honourable leaders. Since then Egypt has always sensed when new leadership was needed, from the time of Cleopatra, who so yearned for Mark Antony to rule both her heart and her destiny. Sadly, we were to see little of Ancient Greek nobility. We had struck a bargain with a carriage-driver who elected himself our guide, taking us to those parts of the city he believed to be suitable for Europeans and avoiding most of the Arab quarters. 'Very dirty,' he would say. 'Very bad. Not *nedif*.' He was a man of about my age, with large frank brown eyes, a small, neatly trimmed beard, a fez and a European linen jacket worn over the local trousers which, Captain

Quelch had told me, were commonly called *shitcatchers*. There was nothing to do but to give ourselves up to our Oriental Chingachgook, who eventually drew the carriage to a halt in a large and impressive square. 'Place Mohammed Ali,' he told us. 'Good European shops. I will wait for you here.' He demanded no money and, after helping us down, lit himself a thin cigarette then settled whistling on the steps of his carriage. I was careful to make sure I would find him again, across from a large equestrian statue, presumably of the hero himself, which graced the well-ordered flower gardens. This wide square was flanked by a number of official-looking buildings in the usual European styles, a Gothic church and what I took to be a bank, on the same lines as the church. Elsewhere were glittering cafés whose décor and elegance could rival anything in Paris, where a grand pallor of European ladies and gentlemen took tea and a murmuring interest in other Europeans moving with the grace of so many fine yachts about their business. I became increasingly impressed by the prevailing aura of calm and good taste, and when we entered the Rue Sharif Pasha we were all astonished to find it lined with the shops one might normally encounter in only the greatest of European capitals. I could not help but be taken back to Petersburg and the wonderful months of freedom in the early days of the War. Odessa in her splendid confidence had been rich and happy. When I spoke of these things to Esmé, I was a little disappointed that she gave me a fraction of the attention she gave to the contents of the store windows. By the time the sun was flooding, blood-red, upon the evening roofs, we had visited three dress-shops, a hat-shop and a shoe-shop and Esmé was satiated with silks, beads and ostrich-feathers – at least until we reached Cairo. I could not begrudge my darling these few indulgences. She must still remember my betrayal of her. Yet so naturally gracious was she that she never reminded me of that moment when, arriving on a foreign shore, she had scanned the rows of waiting faces and failed to find mine.

It was almost sunset by the time we returned to our faithful cab-driver. Yacob helped put Esmé's purchases into the carriage with us and then, chatting the while in a mixture of Arabic, French and English, took us smartly back to our hotel. Esmé had the generalised air of affection of one who has fulfilled her every immediate ambition, and a gentle smile would come to my angel when she recalled some particularly attractive gown she had seen or piece of jewellery she hoped one day to own. I envied her this uncomplicated pleasure. That day, as so often in the past, I imagined myself a parent living through his child. It was marvellous that, with the aid of a few sovereigns, such transcendental happiness could be brought to the girl I loved. The very air we breathed smelled of honey, that evening scent of hyacinths, and stocks, and roses which the British transplanted to so many ancient capitals. We watched the sky turn to deep violet, a houri's eyes, over a sea turned scarlet as her lips by the setting sun and, when our carriage reined in to allow the passage of a band of kilted Highlanders marching back from some musical performance, Esmé flung her soft little arms around me and kissed me with lips tender and trembling as a baby's and said I was the only man she could ever truly love. 'We were born for each other,' she said. 'We own each other, you and I, my darling Max, *mon cher ami, mein cher papa*.' And she turned her head to the darkening sea to laugh, as if fearful suddenly of the depths of her own emotion. She shivered. It was becoming too cool. 'Let us go back,' she said.

I shall always remember Alexandria as the evening loses its heat and a wind begins to stir the palms and cedars of the corniche, when her lights appear, one by one, cluster by cluster, like jewels gracing some mighty dowager, as the scents of the sea and the desert mingle and the carriage trots on through streets grown silent for a moment, perhaps awaiting the transition from day to night, as if that transition is not inevitable, and I remember a moment of exquisite happiness when my darling called me her friend.

I have known only a few such moments in my life. I have learned to value them and not regret their passing. I am so grateful for love.

Birds die within me, one by one.

Vögel füllen meyn Brust. Vögel sterben in mir. Einer nach dem anderen.

What is there to do about it?

TWELVE

LAND OF RUINS, and of dreams, and death; land of
dust and ghosts. Here all the great civilisations of the earth
were born and here they come to die. Here, the British Empire
perished, without honour, without nobility, without friends,
like the Greeks, the Romans, the Turks and the French
before them. For the British, too, inhaled the dusty seeds
of Carthage and found them sweet and carried them home to
England where, as Rosebay Willow Herb was once Pompei's
Fireweed, the seed was given a more familiar domestic name
and soon took hold. There are two lessons that temporal
empires never learn. The first: It is self-destruction to march
against Moscow. The second: Never annex Egypt. Napoleon,
Alexander's only military and philosophical equal, might have
survived if he had made only one of those mistakes. I hold no
brief for the 'Curse of the Mummy's Tomb', the myth which
had brought us to Egypt in the first place, but belief in such
curses reflects a deeper truth. Any other nation which tries to
tamper in the affairs of Egypt attracts a curse. She is a fierce
old mother and she punishes interference in her enjoyment of
her declining years; especially she punishes those who would
wish to 'revive' her. She is too tired for revival. She wishes
only to be left alone, to live in her memories and the remains
of her glory. By her own scale, she could live at least another
thousand years.

Much of this Professor Quelch explained to me next morning as we walked to the special platform of Robert Stephenson's magnificent railway station (the only monuments the British ever raised to rival the temples and tombs of the Pharaohs). I was a little the worse for wear. I had enjoyed many glasses of port with those fine English *chevaliers* of His Majesty's Protective Government, it being Christmas Day. They, of course, were granted leave for that peculiarly English holiday, Boxing Day, in which all able-bodied men appear on their village greens and engage in violent fisticuffs. At that moment I was never more glad, as I made my dazed way through the confusion of beggars, porters, guides and the sellers of every conceivable kind of fakery, that I had not been born an Englishman. I pitied my comrades of the previous night their sporting ordeal. But perhaps they were made of heartier stuff and were already preparing for the fight with an enthusiasm which in another race would be unquestionably sexual? Certainly many of their repressions were set aside that night and their language as well as their anecdotes became increasingly colourful, so that Grace the Hairdresser and Wolf Seaman made their excuses and left. I grew nostalgic, I told them, for the mess of my old brigade. I told them how I had belonged to one of the last Cossack regiments to stand against the Reds. I described the Red atrocities in Kiev and Odessa. I said how cheap life had become, how the most beautiful girls of good homes were prepared to prostitute themselves for a twist of salt or a handful of potatoes. They believed, they said, that Odessa sounded better than Port Said. Port Said was said to be even more of a sink of iniquity than Alexandria, the flourishing centre of a white slave-trade into Africa and the Middle East about which little could be done, since none had sufficient authority over either the whoremasters or their human cattle. One learned to live with such things, they murmured, and thanked God that they had nothing like it to contend with in England. They spoke too soon! That was before the disease had been brought home. Today half of London is indistinguishable from the filthiest souks of the Levant and young girls and boys hawk the most perverse pleasures quite openly. My acquaintances in the Egyptian police would have been horrified by what I see

189

every day in the Portobello Road. And it is so familiar to us that nobody even mentions it any more. When will they tire of their 'progress' and see it for what it is? Year by year the beast grows; year by year it becomes harder to find common justice, common kindness and humanity. Where will it end?

Professor Quelch, who had not attended the dinner, told me he was certain that some of the English police were now quite as corrupt as the Egyptian. 'Bribery is rife in certain departments. I have it on the best authority.' When I mentioned the white slave-trade, he shrugged. It continued to prosper partly because the chief men in the business were protected by high-ranking officers who received a share of the profits and their pick of the boys and girls. 'Of course, most of the high-ranking British officers are ignorant of this. They believe everything's in order. Besides, they know how difficult it is to control the European women and their pimps. The police can only enter a brothel, for instance, accompanied by a representative of the country of which the madam is a national. Every time the police get hold of the appropriate consular official, the nationality of the madam changes. They tried to round up the pimps a few years ago. In Cairo they have their own Pasha, a grotesque individual by the name of Ibrahim el-Ghar'bi, a fat, massive nigger who dresses like a houri out of the Arabian nights. I know him quite well. He's a man of considerable wit and education. If, my dear boy, you have any "special requests", then el-Ghar'bi is the chap for you.'

I told him that I had no need of such services, but I was becoming impressed by the profundity of Malcolm Quelch's knowledge of Egypt and her customs, old and new. I now fully understood why Captain Quelch had been so determined to have his brother look after us.

As we walked beside the great green and gold train towards the first-class compartments, Quelch raised for a second time the matter of his fees. 'There has been no agreement, as yet. I was wondering who to approach. Who, as it were, is our quartermaster?'

I believed Captain Quelch had already agreed fees with Seaman. I was sure the professor could be paid on any basis he chose.

190

'As a rule,' smiling, he pointed to our carriage with his cane, 'I arrange for my fee to be forthcoming on a daily basis for an agreed period of time. If, for some reason, you should break that agreement, then I am to be paid the full amount I should have earned. Since you were recommended by my brother, I had a fee of three guineas a day in mind. All found, of course.'

This seemed reasonable to me. Quelch was also to act as a technical adviser and historical consultant when we began filming. He was clearly flattered to learn he would receive a credit.

'And I would require some sort of letter making it clear to all concerned that I am part of your company.' He made a nervous, dismissive gesture. 'To keep everything above-board, you know.'

I had not heard of an illicit trade in archaeological information, but I assured Quelch that Seaman was bound to meet all his requirements. Even that unimaginative Swede would be able to see that Quelch was going to be of enormous value to us, especially when it came to negotiating with Egyptian officials who were, Quelch and the other English people had told us, growing increasingly 'bolshy'. 'Since we started giving in to them, there's been virtual anarchy.' He referred to the nationalists of the so-called Wafd, who had gained soft-hearted concessions from their protectors after considerable rioting in the streets which only stopped when the British were forced to shoot a few of the thousands demonstrating against them. He was about to say more when the green and gold locomotive let forth a vast, manly sigh, an awakening giant; the pace of loaders, guards and conductors suddenly doubled as they rushed to their positions and the last-minute passengers, some arguing violently with their night-shirted guides and porters, began to arrange themselves on board. Wicker luggage was forced through doors and windows. Mothers and nannies wailed or screamed for lost children; lost children responded in kind and husbands and wives shouted last-minute orders to their departing spouses. I was glad that a special carriage had been ordered for us and that we should not have to compete against the stink and the pressure of weather-beaten English matrons, ill-natured Egyptian businessmen and soldiers, both white and native, who fought to get the best possible positions for themselves before the train started. The rest of our party was already aboard, having arrived by bus from the hotel. Quelch and I had, at his insistence, visited Pompey's Pillar, a rather unremarkable piece of polished granite erected in memory of an earlier and less lucky colonialist, whereupon he had mentioned his fees for the first time. I realised he was using this opportunity to raise the question as delicately as possible and assured him I would speak to Seaman.

Of our party, only Mrs Cornelius was honestly glad to be on the move again. Seaman kept to himself at the far end of the opulent carriage, with the hung-over film-crew, wincing at the jingling chandeliers, between ourselves and himself. He stared through the windows as if already planning his first shots. I asked Mrs Cornelius what was wrong but she insisted he was merely moody. ' 'E's offen like this when 'e's startin' a picture. On *'Er 'Usband's Mistress* 'e 'ardly said two words ter me, even when I was s'posed to be in front o' ther bloody camera. Or on me 'ands an' knees wiv Mr Willy up me bloody backside. It's restful in a way, though.'

In spite of this I went up to the front and sat down across from Seaman who turned on me eyes so full of loathing that I was startled. 'My God,' I said, 'what have I done? Shot your favourite dog?'

He apologised. He was already, he said, imagining me in my rôle as the High Priest who seduces Mrs Cornelius away from her duties and brings about the chain of events culminating, thousands of years later, in the tragic death of two modern lovers. I had written the part myself. I reminded him that I saw the High Priest as a victim as well as a villain. The point of my scenario was that Fate has no heroes or heroines, no favourites. However, there would be ample time to debate the interpretation of the rôle. I mentioned my chief reason for interrupting him, the matter of Quelch's fees. Seaman frowned. 'You're sure we need him? He seems a charlatan. No better than his brother.'

I refused to respond to this unreasonable assessment, save to say that I had every assurance that Quelch was ideal for us. We would be hard-put to find someone of his expertise and general usefulness at less than thirty guineas a week. He shrugged at this, promising absently to draw up the necessary letter. Meanwhile, Quelch could have his first couple of days' pay as soon as Seaman contacted Cook's in Cairo, with whom Goldfish had already made an arrangement. I returned to our group. Mrs Cornelius had attached herself to Professor Quelch while Esmé, festooned with her purchases of the past two days, sat sipping a pensive glass of lemonade brought to her by our own tarbooshed steward, whose name he told us was Joseph. He was a Copt, with healthy light-brown skin and almond eyes, scarcely more than fifteen, I would have guessed, and with the cheerful disposition, the dignified manner of many Egyptian Christians, in complete contrast to the rabble we had encountered everywhere in Alexandria. His nails, for instance, might have been manicured in one of Rue Sharif Pasha's exclusive salons. He positively reeked of strong soap and rosewater. Lunch, he said, would be at 12.30 and he showed us the folding tables that could be raised between our seats. Privately, I reflected on the irony of my situation. It had not been long since I had been riding *under* such trains, or lain hidden in goods wagons praying that the railroad bulls would not find me! All my life I have known heights and depths. I am not sure I could say I regret such extremes of experience. They have taught me, at least, a certain humility and encouraged me to identify with the underdog.

Somewhat off-handedly, Esmé asked Professor Quelch how long he had lived in Egypt.

'Since the beginning of the War, dear mademoiselle. It was the War which brought me here, in fact. I was attached to British Intelligence. I dealt chiefly with the Turkish underground in Cairo.' He dropped his voice to a throaty whisper, giving his remarks a mystery and significance which meant little to us.

'Don't you adore it?' Dreamily, Esmé stared out at the bright leafy streets of the passing suburbs.

Professor Quelch's smile was forgiving. 'Egypt may be a country that one is predisposed to adore, mademoiselle, but adoration, in the face of the facts, changes very soon to reaction, even to detestation, for there is much in Egypt that evokes material, and not merely theoretical, detestation! You have arrived here in the winter when the climate is at its best. Spring, summer and autumn, however, are an endless trial! They are detestable. The insects are detestable the whole year through, and lethal in the hot weather. What's more Cairo, in the spring, is infested by even more detestable dust-raising winds. A year, and you will detest all you now find attractive.'

'You are a cynic, m'sieu!' laughed my child.

'Far from it, mademoiselle. When one is not plagued by the weather and the wild-life, one has the common Cairene to deal with. I refer not to the native of the countryside, nor to the better-class Egyptian – many of these, of either kind, are worthy and decent people, with many virtues; but what visitor ever makes their acquaintance? No, I mean the Cairo native of the lower class. Of him, mademoiselle, there is little good to be said. He is a noisy, rude, excitable pestilence. The cosmopolitan conditions of Cairo life, combined with the natural tolerance and justice of the régime he has enjoyed for so long, have not tended to improve him. It is safe to say that the average European (we must except the English, whose business it is to like the native) abhors him. And he returns the sentiment in most cases. I will grant you he is at his most trying in the more European parts of the city. To the east and to the south of Cairo (his own haunts) it must be granted he is usually more dignified, quieter, polite and helpful. But the foreign atmosphere seems to throw him off balance. Egypt is not in itself a white man's country and so conditions for white men are abnormal and artificial.'

'But ther *sights*!' said Mrs Cornelius attempting to lighten the proceedings. 'Yer gotta grant the sights, prof!'

He accepted this. 'Perhaps. In my view the scenery and the elements, if one may so call them, of the country are also artificial. The Delta is a large market-garden, intersected by canals. Upper Egypt is a market-garden on either side of the Nile. The rest is the rock and sand of the desert. And the features of the country are not, I find, in themselves attractive. When you have seen a village, a village mosque, a grove of palms, the desert hills, processions of men on camels, and a few other such things, you have seen about all there is to see, and everything becomes very much the same. *Summa*: it would seem that Egypt is, save for her history and her art, a distinctly uninteresting and even detestable country.'

'Then why do so many people visit Egypt?' Esmé's question was almost innocent.

Professor Quelch had a ready answer for her. 'White men come to Egypt for their work. They are naturally disposed to make the best of where they work. They are not going to say there is nothing in Egypt for them, so they say the scenery is marvellous. And others believe them. But, believe *me*, mademoiselle, Egypt is an entirely artificial land. Europe can be exquisite. England is sacred to those who know her. Compared to Europe Egypt has nothing save the beauty that may be found in the disposition of hills and water and fields. What dreams can you find on an Egyptian hillside, or in an Egyptian cotton-field or in an Egyptian canal? You may find the fullest force of solitude, but it is objective, never subjective. You may admire it, but you cannot enter into it unless you choose to surrender yourself to it without condition.'

'It looks orlright ter me,' said Mrs Cornelius doubtfully. 'That sunset larst night was a joy ter be'old.'

Professor Quelch nodded as if in agreement, then leaned forward to speak in an authoritative murmur. 'The beauty of Egypt, Miss Cornish, depends upon illusion. The theatrical illusion of the fitting moment, the accident of disposition. You, of all people, surely understand the reasons how one can see beauty in anything that is wholly man-made. You must see what beauty you can in Egypt and be thankful for it. My father, the Reverend Quelch of Sevenoaks, although he never visited Egypt, wrote an excellent book on Islamic architecture in which he pointed out the flaws and fallacies of such buildings, showing how the infirmities of the Moorish arch, for instance, reflect the moral sand, as it were, on which Islam itself is built.'

Esmé and Mrs Cornelius were growing visibly bored with Quelch's idiosyncratic judgements. We had as yet seen nothing to support his arguments, but one doubtless had to live in Egypt a number of years before one understood him. He was, he said, an author himself. He had written on the subject of

Egypt and been published in England. I asked him for titles. He was modest. He said he used a pseudonym. He had also been published by several Cairo firms and felt he had contributed substantially to the subject of aesthetics. Mrs Cornelius, challenged by this one gesture of discretion, insisted that he tell her under which name he published. Eventually, his entire angular face growing a deep and alarming red, he admitted that his best-known *nom-de-plume* was 'René France'. He admitted his feeling that such a name gave authority to pronouncements which 'Quelch' did not. We approved his choice and told him that we would look out for his books the moment we arrived in Cairo. At this, he said he would be glad to help us obtain copies. He was sure he could get any title we wanted at a substantial trade discount.

Esmé remarked in French that the professor was clearly no romantic. He answered with a shrug.

'I assure you, mademoiselle, that you will find the beauty of Egypt *brille par son absence*. Primarily it is the invention of the last century's more sensational painters, exploiting our European greed for the exotic.'

These were sentiments unacceptable to almost any woman and to the majority of men. We had come to Egypt to film the exotic and to make an art of it. We did not wish to hear Professor Quelch's cynical assessment of a country he admittedly knew very well. I did my best to change the subject. Even at that age I understood the plurality of human nature and how so many apparently conflicting views can exist quite cheerfully in one individual. Thus it is unjust to make immediate judgements upon one's fellows. I am uneasy with the way youngsters these days so readily condemn or praise people they have never met, as if they were their own family. I have learned to bide my time. I judge people not by their opinions or how they present themselves, but by their actions. Finally, the only truth is in action, when they understand how their actions have effect. I judge by how they work to understand and control their actions, how careful they are not to do major harm to others. If all they have learned in life is how to justify those actions, no matter how subtly, then I grow quickly irritated with their company. The world is a dull enough place, these days, without having to listen to an old fraud inventing the reasons he was morally obliged to steal some other old fraud's chickens. *Circulus in probando* as one of the Quelches would say. *Iz doz mikh? Ikh farshtey. Ikh red nit keyn 'philosophiespielen'*.

'What well-ordered streets Alexandria has.' I nodded towards the suburbs.

'As artificial as the rest of Egypt,' Quelch maintained relentlessly and waved with contempt towards the vivid David Roberts postcards which Esmé had purchased at the hotel and which she now presented as proof against his argument. 'Exactly what I have said. Those colours were never so vivid, those ruins never so artfully re-arranged. Roberts was out here for a year. Before he came he had discovered that a career could be made from a special subject. Thus he lived for the rest of his life on sketches he had made in his youth. Even at the time those sketches were exaggerated, fanciful. If that is the Egypt you want, *p'tite ma'mselle*, no doubt your rose-coloured glasses will provide it. But do not be disappointed if the grandeur of Roberts's fantasy is not quite matched by the squalor of the actuality.'

'But that is only Cairo,' I argued. 'Further up-river it is less spoiled, perhaps?'

'Less spoiled? Is an old harlot *less spoiled* because she services a handful fewer soldiers? Egypt, Herr Peters, has been spoiled by a succession of conquerors; by Bedouin savages, by Greeks, Romans and Jews, by Christians, pagan Arabs, Moslems, Turks, Italians, Frenchmen. And now the English, with their nostalgia for anything faded and valueless, are here to offer romantic overtures to the crone! Every passing footsoldier in history has left his urine and his initials somewhere on some proud Egyptian monument. Foreign dams have poisoned the Nile and infected the *fellaheen*, who can no longer work and so smoke hashish to help them forget their miseries. As in China, the British managed, in a matter of decades, to destroy Egypt's last important resource: her hardy, cheerful working people. Now she must survive only because she provides a quick route to India for our Empire's peace-keeper, good old Tommy Atkins.'

Mrs Cornelius chuckled. 'Yore soundin' more like a bloody bolshevik orl ther time, prof!'

'My views are indeed somewhat radical,' he agreed. 'But I prefer to think of them as independently arrived at. I am not, I think, spouting mimicry, madam.'

'Oh, yore orl right!' she said, and held out her glass to Joseph for another cocktail. 'I must say I'm glad ter be orf that effin' boat. Know any songs, perfessor? Ovver than ther *Red Flag*, that is?'

Normally this would have served to have broken any ice, changed the topic and got us all into a more relaxed mood, but Professor Quelch was resistant to my old friend's social powers. He drew back in his seat and pursed those large thin lips under the promontory of his nose so that he began to resemble, in profile, one of the stranger birds said to wade in the up-river reeds.

Mrs Cornelius did not follow this line. For some reason she liked Quelch and wanted to see the best in him. She leaned forward and patted his knee. 'Didn't mean ter get up yer nostrils, prof. Go on wiv wot yer wos sayin', abart the Imperialists an' that.'

He responded with a small smile, his cheeks softening and sagging. 'I am not attacking Imperialism, madam. Merely describing its realities. An Empire is not maintained by kind words and a fatherly manner, as the *Boy's Own Paper* insists. It is maintained by force. Sometimes by terror. Usually only by the hint of terror. It's rather like most marriages, in that respect.'

So much bitterness did he express in this last remark that Mrs Cornelius became instantly curious. Even Esmé looked up from her toys. But Mrs Cornelius knew enough not to pursue the matter immediately. I watched with fascination as she charmed and calmed him. With a mixture of flattery, wit and gesture, she brought the leathery skin to a sort of glossy glow, the nearest it had been in many years to the bloom of youth. Within half-an-hour he was trying to recall the words of *It Reely Woz a Wery Pretty Garden*. I was full of loving admiration at my friend's ability to discover the best in people. Soon he began to speak with some lyricism about his childhood in Kent, his envy of his brothers, who lived so often in a world of their own, his loneliness at home, his enjoyment of school. He had been sent to some famous establishment on the coast not far from where he was born and from there had gone to Cambridge where, in the family tradition, he had read Classics. 'I am an archaeologist by vocation,' he told us with some pride, 'not, as it were, by degree.' Divinity, he said, had never attracted him.

Mrs Cornelius, asking him if he knew London, saw him pause and begin to fade. Some harsh memory, some unwanted recollection. Quickly, she brought him back to the sunshine again, to ask him what he thought of China and India, where he had gone shortly after leaving England for the last time. His dismissive answers were brief and witty. He had enjoyed his time with the bank in Macao, he said. The Portuguese were very easy to work with. He had been lucky, sharing quarters with a cultured Lisbonite enduring a spell in the family business before returning to the Portuguese capital and a desk he would never use. 'Manuel is a celebrated poet now. But like so many people these days he involved himself in politics. A dangerous game in the modern world. Where politics was once a worthwhile occupation for gentlemen, even in England the professional politician now holds sway. It's the death of democracy, of disinterested representation. Their only alternative is mob rule. One day soon London will be like Alexandria. And serve her right.'

Again that wave of wounded outrage bandaged by dismissive cynicism.

'Are you sure you won't 'ave a drink, love,' said Mrs Cornelius. 'Maybe just a lemonade?'

Like an old, abandoned cat gradually being reminded of the pleasures of the fireside, of regular meals and a loving hand upon his fur, he allowed himself to be coaxed. Even I, watching this performance, felt bathed by the same warmth, embraced by the same intensity of interest emanating from Mrs Cornelius. She was an Earth goddess. She was Isis.

'I began life as something of a Graecophile.' The lemonade in his thin fist, Quelch folded himself like a stick-insect joint

199

by joint back into his seat. 'But Athens has become impossible since the War.'

'It reelly 'as, 'asn't it?' Mrs Cornelius convinced us all that she had known Athens since the beginning of Time. She had visited the city once, I believe, with her Persian playboy.

'And after all that terrible business around Lawrence. The scandal and so on. Well, it was hushed up, of course, but that didn't stop people here talking. I tried to get a publisher interested. There are several who do my little pamphlets, and I wrote to Secker in London, but apparently these days he is only interested in elegant fictions. They're what pay, I suppose. Ecstatic texts by followers of Goethe and Freud. You know the sort of thing.'

'Awful,' she agreed.

Esmé was watching Mrs Cornelius in a new way, almost like a tennis-player watching a fellow sportswoman's serve. I remained filled with disappointment that these two wonderful women could not be friends. It was not as if they competed for the same man! Esmé had me. Mrs Cornelius had Wolf Seaman, who currently cast the occasional gloomy glare along the carriage's sun-dappled luxury as our train left Alexandria behind to begin the journey across the fields, marshes and canals of the peninsula, where wild birds were startled by our loco's arrogant bark and old men straightened up from ancient wooden ploughs to display fleshless arms and toothless grins. I sympathised with the wretches doomed to such an existence, when even the advent of the Cairo Express was more interesting than any other event in their lives. Yet the success of our cinema was based on such people, all over the world. At last the illiterate mass possessed a great art form of its own! It is no wonder that the most prolific cinema industries in the world are based in Egypt, Hong Kong and India. And it has become a means of controlling us. Now the peasant has no incentive to read at all. He finds the titles merely diverting. That is why the tycoons and their stooges make so much of violent action being the natural expression for film. It is no more the 'natural' function of film than it is of the novel. We have made an aesthetic theory from the realities of commercial necessity and political chicanery. Now the new directors in Hollywood can explain in the language of academia why the husband is knifed, the wife raped and the villain hunted down and killed during a car chase. I have asked the Cornelius girl if the opposite of 'free speech' is 'imprisoned speech' – or perhaps 'imprisoning speech'. It is the kind of speech used to justify and maintain opinions no longer of relevant use or moral value in the world. We imprison ourselves by means of words far more frequently than we free ourselves. *Vi heyst dos? Ikh red nit keyn 'popsprecht'. Tsidiz doz der rikhtiker pshat?* I watch these TV programmes. Every night I have to listen to the English explaining why they are superior to everyone else in the world. Turkish television is not, I would guess, so different now.

I asked Esmé to show me her postcards, the little treasures she had bought for a few piastres from the various sellers of antiques manufactured in Pharaonic Birmingham and the Eleventh Dynasty's factories along the Upper Ruhr. She had a little brass ibex, the bust of some nameless queen, a black cat of lacquered stone. She handled them with the delicacy and pleasure of some Egyptologist coming at last upon the treasures of Rameses II and for her they clearly had at least the same value. Esmé's simple enjoyment and Mrs Cornelius's enthusiasm were bringing me a happiness I had not experienced for some time. I began to feel that America had restricted me, that I had forgotten the attractions and advantages of Europe and, now, the Middle East. Russia became a torture-chamber and a graveyard. The Comintern butchers struggled amongst themselves for Lenin's mantle and spilled still more blood in the process. But at least there were parts of Europe, such as Italy, which were reviving, finding new idealism and hope, new strength to continue the work so many in those days knew to be our destiny. I do not say that I condone every one of Mussolini's actions, but he was setting an example to the rest of Europe in the hope they might decide to follow. Other nations were sinking into fashionable despair, reading self-indulgent novels and watching introspective plays, writing music no one wished to hear, poetry no one could understand, painting pictures reflecting only the hideous turmoil of their uncertain souls. For me this lassitude was generally lacking in America. But that she lacked one thing did not mean she automatically possessed another. I had found vitality there, and optimism and political courage, I had found wealth and good friends, but I had forgotten what it was to live in a land where every tree and hill bore some reference to mankind's urge to tame its own nature and the world around it. Then America was truly called the New World and it was a new coin struck in the currency of Hope. How valuable that currency might have become! Of course it did not happen. The coin of American idealism is worthless now. America became what I most feared. Washington is no longer the capital of the United States. New York rules the entire continent. Michob Ader need no longer fear immortality. Now he has the most powerful nation on Earth to comfort him. There Christ is conquered, yet elsewhere Christ is merely sleeping. He is worshipped and remembered by the Bolshevik's enslaved millions. Christ is simply awaiting the moment of His return. They say the Second Coming is a thousand years late, but we shall now see it in the year 2000. Then I shall be a hundred years old or perhaps dead. How is it one Power pretends to testify for God and yet is increasingly brought under the rule of Satan, while the other claims it has abolished God, yet cannot destroy the love and the need of its people for Christ? Which, I ask any of you, is the strongest Church, the true Church? Could it, after all, be the first and oldest Church, the Byzantine Church, ever closest to the Source, to the origins of our history? I will let the Baptists and the Presbyterians explain how their Church has become a tool of Carthage while the Church of Greece remains the last great challenger to Satan's persuasions. In 1926, of course, I had not returned to the Church and remained open-minded on this subject as well as on many others. My only certainty was in my own vocation, my need to help ease the suffering of all mankind by whatever means were available to me, whether through the miracle of engineering or through the exercise of my artistic gifts. Mrs Cornelius certainly recognised this in me, just as she recognised in Malcolm Quelch a cruelly tormented human being whose love of the world had been associated, perhaps, with the love of a certain woman. Some London beauty who had rejected him, or ruined him? This is what women can frequently see in a man that another man cannot. I was to be grateful, always, for the insights of women. If they made my life both harder and easier they always enriched it. I cannot always understand the arguments of the feminists. Like them, I love women. I admire women. I believe women have many virtues which men do not, many qualities which men cannot ever possess. On innumerable occasions they have been both a comfort and an inspiration to me. Sometimes, it is true, a woman can be a burden or a nuisance, perhaps a little bit of a strain, when she wants attention at a time you cannot give it. Does that make me an enslaver of women? A monster? I hope not. I was raised to respect and honour women. Yet this somehow makes me worse than some hippy journalist who looks like an extra from *The Squaw Man* carrying around on his arm some 'chick' who looks herself like the original squaw! This is progress? I saw a great deal of similar progress in Cairo.

The luncheon tables were raised. We passed through flat, grey country which certainly fulfilled all Professor Quelch's remarks about the dullness of Egypt. The fields were relieved by a few oxen, the occasional donkey and its driver, some brown children and women bent over their crops, a thatched hut or two and sometimes a mud village. More rarely were the modern structures of authority to be seen, for the British maintained the policy which the police today call 'low-profile'. They were already promising the natives full autonomy and self-government within the Commonwealth. Perhaps they had to. The War had depleted their manpower. It was becoming considerably more expensive to maintain an empire.

'We've gone from gunboat diplomacy to revolver diplomacy in a couple of generations.' Malcolm Quelch demonstrated how to fill the local pitta bread with *foul* and take it into one's mouth. 'Soon all we'll have is chocolate-box diplomacy! And we all know how far that gets you, dearie!'

Mrs Cornelius lifted the dripping pitta up to her lovely mouth. Her eyes gave him her full attention. 'A nice box of chocolates always worked with me,' she said. Her mouth closed over the *hors d'oeuvre*, some of which dripped down her pink chin. She dabbed at it with a dainty finger. 'But I suppose you'd fink me a bit old-fashioned.' She sucked her finger.

In another Malcolm Quelch's gesture might have been courtly, but the professor's muscles were unused to so much spontaneity and his bewildered spasm jerked his glass of lemonade solidly into his lap. As his white trousers spread with yellow, he slowly cranked fastidious hands to Heaven. 'Ugh!'

'Oh, blimey!' Mrs Cornelius was at once ready with her napkin. 'Pore fing! Don't worry. It's not a tragedy.'

Malcolm Quelch did not respond to her. Instead, arms still in an attitude of surrender, he stared hopelessly down into his water-logged crotch, where pieces of ice glinted and winked.

Then, with the air of a man who has received some unequivocal signal from an unsympathetic God, Quelch fell back with a resigned sigh as Mrs Cornelius dabbed genteelly at his lap.

THIRTEEN

THE MIGHTIEST CITY in Africa, Cairo smells of coffee, mint, sewage, camel-dung and raw saffron; of jasmine, patchouli and musk; of lilac and roses; of kerosene and motor oil. And she smells of the far desert and of the deep Nile. She smells of ancient bones.

Through alleys and boulevards crowded with the monuments of five thousand years and a dozen conquests, each individual, be they European, Oriental, African or Native, carries upon their person a certain mixture of scents: of sweat, rosewater, starched linen, carbolic soap, tobacco, incense, macassar oil, garlic – borne on Parisian frock, Savile-Row suit, flowing *gelabea* or black *chaddurah*. A flux of trams and trucks and limousines, donkeys, camels, mules and horses, flows back and forth across the bridges spanning these narrower reaches of the Nile between Old Cairo and Gizah. This constantly moving flow of people and vehicles pours into the twitterns and parades of that infinitely tangled knot of streets until they are filled to capacity. Outside every mosque, every church, synagogue and shrine, squabbling men, youths and children scramble to sell you some tawdry fake to remind you forever of the city the great Arab poet called the City of the Book, because here, through the centuries in relative harmony, have co-existed the Jews, Christians and Moslems who share a common testament.

'Cairo is the apex of this whole land,' declared Malcolm

Quelch. 'She is unlike the rest of Egypt yet she contains elements of everything.' He paused to peer through our window at the busy boulevard which, were it not for palms and tarbooshes, might have been Paris or Berlin. Cairo was the most reassuringly civilised-looking city I had known since leaving Paris. Any doubts about venturing into this hub, this nerve-centre of intellectual and fanatical Islam, were thoroughly dispelled. Wahabim or Wafd, those zealots dare not expose their crazy eyes to the light of the Cairene day.

On Professor Quelch's advice we had chosen not to stay at Shepheard's well-known hotel, where Cook's had an office and to which every naive tourist aspired. There is always just such an hotel in every city, soon deserted by those who made its reputation. We were in fact beyond the trees and flowers of Ezebekiya Square at the Continental, an altogether more pleasant and restful place than Shepheard's, which, as Professor Quelch pointed out, was forever packed night and day with people who would not feel their visit was complete without visiting the pyramids, taking afternoon tea in the restaurant or sipping a cocktail at the long bar. One was always coming across ill-mannered sightseers in the corridors who had failed to resist an urge to explore. 'And there's also an unfortunate semi-bohemian element,' Quelch added priggishly. 'Both conform to type. If they did not insist on their individuality, one might forgive them more easily their folly.' The Continental, he said, reminded him of the best class of Broadstairs hotel, where he had holidayed as a child. For a moment a wistful expression crossed his hatchet face as if in his mind's eye the Sahara were transformed to the Kentish sands and in his mind's hands he clutched a red tin bucket and spade.

We had become fairly good friends and were sharing a room at the hotel, but that particular bond which had existed between his brother and myself was simply not there. Malcolm Quelch lacked both Maurice's charm and optimism, his gentlemanly ability to put almost everyone immediately at their ease. I still missed the captain's dry, easy wit, his enthusiasm for literature and the arts, his determination to enjoy every experience. Perhaps I had a tendency to hero-worship in those days. I had never known a father. Mrs Cornelius was always linked in my mind with my mother but Captain Quelch had, by a subtle process I could not understand, become something of a father. History (a Marxist's euphemism for this century's appalling triumph of human evil) had robbed me of all my family, as well as my sweetheart. Mine had been a violent and terrifying progress into manhood and I had survived with only my life, my talents, and a pair of Georgian pistols, to begin the building of a new future. I wish that I had been able to settle, as I had originally planned, in Paris or London, in those hopeful years before the Depression, before the War. I might have founded a proper engineering business. We would have built from small inventions up to the larger ones, as the public's confidence in my abilities grew. Within ten years I would have become the greatest inventor-engineer since Brunel or Edison, with my own company, with branches in every Western country; a vast empire of technical resources. A knighthood would have been inevitable. Britain would take a firmer grip on her Empire, her Christian responsibilities, and commission the first of my great flying cities! Instead I remain unhonoured, an outcast from the world of science and the intellect, seeing all I dreamed of stolen, devalued, misused. Towards the end of the War I had a notion of a kind of stove which could use radio waves to heat food, cooking it in a fraction of the normal time. I called it my 'Radio Stove' and talked about it enthusiastically with the airmen on leave in the Portobello Star, fellows with sufficient technical literacy to be stimulating, intelligent company. More than enough technical understanding, it emerged, to take my ideas for their own and apply them to the profitable new business of cooking plastics! A perfect example of that abuse of an idea! I had hoped to benefit the busy housewife. In my ideal future a Pyatnitski Radio Stove would grace every home, the greatest labour-saving boon since the Hoover. But it is some while since I expected to discover any justice in this world. A parent might have helped me avoid the pitfalls of my career. As it was I had Kolya to help me for a little, and Captain Quelch and, of course, Mrs Cornelius, but no permanent guiding hand to take the tiller, as it were, when my bewildered soul was flung upon the conflicting currents of a singularly threatening century. I should be proud, they say, to have survived so well. I escaped the carnage of the Stalin years, the hysteria of the Nazis when they began indiscriminately to arrest anyone suspected of being a Jew. And it is for these two things that I thank God most. God alone provided me with the courage, the brains and the skills to save myself from the final humiliation and degradation, or at least from death. Professor Quelch often remarked that it was 'one of God's ironies. He bestows his gifts of intelligence and sensitivity upon us and then fails to provide us with the means to make the fullest use of those gifts. This surely is the crux of the human condition?' He, too, had been cheated of his inheritance. His whole family had been ruined by a speculating and dishonest lawyer. The family was related to the Mauleverers on the distaff side. 'We were never, in the past thousand years, anything but uncommon stock.' There being a dearth of university positions for archaeologists like himself, men with Classics degrees, he intended never to fall into a backwater like his brother in England. 'Reigning over an empire of grubby thirteen-year-olds scarcely a stone's throw from where we were born. My hat! I can't believe he's happy. What a fate, eh?' I gave him the confirmation he seemed to demand, but I thought I detected a note of envy. Wanting desperately to be the adventurer his brother was, his temperament was nonetheless closer to the more conservative twin's. This seemed to me the central paradox of his character. I could see him leading crocodiles of Egyptian schoolboys in their little grey English-style uniforms up to the pyramids on a Saturday afternoon to lecture on the glories of their mutual past in which the British Empire and the Egyptian became strangely blended, as perhaps they had done in Ptolemy's time, or in Augustus's time, or even, just possibly, in the time of Suleiman, when the Arabian Empire was at its most powerful, its most opulent and its most liberal, when it carried the light of science, literature and the natural arts across the Mediterranean and gave Europe her mathematics, scientific instruments, alchemical and medical lore. And all this in spite of Islam! Only as the true expense of maintaining an empire manifested itself did the Moors and their co-religionists again take to squabbling amongst themselves and, having no means of moving beyond this stage of their social development, began that irregular decay into their present barbarism. Those people once envied for their decorative arts, their music, their learning, their poetry and the tolerance of their rule, became known as the world's cruellest people, the scum of the Barbary Coast, without honour, cleanliness or conviction. And this was their shame; for they had been better and known better. Here in Cairo the dead hand of the Turk had fallen upon a once-vigorous people and it had lain there too long. To be fair, Egyptians had recovered much of their former self-esteem. The British had already granted them independence with the sole provision that a peacekeeping and administrative force be maintained in order to protect their commercial interests in the Suez Canal. The British in those days were still mainly from the old mould. They were fully aware of their Christian responsibilities to the 'lesser breeds without the Law'. Today it is unfashionable to accept responsibility for our less privileged brothers. Then it was our duty to offer a helping hand, to pass on the wisdom of our experience, to demonstrate, without any other kind of coercion, the benefits and beauties of the Christian faith. I hardly think this is an ignoble notion. Good, brave men died in its service, as did good, brave women. It is in the nature of the generous Christian to want to spread the word throughout the globe, especially in the dark places, the cruel and evil places, where the Light of Christ is the only means of driving away the devil and his minions. If this is 'imperialism' then, yes, I am an imperialist. If this is 'racialism', then, yes, I am a racialist. I am content to leave that judgement to posterity! If, that is, anyone can still read or think when the country's Dark Age is over! This is the time of the Beast, when all conscience and morality are powerless and those who still dare claim Christ's birthright are derided.

That first evening in Cairo, I remember, I was dazed by the heat and the complexity of the vast overcrowded city, by the dense blend of exotic and familiar, of slender, pale fairy-tale towers and domes, of dark green tapering poplars and spreading cedars, of palms, of massive churches so strangely similar to those in my native country, of vividly-dressed Coptic women whose beauty was incomparable, almost alarming. I remember the blue air of the moonlit starry sky, a powerful sense of the great brooding sands lying all about us; there were perpetual stirrings in the streets, even when they seemed deserted, sudden echoes in high-walled alleys, warrens which could never be mapped, for Cairo is a city of worlds within worlds, of mazes within mazes and cisterns within cisterns, vaults leading to other vaults and caverns boring further and further into a past that set its stamp here before even the Pharaohs rose to dominate Egypt and, after five millennia, left, some think, more of their knowledge unrecorded than recorded. German and Russian scientists now have evidence they came to the Earth in their own flying cities, from another planet. It is the only way they know to explain the sudden flowering of civilisation on the green banks of a great African river. How else are we to accept the engineering miracles, the longevity of their Empire? I have never been entirely sure what to think of these theories. I agree it is hard to believe such a refined people emerged from the dust and mud of the Nile Delta. I read a piece by Evelyn Waugh on the subject and wrote to her, but never received a reply. I met her again much later at the Royal Society of Literature. By that time she was permanently dressing as a man and had grown plumply repulsive, though had yet to adopt the famous monocle. She could pose as a *man*, said J.B. Priestley, in whose honour the party was, but she would never convince anyone that she was a *gentleman*. I laughed so heartily at this that the Bard of Bradford – with a jolly 'bugger the little snob' – offered me a drop of whisky from his own bottle (the rest of us had only sherry); a mark, I was told, of considerable approval. I had gone to the party with Obtulowitz, the airman-poet, whose latest girlfriend had just been interned. If 'Mr' Waugh had read my letter she did not acknowledge it. She was unnecessarily rude when I broached the subject again and offered me the opinion that the only worthwhile thing to come out of Egypt was a cigarette and a style of kinema architecture. Perhaps she wanted me to invite her to the pictures. She brandished an empty holder. Maybe she only wanted me to offer her an exotic fag. This reminded me again of that first night in Cairo, at the nightclub Quelch took me to which reminded me powerfully of The Harlequin's Retreat in Petersburg, a place of rabid perversity whose customers were devoted to every queer taste, in dress and no doubt in their sexual appetites. Quelch was surprised, he said, at my discomfort. He had understood from his brother that I was a man of the world. Of the world, I told him, most certainly. Of the *demi-monde*, I was not so sure. Quelch became a little impatient at this. In his view the club was the best place for cocktails as well as gossip, but if I felt ill at ease, he would be glad to take me somewhere a little less crowded. 'Though you might find it a little less *sympatica*!' This somewhat cryptic statement was never to be explained. We returned to the bar of the Savoy Hotel where we were almost the only people not in uniform and where it became quickly clear one was better served if one's name were known to the staff. Realising I had done Quelch a disservice I was about to suggest we return to The Crooked Path when I recognised one of the men who had stepped into the bar. A little deeper tanned, his features as fleshless as ever, his handsome head crowned with rather more grey than when I had last seen him, Major Nye was in civilian evening clothes. The moment I signalled to him from where Quelch and I sat rather uncomfortably in cane chairs to one side of the bar, he approached with every sign of pleasure. 'My dear old chap. How on earth did you manage to turn up in Cairo? I'd heard you were in the United States these days. By the way,' dropping his voice, 'no reminiscences, eh? I'm here on the quiet, rather. What?' Naturally, I respected his *incognito* and merely introduced him to Malcolm Quelch as an old acquaintance from my soldiering days with the Army of the Don. Apologising for having a dinner engagement, Nye asked after Mrs Cornelius and was visibly moved to learn she was also in Cairo. I remained discreet. After insisting on ordering us some more cocktails from a noticeably more agreeable steward, he said he would send a message to my hotel. We would meet again as soon as he had a better idea of his appointments. He had only been back from India a week when London had sent him on here and he was still a bit of a new boy. Naturally I understood him to be on government work and did not press him for details. Mrs Cornelius, I said, would be delighted to know he was in Cairo. He did not, however, seem to share my certainty.

When Major Nye had gone to keep his date, Malcolm Quelch himself proposed that we should revisit The Crooked Path. I agreed to return with him to the club but if I still felt ill-at-ease I would be perfectly happy to leave him there and take a cab back to the hotel. As our one-horse *kalash* bore us through the cool sibilance of Cairo's midnight streets, he murmured that his brother had mentioned 'a certain *penchant pour la neige*'. In some surprise, I admitted a connoisseur's taste for specific *drogues blanches*.

I would never have expected to hear from this rather prim man the secret language of the drug fancy. He told me that while he neither approved of cocaine nor used it himself he had grown partial to morphine when wounded in the military hospital of Addis Ababa. He had fought with *El Orans* himself. For much the same reasons as Lawrence he had been commissioned because of his knowledge of the Bedouin and their language. Lawrence was a great man, who romanticised his life so thoroughly he came to believe in the world's legend. 'Well, it's a common enough delusion, I suppose. He'll romanticise his dying moments if he gets the chance. You've read his books, of course.'

That doubtful pleasure was still to come. I am all for sex. But excessive sex coupled with a cloying philosemitism is not, I fear, to my old-fashioned taste. And now, of course, it is the common currency of television! Having no desire to be reminded of those dusty, evil days, I did not go to see the 'biopic'. Some of the Desert Raider's work was later set in England, but the desert was his true inspiration. At heart he remained a tubercular Midlands nancy-boy and was dead, of course, before I ever arrived in England. Or, at least, there was talk of a road accident. In Mexico, I think. Perhaps he really did want anonymity. Certainly Malcolm Quelch maintained that he had that familiar type of sex-drive which, seeking complete lack of emotional attachment, only functions with nameless people. 'He had strong affections, however.' The publication of his early Pit Life tales proves that. I am no philistine and am always prepared to give Art, no matter

212

how unfamiliar, her due. But there is, everyone will agree, a distinct difference between the probing finger of truth and the vulgarisation of mere pornography!

The Crooked Path, now more familiar, had become less unattractive, especially after one of Quelch's friends suggested that I suck upon the ivory mouthpiece of a *goza*, the water-cooled *hashish* pipe. As a rule I had a deep suspicion of narcotics, but was willing to relax my guard in a company which, no matter what its degenerate appetites, was considerably more tolerant, welcoming and better-mannered than I had recently enjoyed at the Savoy. I purchased some first-class *neige* from a pretty young woman in a blue shot-silk 'flapper' dress whose fashionable page-boy haircut resembled the traditional coiffure of the Egyptian dead. Her faintly green make-up added further to the impression that some deceased Emperor's handmaiden had taken the evening off to sell cocaine in a European nightclub. Apart from some long-haired boys in excessively loose cotton lounge-suits, some, depending upon the tastes of their masters, with make-up and earrings, there were few natives here. Even the waiters were Greeks from Alexandria, or so they all claimed. The blood has mixed so thoroughly in the cities that it is impossible to tell one race from another, except by what they claim for themselves. And people think the South African government is mad!

The increasing attraction of The Crooked Path reminded me how easily and to my detriment I had slipped into bohemian living in St Petersburg, and I drew on my usual resources of self-discipline to leave Quelch in the company of a transvestite, clearly an old friend, and take a *kalash* back to our hotel. Halfway before I reached the Continental I had been asked for *baksheesh* in return for graphically mimed services by a score of little boys, a group of youths, two whores and the driver of my cab. I waved the rest away but suffered the boys through the gaudy streets of the Wasa'a district which even at that hour remained brilliantly lit with a mixture of stained-glass oil-lamps, electrics, naphtha and candles. Each little garish hovel offered the delights of Paradise and the temptations of Hell. Women of every European nation graphically advertised their charms and skill while their negro pimps, their Greek 'protectors',

213

their Italian *capos*, whispered to you of unspeakable gratification and the smell of their perfume made you drunk on the heat of your own blood; yet you knew they promised only profound hunger. I had known that hunger in Odessa; again in Kiev and Constantinople. But here, it gnawed more fiercely than ever. I sensed the softness of professionally yielding flesh; flesh that was never angered, never shocked; flesh that had no morality, merely a price; flesh that could take without surprise the demands one dare not make of even the most obliging and loving sweetheart. And somewhere it seemed to me I heard the wild, vicious whistling of a whip; a whip I myself wielded; a whip that was wielded upon me. My own flesh became nameless until all that filled my universe was pain, lust, more pain and a draining, terrible satisfaction.

'They use their bloody whips a good deal too bloody much,' said Mrs Cornelius next morning, when I found her in the dining-room alone at breakfast. The large, net-curtained windows looked out upon wonderful landscaped gardens and a passing four-wheeler. Ezebekiya Square was the very centre of the European quarter. 'It makes yer wanna walk everywhere, dunnit, Ivan?' She and Seaman had gone to dinner that evening with Goldfish's local representative. The Egyptian market was one of the most rapidly growing of all. Sir Ranalf Steeton, a cousin of Storrs Pasha, the immediate power in Egypt, was now principal agent for all the major British, French and American studios. He had also done some work as an independent producer, chiefly, he had told Mrs Cornelius, for the tourist market in Cairo and Port Said. ' 'E reckons 'e's a plain, blunt Yorkshireman 'oo don't like ter beat abart ther bush,' she said over her fried eggs and trimmings, 'but 'e sahnds like ther usual posh toff wot's 'ad ter find a job o' work, nar the butler's votin' Labour an' wants 'is larst ten years' back wages. Anyway, 'e wos tellin' us that Cairo's *the* flash place ter be at ther mo'. Becos o' Tutenkhamun an' that. There's plenty o' money 'ere an' lots to be made, 'e sez. But it's bringin' wot 'e corls undesirables in. Conmen an' stuff. So wotch yer bloody wallet, Ivan. Yore the first ter fall fer a line y'd be ashamed of if it woz one o' yer own!'

This was my opportunity to mention my meeting with Major

Nye. She brightened at the name. 'Loverly ol' geezer. I 'ad a soft spot fer 'im. 'E understood me. Even when I wanted ter go back on ther stage.'

'He seemed to think you might not be happy to see him.'

' 'Appy? I'm ecstatic. I did 'ave ter borrer a few quid ter set meself up an' I 'aven't 'ad ther chance ter pay 'im back yet, but thass orl water under the bridge, eh, Ive?'

The English major was evidently in love with her and was terrified she would again reject him. He thought of the money only as a barrier he had unwittingly thrown between them.

'Anyway,' she added, 'it turned art ter be a decent littel inves'ment orl in orl. I'll get Wolfy ter write 'im a cheque as a sub on me wages. Did 'e say wot 'e wos doin' 'ere?'

It was my belief he was on secret government business, probably in relation to the bandit problem. Acting as usual under the banners of 'nationalism', they had assassinated a couple of officials and ineptly blown up a few administrative and military buildings. No sane Egyptian condoned them. The king himself condemned these activities. Personally he favoured his country's complete absorption into the fabric of the British Empire, where conditions for the common man would inevitably improve together with his own security. Islam, as is perpetually demonstrated today, habitually selects new leaders through a succession of murderous betrayals, rather than by the less dramatic and more prolonged methods of the West. Fanatics like the Wafd's Roshdi threatened not only the king's life but the lives of his entire family. The king knew as thoroughly as anyone that the rule of Law was synonymous with British rule and that the moment His Majesty's advisers left, his country would revert to the blood-feuding characterising all those countries which had known only enslavement to Turkey or Baghdad or, in modern times, the Great Powers. How right he was to look at his choices and thankfully link his fortunes with the British! It takes an Arab to understand who makes the best master. He is used only to masters. It is all he can himself aspire to.

' 'E was with some sort o' special police, larst I 'eard,'

she said. 'A kind of elevated copper. Ter do wiv drugs or somefink. Y'd better wotch yer step, young Ivan.'

I told her I did not think I had much to fear from a white man.

'Cairo's ther world's drug capital these days,' she continued. 'Opium an' *keef* from Lebanon an' Syria. Cocaine from Bulgaria, mostly. Morphine an' heroin from orl over. Sir Ranny reckons ther big in'ernational racketeers're gettin' in'erested in Cairo. The p'lice fink they got it under control. They fink an 'eavier fine and roundin' up a few dealers an' 'ores 'as solved it.' She laughed. 'I'll tell yer, Ivan, wiv orl these crooks abart I'm on'y too pleased to be legit. Iss bad enough in bloody Whitechapel or Notting Dale when ther big crooks start fightin' amongst themselves.'

I now understood exactly why both Stavisky and Major Nye were interested in this part of the world. Such a vast volume of tourist traffic would allow the, perhaps unconscious, travellers to carry the dope to where, of course, a large European market was willing to pay generous local prices. As well as the Egyptian upper classes who were all connoisseurs, the poor *fellaheen* made up the basic market for *hasheesh* and horribly adulterated heroin. I had already heard stories in The Crooked Path about the old woman near the Khalifa cemeteries who had discovered that ancient human skulls could be ground into a fine enough powder to 'cut' the heroin used by the area's quarrymen and carters. The creature who told me this found it amusing that they were snorting the skulls of their own ancestors back into their living brains. I had merely been a little sickened by the anecdote.

'I bet ther major's 'ere on account o' ther drugs.' Mrs Cornelius reached with conviction to the rack for another slice of toast. 'That'll be it.'

Privately I was in full agreement with Authority's efforts to wipe out the trade in so-called 'black' drugs – the opium and *hasheesh* draining the energies of working people – but it seemed unsophisticated to ascribe the same life-sapping qualities to cocaine, for instance, which was ever a boon and a source of energy, a stimulant to the imagination. As for morphine, to make it unavailable to the likes of ex-servicemen like Quelch, needing to kill the pain of old wounds, was positively inhuman. There had to be selection and moderation in the control of drugs just as there was with alcohol, for instance. I found the whole subject distasteful, so asked gracefully after our great director.

'Wolfy got up early ter go out ter give ther pyramids ther once-over. 'E wants ter get down ter work as soon as poss. In that I'd agree wiv 'im. I'm bored art o' me pants, Ivan. It'll be a relief ter 'ave me nose ter the powder-puff again!' And she laughed heartily at that and could not stop even when a sallow Quelch came almost surreptitiously into the restaurant, caught my eye reluctantly and then even more reluctantly advanced upon our table. I pulled back a chair for him. Slowly, in that deliberate way he had of re-ordering his limbs into a new position, he lowered himself to join us.

He was afraid I would embarrass him. He had not been in his bed when I rose that morning and came in as I was leaving. He had mumbled that he had only had time for a quick wash and change of clothes. He had no reason to distrust my discretion and as this came clear he even managed a small smile when Mrs Cornelius suggested that the sausages were a bit 'funny-tastin' ' and might be 'strickly Moslem', made from camel meat. Again she demonstrated her power to lift the ill-humour of someone whom she liked. Her effort, however, was not of quite the intensity it had been on yesterday's train. I suspected her energies to be a little more widely distributed now. She called him a gay dog. She laughed and said I had told her he had not come home until after nine o'clock that night. 'You've bin 'angin' rahnd them museums an' libraries again, 'aven't yer, prof?'

He was happy to give some vague sign of acquiescence and even giggle as if she had somehow put her finger on his most terrible vice. My understanding of his character was growing with almost every passing hour! At a suitable time, perhaps when we were on the ship back to Los Angeles, I might indeed tell Mrs Cornelius that I had last seen her 'innocent' full of dope and ginger ale in the arms of an extravagantly dressed Albanian transvestite while he quoted excitedly from the more sensational passages of Juvenal! Pinching his cheek

217

with the air of a fond mother who would be happier if her boy were just a little more manly, Mrs Cornelius finished her saucer of tea and rose from the table. 'I'll leave you two norty boys ter tork abart the Redline togevver.' Referring jokingly to the district 'redlined' by the British for licensed brothels, she did not guess it was where Quelch and I had actually spent the better part of the evening. Meanwhile, our encounter at the Savoy offered sufficient explanation as to our whereabouts of the previous evening.

'Our reputations, dear boy, remain intact,' hissed Malcolm Quelch with a wink containing something of his brother's devil-may-care insouciance, but the expression faded almost at once, as if he realised he had been in danger of revealing something to me. His features seemed visibly to narrow. 'It would not do to disturb the lady's feelings.'

For my part I did not offer any opinion. He could do very little to disturb that particular lady's feelings! My friend was a woman of the world. Like me, she had lived by her wits throughout the entire period of the Bolshevik War. In those circumstances one very quickly learns to adapt. The Cornelius boy has a phrase I believe he has borrowed from one of his pop tunes. He says we must all 'ride with the tide and go with the flow'. But I have no time for his washing-machine analogies. In certain terrible circumstances, it is true, the human being will adapt in order to survive. But might it not be our duty to ensure that the terrible circumstances themselves do not occur? Unless we learn to control our appetites we are doomed forever to be in the power of random Nature. This new romantic movement that talks about 'ontology' and 'ecology' instead of the *Zeitgeist* is merely another celebration of the irrationalism Jean-Jacques Rousseau turned to such a handsome profit while incidentally offering a posthumous blessing to the Terror – indeed, to a series of Terrors, some of which we are still enjoying! Has not this century seen enough of such tainted ideals?

It was almost noon before Quelch and I left the table, returning to our room where he would instruct me in some of the more important Egyptian symbols I might incorporate into my designs. I was in this, as in everything I did, consci-entious to the point of obsession. I had already accumulated a great sheaf of designs, both of costumes and sets, and my script was ready for shooting. Though my own part would not be a starring one, I felt it would counter any suggestion that I was a mere 'programmer' idol and show me in my best light as a dramatic actor. I was still reluctant to include Esmé, but Seaman had insisted upon it. I could only agree with him that Esmé's death would probably bring the audience to tears in the final reel and there were after all only two scenes where she appeared with Mrs Cornelius. Thus I combined talent with strategy, diplomacy with humanity, to help create a film to justify everything D.W. Griffith ever taught us – a romantic, stirring spectacle with a strong moral tone. That was what audiences had come to demand and it was what I could cheerfully give them. Today's cinema has lost the willingness to combine those two key elements. What is the surprise if it is thus losing its audiences? Even in Weimar's most decadent days we could be uplifted by a moving tale. There is certainly nothing amoral about *Die Erdgeiste*. Our movie had my full commitment on both levels. I became more and more absorbed in the realisation of my great story, in which the ancient and modern were (as in Griffith's masterful *Intolerance* or De Mille's *Ten Commandments*) held up as mirrors, one to the other. I began to feel it was almost 'in the can'.

Naturally enough, it was at this point that Professor Quelch and I, ascending from the lobby, stepped from the electric elevator to the soft carpet of our floor to be confronted by a Wolf Seaman who had clearly caught the sun and had hay fever. He was burning red. There were tears in his eyes. I suggested he should lie down. I would send someone to him. Perhaps he required a doctor. He spoke in incoherent, guttural Swedish. I could understand hardly a word. In his hand he held a crumpled buff form, obviously a telegram. After we had taken him back to his room and ordered him a large gin and tonic, he was able to tell us that he had stopped at Sir Ranalf Steeton's office on the way back from the pyramids. Sir Ranalf had been hoping to see him. He had accepted a cable from Goldfish on Seaman's behalf. At last the Swede permitted me to examine the wire. I remember it clearly:

WHERE ARE YOU STOP   IF NOT THERE INFORM ME
IMMEDIATELY OF WHEREABOUTS STOP   STOP ALL PRODUC-
TION   STOP   WHERE IS YOUR STAR SINCE CHERBOURG STOP
AWAIT FURTHER INSTRUCTIONS STOP   PS HAS HE GONE TO
TANGIER STOP S.G.

Seaman was baffled. I, of course, understood something of
Goldfish's bewilderment and, I suspect, anger. In my obsessions with my own problems I had forgotten to pass on the
earlier message to remain in Alexandria until our new star
arrived. Clearly the star had arrived and, finding us gone,
with Goldfish's steamer getting ready to depart for Tangier,
where Captain Quelch had further business, had decided to
take passage on the *Hope Dempsey*.

I advised Seaman to relax. This was just another of Goldfish's
self-contradicting cables. He sent them when he was bored.
Tomorrow would bring us a further wire countermanding
everything in the previous one. We should proceed as normal
and begin shooting tomorrow.

'That would be wonderful,' said Seaman with that heavy
tone he intended for irony, 'if Sir Ranalf Steeton did not
have to authorise all our bank orders. We have no money,
gentlemen. We cannot pay crew, actors or our hotel without
Steeton's authority. We have only the money we carry. And
Steeton's master is Goldfish. He must do as Goldfish commands. I respect him for that.'

'But tomorrow or the next day Goldfish will be asking us
why we have no "footage",' I said. 'We shall waste time if we
pay too much attention to this cable.'

'He has never been so adamant.'

'You have never understood him to be so,' I coolly pointed
out. Thus, little by little, I was able to calm the Swede long
enough to get his agreement not to inform the others. It would
cause unnecessary alarm. Meanwhile, we would begin shooting
as planned, early the next morning when the sun's rising above
the pyramids would be the backdrop to the first love-scene
between myself and Mrs Cornelius.

Our story must become an actuality! Mrs Cornelius and I

220

would appear in a prologue where, as modern lovers doomed by society's rules to separate, we meet, ostensibly for the last time, and embrace beneath the stern and battered features of the Great Sphinx; I, Bobby Sullivan, the playboy, apparently debonair and fancy-free; she, Colleen Gay, the débutante, engaged to a titled man of honour and probity whose heart and reputation she dare not and will not threaten. Our story would then sweep back in time some three thousand years, to the age of the Boy King. Now 'Colleen Gay' is unhappily betrothed to the sickly child whom she loved as a brother and to whose cause she is committed. I, too, as the new young High Priest, am loyal to the Boy Emperor. However, there is another, namely Esmé's Cleopatra, who also loves me and is prepared to bring down the entire dynasty to further her own petty ends. When Tutenkhamun is poisoned, we, of course, are blamed. A motive is obvious in our almost unendurable love. Wolf Seaman had found the story moving and he was sure it would appeal to the audience jaded by his sexual comedies.

Even Goldfish had known this could be the movie play of the decade, one which would heighten his reputation, more, even, than *The Squaw Man*. He, better than any, understood the value of a strong moral where heroic self-sacrifice, preferably from both male and female leads, is the turning-point of a tale in which virtue is finally rewarded.

Several times, Seaman wavered. Professor Quelch, doubtless concerned about his fees, lent his voice to mine, pointing out that only he knew the great secret places in the desert, the old temples and tombs which would best serve our story. The combination of authentic locales, strong scholarship, a powerful script and wonderful actors would be bound, under Seaman's inspired direction, to win a vast world audience.

Seaman needed audiences. His old brand of pessimistic irony was no longer finding favour with a public regaining its pre-war optimism. *Flame of the Desert* would attract the kind of universal success he needed. That success was his only motive. Genuine artistic integrity destroyed Griffith's career, but Seaman had his eye forever on the market. Within another ten years he would be making his fortune on Lash LaRue, Tim

Holt and Sunset Carson, adventures which a greedy public demanded in vast quantities. He knew pretty clearly where he was going!

It took Quelch and me the rest of the afternoon to restore Seaman's confidence and remind him that his crew awaited orders to begin a shooting schedule. With the help of several more gins he pulled himself together and by six o'clock was the centre of attention in the small meeting-room we had hired to discuss the next day's work. Even Esmé attended, sitting near the front in one of her loveliest cream lace outfits. The sight of her seemed to restore Seaman's confidence further and when he came to address us on our duties and responsibilities he was able to do so with a certain authority.

I must admit that secretly I was, from time to time, faint with anxiety, fearing the end of all my ambitions. Indeed by the time dinner was over my anxiety had become almost uncontrollable. Under normal circumstances cocaine is a wonderful means of recovering myself, but it was not effective then. I had little experience of dealing with such feelings. Anxiety came to me later in life than to many. Childhood and adolescence were virtually free of worry and it was only after I began to understand my responsibility for others that I experienced real anxiety. Whereupon I knew only one means of releasing myself from its grip: through the pursuit of sexual gratification. I had this in common with Clara Bow. Until recently careless lust rid me entirely of my fears. But since 1940 I chiefly used local prostitutes from Colville Terrace and Powys Square. They had no expectations of me. I had none of them. There is nothing but pain to be gained from attachments to the women one uses for the Release of the Beast, as I call it. In 1926 I had not yet learned that lesson and, when dinner was over, addressed Esmé on the matter. It was now perfectly safe for me to visit her in her room. With Wolf Seaman, Mrs Cornelius planned to be at Sir Ranalf Steeton's for the rest of the evening. Esmé was feeling tired. I told her I would bring something to make her more wakeful. At length, almost as if she were wearying of the debate, she agreed to receive me.

By the time I arrived in her room, I was determined to

make up to my darling for all those long months of unfulfilled desire. That night I planned to show her no mercy. That night, I discovered, she expected none.

FOURTEEN

JE LA PRIS SAUVAGEMENT! *Elle pleurait, grognait, criait. Je la griffai jusqu'au sang. Je la mordis. Je la pénétrai et le sang coula encore. Mais cela ne suffit pas à me rassasier . . .*
The rest was never a memory, simply an impression from which, at length, I stole away. I had made Esmé my own again. My mark was upon her. I had seen a new respect in her eyes. *Ses yeux paraissaient de cuivre incandescent, sa chevelure lui faisait comme un halo de flammes, son corps était couvert d'égratignures, d'empreintes laissées par mes dents et de marques voluptueuses . . .* And my anxieties were vanished, as were hers. We had achieved mutual release. I do not regret all that. It was an act of confirmation. One must experience it to understand it. It was a shame, after so much exertion, that my little girl was wanted for work that morning. As we boarded the hired coach to drive out to the Mena Palace Hotel, where we would organise ourselves before the day's shooting began, both Wolf Seaman and O.K. Radonic regarded us with a kind of distant curiosity, while Mrs Cornelius even exuded a certain disapproval. None of that upset me. I am one who follows the Master. I fly like a Hawk. I cackle like the Goose. O Sovereign of all Gods delivered from that God who liveth upon the damned. I was restored to my old power and was fully a man again. I had proven my control over my own life and intended very firmly to continue with that control. I would

224

not be diverted from my ambitions.

I had already confided some of this to Quelch as we prepared for the morning and he became positively fervid in support of my new determination. 'We are all the slaves of Fate, dear boy. But it's up to us to do our best and pretend that this is not so; to take up the reins of our own runaway chariot or die in the attempt! *Abusus non tollit usum.* That is my answer to those who would judge us.' He had placed a friendly hand upon my shoulder as I shaved. 'It is a motto well suited to this awful country which, I fear, is inclined to bring out all kinds of dormant or unimagined passions in the sexes. The residents here always recognised the danger. That is why it is so important to keep up appearances. *Non nobis sed omnibus.* But this is a rule you and I must take as it comes. We are not, after all, what they would even consider, I suspect, as *omnibus.*' The tone of the older man, rather than his words, was comforting.

Malcolm Quelch was beginning to reveal depths unlike his brother's yet just as mysterious and fascinating. His understanding of the Beast was oddly tolerant, like that of a clergyman confident in his own faith and the triumph of the Holy Ghost over Satan and His armies, even accepting of those times when he himself was in the power of the Beast. The Beast is within all of us. It is our gift from God that we learn to tame the Beast by any means we choose. Rasputin understood this. Quelch confided his ideas of God as we travelled side by side into the west, where the great ruins lay, famous and, like all great works, untarnished by familiarity. The reality was stupendous.

It was when we had changed from the car to the little open tram which carried us up the line through the sand on the last stages of our route that I was suddenly aware of the pyramids' colossal size! I realised why it is not possible to take a picture of the pyramid that does not diminish it since one has to step back a considerable distance to include any idea of its shape and by that means lose the scale. We were fleas upon the remains of Pride; grubs crawling at the feet of the Gods. Never before have I known such awe as when I contemplated the enormous power of an individual able to dedicate the lives and resources

225

of his entire nation to the construction of his own monument! Only Stalin has since known such total might.

'I must say,' Mrs Cornelius strolls up to join us, content beneath her parasol, 'they ain't a disappointment.' With the satisfaction of a housewife who has seen the rising of a perfect pie she peers benignly upon the Great Pyramid of Cheops.

Behind us the film crew are unloading their equipment, observed by crowds of local hucksters and beggars controlled by our own private guards – burly men who gathered the skirts of their white *gelabeas* about them, using their long bamboo canes liberally and without anger upon an undismayed flock momentarily contenting itself with imprecations, wailed pleadings, filthy insults and the offer to sell any one of us anything our hearts or our lusts had ever remotely desired.

Wincing a little, Esmé moves closer to me. She has been sharing for a moment a seat with Seaman. She insisted on coming. I eventually agreed she should continue, to further her career. Our future after all is by no means as certain as it was. Seaman is begging every one of us to give of our best today, since Sir Ranalf Steeton will be driving out later to see how we work. He does not explain that Steeton's word to Goldfish might bless the production again. Much as I am unhappy with Esmé's acting ambitions, it was never in my nature to force another human being to a course of action that does not suit them. As Malcolm Quelch frequently remarks, what one did in one's own bedroom was a matter of personal taste; what one did in one's drawing-room must always be a matter of social probity.

I was thoroughly confident in Esmé's love and respect for me and trusted her completely, in spite of Mrs Cornelius's untypically jealous behaviour which had led her earlier that morning to ask me if I intended to start up as a full-time pimp in Cairo. I told her, rather stiffly, that there was a fairly large difference between a pimp and, for instance, an agent. I saw nothing wrong with a man encouraging his fiancée to follow a career. Most men would, I said significantly, be jealous of their sweetheart's desire for success. And yet, as events were to show, Mrs Cornelius might have had at least a glimmer of honest concern for her rival, some intimation of the danger which lay ahead of us all. *Tel de l'acier en fusion, mon sperme emplit son anus. Je vous aime toutes les deux. Il n'y a aucun mal à être en vie. Wir steckten in einer Maschine, die weissglühend and weich war, die jedoch härtesten Stahl zerquetscht hätte. Das Mahlwerk serrieb uns. Blut spritze. Blut spritze. Sie wollten Vergeltung, den Tod. Sie baten um Gott, um den gnädigen, strafenden Jesus, der in dieser Stunde der Offenbarung über sie gekommen war. Plötzlich war ich missgelaunt . . .*

Le sang jaillissait. I have no further memory.

Sweet. I did love. Sweet, sweet. I did love. Sweet. There is no more sweet, sweet. I did love.

A kite, some scout for her fellow-scavengers, flared her wing feathers high overhead, about half-way to the peak of the pyramid, and the telescopes of a score of bird-watchers swung to observe her. We had arrived at the exact same moment as a Cook's Tour of the British Ornithological Society, 'Here to spot Egyptian exotics and familiar wintering friends!' The tour, I was told by an excited matron, would also include visits to the principal sites of antiquity. She handed me a neatly folded blue and white brochure couched in prose worthy of Ouida. Before she was politely moved on by one of the crew, I returned her leaflet and gave my attention to the camera and our director who, like most of us, had donned his comfortable riding clothes. The cameraman's boy was even wearing khaki shorts, while O. K. Radonic sported a suit of loud yellow golfing pyjamas he had bought the previous day, he told us, at Davis, Bryan and Company in West Street. The clothiers was famous in Serbia for the fineness of its English cut. On a British officer, perhaps, the golfing pyjamas might have looked almost elegant. On Radonic they looked as if he had borrowed a seaside pierrot suit several sizes too large for him. But the cameraman seemed pleased with his purchase and wore the outfit with the air of one who is at last perfectly *à la mode*.

A tent had been erected for Grace and his boxes. He would also help the actors dress. He had acquired, at Seaman's suggestion, a little, round-faced Jewess as his assistant. She had some experience of the European beauty salon at Shepheard's. She seemed competent, if surly. Speaking only Hebrew, Arabic and some French, she was of not much use to the rest of us. Happily Grace proved to be familiar with French and Hebrew and even seemed to have picked up a few words of Arabic. My anxieties, already 'grounded' by the activities of the night before, were almost completely forgotten as I saw we were building a useful team able to work with the camaraderie which makes for greater efficiency and improved artistic quality.

Malcolm Quelch, Esmé and I were not needed for at least half-an-hour while Seaman took readings and made judgements concerning light and focus, so we decided to stroll around the base of the pyramids. Quelch, used to the children and old men who begged from us, struck about him smartly with his malacca, a thin, amused smile on his face, as if he teased dangerous dogs. Cairo was out of sight and the only buildings were a few huts, the only traffic some ancient camels used to give rides to tourists. Out of all those rose the confident walls of the Mena Palace Hotel, a sprawling building in what Quelch called the 'Swiss Egyptian' style. The guides now claimed it as the hunting-lodge of King Faud's ancestors. 'These people are paying for Romance, dear friend, not Truth. One has to give the customer what she wants, I suppose. I try to educate them to the facts of Egypt, but they simply refuse to listen. Some of them become genuinely outraged. I can be attacked at any time for mentioning some perfectly ordinary reality. Did you want to climb up? These chaps will help you.' He tapped an affectionate cane upon a couple of native bottoms. The men grinned and pointed upwards along the flanks of the astonishing edifice where, because of uneven stones, it was possible to scale the pyramid all the way to the top. Several tourists were being pushed and pulled by muscular *fellaheen* as I watched. I had not really been prepared for this mixture of casual use and monumental grandeur. Even the mobs of tourists and jostling *fellaheen*, the tramway, donkeys and rickshaws failed to diminish them. As a hundred Brownies clicked and recorded a hundred identical memories, Malcolm Quelch paused to watch a German party as it was helped aboard its camels for a turn around the Sphynx. 'Do you think anything is being broadened other than their already broad behinds?' he speculated. 'Or will they go home, as I suspect, confirmed in their conformity and xenophobia? We are in danger, as the world grows wider and more available to us in all its considerable variety, of becoming increasingly parochial and insular, even of embracing simplistic systems of ideas, like immigrant Jews, like American pilgrims, as a barrier against so much uncontrollable data. Bewildered men, trained to manipulate the universe, must first instil a fear of the "outside" in their families and then define the universe, making it something they can control, drawing up a system of values merely to justify maintaining power over the only *creatures* they can control, their wives and children. This, of course, is the central point to any understanding of Islam. It explains why the Arab will never progress under his own initiative. He has developed a religion, out of the original creed, which makes him ideally suited to be a client of more powerful states and peoples. Always somebody's slave. It is what he has been bred for. It is almost a crime to offer him anything else. What are these so-called "free Egyptian elections" going to achieve? They demand as a right what the British earned through centuries of experience. Yet had the British never come here, the Arabs could not have conceived of the notion of freedom in the first place! They sneer at us, call us corrupt, tell us we are cruel conquerors. And it is we who brought them the notions of the European enlightenment! But will this produce an Arab enlightenment? I doubt it. Theirs is a religion which thrives on ignorance and belongs to the darkness. No further Enlightenment can come through Islam. It's a dead end. These chaps must eventually make a choice between perpetual poverty and illiteracy, proud, sublime insensitivity and, if not Christianity, at least a form of secular humanism. One or the other – possibly both – will free them. *Solve vincia reis, profer lumen caecis.*' He paused, as if taking control of something in himself of which he disapproved. 'I have unfortunately inherited a touch of my grandfather's messianism. My father, on the other hand, an altogether gentler person, did not really prepare us for the world. Grandpa Quelch's fire and brimstone has rather more to do with the actuality of life's vicissitudes, don't you think?' He led Esmé and myself around a gigantic corner, out of sight of our crew and the majority of sweating *Burgers* and *Hausfraus*, successful caterers from the

Bronx and cattlemen from the Brazos, dowagers and doctors from Dijon and Delft, bored children, and ecstatic maidens jotting purple lines in palm-sized notebooks. It occurred to me, as we looked upon the barren solitude of the Western Desert, that we might easily be upon a desolated planet Mars marvelling at the grave-markers of a race of giants. Might not those beautiful, untypical Pharaohs and their queens have descended in spaceships from the dying planet? Such ideas are now the stuff of cheap science fiction and nonsensical attempts to prove not only that we were once ruled by a benign race from the stars but that the Earth is actually flat. I have attended their meetings at the Church Hall. Mrs Cornelius was very interested in the telepathic aspects of their beliefs and I must admit I have always kept an open mind on the subject. She had several stories of *'psychic phone omina'* as she called them. She had as little success as myself in getting someone interested in her ideas. She had, she said, 'put it to them bland bastards at the BBC but they're so bloody busy keepin' mellow frough a mixture of buggery and booze they don't 'ave time ter fink abaht reality.' I said that since they truly believed they had both defined and accepted reality, anything outside their definitions was therefore not real. I had the same trouble with *Titbits* magazine. The man interviewed me about my theories and then went back and published a story which presented perfectly sound notions in a mocking manner. They make what they do not understand into a farce so as not to consider the actual implications. Even the picture of me was altered. Neither was I flattered by a caption stating that 'Mad Scientist Max Reveals Sphynx's Secrets.' These people have no respect for themselves or anyone else. I would say to them *Ihtarim Nafsak!* This is something the Bedouin still know. True men are judged not by their wealth but by the approval they command from their peers and the admiring fear they engender in their enemies. No one can admire or approve of those Fleet Street gutter-rats. I told Mrs Cornelius she should not sink to their level.

Tugging my hand, Esmé made us fall back a short distance behind Professor Quelch. She leaned her little hip against my thigh. She had a compliant, dreaming softness I had known for a while in Constantinople. I found her mood both fascinating and alarming. She was, once again, suddenly offering me the whole responsibility for her fate, her very life and soul. Flattering as it was, this did not entirely suit me. I was scarcely more than a youth and not ready to transform myself into any woman's tower of strength. While I was quite prepared to look after my little girl and cherish her I did not wish to become, as it were, her cause. There is a considerable strain involved in being another person's ideal. I loved Esmé as a daughter, a sister, a wife, *meyn angel, meyn alts!* She was everything I had ever wanted. Yet, still I could not trust a Fate which had already snatched her from me, in different incarnations, four times. I yearned to commit myself wholly to her. I knew I must do so if ever she was to believe in my devotion, yet it was almost as if I wanted to put a distance between us again. I had always known *how* to master her, yet I feared to master her. Even the Marquis de Sade understood that the slave is not the only prisoner; sometimes the slave owns the master more thoroughly than the world can ever guess. I have known humiliation. I understand it. But I never became a *Musselman*. *J'entendis l'horrible fouet de Grishenko siffler dans l'air lugubre et gris. Nous criâmes au même moment.*

Malcolm Quelch raised his hand to an acquaintance, a gauze-draped woman of middle years, as she drew across the sandy slabs a charge of straw-hatted schoolchildren, doubtless the daughters of diplomats and soldiers, who moved with the familiar reluctant tread I had observed in the museums of Kiev and Paris, their navy-blue pleated skirts swinging in unison and reminding me of a party of Scots I had seen during the last stages of the Civil War, when the Whites and their allies were falling back to Odessa. My own little girl was scarcely older than they. I wondered if I should not consider asking Major Nye's help in finding a good English boarding-school where she could learn the lessons of normality and moral rectitude which would turn her into a perfect wife for a man of affairs. However, Esmé's explicit remarks about these children were not in any way suitable and I was only glad that Quelch's grasp of vernacular Turkish was less than perfect.

'And how are you finding Cairo, dear mademoiselle?' Politely our professor turned to include himself in the conversation.

'It is very pretty,' she said. 'Especially the mosques.' She flicked a fly from her blue and white parasol. 'And the lovely trees and so on.'

'Cairo, my dear young woman, is a City of Illusion.' He paused to watch the schoolgirls racing towards an Italian ice-cream cart almost identical to those I used to see on the beach at Arcadia. I came ashore in Arcadia, from the Oertz when she crashed in the sea, but the carts and the bands and the pretty girls had all gone. Only the Jew met me and took me to his house. He said he worked on a newspaper in Odessa. He had been born in Odessa, he said. This did not surprise me. 'And we can find in that city all the beauty of Illusion. But Cairo is also a frontier-town, sweet dear mademoiselle, with the familiar characteristic of such a town.'

'A frontier to what?' enquired my little one with honest curiosity.

'To the past, I suppose. The North is exhausted, but the South awaits us. Are you interested in the past, mademoiselle?'

'I am too young for the past, in the main,' she said. 'My interest is principally for the here and now.'

'This is the generation of the wilful Modern Girl, I fear.' Malcolm Quelch spoke to me in English. And he winked to show that he had made a joke. I assured him in the same language that Esmé was the very model of virtue and that he was not to judge her by either her fashionable clothes or her apparent vapidity. And Esmé, hating to be excluded by a language of which she had only the prettiest rudiments, asked in French if it were not yet time for lunch. Professor Quelch informed her that it was only nine-thirty and that at twelve, he understood, they would be bringing us out a buffet from the hotel. 'The food is excellent. They have nothing but British-trained chefs.'

Understanding this much, Esmé darted me a look of sardonic despair. Professor Quelch, propped upon one of the lower stones, asked if she were unwell. She merely began to hop about in the loose sand, eventually removing one of her little high-heeled slippers. 'My shoe,' she said. 'It is full of this awful stuff. Are we almost gone round?'

232

'Not yet, I fear, charming lady. We have two more golden sides to negotiate before we shall catch sight of our friends.'

'Oh, Maxim!' Still hopping, my darling pointed at two men stalking by supporting a battered chair on their shoulders. I was obliged to negotiate a price with the ruffians to carry my child in our wake as Quelch and I continued to walk. I explained to him, as if sharing a secret, that Esmé had experienced a restless night and was still tired. Quelch took my meaning. A bond was growing between us. It was of a different order to the wholesome comradeship existing between his brother and me, yet I did not resist it. My respect for Quelch's experience and scholarship was considerable and I was honoured he should be prepared to share it with me.

'The Copts and not the Arabs are the original sons of this land.' He indicated some chipped slogan from an earlier millennium. 'What a paradox it all is. Even the Prophet did not consider Christianity the foe of Islam. On the whole the Moslems are the real aliens and the Copts the real aborigines. The Coptic Christians are today not loved by their Moslem fellow-citizens, despite fine speeches by eloquent young men about the brotherhood of all Egyptians united against the Wicked Foreigner!' He glared almost cunningly at me from the edge of his eye as we turned the third corner. 'Are you interested in paradox, Mr Peters?'

I said that as an engineer I was interested in the resolution of apparent paradox.

'Then you are a man of your times!' He laughed, the sound of a bolt being drawn after years of disuse. 'I am afraid that I *have* accepted the irrational. It is almost the norm, these days. But you are still young enough to think you can mould the world into something better than it is.' He had grown suddenly more effusive. 'The God of Christ is *ipso facto* the God of Chance.' He put his arm around my shoulders, patting me as an older brother might, offering encouragement and approval. Perhaps he, the youngest, had always wanted a relationship where for once he might command. I think he looked for that in me. He was a man desperately needing a protégé, while I still longed for a mentor. Perhaps I let Quelch too easily influence me for a time, to my eventual regret.

We turned the fourth corner and came up behind our colleagues. Watched by a throng of local hucksters, they had gathered about a large touring car. They were sipping lemonade proffered by an impeccably costumed servant in a tarboosh. Seated in the back seat of the great Mercedes was a small, swarthy man in a white satin suit and a gleaming panama which he lifted as Esmé rode in upon her ramshackle palanquin and was lowered to the dust. 'Meet the boss,' said Mrs C., introducing us to Sir Ranalf Steeton, in whose hands our immediate destiny now lay. We greeted him with the enthusiasm of shipwrecked passengers apprised of rescue. As he shook hands with Esmé he returned our enthusiasm twofold. 'I say, what a stunner! This must be our other lovely star! Do join me in the car, ladies. I must learn everything about you.'

I walked away from Mrs Cornelius and my Esmé as they simpered beside Sir Ranalf. He was in the hands of professionals. I could rely on them to do their work and was content to let them make whatever possible gains they could for us. Wolf Seaman, unbuttoning his shirt, had turned bright red and pretended to tackle some problem with the camera. When I pointed out that our girls were currently our greatest asset he said something waspish about his talent being the best thing we had and he was about to expand on this when the car's horn brought us back, smiling and manfully agreeable, to Sir Ranalf, whose orderly had finished handing out the packed lunches and those awful bottles of Bass. 'I'm so sorry I can't have you to luncheon at the Mena Palace,' said the little man bending to kiss Mrs Cornelius's dainty, pink hand with his own dainty pink lips. 'But we shall arrange something soon.'

'You have yet to hear from our masters in Hollywood, I take it?' Seaman wanted to know.

'I fear so, dear boy. It's the holidays, do you see? Everyone's in Florida or Vermont or wherever it is you chaps go at Christmas and the New Year. Valentino apparently left Le Havre on January 16th. I've sent to Alexandria and apparently Mr Barrymore walked out of his hotel and has not been seen for a couple of days. There is some suggestion that he transferred from the *Hope Dempsey* to Lord Witney's yacht which was going to Corfu for the Hogmanay.'

234

'Barrymore?' said Mrs Cornelius, poised upon the running-board. 'Wot?'

'Your missing leading man, sweet lady. I'm most awfully sorry, but you were supposed to meet him, you see, in Alex. They were afraid he would get lost if you weren't all there together. Apparently a wire went astray.'

'There wos so many,' she said.

'Is it John or Lionel?' Esmé was cautious.

'I only know it isn't Ethel. But it would not be the first time John has sent a substitute while he goes about his own business. He is, I gather, something of a prankster.' His little, precise voice had its own peculiar melody, like the warbling of a self-contained canary, and it softened oddly when he addressed women, as if he sought to mesmerise them. I had never heard quite such a voice and I did not find it particularly pleasant. It seemed to me that Mrs Cornelius was rather repelled by him but made a considerable effort to be agreeable. Clearly, she was relieved when she could make her departure. It was left to Esmé to prove herself a most remarkable actress, with her display of reluctant separation from a man she found of consummate fascination. For his part he squeezed her hand, pinched her cheek, murmured a compliment in her tiny pink ear and let her slip slowly from him before swinging his chubby body from the rear seat to the front and, with an impatient wave, directing his driver back to Cairo.

As soon as the car was out of sight, Esmé linked her arm in mine. 'Is it true we shall have no proper luncheon today?' She stared with distaste at the remaining boxes in the hamper.

Seaman stopped with a sigh to pick up his portion. 'I suspect we are on probation. At least until we hear from Hollywood. Sir Ranalf told me privately before he left I was not to worry about anything. He is genuinely on our side, I think.'

Mrs Cornelius looked at him with wondering sympathy. 'That little porker's a greedy bastard, mark my words. 'E's art fer hisself an' 'e's orlready makin' the most o' this. 'E's up ter somefink. Come on. Let's git shootin' before it's too bloody 'ot an' orl me effin make-up runs again!'

235

I watched the two women retreat to their costumes, unhappy tent-mates, calling for Grace and the Jewess.

Malcolm Quelch had found himself a folding chair and a garden umbrella. He sat some distance off with his lunch on his lap, observing the little natives as they ran about our perimeter shrieking with excitement, sticking out their tongues and occasionally pointing to their arses in a manner which was either inviting or insulting, it was impossible to guess. Quelch's attitude was innocent and avuncular, but if any boy came too close he did not miss the chance to whack him smartly with his cane. Meanwhile Seaman was working himself up into the peculiar frenzy with which he normally directed studio flapper parties and which seemed oddly inappropriate here, hands waving and shrieking as wildly as our surrounding audience. Radonic, ballooning vivid lemon behind his camera, took readings off his grip and, having made-up and dressed, I busied myself with the trial scene, our opening shot where Mrs Cornelius and myself embrace against the background of the pyramids and Esmé strolls by to glance idly at me – an action which of course will have considerably greater significance later in the story. For these shots it did not matter if the watching crowd behaved in any way it pleased, but if the footage proved usable, we would employ it in the editing. If not, it would still give us needed information. I knew an immediate sense of elation as the ladies emerged in their special frocks, Esmé in deep blue, Mrs Cornelius in pale pink, a cloudscape of undulating feathers, lace and silk, to stop at last before me, to glance towards the camera and the whining, scowling Scandinavian who, with nervous hands upon the cameraman's careless shoulders, was whispering complicated instructions in his native tongue, of which Radonic had not a syllable. Mrs Cornelius turned fabulous powder, mascara and rouge upon me so suddenly that a sharp, delicious *frisson* stabbed through my whole body. I moved dreamily into her embrace, my eye-shadow so weighting my lids that I was forced to raise them very slowly to stare into her exquisite blue eyes, automatically mouthing the lines which came from Seaman's shriek of 'Action'.

BOBBY: I know that I have loved you since the world began.

IRENE: And we shall love each other until the world shall end.

This was my epiphany. It was as if I had reached the quintessential moment of my existence, from which radiated all the possibilities of past, present and future. Behind me were the wars, the turbulence and terrible cruelties, the filth and the bloody corpses of the century's struggles; ahead lay a silver and gold vision, the ethereal splendour of my independent flying republics, my healthy, handsome citizens in a cleaner, more rational world, with sentimentality abolished and self-respect made the rule. It was as if all the promises of my life were to be fulfilled and every disappointment and betrayal redeemed! It was almost as if I had been sent a heavenly sign, an affirmation and a confirmation of my noblest ideals. I was so close I could barely control my trembling. Her perfume was sweet as morning roses, her flesh so wonderfully soft it was scarcely flesh at all, her body radiating such sensuality I could barely control the shivering of my blood. Esmé was momentarily forgotten. Mrs Cornelius was my Goddess, my Muse, the great constant of my life, my Guardian Angel, the one friend who always cared for me (up or down, right or wrong), who shared so much of my vision and respected the wholesome idealism behind it, the hatred not of other peoples, but of confusion, of mongrelism. The love of my own culture and people is a fundamental of my life. She shared my distaste for lies and hypocrisy, my admiration for nobility, self-sacrifice and courage in all its forms, my willingness to extend a helping hand to anyone who wished to better himself, black, white, olive or yellow, so long as each accepted his equal responsibilities in the order of things. The simple moral lessons of my Russian childhood are not, I think, inappropriate to these chaotic times! Neither are they limited to the Slav. Nordic peoples share them in one form or another and they exist where Christians have left their mark, in Italy, Spain and, still, sometimes, in Greece, the centre of all our learning and our pride. They are the ideals of the Enlightenment, of the Age of Science, and if I alone still

237

hope to convince the world of their message, and point to the road to our salvation, this does not, I hope, make me mad. I continue to speak for my people, for my past, for honest patriotism. Love of country, respect for one's own culture surely helps us understand another's emotions for the things he calls his own? The tribes of Europe might have co-existed peacefully for centuries had not the tribes of Oriental Africa, with their alien allegiances, observed our wealth and power and hungered for it. Let Palestine take her Jews and Morocco her Moors. I have no quarrel with them while they remain firmly on their own side of the Mittel Sea. My inventions and ideas would benefit everybody. I yearned to share my genius with the world. What a different place it would be today! This is the understanding I had in common with Mrs Cornelius. With me she is the only one left alive who knows how perfect was our lost future. I grieve for it, still.

'Yer did yer level best ter make it work, Ivan.' She is still beautiful, seated in her ancient armchair, all her memories piled around her. 'It ain't yore fault if ther effin' world wosn't up ter yer expectations. It's the same wiv kids. Take it as it bloody comes, I say. One effin' day at an effin' time.'

She was a fantastic legend – yielding in my arms. I gasped. The joy was almost anguish. Esmé went by and her eye met mine. She smiled. I returned my gaze to Mrs Cornelius, holding her with all the passion of the years until the 'Cut!' I most dreaded and she was fanning herself with her feathers, pursing her perfect lips to blow air up into her face and calling enthusiastically for a beer. 'Phew! This ain't the wevver for 'uggies and smarmies is it, Ive?'

Hardly able to breathe, let alone speak, I indicated that I agreed with her, but secretly I was nurturing the ambience. If Goldfish's erratic temper permitted no other take, I had at least recorded the fulfilled ambition of those many years! Finally I had held the quintessence of all women (the woman who had been my wife) sober, in my arms for one infinitely thrilling moment! I think Esmé, strolling smoothly through her own part, sympathised, as women can, with my profound physical and intellectual pleasure; something she herself could never quite inspire. Though she satisfied my noblest longings and my every ideal of womanly perfection, though Esmé understood my soul, and my most primitive desires, only Mrs Cornelius really understood my heart.

'OK shot! OK shot!' Radonic, in vivid cotton, raised his thumb, his highest praise. Wiping his forehead, Wolf Seaman's lugubrious features had an expression of faint astonishment. We all knew we had recorded a moment of screen magic.

It was later, as I vomited into the sand at the base of the Great Pyramid, that I realised with surprise that I had caught the sun.

FIFTEEN

OUR STORY BEGAN to take shape at last and, recovering slowly from my mild sunstroke, I was euphorically self-assured, anticipating our movie play's glorious resolution, which would echo the prologue and the central scene in the burial chamber (I was now sketching the clearly visualised final draft). A somewhat schematic writer, I possessed classical skills perfect for a romantic narrative needing a certain detachment lest it be plunged into bathos. Filming was going smoothly, with Sir Ranalf Steeton underwriting our expenses from his own pocket, and we were grateful for this display of confidence. On my birthday, the fourteenth of January 1926, in full Egyptian costume, I embraced Mrs Cornelius once more, but she was ill at ease in so little clothing and we looked forward to shooting the scene again later. It had become obvious even to our patron, Sir Ranalf, that we needed fresh locations. Memphis having proved less ruin than aura, and Sakkarah merely unimpressive, we jumped at Steeton's suggestion that as soon as it could be arranged we take a steamboat up the Nile to Luxor and the famous monuments of Karnak, the centre of the great Theban Empire where we should at this time find fewer tourists and, as Malcolm Quelch said in an aside to me, far fewer distractions. 'The land of the Hawk, my dear boy, where people can trace their ancestry back to the beginning of Time. Of course, you must be hugely imaginative to get anything from the place at all. Basically it is a ramshackle Arab settlement pitched upon the ruins of an earlier and superior civilisation like a fungus on a dying oak, hardly a town at all.' Perhaps because he was now assured of regular wages and was consequently consuming morphine rather generously, he had grown more expansive. He was able to obtain both his own drug and mine in substantial quantities. Indeed, it soon became clear to me that he was discreetly supplying half the team. I did not blame him if he made a small profit, given that he risked up to a year in prison and a stiff fine if he was caught. I told him I was concerned only for him. He assured me it was almost impossible for the British police to conceive of a middle-class Englishman having anything to do with drugs and the Egyptian police had the sense or the greed to leave him well alone. 'It's only the dagos and the natives who get picked up, dear boy, and most of those with any influence or money are soon sent substitutes or bought free. As far as the good Russell Pasha is concerned the drug trade is a filthy native appanage.' Bertrand Russell was at that time the Cairo police chief.

It gave me a rather dishonourable thrill to spend an evening in Major Nye's company. I never mentioned this to Quelch, for fear of disturbing him. The major had asked me to be his go-between and I had a little reluctantly acted as message-bearer for both him and Mrs Cornelius.

He was not, it emerged, pursuing the drug traffic but following a lead British Intelligence had received concerning the arms trade. That was in the days when selling arms to Arabs was still not respectable and was called gun-running. I gathered he was working for the Government of India. 'Through some loopholes in former treaties we can't stop Muscat importing firearms. Muscat therefore is as flourishing a market for whole-sale gun-merchants as Baghdad is for sweetmeat sellers and curio dealers! You can buy as many rifles and boxes of ammo as you can afford. The only problem you have then is getting it to your next destination. Once the stuff is across the Oman Gulf and reaches Persia it can't legally be confiscated. The Indian government instituted a sea patrol out of Jashk on the Persian coast. Most of those guns are going into Afghanistan. Naturally, we want to stop 'em.' But he would not elaborate, although he spoke at another time of going by gunboat into the Gulf to board a native dhow. He had taken from the Jashk barracks half-a-dozen sepoys, in charge of a subahdar and a half-caste Baluchi as interpreter. By some accident of fate they had stopped not a gun-runner but a slaver. 'Bodies packed like maggots in the hold. We let 'em come up, but the stench was dreadful. Blacks mainly, and a couple of Asiatic women from God knows where.'

We had not heard from Goldfish in weeks, which somewhat surprised me since earlier he had managed to send an average of two cables a day. Eventually we taxed the head of our Egyptian office. Sir Ranalf was massively apologetic. He had wired several queries, he said, but Goldfish still seemed to be away. What was more, the missing actor had last been seen at Cherbourg on January 13, had not been found in Cyprus and there was some talk of his having fallen overboard. This news threatened to dissipate my sense of well-being, but I recovered as much of it as I could and was glad when early one morning the porter came to take me and my baggage to the quayside and the paddle-steamer *Nil Atari*, already sighing and gasping in a ladylike way as her boilers were fired. The old mahogany and time-polished brass, her sturdy hull, quivered as we made our way through the usual pleading rabble to the gangplank guarded by Nubian youths wearing dark blue and red uniforms in the local style. Sir Ranalf Steeton was waiting for us on the arrival deck. He wanted, he said, to tell us the news himself. When we had found our cabins we should assemble on the bar deck where he would make a little speech to the whole team.

Although small, our cabins were very solidly built from the best woods, with fittings of brass and chrome and mother-of-pearl and everything neatly stowable, under bunks, above cupboards, within mirrors. It was possible to secrete one's treasures in a hundred unlikely crannies. The horsehair mattresses were first-class and a reassuring smell of Pine disinfectant permeated everything. A place is never clean to a Briton unless it smells of his native fir. I have observed this in some of the filthiest homes in the kingdom: the dirtier the floor, the more it reeks of the Scottish wilderness. So powerful was this resinous charm against infection in the British psyche that I still find myself deeply reassured by it, especially if ill. Mrs Cornelius, as she grew to count the years, paid less attention than most to what she called 'fussy 'ousekeepin' '. The smell of damp and mildew (as well as the unfortunate problems of her drains and the sewer which never recovered from next-door's Flying Bomb) grew to be unmanageable in the end. But for many years a good, strong whiff of Pine allowed me to take my tea with confidence.

The boat's top deck lay under an awning like an outdoor ballroom, with a piano and a bar at the bow end, backing on to the wheelhouse and behind that the great stirring blades of the paddles. It was here that Sir Ranalf addressed us, wringing his little hands as he waited for O.K. Radonic and Grace (reluctantly sharing a cabin) to join us.

Some of us leaned against the bar or the piano. Others had taken lounge-chairs or simply preferred to stand back against the railings as the ship rocked gently in the wake of a passing police launch and Old Cairo ululated from the far bank.

'Fair ladies, gentle *chevaliers* all,' began Sir Ranalf with that odd choice of forms which I understood was called Olde Worlde in England and was now chiefly associated with followers of Shelley. There had never been much discussion of PreRaphaelite or *Yellow Book* tendencies in my own *Pearson's* and *Strand*s, which meant that for years I remained oddly innocent of references most English and Americans find excitingly or disgustingly obvious, depending upon their tastes and dispositions. 'My dear colleagues,' he continued. 'My news from the United States is, like the *News from Persifiloum* in the Wheldrake poem, of a disappointing rather than a tragic nature. I must tell you at once, sweet mortals, that our mutual master, Mr Samuel "Gold-wynn", has withdrawn all support from *The Nile Remembers*. He has washed his hands of you. He claims to know nothing of the *Hope Dempsey*.' At our expressions of dismay he released his hands and chuckled. 'However, I will not play cat-and-mouse with you, hearty lads and noble lasses, but inform you that nothing is lost! Nothing at all!'

It was my turn to consider Sir Ranalf's sanity and wonder if he were not after all one of those many English eccentrics whose instability goes unnoticed in Egypt or India where chaos is always barely held in check and the more bizarre expressions of the human beast's lusty appetites are given full rein.

'I have been in frequent communication with our "Tsar", as they say, and he is emphatic. Without major players an epic on its own is no longer enough. *Ben Hur*, he says, has proved that much. Everyone's doing epics now, don't you know. He is "cutting his losses", he says. I believe he is about to go into partnership with United Artists. So whether our "star" really did turn up or whether he never intended to leave Hollywood but lay low and relaxed at home, we shall never know.'

'No word, then, of Barrymore?' enquired an anxious Swede.

'None. I think it is probably immaterial now. We can keep our fingers crossed, of course, and hope to tiddlypop that he has discovered our whereabouts and is on his way, but meanwhile time really is money in the kinema profession, as you know, so I think you should just carry on as you were – only this time, my courtly squires and lovely demoiselles, I am your new angel, your producer. You are now working for Cinema Anglo-Cosmopolitain. You'll receive regular weekly salaries, the best in Egypt, and we shall produce only the most artistic films!'

He went on to explain how Egypt was the apex of the international film business. From here movie-plays were exported all over the world, even to America. Up to now Sir Ranalf had not been able to assemble a team to make the quality of pictures he demanded, but now, to our mutual profit, here was the golden opportunity!

I, for one, was particularly relieved. It seemed I again detected the hand of a benign god. Not only were our salaries saved but our integrity also. I turned to share my joy with Quelch. He was unimpressed, and Mrs Cornelius reflected his reaction. But the rest seemed moderately agreeable to see how the plan worked out.

'I have already, don't you know, had a word with Mr Seaman who will explain any details of our contract, but I think, under the circumstances, you'll find it pretty decent, sweet fellows, fair ladies.' And he leaned to chuck my Esmé under her little chin. 'I wish you Godspeed for Luxor. You need not fear a lack of interest. As soon as you berth there I shall take the railway to join you. Meanwhile, *this* is your hotel! Every facility and servant is at your disposal. They are up-river Nubians, chiefly, and therefore good, docile, cheerful workers. You need fear nothing of thievery or any other form of banditry. You may leave your cabins unlocked, your valuables wherever you care to put them. It has been said before – and I repeat with approval – Islam has a rather more positive way with criminals than we in the West. Perhaps we could learn from their forms of discipline. Be that as it may you have, if it does not seem indelicate to suggest, only to mistrust each other.' With that, he departed, our miniature Henry V, from the bar. Descending to the main deck by means of a carpeted stairway, Sir Ranalf strode with chubby dignity across the gangplank, up concrete steps to the quayside and into his noble Mercedes.

'I can't help feeling suspicious of an English chap who sports a Boche car.' Malcolm Quelch scowled after the departing producer. Mrs Cornelius put her arm through his. 'I noo yer 'ad yer 'ead screwed on right, prof. 'E's a tricky bugger. Did ya recognise 'im from somewhere?' A shy, flattered schoolboy, Quelch allowed her to lead him slowly to the rear of the deck to watch the casting-off procedures of our muscular 'fellahs'.

The city still held some of her blue dawn haze, turning to pink-gold glaze where it met the sky, and, with her tall silhouetted trees and towers, her pale domes and glittering crenellations, possessed for a moment the air of fabulous romance the tourists so longed to find and which their agreeable guides so poorly understood. It was pleasant to enjoy the skyline's beauty without having to block out Malcolm Quelch's dampening realism. The noise of the surrounding paddle-wheelers and motor launches readying themselves for their work slowly drew my attention until I was watching with fascination the brown barefoot boys and men running back and forth through the morning air, shouting orders, slipping lines, pushing off, starting engines, and when I looked back at Old Cairo it was once again the same dusty, modern Europeanate city I had first seen from the railway station, its solid neo-Classical buildings proclaiming the latest followers of Alexander and the Ptolemys working to create stability out of this confusion of creeds and races. In those days there were many of us who still looked to the British Empire as a force for peace and order in the world. The Germans always admired the British. No one was more astonished than Hitler when they sided with the Bolsheviks and, achieving his ruin, achieved their own into the bargain! Who could have predicted such a will to self-destruction?

From a moored *felucca*, the white-sailed swan of the Nile, came the rhythm of a drum, the yodelling of a native violin and clarinet, as some ceremonial party stepped aboard, the men in dark European suits wearing garlands of pink flowers, the women in enough gold, blue and cerise to make an Odessa wedding look dowdy.

Esmé came back to me, seeming a little wan as she sipped from the glass of Vichy water a Nubian boy brought her. She had on her pale green silk. 'What are they doing, Maxim?' Her attitude towards me had changed radically now we again enjoyed the pleasures of man and wife. The mixture of terror and lust, which produces that adrenalin best released in urgent sexual activity, had momentarily taken us in its power and she had developed a peculiar clinging quality which I found flattering and perhaps a trifle alarming. I placed my arm around her little shoulders and told her I guessed they were celebrating a marriage, though it was unclear which particular day of the ceremony they had reached. As we stood together watching the boat, still shuddering and squealing with the sounds of Africa, I reflected that it was not the prospect of marriage I feared, but the threat of betrayal. I was sure Esmé would not betray me but feared that Fate might again conspire to take my darling from me. In the past days I had developed a creeping sense of dread which even Quelch's comforting junk could not dispel. My attachment to Esmé was deep and enduring. Our mutual sexual satisfaction had peaked, I think, during those days of sublime equality. I could only enjoy such fearful pleasures if they were mutually demanded, when, as it were, the *Yin* and the *Yang* achieved their ultimate expression, when the fundamental male and quintessential female found total harmony. This power is only satisfying when it is mutually experienced. I believe it is wrong merely to use women for this particular release (though I must admit there is a certain type of female who almost demands it). After all, I say to Mrs Cornelius, women are the only other sentient creatures on earth! Mrs Cornelius had no brief for Suffragism on the basis that she did not want 'ther right ter vote fer ther same bunch o' wankers thass in orlready'. I say that women are half the population of the earth. It is as much man's responsibility to protect women from the beast that lurks in all men, and which he controls in himself, as it is for women to take care and not arouse that beast. I have fifty per cent of the burden, I say to her, 'and you have the other fifty per cent.'

She disagrees. She is no feminist. 'Orl I can say is, Ivan, that you keep yore little John Willy in yore bloody trousers or risk, pardon my French, an 'undred per cent bollock loss!' In some ways her views are too conservative for me. My thinking has always tended towards the radical. There is little point in trying to reason with most women when it comes to matters of rational behaviour. They are creatures of impulse and I suppose we would be mad to want them any other way.

Esmé pointed to where a brown-necked raven glided in the sky overhead, searching the debris along the bank for some titbit. 'Is it an eagle, Maxim?'

Amused, I told her that only she could see such beauty in a carrion bird. She insisted it was still beautiful. I marvelled silently at that ability women have to look upon something ordinary, even lowly, and make of it an object both noble and desired. Valentino is an example. The raven spread his wings to perch for a moment upon our tasselled roof, just above the wheelhouse where the plump Egyptian captain, important in his grubby whites, and his laughing, bare-chested Nubian mate directed our final casting-off, moving us further towards mid-stream, our paddles slapping against the tide until my view of the city was almost completely obscured by a billowing white spray.

Within half-an-hour we were leaving Cairo behind, looking out across wide fields, an endless game of noughts and crosses produced by dozens of narrow canals. The rural scenery had scarcely changed since the Pharaohs raised their first great pyramids. Beyond the palm groves the fields were a vivid green and yellow patchwork of corn and cotton, while at the

247

wells and locks old camels circled endlessly, moving the water in which all our destinies had been born.

For a while the Egyptian wedding-boat sailed in our wake, its occupants waving and smiling and offering us mysterious salutes, but then a gust of wind caught the tall sail and sent the *felucca* almost at a complete right-angle, narrowly missing our port wheel which continued its relentless gushing and groaning, sounding for all the world like a camel of the river, ill-tempered and sturdy. The *felucca* veered away, its occupants roaring with laughter at their close brush with an appalling death!

Mrs Cornelius returned, cocktail in one hand, and in the other a grinning Professor Quelch. She opened her wonderful mouth and screamed hilariously, 'Yer c'n be a norty littel boy when yer wanna be, carn't yer, Morry?' He had her complete drunken approval and was close to winning her sober blessing, too. She had a soft spot for the people she called the 'walking wounded' of the world.

We were passing palm-lined levees now, raised against the flood, the date orchards, the figs and the olives French and English managers restored to Egypt, and as I turned to look at the distant shore to port I was surprised to see a native in a very well-cut European suit, a crimson tarboosh on his impeccable head, climbing up the stair to the open deck. He bowed and salaamed to the ladies and advanced towards us with his hand outstretched. I saw Quelch respond as I did, but there was nothing to do but shake it. Quelch became oddly formal and made a bitter to-do of introductions. We were introduced to Ali Pasha Khamsa whom I immediately recognised from several issues of *The Times of Egypt* as, under a different name, a highly-placed member of the Wafd, the recently 'independent' parliament of Egypt!

I realised that he was the better breed of pale, round-faced Egyptian, uncorrupted by Semitic or negro blood. No matter what my opinion of his politics, I felt an immediate respect for him, regretting my hasty judgement. Since those days, I have learned to know a man by his actions, not by the colour of his skin or his creed. There are, for instance, Nile-dwelling *fellaheen* whose blood is that of those who created the first literary writing, the first temples and tombs. It is scarcely their fault that alien invaders came to rob them of their inheritance and their beloved Christianity and if they have degenerated it has been through the efforts of the Jewish and Arab drug-dealers who have found it profitable to sap these hardy men of their energies, already debilitated from waters poisoned by imperfect British engineering. The British were the first to agree that the dam had unfortunate side-effects. They argued that they were doing their best to control the problem, yet refused to see how they had helped to create it. This was often the genius of the British abroad and at home. Their philosemitism was their particular ruin. I still believe they held the key to the way forward. Even 'Socialist Herbert' Wells understood the duties the British began to ignore in those terrible, self-doubting years immediately following the Great War. The spectre of Bolshevism terrified them. Only in England was it unexpected! Wells's hero in *Things to Come* proudly predicts a future where Man will conquer Chaos throughout the Universe – and only then will he begin to learn! How close this was to my own frustrated vision. Now I have learned that Chaos is God's creation and it is our duty merely to order our own part of the universe. Perhaps we were all too slow to accept responsibility. I cannot blame the British Empire, nor the American, nor Hitler, nor Mussolini, without accepting some blame myself.

Ali Pasha Khamsa had been educated in England at a school whose name I did not recognise but which clearly gave Professor Quelch some pause. I received the impression that Quelch's education, though honourably thorough, lacked the excellence of Mr Khamsa's. The Egyptian also had a degree from Cambridge. We were therefore a little uncertain how next to proceed but, needless to say, it was Mrs Cornelius who broke the ice, linked her arms in Mr Khamsa's and Professor Quelch's and chuckled, 'Ain't I a lucky lady, now, ter be entertained by two such brainy and 'andsome gents.' She led them off, slightly startled sheep, and again Esmé and I were alone.

The Egyptian's presence had made her uncomfortable. 'He reminds me of those Turkish officers. They were bastards to all the girls.'

A little sharply I told her to forget her Constantinople life. She would soon be my wife and a film star in her own right. She had been born in Otranto, with Doctor Gastaggagli presiding. Before that, I reminded her, there was only the inchoate miasma of pre-existence. She lowered her eyes, admonished. 'I'm sorry, Maxim.' Of course I forgave her at once.

Drawn by a sturdy sailing-boat, a string of barges went by, the sacking tight across their mounded cargo bringing to mind a shoal of primitive river monsters advancing to devour the distant city. Seaman strolled over from the bar where he had been talking to Radonic. 'It seems we are not to be saved by *Ben Hur*, after all. Although it has made a considerable profit, it has made none for our former master. He has lost heart, I would guess, for historical subjects, at least temporarily, and has found an excuse to withdraw his support. Thank God for Sir Ranalf! The native gentleman, by the way, is some sort of business colleague of Steeton's. He's only going as far as El-Wasta and from there will take the train up to Medinet el-Fayoum where I gather he will address a public meeting. I think he's going by boat to get a rest from his duties. He's an important "big-wig", you know, in the Egyptian government. It's through him we received permission to film almost anywhere we like. Even the British can't pull strings like that, as a rule.'

Only then did it occur to me to wonder what kind of compromise Wolf Seaman himself had made in order to secure his own ambitions. While I believed in the ideals expressed by our new producer, it now seemed to me that Seaman's explanation of our passenger's presence aboard was somewhat defensive. Was he justifying a secret arrangement with Sir Ranalf? It did not greatly concern me what Seaman gave up or promised, so long as our film was made to the highest standards and we received our salaries. When it was completed I would return to the US with Esmé and challenge Hever to do his worst!

'You are so clever, Wolfy.' My darling was an admiring schoolgirl. 'None of this would be possible without you.'

'Steeton is an agreeable fellow.' Smiling down at her he passed a modest hand through his curly hair. 'And I intend to make our movie, little fawn, never fear.' With a sigh he stepped up to the rail and stood beside me. Together we looked towards some distant ruin. 'It will tell the true story of mankind,' he continued. 'How we strive in so many ways to avoid the fact of death. The variety of ways in which we avoid the inevitability of unbearable loss. Unlike ourselves, the Egyptians refused to remove themselves from that central fact. They built their entire civilisation around it. As a result it lasted the longest of them all. Empires like the British, or especially the American, build their culture on the very opposite idea. Their people devote themselves to avoiding and ignoring the fact of death. Well, *Death in the Pyramids* will force the world to look upon its folly and to bow its head in shame.'

'They will love it!' Esmé turned away from where she had been admiring a group of little boys bathing in the shallows. 'It will pack them in, darling Wolfy.'

And turning again, so that only I could see her this time, she delivered a wink of such ironic intelligence I realised with delight the depths to my darling I had yet to explore.

Separating themselves from Mrs Cornelius and O.K. Radonic (newly nicknamed The Yellow Kid) Professor Quelch and Ali Pasha Khamsa, now getting on like fire-engines, rejoined us.

'*Actum ne agas,*' the Egyptian was saying.

'But how can we avoid it, my dear sir?' Professor Quelch moved delicately upwind of Ali Pasha Khamsa's cigarette.

'That is what we're in the process of discovering. The fashion in Europe today is to pamper and adopt the Jews, but there are a few men of vision who see the dangers of that policy. Have you heard of Adolf Hitler? He's a German very much in the news there. A follower of Mussolini's, I understand, with a positive approach to his country's real problems. A genuine intellectual activist. You read German, do you, Professor Quelch?'

'Only inexpertly.'

'I've seen a lot about these socialists in the *Berliner Zeitung,*' Seaman joined in. He had always shown a preference for the German newspapers. 'It's rather alarming, isn't it?'

'Oh, they are scarcely socialists in the old sense. This new kind is dedicated to the destruction of Zionist Bolshevism. A good many people in Egypt are following this chap's activities. He could teach us all a thing or two.'

And that was how I came first to hear of Hitler, in the early days of his success, when he still controlled his party. It was painful to see such a fine man brought low by his own *hubris*. Some day, if there is a future left to us, a playwright will take Hitler's story as a subject and show Germany's Führer as the noble, flawed, tragic hero that he was. I mourn my own lost opportunities, but how *he* must have mourned in those last moments, when Berlin was falling to the Bolshevik guns! It would take a Wagner to do that tragedy justice.

'You are a Muslim, Ali Pasha?' Seaman was hesitant.

'Good heavens, my dear sir, nothing so old-fashioned! I am a secular humanist by persuasion. But it is best to keep one's religion to oneself in democratic Egypt. We are still in some ways a very backward country. There is much to do. Industrialisation is, of course, of chief importance.'

'And you support land reforms?' Quelch's question had a significance I barely understood. Ali Pasha Khamsa was amused. 'I have nothing against the rich, Professor Quelch, if that's what you'd like to know. I wish all my people were rich. I respect, as thoroughly as anyone, a hard-working man's right to do well for himself. There are ways to expand our agriculture so everyone could become a prosperous farmer. I believe this can be achieved through engineering, not social regimentation.'

'You really are a chap after my own heart.' Malcolm Quelch raised a salute. 'Mr Peters, you must tell Ali Pasha all about your inventions and your ideas for "turning the desert green". This young man, sir, is an engineering genius. He has already built several flying-machines and a dynamite car. Let him describe to you the astonishing marvel of his aerial turbine!'

'Egypt has great need of engineers.' The politician looked speculatively at me. 'Especially American engineers.'

I explained to him that I was only American by adoption. I was actually Russian, forced from my homeland by the Reds. He expressed sympathy and enthusiasm. 'So much the better. If there is ever a revolution here, Mr Peters, believe me it will not be a Red one!'

Again I was learning not to judge a man by superficials. Ali Pasha Khamsa was anxious to listen to my ideas. I was soon expanding on my dreams of vehicles especially designed

252

to cross vast areas of desert, of others for automatically digging canals for hundreds of miles, irrigating land which had not known fertility since Time was first recorded. I was quick to tell him, however, that I did not share his general distaste for the Jewish race. There were those among them of the most virtuous type. I myself owed my life to a Jew. But there was no persuading him. I lacked, he said, daily experience of the race. His people had had to contend with their cunning for centuries. 'Islam has been singularly tolerant to the Hebrews. But there is no pleasing them. Zionists are taking over the British parliament, demanding Palestine for themselves. No longer content with milking us of our money, they now demand free land! Land which at no time belonged to them. Soon, we fear, the British will give them Egypt itself! This will be my subject in Medinet el-Fayoum.'

Emphatically I assured him the British could not possibly betray Egypt's trust.

1948 was to prove how wrong I had been in those days of my innocent idealism.

SIXTEEN

I SAW THE GOAT. I saw Him first in Odessa. I saw Him again in Oregon where the dead live in caves hidden amongst the mountains. I saw the Goat. He tempted me. He put a piece of metal in my stomach. *Die iron strudel.* It was His joke. He showed me my sister Esmé and told me she was my daughter. He said He would make her my wife. He promised power over them all. The Power of the Untrammelled Beast. Where He was not recognised was where He was best employed. The Devil was tired. He had worked long for this day. I met the Goat in Aswan, upon the ruins of a conquered Christianity. The Cow and the Ram came to witness my humiliation and my grief. What justice condemned me to their cruel control? If I could not believe God directed the world, I could only pray Christ remained to guide us. Satan reaches us through our most vulnerable and tenuous idealism; our faith in the future. That is how He conquered Russia and brought down His capering triumphant hooves upon the ruins of Berlin, upon the fallen bastions of our beliefs. Hitler turned his back on Christ, just as Napoleon had done before him. And so Satan, weary and sated as He was, came to sit upon the piled thrones of Europe and watch with grim ambivalence the destruction of what He had once most desired. Those modern Parsifals who took sword against Bolshevism are all dead now. Not one was killed in honest combat. All were betrayed from within. I was betrayed from within. There is a piece of metal in my stomach. Sometimes it feels like an iron Star of David. Was it in the bread the Jew made me swallow? What did I pay him? A Jew will never give you something for nothing. What did he want from me? He saved my life in Odessa, in Arcadia. What did I pay for this service? His hands were gentle. I loved him. *Stadt der schlafenden Ziegen; Stadt des Verbrechens; Stadt der meckernden Krähen; die gerissenen Kunden liegen in den Gassen auf der Lauer die kleinen Vögel seinen trügerische Lieder. Die Synagogen brennen. O, Rosie, mi siostra! Zu är meyn zeitmädchen, meyn vor . . . Im der Vatican* He lolls in an attitude of bored familiarity while His subjects queue to kiss His gloved paw. This affords Him no further amusement. Must He corrupt and destroy everything in order to escape the fact of His own agonised sundering from Grace? His is the worst torment of all, for He has already known a state of oneness with God. That state is now denied Him, as it is denied no other. We can only guess at the enormity of that loss. Is it any surprise that this fallen Immortal prefers to distract Himself from this unimaginable anguish by devising fresh trials and defeats for mankind? What would any of us do in His place? I thought I had left Him behind me in Odessa, in the bloody streets of Slobodka, where bloated dogs pant, replete, amongst the corpses of slaughtered Jews. There seemed no justice in His pursuit of me. I did not know then that I had been chosen by God to bring a particular gospel to this Age of Science. I was innocent. I was afraid.

I journey to a place where souls are weighed, when benevolent Anubis weighs our sins.

Ali Pasha Khamsa shook my hand before he chanced the bouncing plank stretching from our boat to the muddy bank where local porters stood ready to support him if he slipped. '*Nigra sum sed formosa, filiae Jerusalem,*' he said as he left. I believe it was a mild, and civilised, admonition to me for my initial reaction to him. I accepted this with good humour and told him that I was sure we would meet again. Even now I cannot believe, when I see the television pictures, that this man was the same Sadat who has been so instrumental in betraying his country to Israel. That cold claw struck at my stomach and seized my heart. I had a brother in Odessa. He was a good Jew. Such creatures can exist. I am in too much pain now. But I shall not always suffer. There is a white road down which I ride and the road ends at the sea, at a green cliff, and when I reach the end of the white road my horse lifts easily into the air and we fly towards Byzantium, to be reunited with my Emperor and my God. My plane is called *The Dragonfly*. It is my own machine. It is delicate. I have made flight ethereal, as beautiful as Man first envisioned it. I have not reduced it to those lumbering metal tubes carrying their human baggage from city to city like so many sacks of grain. My plane was called *The Angel*. Silver and gold, she sang a low musical note as she progressed through the sky. She would fill the air with her marvellous, shimmering wings. My plane was called *The Owl*. She would carry wisdom and peace to the world. She would swoop and thrust and hover and at night you would hear only the soft passage of her body through the darkness. They were all in my catalogue. I could make them to special order. Each one would be designed for the individual who would fly her. They would reflect the personality of the aeronaut. They would be a fulfilment, a completion.

In the early pallor of a Nile dawn, with mist still folded about our rigging, when I walked by myself on deck, unable to sleep for Quelch's peculiar cries describing some unnameable need, I saw what I guessed to be a pelican diving into the deep water ahead, to re-emerge with a silver-dripping beak weighty with fish. That noble bird's self-sacrifice was so great she fed her young with flesh plucked from her own breast. She had long been a symbol of Christian charity, carried upon the shields and crests of Christian knights, carried, indeed, as far as Jerusalem. At last I understood something of the bird's symbolism. I watched her soar away to the west followed by the long shadows of the rising sun which gave palms, ruins, villages, fields, a peculiar two-dimensional appearance as if, for an instant, we had caught sight of another reality, another Earth, beyond our own, or perhaps merely a singularly artistic set. I had never in my life witnessed such extraordinary beauty, such depths and grades of colour in a vastly widened spectrum, such intensity of light, a smell of such subtle fecundity I could honestly believe I had arrived at the birthplace of the world. The Nile Valley was all that remained of a lush Sahara. Was this not the site of Paradise itself? I remembered a story from a gypsy when Esmé and I visited that camp in the gorge outside Kiev before the War. She believed that when Adam and Eve had been expelled from the Garden it withered away for lack of human beings to celebrate it and so became the great Sahara. Paradise, the gypsy woman said, can only exist if people positively want it to exist. I remember her words nowadays, when I encounter caution and lack of imagination at every turn. Can they not realise it requires just a little courage and self-respect to grasp the key to Paradise? I am not the only one who held it out to them in those decades of our world's collapse when we witnessed the rapid dissolution of the great Christian European Empires. The Road to Paradise, Rasputin told us, lies through the Valley of Sin. Such ideas were common in Petersburg during my student years. I was as infected by them as anyone. We are social creatures, after all, and enjoy the approval of our peers. Only when we learn true self-respect do we become fully uncaring of disapproval. This is what we learn as Christians; what I understood (but without words in those days) as I watched the pelican climbing away into the blue-grey distance, the quintessential symbol of female purity. My plane was called *The Pelican*, which is the enemy of the Goat.

'Why is it,' asked Professor Quelch, pursuing me later to the upper deck where I sat in a lounger sketching a design I was considering for a new high-speed troop transporter able in days to move regiments through the Suez Canal to the Empire's key points, 'that the river always smells of roasting meat at this time in the morning, when we are informed by every bleeding heart that the *fellaheen* live on a handful of maize?'

I told him I smelled only what I took to be sewage and he admitted, with ill grace, that his own senses were these days blunted a little. 'But I usually thank God for that.' He further admitted that perhaps he had caught a whiff of our own little galley. He seemed anxious to keep from even the mildest disagreement and I wondered if there was a motive in this, for I knew him to be habitually and happily contentious. 'I'm rather glad our friend Khamsa is gone, aren't you?'

I said that I had been enjoying our conversation. I was always glad to hear another viewpoint.

'Even when most of it is a blatant lie?' Professor Quelch gave up trying to repress his natural aggressiveness. 'All *khamsa* means is that he is one of the Inner Five of the Moslem Brotherhood.'

At this, I folded up my pad and laughed openly. 'Really, old chap! He's a convinced agnostic. You heard him say so.'

'I heard him lie, certainly. Believe me, Peters, that man has sworn on the Koran and a revolver to uphold the honour of Islam against all who attack or humiliate her. It is the most influential Secret Society in the East, which abounds with such societies. They are said to be responsible for the majority of important political killings.'

I suggested this was unfounded speculation on his part. My impression of Ali Pasha Khamsa was of having shared the company of a gentleman.

'That is indeed what is so dangerous about him, Peters, old man.'

Wolf Seaman came labouring up the staircase in his running costume and, with a faltering wave, took a last turn around our deck before leaning, with some high, indistinguishable noise, against the bar. 'Good morning,' he managed, after a pause.

We approached him. 'Good morning, old chap.' Quelch looked him over carefully. '*Venienti occurrite morbo*, eh?'

'I lack your Latin, professor. But yes, it is so. I believe a truly fit man is never sick. You are up, both of you, unusually early.' He paused to take another great gasp, but there was a resentful, proprietorial air to the remark as if he had not only the lease of the deck for his own personal use but also of this particular hour. Although common in Swedes I have noticed this trait chiefly in Germans, who travel these days in large numbers and always complain of the crowds. Is there in this habit some secret to the rest of their behaviour? Perhaps it is a dichotomy, perhaps a paradox? I am not sure.

The sun was above the horizon and her dramatic shadows had shrunk so that surrounding land and patient river resumed a more familiar perspective. Our director drew a brave breath and expanded himself proudly for a while.

'We were discussing the passenger who recently departed.' Quelch yawned. 'I expressed an opinion which seemed to shock young Peters.'

I had not wanted to pursue the issue. 'Surprised me,' I said. 'Only, after all, there is no evidence.'

'Of what?' enquired Seaman with a rush of expelled air.

'That he's involved in politics.'

'The Moslem Brotherhood, actually,' added Quelch, and I gave up any attempt to steer the conversation to a pleasanter and less spectacular subject.

'I'd remind you,' Seaman rubbed importantly at a muscle in his leg, 'that the gentleman is a very close friend of our new "angel", Sir Ranalf Steeton.'

'Then,' said Quelch, 'Sir Ranalf must be warned. I assure you, I recognised him. A couple of days were enough to be certain who he was.'

'Don't be an ass.' Seaman found him preposterous. 'Sir Ranalf's all right. He's accepted by them. They trust him. That's how we get so much co-operation.' He was contending now with his cramps and spoke with a certain harshness.

Quelch laughed through his nose; a cold, demeaning sound. 'Sir Ranalf is not a traitor, Mr Seaman.'

'Of course he isn't!' Seaman lowered his foot to the deck and straightened his back with a sigh. 'He's a businessman. National Security isn't involved.' He had assumed the soothing tone he normally reserved for a temperamental star.

'In all the years of our association, he has never hinted . . .' Quelch shook a baffled head.

'He's not exactly one of them, Professor Quelch. But he is party to some of their secrets. I suspect Sir Ranalf Steeton to be a very brave man. I need say no more, eh?'

The clever Swede had found the perfect means of silencing an Englishman: a call upon his patriotic discretion. There was nothing of which an Englishman was prouder than in saying nothing about something about which he knew nothing. Here was a most satisfying illusion of favoured status, of power. And it was not confined to the men. During the War British women throve on it. They frequently had nothing else, but it was enough for them. I remember their efficient, confident voices. All a man had to do to finish a love affair was to murmur the words 'Top Secret'. They were born to this service. It is no wonder the typical British mouth is thin and capable of little movement.

To their delight, men have discovered that the less they say the more attractive they are. Indeed, Mrs Cornelius used to declare that she didn't mind blokes so long as they kept their bullshit to themselves. But in the end, she said, she had given up hoping. 'No bullshit – complete silence.'

She joined us downstairs in the boat's little restaurant. I had pushed back our window's lace curtains to see some ducks squabbling in the nearby reeds and now watched while Professor Quelch instructed one of our Nubian boys as to the exact, and somewhat large, portions he required of ham, eggs, bacon, sausages, tomatoes, mushrooms, fried potatoes, kedgeree, kippers and fried bread, all of which, he confided to me, as the boy carefully piled the food upon two plates before him, were a bit substandard if one had enjoyed the real thing in England. 'Here, the cuisine goes through what I call a river-change. It frequently looks or even smells right, but there is a difference of taste. I suspect it is the use of oil rather than good Home-Counties butter.'

For my own part I contented myself with a small rack of dry, crumbling toast and some almost liquid marmalade.

I told Mrs Cornelius how I had risen early that morning thinking we had crossed into another dimension of the world, perhaps into the netherworld. She shook her tolerant head at me while Professor Quelch declared sardonically: '*The world hath turned the man mad, this good man mad*, as Wheldrake has it in his *Martin Azuratt, the Alchemist of Leeds*. Now there's a fine play you might consider filming, Mr Seaman.'

Seaman just at that moment had filled his mouth with a buttered roll and could only grunt.

'You'll play the leading rôle, Peters. You'd be perfect in it. And Esmé – Miss Gay – could be the mayor's beautiful daughter, a victim of unthinking male rivalry. It is a marvellously uplifting story. We must ask Sir Ranalf to consider it as an early subject for our new company.'

Seaman was not much pleased at Quelch's assuming he was

on our permanent strength, but the Swede was still struggling to speak. He began to turn red. I was reaching to bang him on the back when Esmé, in a scented billow of blue and white, entered and he swallowed suddenly. The gentlemen got to their feet. Esmé curtseyed and smiled. Her glance to me was full of shared secrets. Sitting down with her back to the window she dipped dainty fingers towards the bread basket.

'It is so pretty out there. I saw some lovely birds.'

I asked if she had seen a pelican, but she shook her head. 'Just a few little birds, you know. And those wonderful palms. Isn't the weather warm? Who would think it was March?'

'So it is!' Mrs Cornelius was delighted. 'It's Wolfy's birfday, soon. We'll 'ave ter 'ave a Easter party! It might resurrect yer, yer pore barstard.' She guffawed.

Quelch asked the day. It was, by the British calendar, March 14. We were due to arrive in Luxor in three more days. 'That will be perfect,' he said.

'And shall it be a masque?' asked Esmé. 'A fancy-dress?'

Seaman shrugged. He was deeply embarrassed, burning scarlet. 'I'm not sure that Grace will allow our properties to be used . . .'

'It's easy enough to dress up as Arabs,' Mrs Cornelius escalated her enthusiasm. 'We've orl got sheets on our beds, I 'ope. We'll make the most o' wot's arahnd.'

I was captured by their enthusiasm, though I suspected some of it had to do with the element of boredom which so often overtakes shipboard life, leading to childish pranks and unsuitable couplings. It had been some while since I had properly celebrated Easter, so I began to look forward to the party. Indeed, anticipation helped relieve the slightly morbid sense of dread gathering at the farther corners of my mind. It was impossible to tell the origins of this dread, though the iconography of the landscape forever reminded me of Hades. I was not reconciled, in those days, to the Fact of Death. I was impatient to make my mark in this world. I would leave it to the priests to worry about the afterlife. Old age brings either wisdom or defeat, I am not sure which.

Esmé and I now found plenty of time together, since Mrs Cornelius had made Professor Quelch and, occasionally, Wolf

Seaman, into card-players, together with Radonic and Chief Sri Harold. We had all by now become active at night and saw the dawn as a preliminary to sleeping until lunch-time, when we would all gradually congregate in the restaurant as if we had not seen a soul since dinner the night before. Something in the dry Egyptian air combined with our cocaine to bring Esmé and me unimagined sensations and delights. We became obsessed with exploring them. Only when the intensity began to drop did I turn to less energetic pleasures rather than, as so many tyros do, attempt somehow to boost sensation with sordid games and pornographic postcards. For me, to patronise these Sex Shops would be a sign of failure.

I celebrate sexuality with women on their own terms, and I have willingly explored those terms to the fullest extent. That is why they trusted me. Today there are no ways of knowing how to trust a man. These *Mayday*s and *Pentaxe*s promise too much and fulfil no one; creating a hunger for a non-existent food which, if it did indeed exist, would anyway be a coarse and inferior alternative to food already available. If we are patient, giving, willing to learn, willing to be malleable sometimes and to be masterful at others, so we shall taste the food of the gods, the food of quintessential human love. This, in those noisy nights, is what I taught Esmé, and the nights became tranquil again. There is an exquisite and particular harmony in savouring the past and predicating the future. Much of this, I admit, I learned from my Baroness and from other dear comrades whom a friend would not name in the current climate. By the middle of the 30s we had learned discretion and lost our innocence. By the 40s we had discovered the delicate pleasures of restraint and sacrifice, of brevity. By the 50s these things had become mere habits and everyone had forgotten the reason for their creation; they were rejected in the 60s as being of no value whatsoever and everything was sudden Licence. Their newspapers are the work of mad spiders, of psychopathic sex criminals, of irresponsible hooligans, of repressed middle-class children whose fathers and uncles and older brothers are daily bread to the specialist prostitutes of Colville Terrace and Talbot Road. Sometimes they run into one another, the Portobello hippy indulging some infected North African narcotic and publicly groping his bewildered PreRaphaelite concubine, and his father, just popping out from Madame Lash's Chamber of Desire. They tell me there is a difference. I cannot see it. One by one they surrender to the Power of the Beast. Do they see virtue in infecting the public with their own filthy ikons, their shameful desires and social diseases? These papers hold up every form of torture and humiliation as an extension of human sexuality. And you say the Goat does not stretch His hairy body across Portobello's rotting slates and look down on that agitated human flux which might have spilled from some Islamic slum, and laugh through His pain? Achieve even, perhaps, a modicum of pleasure? Can this be what all great civilisations come to? A people which brought the *Pax Britannica* to half the globe and won the right to plant the flag of Christendom in the very heart of Arabia, carrying it into Mecca itself and destroying the very roots of our present disease. Instead, horribly, Britain fell in love with Arabia as she fell in love with the Jews. She loved all Semites. And then she was torn between two rivals. Which to choose? She did what every *femme fatale* has done since the time of Eve: she compromised; she vacillated. She should have turned her back on them both and recovered her matronly self-respect. Everyone thought she would. Especially the Germans, who would otherwise never have gone to war. And when the British socialist parliament stated quite clearly where their new loyalties lay, what choice had she but to make a treaty with the Bolsheviks? The date of their shame is May 23, 1939, when they made an independent state of Palestine. That some Jews attacked this declaration, as well as Arabs, is an indication that there are sane people even amongst our opponents. Britain had become a Jew's whore, servicing the Arab trade. Hitler saw it as his duty to save the British Empire. But he reckoned without her new Uncle, Sam, who now clutched the purse-strings of more than one nation. How could he know so many Christian lands had already fallen to the strutting carrion released from their old restraints by the violence of War and Revolution? How could he know that he was to be betrayed by everyone he had counted on, even Mussolini? I am no apologist for Hitler. I do not condone his excesses or, indeed, many of his methods; but neither do I blame him alone for the entire collapse of the world into thinly-disguised barbarism. He was badly served. He trusted too many of the wrong people. Churchill shared my views. He confided as much to Mrs Cornelius on that night she still refers to as when 'me an' littel Winny 'ad a bit o' fun tergever', some time during 1944, if that was when we began to get the V1 rockets. It was that same week I saw Brodmann coming out of Downing Street and standing beside the sandbags to strike an illegal match for his cigarette. He was dressed as an ARP Warden, with the white webbing and lamp. It was twilight, the trees were black, like cracks in grey glass. Just as I started across Whitehall to buttonhole him, the siren went off and we were rushed to the evil-smelling shelters. I think that if I were to murder anyone, it would be Brodmann. How he mocks me with his knowledge. He is the only living witness to my shame. I can come to terms with the shame. I have learned I should not blame myself. But I always hated recalling that Brodmann, a renegade Jew, the worst example of his race, had seen what he saw in the Cossack camp before I was given Yermeloff's pistols. It is no worse, I admit, than what Quelch observed later – what little he observed – but Quelch is dead. The *Palmach* did not keep hostages beyond their usefulness. It is all blood down the gutter now, as we used to say in Slobodka. I cannot speak of any of this, however, without shivering. My whole body cries out for me to stop. It is self-torture. My hands refuse to hold the pen. My head refuses language.

My plane was called *The Hawk*. She sailed above the world. She sailed through history. She sailed through time.

They say in the papers that we are on the edge of a new Ice Age. Will it cleanse or will it merely preserve the world, I wonder? Was that miserable conflict, which ended in 1945, not our Ragnarok?

My ship is called *The Rose*. With dawn light turning her silver-green fins to shimmering pink, she rises into a golden sky touched by the faintest bands of blue and grey. She could have been the first of a fleet – the mother of my flying cities, my new Byzantium.

By stopping the spread of Hellenism through the Semitic

world the Jews paved a way for crueller, more primitive Islam. The Jews did not kill Christ; they merely halted His progress. And paid a price, I agree, for so doing. Well, we are all wiser at last. Now is the time to recognise differences, go our separate ways. By all means let the Jews forge a homeland for themselves in Africa – but not at Gentile expense! How do we profit from our support of Israel? Why do we support her? There is one obvious answer to this question, one answer the Arab himself frequently offers, loudly and unequivocally, to the world: Now Jews control everything.

Even Mrs Cornelius refuses to take my point. I rarely discuss politics with her, of course. Now she proffers me the newspapers which tell us each year who are the richest people in the world and she says they are all Anglo-Saxons or Greeks or Swiss. The Queen is richer than anyone else in the world. 'And is the Queen a Jew?' she asks me.

'Maybe,' I tell her.

I rule nothing out.

SEVENTEEN

EVERYTHING MAN EVER IMAGINED can through our wills be made reality. That is my Faith. That was God's final message to the world. It is the message His son incorporates and holds in holy responsibility. This is the doctrine on which my reborn Church of Byzantium shall be based. She will not be a Church who restricts and formulates. She will be a truly Greek church, expansive and all-embracing. FOR THE WORD WAS MADE ACTUAL. I say this to you, brothers and sisters, and to you who would count yourselves my enemies: We are upon this earth to serve and honour God, and to redeem the Spirit of His Son, Our Lord Jesus Christ, and make His Word ACTUAL. Jesus brought a simple message to the world – Love One Another. Put down your arms; settle your differences with honest reasoning, not lies and guns. We are none of us perfect until we are reunited with God in Paradise, through the message and example of Jesus Christ, His Son.

Science is God's blessed gift to us, so that we may better understand His Word and learn to do His bidding. I know this now. It sustains me through all my disappointments, not least the way I am now forced to make a living. I was repairing bicycles for a long time. And little engines of various sorts, up in the arcade past Ladbroke Road. Now the fur coats. I had started attending St Constantine's in Bayswater. For too many years I had avoided the consolations of religion. To be absolutely honest, I think I feared religion. Today I believe in God and the tenets of the Christian religion. A godless nation cannot prosper. But mine is not what the eldest Cornelius boy calls 'fundamentalism'. Unless it is 'fundamentalism' to believe in God and His Word! *Klyatvoy tyazhkoyu, klyatvoy strashnoyu* . . .

I used to meet an émigré called Gerhardie who wrote novels. He had been successful, he said, before the War. We frequented the same art bookshop in Holland Street. We had interests in common with the proprietor, an academic, I understood, originally from Athens.

'One must control the page as one controls a woman.' It was Gerhardie's favourite phrase. We walked together in Holland Park at four o'clock on a wonderful summer afternoon. That park is a godsend to lovers of beauty who cannot live all the time in fine surroundings or touch rarity with familiar fingers. 'One must appear to let it have its head, but one must always be exerting the subtlest of guidance. This is the exquisite pleasure of real power enjoyed for its own sake.'

He was writing a story about a dog which has the intellect of an Einstein. But he still couples with bitches, sniffs turds and pisses on lamp-posts. When challenged on this he insists, 'I might possess the mind of a man but I must still uphold my honour and dignity as a dog.'

His books were, he said, a little like P. G. Wodehouse's, though more Russian. I took some of them out of the library. Modish things, with little perceptible plot, and observations which were barely fresh when offered to their fashionable 1920s audience, they were on the same lines as John Cowper Powys. I took them back the next day. At least 'Mister' Waugh had the taste to keep her dress-shop offerings relatively brief. I was able to tell my acquaintance that his books seemed 'more substantial' than Waugh's and he agreed. He thought this was because for his part he had always enjoyed masculine appetites. His prose, he felt, had a more robust, continental quality to it, and he was not quite the narrow moralist. He was writing a new one, to be called *Lemmings and Wrens*, about creatures whose tempers are disproportionate to their power. 'I was wondering if I shouldn't add in gorillas, but there are difficulties, of course, with all this extra perspective.' We stopped meeting at Holland Street. I think they had some trouble with the police. There is another Greek runs it now, they say is a hunchback, but I have never seen him in there. My literary acquaintance became even more reclusive. I had hoped to find him at the church, whose services I had recommended. The choir is adequate. For a while I used the Anglican St Mary's at the end of Church Street, but there was a commotion, I do not remember the cause, and I felt no call to return to their bloodless fold.

I remember another great literary name of the forties and fifties, Hank Janson, telling me in the Mandrake Club that he sometimes imagined himself some slugular queen, continuing to breed entirely by intuition. All but mindless now, he had become a creature so specialised he could write his novels entirely without conscious thought. 'Is this dangerous?' he asked me. In the end he had to go to Spain because of the ridiculous British obscenity laws which allow a woman to be tied up and tortured in public but not to fondle her lover's penis. 'My covers were the nastiest things about those books. That and a bit of fladge. You can't say "knickers" these days without some bluestocking taking the sheepshears to your knackers.' I gave him the addresses of friends. That was in the days when the Falange kept strict discipline and Spain was the cheapest, safest nation in Europe. No longer, they tell me. The moment Franco's hand slipped from the tiller the ship of state was doomed, prey to fresh invasion from Moor and Christian alike. Already the mark of atheism can be seen everywhere, especially in the architecture of the Costa del Sol and Nova Palma. This cheap, careless brutalism, as they proudly term it, is academic rubbish. It has nothing to do with what people require from buildings. They want human scale. Architecture is the greatest of arts, our most sublime acknowledgement of God's purpose.

Once it was our Church determined the aesthetics of our buildings. Then honest, god-fearing merchants imitated them, perhaps with a greater eye to practicality. Kings built their monuments and princes their dynastic piles. All by way of offering to God and to their fellow-men the confirmation of their good fortune, their thanks. Those who did not build thus were soon judged atheistic misers by Nobles, Church and State alike, and gained neither friends nor honour in the Commonwealth. I do not believe it is atavistic to pine for the Golden Age. The great buildings of Asia Minor retain their mighty authority, even as ruins, because they were raised to the glory of an unchallenged Faith. Those tawny red ruins distant against an ever-demanding sun: you could smell their age even as our boat slid past them, sailing into the pearly core of the mightiest Egyptian empire, which Homer called 'hundred-gated Thebes'.

'*Fons et origo,*' intones Quelch, '*fons lacrimarum!*' as we remark some unostentatious tomb or temple, the limestone framed by deep vermilion hills, by yellow-green palms. 'Typically and terribly picturesque,' says Quelch with that sneer I no longer believe. I wish I understood the reason for his defences. I think some peculiar sense of honour, a quasi-religious understanding of Free Will, forbids his telling me why he denigrates and shuts out so much. But, of course, there is something else he is hiding.

Quelch professed boredom with it, but for me Egypt was unique, almost a different planet, forever astonishing me with her gentian waters, her gashes of ochre vivid against the deep canary of the rocks, the lush emerald and jade of her palms and fields, her pale old stones worn by the winds of centuries, staring out of her unimaginably distant past, the tall, triangular white of bellying *felucca* sails, her little grey-brown donkeys and her creamy amber camels on the banks, her healthy children, the colour of *café au lait*, who ran along the river path calling out to us, her brightly veiled women who stopped to wave; her smiling men in tarboosh or turban. Quelch saw all this as squalid, boring or irritating and spent most of his time on deck reading a pocket edition of *Simplicissimus* in the suppressed Wheldrake translation which he had found in Cairo. He had a taste, he said, for the knockabout school of German romance, its men dressing up as women, its frequent whacking of servants, its impossible coincidences and extraordinary urinations. That this antiquated form of humour still had an appreciative audience was demonstrated from time to time by the peculiarly strained noises escaping my travelling companion, even at night in the dark, when he recalled some particularly hilarious episode, frequently involving a peasant girl, a pistol, a common domestic animal (usually a pig) and occasionally a Jew. Unlike most people, Quelch declared, his appreciation of German culture did not stop at Beethoven and Goethe.

We each of us now had cheques in our pockets drawn on Sir Ranalf's Anglo-International Moving Picture Company account, and gone was any suspicion from our minds that our new producer was not a gentleman.

'Sir Ranalf,' Seaman insisted one afternoon as we sat under the awning drinking bitters and soda, 'is your grand Old English squire. We have them in Sweden, too. The kind of well-bred yeoman who, disturbing a nesting partridge in a cornfield, allows her, as a consequence, to lead him away from her eggs. Having reassured her that he has been thoroughly deceived, he will lift his hat and say "I'm sorry to have inconvenienced you, madam," and continue his way by a different route. I made a film on the subject before I came to America, but they said it was too long. They cut it to ribbons.'

'Quite a step from rural symbolism to smart society.' Professor Quelch lifted his nose against the breeze from our *punkah*.

'Not quite so different, you know. I am telling the same stories, the same morals, but in a slightly different context.'

'Wiv more sex.' Mrs Cornelius leans luxuriously across the top of his lounger to take a sip from his glass. She is lightly swathed in apple-green silk, with an apple-blossom border, a Gainsborough hat and a great wave of 'English Garden'. 'More love interest, as they corl it.' She kissed his small, but distinct, bald spot. 'It's wot they pays ter see, eh, Wolfy-boy? A flash o' this, a hint o' that.'

'They get a strong, uplifting moral.' Gradually he resumes that cool manner which always comes when his dignity is offended. Seaman hates any questioning of his artistic motives. Mrs Cornelius does little else but mock them. She is moved, she admits privately to me, chiefly by boredom from having to listen to his monologues in the bedroom when she would, if she had not felt paralysed, have flung herself from a window rather than hear another note of his trumpet-blowing. His genius, his mission to the world, his early brilliance, his prizes and his fine reviews were familiar to Mrs Cornelius not, she said, so much in the words but in the way you remember a particularly horrible noise, like a neighbour's creaking mangle. I sympathised with her. We have many such windbags in Russia. I have spent my life avoiding them.

'Besides,' she says. ' 'E's such an easy bloody target, i'n' 'e?'

I feel rather sorry for him and hasten to tell him I think our story will have all the moral uplift possible to pump into a modern motion picture, yet it must speak to the hearts of a popular audience. We will give them romance, spectacle, tragedy, laughter, tears, a story that cannot fail to engross them, 'a message that celebrates modern love, that champions understanding and rationality!' This more than placates him and he even smiles a little when Mrs Cornelius pats his hand.

Esmé returns from the forward deck where she has been sitting under her sunshade. Never prettier than now, she is the epitome of my childhood sweetheart. 'We were saying how wonderful our film is going to be.' I kiss her lightly on the forehead.

Seaman turns to leave. She stays him.

'Oh, yes, Wolfy, dear, it will make us all marvellously rich and we will become millionaires. I was thinking, just then, what to spend my money on when we get back to Hollywood. A big house first, yes?'

'Our own Pickfair,' I promise. And so extraordinary are our surroundings that I immediately visualise, even to the smell of our roses, the home we would build in Beverly Hills. My ship is called *Der Heim*. She is a city of 100,000 people – artisans, artists, professionals, intellectuals, academics of all kinds. Her delicate towers shine bright as gold, bright as silver, bright as new-tempered steel. *Meyn shif ist meyn sheyvet, meyn shtetl.* My ship is my monument to God, my expression of His Will, my understanding of our ultimate purpose upon the Earth, which is to rise, in every sense, *above* the Earth. Let their skeletal arms lift and fall in the mud and blood of their ruined planet, where they gasp for air and beg for a quick death as they slaughter anything that lives and with such great enthusiasm do the work of their master, Satan. Our pain distracts Satan from His own. Satan it is who makes us suffer, not Christ. They will not accept this.

Mrs Cornelius says I should not brood so much on these things. She insists on my accompanying her to The Blenheim Arms where she meets her friends, the schoolmistress and the clergyman. Then, while I drink their inferior vodka, she proceeds to demonstrate how I should be forgetting my grievances in a Knees-up. I have no instinct for the Knees-up. It is not my national dance.

The temperature increases noticeably as we move up-river. It is dry, desert heat and does not greatly inconvenience the men but the ladies find it irksome. They are not allowed to wear sun-suits or swimming-dresses on deck because of the disturbance so much naked European femininity will cause amongst the crew (not to mention any passing native boat or spectator from the shore). We would attract, Professor Quelch assures us, the very worst sort of Arab attention, from the filthiest catcalling to imanic fulminations against the spawn of Jezebel. The imans, already causing a great deal of trouble in the rural communities, supporting Wafdist extremists whose policy of murder and terror works well in more remote settlements.

The weather irritates Mrs Cornelius in particular. 'It makes me sweat like an effin' pig, Ive. I need ter be in somefink cooler – like a bar seat at the Oyster Room in Piccadilly Circus. English people weren't meant ter take so much roastin'.'

I suggest she will not notice the heat once we are working again. Our desultory rehearsals, usually in the vacated dining-room when not occupied, had been more a means of passing time than a means of perfecting what was, we felt, already perfect. Contemplating the muscular subtlety and strength of our 'photoplay', I knew I was on the brink of creating a film D.W. Griffith himself would recognise as great. Coming home to Hollywood I could display it with pride and then there would be no more 'trousers'! Other directors would fight for our services. We would be a force as great as United Artists. Douglas Fairbanks had been made a star overnight by Anita Loos. There is no reason why I should not make Mrs Cornelius and 'Irené Gay' stars. The power of the director in these matters is always overestimated. Those elevated studio-hands have convinced the gullible public that they alone are responsible for all that is wonderful on screen, that the producers and the rest are responsible for all that is bad! That was never my own experience. For one thing producers usually have a great deal more common sense, while writers and set designers hate to waste time or money.

But Mrs Cornelius is in poor temper and will not, this time, be mollified. What's more, she announces, she finds the food less and less to her taste. If she is forced to eat one more fish that looks as if it would rather eat her she intends to become a vegetarian. The food is excellent, if more to my subtle Ukrainian appetite. I came to enjoy Turkish cuisine in Constantinople and discovered how well the Egyptians had learned from their masters! If the Levant owes nothing else to the Turks, it must forever thank them for their *brik*, their *pastilla*. My taste for corn and various beans is another preference baffling to Mrs Cornelius; neither does she have much relish for rice, especially with her fish. The fish is incomplete without the chip, she insists, just as pie is not a real pie without gravy. The baby eels are inferior to those of Whitechapel while the schnitzels and beefsteaks would, she assures me, be hurled at the wall by the diners of Aldgate or Notting Dale. On hearing this, Professor Quelch opens an eye and rises from the rainbow canvas of his chair to announce that it was very often possible to get a better meal for a shilling in Stepney than for a fiver in the West End. Certainly, if we were judging food by Mayfair standards, ours is more than adequate. Growing sentimental for her ancestral pie-shops and ale-houses, Mrs Cornelius asks him if he knows Sammy's in Whitechapel. It is famous, she prompts, in the East End. Professor Quelch reminisces vaguely of delicious chops and sausages and thinks he might have eaten some exceptional eels there.

'Sammy never did eels.' She frowns. ' 'E wos strictly pie an' mash, chops an' mash, sausages an' mash. The eel-shop was Tafler's next door. I never fancied 'is likker. Wot wos it yer wos doin' in ther East End, prof? Mish'nry work wos it?'

'An uncle of mine took an interest in the orphaned boys.'

Esmé, chewing on a straw, casts uncomprehending eyes upon the palm-lined banks. Her thoughts are in some more urban paradise. Mrs Cornelius asks after one or two acquaintances in the various dockland missions, but he shakes his lifted head. 'I have not been back in England since before the War, *cara madonna*. I really don't think there's anything to go back for, do you? The socialists are giving away the Empire! Ireland's the thin end of the wedge.'

'Well, everywhere 'as its ups and darns, prof.' Mrs Cornelius's discomfort is swiftly forgotten. She sips an early gin. 'One door closes, anovver opens. You lose somefink 'ere, yer gain somefink there. Thass life.' She smacked optimistic carmine.

'I happen to believe certain standards existed before the War and are worth hanging on to,' he pronounces almost balefully – Luther summoning good Immaneus for the whore of Babylon.

But she agrees with him. 'It's a changin' world, though, perfesser, an' it's best ter change wiv it. Any ovver way's barmy, doncher fink? I wouldn't mind seein' wot it wos like again.' She grows nostalgic for London since she found old copies of *The Tatler* and *The Play Pictorial* in the little niche that serves us for a library and working-room. She is like a migratory animal which, at certain times, feels an instinctive pull towards its home territory. 'An' meetin' ol' Major Nye like that, wiv orl 'is noos of the 'alls an' everythin', I orlmos' teared up, yer know.' This is the first time she has referred to the evening before we left Cairo and her single dinner with the Major. Obviously he had asked her to say nothing and I had respected her silence.

'Nye's coming to Luxor?' Professor Quelch is alert. 'Dear lady? That's the police chap?'

'Don' worry, prof. 'E 'asn't come ter take yer 'ome. The socialists won't be able ter 'urt ya. Besides 'e's not 'ere fer ther dope.' She reaches to pat his sallow cheek. 'Picked art yer costume yet?' The next day was Seaman's birthday. As a concession, the Swede had authorised a limited use of the props basket. The main costumes, for the leading actors, could not be used, but there were considerable numbers of slave and soldier outfits in which it was proposed we dress the locals once we were filming again in Karnak. In our first scene the ancient city would come to life in a reverse dissolve. Ali Pasha Khamsa had recommended a family of skilled plaster-casters who would recreate the monuments of Ramesid Egypt as they had been at the height of their glory. This weary land of ruins would flourish again. It would be our tribute to the ancient world's master-builders. How the natives would marvel when they saw their own past reborn! But would they feel pride or shame?

Esmé had been fascinated to watch the few rushes in which she had appeared. She admitted she had fallen in love with herself. We laughed about it. 'Now we have something else in common,' I said. Sir Ranalf Steeton had equipped the boat with its own darkroom and viewing-saloon, a projector already firmly in place for us, and even some films to look at if we wished. I watched a few. They were low-grade things, unmistakably British or local in origin, involving frequent loss of clothing. I had never been fond of Chaplin, let alone these badly-shot imitations, but the other men seemed to enjoy them. I was not surprised. They were almost all first- or second-generation peasants from the backward European nations. A turd on a top-hat would have been the epitome of sophisticated comedy. Today they would make a perfect audience for the Andy Warhoon comedy-Western I was forced to watch at the Essoldo last week. *Thark* at the Whitehall was another such fairground entertainment. Mrs Cornelius loved it. I pointed to the rest of the audience and told her to note the straws in their hair. We might have been gathered around a village marketplace watching one itinerant peasant belabour another with a blown-up pig's bladder. The British genius is for making the banal and vulgar respectable. It is the secret of British television and why Benny Hill is watched round the world. The most splendid triumph of British philistinism came when the BBC discovered at last the lowest common denominator and blessed it as Art. P.J. Proby only understood part of the equation when he exposed his bottom to the teenage eye. Nobody would have minded if he had been wearing a dog-collar and a pair of *pince-nez*. Within a few years he would have received a knighthood, another Attenborough.

I have watched all the careerists. In Bolshevik Russia, in Paris, in the literary and scientific communities, in Fascist Italy and Socialist Britain, in Berlin and in Hollywood they climbed by means of familiar ambition. I am no stranger to their strategies. However, my own pride refuses to let me employ such techniques. I remain, I suppose, too much of an idealistic individual.

Women recognise this. It is why some of them find me dangerous. Even Esmé said so more than once and Mrs Cornelius confirmed my girl's opinion. 'If ya weren't so dumb ya'd be dangerous.' She meant that my own good nature was frequently my downfall. She has never belittled my intellect.

The ardour of reconquest abated, I passed some time in reading to my little girl from the books we had found on board. My favourite was an English translation of *Salammbô*. How right was Kingsley Amis when he remarked that this, rather than *Madame Bovary*, was Flaubert's masterpiece. It is much more colourful. Flaubert read a thousand books for every chapter of his own. His research for that other, far more depressing novel, was minimal. It was through this exquisite romance that Esmé and I became acquainted with the depths and complexities of Carthage, although in those days I was naive enough to believe the book no more than a piece of wonderful fiction. Insufficient has been written about Flaubert's gift of prophecy.

We scarcely progressed a hundred pages before the eve of Seaman's birthday. Increasingly, Esmé would take the book gently from my hand and kiss me, suggesting that we pass the time in some other way. A gentleman always, I was unable to refuse her, though as our various fantasies became less able to arouse me, I was drawn more and more towards the Frenchman's history. My sense of foreboding would not abate. At night I took to smoking Quelch's *kif* in an effort to calm my racing heart. While I have deep reservations about all narcotics, as opposed to specific stimulants, I found for a while a unique pleasure in absorbing myself in *Salammbô* on the deck of a boat moving steadily into Africa. The brilliant descriptions of the book were mirrored in the reality. This in turn was enhanced by the effects of the *hasheesh*. But all this was still not enough to drive away my unspecific terrors, my half-sensed ghosts. It reminded me of some of the worst episodes in De Quincey. I breathed jewelled air, surrounded by exotically scented wonders and deliciously erotic sensations, but somewhere in the shadows I glimpsed the face of a goat, winking from garnet eyes, grinning through yellowed teeth; a senile goat whose only distinguishable quality was an air of implacable malice. For some reason I was reminded of Yermeloff, the Cossack camp and the night Brodmann saw me with Grishenko. Esmé! Esmé! Little teeth suck the marrow from my bones. They brand my flesh; they put their twin marks upon me, the Mark of Death and the Mark of Shame. Those camps all stink of fear. I refused to become a *Musselman*. They did their worst in Kiev and Oregon and Hannibal, in Aswan and Sachsenhausen. Most of them are dead now and I am still alive. If I had been born in Hellenistic times there is an operation I could have had which would have undone my father's hygienic decision and enabled me to put behind me a confused and crowded past, whose fictions and distortions would have taken a further lifetime to untangle. My own vision was a clear, uncluttered vision of the Future. The past became my enemy. I could have saved us all, Esmé. I could have shown you Paradise. It is not true that I am *filius nullius*. I am related to the most distinguished blood in Russia. Those great, scattered families represent the heart and soul of our country. I carry their secrets with me. I have never betrayed them. *Ikh veys nit. Ikh bin dorshtik. Ikh bin hungerik. Ikh bin an Amerikaner. Vos iz dos? Ikh farshtey nit.* I saw the film about the heroes of Kiev. It was in 'Sovcolour' and 'Sovscope' and was made by a 'Sovdirector' with 'Sovactors', yet it conveyed much of the force of those old legends, the stories of our fights against the brute hordes of Asia Minor. I had a great relish for films until it became the fashion to depress us all the time. And they wonder where their audiences went! Why their cinemas turned into bingo halls! They blamed the public for staying away. In this, at least, they had the truth. Who in their right mind, having spent a long day in a factory or an office, can relax in the dark watching an inferior and inaccurate account of life in an office or a factory? Do not mistake me – a musical or a Western or a romance are fantasy, but these new melodramas are merely unreal. In the International Cinema, Westbourne Grove, I watched *The L-Shaped Room*, set in Notting Hill. The theatre filled with spontaneous laughter as we enjoyed the profound inaccuracies of character and scene. Like most of the audience, I left half-way through. We wanted our lives made legend, not merely sentimentalised and thus enfeebled. This was the message of *The Great Escape*?

Esmé made me close my eyes and then admire her costume. She had taken one of the *houri* outfits. To the blossoming scarlet trousers, metallic breastcups, and gauzy accessories she added a pretty veil which, if anything, enhanced her beauty. I told her she looked wonderful but warned her against wearing such revealing clothes during the day. On the night of the party, when we were all dressed up, there would hardly be problems. She pouted. She thought I would be stimulated by having a slave-girl of my own, but I was not, I gently pointed out, the kind of man who needs public confirmation of a conquest. Then, understanding I had hurt her feelings, I quickly added that since she was already the most beautiful girl in Egypt I was afraid some powerful Pasha would cast lustful eyes upon her and demand she be captured for his *harem*. While this flattered and consoled her, I still insisted it was imprudent of her to wear the costume out of context. For my own part I was to dress as a Wahabi warrior, in simple black and white, but sporting the dark glasses which those tribesmen wore as a mark of their civilised dignity, while Captain Quelch had settled on Rameses II and Mrs Cornelius would be our Cleopatra, some general Ptolemaic consort rather than that most famous Egyptian queen. To swell the feminine ranks, Grace had decided upon Nefertiti. Only Seaman himself, our birthday boy, refused these childish excitements as if he felt it was his duty to maintain an appropriate directorial *gravitas*.

When he emerged at lunchtime on his birthday, a small group of us had already gathered at the bar to sing the English birthday song and insist on his drinking a special cocktail which Mrs Cornelius had ordered. Very rapidly he began to enjoy our company and, for a change, we his. I remember little of the afternoon, save that I became at one point emotional and wept for a while. Professor Quelch and Mrs Cornelius helped me back to my cabin and I slept until Quelch, his exposed flesh darkened by a solution of Mars Oil and cooking butter, woke me to say that it was after seven and the party itself was due to begin at eight. A little cocaine brought me back to the world and after a brisk shower I was ready to slip into my simple *gelabea*, burnoose and set of false whiskers fixed to my chin by gum arabic. As I stepped into the passage, one of our Nubians caught sight of me and addressed me in his native tongue. When I asked him to translate he laughed and apologised. He had taken me for one of those Wahabim barbarians, he said. 'I had thought us captured, effendi.' I was still a little the worse for the cocktails but this restored my spirits as I made my way up to the deck. Like pantomime conspirators we gathered around a small table on which sat an enormous iced cake blazing with candles. How they managed to get the chef to bake and then decorate this work of art I do not know! While the pastry itself was somewhat oversweet and the icing a riot of local geometric designs, calligraphy and pidgin English, Seaman seemed deeply moved by this expression of kindness and was weeping as he poised his knife.

Esmé, a dream in her slave-girl pantaloons and flimsy silks, made a delicious *frou-frou* whenever she moved and it was clear our Nubians were gripped not by lechery but by adoration. She was a little goddess to Mrs Cornelius's magnificent Queen. Both women sported extravagant peacock-feather headdresses at least a foot higher than Pola Negri's. They swayed at alarming angles through the course of the evening as we danced to the music of O. K. Radonic's portable phonograph. Since women were in short supply, we cheerfully agreed that each man should take his turn. If he became impatient, we said, then he was more than welcome to ask Grace for a pirouette or two around the deck. As the evening wore on, more than one of us gave in to boredom and Grace was rarely without a partner, albeit a somewhat drunken one. Professor Quelch, heroically teetotal, had grown expansive in his rôle and attached himself to Esmé, promising her 'the finest tomb in Egypt' if she would only permit him a kiss. She found him amusing. She would gladly give him a kiss before the tomb. I think it was Esmé who first saw the lights of Luxor ahead, a scattering of electric bulbs and oil-lamps in the forward blackness. Professor Quelch raised his eyes from her tiny chest and licked his lips, sniffing deeply. 'No question of it. That's Luxor.' He straightened to accept from one of our boys a glass of Vichy and a slice of cake. 'You can smell the sewage from here.' Then he got to his feet, raised his paper wig to Esmé, and drew the boy into the shadows.

All I could smell was jasmine. Under the awning, by the piano, Wolf Seaman had begun to play some repetitive Scandinavian polka and sing mournfully to Sri Harold Kramp in his native tongue. From time to time he darted wounded and significant looks at Mrs Cornelius, who, having pursued Malcolm Quelch and the boy below decks, now returned, grinning to herself. Grace, overwhelmed by excitement and alcohol, was puking over the rail and O. K. Radonic was waltzing with our captain, Yussef al-Sharkiya, a gargling fat man who held a cigar in one grubby hand and a defiant glass of whisky in the other. Our Charon had a faded blue *gelabea*, a dirty white turban, a pair of sandals made from tyre-rubber and lips permanently stained from the nuts he chewed. Earlier that week he had approached me with effusive good humour, making some mysterious proposal. When I failed to understand him, he had withdrawn in disgust; thereafter speaking to me only in the most formal terms while having nothing but greasy smiles for most of the others. I believe he had somehow lost face with me and was embarrassed. I had no notion, however, of the circumstances or the cause. Resting for a moment in a chair near the port rail I watched Captain Yussef cast glances of extraordinary heat at Mrs Cornelius and, had I been a little more sober, would have offered him some sharp admonishment. I already knew such men frequently lusted to possess a beautiful European woman but those around us were generally discreet with their fantasies. The captain, his habitual caution banished by unfamiliar alcohol, was now incapable of hiding his disgusting longings. Soon even Mrs Cornelius herself noticed his glances and wagged a chiding finger. She wished no man to get into trouble on her account. Returning from the lavatory, Esmé suggested we dance. I summoned as much of my resources as were left and once again took the floor, uncertain whether to follow Radonic's groaning, wound-down *Am I Blue?* or the erratic chords of Seaman's Nordic *folklorique*. Meanwhile, from somewhere amidships, I thought I detected the tumbling rhythms and twanging catgut of a Nubian concert, as our servants celebrated the director's nativity and our saviour's sacrifice in their own quarters. The steam-whistle's vast bellow drowned all of this suddenly when the captain returned to his wheelhouse, intent on alerting Luxor to our imminence. There was a stirring of comic Bedouin, fanciful Pharaonic dignitaries, caricatures of tarbooshed Cairenes and Theban soldiery as members of our party understood the signal to mean we were sinking and ran about shouting loudly before being calmed. Esmé became urgent, drunkenly eager, leading me below decks to my cabin forward. We reached it. She was already sinking to her knees before me. To my angry frustration, my door was stuck. It did not occur to me that the cabin was anything but empty as I put my shoulder to the panel and flung my weight to smash the lock, exposing my angel to the nightmarish sight of Professor Malcolm Quelch lifting a red and terrified mouth from the rampant genitals of our youngest Nubian.

EIGHTEEN

LUXOR IS DOMINATED by her two greatest monuments. The dreaming ruins of Karnak and the confident edifice of the Winter Palace Hotel dwarf a miscellany of native houses, official buildings and hovels, the modern village. The hotel is the magnificent pride of all Englishmen and the envy of every other race; she is fully worthy of the ancient city. A huge white building, her wide, winding twin stairways to the long outer terrace dominate the river-front and look directly across to distant Theban mountains. From her flowery balconies you can see ancient temples, the dim battlements of Medinet Habu and the twin colossi who are all that remain of the lost temple of Amenhotep. Then come the dusty terraces of Deir el Bahari. Between these, on the cliff-side, is a curving honeycomb of nobles' tombs. Then the great shoulder of the hill hides the Valley of the Kings, beyond which is the wide, unwelcoming desert and the hostile borderlands where wild Bedouin still rove and raid.

The hotel's great garden faces east. One can almost forget Egypt, taking one's meals in the company of other upper-class Europeans. With its imported shrubs and its tall walls, the Winter Palace is magically self-contained. All one sees of Luxor are the far-off eastern hills, blue and translucent as chalcedony in the morning light. The gardens boast every kind of familiar English flower – roses, carnations, pansies, irises, geraniums

– surrounded by smooth green lawns as sweet-smelling as any English cricket pitch, constantly tended by impeccably uniformed gardeners.

'Luxor is the soul of Egypt,' Malcolm Quelch insists. We sip our afternoon Darjeeling. (I had slammed the broken door swiftly that night but was convinced he had in that instant seen us both. He had chosen to pretend amnesia, perhaps to save us all embarrassment. Save for a single passing reference to his two years of medical training with the army and his willingness to use his skills to help any native who might be in discomfort, he did not attempt to explain the affair. Indirectly, I had let him know I was a man of the world and that Esmé had no notion of the world at all.) 'Karnak is perfectly fitted for a great city, don't you think? On the east we have the long stretch of rich plain, a shadowy changing green reaching to the very foot of the hills! To the west we have that wonderful view of the western plain. Then, between east and west is our sinuous Nile!'

With Esmé I had already taken to renting a *kalash* to explore the vicinity. We had trotted beside fair fields, dotted with palm thickets, through hills which rose low to the south before suddenly towering, knife-edged, to the Red Mountain – that huge and fantastic outcrop, scarred white as Odysseus's old wound by a pathway descending from the ridge. 'That mountain is as the ghost of the greatness of Thebes,' declared Quelch, drawing closer, 'as a liss of the Earth-gods, as a thunder-cloud advancing out of an open sky! Whether it be close upon you, grim, brown-red, hot, arid, impenetrable, rugged against all time – or far away, a mass of shimmering rose with paths of faint blue shadow in the early morning! And it is always immense and immediate, my dear friends, upon all things and all men!'

He has become emphatically lyrical since we disembarked. Far from avoiding Esmé or myself, he takes to seeking us out, as if needing to impose upon that graphic moment a different image of himself which we can respect and which might even erase all memory of it. His manner is more urbane, and increasingly avuncular. 'No Ptolemy, no Roman, no Frenchman ever built anything as magnificent and practical as this hotel,' continues Quelch as I begin to consider escape. 'Monsieur Pierre Loti, in that peevish and decadent epitome of Anglophobia which he entitled *The Death of Philae*, murmurs fretfully against this hotel, you know. But don't you find it has a fine presence? It dwarfs the modern village to forgetfulness. That alone is surely a valuable quality? I have said all this in my book. I was flattered to receive a personal letter from Thomas Cook's and, before the War, could sign for anything I pleased at the bar or in the restaurant. The War lowered the tone of so much. What sort of Will was it that drove us to such terrible self-destruction?'

I admit it is a question I often ask. I hope to answer it through one of the photoplays I will write for our new company. *The Folly* would be set in a French garden invaded by soldiers of every country. Quelch thought that Sir Ranalf Steeton would leap at the idea – 'especially if you include some love-interest. A young lady violated by the Boche, for instance.'

I intended my film to be above mere nationalism and felt Sir Ranalf must appreciate the universal appeal of my idea. He was after all dedicated to making pictures with an international flavour. He had affirmed this when he arrived on the train from Cairo, accompanied by three servants and a large amount of luggage. He had taken almost half a floor in the Winter Palace. Some of the rooms were for our film-making purposes, but I had the impression that servants, rather than Sir Ranalf, had been forced into more cramped accommodation.

Most of us were not, in fact, staying there, but retained our rooms on the moored boat, dining by special arrangement at the hotel. A modest account was kept in the company name and we received envelopes of cash for small transactions, but few of us felt any urge to buy souvenirs so had very few immediate needs. Accounts opened in our names by Sir Ranalf in the United Egyptian Bank received the bulk of our fees.

'*When the May blooms red 'midst the green of the glade and the white May spreads and the white flowers fade, I shall recall our trysting plait, and seek the heart of the hawthorn's stem to find our winding brands again,*' quoted Quelch by way of a companionable reference to a favourite Wheldrake, *Love in the Dale*, and with a gesture both romantic and mechanical rose to greet Mrs Cornelius who strode towards us through the garden followed by four little boys in bleached linen, their heads piled with what were evidently her purchases. 'Good heavens, Mrs Cornelius! Have you a private income? Where on earth did you come by the cash? Or is it all on credit?'

'Not me, perfessor!' She laughed without rancour. 'It's not ser diff'rent 'ere from Petticoat Lane. Ain't yer 'eard o' the barter system? I got the 'ole bloody lot fer a silk petticoat that wos a size too small fer me, an' an 'at that wos a size too big. Some local lady's gonna look ther pride o' the 'arem ternight!' And, passing us with a wink, she gave the boys kindly instructions in simple Arabic.

Quelch at least pretended to be amused. I understood that he seemed at his easiest when actually at his most anxious. '*Fas est et ab hoste doceri*, as Ovid tells us. I must see what unwanted articles I have in my own wardrobe. Perhaps one of the native sheikhs would care for a pair of excellent galoshes?'

I did not in those days understand 'galoshes' and he was irritated by my query. 'Actually,' he continued with a sudden change of mood, 'I suppose it's a bit *infra dig* for a white man to bargain with the natives in that way.'

I said I saw no harm in it.

'Well, perhaps just for the British. A foreigner, after all . . . A Russian.' His smile threatened to disappear into his head. 'A sort of neutral. No offence. The only English people who do that sort of thing in Cairo are the drunkards, the worn-out whores and the deserters. And, of course,' he lowered his voice, 'the *nouveau-riche touristas*.'

Until then I had not cared about my lack of spending money but, since Cook's were unable to provide us with suitable cheques for our accounts in Port Said, I now saw a way to obtaining a few souvenirs. In our business transactions Quelch had been generous in his acceptance of IOUs from us all, and knew he would be repaid as soon as we returned to Cairo. In spite of his warnings about 'face' I nonetheless determined to find some more or less honest antiquarian and barter perhaps some of my jade and amber cigarette-holders for some mementos. I suspected Quelch's own willingness to extend credit had much to do with wishing to ingratiate himself with us and gain a permanent situation in our company. Thus he made himself especially agreeable with me. I guessed he feared his secret would become generally known, so he seemed eager to be of help. I had in mind an Egyptian collar for my little girl and an elegant statue of Anubis, the jackal. Quelch expressed considerable approval of my taste but was pessimistic as to my chances of finding any original, though new tombs were always being sought by those who resented the Egyptian Society's imperialist monopoly on antiquities. 'Egypt exists because others honour her dead,' he reflected. 'Indeed, Egyptians honour *only* death. Nothing else is sacred to them. All they have left to sell is the contents of their tombs, and the manufactured replicas they bury for a year or so to give them the authentic suggestion of the Pit. What a peculiar heritage, Mr Peters! Do all old empires come to this? Will Russia and Britain one day have nothing to sell the world but their graveyards, their statues and their museums?'

I found his remarks fatuous at the time. The Bolsheviks' current encouragement of the package tour and the sightseeing bus has vindicated Quelch in this at least, while it is obvious whenever I look out of my window how readily the hub of the British Empire has degenerated into a nation of shrieking street-arabs hawking the synthetic ikons of their exhausted glory.

Fifty years ago I was like any tourist. I wanted a good-quality souvenir of my visit. True, the film itself would of course ultimately be the best memento, but I itched to do a little bargaining. I remembered I had also accumulated a large variety of silk ties and handkerchiefs in the latest 'jazz' styles. I returned to where the *Nil Atari* was moored a little west of the hotel's quay, to find the tradeable haberdashery and smokers' accessories in my stowage. I then went back to the corniche, walking slowly down to the *souk* clustered at the very bases of Karnak's ancient pillars, where a mosque had grown almost organically from ruins whose stones were used in its own nativity. This blend of architecture and scenery, the miscellaneous crowd representing a host of trades, professions and costumes, a glimpse of almost four thousand years of mankind's history, was perhaps a symbol, as Quelch had implied, of every imperial fate. It was oddly sweet to look upon temples where people had worshipped the living Osiris, Amon, Set and Isis, in the blind faith of absolute belief. All manner of other momentary favourites, local deities, animals and the great Ra, were alive beneath Egypt's eternal sun, the true source of her Glory. I looked at Coptic churches carved from the ruins of chapels originally dedicated to Horus and Sekhmet. Those early Christians believed they put the holy mark of God on the works of Satan. The warlike followers of Mohammed, who had next imposed their grim morality upon these buildings, hacked at the wholesome signs of gender and fertility until they became obscene. I inhaled the smell of the desert, the water, the palms, the spices, fabrics and aromatic woods; the less pleasant smells of human bodies and sewage. I would look suddenly into green or blue eyes staring from faces which might have belonged to hawkers or scribes or field-hands of the Eleventh Dynasty. I absorbed by touch and taste and scent, through my eyes and ears, the layered centuries of a capital which had ruled the mightiest empire of the ancient world. I did this as a welcome stranger at whom everyone smiled and offered their goods. I plunged into the embracing crowd as I might plunge into the legendary Pool of Time. This last was, for me at least, the sweetest of Luxor's temptations.

Thrusting through narrow lanes of stalls and chattering salesmen, whose dark, sardonic eyes regarded me with a thousand separate calculations or were as frankly curious as their veiled women, hanging over balconies which perched crazily atop awnings, sometimes leaning to form archways for muddy alleys paved with old coffee-cans and excavated uneven stones sticking like hags' teeth from the dirt to snag a camel's hoof or trip a running child, I was at once absorbed. I lost sense of passing time. I grew increasingly fascinated, not with the variety of goods (save for the local foodstuffs they issued largely from the same rather unvaried cornucopia producing manufactured antiquities and poorly-printed pornography) but by the lack of urgency with which these people conducted their business.

They say the Arab has nothing to spend but time. But that glib phrase scarcely described the value these people placed on the formalities and pleasures of conversation and barter. In Odessa's Slobodka, too, there were important rituals involved in the buying, selling and trading of goods and services: this often in lieu of any other entertainment. Bargaining was clearly of greater importance to Luxor's citizens than profit and doubtless it had been the same to her founders. Locally, certain histrionic gifts were much appreciated, highly applauded and well rewarded. The better a merchant's pantomime of poverty, despair and sheer frustration with another's stupidity, the more he was patronised. A culture which denies its people so many casual pleasures has created pleasure – even art – from the ordinary functions of daily life. Here the aesthetics of argument are displayed and criticised in the little cafés where men drink tea, or coffee, or smoke from the communal 'hookah' every proprietor provides. They comment on matters of the day – perhaps observing a group of drunken English soldiers shouldering their way through the mobs, shouting obscenities as they go, or making some amused comment upon the baffled crocodile of tourists brought to taste the realities of modern life and make trembling purchases at shops and stalls already come to some previous arrangement with their particular dragoman. The more refined people wear pale European suits and tarbooshes and read copies of *The Egyptian Gazette* or *La Vie Parisienne* as they sit in little chairs outside their premises filled with superb objects identical to those made thousands of years ago, carved by hands through which flows the blood of the original artists. There were people for sale in there, moreover, creatures of every age and trained in every humiliation. Slavery, when not an open part of a society, when it is made shameful and criminal and secret, becomes a dark thing. I heard this argument many times in the Muslim world and appreciated its logic, but I could not approve. The men in the *souk*'s shadows whisper to me, displaying an intimate knowledge of my desires. They offer me all they know to be forbidden. But I push them away. They offer me disease and death, I say. They offer me shame. *Shuft, effendi. Shuft, shuft, effendi. Murhuuba, aiwa?* They touched me; they grinned and made smacking noises with their lips. They made little gasping sounds and they winked and flirted. This was not what I had come for, I told them. *La, la! U'al! Imshi! Imshi!* But they were relentless. They had an idea that a lone European only came to the *souk* seeking sexual digression. While I did not find this especially offensive, I grew impatient with their persistence. Attempting to avoid a rouged boy, I found myself in a little cul-de-sac formed by three tall houses, their walls covered with awnings shadowing stalls selling fish over which black masses of flies crawled like a heaving canopy. I turned to seek a way out, pushing through the youths and little boys whose hands clutched at my arms, their opportunist nails digging into my flesh. Behind me, as if following me, I saw a tall European, wearing a rich *gelabea* and a *kefta*. His deeply tanned face was alight with laughter at my plight. His teeth were white, as startling as his eyes and as familiar as his hands which now quickly pulled the veil about his lower features before he wheeled about. I was still in a state of profound shock. I saw him move swiftly to merge with the crowd. Almost sick with disbelief I found the use of my limbs and paid no attention to the squealing children who still picked at my clothing and my person.

'Kolya!' I cried at last, stumbling forward. 'Kolya!'

It was none other than my oldest and closest friend, my teacher, my exemplar! Shura had said he was in Egypt, on a mission for his new employer. Why had he followed me? Certainly he had recognised me. There was therefore some good reason why he did not wish me to know him. He could easily be working not for Stavisky at all but for a foreign government.

The little boys were brushed aside, the begging girls smacked back as with sudden unthinking energy I continued in hasty pursuit of my friend. I did not consider at that moment his good reasons for not wishing to meet. Separation from Kolya had been an agony I had feared to admit and now here was a chance to be free of it. This friend and evangelist of my youth had been, in so many ways, the creator of my adult self. I had despaired ever to experience again his languid, aristocratic ambience, his perfect poise and diction, his amusement with the world and all its works! I longed to know why he was separated from his wife, that bloodless Frenchwoman who, I suspect, had been behind my own undoing. How long was he in Egypt? Where and when would it be possible to meet? Of course he would not be as eager to see me, but I never doubted his affection, perhaps even his love, for me. I was certain I had seen pleasure in his eyes for a small instant. I could still see the vivid *gelabea* ahead until, like a conjurer dismissing an illusion, he had swirled himself into the agitated body of the crowd and vanished. The truth of Professor Quelch's assertion was becoming rapidly apparent. Egypt was indeed a land of illusion and hallucination; she depended on both for her survival. Yet that moment's recognition had been no insubstantial mirage. Even with its deep tan, his handsome face could not be mistaken. I knew every line of it and remembered every gesture, every muscle, every tiny movement of his body. Forcing my way on, careless of all protests, I looked desperately for the blue and gold *gelabea*, the dark blue headdress, but they had vanished. I might as well pursue a genie on the desert wind as hope to find my friend in any of the surrounding warrens. My next desperate thought was to try the cafés fringing the *souk*. These were frequented chiefly by Europeans but I could find neither a tall 'Arab' nor Count Nikolai Petroff in more conventional dress. My next thought was to try the hotels, starting with the Winter Palace, the most likely. I called for a child, offering it a coin to lead me out of the maze. Only then did I realise that my little bag of ties and cigarette-holders had gone. The boy was an honest guide and I was soon in the lobby of the Winter Palace. I searched every corner, before dashing into the garden as tea was being served. I could not find Kolya but Mrs Cornelius and Esmé, in the shade of a large palm, were sharing a glittering table and a pot of Earl Grey. It was a pleasure to see them comrades at last and I wanted to tell Mrs Cornelius my splendid news yet hesitated to interrupt the start of a greater understanding between the two women. So, suppressing my natural eagerness, I passed discreetly behind them and, while I had not planned to eavesdrop, overheard a fragment of conversation.

' 'E'd pull 'is socks off fer ya any time you wos ter say,'

Mrs Cornelius declared. 'Them blokes is orlways a bit weird, though. Take my word for it. It's the schools. I'll admit, 'e makes me shudder orl over. Me ol' mum warned me abart 'em. Chilly-arses, she corled 'em. Wot ever they wos doin' to yer, she reckoned, their bums never got warm.'

'Sir Ranalf is an English gentleman, I think.' Esmé had not entirely caught Mrs Cornelius's drift. 'He is a wealthy man. Of course I do not find him attractive, but Maxim has said one must be agreeable.'

'Indeed, that is true, little sweetheart.' I leaned to kiss my startled little girl. 'Is there a point, Mrs Cornelius, to alienating the man upon whom all our fortunes now depend? We must surely be diplomatic.'

'There's a diff'rence, in my opinion, between diplomacy an' total surrendah.' She shrugged, dismissing the topic.

I was not at that point especially interested in these social nuances. 'I have astonishing news, Mrs Cornelius! I have seen my old friend – our old friend, Esmé – Count Nikolai Petroff!'

'Kolya!' Esmé's eyes grew large first with delight and then, I thought, with alarm. She frowned. 'Why is he here? With Sir Ranalf?'

'He has nothing to do with Sir Ranalf. Shura mentioned his business in Cairo. I told you.'

'He was not in Tripoli?'

'No – in Alexandria. And now in Luxor. I will ask at the desk to see if he is staying here. Won't it be marvellous if he is!'

Esmé seemed confused and before she could reply burst suddenly into smiles at someone else's approach from behind me. 'Sir Ranalf! How pleasant!'

'My dear! My dears! My good companions! How perfectly wonderful to find you all together! My three stars! I have come to ask a favour.' The weighty baronet paused to mop beneath his hat.

Mrs Cornelius withdrew into a cloud of perfumed pink silk, her cloche casting a shadow, like a veil, across her face until only her narrowed eyes were faintly distinguishable. Seemingly oblivious of her dislike Sir Ranalf again raised his panama, put away his handkerchief, kissed their fingers and clapped me upon my shoulder. For my part, I was impatient to leave, to discover Kolya's whereabouts. 'I have just come from our good Director's company.' Sir Ranalf waved a chubby hand to indicate how he had been communing with the somewhat difficult genius. 'And we are to begin shooting tomorrow in the Valley of the Kings. Which means we must all be up by five in the morning and, I fear, on our way by six.'

'For the light, I suppose,' said Esmé with a miserable gasp.

'My tender bud – for the *heat*! It will be unbearable by ten. Only the natives work after lunch. The light? The light is always perfect. Thanks to our influential friends we have received special permission to film in the Valley and its surrounds. This means we will not be troubled by random tourists. Some of my business partners in town have been of considerable help to us.'

Until now we had been unaware of Sir Ranalf's partners, but were not particularly surprised to hear of them. His understanding of the politics and customs of this country was considerable and no doubt he had diplomatically included some local members of the Egyptian Society on his board, so ensuring us a *carte blanche* amongst the monuments. Our affairs were in the hands of a clever and practical man who, for all his dandyism and his affectation, clearly had a cool brain. I saw him as one of those people who like to present a misleading idea of themselves to the world. Mrs Cornelius, after all, supplied no evidence for her prejudice against him and I had not yet learned how much to respect her judgement. Today, I would follow it without question. Then, I was merely uncomfortable when she sniffed at Sir Ranalf's statement that he was in a dilemma for the evening. He needed, he said, a female escort, someone to impress his partners with her wit, beauty and talent. His smile upon my little girl was the smile of a good-hearted patriarch. 'We have to be up early tomorrow, of course, so the night would not go on for very long.' He turned humorously pleading eyes to me. 'I would bring her back before midnight, good Sir Max, I promise. She would be such an asset! She could double our budget.'

My mind upon Kolya, I was only too pleased to be relieved

of my sweetheart's company. After all, it might take me all evening to find Kolya.

'It would make such a wonderful impression, if I could introduce my friends to our leading lady.' He bowed. This brought Mrs Cornelius to her feet with a disgusted snort to rival a camel's. 'I think I'll go back ter me cabin an' git art o' these cloves,' she said. 'It's really gettin' a bit niffy, orl in orl, doncha fink, Ivan?'

I wished I had given her more support, but I was in her wake, heading for the reception desk, as she moved with dignified fury towards the electric lift. I understood her fury. She, not Esmé, was the featured star. Now she saw she had lost her last chance to appear in a romance with Barrymore, Gilbert or Valentino. Doubtless because of confusing messages from Goldfish, Sir Ranalf seemed a little unclear about the man's identity. Irené Gay's part would be nothing like as large as Gloria Cornish's. While I had every sympathy for Mrs Cornelius, my attention was still upon my missing comrade and I did not want to lose my momentum. By the time the receptionist was able to check the register for me and tell me with fulsome regret that Prince Petroff was not yet with the Winter Palace, Mrs Cornelius was gone. I turned back to ask where a gentleman might otherwise stay and after a pause it was suggested I try the Karnak or, failing that, perhaps the Grand.

Luxor is not a large town and consists primarily of her ruins and her tourist establishments. Most of the good hotels were close to one another along the corniche and it took no more than half-an-hour to enquire if they had Kolya as a guest. Soon it became clear that even if he were staying in Luxor, my old comrade was not registered under his own name. It then occurred to me he might well be staying with one of the British officials so I set off for the Consulate. This proved to be a fairly unremarkable house surrounded by a high wall. When I asked at the gate for the Consul, I was told he would not be available until the next day. When I asked if they had any news of a Count Nikolai Petroff the concierge scratched his head and let his jaw hang in a pantomime of idiocy which was the local way of bringing a line of enquiry to a halt. I told him I could not come back tomorrow morning, that I would be working, but this failed to impress him. Eventually I returned to the centre of the town to ask after my friend at the smaller pensions until an English police sergeant, who had been chatting with the Greek proprietor of a small rooming-house behind the Telegraph Office, had a joke with me about looking for a Russian spy, at which point I realised I was in danger of betraying my friend. I decided instead to seek Sir Ranalf Steeton's help and refrained from visiting every steamboat moored at the various quays along the corniche. By now it was dark and most of the shops had closed. There was some sort of curfew the British insisted upon, although the cafés and more respectable places were allowed to remain open, their candle-lanterns and oil-lamps casting a wonderful glow across the little alleys and cobbled squares. A sort of lazy tranquillity settled upon the town and by ten o'clock the tourists were gone and the only white faces belonged to a few soldiers on leave. The cafés remained full of local men and I chose one of the cleanest whose view of the street went down as far as the corniche and the green glow of the river. I ordered coffee of the thick, sweet Turkish type, and forced myself to relax, to watch. But Kolya still did not pass by. Reluctant to get into conversation, I was nonetheless eventually joined by two fluent Egyptian English-speakers, in well-cut suits and neat tarbooshes. They were from Alexandria, with business in Aswan, and had a scheme to reproduce the ruins of Luxor in a special park in Cairo, 'for those tourists without the time to go up the Nile'. This scheme has been initiated since in Italy and Greece, but the Egyptian Government, such as it was, never displayed much initiative in encouraging local enterprise. They preferred merely to talk, to engage in empty rhetoric blaming all their ills on the British as earlier they had blamed the Turks. Suez was the last attempt of a British government to follow the urges of idealism rather than expediency, but the Egyptian had to extend the blame to a more general conspiracy of 'imperialists'. Their flirtations with the Bolsheviks were, I suppose, inevitable. But these people make and break alliances faster than a Borgia prince – faster, indeed, than Adolf Hitler, whose example they all once sought to follow. That was never a quality of Hitler's I admired.

These well-bred natives assured me they were more interested in public works than personal power, yet to join the Wafd you had to be interested in power. 'Once they have challenged the British successfully, they will challenge the King and his ministers and eventually set up their own dynasty. Confrontation is all they understand. We need more politicians of the English sort, whose chief interest is in public hygiene, street lighting and decent burial for the poor. Dull fellows, perhaps, but usually effective, what?' This was Mr Ahmed Mustafa. With his companion, Mr Mahareb Todrus, he had spent two years in England – 'for languages and business'. They believed themselves very decently treated, they said, and were gratified to discover that most English people of the better class could easily distinguish an Egyptian from a nigger. They were fortunate in that they were well-connected. Their uncle Yussef was a frequent visitor to Buckingham Palace and Ten Downing Street and, of course, this gave them an entrée into the very best Belgravian society. 'Trade is a great demolisher of the class system, don't you think?'

What, they asked, was my own business in Luxor? It was twofold, I said. I was here to meet a friend, a tall Slavic gentleman, perhaps given to Arab dress. I was a writer and actor with a film company beginning work here tomorrow. They were impressed. 'Is it a thriller? Do you know Sexton Blake?' They already knew Steeton's name and were flattered to have the ear of someone like myself who could perhaps advise them on their own rather insignificant projects. They supposed they too might also be considered a branch of the theatrical profession. I said I would be happy to help them on some other occasion. My priority, that evening, however, was to find my friend. At this these two good-hearted souls determined to help me. Realising the advantage of companions who could speak fluent English, Arabic and perhaps certain local dialects, I accepted, although it was already beginning to nag at my conscience that Kolya might have a reason for not wishing to be seen by me. As we departed the first of several bars, I told my acquaintances that it would probably be best if we left our quest for another time, but they were by now insistent. With that attitude of daring only Muslims possess when reaching a hand towards alcohol, they had downed several glasses of the local brandy. It occurred to me, even then, that no other religion so clearly reflects the prejudices of a single neurotic semi-barbaric bigot. One only achieves 'submission', it appears, by means of 'repression'. Or is submission what they secretly seek, all of them, by means of challenge and confrontation, like a sado-masochistic marriage? Islam is the religion of a people fundamentally addicted to defeat. And we all know how dangerous such a religion is when a well-meaning power makes the gestures of compromise rather than threat. I have written to the Foreign Office about this. The world would be a very different place today if France and Britain had held to their original plans over Suez. The *fellaheen* do not much notice the faces within the uniforms.

The drunker my native comrades became, the darker and danker the bars they sought out. I think they were trying to find a particular kind of brothel, but it was not clear to me what they wanted. They assured me, however, that Count Petroff was bound to be in such a place. Europeans, in particular, liked these establishments. People, they said, would be less cautious of me if I asked its location. They themselves might be mistaken for officials. The bar was never discovered. It was almost dawn when I came suddenly to my senses. I had not only been stupid but selfish in spreading Kolya's name all over Luxor. My companions were by now completely incoherent and although I knew we were somewhere on the outskirts of the town, it should not be hard to get back to the corniche and the Winter Palace. If necessary I would stop the nearest *kalash*. Those horse-drawn taxis are still, I hear, a basis of Egyptian city-life. The streets were lit only by the faint pearl of the approaching dawn, and chiefly populated by dogs and cats who emerged every night in bestial pantomime of the human day. I could imagine them bickering and bartering and howling over some rotten scrap, some fly-fouled morsel in imitation of rituals their masters performed over a piece of fresh-cast junk or some wretched donkey splattered in mud to disguise its disease. Yet these night-time denizens were altogether better-mannered and none tried to bar my way. At length, I recognised the spire of a mosque in the sky ahead.

I could not be far from the Temple of Luxor where I could find my way back to the hotel. Perhaps Kolya was hiding in a Moslem *musrum*. What deep disguise had my friend adopted so that he could pass at will into forbidden sanctuaries of the Faithful? I was growing sleepy and my eyes were blurred. The various concoctions imbibed with my Egyptian friends were taking their toll. My legs were weak and inclined to directions of their own, but my brain was still in control and I set a determined course for the mosque, even scaling a high wall in order to keep my bearings rather than go round it and risk losing sight of the only building I recognised. I got over the wall with ease and found myself in a cubist moonscape. As the dawn turned to pale blue I saw that the crazy angles were formed by blocks of masonry left by everyone who had ever systematically destroyed the place in search of building materials, treasure, or immortal glory. As I stumbled over the blocks I made out the taller pillars of the temple itself and stepped, I thought, on firm ground to trip instead and fall forward with a loud cry of pained surprise onto a broken pillar lying where Time or some passing vandal had left it. Echoed through the temple, my cry was transmogrified into a strange, almost sweet note of mingled innocence and grief, as if a child mourned its imminent death. This version of my own voice sent a terrifying shudder through me. My heart began to beat rapidly as panic came, and I scrambled to my feet and ran up a long avenue of shadowy sphinxes towards a gate which I vaulted while a drowsy nightwatchman shouted after me in outraged Arabic. The dawn was now shading to pink across the river and the palms grew from black to the deepest green while birdsong surged from the town's every cranny. The water grew paler and richer, its colours seen through a subtle mist where waterbirds hunted and shouted in the stillness, where two or three white sails already bent to the faintest of cool breezes. The steps of the Winter Palace were transformed to some dream of ancient wonder. I heard the muezzin begin the calling of the first prayer. I would come to know it by heart. *Allah akhbar, Allah akhbar. Ash'had an la ilah illa 'llah we-Muhammad rasul Allah. Ash'had an la ilah illa 'llah we-Muhammad rasul Allah. Hay'y ila s'salat hay'y ila l-felah. Hay'y ila s'salat hay'y ila l'felah.*

Es-salat kher min en-num. Es-salat kher min en-num. Allah akhbar. Allah akhbar. La 'llah illa 'llah. Prayer is better than sleep. There is no god but God. I might have argued with the first sentiment as I entered the hotel in time to see all my colleagues, even Esmé, arrived and ready to take their breakfast. Reminded of my professional duties, I had time to return to the boat, bathe, change my clothes, equip myself with plenty of Professor Quelch's finest cocaine, return at some speed to the hotel and even take a cup of coffee and a piece of toast before we all departed, in high excitement, for the ferry which awaited us at the hotel's private quay.

As we selected places on the polished oak bench seats under the launch's awning, Esmé came to settle her warm little body against mine. She was at her sweetest this morning and did much to dispel my mood of fatalistic gloom at the dawning realisation that I was to begin work in enormous heat having failed to get even a moment's sleep. 'I hope you did not miss me, darling,' she said. I felt a pang of guilt. I assured her that, of course, I longed for her, but sometimes duty took precedence over personal needs. She frowned for a moment before she shrugged and began to sing a little song she had learned in Paris. For some reason this caused Mrs Cornelius to raise her eyebrows as she nodded good-morning to us on her way to the back of the boat where, she said, she could stretch out a bit and get the best of the morning sun before it threatened to touch her. The sun, in those days, was a serious threat to the complexion. It is only in recent years, with the rise of the Beach Bunny in a mongrelised Los Angeles, that the Tan has become a sign of health, wealth and sexual prowess. I wonder why the Americans got rid of the Mexicans in the first place when they now spend their leisure trying to make themselves look indistinguishable from them! This is what I mean when I say standards are slipping in every sector of human life. I remember when Watts was a pretty little village of neat lawns and flowers. Now, I understand, it is a warren of burning tenements with every available space filled with bizarre sculptures in place of trees, where negroes lope, hyped on heroin and rock and roll, performing primaeval rituals of puberty and manhood, of magic, and hunting and murderous revenge. It is hard to believe it could alter so much in a matter of twenty-five years! I spoke to an American I met in the Portobello Road. His opinion was that the slaves not only should not have been freed but did not want to be free. The worker bee, he told me, dies if it cannot work. The negro goes mad. He was, I gather, a famous writer and editor in his own country. He was over here for a Convention, he said. This was in 1965. I do not know what kind of Convention. Perhaps a Convention of Sane People! That would be an original idea. But we know they had no effect so far upon the world.

It seemed that Esmé had also had a poor night, perhaps pining for me. I felt sorry for her. While I had embarked on a harebrained personal chase, she had been working to help our company. Did Mrs Cornelius appreciate how much all our fortunes depended upon my little girl? I remember that the ferry ride was conducted in a mood of general conviviality, especially since our crew was growing increasingly more anxious to complete their work and get back to Hollywood. They had had enough, they said, of the local colour. Most had had bouts of dysentery. Professor Quelch made some dry joke about 'crossing the River of Death' while Seaman, who was better read in Egyptology than the rest of us, looked about him and asked where 'Turnface the Ferryman' had got to. I believe he referred to Sir Ranalf. We were all in high spirits as we disembarked and mounted the donkeys which were to take us to the valley of the Tombs. Helped by courteous boys we mounted the little animals, surprised to discover that their saddles were relatively comfortable. Suddenly we were trotting up a long, dirt road into a low line of hills, the burial caves of the pharaohs and their favourites. It was already warm. I was glad of my wide-brimmed straw hat, my dark glasses. We had not gone half-an-hour, with the dust of the road beginning to rise like mist behind us, obscuring our view of a distant line of tourists, before I had the urge to remove my jacket, but decorum disallowed me from taking it off until I saw others doing the same. Behind us the Nile had become a path of grey silver through the red-brown clay, through the dark yellows and the untidy clumps of green, of rocks and palms, while Luxor was a ghost on the far shore, distance as usual undoing the damages of time. My little girl, prettily sidesaddle on a donkey more her size than mine, seemed entirely at her ease, jogging at the rear, chatting to Professor Quelch, while Mrs Cornelius rode beside me, a billowing cloud of white linen and lace. A sunshade over one shoulder, a gloved hand upon her donkey's pommel, she could not maintain her ill-temper but shrieked with pleasure every time the donkey's hooves struck an uneven part of the path. 'Y'd pay an effin' fortune for a ride like this at Margate!' But she admitted she would be relieved when we got to what she was insisting on calling 'Tooting Common'. His long legs brushing the ground, Wolf Seaman bounced moodily in her wake, glancing at his watch and looking up at the sun, while the rest of the crew trailed back along the path, commenting on the scenery and waving away the occasional group of children who appeared from nowhere to offer us reed fans, straw scorpions, huge living lizards harnessed with string or the usual figures of Bast and Osiris. I began to think the whole area hid a troglo-dytic city, a warren of caves where these children skulked and their goods were manufactured. Could that barren landscape deceive the eye and support human life in subterranean tunnels? Was all of Egypt living, literally, with its dead? But I knew this to be fanciful. The villages were behind us and to one side. That was where the bony children originated. Everything else here was dedicated to Death and the Netherworld. How careful had these people been to ensure their immortality! How vulner-able, in the end, that immortality was proven! When the day came for the souls of the dead to return to their bodies, there would be nothing for them to occupy but the temporal forms of huge German *Hausfrau*s in sturdy cotton walking-suits or slender French homosexuals in the latest Paris cut. One could imagine them feeling a certain amount of confusion.

The Valley of the Kings is itself a somewhat disappointing sight. It was, after all, picked for its isolation rather than its beauty. It is a wide, shallow *wadi* in the walls of which, over the centuries, tombs were bored and into these tombs had been placed the mummies of kings, some of which survived until the twentieth century when, with our more sophisticated methods, we succeeded in disturbing the rest of what were probably the last untroubled dead. Cook's and the Egyptian Society had built sets of iron or wooden stairs to some tombs so that the thousands of tourists who came here every year to peer, without much interest, at what the looters had spared (mostly wall-paintings) and giggle or gape at the oddness of it all, might save themselves even the discomfort of a modest scramble. There were only a few tourists here before us, most of whom belonged to Thackeray's German Touring Group which had pitched its tents overnight, perhaps in the delicious hope that the spirits of Tutenkhamun or Horemheb might be tempted to return to earth by the smell of canned frankfurters and sauerkraut. These Germans did not look as if they had seen ghosts and as we approached were finishing a hearty selection of breakfast meats. O. K. Radonic, who was our best German-speaker, went up to explain what would be happening, asking merely that they did not stray into camera-shot. I noticed that many of the campers had been looking rather sullen and actually cheered up at his news, taking rather more interest in our Company than in the ringing tones of Miss Vronwy Nurture who addressed them, in clear, precise schoolroom English, on the lineage of the Egyptian God-Emperors. Even in Germany, that bastion of culture, there are those who would rather watch a modern movie crew at work than absorb the wisdom and revelations of ancient stones or admire the beauty of an unnamed artist whose skills were dedicated only to an unearthly posterity.

There would be time to inspect the tombs later, said Seaman. For the moment he wanted some good outside shots. Later that afternoon, Sir Ranalf would send a party of *fellaheen* to us. These we would dress as slaves to carry the mummy into the tomb. We had not yet decided whose tomb to use. Radonic said we seemed to have come a long way to get a take we could have gotten better in Death Valley. Seaman, who had invested so much of his reputation in this film, asked him pompously not to display his philistinism but just to turn the camera when he was commanded. Radonic, who had been losing patience with Seaman as his boredom increased, told him there was only one place he was prepared to point his camera at that moment whereupon Seaman began to utter his familiar self-pitying squawks, like a gannet discovering a damaged nest.

' 'E's started early,' observed Mrs Cornelius with a placid smile. 'I 'ope that means we finish early, too. It's gonna get effin' 'ot soon, Ivan.'

There came, as if in concert, a high-pitched wailing from the entrance of the valley where an enormous dust-cloud began to thrash upwards obscuring the sun. The children dropped back, knowing an *afrit* when they saw one. The wail dropped to a roar and then a cough, almost lion-like, as through the dispersing sand came a monstrous Rolls Royce half-track, the kind I had last seen abandoned on the Odessa road as we retreated to the sea. This one was not camouflaged but vivid with scarlet and yellow livery, with a great Ibis in outline above a motto reading *Flectere si nequeo superos, Acheronta movebo* scrolled in elegant Gothic and above its head the angular words EGYPTIAN UNIVERSAL MOVING PICTURE CO. Sir Ranalf Steeton himself sat at the wheel while behind him two servants held tightly to a rope-lashed mummy-case poking at an uneasy angle across two sets of back seats.

As it rolled to a rasping halt its tracks threw up a huge curtain of sand, which fell back to half-bury the Thackeray camp. 'Don't worry, sweet lads and lasses,' Sir Ranalf assured us as he dusted his own coat free of the beige-coloured dust. 'I've seen them here before.' He glanced up briefly as the campers flapped over collapsed canvas. 'They're only Krauts. Well, what do you think? Isn't she a beauty? The real McCoy, too, though I'm not so sure she's a Queen exactly. Will she do? The slaves are coming by a separate route.' And with a rap of his cane upon the mummy-case the little man, almost a pantomime pig in tropical whites, crossed the sands to help my Esmé free herself from her donkey, to flick a wisp of cotton from where it had caught on the saddle, to kiss her upon the cheeks and to pat her little head while Mrs Cornelius (dismounting with all the easy skill and grace of Buck Jones about to confront troublesome rustlers) called out to nobody in particular, 'It's orl right everybody, ther bloody star's passed 'er ordishun.'

If she thought to alert me to anything, she failed. Instead I was shocked and upset by this unseemly display of petty jealousy and spite from a woman whose integrity and judgement

I habitually respected above all others. As she strode towards Professor Quelch, he looked almost in panic from her to Sir Ranalf. She paused beside him, clearly expecting moral support, but he peered over her shoulder and smiled apologetically at an expectant Steeton, who showed evident satisfaction at this display of equivocation. I wondered what had caused Quelch to change allegiances. As Mrs Cornelius stalked disgustedly across the sand in my direction I, too, found myself offering a placatory grin to our new master. And in betraying Mrs Cornelius, just for that instant, I knew in my heart I had betrayed myself.

NINETEEN

WHAT I EXPRESS IN SADNESS, she expresses in anger; but the pain is the same, the pain of watching people destroy themselves, destroying any hope for their children. 'Yer carn't save ev'rybody, Ive,' says Mrs Cornelius. Yet I thought I had found a way. 'They 'ave ter make their own mistakes,' she says. Sometimes she falls prey to that careless tolerance which is her caste's bane but which the middle-class idealise as its greatest virtue. Their myth of the British sense of fair play is their most effective means of maintaining a status quo favouring an élite. If there was anything wrong with what they were doing, they say, the people would complain. Everyone knows the British will only complain about the weather to which their combined creative intellects have failed to make a jot of difference. And yet they are always surprised by it. They have a myth of snowy winters and hot summers, imprinted from childhood Annuals. What is more they have been conditioned so thoroughly to a Stoic conceit, wherein suffering is morally superior to pleasure, that they are now the chief guardians of their own confinement. I see this clearly. Anyone could. Observing the truth does not make me a Communist! It is easy enough to identify the disease but far harder to agree on a cure. This is what neither side will ever understand. I am not a fool. I know what it means to take an independent position in life. People do not appreciate the consequent pain and the loneliness of that position, the contempt and insulting threats one frequently endures. I do not think this is 'amoral', as those women say. Nor is it immoral. I am a man of profound and subtle conscience. Only a moron would disagree that it is not always possible to be sure of the best course of action. Why make politics confrontational? One cannot solve every moral dilemma in an instant. Am I the only man on earth who is naturally tolerant and unbiased? Who likes to weigh all arguments?

Why should I feel guilt because I refuse to march through the streets of Paris side by side with some semi-literate student? Does it make me a monster because I have actually seen the red flag flying over vanquished courts and parliaments and understood its immediate meaning? Why are the agents of Terror such figures of romance to the young? Bonnie and Clyde? I saw the movie. During their hey-day, ask anyone, it was no fun to step in their path.

Though lighting problems made it impossible to film just then in the tombs, our photoplay progressed fairly well during that first fortnight and the basic story was soon 'in the can'. Sir Ranalf assured us that we should eventually receive a generator or, failing that, he would seek permission to shoot what we needed in the complexes of Karnak. The rest, he said, could be reconstructed in the studio. I still had my chief love scene to enact with Mrs Cornelius in the tomb. We would die in each other's arms, to be resurrected centuries later as the young lovers of the opening. Then I must perform what we called 'the seduction scene' with Esmé when, for a few brief days, I had to fall under her spell, almost betraying my love for Mrs Cornelius. Few – even Wolf Seaman himself – denied this was my greatest acting achievement. If I never acted again the world would remember this film for the passion and sensuality I was able to bring to it! A monument, a testimony to my love and my aspiration, even should I die the day it was completed. This film would be seen in every picture-house in the world. Cornish and Peters would be as famous as Garbo and Gilbert. We performed our parts in the blazing sun, with an audience of grubby German tourists, local children and tarbooshed guides. They applauded every gesture

305

and embrace. The lack of sleep and the sapping heat meant we resorted increasingly to our cocaine, of which our 'technical producer' Malcolm Quelch had an endless supply. Sir Ranalf Steeton expressed gargantuan delight in our achievements. *Desert Passions* would set new records at box-offices across Europe and America. During the day he now insisted upon Esmé accompanying him wherever he went. She was his 'sweet little kiddy', his 'perfect girl'. At the time, I found cloying and unnatural these affected pronouncements of an older man for the charms of young flesh. Yet Esmé explained how important it was to keep his goodwill. She had overheard him praising the merits of the film to his partners, who were all Egyptians. She thought they expected something more sensational. By now I had seen a few examples of the local shadowy melodramas. I told her our own film was so much above those that there was no point in making a comparison. Egyptian 'thrillers' scarcely travelled out of their country, let alone to America. But I understood the importance of encouraging our producer not to drop artistic standards for short-sighted commercial gains, so I permitted my girl her time with the Englishman when, on more than one occasion, she attended meetings and helped reassure his partners as to the nobility and certain financial success of our venture. If any other relationship was developing between Sir Ranalf and my girl I did not detect it, although I must admit I suppressed suspicions now and again. I thought often of Kolya and I was desperate to ensure that my scenes with Mrs Cornelius would be as perfect as possible. I must admit I did not give as much time to my little girl as she deserved. It is folly to neglect a perfect flower, as we used to say in Kiev. Without appreciation, such a flower fades or is plucked by another. I blame myself as much as anyone. Sir Ranalf Steeton plucked my flower, but I do not think I was to blame for most of what followed. I suppose, too, I should not blame Esmé for feeling a certain jealousy while she watched those powerful scenes between my old friend and myself, though it was always clear we were platonic comrades off-screen. While Seaman did not suspect me, he was on the other hand deeply suspicious of Professor Quelch. Mrs Cornelius seemed the only person able to get a smile from the old boy. Quelch grew almost foolishly relaxed in her company and said he thought she was the most amusing companion he had ever known.

Another distraction was the general attitude of the crew. Grace was almost constantly in a state of bridling offence and disappeared one night, apparently with a Greek soldier on leave, while O.K. Radonic clearly had no respect for the director or sympathy with the story. He spent most of his time looking for cigars, operating his camera only when forced to do so, and displaying all the signs of the heat fatigue which eventually brought him down. He was taken to the Hungarian doctor in Luxor and was declared unfit to work. Seaman solved the problem by turning the camera himself until our two lighting people deserted with a pair of wealthy Swedish women they had met in Tutenkhamun's tomb. We began to look less like a film company than a small dramatic troupe, yet the beaming Sir Ranalf was undismayed by anything! He assured us that new staff would soon be entrained from Cairo. He knew only the best Egyptian film professionals and could easily get skilled technical staff from Italy if necessary. Eventually we were joined by an Alexandrine Greek, who was impressed by what he called our 'modern' equipment, but showed himself a competent enough cameraman under Seaman's direction. Two more Greeks and several Copts followed until we had a full complement again, although Seaman moaned constantly about their incompetence and laziness. The Copts, discovering Esmé to be fluent in Turkish, spent most of their time chatting with her. She was soon on excellent terms with them until Sir Ranalf objected. Her friendliness was not good for discipline. We should keep a proper distance.

Finding himself with only moderately expert help, Seaman grew increasingly distracted. Few of the team spoke English, one spoke a little German and Seaman was forced to rely on those of us with French to translate the simplest instructions. Eventually, when I was unable to fix the run-down old generator brought to us to power our lights, he announced he could no longer work in such conditions. We had set up our camera in Tutenkhamun's tomb, a rather chilly, narrow place for a king to be buried, with tiny chambers and unimpressive paintings like bad comic strips. None possessed the beauty or the inspiration

I had seen in other tombs and temples where it was impossible not to become familiar with ancient Egyptian art. Eventually the two-dimensional form seemed perfectly natural to me and it was easily possible to distinguish sublime from crude. There were wonderful bas-reliefs and tomb paintings, temple art and monumental sculpture, but there were also, thousands of years on, wretched copies of the great originals, heartless academic facsimiles, just as exist in our own world. Age does not improve bad art. There are never many great artists alive at any one time and Tutenkhamun's fame appears to rest on his gold and his physical beauty rather than upon the magnificent workmanship of his burial goods, the artistry of his tomb's paintings. They believed the tomb was really meant for a minister, but that the boy king died suddenly and it would have taken too long to quarry a fresh tomb from the rocks of the Wadi el Mulak. The stars in the dark roof were lifeless; the blue, green and red figures in procession on the walls seemed without direction. I found the place depressing. But that, I suppose, is the nature of tombs. I do not share the public's fascination with such places. While everyone else spent their free time exploring the various resting-places of the much-disturbed dead, I contented myself with sketching designs for a new project in which I hoped to interest Sir Ranalf. I had conceived the idea some months earlier. I called it my Desert Liner. Finally the patient camel would be discarded as 'the ship of the desert' in favour of a gigantic motor! My vehicle would carry passengers across the dreaded Sahara Desert in the comfort and luxury they enjoyed on an ocean liner. I showed the plans to Sir Ranalf one afternoon as he sat in his car watching Esmé playing cricket with the Alexandrine, Mrs Cornelius and Professor Quelch. 'Howzat!' he would cry, and, 'Well caught!'

'My Desert Liner,' I told him, 'will have its dining-saloon, recreation-room, look-out deck, state-rooms and other comforts. A fleet of them could easily be built. The prototype would be a hundred and thirty feet long. She would be forty-two feet high from the bottom of the wheels to the top of the upper deck, and twenty-six feet wide. In general arrangement she will closely resemble a passenger steamship, with the exception that she will run on wheels of colossal dimensions!'

'Splendid!' said Sir Ranalf. 'Astonishing! Go on, brave sorcerer! Prithee, tell me the rest of thy tale!'

'The wheels will measure thirty-nine feet in diameter,' I explained. 'As you can see here, by the employment of an ingenious (you'll forgive my pride) compensating mechanism they hold closely to the sand and soil in every possible position. This means the hull of the ship is kept always at a comfortable level. Whatever the relative position of the wheels may be, the hull remains steady!'

Clearly surprised by my engineering vision, Sir Ranalf nodded his plump head. 'But what would power such a monster, my boy? The engine would have to be huge! The weight! The weight!'

I was ready for this. 'It will be driven by two Diesel motors of four hundred and fifty horse-power, of which the second is kept in reserve. Two dynamos furnish light and electromotive force. Steering is effected by means of this hydraulic apparatus.' I folded back the plan to display it.

'You should patent this, brilliant youth!' Then some action of the cricket game caught my patron's attention and he let out a mysterious gasp.

'The machine is built to ascend grades of thirty degrees. Steep hills are very numerous, as you know, in the Sahara. Great speed has not been my aim because the friction of the sand on the wheels will generate tremendous heat, some of which, admittedly, I can convert for a variety of purposes. The ship will travel at about nineteen miles an hour.'

'So slow!'

'Faster than a camel, Sir Ranalf! It will carry a hundred and fifty people, including passengers and crew members, two hundred tons of merchandise, oil and water and a supply of fuel sufficient for a journey of ten to twelve thousand miles without replenishment. The vehicle will be more than able to cover the greatest desert surfaces in the world!' There would be four decks, I explained. The upper deck held the control cabin, the wireless cabin, the cabins of the commander and three officers, two-berth passenger cabins plus four cabins de luxe. On this deck, as I showed on my plans, would be the washrooms, an office, a baggage-room, and a large promenade

sheltered by a roof from the sun's burning rays. The two inter-
mediate decks would contain cabins, the dining-saloon, the kitchen, the reading-room, the smoking-room and more baggage-
rooms. I showed him where I had sketched the two derricks,
weighing 2,000 pounds each, which could be fitted on either
side for the handling of baggage and cargo. I was particularly
pleased with a novel and important feature. My land-ship would
have a cooling-room always maintaining artificially low tem-
peratures. Here passengers overcome by the desert heat could
rest and recover. The extreme clearness of the desert air
allowed the sun's rays, as we had all grown painfully aware,
extraordinarily powerful penetration. Exposure to them was, of
course, dangerous, since they penetrated the brain and spinal
cord (the practical reason why, I reminded him, Arabs had
always worn heavy turbans over heads and necks).

The pretty sportsters screamed and giggled and began,
inexpertly, to make runs. Sir Ranalf's interest in the cricket
became intense. I had never understood the British enthusiasm
for this mysterious game. Whenever I could catch his attention
I continued to explain how I had reserved the lower decks
for merchandise, the helmsman's cabin, the motor-room, the
repair-room, the water and fuel reservoirs. 'If you want to put
this to your business partners, the discussion will naturally arise
as to the merits in conquering sandy wastes of a small motor
vehicle over this "land leviathan". Well, Sir Ranalf, as we have
all read in *The Egyptian Gazette*, recent proof is provided that
specially constructed small cars, such as your own, can cross the
Sahara! But you will also have read that they are subjected to
enormous dangers, including wild desert tribes!'

'The desert, it's true, my dear chap, is crammed with
hazards. Those heathen fellows were Tripoli Berbers mostly,
I suspect. The British police are powerless of course. Well run,
pretty demoiselle!'

'You will appreciate, Sir Ranalf, the superiority of my
Desert Liner over the desert motor-car. A freight Desert Liner
of three hundred and fifty tons would cost about twenty-six
thousand pounds. Forty motor-trucks would cost, say, five
hundred pounds apiece. Armed with Bofors and Bannings my
liner costs about six thousand pounds more than the trucks,

yet the *running expenses* of forty motor-trucks on a dirt-track without tank stations would be considerably higher than that of my luxury cruiser of the dunes. Each truck would require at least two chauffeurs, for instance, making a minimum staff of eighty men. A crew of twenty is sufficient to run and man my liner! The population of wild desert tribes is reckoned at some three and a half million. Wild beasts are another common danger. Where trucks would have to make camp and guard against these threats, my liner ploughs on day and night without a halt. Thomas Cook should be especially interested.'

'Howzat! Ha! Ha! Howzat! Cook?' Sir Ranalf glared at me almost in alarm. 'Oh, no! We'll sort something out without involving them. My partner in Aswan is always interested in daring new notions. I am sure he would love to back you to the hilt. And there are others I know in Alexandria and Cairo. Perhaps even here in Luxor. See me later, famous bard, and I shall be delighted to help you find someone for your ship!' His eyes wandered again to the willow and the leather. 'A scheme, my handsome mechanic, worthy of the Suez Canal and all who built her! I am mightily impressed.' And then he could resist the contest no longer and went rolling and panting through the dust to snatch the bat from Esmé's hands and call an incoherent challenge to Professor Quelch who, thoughtfully rubbing his ball upon his bottom, began the long stroll backwards which was a special feature of this game.

Everyone who knew me in 1926 knew where Bischoff of Kiel got his plans, lock, stock and barrel when he announced the building of the *Countess Marianna*. As it was, the Nazis scratched all Bischoff's experiments and research when they came to power. I understood Hitler's decision, but he was already growing into another short-sighted politician. Thanks to their ideology they needed to show the public immediate gains. As with Stalin, life, dignity, spirit, everything was sacrificed. Goebbels was right. He and his friends were, indeed, temperamental opposites of the patient Jew. Seaman was himself very Teutonic and determined. The Slav possesses both virtues, which is why he survives so successfully through history's ups and downs, resisting all outside conquerors.

My patience saved me undue exertion, whereas Seaman

grew increasingly frustrated at the antics of his inefficient crew and at Sir Ranalf's interference. With the second problem, I sympathised. I had explained to Sir Ranalf how a producer's function is to be the efficient medium of the artist's creativity, but he had tasted previously unguessed-at power and wanted to embrace it forever. Did the film have sufficient 'authority'? Sir Ranalf mused. When we did not follow his reasoning, he explained that so far we had to take too much in the film for granted. The characters needed deepening.

As a team we united against him. We were not sure what he meant by 'deepening', we said. All the actors, even Esmé, had given extremely good performances. They were real people on the screen, with whom other real people could identify.

'But not *everyone*!' Sir Ranalf insisted the film have as universal an appeal as possible. He was not sure he really *believed*, for instance, that Esmé was actually a voluptuously sensual temptress. I was offended by this. Our rushes showed Esmé to be thoroughly sexual. Clara Bow herself had said as much about Esmé.

'But do we believe she could seduce the greatest priest in Egypt, the noblest of men, your good self, Ah-ke-tep! You are the mightiest engineering genius the world had ever known, sweet esquire, Rameses the Second's most powerful architect!'

He had no need to butter my parsnips. Better than any I understood my story's symbolism! I could not deny, for instance, a certain autobiographical strain. Yet I was puzzled by his body language. I was reminded of a semaphoring squid.

'I think we should show Ru-a-na in a scene of her own. Where she reveals her charms to you.' He cleared his throat.

'Wot?'

Mrs Cornelius came ploughing through the dust to gulp refreshment. She had been on a camel most of the morning and unlike myself had no affinity for the animal. 'Dirt?'

'A scene of artistic nudity.' Sir Ranalf ignored Mrs Cornelius, fuming and scarlet, behind him.

'Wot the effin' butler sor!' she declared. 'I noo you wos a twisted ticket, Rannie. Someone tol' me yer made yer pile in dirty pictures!'

312

'Really, my dear Queen of the Nile, I assure you I speak for the whole of Europe, where the nude scene is an accepted convention of the medium. In America, where prudishness reigns, I would agree that is not so. But surely you, as cosmopolitans, understand that I demand nothing unworthy of your great talents?'

'Too effin' right, chum.' Mrs Cornelius drew me forcefully on, speaking in a rapid whisper. 'I've 'ad enuff, Ive. This bastard's up ter somefink filfy, I c'n smell it. Git art, nar. Take an ol' trouper's tip.' And, laying her pink finger alongside her delicious nose, she informed me she had been in touch with Major Nye in Cairo. 'Me an' ther major are chums again, since that larst night. 'E sent a ticket, firs' class. *An'* I gotta bit o' spendin' money. I've reelly 'ad enuff o' this, Ive. Next fing yer know I'll be on some bloody pilgrim boat off ter ther bloody Sultan's 'areem. God knows wot they'll do wiv *you*!' And she smiled, though her grip on my arm was urgent. I had rarely known her so positive. Yet she was asking me to give up the project of a lifetime. I needed to see my film completed. True, all our main scenes were 'in the can', and we had only to shoot a few more interiors, which could be 'faked'; but I needed her with me! I begged her to remain. We would insist on complete control over any doubtful material. 'It's *orl* bloody doubtful, Ivan. You know as well as I do wot that bunch o' Bubbles an' Eye-ties do fer a livin'. Git on ther bloody train, Ive. Same time as me.'

I trusted her instincts, but my loyalty to Esmé and my art was greater than my fear. This loyalty, of course, was completely misplaced. I have never ceased to curse my own folly, though she never once reminded me of that warning, in all my years in England. I told her I would consider her suggestions. I would let Esmé decide (I could not, after all, abandon her). There was also the question of Sir Ranalf's partners investing in my Desert Liner. I had more than one career established in Egypt – then a country ripe for every kind of development. Surely I could trust men whose self-interest was identical to mine? I did not know then how many of those business people prefer to talk than act. (Unless of the most hysterical and irresponsible types they are racially conditioned to inactivity.

The blood feud and the football match is all that engages them.)

During that boiling May I could see my chance of fame returning. Already history had rolled over my hopes and destroyed a career in Russia, another in Turkey, another in France. It threatened yet another in America. But now I had the chance to redeem everything. Here were wealthy potentates with private fortunes for developing ideas. I would point out the military as well as civilian use of my Desert Liner. Such a juggernaut at the heart of their armies would ensure British dominion over the entire desert as far away as their deeper African possessions.

Mrs Cornelius wished me to abandon that dream (as well as the dream of our screen union) together with my salary and my fiancée? How could I listen? Yet, so great even then was my belief in my old friend that I was prepared to consider flight, as long as Esmé would come with me. By now others were glancing curiously in our direction. Mrs Cornelius became evasive. 'Well, 'ave a good time wiv it, Ive. Don' ketch cold.' And she stormed towards her tent.

That evening we returned to Luxor and prepared for our evening meal aboard the boat. As soon as I could I took Esmé aside to tell her urgently that she should not do the scene Sir Ranalf suggested. At the station I would get us tickets for Alexandria. From there we would go to Italy, where we had friends. It would not be long before we were returning to America. I said nothing of my own reservations.

To my relief she would have none of my sacrifice! 'You have set such store by this, Dimka. I could not let you abandon it. I understand the scene is necessary to the success of the movie.' She giggled. 'After all, my darling, I am not unused to a few appreciative male eyes.'

I told her, 'That bad time in your life is a forgotten dream. I promised you need never suffer such awfulness again.'

'Oh, Dimka, sweetie, it is *fun*,' she said. 'It's just a jolly game. Sir Ranalf will explain. You mustn't be so stuffy, darling.'

I was, I admitted, the product of a more upright age, yet I did not wish to seem unadventurous in my darling's eyes. I required her voluntary obedience. I smiled at her jokes about my 'stern, old-fashioned face'. She had won me! I saw how, through art, she would not demean herself. I had to add something in reference to Mrs Cornelius's observation. Foreigners would feast, I said, upon her form.

She laughed. 'None of them Moslems, Dimka dear.'

Then Wolf Seaman joined us, a bulky vibrating tower, and explained with lugubrious intensity how our film would shock no one in Europe. Without those scenes the story would lack a certain impact. Let us do this, he begged, for the sake of perfection. He did not know of course that Mrs Cornelius, whom he still referred to as his fiancée, was leaving. I made up my own mind. I sought my friend in the cocktail lounge and drew her from the bar into a quiet corner of the deck. With trembling voice I begged her to remain long enough to complete the tomb scene. She was adamant. 'When I git a sniff o' somefink narsty, Ive, I'm on me bike. This littel set-up's gettin' def'nitely niffy. I'm orf while the goin's good an' ya'd better scarper, too. Mum's ther word, eh?'

Of course, I could not betray her. I bowed. I kissed her hand. Then I returned, with some reluctance, to what remained of our fold.

Mrs Cornelius's disappearance was discovered next morning, as we set up our shots beside the Colossi of Memnon, those strange guardians of a lost road to the barren valleys of the dead. I retired as quickly as possible to the little Greek café across the way, which catered to passing tourists. Sitting in the shade with a cup of Lipton's, I listened to Seaman bellowing as loudly as those legendary Colossi whose voices had howled above the desert winds even when Caesar came here to marvel at the monuments to a conquered past. Seaman delivered a manifesto on the nature of art, the artist, his rôle and rights, his need for order, his own need for us to work as hard as he did, his understanding that punctuality was the backbone of a good movie play. They believed Gloria Cornish had remained behind in Luxor, but I had looked from my window early that morning and seen her, aided by tip-toeing Nubians, heading for the *kalash* stand at the top of the mooring steps. She was taking the early train to Cairo and would return to England with Major Nye, re-assess her career, and perhaps rejoin me in Hollywood later. She could easily get a job in England on the strength of *Social Follies* and *Lady Lorequer* alone. By eleven Sir Ranalf arrived, summoned by Seaman. At first our master seemed as angry as his director but then he had composed himself, going about with his usual authority, calming everyone, white or native alike. It was not, he said, an important issue. Our main footage was shot. Esmé could take a slightly stronger part. No actress, he was sure, and he touched his fingertips to her face, would refuse such a chance. Esmé flushed with pleasure. I must admit I became a little jealous. I left my place in the shade and strode up the path towards them, calling out, 'Miss Cornish will be ready for us soon, I am sure. Meanwhile, I should remind you, gentlemen, that the story is mine. I will accept no interference. No dilutions.' Had Sir Ranalf, too, seen Mrs Cornelius on her way to the station? Perhaps while he glanced idly from the window of his hotel, overlooking our boat? He did not say. He was all soft reassurance, affirming our story as a model of the literary art. There was no question of interfering with its fundamentals. But he was a showman – a kind of window-dresser. It was his job to make sure the public would come to see our picture. If they did not come, my message would never be heard. This was a reasonable argument. I was relieved to hear it put this way. Then Sir Ranalf began the rather more difficult task of calming Seaman, who claimed he could not work without his star's presence. Eventually it was agreed that we shoot all the scenes, with 'Irené Gay' heavily veiled, standing in for Gloria Cornish who would be with us the next day when we could shoot a few more scenes. Sir Ranalf reminded us that time was money and since this solution would cost more, no doubt we thought his acceptance exceptionally generous.

Mrs Cornelius did not turn up, of course. After a couple of days, Sir Ranalf's people established that she had boarded the Cairo Express. Whereupon Seaman returned to his cabin and refused to come out. When he did emerge next day he seemed chastened. Sir Ranalf had visited him in the night and brought him to his senses. Thereafter, he was a far more agreeable man. Indeed, his control over the film was almost too light, even lacklustre, on occasions.

The nude scene was tastefully accomplished by daylight amongst the ruins of Karnak. There were, of course, no witnesses amongst the general public and, moreover, the majority of our crew was banned from participating. As Esmé stripped her silks from her body, her eyes yearning towards me, I must admit I was moved to my deepest masculinity. This display aroused an unexpected lust. The beast leaped to fill my skin; a sensation in its own way more intense than those almost savage days of lovemaking experiment in Cairo. The scene could not have been better and was unquestionably of the most superior artistic merit. Seaman was thoroughly satisfied with our work. Esmé, with good humour and her *Erdgeist*'s love of nudity and natural freedom, made me understand how I had indeed been unnecessarily stuffy. That night my little girl and I continued our scene unobserved. Free from other eyes, she became uninhibited, inventive.

When, next day, Seaman assembled us near the Sacred Pool and casually required my darling to remove her clothing and seem about to swim, I remained relaxed. There had, I accepted, to be continuity. Karnak, that bastion of a savage intellectualism, of a profoundly pagan art, helped establish in us a new mood. It had grown so hot that most of us were already wearing as little as possible, no more than a pair of shorts, a singlet and our lightest boots. This semi-nudity contributed to a mood of moral looseness which, with the slow pace of Luxor's days, the high quality of the cocaine and the *kif*, was extremely seductive. I was young and relatively inexperienced. I do not blame myself for relaxing my standards a little. Perhaps, even by then, I could not have escaped. Now we had lights, so that we could shoot in the shadows of the temples, amongst the great pylons. We laid Esmé out upon a great fallen slab, stretched for sacrifice. And I, the priest of Ra, was supposed to raise my knife over her lovely, screaming head. I discussed this scene with Malcolm Quelch. I had an artistic, as well as an historical, problem. Surely there had been no such sacrifices made at that time? He said there was such a thing as imaginative human licence. I asked him if he meant 'artistic licence' and he said he did. He had become extremely off-hand in the past week.

Our days now had a peculiar, hermetic quality. We filmed in enclosures, in alcoves, in ruined chapels, among Karnak's tall, knowing pillars which had witnessed all human folly, all human greed, all lust and dark, unnatural need. My inhibitions indeed seemed stupid in the presence of all this hot African sensuality. I was giving myself up to the past, to a barbaric civilisation that had grown old, tolerant and yet was still greedy for human feeling, for the thrill of flesh against flesh, the touch of a fingertip upon a nipple, the rush of blood and heat, the gasping desire, the stink of sweat and sex. Watching Esmé spreadeagled and perspiring on that rock I conceived such an almost uncontrollable desire for her I yelled with astonishment when Sir Ranalf's friendly hand fell upon my naked shoulder. 'Isn't she lovely, old boy? Such a deliciously natural young lady, don't you know. Well, we should *all* know. Those things we do in secret!' And he chuckled. I was offended. 'What do you know of my private life?' At once he became an avuncular tomcat. 'Only what our little darling has told me,' he purred. And, of course, it was then I knew she had betrayed me.

My emotion at that realisation is indescribable. Though I hated them both my lust for her had never been greater. Had I always hated her, always mistaken one intense emotion for another? Had I ever loved her? I became horribly confused. That dreadful passion threatened to engulf and activate my entire being. I was grasped by the twin fists of lust and rage.

My Esmé was a whore! She had been fucked so many times she had calluses on her cunt. *They aren't a bad bunch, the soldiers I'm with.* Why had she betrayed me? She was my angel. *Meyn batayt, meyn doppelgänger.* It was my duty to rescue her. Yet I had so many other duties, not least to Art and to Science. To the Future.

'Esmé?' I moved to where she lay, chained and ready for sacrifice. 'Sir Ranalf has confessed.' I turned to still the cameras. This was not, I said quietly, a scene for the public view.

Her voice was a little sleepy, as if she had been dozing while waiting for the take. 'But you told me it was all right, Dimka.'

Now, of course, I understood my own thoughtlessness. For all her exotic past my little girl was not trained in the ways of the larger world. I had protected her for too long. I softened. 'I had not meant – '

'Really, my dear Childe Max! As a man of the world!' It was Sir Ranalf who had taken advantage of us. My respect for the man vanished in an instant. I turned. 'How could you?'

'My dear little knight-errant, don't be cross! We're all innocent bucolic lads and lasses here together, enjoying a little bit of pagan pleasure for the short years we are upon this Earth. What harm was meant, sweet Orpheus? These are games, no more! Natural games, you know, as between little boys and girls. Between chums and chumesses, eh? Yum, yum!' And he placed his warm fingers on my arm to pat it. 'No secret nastiness was intended. We are not the humdrum sort enchained and limited by awful, useless emotions of jealousy and possessiveness, surely? I had you down, dear Sir Galahad, for a Shelleyan like myself. A worshipper of all that is natural.'

Again, I was made to feel both inhumane and unsophisticated. An intolerable bigot. I blushed and cleared my throat. 'I had not quite understood,' I said. 'It was a shock – '

'Of course it was! I'm so very deeply sorry, dear, old pal. I thought all this was happening with your consent. I knew – '

'Whereas I did not!' But, hard as I strove for sophisticated acceptance, I was close to tears. So many different emotions flooded through me.

'You will of course remember your professional commitment.'

I could not answer at once. My groin flashed white-hot. Seaman now joined us, followed by Quelch, who was now forever at the director's shoulder. Perhaps as Mrs Cornelius had done a little earlier, I looked to Quelch for sympathy but he returned my glance with the same shifty warmth I interpreted as continuing embarrassment at my witnessing his Eastertime fellatial diversion. And Seaman seemed entirely without energy. His 'Can I help?' was almost timid.

'We need you to persuade our baffled chum that what we demand is within the bounds of artistic good taste.' Sir Ranalf was affable. 'Really, there are pictures hanging in perfectly respectable Birmingham villas more suggestive than our little scene.'

'It's a question of conviction,' said Seaman. 'We need to startle them.'

'We need to persuade the audience, you see, of the absolute authority of our *mise-en-scène*.'

As they talked we smoked a little *kif* and I began to understand what they were driving at. I recalled that I had read how many Egyptians went naked during festivals and special periods of worship. But not, surely, in such circumstances? I looked to Quelch who spread his hands. 'I think, as I said earlier, that some licence . . .'

'But, of course, it would help if you, too, could get a little closer to nature, to the olden times. Don't you agree, Herr Seaman? Dear Maxie should divest himself of his own little kilt and perhaps substitute a tasteful ceremonial apron?'

I, of course, refused. At this rate what would be the difference, I asked, between our film and a piece of commercial pornography?

'They have *nothing* in common,' Sir Ranalf assured me in some outrage. 'Our great moral work will stand as one of the milestones in the history of dramatic representation. It will be the *Hamlet*, the Pinero, the *Birth of a Nation* of its time. Because we dared, dear Maxie. Because we *dared* . . .'

But I was still unconvinced of any authentic reason to undress. The chance that my father's 'hygienic' operation might be detected and the obvious appalling conclusions drawn was, I must admit, my chief fear. Again Malcolm Quelch was commissioned to take me aside to mention certain precedents in certain paintings, the great myths of fertility and rebirth we hoped to examine through our film. In another part of the temple he helped me light another calming pipe and soothed me with his scholarship, his talk of high aspiration, of the world's attention. 'This could be your guarantee of immortality.' He helped with a match to coax a flame. The *kif* was especially pungent and I think now that he had made what was known as a cocktail, perhaps with opium and something else. It had the effect of bringing me back to my deep self, my fundamental beliefs, my sense of self-worth. This would, he murmured, be merely the means to an end. When *The Follies of a Pharaoh* made me world-famous every other reward would fall into my lap. At this point I became convinced, yet still insisted I must have my own little changing-space, a curtain drawn across a corner of the ruin. Quelch agreed. He helped me as, a little unsteadily, I disrobed. Then, in 'ritual apron' and the rest of my rather gorgeous costume, I presented myself again upon the set.

I had not expected to find another figure standing with Steeton in the shadows of the pylons. An enormous bulbous negress, a gauzy veil scarcely hiding her huge lips and flat nose, blinked extraordinarily long eyelashes, like a cow's. From the way she met my glance she clearly believed herself attractive. Was she some sort of nurse brought to give proper decorum to the scene? Eventually Sir Ranalf came over to murmur that this was a 'very highly placed personage who could finance all our ambitions'. I was dreamy by now from the pipe and I smiled and bowed to the negress, whose response was to withdraw almost coquettishly into the deeper shadows. It did not for a second occur to me who or what she might actually be.

Her own first glimpse of the woman seemed to startle Esmé, who moved cautiously on the slab, as if testing her bonds. But then she looked to me and seemed reassured. I guessed from her manner that she had already encountered the negress with Sir Ranalf at one of the 'meetings' I had innocently encouraged her to attend.

My anger surged back. I stepped forward, calling out to Seaman. 'Can we start them rolling, soon, Mr Director? I have other duties, you know, besides acting the leading part and writing the scenario.'

Seaman scuttled towards the camera and placed his hand on the poker-faced Greek who stood ready to turn the crank. Checking lights and angles in only a fraction of his normal time he nodded to me with a shout of 'Action'.

Knife in hand, I advance towards my treacherous child. O, how I have worked for her, lived for her, suffered such agonies for her. And this is to be my reward! Reminded of my own folly, of the fruitless idealism that tried to turn a dungheap weed into a perfect rose, now all I wish is to ravage her, to terrify her until she begs for my forgiveness. I long to hurt her in every fibre of her being as I had never hurt her before. I am not proud of these feelings, but they are any man's normal emotions in the circumstances and I have never been one to resist the truth. The drugs brought a drumming to my ears. It was as if the bodies of a huge crowd pressed close around me, their humid breath upon my back, their dreamy eyes upon my every action. They were willing me to take vengeance, to take vengeance for them, for every act of betrayal Woman ever served on Man since Eve betrayed Adam, since God expelled them from the Garden.

Seaman's voice grows suddenly animated, as it does only when he knows he has a singular shot. 'That's it! That's wonderful! You go towards her. You love her. You hate her. You want to kill her. You want to save her. She is yours. She is everyone's. You are expected to sacrifice her. That's right. You raise the knife. Good. But your hand stays. You cannot move. You cannot bring yourself to kill her – not before you have ravaged her. Yes. You will rape her. You will take her. You are heedless of her cries. Of her struggles. This is what she offered you. What she owes you. This is the debt you will now claim – and then appease the gods with her blood.'

Bile rose in my mouth. I was terrified, certain I must vomit, yet I was completely committed to the scene, knowing what an incredible sensation it would create on screen. I flung my body on hers. Peering into her terrified eyes, I realised that she too was drugged and was genuinely afraid of something. I pulled back. I leaned to spit into the sand at the base of the rock.

'Cut!' cried Seaman.

We would try another take, he said, later. Perhaps tomorrow, when we had seen the rushes. I apologised for my condition. The heat was proving too much for me again. Sir Ranalf was solicitous. 'We must get you back to the boat, dear little chummy. You were *wonderful*. It must have drained so much out of you. But this is how we will make our film not merely good, you know, but great.'

I remained for the rest of the evening and the night in my cabin, sleeping and dreaming. The image of my chained fiancée recurred frequently and with it that same swamping, horrible lust, a kind of bleakness. Then I would recall the image of that huge negress. What was she? A princess of the ruling blood? Some royal shame? Or a mere brothel-keeper? She had seemed to approve of me. The pale delicacy of my spreadeagled child and the engulfing embrace of the negress merged in a single sudden sensation gripped my genitals and caused me to wake gasping for breath, crying out. I was alone in my cabin as it rocked gently on the water. Outside, far away, came the call of a jackal to its mate. The dreams did not stop. I had soaked my sheets.

Next morning I was aroused by a cheerful Quelch. 'Come along to the viewing-room, dear boy. You did wonderfully. It's all developed and ready to watch.'

Still bleary from the opium, I allowed him to help me wash and get my clothes on. Then I followed on padding feet through the hot, yellow daylight to the stern where the company was already seated in semi-darkness waiting for Seaman's projector to roll. The rushes appeared, flickered, focused and gave us very suddenly three powerful minutes. Now I saw why everyone was so excited. They were incredible shots. All my fierce lust and rage and hatred had been captured. Esmé's terror had been genuine. There had never been scenes to rival these in the power of their emotional statement! I was at once perturbed and proud. Surely this ravishment would do for me what Valentino's tango did for him. 'And yet,' said Sir Ranalf, after they had all congratulated us, 'we still have a little way to go before our movie reaches its perfect peak!' I said I thought we had reached the pinnacle. But he laughed heartily. 'No, dear, dear chum, we have hardly begun to climb! Isn't that so, Professor Quelch?'

'Indeed. We are still, as it were, in the foothills of the ecstatic element of our film. The metaphysical element, shall we say. After all we are seeking to record the insubstantial, the indescribable!'

The English have always had a singular admiration for the insubstantial in everything but religion. Their composers and their painters, their fashionable writers, they are all so happy to substitute mysticism for experience. It is not quite the same thing as our Russian 'soul'. However, I was convinced. The scenes possessed artistic and intellectual authority. I began to feel quite proud of what everyone but myself and Esmé described as my acting.

'And, too, remember we have Dame Commerce to placate,' added Sir Ranalf, shaking his head at the crudeness of our world. I wondered if he referred to the negress. 'We must ensure that we have enough properly sentimental scenes as well as, I think, a few more "fun scenes". To give substance to our spectrum, you know. To show that no aspect of human life is left unexamined. This afternoon, Maxie, my good fellow, I want you to consider, perhaps, ripping aside your ritual apron as you advance on the helpless vampire. It will not be photographed directly, of course, but it will help with the ambience, will it not, Mr Seaman?'

Seaman nodded silently from where he sat huddled in his chair. He had achieved the best scene of his career, yet for some reason he was discontented.

I refused Sir Ranalf's suggestion. 'I have to consider my reputation,' I said. 'I am not sure the engineering world would trust a man who showed his bare bottom to the kinema public.'

They laughed at this. The public would receive only a hint! Of course, I would have a perfect right to see the rushes. I would note how subtle the shots would be.

In spite of my deep desire to continue with the film, I could not bring myself to agree. Paramount in my mind was my need to get our footage safely back to America and edit it properly. Only if it won the approval of America would it be a true success. The more intimate scenes would not appear in the United States version but their rumour would attract millions. It was also probably true that the rest of the world would not respond prudishly to such natural portraits which were almost necessary for a film's success, in France, for instance. Yet what held me back was the dilemma of my shame – or rather my father's shame – my missing foreskin, removed for hygienic reasons almost before I was sentient. Again, with good grace, I refused to accept their logic.

Sir Ranalf seemed only a trifle disappointed. 'Just as you

like, dear chappy. I take it, however, that you aren't averse to turning up for some extra shots this afternoon?'

I told him, with perfect truth, that this film meant everything to me. I would do nothing to harm it.

When Sir Ranalf took Esmé back to the Winter Palace for lunch I was rather relieved. It was difficult at present to face her in real life, our rôles had grown so intense. Profoundly disturbed and thoroughly confused, I was grateful when Professor Quelch showed some of his brother's old affection for me and suggested we try another pipe or two before work began.

'To calm you down, old boy. You want to be on your best form, don't you? And it certainly worked yesterday. What superb shots they were!'

We sat together in the cabin we shared while Quelch read to me from Browning and some more modern writers. But it was impossible to give my attention to the written word. I struggled to find a language to describe my dilemma. At last I admitted that, while I had every understanding of their logic and needs, I wanted neither Esmé nor myself to perform further nude scenes. 'It is not what we mean, it is how it will be interpreted,' I said. Quelch dismissed this. He assured me that only certain bluestockings in America would object while in Europe I would become a household name. An honoured artist! A great engineer! But I remained uncertain. There was another problem, I said; a question of my operation. He became sympathetic. He did not know I was bothered by such a thing. A scar? He did not recall a scar. The scar, I said, was secret and indelible. And then, because I had borne this lonely burden on my soul for so long, I told him how my father, a socialist, a physician and a Modern Man, had performed the barbaric surgery which was to dog me all my days and which more than once had almost cost me my life. Quelch was deeply understanding. He had heard of the operation. Children in England were given it all the time, these days. He understood it even to be fashionable amongst the lower classes. I was foolish to worry. This was not a stigma. Everyone would understand. 'Besides,' he laughed, 'your bald gentleman would go quite unnoticed in this country, don't you know!'

This was far from being any consolation! But he went on to tell me how such a thing meant nothing outside Ukraine these days, that it was quaintly old-fashioned of me to worry. Nobody would take me for something I was not. This was the time to put all such stupid thoughts and fears behind me. 'After all, my dear Peters, *fortuna favet fortibus!*'

Fortuna favet fatuis, they say also. Would that I had been the fool Fortune favoured!

That evening I came to the set in my light overcoat. I had already donned my costume so that I need not risk further awkwardness. I was a little bleary. Some of the earlier details of that evening have gone but I know we were to re-enact the scene in a 'tomb' created in a small ruined Coptic chapel on the outskirts of town, its walls freshly covered with paintings supposed to depict the life and death-journey of our mythical Queen. Esmé will be chained into the coffin in place of the mummy. It will be her fate to be sealed there forever, fulfilling her ambition to take the place of the queen she dared challenge. We will shoot alternative scenes. In one I will stab her. In the other I will reach longingly towards her lips, my body tensed as if I mean to release her. Then I will crush one kiss upon her and turn to flee down the rather ramshackle cardboard corridor representing the tunnel from the tomb. Again I am brought to an Esmé already stretched upon the slab, her legs pressed against the warm stone, her wonderful little body writhing in the most lifelike display of terror. I am proud of her. I am aroused. I have never felt such a peculiar power. I never wanted it. But it will not leave me. The beast stirs and stretches within me. There is metal in our womb. I draw back, conscious of the electric ambience. I turn to Seaman. 'I cannot,' I say.

'You must.' His voice is quiet and urgent. There seems to be fear in it. 'You must.'

I begin to shake. Sir Ranalf comes up. 'My poor dear old fellow, are you sickly?'

I cannot do the scene at all. I will never do it. He asks if I am nervous. I do not know. I am trembling. Sir Ranalf speaks more soothing words. He gives me into the professor's care. Morphine and cocaine help me get a grip on myself. Now

I feel very guilty. I have not been professional. It is completely against my self-interest to let down my potential patron.

When I return to the set, Esmé is calmer. Her eyes are closed and she pants almost in natural sleep. Distanced, she becomes another creature, a lovely animal, even more desirable. Now I am much steadier, almost gay, as I adjust my costume, let the Ethiopian put finishing touches to my make-up and advance towards the altar. All the gods of Egypt are looking down on me. As Seaman rolls the camera I stare in sudden awe at Horus and Anubis and Osiris and Isis, at Mut and Set and Thoth and the hosts of animal-headed demigods surrounding us. Beast blends with man, woman with beast. I feel the power of the beast in me. I feel that terrible power which can inhabit every one of us who invites it in but which it is our duty to control. I would have controlled it. I have controlled it since. Then Esmé begins to cry, a strange little sound, a dreaming sound, and I turn to see her face shift through a dozen expressions, almost as if a series of masks emerges, one beneath another, and her eyes open and she smiles at me. She thinks I can save her.

'Now, Maxie, now!' whispers Sir Ranalf from somewhere behind Seaman. 'You do not know whether to kill her or whether to ravage her. You are torn. The knife is in your hand! But you cannot immediately kill one whom you have loved so passionately. How to take your final revenge?'

And I press myself upon her, kissing her, fondling her, thrusting my body upon her soft, shivering flesh. Her cries are now almost guttural and they frighten me. I continue to kiss her and caress her, but slowly my inspiration again fails me. I stand up, my leg steadied against the rasping granite, and tell them that I will do no more.

'But that is not possible.'

It is the negress who speaks. A deep, vibrant voice; gorgeously sensual. 'We must have our rape, I think, or there will be no proper resolution. And the public demands resolution.'

I do not understand her. I hear Sir Ranalf in urgent conversation with her, but cannot make out the words. She is adamant. Sir Ranalf comes up to me. 'My sweet boy, this is our most important backer. It would be very foolish of any one of us to give offence to such a personage. If you could please find the inspiration from somewhere, I would be deeply obliged.'

I stand there and shake my head. Suddenly the negress advances, a pillar of swirling vividly-coloured silks and rolling black flesh, she walks with the deliberation of a colossus.

A gusty sigh escapes the creature. Her rich voice is now full of sadness. 'I had hoped to be associated with one of the century's great picture-plays. The rape will provide the catharsis. The resolution. You understand Freud?'

I say I am not prepared to pretend to rape my girl.

'We did not suggest that you pretend.' The negress's bulk moves as if to silent laughter.

'Then I will act no further.' I am barely able to focus on the creature. From her radiates an aura of extraordinary power. Her eyes refuse any disobedience. Yet I stand my ground. For my girl. For myself.

'This is deeply shame-making, dear boy,' murmurs Sir Ranalf from behind his partner. 'It is so important for us all to achieve this.'

'What you are asking, however, is too much.' My lips are dry, my words sluggish. 'Esmé and I will return to Cairo in the morning. I believe you have genuinely frightened her.' I reach backwards to clutch for her grateful fingers. 'This has all gone too far.'

' Very well,' Sir Ranalf turns away with a small shrug. 'Once your debts are cleared up and everything else sorted out, you can be on your way.'

'You can have every penny of my wages.' I am cool. 'All I want is a ticket home for Esmé and myself.' I speak clearly. My demands are exact. I refuse compromise.

'Sweet boy, I fear your back wages, generous as they were by Egyptian standards, are not enough to cover your IOUs.' Sir Ranalf's tone is one of deep regret. 'Not so?' And he turns blue, enquiring eyes upon his backer.

The negress waves a confirming hand.

I cannot read their signs.

'Professor Quelch will explain.' Sir Ranalf is curt.

'I got behind with my own bills, I fear, dear boy. My hands

are tied. *Felix qui potuit rerum cognoscere causas*, you might say. Your IOUs were my only collateral.'

Sir Ranalf clarifies Quelch's meaning. Esmé and I owe some £2,500 in back debts. Our salaries would yield perhaps £500. Accommodation costs have also been deducted, as well as local taxes, bar bills and so on. There is also a question of a dishonoured contract. 'It is very simple,' he says. 'If you wish to leave the project, merely pay your bills, reimburse us for your expenses and go.'

'But what of our film?'

'You may have what has been shot, I suppose.'

'The negative as well?'

'If you can reach agreement with Mr Seaman.' But when I look at him Seaman withdraws. I realise he has already made his own irreversible compromises.

'We should leave.' This from Esmé. I turn back to her. She moves her drugged hands in the chains. 'We must get home, Maxim. To America. It was my fault. Help me.'

I do not know whether to blame her for all this or whether to take her in my arms and comfort her. It is clear, however, that we are for the moment trapped. All I can do now is bide my time until we can escape. Tomorrow I will seek the help of the American Consul.

'We will leave,' I determined, still bleary.

'We shall keep the film, I understand, as security.' This is the negress. I cannot bear the idea of my naked Esmé becoming her property. I cannot think clearly. I stand there, trying to determine the best course of action.

'You must make a decision, Maxim. You must make a decision.' Never before have I heard such urgency in her voice.

'But the film is ours. We are its creators!'

'I am afraid that as the producer I must confirm it belongs to my company,' said Sir Ranalf. 'And our friend here, of course, is our major shareholder.'

'I own you all, I think.' A thin smile plays behind the negress's veil. 'I think so. But we need not quarrel. You will be good, I know.'

Esmé whispers to me again. She must escape. She must

329

get to Cairo. I have so many duties. I have a duty to our film. She will not respect me if I abandon it. After all, her chances of fame are also linked to it. We need only return to Hollywood and our fortunes are made. But we have no money here. I look towards Quelch. There is a suggestion of guilty triumph in his eyes and it occurs to me he could actually be chief architect of our predicament. Has he nursed some dreadful plan of vengeance since Esmé and I, the only witnesses, inadvertently stumbled upon him and the Nubian boy?

'We can compromise.' Sir Ranalf is persuasive. 'We can still be friends and comrades. After all, we have the basics of a jolly good film!'

'But he must rape the girl.' The negress speaks quietly, in a tone of threatening finality.

'Yes, yes, of course.'

I turn to test Esmé's bonds. She is chained firmly to the slab. I understand something of the trap into which we are falling, yet I can see no easy way out.

'Decide, Maxim!' She is desperate with tension. But how can I decide? After all, she betrayed me. She was nothing but a little whore I rescued from Constantinople's gutters. What did I owe her? Up to now she had already enjoyed a far superior life with me than any she might have expected. She was born a whore. Let her suffer the fate of a whore.

Within me my love for my angel, my sister, my rose burns as strong as ever. But I cannot let this inform my common sense.

'Yes. You really must make up your mind.' Sir Ranalf clearly fears the negress. 'After all, you're not exactly on the right side of the law now, are you, dears? Drugs and prostitution are both crimes in Egypt, ha, ha! The authorities would be deeply shocked to find a white man doing business in both.'

Sir Ranalf is of course describing himself but he is too well-protected to be caught, whereas Esmé and I are already on film. Quelch will doubtless turn State's evidence to convict us of our drug-using. Worse, without money we have no guarantee we would ever get out of Cairo again. Had the negress bought

330

or merely taken Quelch's IOUs? Clearly she had a firm hold over both Sir Ranalf and the professor while I had no friends here. Common sense said that Kolya had long since gone on about his business and was by now back in Algiers.

'Consider your assets.' The negress is persuasive, impatient. 'What do you own? A pretty fiancée and a young, healthy body? You also have brains and talent. But these are rather tenuous things. What can you sell me for two thousand five hundred pounds?'

'My talent, apparently.' I am growing steadily more frightened. 'And my designs. I am an engineer. There are many other things I can do.'

'Certainly. So there is no quarrel between us! If you wish to dissolve your partnership with us, that will be absolutely agreeable. If you are unhappy, you should not stay against your will. So, let us say the girl is worth two and a half thousand and call it even. She will be happy with us. That will discharge your whole debt. What do you say?'

The suggestion is loathsome. I am in their power for the moment but I retain my integrity.

From behind me Esmé still murmurs, begging me to make a decision. But it is impossible. I have no worthwhile choices. I am confused by the shocking suddenness of their threats, by the narcotics Quelch has pumped into me. It is true, I have a duty to the film, but I have a duty to my own destiny. She, after all, has already broken her trust. What does it matter if we indulge in a few moments of animal high spirits for the camera? The film will still be a great one. The world will see Gloria Cornish in my embrace. We have already found immortality. Esmé is calmer now. Her breasts rise and fall very slowly; her eyes, dark with emotion, stare mindlessly up at me.

There are no better alternatives. I can only make a decision based on the least harmful choices presented to me. Once more I know what it means to be powerless and without an embassy. I am alone. I have no rights and am forced to fall back upon my own resources. Expediency demands the only possible decision: 'Very well.' I lay a firm fist upon my hip and hold up my head with all possible dignity. 'I will play the rape scene.'

My statement is received with general applause by everyone save Quelch who stares at me from eyes darkening with a joyful intensity; as if our terrible compromise is the result of his own wicked engineering; as if he believes he rights some singular wrong performed by us upon himself. A malevolent automaton, a *Golem*, he smiles at me from the shadows. I look urgently for Seaman. He might now be my only ally, my last link with Hollywood and safety, but he has vanished. Sir Ranalf shrugs and smiles. For the time being he will direct the film himself. (I heard that Seaman left the next morning and eventually returned to Sweden, from there to Hollywood where he resumed his career.) Once I was naked Sir Ranalf expressed his delight. Circumcision, he assures me, was practised by high-born Egyptians. It was a sign of nobility. It is important to establish our authority, to have our details as authentic as possible. *Abraham, der als erster seiner eigenen Menschlichkeit ein Opfer brachte: Wo traf dein Messer deinen vertrauensvollen Sohn? Alte, geliebte, furchttreifende Sumer. Leugne den Juden, und du leugnest Vergangenheit.* There was a time when the Hebrews were feared by Egypt, and by Greece and by Rome, before they cultivated their insidious, all-destroying fatalism, a philosophy which makes a virtue out of defeat and dissipation. For this, I suppose, we must also blame Vespasian. It became *richtung-gas* . . .

I perform the rape. Thoth and Isis look down in sad disgust but the Englishman is all celebration. 'Well done, Maxie. Oh, sweet boy, well *done!*' And Esmé weeps quite silently. The tactful camera will not detect it. It seems as if she is smiling. *Bar'd shadeed.* It is cold. There is a piece of metal in my heart. I cannot get rid of it. They say we are at the beginning of a new Ice Age. Now only ice can cleanse the world. Then the fires and then the sea. After Ragnarok the world shall renew and perfect herself.

Not only Nazis accept this.

All evil dies there an endless death, while goodness riseth from that great world-fire, purified at last, to a life far higher, better, nobler than the past . . . I understand that Moslems have some similar belief in the purification of the world through battle, death and rebirth. There is an attractive singularity to such notions. I am drawn to them myself. They are not, in essence, unChristian. Some perfectly reasonable people are convinced that a nuclear holocaust is now our only hope.

Again, next day, I perform the rape scene. I achieve this by turning my terror and hatred into love. It is easier to do than I imagined. I have no time in which to consider spiritual profit and loss. Only the moment becomes important. This is not an uncommon response, I gather.

Perhaps I think of Lif and Lifthrasir hiding in Mimir's forest, sleeping in peaceful unconsciousness of the world's destruction, until the time shall come when we can take possession of a regenerated earth? What fundamental wisdoms remain in those ancient stones? What lessons are there to be learned from that land of the waiting dead and old, still vibrant power? The Sahara obscures swiftly, but what it obscures it also preserves! Here is a world of secret magic, which could be brought to life by a random breath of wind; here the worlds of the here-and-now intersect with the worlds of the spirit and the stars. Here lie hidden long-gone ambitions, immortal yearnings that were never fully stilled, great and monumental dreams; here sleeps a living culture of archetypal loves and hatreds, where death is celebrated as the best and richest of all adventures and a host of gods, goddesses and demi-gods greet and welcome one's new-fleshed soul. It is so easy to become confused between the realities and the imaginings of the ancients. They say there is a lush forest existing below the desert where the souls of the dead wait patiently for judgement. I, who am Osiris, am Yesterday and the kinsman of the Morrow . . . May your knives not impede me; may I not fall into your abattoir. For I know your names. My course upon earth is with Ra and my fair goal is with Osiris. Let not my offerings be in your disfavour upon your altars. I am one who follows the Master. I fly like a Hawk. I cackle like the Goose. I move eternally as Nehebkau. O Sovereign of All Gods, deliver me from that god who liveth upon the damned, whose face is that of a hound, but whose skin is that of a man, devouring shades, digesting human hearts and voiding ordure. One seeth him not. Deliver me from that god who seizeth upon souls, who consumes all filth and corruption in the darkness or in the light. All those who fear him are powerless. This god is Set, who is also Sekhet, the goddess. Sekhet is called 'the Eye of Ra' and is the instrument of mankind's destruction. Deliver me from that god that is both male and female. May I not fall under their knives, may I not sit within their dungeons, may I not come to their places of extermination, may there be done to me none of those things which the gods abominate. It was what Quelch gave me before he abandoned us, that *Book of the Dead*. 'It might prove useful to you,' he had said.

There is more work for me, says Sir Ranalf. I am a star, he says. I am a genius. I am a natural. Who would have suspected such talent? Al-Habashiya, the negress, has instructed him to convey her approval. I know how and why I must earn more. I become weak. I think they are feeding me native food. I cannot hold it in. I continue to perform the rape scene. I rape her anus. I rape her mouth. I have no choice. If I am to rescue her and myself then I can only comply with their demands until the moment comes when we can both escape.

She does not understand.

She thinks I have betrayed her.

TWENTY

MY SHIP is called *The Ship of Death* and she cannot fly. She drifts upon an infinite river of black mercury, beneath high shadowed arches as in some vast Stamboul cistern. She is crewed by the damned, steered by a blind man, captained by the *Turnface*. I perform the rituals of the dead. I perform the rituals of submission and remorse. By careful repetition I shall make my way through to that better world where every earthly dream is perpetually fulfilled.

I journey to the place where souls are weighed, where benevolent Anubis weighs our sins, the jackal weighs our sins. The dead have no choices.

I had no choices. They took us to where the darkness was. The darkness had a thick, vital quality, a great, slow intelligence at once malevolent and amused, at once agonised and triumphant; a sublime intelligence gone quite mad with grief and loss; as though it were, in the entire universe, the last of its species, grown selfish and utterly alone, without mercy or concern for any other living thing.

Here was Death personified. Here was pure Evil. Its name was Satan. Its name was Set. A nihilistic essence, it was at its most seductive in the person of its female avatar, the lioness-goddess Sekhmet, the Destroyer. They put a headdress on my little girl, some *rosbif*'s moth-eaten trophy, a snarling civet, and they called her Sekhmet, the evil one, whom I must vanquish with my magic, my manhood, for they made me a god. First I was Horus, the Hawk, son of Osiris, brother to Anubis the weigher of souls. Then every day I was resurrected as a new god. Every day my girl was freshly vanquished. It was our art, perhaps, but only the night world would ever applaud it. I knew about these films. Most of the time our directors, so long as we obeyed them in all other ways, let us wear our masks. They were contemptuously knowing; they understood that every day the concessions grew fewer and we were descending deeper into their world, became more thoroughly their creatures. I schemed to steal the films. Next they began to ration everything, our food, our drugs. We became disorientated and light-headed. There were naphtha flares fluttering amongst the electrics, the powerful scent of jasmine and roses, long black figures crawling between the columns, a stink of cheap tobacco and sweat. I wished them lingering deaths but we could not eat without their goodwill, we could not sustain ourselves. We could not live. They made us smile for them.

The negress was treated with increasing respect by everyone and it was soon clear that it was she to whom they all, even Sir Ranalf, deferred. She was always a faintly stirring presence in the darkness. Was she perhaps the darkness itself? Its human form? She stank of everything I most feared. With great respect they called her al-Habashiya, but I did not know what it meant. I would be taught only one name for her. The only name I would ever be permitted to utter. But that would come later. For many weeks I performed the rape scene. I became very weary and could not stop weeping. Eventually they took pity on me and let me rest while some of the crew did my work for me. But al-Habashiya insisted I remain present in the scene. 'It will make for better continuity.' Sir Ranalf's eyes now stared all the time from red sockets and he had taken to wearing Seaman's old wardrobe, most of which fitted very badly.

Occasionally I saw Quelch but he no longer looked at me. He did not seem satisfied with recent events and he had a haunted appearance as if he, too, longed to escape. Once, I recall, al-Habashiya offered to have him whipped and left naked outside the local barracks, a punishment normally reserved for blacks. *Min darab el-walad es-saghir? Wahid Rumi nizil min el-Quads. Er-ragil misikni min idu. Fahimtush entu kelami? Ana kayebt gawab* . . .

My ship is called *The Sun*, the source of all life. My ship is *Ra*, light of the day, brother to the moon. Gold married to silver in that forbidden crucible. My ship is called *The Unknown World*. Two lions guard her – one is called *Yesterday* and the other *Today*. The lioness is their mother, Sekhmet, Mother of Time, fierce Hater of Life. Her chariot is a fiery disc. She flies swiftly above the Nile, destroying all she detects. They say on the radio that Haydn was always jealous of Beethoven. I understand this. So many were jealous of my own genius.

I would not become a *Musselman*. *Wer Jude ist, bestimme ich. Mein Kampf* makes me sick. I could never read it. Yet Adolf Hitler was a brilliant man. He inscribed a copy to Clara Bow, hoping she enjoyed reading it as much as he enjoyed writing it. Poor Clara went mad, I heard, on some remote ranch, with a cowboy. I think *Mein Kampf* contained a truth I dared not face. Facing that truth drove Hitler mad. I did not wish to suffer the same fate. Let sleeping dogs lie, I said. Perhaps I was young. How could I blame myself? Such guilt is useless. It has no purpose. I, after all, was the one betrayed. *Eindee haadha – ma eindee shee – haadha dharooree li-amalee* . . . *Wayn shantati – wayn shantati – wayn shantati* . . . They would tell me so little, even when I begged. I asked for my luggage, my plans, my books, my personal goods. They said my things were still in Luxor. They had been put in Sir Ranalf's care at the Winter Palace. I dared not mention my only valuables, Yermeloff's black and silver Georgian pistols, symbols of my Cossack heritage. I prayed they would not find them where I had hidden them in the Gladstone's bottom, beneath work materials, notes and designs, *mayn teatrumsketches*, and the details of my Desert Liner! They were, I will admit, by then becoming decreasingly important in my mind for they all existed in the world of the living. Esmé and I now inhabited the world of the dead; ordered to mime the functions of life to earn our sleep, our food, the very drugs enabling us still to perform the rape scene. The drugs relieved some of the

337

pain. It was clear we would never earn enough to pay back our debts. Though I could easily wean myself of any craving, I knew it would be impossible for her. Therefore I saw no point in refusing what was offered until such time as escape was possible. So we became the lady and the butler, the newly-weds, the slave-market, the office couple. We played many parts but with a certain sameness of plot. The more elaborate Sir Ranalf's demands upon us, the closer did al-Habashiya move her couch from the shadows to the set. Every day she watched us with mounting interest. She was a fleshy heavy darkness with burning eyes, gasping weightily, smacking red lips, until soon she was almost within the scene herself, exuding a sense of greedy urgency, then she would fall back and something would be purred in Arabic. Sir Ranalf would suggest a different angle.

They said they needed new backgrounds where we were less likely to be interrupted. They took us to a ruined Coptic chapel in the remote Western Desert. In the shelter of a wind-smoothed crenellated wall, al-Habashiya had pitched her gorgeous tent with all the proud display of a wealthy *Bedawi*.

The chapel was unknown to archaeologists, Sir Ranalf assured us, because it did not serve a camel route.

There was however a well where two etiolated palm trees stretched high into the arching clarity of the sky. In the distance the desert was broken by a ridge of muddy slate. We sat silently together, Esmé and I, while al-Habashiya shared a glass of sherbet with Quelch and Sir Ranalf. They stretched on couches arranged to enjoy the sunset better. We sat at their feet on the carpeted sand. 'In Bi'r Tefawi,' murmured al-Habashiya, 'I have a villa and a garden. It is more peaceful there. I live in seclusion these days, though once, Professor Quelch, as you know, I ruled Cairo – or at least the Wasa'a and its environs. But then they arrested me.' She drew lusciously upon her *hukah*. 'I was put, eventually, into jail. It was not unpleasant. I was lucky enough to have friends there. But Russell Pasha himself had made up his mind to set an example. I was arrested again. They tried to confiscate my business interests. Russell Pasha was not then prepared to come to any sort of agreement, so I was forced to die in prison. I had no trouble arranging it. But I am used to a city. Exiled to the provinces one grows easily bored. It is very hard to kill so many hours.'

In the first months of my captivity this was one of the longest speeches al-Habashiya was ever to make in my presence.

I recalled Quelch's stories of a creature who had sat unmoving all day on a bench in the Shari Abd-el-Khaliq, yet had controlled rigidly every aspect of Cairo's vice. I remembered too that he was a transvestite negro of enormous size, who always dressed as a woman and veiled himself in white and would stretch jewelled fingers to be kissed by some passing servitor. Every Arab of the quarter was owned in some way by that grotesque. A silent, ebony idol, Quelch had said, more powerful than the king himself. Cairo's most successful brothel-keeper, pimp, drug-dealer and white-slaver, a major partner behind half the 'theatrical booking agencies' in the East. And yet beautiful, Quelch told me. Once he had seen the negro's face. Everyone who knew him agreed he was, despite his bulk, the loveliest transvestite they had ever seen.

For us all, however, al-Habashiya, if it were the same creature, remained veiled, mysteriously feminine. Those were the early days of our serfdom, when it seemed we must soon be released. They never raised their voices. They always spoke humorously. They merely offered us choices. Certain choices were good ones and we were praised for making them. Certain choices were bad and we were punished.

The injustice of this did not outrage me for long. I came to understand that I had entered a dream-time I must endure until I could wake and return to the reality and security I had known before. It was my only alternative to death. I came to appreciate Goethe's notions of joyful revelation through pain, hardship and humiliation. I am, moreover, not of a suicidal disposition. Indeed, I am by nature an optimist. Is this Jewish?

The Future is Order, Security, Strength. On this we all agreed. But the Future is Beauty, Tolerance, Liberty, also, I said. Those will come later, they told me. That was when I lost my faith in the Nazis.

I was 'too much of an idealist'. They still say so. Mrs Cornelius tried to convince me of this, on the Berlin tram, shortly before my arrest. She sent me clotted cream from Cornwall. By then I was on the Isle of Man. When I received it it was rancid. After that the rationing got worse. I was back in London in time for the Blitz. 'They didn't wan'cha ter miss nuffink, Ivan,' yelled Mrs Cornelius on that first weekend together as we huddled outside a crowded makeshift air-raid shelter while the world turned to howling, heaving red and black and from above and all sides of us came the drone of engines, the banging of guns. Britain had expected to lose, you see, like Poland or Czechoslovakia or France. She had prepared London for siege, not for victory. They say Churchill was the last to accept that we survived the Battle of Britain. Even he was infected by that new, corrosive defeatism which comes from only one insidious source!

Even in those days Mrs Cornelius was coughing badly. Her cough was almost terrifying when I first heard it. It brought back the sound of my mother's coughing, her retching and heaving over the washstand, as I waited patiently for Mrs Cornelius to come out of her bathroom. The rhythm and volume of their coughing fits was identical.

There are some memories which accompany such associations – bad ones, which I will not allow to emerge, because to dwell on them is pointless – and sweet ones, of summer gardens and happy outings, of the flowery fields around Kiev, the distinctive lavender scent of my mother's best coat; the gorges, the woods, the old yellow streets and sturdy timber houses under gentle trees, of the busy Kreshchatik Boulevard with its scintillating store displays, its window-boxes and decorative baskets, the rich smell of the cafés and the chandlers' shops; all the nooks and crannies of a true city, long in the building, making little shadowy places, safe places, caves and hollows and enclosures and sharp corners and mysteries in every sidestreet, grown naturally over centuries like a vast, wonderful shrub, thoroughly-rooted and profoundly implanted with the pattern of the past, for the memory of Kiev is the memory of the Slavic people, those warriors of the Eastern marches, the bastion of Christ against the ferocious and envying Mongol. This is why we understand so well what is happening today. Yet still you refuse to listen. You think you have a kind of

340

peace? A pact with Carthage? Believe me, you have the Slav to thank for that. When he falls, as he must eventually fall, unless Christ sends a miracle, then it is an end to the old world. I would not wish to live in the mongrel, unruly new. Has Chaos already conquered? My ship is called *Novaya Kieva, Novaya Mira*, SHE IS THE *Tsargrad*, THE CITADEL OF OUR RACE AND OUR FAITH! They tried to make me a Jew, a *Musselman*, their dog, but I deceived them. I was only acting. I performed the rape scene.

They took us step by step into the Land of the Dead. We licked our lips; then we rolled our eyes; then we grinned at the camera; and then we did everything again. As *Sin of the Sheikh* reached artistic unity the noble gods of Egypt, in crude replica, peered in alien distaste from alcoves once honouring saints. Step by step they coaxed and threatened us into the Land of the Dead, where in grotesque pantomime of the living, we endlessly performed our rape scene, where al-Habashiya, Queen of the Damned, would laugh and clap as a proud parent applauds her children. And one day she makes us come to her in her perfumed inner pavilion where eunuchs and hermaphrodites wait on all her needs. *Would you now become a Musselman?* No, I would not become a *Musselman*. *Then you must be a Jew. Sweet little darling Jew-puppy. Soft little Yiddy-widdy dinkums*. This was how He rationalised His rape of me. That tide of black fat was never still, it flowed over me, it threatened to suffocate me, and yet there was a terrible hardness in it, as if at some point the tension would burst to reveal razor-sharp steel gashing through bloody flesh, the spring of its overwound energy, to destroy me. To cut me into nameless strips of meat. That fat black tide dragged me into a darkness worse than any pain. *Little greasy Jewboy whore, momma's darling, sweet darling arse. Obedient little cocksucking Jewboy filth garbage muck fuck English Jewboy whore bitch*. She said was I a Moslem or a Jew? I said, a Christian. No, she said, a Moslem or a Jew? She told me what a Moslem must eat. She told me what a Jew could eat. A Jew, I said. I will be a Jew. There was a piece of metal in my womb.

They say the icecaps are heating up because of our industry.

What an irony should Stephenson's engine prove the direct linear cause of Alexandria drowning forever beneath the Mediterranean! The science of our Enlightenment drowning all that was ever of value to us. Is this any destiny I should be party to? Нет, нет, нет, я делаю. لا . . . كذ. How much more must I answer 'guilty'? I am guilty of nothing. Unless I am guilty of wanting to improve the world! This is a crime?

They were offered my new Jerusalem, my new Rome, my new Byzantium, my flying cities of silver filigreed with gold, my glorious towers, my Eden, my independence of thought and movement, the ultimate democracies. But what did they settle for? Harold Wilson, Lyndon Johnson, Ho Chi Minh and the Beatles!

Yet in spite of every vicissitude I refuse to forget my true destiny. If I am the light and inspiration of Europe, I am also the secret protector of our civilisation, the scribe of our victories and our honour. I am Thoth. I am Anubis, recorder and guide in these days of our dying. Jane Austen does not impress me since she agreed to the rôle of a slut in that film called after some Dutchman's surname. I saw it again last week. As Cleopatra she could have ruled my heart forever. But I am a stupid, chivalrous old Slav of a forgotten era. Anything I say is misinterpreted by that filthy-minded scum. I merely held her, after all, as I explained. I said nothing bad. My intentions were perfectly loving. *Ach, Esmé, mein liebschen, mayn naches!* What could I do to harm you? I was your brother, your father, your husband, your lover, even your mother! I was all these things. I cared for you when you were sick. Only I was all these things. Why would God take you from me? I still blame myself a little for that, but ironically this is not the guilt they would have me bear. They would rather blame me for the genocide! For all those millions of Slavs and Gypsies and Celts and Jews? I think not. If they had listened to me I could have saved every single soul of them.

But they traded with the Bolsheviks, they placated them, they made a friend of Uncle Joe. What did they expect next? That a mad dog should suddenly become a loyal old pal? That you could sleep beside him and not be amazed if your throat was not torn out by morning? I would have brought Light and

Peace to our starving darkness. Hitler would have ruled a world of simple decency and benign opportunity, where natural selection would ultimately produce a perfect citizen living in a city worthy of the Nazi dream. But their Final Solution weakened their authority in many eyes. I am the first to admit it. I have seen Alexander's body in its secret tomb. God showed me where it was hidden. God said Alexander belonged to Him now. That mighty Greek, the great evangelist for Christ, came to Egypt and established the first truly civilised city, which became the greatest in the world. The Greeks took the best from Egypt and Assyria, discarding the cruel barbaric decadence of those first noble Semites whom heartless ambition brought low. It is the fate of the Jew to fall victim to his own marvellous invention. Some call that city the birthplace of our Church, where St Mark converted the first Jew to Christianity in AD 45. *Volvitur vota*, as Quelch might have said.

I begged the Englishman to get a message to Goldfish. He said it was more than his life was worth. He gave me a dark red volume, a *Book of the Dead*. I was bitter. I said he had sold me into slavery. He avoided the accusation. 'You people must be used to that sort of thing by now,' he said. It was a meaningless remark. He pointed to the low hills. 'There's a railway line about a day's walk that way. You could almost certainly reach it if you went on your own.' Of course, he knew I would not leave Esmé, that she was still my responsibility. He was taunting me, he was delighting in my downfall. That evening I was whipped. I said I was a Jew. And Esmé was a whore, my sister, my rose. There was metal in my womb. I called an androgynous nigger musselman my mother and I asked it to forgive me. I told my mother that Esmé was a whore, a bad girl. It was one of the games she made us play. Anyway, what would you do if offered a choice between humiliating death and humiliating life? Life or death? Which would you choose? Some in those camps chose death. They wanted it to be over. But that is not my nature. I am more of an optimist. You betrayed me, Esmé. You gave away our child. You sold our little girl. Did you care that you hurt me? *When kunte, Esmé? When kunte? Muta-assef jiddan. Bar'd shadeed.* That false place of death. What did it matter if I admitted my sins? It was all false; nothing

343

was as it had seemed. Quelch's pronouncements on Egypt were proven. The world was false, a second-rate fantasy, a faded dream. Dust lay everywhere. We had arrived at dust. Yet the blood in our bodies still circulated. The limbs of our bodies still performed. Al-Habashiya still applauded and praised us and made me lay my head on his thigh while he fondled Esmé and played ecstatic Cairene hymns on his ornate gramophone. He promised he would find some Mozart for us. It was the same in Sachsenhausen. Mozart was supposed to make up for everything. I wore a black triangle, then. I was an engineer, I said. It was a concession, we said. Al-Habashiya stroked my head and cooed. *Vögel füllen mayn Brust. Vögel picken innen singen für die Freiheit. Mein Imperium, eine Seele. Vögel sterben in mir. Einer nach dem anderen. Mayn gutten yung yusen.* He stroked my head and called me his good little orphan, his sweet little Jewboy. It was better to obey than to endure that prolonged pain or agonising death. Esmé understood this better than I. It is how she too survived.

All those human bodies ploughed like bloody chaff into the furrows of barren fields. Was Esmé among them? I have a boy, she said. He's a soldier. Did they ever understand what they took? Soulless themselves, they did not even recognise what they had stolen. They threw it away. They ploughed it under. But Russians know the truth. Every inch of Russian soil is nurtured by the souls of martyred millions who, down the centuries, defended their homeland. I spoke of this to Dr Jay in the hospital after they had examined my head. What makes the Jews so special, I asked. He agreed with me. He said he could find nothing physically wrong with me. Four days later I was free on the streets of Streatham. But I could no longer fly.

Kites rise from the mountains, from the *Totenbergen*, and red dust clogs my throat. You must get away from here, Maxim, she said. The people here are not *sympatica*. I think Brodmann had come to Luxor. I think I had seen him standing below the great clock in the railway station. He said he was English and that his name was Penny, but I guessed it was Brodmann. I was obsessed with Kolya. I was still looking for him. Al-Habashiya gave me some pyjamas. 'Some stripes for you,' she said. They were black and white. I saw Brodmann in Sachsenhausen. I recognised him and shouted at him. He answered with a hesitantly raised hand. What a superb actor that monster was! *Binit an-san!* But should I blame him? This century demands we join in a charade; it decrees the parts we play. It is only acting, I tell her. It is not really us. The pyjamas make my eyes shudder. The stripes stretch before me, merge and swirl and break open, like fragments of some vast psychic map.

I would not become a *Musselman. Negra y blanco, noire et blanc.* I lost you in the desert, Esmé. What brute makes use of you? Mrs Cornelius says she doubtless landed on her feet. 'She was lucky enough for a while, Ivan. She never 'ad no talent. Still, neiver did I, reelly.'

She was a great actress, I told her. 'Your talent is recorded for posterity.' This amused her. 'Wot? In an ol' can in a closed-down fleapit somewhere artside Darjeeling? Come orf it, Ive! Not exac'ly wot *I* corl immortality. I'll take me chances in 'eaven, rahver.' She was too tactful to mention our Egyptian adventure.

My friend pretended to a kind of primitive pantheism, but she was a Christian at heart. In 1969, moved no doubt by a profound piety she did her best to hide, she took up a position as caretaker in St Andrews, round the corner. But she found that cleaning on a Monday got her down. 'Pews! Ya c'n tell why they was corled *pews*, orl right. Some o' them worshippers must never wipe their arses!'

What do they do to me with their instruments? Those spikes! Those pyramids! My stripes! That golden ship comes to me out of a sky the colour of blue silver. Tomorrow the hawk will fly, I tell her. Oh, this filthy tide flows over me. There is a black sun warming me. Deprived of sleep, I dream most of the time. I dream of a future. They would murder you, Rosie. You are too intelligent for them. Mr Mix always insisted you were too good even for me. But I was better than Franco, you said, though he never took up much of your time. It was the same, you said, with Mussolini. As for Hitler, you kept silent. It was your ambition to sleep with every dictator in Europe, but you were not sure if you had fucked Stalin or just an understudy.

'They are always so busy with details.' You were fascinated with their power. You studied it as others study volcanos, moving further and further towards the rim until directly confronting the destructive heart. You slept with Franco by mistake. At that time he was only a colonel in an obscure garrison. We flew together, Rosie.

I performed the rape scene. I was tired, I said. I needed more cocaine. It was not good for me, she said. Separate the Jewboy's legs. And she would descend, like a warm blanket of flesh, to enfold my body. Only later would there be much pain and the terrible smells. I recall her schoolgirl giggling at my antics to get free. There! You are not tired at all, she said.

Sekhet comes with a knife in her hand for she is the Eye of Ra and her task is to destroy mankind. You betrayed me, Esmé. You gave away my little girl. I lost something in that *shtetl*. I am still not sure what it was. *Bedauernswerte arme Teufel, diese Jude. Ich fing an zu frösteln. Meine Selbstkontrolle liess nach. Ich brachte Kokain. Ich kämpfe unter uberhaupt keiner Fahne! Ich stehe für mich allein ein.* I had a similar experience in Prague. Who wants such charity? *Höher und höher stieg ich uber der Schlucht, bis ich ganz Kiew unter mir sehen könnte, dahinter den Dnjepr, der sich der Steppe entgegenwand und auf seinem Weg zum Ocean den Saporoschijischen Fällen entgegenströmte. Ich könnte Wälder, Dörfer und Berge sehen. Und als ich wieder nach unten sank, sah ich Esmé, rot und weiss, die mich . . .* I flew, Esmé. Above the Babi Gorge. I loved you. You were my daughter, my friend, my wife. You were my childhood and my hope.

I performed the rape scene. He showed me how to make her scream so that on film it would look as if she were beside herself with passion, whereupon I was subjected to the same infamies while a second reel was shot. They were things a man should never suffer. He made me both a Jew and a woman. Whenever I could I reminded myself, through all the torment and the abuse, that I was neither. I was a true Cossack, a Lord of the Earth. I was Kiev. I was the sound of cavalry through the Podol. I was power, I had ultimate control over my own destiny. I was a scientist, an engineer. I could control the world and I could set the world free! I am a Jew, I said. Yes, I am

Jewboy scum, but though my lips sounded the word my heart said 'Cossack', my soul said 'Engineer'.

There was humour in those places, even between tormented and tormentor. We all shared amusement at our antics to stay alive. We connived at those appalling experiments in human cruelty not because we were any of us evil but because it was the only diversion available to us. To relieve our fear we told one another jokes about our own imminent deaths and dismemberment. We participated in horror for its own sake. But I do not believe many of us were to blame. Our needs had not been for death, but for hope and for life. We gave power to men who had unequivocally promised us those things. If we wondered at their promises we did not challenge them with any great passion or suspicion. We had offered up in trust to them everything we valued, everything that was good. They were not simply collecting second-hand clothes. They wanted everything we possessed so that they could prove it was worthless. They were so greedy, those few. Yet great empires do not grow through greed, I said. They grow through need, gradually and through historical necessity. Those who would forge an empire in a few years are always thwarted. They always die, dishonoured by their own nations. Great empires do not flourish on war but on industry, trade and curiosity. Enlightenment follows such empires. Whatever inequalities they exploit, eventually they develop the idea of equality, of institutional democracy. Captain Quelch was that kind of old-fashioned imperialist. We met again on the Isle of Man, in 1940. He had suffered a great deal and had changed his name. His first words to me were 'Hello, old man. How's your sex-life?' He had roared and embraced me, his face glowing with pleasure. I thought Seryozha was there, too, but sometimes I get the camps mixed up.

My main complaint against the Jews was their vulgarity. Ironically this loud, garish, uncontrollable, expansive race when brought to heel, and those wild, restless brains restrained, becomes even more overheated. In the frustration of their restrictions they become completely mad. This explains the outpourings of Marx and Freud, for instance. If left alone, I told Hitler, they merely quarrel amongst themselves and offer

347

no threat to anyone. To me isolation seemed the best strategy. Hitler called me a Jew-lover. I thought he was joking. Two days afterwards I was discreetly arrested. Goering himself admitted it was a mistake. Later my engineering expertise, my natural wits and a certain amount of good fortune, earned me my freedom. We did not *all* die in those camps!

I have known passion and joy, the love of men and women. I have known success and I have seen a good deal of the world. I have known them all again, since 1926. So was my choice not the best possible choice? I am alive, *nicht wahr?*

My master said the English called her a pervert, did I know the word? I did. Was a pervert, she asked, worse than a Jew? No, Master, I said, a Jew is worse than a pervert. Was a Jew worse than a nigger? Yes, Master, a Jew is worse than a nigger. This was one of our jokes. And what are you, she said. I am worse than a Jew, I said. No matter, she played with my ears, I still love you. Then we would laugh together. Call me momma, al-Habashiya would say, reaching for one of her instruments, call me momma, dirty little Jewboy sweetheart. *Momma! Momma!* I was a Jew and Esmé was a whore. She still belongs to you, al-Habashiya was smiling. She is still yours. I hope so, I said. Oh, yes, she is still yours. Why, if you wanted to you could trade her with the *Bedawi* and become very rich. You could do it whenever you wished. Esmé smiled at her. We both smiled. We all smiled. She was my sister, my rose; but her innocence was gone. O, Esmé, how I wish you had not betrayed me. I did everything for you. I would have travelled wherever you desired. I would have made you my Queen. But perhaps you are no more to blame than I. We all have our moments of weakness. It did not change my love for you. I had no choice. I thought I would free us both. My Master says she must be worth, well, at least your drugs bill. You could sell her to me. I could pay your bill for you. Then we would be square on the matter. My Master's beautiful lips are encouraging. Perhaps I could get to the police in Luxor? I do not care what happens to us so long as we get free of al-Habashiya. I do the best I can for us both. I agree to sell her to al-Habashiya. She now belongs to you, I say. I watch while she puts the sign of life on her inner thigh, branding the scarab on her. They all have it, if they are mine, she says.

I have discharged my debt. Now let me go to Cairo.

No, she says, we are going to Aswan. I have a large house and a beautiful garden. I am a respectable Egyptian dowager. Everyone knows me. If you are well-behaved, perhaps I will tell them you are my adopted son.

I am free of the debt. Let me go! Please, Master, let me go. But you are not yet out of debt, she says. You remain my property until you pay off your living expenses, your ongoing supplies of drugs, et cetera. I am, I think, generous in these matters of unpaid bills, at least while you remain in my charge.

I had not thought it possible for my despair to increase. We took the boat up to Aswan. Sir Ranalf was aboard but Quelch was no longer with us. Sir Ranalf was greatly irritated by this, doubtless missing civilised company since he and I were no longer allowed to communicate except when the camera was running. We spent the voyage, the three of us, in the viewing-room and watched while, over and over again, I performed the rape scene. The next night there was just myself and al-Habashiya. At length I dared ask where Esmé was. Al-Habashiya was casual. She had been 'sold on', she said. She would doubtless fetch a handsome profit for someone in the Far East trade. Then my Master used me in my mouth while in black and white the rape scene flickered over us like the bleak lights of Hell.

I have never forgotten how cold and grey it was on the Isle of Man. I think there can be few camps as gloomy.

When I met Captain Quelch again he was a frail man, bent by scoliosis, but he retained his sense of humour. It was Quelch who told me of his younger brother's fate and mentioned that he was sure he had seen Esmé on one of his runs along the coast near Shanghai. He was interned because he had been captured aboard a Japanese destroyer. There had scarcely been, he told me, any point in getting on the wrong side of them. 'What the Japs do to the Chinks is no concern of mine. I don't think the chaps in Whitehall believe I'm a traitor. Yes, I saw that little girl of yours – I would swear it was her, though the hair was a bit brighter and the make-up a bit thicker, and I think she recognised me. Anyway, it was in a bar in Macao, just before Pearl Harbor. Esmé wasn't her name. She had some sort of nickname, I think. Coasters often get called by a nickname. Everyone seems to prefer it.'

When I asked he told me a coaster was a girl who lived by her wits up and down the West China coast. She had not, he assured me, seemed to be doing that badly. 'She was showing a few signs of wear and tear, you know.' But I will never be sure it was Esmé. Which Esmé had he seen? It was pleasant to think, however, that no great harm was done.

The high walls of the house near B'ir Tefawi, some miles from Aswan, were heavily but discreetly guarded. The gardens were beautiful, watered by a special system all the way from the oasis and shaded just enough so that the sun did not destroy them. As in most Arab gardens of this quality there were tiled fountains, though al-Habashiya had a preference, she said, for English flowers. There were poppies and roses, geraniums and hibiscus, most of them maintained by expensive fertilisers. The walls were white, trimmed in royal blue. Through the great part of the day I remained in the deepest chambers. Here I discovered I was not the only foreigner in al-Habashiya's collection. They were all, however, male, female or neuter, completely addicted to morphine. I pitied them, knowing I could never succumb to a narcotic as they had. It is not in my metabolism. I must admit I found most of them despicable, even when I discovered how the younger ones had all been blinded or had been subjected to disgusting surgery. This increased my alarm and I determined to escape at my first opportunity, even though I was now beyond the edge of any kind of civilisation. Indeed, all my fellow-prisoners were quick to tell me how I was beyond any form of salvation. Most of the horizon seen from the roof of the house was Nubia.

My Master found it amusing, during those first days, to have me coupled with every other creature in his collection. It was, he said, the best way of getting to know people. Sir Ranalf sometimes came and went. I think he was organising the distribution of various commodities, including the films and still photographs. I prayed they would not use our footage with Mrs Cornelius. (I learned later that this had gone with

Quelch who, typically, stole the only commercially worthless reels! Al-Habashiya asked me if I didn't find it a capital joke and we laughed.)

My Master had a whim one day to play the gramophone again. He asked me if I were an aficionado of music. He adored Beethoven but he had particular fondness he said for the English moderns. Did I like Elgar? I had not heard of him. Now I am familiar with them all. I cannot bear them, perhaps because of the associations. Holst, Delius, Williams, Britten and the rest are all the same. Sentimental mystic bum-boys producing formless rubbish worse even than the French! Make no mistake, I give the same time to Ravel and Debussy. Tchaikovsky was the last great composer. All the rest is nonsense. I wish I could find a copy of *Song of the Nile*. I advertised for it in the *Gazette* but the only answers I had were from 'fans' full of nostalgia for a non-existent past.

One cold night I am taken to the large courtyard and the building called The Temple. It is decorated in some bastard, chiefly Ptolemaic, style and dedicated to the lioness and the crocodile, the female and male forms of Set. There is an altar shaped like a couch, covered in fabric whose dark designs seem to my untrained eye more alchemical than Egyptian (perhaps the vestments of some Masonic Lodge) and behind this a great, tall throne surmounted by the head of a serpent, which is another form of Set. Thick candles cast fitful light, their tallow impaled upon ornate iron sticks and the thick yellow wax dripping heavily, as if stalagmites form in a cave. Before the altar fumes a red-hot brazier in which is placed a single iron. Al-Habashiya enters and sits carefully down in the throne, arranging fastidious silks as always, but now upon my Master's head is the crown of Upper and Lower Egypt, the wig and false beard of the Pharaoh, and al-Habashiya's beauty is extraordinarily enhanced, grown vastly alien like the strangest of Akhenaton's breed, the flesh beneath the silks wrapped in white gauze through which the dark brown fat rolls and ripples as if composed of a thousand other bodies, all struggling to be free. I have been fasted and I am glad of it, for I want to vomit. My terror has come back at the moment I thought I had learned to exist beyond it, separate from it, obedient enough to keep

351

the worst pain at bay. I had not expected the agony to increase.

When the iron was put to my shoulder, the mark of the scarab, it was of little consequence. I was already contemplating an even more terrifying future. Today you can hardly see it. People think it is a birthmark, a tattoo, a scar. I tell them it is something I got at sea.

'From this time on,' says the hermaphrodite, 'you will address me as God. Do you understand me?' Al-Habashiya uses the English word.

'Yes, God,' I reply. Acquiescence is the only defence against inevitable horror. I did not think it blasphemy. In those days I had a more secular bent. In the camps, too, one had to lose such refinements.

God says He is pleased with me. He says I am thoroughly submissive and obedient. It is, He says, the Jew's natural state. Surely I now feel that certainty of truth, deep in my soul, that resonance telling me I am fulfilling my properly ordained rôle in life. Yes, God, I am dutiful. I am fulfilled. I do not know if this is true or not. Sekhet is called the Eye of Ra, the Destroyer of Men. A pitiless lioness, she has no mercy. Her cold claws reach into your breast and clutch your heart. She says she is Set. She manifests herself as Set and becomes a male crocodile. That night we explore new depths of fear and humiliation and the snapping fangs seemed to draw back in a great grin but the darkness, though it grows very strong, is now familiar to me. I am almost part of it. Two are injured, a girl and a boy. God explains that He is the only healer and today He chooses to let them die. They are left in the garden to die. They are there for days. The flies become a nuisance.

God takes me to the garden where, on green lawns, little daisies and wild flowers blossom, a summer meadow where the eunuchs and the hermaphrodites and the blind girls and boys play. 'What kind of religion dismisses the natural world in all her beauty and variety to praise an invisible world which it claims to be better than this?' God has developed a habit of discoursing on comparative religions and on occasion His tone becomes somewhat hectoring, defending the Moslem faith while ascribing to Himself a pagan divinity. 'What could be better than the world I have created here?' He adds. He is massive in green and blue silks, a monstrous scarlet turban. 'What is more like paradise than a tranquil English country garden in the glory of summer? What better can one do for oneself than provide some little sanctuary like this. Lie back for a moment against those roses.' And while my back grows bloody from the thorns He uses me casually amongst His flowers, crushing me down amongst the nasturtiums, lilies and sunflowers – red, blue and yellow – green and blazing orange in the poppies – while the tranquil water plays – while the eunuchs and hermaphrodites whisper like the last of the summer's wheat and the blind boys and girls smile into a blank future. And yet because there is hope in all beauty I remember that perfume, I recall those crushed leaves with all the pleasure of childhood nostalgia, the broken stems and scattered petals spreading across the tiles like wedding confetti (and our audience the ululating guests) while the damp, red earth, the old, almost lifeless earth, sustained only by Man's constant nurturing, that dank mould clings to our bodies and enters our mouths as it entered the mouths of thousands before us, and clings to our flesh as it clung to the flesh of the dead, so many dead. And my body is bent over shrubbery of subtle greens and pinks and dark yellows, of white flowers with little scatterings of brown-red and myriad shades and shapes of green against the blue of a cloudless African sky. And you would condemn me if now I understand no other reality? What else can I know? I am the property of a god in some forgotten corner of Paradise where only He determines what should be called pleasure and what should count as pain, on what deserves to exist and what should be wiped out. I tell Him I am in anguish. He tells me I am not. I have no choice but to accept this and eventually grow as mad as God. I become a complement to God's utterly lonely pursuits as bleakly He vanquishes boredom sometimes for hours, sometimes only for minutes when my pleasure or my pain is at its most intense. I can no longer distinguish these things, for my mind has left my body. I begin to suspect that God, too, feels little contact with His gigantic bulk and knows we are joined in a pact not to curb this condition but rather to maintain it. He hates His own flesh. This condition becomes our principal addiction, our mutual escape, and I begin to forget entirely the cause of my pain or my desire to escape. We grow together. My only reason for God's permitting me to exist is that I am inventive in finding ways to relieve God's *ennui*. There is a state of terror so absolute that it becomes an unconscious way of life. One exists in that state just as one might exist in a hostile geographical environment, on familiar terms with it, but never free of it. One performs the functions necessary to one's survival but thought, as it is generally understood, disappears completely. One becomes a rapid instinctive reactor to familiar stimuli and, when unfamiliar, one adapts very quickly to learn what one must do to remain alive. I have known this high terror only a few times, in Russia, in America, in Egypt and in Germany. It would be obscene to pass moral judgement on anyone who was ever exposed to it. It amused God to explain how the subject (myself, for instance) was taught obedience by providing him or her with a series of narrowing choices. This, of course, was the scientific principle by which discipline and order in the camps was maintained. After my first arrest I witnessed it personally. God had one of the blind girls killed. He said it was a punishment and we must all watch her through the hours of her dying, but I think He was demonstrating something else, perhaps for me. I think I understood what I must do, but God would not tell me. This is another means by which you are controlled, He said. By uncertainty. From time to time, therefore, He changed the rules. We had to learn the new ones very quickly. I was terrified He would grow bored with me, as He had grown, He implied, with the blind girl. She was useless, He said. He asked me if I could guess why He felt secure enough to tell me these things, to discuss the nature of His power over me and the nature of my will to serve Him. It is because You are God, I said. But I was wrong. He slapped my face impatiently and grew angry because I could not weep. There are no tears left in you. You are drying up, little Jew-angel. We must make you more interesting. Under the surgery you will begin to guess why I feel so secure. I am so glad you are intelligent. Most of these creatures, they hardly understand a word I say. I might as well talk to myself. But then you are part of myself, aren't you, sweet, filthy Jewshit?

And I must whisper that I love Her, that I love my mother, my goddess, Sekhet, who yearns with such bitter longing for Her own death and the death of the world. Yet still I am not ready to serve Her in the next world, She says. I have yet to yearn for death as She yearns for it, to want it more than life. God promises me the time will inevitably come to me as it comes to all Her creatures. It had come to the blind girl, God said. She had wanted to die. At any rate, towards the end. As we laugh at this I realise my own time has become finite.

Are you ready, says God, for your conscience to be weighed? I am not ready, I say. I still have no wish to die. God will be patient. But I will not become a *Musselman*. The thought of dying before my body dies is obscene. What is more, I have a secret which I doubt my fellow creatures possess – I have previous experience of miraculous salvation. I am not, as yet, completely bereft of hope. God understands this without being irritated. God will leave me with a little delicate thread of hope until it suits Him to take it away. It is part of His scientific method. It is the mark of our century that we have turned everything, including human anguish, into a science. We would joke sometimes about my impending death and what moment God would choose to blow away the last of my hope like a dandelion spore upon the breeze, delicately, perhaps without my even noticing.

God had me dress as a girl and attend Him when He received Sir Ranalf. The little man was breathless and made a weak joke concerning the heat. 'I think the arrangements are in order at last. These people are quite impossible. He's with me now. Shall I bring him in?'

You are very informal, Sir Ranalf, said God. Sir Ranalf became embarrassed. 'I'm frightfully sorry. Those awful camels. I really never can get used to them.' He had not looked at me at all, perhaps from nervousness but probably because he had not yet noticed my presence.

Have you met my wife? God asked. Sir Ranalf was nonplussed, peered, glanced away. 'No, indeed, al-Habashiya, I had not. Congratulations, perhaps?' He was told to kiss my hand.

God found this thoroughly amusing, especially since Sir

Ranalf did not begin to recognise me. When God lost interest in the joke, He lost interest in me and I think forgot me. Sir Ranalf was allowed to bring in his visitor, a tall, heavily-veiled *Bedawi* who spoke in gruff Arabic until al-Habashiya, using his high-pitched feminine voice, disclosed a preference for French. Perhaps she had hoped to shame the nomad, whose French was excellent, if a little old-fashioned. There were greetings offered and various goods mentioned, none of interest to me. I was inclined to doze whenever the opportunity was granted. At one point I thought I heard a Russian name, but the accompanying associations were too painful. I turned them away. Mercifully, God eventually leaned sideways so that my head was caught between the pillows and His flesh. After that I heard very little, for I was forbidden to move.

I think God became impatient with them both and dismissed them. He complained. He was monstrously annoyed. Towards evening, before the sun began to drop, He made us all assemble in the tiled courtyard around the fountain. He ordered us to form a mound, climbing one on top of another until we were all groaning with discomfort save for those at the bottom who were still. Laboriously, frequently falling backwards, wheezing and blowing, God began to ascend this hill of miscellaneous limbs, of writhing muscles and organs until He could squat on top, lift His skirts and shit. Time was an enemy I rejected. I do not know how much went by.

One day we returned to the garden. God told me to play with the blind children. He remarked how docile they were. They had all been fitted with artificial eyes of different colours, chiefly blue, which gave the rest of their faces a doll-like quality, especially when they were rouged and mascaraed. All of course had the scarab brand. When God told me to kill one of them, whichever I liked, the choice was mine, I said I had no weapon. He told me to use my hands or my teeth. Pick the smallest, He said, it should be easy. But I could not. And that was God's signal. I had been tried in His eyes. He was about to whisk away the last of my hope. If you like, He said, I will let you pluck out your own eyes. It has been done before. Or would you rather die? I will give you a day or two to choose.

Blind, I knew I would never escape Him. I cursed myself

for my weakness, for the cowardly failure of nerve which had brought about this final assault on my spirit.

I remember that I did not blame God for reducing me to this. I blamed Esmé. I had remained behind in an attempt to save her. She had not even thanked me. I blamed Mucker Hever and Samuel Goldfish, Malcolm Quelch, Wolf Seaman and Sir Ranalf Steeton. I blamed Mrs Cornelius. I blamed the blind boy for not resisting as I tried to squeeze his throat. I blamed myself for a soft-hearted fool. And still I knew I would not choose death.

I begged for paper and to my surprise was granted it, together with a fountain-pen and ink. I was beyond God's mercy but I hoped to entertain Him, to defer His decision so that I could have a little longer with my sight. I prepared a kind of prospectus. I described my inventions, my experience, my skills. I sang my own praises a little, going hard against the grain, but I was desperate. I told Him I could fly. I could show him the plans of my Desert Liner. I quoted poetry in half-a-dozen languages. I described my experiences in Kiev, Petrograd, and Paris, my meetings with film stars in America. My life with the Ku Klux Klan I did not discuss, being uncertain what sort of interpretation God would put on this episode. I wrote out jokes and summarised articles I had read in magazines. I described my childhood, my youthful adventures, my future. That, I thought, would at least convince Him of my sensibilities and might even open a fresh avenue of pleasure for Him. At last God told me to give Him what I had written. God had me stand before Him in His Temple while He read every page, nodding, smacking His lips, murmuring interest, expressing surprise, approval, disbelief and one by one screwing the pages up and tossing them into a brazier. Whenever one missed the brazier He would tell me to pick it up and throw it on the fire before returning to my place. When He had finished He told me to kneel before Him while He masturbated Himself over my face. When He was satisfied He congratulated me on the novelty of my narrative. It had, indeed, given Him pleasure, though of course it was only possible to experience such pleasure once. He produced a long metal rod with an oddly-shaped end and told me to take it to the brazier and push it into the hottest part. That is the instrument which will put out your eyes in the morning, He told me. If you wish to read or write until then, you may do so.

I had nothing but false hope now. I became obsessed with the small *Book of the Dead* Quelch had given me. I began desperately to learn all the words and responses needed to make a successful journey to the other world. God understood the nature of my torment as thoroughly as Paganini understood his violin. By convincing myself of this afterlife's reality, I might find the courage to choose death. I could not sleep. My eyes, refusing to understand that these were their final functioning hours, began to blur and close. My last moments of sight would also be my last moments alone. Tomorrow I would join the others in the pit to be tended by the eunuchs and the hermaphrodites until I was healed or became incurably infected and my face rotted, covered in black flies like a calf's head in a market. I had seen such creatures, still living, in God's garden.

Behold me. I am come to you, void of wrong, without fraud, a harmless one; let me not be declared guilty; let not the issue be against me. I feed upon Righteousness and drink of an Uprightness of Heart. I have done that which man prescribeth and that which pleaseth the gods. I am one whose mouth is pure and whose hands are pure to whom there is said 'Come in peace' by those who look upon him. I am one who glorifieth the gods and who knoweth the things which concern them. I am come and am awaiting that inquisition made of Rightfulness, when the Balance be set upon its stand within the bower of amaranth. I have made myself pure. My front parts are washed, my back parts are pure and my organs steeped in the Tank of Righteousness. There is not a limb in me which is void of Righteousness. I execrate, I execrate. I do not eat it. That which I execrate is dirt. I eat it not, that I may appease my Genius. Let it not enter my stomach, let it not approach to my hands, let me not tread upon it with my sandals. Let me not drink lye, let me not advance blindly into the Netherworld . . .

The effect of this reading was to give me at least a dim

358

understanding of what God had meant when He told me that one day I would long for death as helplessly as He Himself yearned for it. For I am the God of Death and I am not allowed to die. I knew without any doubt that His prediction would come true and that soon I would yearn for death as once I had yearned for a bride. Was this Egypt's whole secret? Was she still a nation for whom the pleasures of life were merely a prefiguring of the pleasures of death? By making death preferable to life, Islam allows every barbarism to flourish. What is this but a deep perversion of the old Egyptian creed?

The book could not distract me. I began to pray for the very death I would tomorrow refuse and was babbling some foolish smattering of Old Slavonic to myself when my door was opened. 'I have several hours, yet,' I pleaded. 'It is not morning.' There was no light behind the figure. He was illuminated entirely by my reading-lamp which cast a warm orange glow over his white linen *thob*, his cream and white silk *zebun* and his rich blue wool *aba*. In such princely nomad finery I guessed him to be God's executioner. I prayed for him to be only an hallucination conjured by my terror.

Then he had pushed back his headcloth to peer hard into my eyes and grin with delight at my astonishment.

'*Kolya?*' (Perhaps this was a finer form of madness than I had understood possible?)

He knelt. He took me in his arms. For a moment an expression almost of compassion crossed his face. Then he frowned. 'Ugh! You stink like a Prussian whore. Get to your feet, Dimka my love. We have to try to reach Libya before the British arrive.'

I asked him where God was. Where were the guards? I began to feel this to be another of God's games. Doubtless He now owned Kolya, too.

But Kolya did not understand my first question. 'The creature's guards were bribed. They were growing nervous at their master's excesses. God? What do you mean? Did you have a vision, Dimka?'

'Al-Habashiya.' I summoned enough courage to whisper the forbidden name. If I dreamed, I could not be harmed further.

'Oh!' He moved his fingers across his chest and then shrugged. He reached down to pull me upright. 'God is dead.'

The scarab is unrecognisable, burnt off in the accident. I do not think I could have lived with it on my body. Even the scar is loathsome. I would not speak of those events, not even to Kolya, who had some idea of what had transpired within God's garden. He had seen the pit, he told me. He had decided to leave it for the authorities to find. They were less likely to pursue al-Habashiya's murderer for long. I began to record this only after Suez. I felt it my duty. People should understand the influence of Carthage. They should know what it is to exist in a world where perverted negroid Semites enjoy the power of life and death over us. All I can do is warn you. I have sent these accounts to every newspaper and radio programme in the country. Most of them ignore me. *Reveille* ran a story but they made fun of me. SAMMY DAVIS JNR SECRET WORLD RULER SAYS POLISH MYSTIC was their headline. You can imagine the rest. Some say I disgust them. Certainly it is disgusting, I agree. It happened to me. They think I am *not* disgusted? I am one of the few who survived with sanity and my speech intact. Without studying evil we cannot resist it and we can so easily be deceived into taking the wrong path.

I told Kolya that God was a darkness to me and that something of myself had grown to love Him. Kolya said that it was always possible to find a little scrap of darkness in one's own soul, some scrap that longs to join the greater darkness and share in the power of its Prince. It is what we mean by Original Sin. His understanding of religious matters was considerable. He had spent some of his youth at a seminary. He understood the Greek creed far more thoroughly than I ever shall. At that time, however, it was of little comfort to me because I was beyond comfort. I was beyond emotion and sensation. Listlessly, I let my friend hurry us through the gates to the waiting camels, who groaned and complained at being awakened so early. He made me mount a tall, pale doe who got to her feet with all the offended grace of a dowager instructed to remove her chair from the park's verge. Then he perched himself on his own beast's hump, tugging on the rather large number of pack animals, goading my animal forward with his long whip and thus propelling us all willy-nilly into the cold night. An oily stink was drifting from the house. It stayed with me for hours. Only as the desert air cleared my lungs did I realise how familiar I had become with the smell of death.

'I sold her to him,' I said. 'She was sold on . . .'

By dawn, out of sight of the house and its surrounding palms, we pressed into the deep dunelands. Kolya said it was our only alternative to capture. The British came and went as they pleased in the Sudan. Beyond Sudan the only place worth going was Kenya, which was also British. Neither of us, he said, would benefit from being interviewed by the British. Besides, he had friends in Libya. He made us pause while he consulted a map and took a compass reading. I, being convinced that this whole episode was a mental escape, some hallucinatory salvation, merely grinned inanely and wondered vaguely when the pain in my eye-sockets would begin to penetrate this glorious madness.

I think that was the point at which I fell from my camel. Next, I was riding across Kolya's pommel while he steadied me with one arm and guided our team with his free hand. Still half-swooning I stared up into his handsome strength. He might have been one of our legendary Slavic heroes. I thought how much he resembled a refined Valentino, and then came a pang of memory for *The Sin of the Sheikh*.

Seeing me wake, Kolya directed my attention to the vastness of the pale dunes ahead, the true Sahara, which the *Bedawi* feared and hated, that most dangerous and unforgiving of oceans, where quicksand could without warning swallow you and everything you owned, sending you to populate the buried city of some forgotten race, to join those who had already marched down the centuries to fill the dead but perfect streets.

'It's to be a long journey, Dimka my dear, before we get to where we have friends.' He sighed. As he stroked my head I became calm, perhaps mesmerised, but the quality of fear was duller. I still believed I was looking upon my executioner, even when he kissed the tips of his fingers and placed them to my lips. 'Ah, Dimka, Dimka!' He regarded with mild exasperation the uncountable miles of pale brown sand. 'So little to say and so much time to say it in!'

We rode without pause until noon, and I still waited for the pain to impinge. It was easy to see how madness could be God's mercy; how peasants still believe the insane to be blessed. Or was I already in Heaven? I determined to appreciate the moment, never hoping it would continue for long. As we set off again, Kolya pointed to one of the bundles bouncing on a pack camel. 'Your valise, Dimka, I think. That's how I first found out you were still here. It was in Steeton's quarters at the Winter Palace. I thought I'd bring it with me. Any good?'

I giggled at this fancy.

The Western Sahara embraces and threatens us with her infinite waves of sand, shifting with implacable slowness. On this Netherworld Sea suddenly looms a great funeral barge, some vivid beast-headed benevolent at her helm, remorselessly rolling towards us, carrying the stark, clean smell of a desert death. If, by chance, I have been released, blind, into the desert, then I am compensated by the steadily improving quality to my mirages! When we next stop to light our evening fire, I open my Gladstone. Here is everything except the main specifications for my Desert Liner. My books, my pistols, some money and other personal things, my whole identity is returned to me. Yet still I refuse to hope that this is anything more than an illusion clouding over the fact of my unbearable blindness.

I hardly wish to consider an even more terrible alternative – that my oldest and greatest male friend has been commissioned to destroy me, as I was instructed to destroy the blind boy.

My ship was called *The Esmé*. Pink as the Egyptian dawn, gold as the Egyptian night, soft and gently warm, her perfume was the scent of life itself. She was the loveliest of all my dreams. She would have risen in the morning, so pure and vigorous, and everyone who saw her would have gasped at her virgin beauty.

My ship was called *The Stolen Soul* and even in her ruined state, everything smashed and scattered and looted, she had an aura of noble vitality; a pure sense that once she had served her people well and with grace.

'If they ever named an effin' ship after you, Ivan,' says Mrs Cornelius, 'they ort ter corl it *Ther Lucky Bastard* . . .'

'Luck, Mrs Cornelius,' I say, 'does not exist. What you describe as luck is a combination of stolen opportunity and honest judgement. There is nothing random about it.'

So it was by virtue of my own sublime instincts, and, I would readily agree, some help from an old friend, that I escaped at last from Paradise.

TWENTY-ONE

I HAD PASSED THROUGH the final gate, the gate to eternal death. Anubis was my friend. I had won a kind of immortality. I was free to wander in the Land of Shades, but my future remained uncertain and my terror would not leave me. I possessed a knowledge I had never wanted and of which I never dare speak. I had been in the presence and the power of purest Evil.

There is an old man, a kind of vagrant who walks up and down the Portobello Road on weekdays, when the market is only fruit and veg. He is sometimes mistaken for me. Even Mrs Cornelius mentions it. He is *Irischer*. I am not insulted. We would call him *rorodivni*. He is, says Father P., what his own ancestors named *da-chearde*, a son of two arts; an oracle. Barnum the Jew says he is a *nebech-meshiach* and gives him a shilling, but I am not sure this is blasphemy. Arabised Berbers of the Tripoli desert might identify him as an *achmak ilahiya* and perhaps also consider him an oracle. And why should he not be one? He declaims only what we fear to whisper. He quotes the Bible. He speaks of God's mercy and how it might be earned.

There is no reason to disbelieve him. His logic is soundly based in conventional theology. Perhaps he is actually the medium for God's voice. And none of us listens. Not even I. But I know when to be silent. In the desert I learned silence and I learned the art of the fool. Otherwise I should not have lived.

He does not seem to care for the Pope. I think they give him something at the Poor Clares across from Mrs Cornelius. He would therefore be a Catholic, perhaps an ex-priest. Those who say God never announces His presence might wish to spend an hour or two with Mr O'Dowd. He speaks not through ritual or parable, but is the direct medium of God's command. And still we do not listen! I saw him with those new nuns who so resemble social workers, with their sensible stockings and skirts and little heels. They are always Irish; they have that screeching, unnatural laugh that needs whisky to make it melodious. They remind me of the *fellaheen* women. I think they keep an eye on him. My friend Miss B., who was once so famous as a dancer, was also a Catholic. She went to the big church near me, which was how we met. All her friends are Irish or Polish, from Hammersmith. She herself lives in Sporting Club Square, West Kensington. I used to go and visit her, but Brodmann put a stop to that.

It was a fine evening in February when Brodmann discovered me again, or, more properly, I learned he had picked up my trail. After tea I had left Miss B.'s eccentrically Ludwigian terracotta mansion, deciding not to use the square's Mandrake Road entrance but to cross the gardens and enjoy the last of the evening light. I had a particular fondness for Sporting Club Square. With her tall wrought-iron railings and surrounding trees, her botanical gardens, the creation of Halifax Begg, offered a sense of sanctuary. By some fluke they had always shut out the busy noise of nearby North End Road and I could easily imagine I sat enjoying the solitude of my own ancestral estate near Kiev. The gardens possess that special sense of well-ordered security one finds so often in Arab courtyards. It was a Monday, at about five o'clock. The sun was setting, a red pulse through the dark branches of the massive oak which sixty years earlier had been the dominant landmark of some Fulham pasture. I smelled grass and evergreens. The pungent fumes of coal-fires seemed to intoxicate two tabby cats chasing each other across the lawns, through ornamental grasses and flower-beds, laurel hedges and waxy botanical oddities. Maintained by a bequest from Begg himself, the little park was as well-kept and as varied in its flora as Derry and Toms Roof Garden, another favourite retreat for meditation and recollection.

A misty stillness filled the whole square with that timeless calm one often used to find in London until her streets filled up with yelling immigrants, middle-class colonists and the anti-social family saloon. In those days during the afternoons only the centre had crowds of people. Most of the square's flats were occupied by middle-aged people who had moved here at a time when the rents were reasonable. Today it is a landmark. All taxi-drivers know it. Tourist buses bring visitors on their way to Earls Court. Each of the mansion blocks is in a different style, many of them daring when raised, but the place is now I believe in a book and up for development. It was just as I approached the ornate north gate, with its cast-iron Imperial Eagles imitated from St Petersburg, that I saw Brodmann. He must have been following me. Perhaps he already knew of my association with Miss B? Or perhaps Miss B. had betrayed me? It was even possible that they had been shadowing her and accidentally found me. It no longer mattered, of course. The inescapable fact was that Brodmann had picked up my trail again. This was just after the War when I was praying he had either been recalled or, better still, killed in the Blitz. I believe he thought I had not recognised him. I took my single advantage and pretended bafflement. He was disguised as a tramp but nothing could hide his leering triumph! My warm reverie was utterly destroyed. My peace of mind was exploded. I felt my hard-won harmony fragmenting into a vacuum. Now, at any moment of his choosing, Brodmann could report me and have me forcibly returned to my homeland. Like those other Cossacks the British lords sent back to Stalin, I faced inevitable torture. This is why I can never reveal certain names, including my own. Those few of us who have survived into natural old age are mutually responsible for one another. To call us Nazis, I said to Brodmann in a note, was the grossest simplification of our political ideals. He never replied. I had hoped to flush him out. Brodmann of course was the real Nazi. He was not the first Nazi Jew I ever met. They are all the same, these communists.

I was never again to enjoy the botanical tranquillity of Sporting Club Square. I caught the 28 from The Seven Stars and looked back to make sure he was not following me. I got off at the Odeon, Westbourne Grove and, rather than risk leading him to my home, I went to the pictures. They were playing a cowboy film in which some ludicrous Billy the Kid saves a town from every kind of villainy. There is a scene in the desert which I recognised as Death Valley, although the buttes and mesas of that landscape have the same sort of confusing similarity one finds in parts of the Libyan Sahara, where one peak can look very much like another. I remember very little of the ride from Bi'r Tefawi to the oasis where we joined a small camel caravan with which, Kolya said, we would journey to Ouenat and from there to al-Khufra where he expected to meet old friends. Al-Khufra was some four hundred miles due west across the Sahara. He advised me to relax as best I could and enjoy the journey. This would be the easiest part.

'But *what* is Khufra?' I had never heard of such a city.

'A great oasis, a junction for the large caravans out of Africa and India. She's six hundred uncrossable miles of desert south-west of Cairo. Nine hundred miles of dunes due west to Ghat and a thousand miles of wasteland and mountains north-west to Tripoli. In short, Dimka dear, Khufra is in the middle of nowhere – and yet you shall see there sights no Christian has witnessed in centuries! Be patient, dear, for at present you are riding first-class. After Khufra the real journey begins.' I asked him what lay after Khufra but all he would say was that he hoped we did not have to go to Ghat.

The others on the caravan called me *al bagl* which means 'the mule', but I did not mind. I was safe from God at last but I retained the habits He had instilled in me. Intellectually I knew this; He could no longer punish me, but my nerves would not accept this. Somehow I had become addicted to others' approval and would serve happily anyone who commanded me. I could not sleep until I knew I had the general goodwill of the whole caravan. Only their cheerful condescension made me feel at ease. Their mockery and their contempt, their affectionate insults, warmed me. In Arabic they sometimes called me 'Father of Fools' but in Tebu their names were usually more cryptic. The Goran tribesmen also had filthier epithets. These haughty blacks chose to assume me Kolya's catamite. Kolya, with his talent for languages, had let it be known that he was an anti-French Syrian *sharif* on the run from the authorities. He even had a blurred newspaper cutting as proof of his credentials. The cutting was from the Parisian yellow press, a gossip column. Since few of them could read in any language, it served to give authority to his claim that he was considered an enemy by the Rumi. Why else would they print his picture? Everyone agreed on this logic.

Between B'ir Tefawi and the first oasis I discovered a thoroughly useful talent. I had a natural skill with camels and, after only a few days, amazed Kolya with my easy seat, my deft control. Was there a part of me that sensed in those landscapes some ancestral homeland? Again I wondered about lost Atlantis. Could the Caucasian Berbers be the remnants of that legendary people? Both spoke a language that was the root of many others. There was no explanation as to how they had come to occupy the Sahara. Had they actually been my Atlantean forebears? Few Berbers were nomads by vocation. They would tell you how they had once lived in magnificent cities, ruling a world. At first I took that to be a reference to their Empire, which had included the Spanish peninsula until the Christian conquests, but later I began to realise they referred to a civilisation more ancient even than Egypt, with whom they also shared their language. The Berbers of our party were inclined to keep themselves apart from Arabs. Did their blood recall a time when these same people were their slaves? And was it common blood that bore in it a knowledge of the years before the oceans drowned Atlantis, before the rise of Carthage in all its luscious and extravagant barbarism? Before Sumer; before Babylon and Assyria and those other neurotic, brooding Semitic Empires whom greedy introspection brought so low? We came to Ouenat, a valley of red rock in a range of eroded mountains, a collection of sun-yellowed scrub and a few miserable saplings growing where rainwater had gathered in brackish pools. Our party had no intention of staying long. The place was thought to shelter *afrit*s and *djinn*s of testy disposition. Now the walls of the valley were steeper, masses of weather-smoothed granite boulders which could dislodge and roll down on us at any moment. Eventually we camped at the base of a cliff and a pool more palatable than most and settled to wait for the main caravan from Furawia and French Equatorial Africa. We waited a week, grumbling and fretting until bit by bit the other caravans began to come in. Yet we still could not set off until we had debated our relative positions in the train and all demands and honour had been properly respected. This involved the offering of *daifa* – the special hospitality of the desert – and the consequent feastings and ceremonies attending the offerings. These were followed by friendly debate between the various elders of the caravans, when they smoked and chatted and, after it seemed we must drink Ouenat dry, they rose, shaking hands, slapping shoulders and laughing to expose their few white fangs in the weathered leather of their faces.

At last we were ready to take the road to al-Khufra, leaving the mountains behind and crossing a plain which glittered with cornelian, flint, mica, agate and obsidian worn by the hooves and sandals of all the animals and men who had passed this way for three thousand years or more. The splintered peaks were below the horizon and the desert widening under the evening sky before Kolya grew at once more light-hearted and more cautious. 'Soon, Dimka, you will understand the real temptations of the desert.' But he refused to expand on this.

Each caravan has its own rhythm, pace and character. Our party now consisted of a miscellaneous collection of Bedouin merchants, Tebu camel-breeders, Sudanese slavers, pilgrims returning from the Haj, and the camp-followers who served us in various ways. Kolya assured me it was nothing compared to the great oasis at Khufra.

In those days, before the half-track conquered all, a caravan was exactly like a train, with connections at various oases for other caravans following a variety of fixed routes. You waited for the next party going in the direction you desired. It was Stavisky's people, he eventually admitted, who were supposed to meet Kolya at al-Khufra, near the Toom road. He would turn over our pack camels to them in exchange for cash. Then, he hoped, we could head for Tripoli. I remarked gloomily that the camels couldn't be worth very much but this only amused him. 'Enough to get us a room and breakfast at Bagnold's, never fear!'

At night our trail across the golden dunes turned to gleaming silver and remained easy to follow. We were rarely far from water. With a good caravan it was a route as uneventful to travel as the railway from Delhi to Bombay. Gradually the desert became what the Bedouin called *sarira*, hard sand, flat, all but featureless and spread with a thin layer of gravel. Later I would come to know the gruelling boredom of caravan life which would teach me the habit of patience. But then my head was filled with an understanding my body still refused to accept. I was free! I had escaped God's punishment. God, Kolya assured me, was slain. It was as if I had passed every test I had tried to learn from my book. I had answered all the questions, made the proper statements of repentance, all the time believing I would still at any moment be struck down, further humiliated and weakened. But I had gone safely through the First Gate and Anubis was my friend. Why should I still be afraid? No rationality would release me from the fear that at any moment God might stand again before me, telling me that I had merely drifted for a short while into a dream. Yet if I dreamed, then I experienced a nightmare within the dream. I was yet to be blinded. I remained terrified of a future which could only be horrific, grotesque and disgusting. I had seen the boy turning in circles with his own living eyes clutched in his bloody fists while al-Habashiya had chuckled softly. I had seen the mutilated girls. So still I capered and giggled, the compliant object of all their foul-mouthed speculation. I even suffered their gross sexual advances. (I have often thought that the reason the British and the Arabs have such a love affair is because each race is as sexually repressed as the other.) Sex, my enemy, continued her tyranny.

I was conditioned to please them. I had earned my life through pleasing them. I had very little capacity for logic at that time. I was at any *fellaheen*'s mercy whenever I was caught alone relieving myself behind a rock or running to fetch a wandering goat on the far side of a dune. But then some of them took to calling me casually, for their own perverse amusement, *al Yehudi*, and I began intellectually, as well as instinctively, to fear for my life again. Then Kolya issued some subtle decree to my tormentors (which I do not think was an appeal to their better natures, but a suggestion they discontinue handling his property). I was grateful for Kolya's intercession, but might have hoped for a more dignified appeal. He did his best, he said. He had, after all, to behave thoroughly like a desert Arab. Anything else would arouse suspicion. I assured myself that I need have no more rational fear of them. Anubis was my friend. If, by God's command, I was already dead, I had nothing at all to lose. Any sensation of life would be a gain. There remained, however, the knowledge that anyone whom the Arab intended to murder was always first cursed with the name of 'Jew' and so the crime became legitimate. It was the same, of course, in parts of Germany, as I discovered to my cost.

God continued to haunt me; her smothering flesh, her organs still threatened my soul. My bowels would knot in agony for the loss of Esmé, my muse; the little goddess who had betrayed me so badly. I had not wanted any of this. I had done everything I could for her.

Within caravans, disputes and quarrels are rarely allowed to blossom into full-blown affairs. A people whose law is the blood feud and who are in constant conflict with the elements cannot afford extra antagonisms. Kolya's words were heeded. My days became happier. What if I had gone from being a Cossack's pet Jew to an Arab's pet Nazrini? I now stood every chance of reclaiming all I had lost. I still had a small fortune in my California bank. In the fullness of time, Kolya would get us to a town with civilised conveniences and I would wire Goldfish with a brief account of the truth. Calling upon our funds, I could return to Los Angeles before the year's end and start my career again without encumbrances. I would look back on these months of inhaling sand and living off brackish water and miscellaneous beans and, no doubt, even I would romanticise it, softening the details, embroidering certain facts until it was suitably similar to *The Desert Song* for the civilised world's demanding sensibilities.

Even the most persistent of my persecutors lost interest in me as we neared al-Khufra which, we were warned, now had a large Italian garrison on the look-out for slavers and gun-runners. The Wormeater's incapacity to distinguish a gun-runner from a blind mule was a source of wild amusement amongst those Arabs who had already experienced Italian occupation. They of course were equally unable to tell an Italian musketeer from a Norwegian matron. One fierce rumour had it that the soldiers had been ordered to erect a Christian church on the site of the oasis's chief mosque. In the mythology of these people Christians were forever hatching complicated (usually extremely petty) plots and spending considerable resources merely to bring insult to the Moslems. It had reminded me of Kentucky, whose people credited the Pope with similar ambitions against their dissenting congregations. As I said to Kolya: Considering the army of crazed zealots which between them the Chief Rabbi, the Pope and the Bishop of Constantinople can rally, it's surprising they have not thought of combining resources before now!

Such racialist paranoia is disgusting. It only clouds the issues and makes us lose sight of the real enemy. 'These Moslems are bound to be touchy,' said Kolya, lapsing into Russian as the bulk of the caravan fell away to our left. 'What would you think if you suddenly realised, in your heart of hearts, that you and your ancestors had backed the wrong religious horse – and were still insisting the useless nag could win the Petersburg Straight? Yet when you listen, in Cairo for instance, to their political ideas, you wonder which came first, the self-destructive religion or the average Arab, who would always rather shoot himself in the foot than not shoot at all!'

It seemed to me that his understanding of Islam was limited, but I said nothing, for I was as anxious to agree with Kolya as I was with the Arabs.

He had by now been accepted as a rebel, a *sharif* (minor noble) and a scholar, while I was identified as his idiot kinsman, employed from the goodness of his heart. This story was thin, but perfectly acceptable to our confederates who rarely demanded the truth of anyone, but felt it a matter of good form for someone to present a lie with grace, wit and dignity.

In the main the Arabs are a tolerant people prepared to take any man at his own value until he proves himself an antagonist. My Arabic being specific and limited, I had no other choice but to accept the idiot rôle.

I was, for those first weeks, incapable of speaking anything but the Arabic God had trained me to speak. Since we had joined the moving sprawl of burdened camels and trudging drivers, following the old trading road from oasis to oasis, up and down dunes as high and steep as the English Pennines, deep into the Western Desert, I dreamed of nothing but God's penis and every night relived my terror, my mouth now bound at my own request for fear that the Bedouin in their nearby tents might discover that a Nazrini had insinuated himself into their company. If they suspected me, I would have been betrayed by a double blasphemy, for which I have since been redeemed, but Kolya quieted me with his familiar soothing ways and turned terror into comfort and comfort into pleasure, until I began to calm. He said I was like a terrified stray, jumping at every sound.

Inta al hob. Inta al hob. I shall never forget her yearning voice, that woman singing from the Bedouin tent. It is you I love. You are the love. I could not tell if she sang to God or to a man. Kolya wept when I asked him this. 'Who can say?' He cleared his throat. 'Can she?' Once or twice he also wept at the thought of my humiliating ordeal but we were both consoled by his opium which we smoked in the traditional style, through the *narghila*. This brought me some rest at last. Little by little I recovered my old personality. So far, I said, the desert lacked the romance I had come to anticipate from Pierre Loti or Karl May. Kolya believed the former too feminine, the latter too masculine. Actually the desert was paradoxically a place where such divisions ceased to exist, where even life and death were blurred, and yet always there was the threat of sudden extinction. He said the desert quickened the senses but offered no easy release. It produced, in a subtle being, an extraordinary state of perpetual piquancy. Fine wine and good cocaine were to a true aesthete, he said, mere substitutes for the desert. I had not until then encountered this epicurean definition of the Sahara. It reminded me that Kolya was truly born a little too late. Sometimes it seemed the flawed genius himself, a slender Oscar Wilde, rode his beautiful aristocratic grey camel at my side. The Arabs, who constituted the bulk of our party (we also had blacks and, of course, the Caucasian Berbers), treated my prince with a certain respect while making comradely fun of his poor riding, saying he had spent too long in the cities with the Franks – now in the desert he would learn to become a true Arab again. They were impressed, however, by his elaborate garments, which he wore with considerable panache. To the Arabs they suggested he had powerful family connections. Contrary to the ridiculous myths which the tourists take out with them, the Arab is as vain as any other man and likes nothing better than posing for a camera or an artist's pencil. It is not the Koran but puritanical tradition, an interpretation of our common Old Testament, that forbids images. The Arab's love of display makes a Neapolitan gigolo's seem like modest shyness. One glance at a French drawing-room wall shows how gladly these people will model. They have learned, too, that the tourist expects to *reward* them for their delicious experience! The Brownie is raised, the hand is held out in demand, the exchange is made and the happy Arab, like his fellow spirits throughout the world, adopts the most romantic and unlikely posture, thus confirming every stereotype which ever put a distance between himself and his equally ordinary brothers around the world. Any picture taken in the Middle East and North Africa bears the unmistakable stamp of this gamecockery, whether it be Haramin posing on their borrowed camels before Giza's pyramids at sunset or Marakshi riders galloping about and letting off their rifles for the benefit of wealthy Europeans watching from the balconies of the Atlantic Hotel. But these are Buffalo Bill's Wild West to the ordinary reality of prairie life. The long dull days of the caravan trek teach the European the thorough lesson of this ordinariness. However, if the average life of a desert warrior is somewhat less stimulating than the daily round of a suburban office worker, the Arab's imagination is more vivid and his vocabulary is on the whole more colourful, resembling the combined invention of a French *sansculotte*, a Russian whore, a Greek cab-driver and an English public-schoolboy, developed through use and habit into an instrument of extraordinarily fluent and specific obscenity. As a people whose chief entertainment is from spoken language it is no surprise they have evolved an oral art no whit less impressive than our own Ukrainian tradition. Such an art cultivates the mind as well as the tongue. It is never a mystery to me that so many poets under Stalin were capable of committing whole volumes of verse to memory. An oral literature depends on intonation. A good Arab story-teller learns the music of discourse and dramatic narrative. He has developed and refined his conventions as Western novelists have developed subtleties of punctuation and grammar. Only on the page is an Arab's story simple. His literary conventions seem theatrical and whimsical only to those who do not understand their function. It is much the same with Shakespeare. I think however my own raving obscenities would have shocked those Arabs. Happily I had vented most of them on Kolya alone in the desert three hundred miles west of Aswan, before we joined the caravan. But I still asked Kolya to bind my mouth and sometimes my limbs at night until, gradually, though I used Arabic, I raved only of God. This was acceptable to the Moslems who became convinced that I was actually some kind of idiot divine. But it was not until we were nearing the great oasis city of Khufra that I trusted myself to sleep only with the aid of the hashish. As slowly the devils were driven out of me I became more comfortable in my consciously-acted part of cheerful fool whom all men sought out, with a kind word and a coin, for the blessing of my sweet smile. I had become, in God's care, a far finer actor than ever I had been in Hollywood.

Gradually the more visible aspects of my terror were brought in check. The Bedouin became familiar. I grew to enjoy their bluff good-heartedness towards any creature not a sworn blood enemy. They are at once less cruel and less noble than the characters of Karl May and the more doting *arabistes* of my boyhood.

Benighted barbarians that they were, the majority showed courtesy and concern for those they accepted. They were like peasants anywhere in the world. Once Kolya saved me from their more amorous notions I received the best of their hospitality, their rough, manly affection. Of course I perceived the irony of my position, yet in my miserable loss of dignity and self-respect I discovered a kind of innocence. In this way I had something in common with the devoted Musselman.

Those qualities we so despised in the camps can, in certain circumstances, be a kind of strength. I remained proudly glad to be free of their worst sexual banter. I remained terrified of sex. Sex had brought me to my present predicament.

They called me the Lucky One, Beloved of Camels and they liked to call me *al Sakhra*, the Hawk, when I flapped my arms for them and imitated the screech of the hunting bird. They said they would catch me an ostrich for a mate. Amongst themselves they continued to indulge in a farrago of boastful reminiscence and slavering anticipation of the women they would fuck in Khufra, where (Kolya told me) only overworked and generally clapped-out old whores would be available to them. They discussed the qualities of Nubians and Jews with all the authority and sophistication of schoolboys in a locker-room. Another irony; while my Bedouin comrades longed for the sexual experience they had never known I longed to forget all that I had ever learned. I wish I could have distributed my wealth of memory to them, scattering amongst a hundred or two the unsought-for sensual knowledge of an unnaturally concentrated lifetime; which might have had the mutually beneficial effect of satisfying their frustrations while saving me the disturbance of their conversation. I was grateful that the Bisharim, the long-skulled Nubian nomads whose forms of religion were a matter of dismay to our few Wahabim, generally spoke their own language but sometimes told stories in Arabic of the Berber women warriors – whole tribes who would set upon a man in the desert and make use of him until he died. They also spoke of the Berbers' general partiality for human blood and the sacrifice of babies, of their hideous methods of torture. I came to realise that to these people a Berber was merely the manifestation of all their unfocused fears. He was to be avoided if possible and traded with only cautiously, for in the art of bargaining he was worse than a Jew. Sometimes the astonishing and complicated racialism of these people was blood-curdling! It was only matched by their sense of commonality. This, as usual, resulted in the notion of 'good' and 'bad' Berbers, Jews, Nazrini or Nubians and so on; that is to say, the ones with whom you got along personally were evidently good; the ones you despised, feared, loathed and were sworn to kill on sight were the ones you would never meet. We have similar notions of our own about Arabs. Such ramshackle logical adjustments do admittedly reduce potential bloodshed and, because it is alert to mysterious danger, makes the average caravan as prey to banditry as the average Pullman. I have yet to meet an Arab or anyone else who would not, if left to his own devices, prefer to talk and trade, in that order, rather than fight. Anyway it is only the unfortunate Jews of the *mellah* who get hurt in any numbers during an Arab war, as one side or another 'takes' a town and performs a little ritual slaughter before riding out again. The Jews themselves seem singularly free from any genuine sense of outrage. It is as if the loss of a few sons, the rape of a few daughters, is some kind of local tax they must pay. Those Jews of the oases make me afraid. I was abandoned to the *shtetl*, but their darkness was worse than the *shtetl*, perhaps because here, in their own birthplace, they had more choice. They had chosen this life! Every honest Arab will agree that even amongst such creatures, with their ostentation and their devotion to usury, you can often find one or two of the noblest type, great craftsmen, intellectuals, artists. But it is not the Jew's love of art the Arab fears. It is the Jew's love of money, his substitute for patriotism. With a love of money comes a quest for security. A quest for security becomes a quest for power, a quest for power becomes a lust for land, and there you have full-fledged Zionist imperialism against which of course the *jihad* is the only effective weapon! Such a Holy War began the Nazi success. Hitler's lowly origins were, in the end, however, his downfall. Someone better educated and better bred might have tackled the Jewish problem with greater moderation. In the end the exterminations lost them the support of many ordinary decent Germans. Herman Goering was the only gentleman in the group but unfortunately had not been well educated. He had found, as it were, his natural level. In another age he would have gradually become the butt of the *Bierkeller*, but, as I have reason to know, he was a good-hearted creature in his own way and had an excellent grasp of engineering principles. Goebbels had more intelligence, but he was incapable of gentlemanly behaviour.

The rituals by which we order and contain our terror of death are as varied as they are immutable. Before we ever dare to re-examine and perhaps change them we defend them by herculean efforts of the imagination, sometimes to the very death we most fear. I remarked on this to Kolya. 'Is there a vicious circle of terror and tyranny which is destined to enslave forever even the most enlightened of us?' He thought this was a pointlessly pessimistic question brought on by my ordeal. He saw in everyone, no matter how degenerate or immoral, a spark of goodness which would always respond to what he called the 'reasoning voice of love'. Only rarely did there emerge a truly terrifying intelligence which could take even that spark of goodness and corrupt it.

I was relieved, when he mentioned this idea, that I had been unable to kill the blind boy. I remember an old rabbi telling me that when he was asked, 'Where was God in Auschwitz?' he would say 'God was there with us, violated and blasphemed. Ask rather – Where was *Man* in Auschwitz?' For my own part, I never became a *Musselman*. I still know exactly what he means.

I told Kolya how Esmé had betrayed me; how I had given up the chance, nevertheless, of escape without her. I still hoped to find who had bought her. He was oddly unsympathetic, but he had not known her as well as I. I was surprised, however, at his next response. 'I doubt if you will ever realise the extent or the nature of her suffering. I would imagine that, perhaps on a level she dare not admit, her anguish is now nearly unbearable.'

I laughed. I might imagine him to be in love with her himself! But now I think he meant, like Mrs Cornelius, that it might have been better if I had never taken her from her Constantinople whorehouse to offer her a future in Hollywood. She did not possess the character for it. But at

378

least she had more than most girls of her type who are merely promised such things!

This was to be the last rigorous step of our journey into the desert. At night, when it grew chill, tents were pitched for almost a mile along the trail and fluttering fires disappeared into infinity. From everywhere came the aroma of cooking, of hot charcoal, of dung and urine, of spices and perfumes, of animals and men. I wondered if it had been like this in the Old West, on a wagon train, or perhaps more closely a great cattle-drive such as the brothers Butch and Hopalong ramrodded into Mexico. I saw it on the television. The cowboy films are the only things that have any real morality, these days. Sometimes I hope in all the Hoot Gibsons and W.S. Harts they will turn up one of mine. But those days are too distant for them. Our work is no longer entertainment, it is now a social archive. They want to forget those old lessons, I suppose. Even John Wayne seems happy to play some Falstaffian lawman in mockery of all he ever stood for, so I do not hold out much hope. The Western no doubt descends into sensational bloodshed, substituting violence for technique, like the detective story, the exotic romance and the chiller.

At this time of year the day's heat was not unbearable; for Russians, used to the most modest summers, we adapted well. We took the precaution of wearing thick headcloths and veils against the glare and dust while we did everything 'Arab-fashion'. We were sparing with all our supplies, even the cocaine. I was surprised at the quantity and quality that he carried. He was amused. He told me mysteriously that the hump of the camel was the choicest part of the beast. Had he murdered al-Habashiya for his drugs? He laughed. 'That fat pervert got into a business dispute with someone who had his measure, that's all. Nobody will mourn him. But yes, I think we are probably both hoping to *escape*, if that was your implication. I need to be my own man again, Dimka dear. I would like to be free of Stavisky and there could be an opportunity in the offing. I could still be his agent. It depends who is waiting for us at al-Khufra. Meanwhile no one will spend much time searching for us, even if they see our tracks. They will not know who we were. The news will travel through the underworld, as it must, and those who do know us will assume us killed in the dispute. There was, you know, quite a quantity of corpses and general shambles in the end. Poor, silly Sir Ranalf was left holding a somewhat messy baby. But he's been a lazy beneficiary of al-Habashiya's bounty for many years. He'll no doubt be paying a proper price for his pleasures.'

I was thinking of the film. There must have been miles of it. Could its origins be identified? Somewhere in the world, even today, my poor, scarred black and white bottom rises and falls between bruised little legs as I perform the rape scene and few who watch will even think the people on the screen are real, will even want to ask how they came to be there. If they watched it today they would be howling with laughter at our quaintness. It makes me wonder if our increasingly abstract society is not wholly the creation of Mr Kodak and his colleagues.

I told Kolya that I would not feel easy until we were in Europe again and all this far behind us. I pointed out that I no longer had any identity papers. 'I left your passport behind deliberately,' he said, 'and changed my own for something more suitable. That gives us a double opportunity.' That night in our tent he showed me a variety of passports he had taken from al-Habashiya's. 'I was looking for money. But he was too old a dog to keep much there. At least we can take our pick of identities now, Dimka dear. I know a man in Tangier who can work wonders with documents.' His hope was to get to Tripoli and from there reach Tangier by ship. From Tangier, with new identities, we could go anywhere we wanted.

The pile of passports disturbed me, recalling a dozen ghoulish images, but I said nothing. Indeed, I still had little urge to speak, even after five weeks in the desert, and publicly contented myself with the grinning gesticulation which so pleased the other travellers. Alone with Kolya, I mostly sat and wept. Frequently, with superb tact, my friend would leave our tent and stroll about in the desert, sometimes for hours at a time, respecting my grief.

The stink and constant bustle of the caravan became a familiar comfort. There was always an incident, usually domestic, always gossip and banter to while away the patient hours, and the five prayers gave a welcome structure to the day as we proceeded at a camel's walk across the hostile waste of sandstone, dust and biting winds, of unwholesome heat and wells gone dry, of yielding dunes and barren *wadi*s on a trek that was for some of us the first stage of a journey the equivalent of a walk from New York to Los Angeles – three thousand miles of desert, of sudden death and infinite boredom. Those extremes created the Arab's unique soul and made him such a frustrating enemy, forever changing sides on a whim; for an Arab is a fatalistic and practical creature used to thousands of years of unchallenged despotism. He is encouraged by his religion to submit, encouraged by his traditions to aspire to power through a cruel despotism, for shame and pride are his poles, and his society demands of him at least a well-advertised display of violence. The Israelis have learned his language. They have given up trying to speak to him in the reasoning vocabularies of America and Germany.

I see parallels all around me. I am not the only one to argue that we ourselves socially are barely out of the Middle Ages, judging by the broad ideas of the *hoi polloi*. Our philosophy – from Aristotle to the present – which has made us so great is meaningless to the man in the street, who benefits, incidentally, from it. Left to his own devices, he would cheerfully drink his beer, whistle his little tunes, study his pools, while his priceless institutions, for which so many sacrificed themselves, his very security as an individual, crumble noisily about his ears. Indeed, I could easily prove that the average *Wahabi*, for all his obnoxious piety, would be able to debate the Greek and French schools more fluently than any modern middle-class Briton!

As the familiarity and sense of security grew, as it became less and less likely that our disguises would be discovered (I had even heard some Hadjizin claiming to have fought beside my '*sharif*' at some *wadi* famous only in their own annals) I grew to appreciate my position. My life in Hollywood, almost certainly in ruins, could be restored; I had escaped an appalling fate with my health and mind intact and I was reunited with my best and oldest friend. I needed time for my mental wounds to heal, for all my nightmares to be banished and my usual cheerful optimism to return in full. By assuming the rôle of a simpleton I found for myself the least demanding persona. When I at last reached Tangier in a couple of months or so I would be fully able to resume my place in the civilised world. My California money could be touched by nobody save myself. Yet I had grown used to the caravan's pace. I had made pleasant acquaintances, including several young women who trusted an idiot far more than any fully-sensed youth. Sometimes I could hardly conceive of any other life, or of wanting any other life. I had come in particular to appreciate the beauty of the camel and to enjoy the subtle meaning of a sunset sky and to take pleasure, as my colloquial Arabic improved, in the story-tellers who moved among us (sometimes with a single laden camel), earning their place with a mixture of traditional tales – including most of Aesop's – misreported world news, snatches of doggerel, prejudice. Ignorant and with a relish for sensation, particularly sexual sensation and local sport, they were, in effect, complete walking tabloid newspapers. For those who preferred more highbrow fare there were a few other *sharif*s ready to debate matters of Koranic law, recite verses from much-loved books, even from the Holy Book itself. Our train grew longer as smaller trains joined us, until it stretched out of sight across the red-gold dunes and valleys of the wide Sahara. Its general mood resembled more closely the mood of an Odessa public holiday in August, of good-humoured determination to make the most of all the hours God granted. As a result they could be the most tolerant and in the main the most honest of people. It was necessary to cultivate these virtues. There was nothing worse, all agreed, than a mood of ill-feeling or mistrust on a caravan which might be together for months. Such a mood could, what was more, be highly dangerous for all.

Compromises were sought first in every sphere of their lives, from trading to surviving – even to war. From this mixture of Bedouin grain merchants, Sudanese traders and Berber camel-buyers, of tribes and races as unique and as far apart in culture and experience as people from Birmingham and Bratislava, in all their clannish specificity of costume and courtesy, was developed a level of social stability, a sense of the individual's responsibility to the common good, that any

Western democracy would envy. This was a world acknowledging few kings or governments, a natural democracy, almost an anarchist ideal. Sadly, though, such perfection is probably only possible in a desert or a vacuum. Why do we in the West believe we have the right to determine what is progress and what is not? We have created the power to destroy the very star around which we whirl. We, surely, are crazy? That, at least, was what I came to believe as I capered and shrieked for the entertainment of grinning Wahabi and chuckling Sudanese. As we moved deeper into Italian Tripolitania we were joined by a small band of blue-veiled Berber Hadjim returning from Mecca, their skin stained deathly grey by the indigo from their robes, so that they might have been a gathering of the dead on the walls of some kingly tomb. They had green or blue eyes, most of them, and the same fine swaggering control of their camels which a Cossack exerts upon his half-wild horse. Their long rifles and spears were slung over their backs; their bandoliers and belts were festooned with knives and the very latest in German automatics and English revolvers. These were the famous Tuareg, regarding themselves as the natural overlords of the Maghribi Sahara, the Land of the West. On their way back to their hidden cities they rode apart from the Arabs and the other Berbers, their cream and golden camels reined in silver and brass, the blue leather decorated with tassels of scarlet and white, the embroidered blankets carefully matching the rest of their costume in a display of magnificent challenge. The weapons, the vivid colour, the workmanship of their harness and clothing, were all a cautionary display of power. This display had its desired effect on their Semitic co-religionists whose chief prayer was that the veiled ones would not take against them or demand tribute for the privilege of their aristocratic company. I threw myself more enthusiastically into my rôle. Western newspapers had frequently reported cases of Europeans slaughtered by these unrulable desert warriors whose women, the Arabs said, went unveiled and worshipped equally with their men. Women even held power in the Tuareg councils and, in certain tribes, rode with their men to war.

But the blue warriors left the caravan as swiftly and as suddenly as they had joined it, disappearing back into the desert long before our camels began to sniff the water of al-Khufra. After they had gone, a prune-skinned handsome old man in a huge white turban considered old-fashioned even by his contemporaries, Achmet al-Imteyas, began to speak of a Tuareg, *al-Khadbani*, the raging one, who for years was the terror of the Sahara from Fezzan to Timbuktu and only in old age was revealed to be a woman, the mother, she boasted, of five sons, the 'husband' of a considerable number of wives and concubines. It was her sons who claimed the Sahara in her name and whose secret city lay somewhere within the Takalakouzet Massif in French West Africa. The Tuareg figured largely in al-Imteyas's tales, usually in some fabulous way and frequently as the personification of supernatural evil, to be feared, avoided and, very occasionally, tricked into releasing some legendary wise-guy (the same Ali Baba who had for instance managed to get a rabbi in Benghazi to pay for a new mosque).

I was doubtless the only one to appreciate al-Imteyas's sole critic, a pale Kurdish deserter from the Imperial Army in Astrakhan who, with a miscellaneous bunch of self-elected outriders, made himself useful to the caravan. Not one of them had a horse worthy of the name. The Kurd spoke mostly in Arabic. Sometimes, when moved to strong emotion and believing everyone but himself ignorant of the language, he would curse or disagree in Russian. 'The Tuareg,' he said in that language, 'like the Turk, controls his empire thanks to the Arab's own profound suspicion of change.'

I wish it had been safe to speak. I would have suggested his scepticism and resentment made him a suitable candidate for the Red Army. I would have suggested he return at once to his homeland, where his fellow-cynics would welcome him! Given his sympathies it was hard to understand why he had left his country to join the hundreds and thousands of Russian subjects scattered across Europe, Asia and America, even down into Africa, even to Australia, in a diaspora of previously unimagined scale. Kurds were always dissatisfied grumblers, like Armenians, but it was pleasant to listen to my native tongue, no matter how barbarously pronounced, and it helped me find further inner peace. Kolya, at this stage, insisted, in his rôle of Syrian renegade, on speaking only French and Arabic. It was important to convince, he said, the Italians.

The greatest comfort of my almost timeless existence was a developing appreciation of our camels, especially Kolya's lovely pale gold doe. Sadly, my affection was never reciprocated. For some reason no camel in the world will ever do anything more than tolerate me. Most hate me on sight. Twice, when wandering in the vicinity of one of the herds, I would be warned by a shout from the drivers and turn to see a beast, its neck stretched out before it, its great yellow teeth bared, its nostrils flaring and eyes glaring, galloping down on me, enraged and infuriated by the very fact of my existence.

As I picked up my ragged *gelabea* and dashed over the rocky ground towards the main party I would see them whooping and ululating, some cheering for me, some for the camel, providing them with enough amusement to keep them in gales of laughter for days. To them my discomfort was almost as funny as the old woman, one of those miscellaneous creatures providing us all with general services, who caught fire and could not be doused. The inept antics of those like myself, who made some attempt to help her, were the chief source of their merriment. Yet they were good-hearted in their own way and one of the Russian deserter's comrades was given a few coins to despatch the hag with a bullet from his Martini. They would have done the same for any creature without hope of survival in the desert. They valued life as readily as men of the civilised world, but the desert has no room for sentimentalists, nor for morbid introspection.

At length the wide shallow valley of Khufra came in sight, a sprawl of townships surrounding a marvellous stretch of blue water. The shuddering greens of the palms, the glittering whitewash of the mosques and houses, the shining oasis itself, were at first almost blinding. I was awed by it but Kolya said the oasis struck him as vulgar, though he admitted it was a scene which a few months earlier he would have gasped at. Even the fine palm-shaded houses and gardens of the wealthy failed to impress. He had cultivated those ascetic desert disciplines which produced the spare beauty of Al-Hambra; he had grown to prefer deeper colours, the textures of red stone and

385

tawny sands, repeated in an infinity of subtle variation like some classical Egyptian melody. The settlements of Zurruk, Talalib and Tollet were spread out across the valley, their myriad shaded stalls selling the bounty of Africa and the Mediterranean, the detritus of Northern Europe and America. Above all this brooded the eroded Libyan mesas, while here and there the orange, white and green banners of Italy flew upon the few bastions of Western civilisation. From these our latter-day Romans, unsupported by the rest of Christendom, attempted to control the growing threat of Carthage which their ancestral blood recognised, respected and feared. Kolya and I avoided the whirling dust of the Italian half-tracks and lorries, their staff cars and their motorbikes. To Kolya their presence was an offence – as if a rowdy party were taking place in a sanctuary. Realising I was a little unnerved by the size of the garrison, Kolya became warily amused. 'They presumably plan to claim the whole of Central Africa for their Empire. Will they raise the new Byzantium in the Congo, do you think, Dimka dear?'

Even then, still lacking most kinds of discrimination, I thought Kolya's remarks in doubtful taste, but he was distracted. His friends had failed to meet him near the Toom road. Approaching the centre of Khufra across from the largest mosque and a comfortable distance from the nearest army post, an agitated Kolya left me in charge of the camels while he went about his business. He was clearly familiar with the town and its satellites. I sat down in the shade of a shrine and whenever anyone addressed me I simply grinned at them and screeched, flapping my arms, *'al Sakhr! al Sakhr!'* while our camels, chiefly from habit, made desultory nips at my person. Kolya returned with a spring in his step, evidently much relieved. 'Stavisky's people went on. By now they've already crossed the Red Sea and are into the Hadjiz. They were carrying too much contraband to risk waiting for me. That's excellent news, Dimka dear.' His smile was wonderful. 'They'll hear rumours of my death. It won't be in anyone's interest to pursue me. Stavisky will write off his losses and forget all about me. Even if he finds out eventually that I'm alive, we'll have disposed of any unwelcome evidence.'

I pointed out, *sotto voce*, to Kolya that we might well be overheard. He shrugged and said, in English, 'We'll ride with the caravan as far as al-Jawf, but we can't risk being recognised by any more of Stavisky's people coming up from Benghazi so we'll have to head further over and get to Tunis, perhaps. I'm going to need a buyer. We'll steer clear of Tripoli and Tangier because someone's bound to spot one of us. That means selling to a local dealer up here, which means going to Zazara, I suppose. Another oasis the authorities deny exists!' He was satisfied with his plan. 'From there, if need be, we can make our way south, following the tropic of Capricorn all the way across the *Sahra al-aksa*!' Even I had heard that such a route was a myth, frequently searched for and never found. Kolya shook his head at this, laughing. 'Everyone knows Zazara and the Darb al-Haramiya here, though they wouldn't admit it to the Rumi. The Darb al-Haramiya is the old Thieves' Road. It's the secret slavers' route out of Chad and French West across the top of the world. The Arabs insist it is the most dangerous trail in the whole Sahara. The Berbers, who are its undisputed masters, call it the Road of Courage.' His smile continued to broaden. 'Isn't it strange, Dimka! It has a thousand names yet appears on no map. That's why it's safe for us. The British and French, for instance, have officially declared its non-existence. The Italians claim to have destroyed it. Are these the responses of men who have failed to control something, I wonder? Sour grapes, as Achmet al-Imteyas might point out.'

I ventured that not one of those names made it sound in any way attractive. I had no further curiosity about any other aspects of the slave-trade. So far we had travelled in easy-going, amicable company. But I had seen the blue-veiled warriors. Such as these would doubtless be our company on the Thieves' Road. How would they receive us?

'They will recognise men of courage,' Kolya informed me with cheerful insouciance. 'After all, there is no route mapped to Zazara. Men must find it for themselves. With a map and a compass.' He held up an old leather case attached to his belt. I admired my friend in so many ways but I must admit I had no great faith in his scout-craft. I believe now he was more desperate than he admitted. He was, I gathered, in the process of stealing a commodity of huge value. Stavisky had a hold over Kolya and had been blackmailing my friend in Paris, perhaps threatening to give him up to the Chekists, now about half the city's émigré population. There had been some trouble, too, over an Apache girl. I did not judge. I, too, have had moments when I have been unable to act like an absolute saint. *Il fallait être idiot ou hypnotisé pour périr dans ces fameux camps. Chacun a toujours être maître de son destin.*

Our journey, which would end, we hoped, in Tangier, had hardly begun. All we knew was that it would not be the leisurely and predictable trek we had so far enjoyed. By now, however, I had learned to respect the desert and never to trust it – the only attitude permitting survival. As yet we had hardly experienced the 'real' desert, that 'abomination of desolation' as Leonard Woolworth had it, although he was referring, I think, to Ur.

Egypt conquered Phoenicia but made the mistake of letting her people settle in Canaan. They had a theory that the 'Philistines' would control the Jews. And of course reckoned without Samson.

Paradoxically relieved to leave the lonely citadel of Christendom behind us, we took up with a party of tall white-robed Sheul making a trading circuit which would bring them back to Chad as wealthy men. They spoke thickly-accented Arabic and bad French. But the blacks were cheerful company for the two weeks it took us to reach al-Jawf, a typical oasis with the usual assemblage of clay hovels, ramshackle places of worship, ragged awnings and rickety stalls, but boasting a collection of Jew merchants who, judging by their relatively rich clothing, possessed the only wealth in the place and with whom Kolya did some discreet business. He disposed of our oldest and weakest camel at a price which surprised and delighted him. When he showed me the purse of gold, my heart sank. Now the Tuareg were bound to attack us. I had been listening to some of the drivers and suggested we follow one of the other routes down as far as Djarba and from there make our way to Tunis, but he said it would be too dangerous. We must be sure never to live in fear once we returned to Europe. Also we could not risk the French and Italian patrols who nowadays habitually covered those roads. The only sensible route for us was the one he had chosen.

I asked him if he was absolutely certain the Darb al-Haramiya existed. He laughed loudly at my question but did not offer a direct reply. He said I should prepare myself. In less than a week we would be making our way into the Sand Sea, *en route* for 'the Lost Oasis'. 'We'll be the first white men ever to see it!'

With good riding-camels and three of our pack animals exchanged for two fresh sturdy beasts we had traded with the Tebu who had brought them to al-Jawf to sell, we allowed the momentum of the next caravan to carry us from the oasis while our prayers were still echoing amongst the eroded hills. Kolya had insisted we needed cover so we were carrying fabrics and clothing, much of it in colours favoured by the Berbers. We now claimed to be Palestinian haberdashers from Haifa. As I had guessed, the Zazara Oasis was not marked on any map, and most believed it a myth, but Kolya's information came, he said, from an Arab slaver in al-Jawf who travelled that way regularly. It lay far into the Sand Sea, a place of lush vegetation and sweet water, hidden by a great rocky overhang so that it could be seen neither from the air nor from the ground. 'He swore it gives the purest water in the world.'

Everyone on the caravan guessed we were planning to go south-west to trade with the Tuareg and to a man declared us both mad. One Sudanese spice-merchant told Kolya he now realised he was 'as foolish as your brother. You are clearly of one blood!' He begged Kolya as a friend not to choose certain death. This caused me to sink into a peculiar, expectant calm from which it was almost impossible to arouse myself. Having failed to convince us to avoid the Thieves' Road, he shrugged and left us to the Will of God, but continued to behave as if he had persuaded us to stay with them and give up all thoughts of the Darb al-Haramiya. This was a form their courtesy took.

Again, I found it remarkable how different were all these people, all of whom were conditioned and moulded by the desert. The Sahara is a pitiless wasteland of sand and rock relieved here and there by peaceful waters and waving fronds of blood-red flowers when the palms and cactus are in bloom, yet places of sanctuary are found even in the most run-down and overpopulated of the oasis townships. It is the basis of the desert nomad's sense of order. Outside is threatening Chaos, uncertain Fate. Within the tribe, within the camp, within the family, within the tent, must be harmony. It is why the Moslem divides his world into Zones of War and Zones of Peace. Their architecture provides havens of tranquillity in the din of the city. They have developed a philosophy which seeks to accommodate the world's realities, not abolish them. This is a fundamental difference between the Christian and the Moslem and especially between the Moslem and the Westernised Jew who has done so much to tinker with the great machinery of our existence. With his 'social experiments' and his theoretical physics, he has led us nowhere but to self-destruction. This the Arab understands; it is what informs his realistic assessment of his old friend, the Jew. Otherwise he has more in common with his Semitic cousin than he has differences. This is the only ironic amusement one can gain from the Arab's superstitious notions of race. Those superstitions, to which he clings with proud insanity, are the rocks against which he dashes even his finest brains, all his ambitions, his yearning desires. Like the natives of New Guinea, he has developed a religion of self-destruction, of perpetual defeat. Sometimes, to me, this Arab seems noble in his quixotic combination of hard common sense and crazed hallucinatory vision. Perhaps Don Quixote has his most profound psychic origins in some Moorish desert where to survive you must also go mad.

These people are tender and kind-hearted. They care for one another. Finally, however, the desert allows room for too much abstract thought, especially when it concerns the outside world. Inevitably the desert gives you the mentality of a hermit, a great tendency to think in terms of broad and simple issues. The hermit comes in from the desert after ten years and he goes to the city's central square. 'I have,' he says, 'a message.' The people gather around him. They send their friends to fetch other friends. They wait, patiently, but with mounting eagerness. And when they are all congregated there, in silent respect, he looks upon them and smiles. 'Love one another,' he says.

It could be that the city complicates issues. The city is a complicated organism after all, the finest creation of mankind. What human mathematics can describe a city? The city's complexities mirror the complexities of God's universe. Yet the nomad has a clarity of vision the city-dweller will never know. That is why our cities must fly; the best of both worlds.

'It makes yer git everyfink art o' proportion, Ivan,' says Mrs Cornelius. 'Like orl big spaces. It wos ther same when we went ter Dartmoor. Or up in Yorkshire. Ya git a littel bit o' news an' yer blow it up too much.' It made me think again of the attitude towards Christians which, say, the Wahabi Arabs have, or indeed, how the Cossack perceives the Jew. Perhaps that was why I sensed such a feeling of belonging in the desert. *Stippi* or *baria'd*, the invariable view has much the same effect on the mind. As I discovered from the Bedouin, the less one sees of a supposed enemy, the more sinister he becomes. Then, of course, one's imagination has done its work. You do not recognise your enemy when you see him. Not all Jews, for instance, are Communist Fifth-Columnists; not all Christians are hypocrites.

I told Kolya I thought the Sudanese had made sense. We should employ a guide. If not a Bisharin some kinsman of the Tuareg, perhaps? But he was adamant. 'The trail is not known. The trail that leads to the trail has been lost. That is why Europeans have failed to locate it. When we find it we shall be establishing our own route. A secret which will give us a permanent advantage if we wish to do further business in this area.' Then he showed me the map the Senussi had helped him draw. It could have been of anything. But he had longitudes and latitudes. 'Once we reach Zazara, there is a well-defined trail again. More than one. Most of the rest, of course, lead to the interior. The slave roads come out of Africa, here and there, out of French West and Rio d'Oro, out of Abyssinia. Almost all black slaves go through Zazara now. From there they can go east to Cairo and the Hadjiz, to Iraq or Syria; west to Tripoli, Algeria and Morocco. The Romans no more invented the road network than they gave us mathematics. We owe both to the Arabs.'

It is true that the Arabs invented algebra. It is also true

that Einstein used algebra to invent the nuclear bomb. A fine example of Arab and Jew working together. *Nicht wahr?*

And who was responsible for the triumph of the primitive decimal system over the subtle duodecimal? The Sumerians, first to celebrate the discovery of their own mental treasure-trove, gave us the flexible mathematics of the dozen, infinitely more manipulable and therefore infinitely better able to represent and examine the world. But it was the rationalising Jews with their tens of this and their tens of that, the Arab's undivided finger, who found a way of narrowing and simplifying our achievements. This numerological imperialism earned its final great victory when Britain fell to that mathematical dullard, Monsieur Dix. Twelve groats to the penny, twelve pennies to the shilling and twelve shillings to the pound would have been 'rationalisation' enough! Without her 'illogical' currency, England was nothing. Use of such currency cultivates a subtlety of mind. The history of this century will record with cruel irony that our worship of Lord Rationality was our most ludicrous folly.

One must, I suppose, blame the French for this. In the hospital it was the same. That psychiatrist told me he was experimenting with cats. The human brain, he said, is like a computer. Oh, certainly! What he meant was he had found a model he could understand. So he promptly called the model Reality. I pointed out to him a simple truth, that the computer is the invention of Man. Man's mind, however, is the invention of God; the former comfortably finite, the latter unfathomable in its infinite variety. And for that the double-six is a better representative than the half-score. We are spurning the heritage of our first great city-builders. God gave them twelve. We have since converted His gift to ten. With our present education standards we shall soon be asking for 'one and one and one' because we no longer know how to count to three. By means of these economies do we slip steadily away from Eden. Shall we ever begin the journey home?

We left our caravan at night, before the morning call to prayer. We were out of sight beyond the rocks as the dawn rose to reveal the flat *daffa*. This waterless and barren plain of unbroken brown monotony eventually gave way to dunes which stood like rollers frozen in time, a memory of when huge rivers had boiled down the shallow dales and everywhere had been green and rich and in these lush lands rose the cities of the people who came before Atlantis, who made laws and developed great arts and sciences and knew peace. Now, with all this unearned wealth, the Arab could easily make his homeland blossom again, see it grow rich with trees and grass, but of course he has made a virtue of his desert necessities. Now his ambition is to create further wastelands wherever he has the opportunity. I do not blame this on the Moslem religion. Persia does not waste her wealth on weapons. 'But an Arab,' as Captain Quelch would say, 'genuinely loves a gun.'

That was why, I think, Kolya had hidden our Lee-Enfields within heavy bales of cloth. Under our robes and general Bedouin impedimenta we carried Webley's revolvers with a dagger or two for outer decoration to show, as the Mozabites say, we had not taken the Woman's Way. A man without weapons was looked upon with considerable suspicion by the Bedouin who, like the American cowboy, tends to wear a gun as a form of sexual identification. Some of the cowboy guns were so old, and in such bad condition, that they lived in terror of ever having to fire one. This was also true, I was told by Buffalo Bill's nephew, himself a famous Circus Master, of the Old Frontier, where a knife, an axe and a bow remained, for many years, the only reliable weapons. Only the rarest of buckaroos sported a good Colts' or a Henry's and was usually loth to employ it in any action which might mark it. Young Cody asked me to imagine how difficult it was for the Chief of Scouts to keep his buckskins, especially the white ones, so clean and bright on the buffalo trail. Constant changes were needed to ensure that the Dandy of the Plains was never dusty. And Custer took a valet with him, said Cody, to the Little Big Horn. Indeed, one legend spoke of the same valet surviving the massacre and attending his new master, Sitting Bull, on his famous Grand Tour of Europe. Wherever he went Texas Jack, for instance, would always take three wagonloads of outfits and a fourth wagon full of weaponry. Kit Carson, called *Pe-he-haska* (Golden Curls) by the Sioux, was known to have escaped at least twice from certain death with the aid of nothing but his manicure set. And, Cody had added, Jim Bridger's Palomino was the best-groomed and sweetest-smelling pony in the whole Arizona territory. He had showed me pictures of all these people. It was true. I had never realised before what emphasis America's great frontiersmen placed upon personal hygiene and smart appearance. Their spacemen are the natural successors to the plainsmen of yore. There is a lesson in this for those boys of today who come into my shop and complain because I have had an overcoat cleaned before I feel I can offer it for sale!

I had taken to Cody when I was still in Hollywood and he had promised, when we next got together, to introduce me to Pecos Bill's hairdresser. Sadly, Fate intervened. I was driven, willy-nilly, into Egypt. The hairdresser, I discovered when Cody and I met again years later, had shortly afterwards been killed by a disappointed customer up in the Texas Panhandle.

One has only to see Mr Dirty Spaghetti Eastwood to see where standards are today! I think it was one of the ways we maintained self-respect in the desert. No matter how gruelling the day's journey and how little sleep we had had during the night, we always maintained a smart appearance.

Neither plain nor dunes revealing the slightest sign of a trail, we proceeded only with the aid of Kolya's inexpert compass while he forever bemoaned his inattention during his army orienteering instruction as a cadet and cursed the British for having no talent for map-making. We were now heading more or less due south, towards the Tropic line. By this means, Kolya believed, we were certain to find Zazara or, if not, one of the slave roads which would lead us to the oasis. Under my friend's baffled guidance I had rarely felt as exposed and vulnerable. With new fatalism, however, I sat comfortably on my camel as she followed Kolya's up and down the great frozen wastes of the red Sand Sea. For some reason my female had been christened 'Uncle Tom' – actually *Um-k'l-Thoum* by Arabs, who cannot pronounce the letter 'T' any better than we can make that discreet throat-clearing sound they use in preference to the 'k' (and not so alien to a Russian as it is to a Briton). Still psychologically escaped into the Land of the Dead, I saw no sign of potential enemies in all the vast world around me. I had the tranquil satisfaction of my own company. I no longer had to caper and squawk to ensure my life. At first I was also glad to lose the burden of the five daily prayers; yet, paradoxically, after we had been moving across the dunes for a while and our pace had become steady, I began to miss the routine and discipline of the call to prayer and would gladly have resumed it. I now realised I had found a peculiar happiness and security with the caravans and felt homesick for them. I prayed our journey through the trackless Sahara would not be long, that we should soon meet another great caravan and travel with that all the way into the Maghrib. I asked Kolya if the Zazara were used only by slavers. 'And drug-smugglers and gun-runners,' he reassured me. 'It will be good to give up a few of our prejudices for a while, eh?'

I protested I had not yet come to think of the people he described as my natural comrades. He grinned at this, remarking on the wonderful sense of piety in the 'convent' of Bi'r Tefawi. I knew instinctively that his sharp tongue betrayed, as they say, a soft conscience. I did not torment him further. My friend was of the Romanoff blood. It pleased him no better than I to consort with the riff-raff. We already had sufficient money, I said, to get a passage back to Genoa or Le Havre. From there we could return to America where I had a small fortune awaiting me. All Kolya could do was remind me that I was now a Spanish citizen, Miguel Juan Gallibasta, resident of Casablanca, born in Pamplona, and a Catholic. He pointed to the passport I had picked. I told him that I had preferred my American passport and would have been willing to take my chances. Free at last of the caravan's security, we came close at that point to bitter quarrelling. Perhaps we allowed ourselves this release of tension knowing that to part now would increase considerably our chances of perishing. Frequently travellers died within a mile or less of the water whose location they had lost. I must admit, it did not seem to me to be an advantage to go from American to Spanish citizenship, especially since I had never set foot in my 'home' country.

How, I asked, would 'Gallibasta' prove himself 'Peters' back in Hollywood? Matters of identity were growing at once more complicated and less secure. The world looked up to an American film star. How could it make a myth of a Moroccan café proprietor? Kolya said that I was worrying over trifles. As soon as I presented myself back in the USA, with a tale of my capture, torture and escape, I would be a bigger hero than ever. My career was assured. I would be able to tour the country on the strength of my adventures. I said that I hoped my adventures would not be illustrated with film.

We were veiled, now, against a fine dust borne on an uncomfortably steady breeze. As yet we had to experience a full-fledged sandstorm. The Sudanese had warned that it was nearing the season of storms. Another reason, I suggested, for picking a different time to find the Lost Oasis. The Arabs adored such tales. Frequently books circulated among them – *Where to find the Buried Gold of Egypt*, *The Sweet Wells of Nubia*, and so on. They believed these much as Americans believed their *National Enquirer* or Australians their *Sun*. They told stories of men who had foolishly set off to look for these places. Even the Nazrini, the Sudanese had said, with their noisy machines, had failed many times to reach Zazara. I was conscious of the ghosts that must flock all around us, wondering how much the sand buried. How many souls had been driven like dew from the sun-withered corpses of men who had risked everything merely to prove the truth of a legend? I remembered the melting snows of Ukraine during the Civil War, that white purity hiding the evidence of a million tragedies, a million violent crimes. Perhaps now we rode over the final remains of all the travellers who had perished here in Africa, from the time of Atlantis to the present?

The ash of those dead Japanese drifts through Annaheim and settles on Pluto's gigantic ears; the ash of Greeks and Egyptians and Arabs and Jews blows back and forth on Mediterranean winds; ash from the Congo and from India and China sweeps across the surface of oceans and continents. There is so much death, so many dead. Every breath we take carries human cells to our lungs, to our blood, to our brains. We can never be free of our ancestors. Perhaps the desert contains nothing else. I fell into the peculiar trance, that state between the sleep of ages and the alertness of the instant, when we come to contemplate the nature of existence and our fulfilment of God's intentions. I blew the sand from my nostrils and spat, occasionally, on the ground. I hated to spit. I hated to lose even my urine or my sweat. I had an instinct to preserve any liquid, no matter how noxious, in the knowledge that it surely had good use in a waterless world. The dunes – great russet drifts in this part of the Sahara – glared in the heat of the day and little rivers of silver ran through them, always the mirage of water, to a point where by the time you actually saw water you had learned to ignore it. This, too, was how desert venturers met their end within very sight of the oasis. Once we passed a litter of camel and other bones, marks of a camp still in the sand, undisturbed for a century, perhaps, and a presentiment of our own slow death. Again I thought of the mummified corpses, the thoroughly preserved bodies of all those others who had sought Zazara and never found it. Why should we be favoured, when God had determined that the Zwaya'im and the Tebu'um, who were native to this region, had perished in the same quest?

My other fear, perhaps a more practical one, considering Kolya's orienteering abilities, was not that we should become irretrievably lost in the desert but that we might turn in a curve and encounter to our embarrassment just the caravan we had quit with such discreet grace. Our discretion, accepting full responsibility for our decision, would have been admired by our companions. They would be suspicious, however, if we returned for no clear reason. I had begun to concoct a suitable tale involving overwhelming Tuareg attack when Kolya interrupted my train of thought with the somewhat unoriginal observation that we might, for all intents and purposes, be traversing the sands of Mars. From my reading of Mr Wells, I said, even the Martians had no great desire to live on their home planet! Why had we to remain any longer than necessary in an environment in which no sane man – or monster – would choose to spend more than a day of his life?

Everything I said amused my friend. Eventually his laughter became so frequent and so loud I suspected he had been too long exposed to the sun and the monotony. Soon I realised that my poor friend had lost his grasp on his reason, that he had probably been insane for some while. Ironically I had linked my fate with that of an obsessed lunatic!

By the fifth day even the few distant bluffs had either disappeared or proved themselves far from unique. We roamed a trackless wilderness and all we knew for certain was the position of the sun and our relation to it. With Kolya cackling and roaring from his uneasy seat on his camel, breaking off occasionally to whistle a few bars from *Lohengrin* or *Tannhäuser* while my own sweet Uncle Tom growled and snapped with re-invigorated foul temper, as if she sensed we should never see water again, I once more reconciled myself to death.

The dust became grit, blowing steadily onto our lacerated faces. Every time I ventured to voice some trepidation Kolya would bark with laughter, informing me we were still in Senussi territory; the Tuareg would not dare attack us here. I would have welcomed a Tuareg, or anyone able to lead us back to a familiar track. Kolya said we were Bedouin now and must think like Bedouin, putting our souls into the hands of Allah. He reminded me that this was what Wagner had done and roared out some chorus from *The Ring*. Allah, I declared under my breath, I would trust rather more readily than my poor, singing fool. I should have stayed in Khufra and waited until I found a caravan heading towards Ghat, I thought, but I knew in my bones the best I could hope for without Kolya's protection would be to become a Senussi slave. (The Senussi were known to be fair, though strict, and tended to adhere to the Koranic system of punishments. Their slaves were known, therefore, for their honesty as well as their plumpness.) I remained grateful to Kolya for his rescue of me from Bi'r Tefawi, but his characteristic over-confidence, a result no doubt of his aristocratic upbringing, was an increasing source of dismay. I gave up attempting to debate these matters with him. He bellowed some phrase from *The Flying Dutchman*. Since he automatically kept goading his mount forward, I let my camel follow him, though I began to regret this when he later took to composing long alliterative verses in Old Slavonic and sang snatches of folksong, or Greek liturgy, availing himself freely of a sudden supply of drugs which he had not previously revealed to me. No doubt he planned to sell these at

Zazara or some other mythical oasis. On the first night we lost a sheepskin of water as two of our pack camels crushed against one another. We still had several more skins and a couple of tin *fantasses* slung over our camels' humps, hidden under our equipment and trading goods. We could survive for at least a week. But the event depressed me. No man on earth can go without water for more than four days whereas a camel, far from plodding into infinity, can never be trusted to survive! Some will trudge for weeks, even years, seemingly the sickliest of animals, giving no hint of weariness; others, young, healthy and pretty, might decide to fall down and die for no apparent reason, their hearts suddenly stopped. My own belief is that the camel, a noble and independent beast by nature, has always been resentful of his rôle as carrier of Man and his goods. One of the few important choices he can still make for himself is his time of death.

Through days of relentless blue, under a sun which increasingly demanded obeisance, under a night of extraordinary, comforting darkness, in which the stars became identified, each an individual, whose intensity changed with the hours, over dune upon dune and rocky pavement or parched *wadi*, we trudged due west into the widest and least-travelled stretches of the Sahara, moving steadily away from any charted or inhabited region, so that we might indeed have accidentally crossed to some incompatible planet!

Ironically, I had ceased at last to be afraid. The desert, our animals, the sky, all had become marvellous and beautiful to my eyes, for I had discovered that composure of spirit which is the mark of every desert gentleman. Karl May described it. I was at one with Death and with God. My fate was already written by Allah. I trusted to the moment. I relished the moment. I was free to wander in the Land of Shades. I was reconciled to my destiny. I had won a kind of immortality. And Anubis was my friend.

TWENTY-TWO

IN THE DESERT God came to me again and I no longer feared Him. We had suffered together, He said. Now He brought me comfort. I had not realised how thoroughly I had learned the habit of prayer, of giving myself up to my creator, of keeping faith in His plans for me. I was convinced that I was lost, that we must die in those endless dunes, but we trudged up one after another, losing our footing in the soft sand. God straightened my shoulders and cleared my eyes. He gave me back the dignity which that other abomination, that quintessence of falsehood, had stolen from me.

The back window of my flat looks out upon a great pollarded elm, protected by city isolation from the Dutch disease which destroyed his rural relatives. He stands like a triumphant giant, his head lowered, the bark of his oddly muscular arms gleaming in the misty sunshine, knotted fists of gnarled wood lifted like a champion's while another thick branch juts from below like a petrified prick. This benign monster stood there, much as he does now, a hundred years ago, before the speculators thought to evict the gypsies and pig-farmers, to get rid of the tanneries and race-track, to clear the way for respectable middle-class London expanding into confident new comforts and sentimentality, begging a suburban tree or two be spared for old times' sake.

Now the enduring elm is for me God's most immediate

symbol and evidence of my own belief in our ultimate redemption. In the desert, as one dies, it is easy to understand how one might worship the Sun, coming to believe it the manifestation of God, beginning that profound progress towards the conception of God as a unity. Nowadays it is not difficult to sympathise with the ancient Slavs, those Franks and Goths who worshipped God in the form of a tree. What is better? To worship God in the form of a Bank? Or even to worship Him in the form of a Temple? I speak, I suppose, as a kind of devil's advocate. But I have never hidden my pantheistic sympathies.

In the city, sometimes, there is only the church or the public building in which to find peace to pray, but the Bedouin can create a tranquil sanctuary virtually from nothing. I have warned Christendom for many years of how Islam carries the barbarous blood of Carthage into the very veins of Europe and America. Yet I am no hater of the desert Arab. In his desert, the Bedouin is a prince, a model of gentlemanly dignity and manly humility. However, in the deadly element of some oil-founded sheikhdom, the traditions of absolute certainty by which he has survived (prospering only through blind luck) will make him everyone's enemy. The noble Bedouin becomes a paranoid aristocrat. The great traditions of the Senussi, which brought law to the Libyan Desert, bring only bloodshed and chaos to Cairo. Jews and Arabs both are never entirely comfortable with political power. It is what makes them such dangerous enemies. Today it is fashionable to sneer at the philosophy of *apartheid*, as if it were a simple matter of black and white. For years the Arab practised it successfully. He had no problems until he himself began to break his own rules. The young today use those words like blunted weapons. They have no idea of the convictions lying behind them.

Until I arrived here I had not known that the British urban peasant is as stuffed with superstition, misinformation, prejudice, raw bigotry, self-deluding self-importance and low cunning as any inhabitant of a Port Said *souk*; he can also be quite as good-hearted, sociable, ferocious in word and kindly in deed as his Arab counterpart.

In Aristotelian terms, as I told the older Cornelius boy,

about the only thing distinguishing the Briton from the Berber is that the Berber washes more frequently. But he is unteachable. Last week he admitted he had never heard of G. H. Teed, who knew more about the British Empire than Kipling! The boy despises his own heritage. Such shame, I told him, is useless. Britain could be a great imperial power again. He laughed at me. He guffawed in the face of his country's finest traditions. Only in a truly decadent country would such irreverence go unchallenged. He says he does not hate me, only what I represent. Myself I represent I say, and God I represent. Is that what you hate? It is a mystery what he finds amusing. Mrs Cornelius has hinted more than once that his father was insane. It seems extraordinary that I was only forty when he was born. Two lifetimes.

Mrs Cornelius insists I was just as obnoxious at their age. I somehow cannot see that.

Saa'atak muta qadima, as they say in Marrakech. She is very defensive of those children and yet they are a tremendous disappointment to her. They showed a few seconds from *Ace Among Aces* on the television a few weeks ago. There we were in the same scene, Max Peters, Gloria Cornish and Lon Chaney – a moment of exquisite camaraderie, of poignant memory. I telephoned Granada to ask if they would let me watch the whole film. They said it came from America. I got the name, something like *When Hollywood Was King*, but I never heard.

There are many people in Hollywood now who suppress the truth about silent pictures. If they did not the public would soon begin to question their talent, their creativity! We are allowed only to laugh at the past or to forget it. This is how they control us. They put joke music in place of dramatic music. I know their strategies and obfuscations. They respect no one. The silent film was a rare art form. The talkers encouraged lazy directors, second-rate actors, just as big budgets were to ruin television. There is something to be said for the discipline of limitation. It was disgusting what they did to Griffith and the rest of us.

The reason I never continued my movie career was because I left Hollywood a silent star but returned to a world where

American English had become the only language permitted an actor. And the Zionists say they care nothing for Imperialism. They took control of everything. Their ambitions are reflected in their films. Look at Hollywood's devotion to Kipling. Kipling's books are loved second to the Bible by Texans. The Jew is the arch-chameleon. The Arabs will tell you the same. One only has to look at the BBC. It is controlled by Jews.

I was talking only the other day to Desmond Reid, the scriptwriter, in Henneky's. He works there. He agrees with me. 'Lefty faggot yids, mate!' His words, not mine. He writes the thrillers. I think he was with Dick Barton, Special Agent. He says I help him with his ideas. Reid was the first professional writer to suggest I order my memoirs for publication. Although he did all the Sexton Blakes in the 50s he never knew G.H. Teed personally. Apparently Teed died in hospital suddenly of a tropical disease before I arrived in England. Teed, I told Reid, was my soul's ease during some of my most trying years. Teed knew a thing or two about world politics. Unlike 'King Kong' Wallace, who wrote against Jews and Anarchists but was probably a secret Zionist and a Mason, George Hamilton Teed possessed the world traveller's sophisticated understanding of English values and of the Englishman's responsibility always to exemplify those values.

Reid says it is no longer permitted to voice such honest, common-sense opinions nowadays.

His own television work suffers, he says, from that kind of censorship. The belief that we have a free press is a nonsense, he says. In many aspects Nazi Germany had a freer press than contemporary Britain.

Our picture was in the *Film Fun*. They said it was Richard Dix and Elizabeth Allen, but that was the remake. Dix never could grow a moustache. It is typical – they care nothing for their history. I have the clipping. I showed it to them. *It's the fine photography and crashes that provide the thrills – Variety. Peters and Cornish are never less than adequate.* 'Oh, let the past bury the past!' Sammy, that fat fryshop Romeo, hangs around Mrs Cornelius and claims to be an old friend from Whitechapel. (This is what the British call 'tolerance' and the rest of us call moral torpor. Through such somnambulism are empires thrown away.) Why does she let him come round? The man has no mind, no soul. Morality must change, I am the first to agree, to suit our conditions. The morality of the Bedouin Arab is as valid to him in his deserts and watering-holes as the morality of the Japanese samurai or the Russian Cossack in his native sphere. Morality, I say, is specific. Virtue is general. To speak for a New Morality is not to speak for *Chaos* but to recognise *Change*. I am over seventy and even I understand that. Perhaps experience has taught us what these spoon-fed hippies can never learn.

This is certainly not the British Empire I was brought up to admire.

In caverns deep beneath the dunes and *sarira* a hundred empires might have come and gone leaving behind no more than a mystery, a few scraps of language, perhaps the trace of a legend, a crumbling pillar. It grew vividly clear how frail were human aspirations and I was sure that very shortly our mummified corpses would add a further numinous stratum to that shifty geology.

Since rescue was unlikely I became doggedly fatalistic, reconciled, like the Bedouin, to my end. This is how some of us survive. Others, when there is little water and they are lost with the nearest human settlement weeks away, retreat, as a saving state of mind, into raving madness: the very alternative Kolya had taken. He now assured me we were on course for Zazara but refused to let me see the compass. 'There's no point in your confusing the issues, Dimka dear.' Anyway, he said, we had passed beyond the material state and would soon enter the golden limbo which lay before the gates of Heaven. We had nothing to fear. He forced more of his excellent cocaine on me. He had at least a kilo.

Soon the only sane company I had was my grumbling camel, Uncle Tom. Kolya continued to develop his obsessions with the theory that not only was Wagner heavily influenced by Arab music but that the composer had been at least a quarter Bedouin. 'We know he experienced his own spiritual struggle in the desert.' He hummed a snatch of *Parsifal*. It is always depressing when a good friend is gripped by such paranoid banalities.

Although we were still not quite out of water, Kolya was drinking and splashing with complete abandon. He claimed that the cocaine which sustained us improved in direct proportion to the amount of liquid consumed. I was only glad that he was at least equally generous with the camels, who were now considerably fitter than either of us.

By now, Kolya, constantly sniffing cocaine and putting himself to sleep with morphine, was red-eyed and pale under his tan. He no longer shaved, or cleaned himself. He defecated quite cheerfully wherever and whenever the urge came, squatting in the sand and humming snatches of *Gotterdämmerung* to prove some lunatic point.

'Thus he sings of a new order, Dimka dearest. How Love, not Power, shall rule the world! Idealism and music combined. We shall worship not some sectarian Old Man, but a universal, all-embracing, all-loving Being! Would you call that genius Pagan? No! His love of God displayed his Senussi heritage! He returned to his desert homeland and found the truth he sought. But he refused Christian piety and rejected Jewish sentimentality as readily as Arab zealotry. That, Dimka sweetheart, is why he looked back to the great gods of a mutual past. Forces which refuse to be limited by modern theology! Dismiss these elements if you will – but they are what informed Wagner's astonishing subtleties of technique, his extraordinary use of narrative and *Leitmotif* that made him the unmatched innovator.

'In the desert Wagner learned the truths our people were in danger of forgetting. He longed to know who his father really was. He became Parsifal, that most pure and holy of knights. He became Saladin, that most godly of leaders. He was Igor as thoroughly as he was Siegfried, Arthur and Charlemagne and El Cid. Our great common heritage, our Mediterranean inheritance, was reborn through Wagner. And why? Because he returned to the womb of our culture. That place where race met race and created the chain-reaction which has not yet stopped. *Al Fakhr*, they called Wagner. The Wise One. The Old Gods pass away and it is time for Man to rule. But is he ready for the responsibility? Can't you hear the echo of the Bedouin drum, the Moorish guitar, in Wotan's final aria?

And he knew his Jew. Like his ancestors, Dimka, he knew his Jew. But this did not make him a bigot.'

I refused to argue with him. My friend was obsessed. A more superstitious person might have thought a *djinn* had taken possession of Prince Nikolai Petroff, but I could recall no moment when this would have been possible.

It was now my turn to weep for my mad friend. Indeed, in that infinity of uncaring sand, with only the pulsing globe of the sun or the cold light of the stars for company, I moaned for him. I shrieked for him. I implored Heaven to bring him back to his senses. I sobbed and I wailed. I begged whatever deity that heard me to answer my prayers. But my imploring wails were addressed to the vast, unhearing heavens. At times like these I envy the atheist. They deny God's existence. Yet sometimes, as then, it occurs to me that while God most certainly exists, He might not in any way comply with the benign image we have made of Him. We are forbidden to make God in our image – for God is most definitely not Man. God is God. Yet, all the same, God might take no more interest in us, His creation, than a cat who grows bored with her kittens. That God cares for us is our presumption. That is what we call Faith. That is the hope we cling to. Such thoughts did little to relieve my sadness, my anxiety, and my wails grew louder.

One morning Kolya was gone, leaving his camel and all his goods behind. He had, as the Bedouin say, 'walked into the desert'. I called to him. I knew the folly of leaving this spot where he could at least follow his own footprints back. I waited a day, calling out his name until my own parched throat could summon little more than a croak, even with the kindly sustenance that cocaine, in moderation, can bring. He did not return. Once I thought I heard a snatch of *The Flying Dutchman* but it was doubtless a trick of the desert. I mourned for him as I stared around at an horizon consisting only of glinting brown dunes, unchanging blue sky and merciless sun. I had never felt so lonely and yet I remained free from fear. Although I was concerned for my friend, who had, after all, saved my life, I was at that moment deeply glad to be free of the Bedouin Wagner.

I had enough water for three days, but Kolya had taken

the compass with him. All I could do was arrange my camels so that one followed another, take note of where the sun rose, and head west in the hope that I would stumble at least upon a *bi'r*, a place in the sand where I could dig for water. I took one of the Lee-Enfields from its oiled paper and fitted in a clip of ammunition. I had always been a good shot, but had little experience of single-handedly fighting off, say, a horde of attacking Gora. As long as I goaded Uncle Tom, using the long camel-whip Kolya had left behind with everything else, the other camels, lacking a dominant male, would follow their herd instinct and fall in behind her. I had little difficulty leading them over the dunes, nor was it difficult to hobble them at night. They seemed as thoroughly aware as I of our danger and our need to keep together. Uncle Tom I rewarded with her favourite treat – a plug of 'Redman' chewing tobacco I had purchased in al-Khufra.

An intelligent camel is one of God's greatest gifts. She is everything a man needs in the desert. And if she is beautiful, as my Uncle Tom, she is a perpetual reminder to us that we are no more nor less important in the sight of God than any of His creatures. As God's creatures we always have some kind of kinship to the beasts – and they to us. The symbiosis, the deep friendship, between Man and animal is as beautiful as any human relationship, and as mutually useful. This is another thing one learns on one's own in the desert. God does not forbid these things. The Bible abounds with examples of this love between Man and his cousins. Noah would have understood.

In the desert nothing stands between Man and God save Man's own self-deceit. Unless you acknowledge God's dominion, you are destroyed. There are simple parables to be learned in the desert. One loses Self, but one gains the Universe. I pray for all souls, all innocent souls who are slaughtered in War. I pray they find sweet happiness in the presence of Jesus, our Saviour and God, our Father. Let them be released from the terrors and humiliations of this world and all its unjust torments. Let the forces of evil wage war amongst themselves while the Godly remain powerless to affect the cause of peace. What was Munich but the last hope of a good man in an evil world? In the end the British betrayed him.

Kolya said religion was the last resort of rogues. Of course that can also be true. But what I would sacrifice to live in an age when God was our *first* resort and the Lord of Peace ruled our hearts and minds!

I have almost given up hope of the New Jerusalem, as the English call it. Eventually, no doubt, Karl Marx will conquer the world, Sigmund Freud will re-interpret it, Albert Einstein will provide it with suitable physics, Stefan Zweig will give us its history, Israel Zangwill will furnish its literature and we shall no longer remember a time when Christian chivalry might have recreated Eden. *Carthago delenda est*. I think not!

A wind brought up burning sand against which I veiled my mouth and eyes, finding it even more difficult to keep to my chosen direction. Her beautiful long lashes and elegant nostrils closed against the razoring wind, Uncle Tom was led up and down the dunes now furious with activity, as if a thousand wakened devils plagued our way. Every so often, through the sighing air, I thought I heard a ghostly *Meistersinger* or Kundry. I would pause and call, but I was never answered. My exposed skin was flayed. My camels, refusing to move further, folded themselves down into the sand. They would have perished, half-buried, if I had not wrapped their heads in cloth and yelled at them to rise, slashing at them with my whip, pleading with them to think of their own safety as well as mine. Then, unveiled, supremely self-contained, Uncle Tom rose at last to set an example. Soon the camels were placidly following Uncle Tom through the whirling fury of the storm. I think they now accepted that their fate was in God's hands. There is a Berber saying: *The great follow the ways of God. The would-be great follow the ways of Satan.* There is considerable truth in this. I came to understand it on the beach at Margate in 1956 when I was, of course, 56 years old. I had just heard the news that the Allied Defence Force had struck to defend a Suez Canal seized by the warlord Nasser. Nasser now has no great support in the Arab world because the Arab wants a just king, not a democracy. Chief of all he wants a successful king he can worship as a manifestation of God on Earth, just as his Sumerian ancestors worshipped their leaders. Unsuccessful leaders, like Abd el-Krim or Raisauli are simply forgotten.

Krim was first defeated the year I entered the Western Desert. As a result, all the scum who had flocked to his standard were scattered some fifteen hundred miles across the *sarira* and dunes, surviving by any means they knew. And most of what they knew involved murder and rapine, especially those Kurdish mercenaries who had been the first to flee. Like Trotsky, Krim had found it expedient to murder or betray some of his own lieutenants, to prove his loyalty to the French who sent him to Paris with his loot. But this is Arab politics. It is their culture. Some might say it is our culture, too. But our own half-conscious tribal customs are never entirely clear to us, I suppose.

The English and Americans always amuse me with their denial that they display such unconscious tribalism. Only true citizens of the world like myself are relatively free of unexamined prejudices. Margate, I sometimes think, was my psychic Waterloo, just as Suez was Dunkirk for the British and the French. It was then I was stunned to realise that the English, after letting Persia seize their oil in 1951, had given up their responsibilities in the Middle East while America had failed to take up the burden. It was the fall of Constantinople all over again.

Parched, down to a few sips of water and all that remained of a kilo of cocaine, together with a little morphine and hashish, I refused to crack. I would not let madness overtake me as it had my poor friend.

A day later, as the storm subsided to a few streamers and dust-devils, I thought I heard distant thunder, rolling as it does, through echoing hills. The camels grew alert and joyful. Here was a promise of rain, or at least water. Sayed the Sudanese had told me that thunderstorms often followed sandstorms. Sometimes they coincided. Sometimes rain came. It was unlikely, I reasoned, that it would rain here, in the dunes, but in shaded limestone hills pools sometimes formed. I summoned my energy, sipped the last of my water, touched some cocaine to my raw gums and led my little caravan towards the sound of thunder.

And there at last, just before sunset, I saw the pale blue horizon broken suddenly by a line of low, rocky hills over which a few wisps of cloud hung, as if glad of any company. I began to shake with joy. I even wept a little, yet was so conscious of losing water that I spread my tears over my face and neck before urging my camels down another dune. The hills were lost from sight, but I had taken their position from the setting sun and would know which way to go as the stars came out.

So, with sun, stars and God as my infallible guides, I came at last to the Lost Oasis of Zazara. She was neither mirage nor legend. But I was not to drink her waters for many more hours.

For a second time I heard rattling thunder from the hills but I paused, suddenly suspicious. From the distance I realised I had heard not a storm but a rapid exchange of rifle fire. My heart sank. Ahead of me some tribal conflict was in session. My arrival might, in time-honoured fashion, make both sides decide to satisfy their honour by burying their differences, killing the stranger and dividing up his goods.

For this reason I approached the hills as the Bedouin had taught me, making a wide arc until I could be sure that I could reach the hills without myself being easily seen. Frequently I paused to rest and listen, a bullet in my Lee-Enfield's breech instantly ready to be fired as a warning to anyone who tried to attack. But obviously the warring parties were busy with their immediate dispute and had not noticed me. Every so often the gunfire would rattle again and then there would be silence, doubtless as the combatants licked their wounds and reconsidered their strategy.

In other circumstances, I would have risked going on, but Zazara was on the Darb al-Haramiya which, all knew, led for thousands of miles back into the Sudan, down into French West Africa, to Chad, to Abyssinia, to Fezzan, Tripolitania, Algeria, Morocco and Rio de Oro. I was at another terminus and could go almost anywhere I wished. My only problem now was how to avoid being robbed and murdered. Once I had taken stock of the terrain I might be able to sneak into the oasis, water my camels, fill my *fantasses* and get

410

out again while the factions were still occupied with their battle.

By now half-crazy with thirst, my body having no patience with my mind's disciplines, I yearned to run into those crumbling hills and seek the water the camels were already trying to sniff.

I would not be able to hold my beasts back for long. Only an experienced camelman can do that. Soon they would begin to trot forward. I would lose control. I decided therefore that it was best to lead them, rather than follow. Uncle Tom, dignified as always, was proceeding at her usual unhurried walk. When she glanced back over her shoulder to make sure her herd was following, her lovely eyes were full of concern, her lips drawn away from her great prehistoric teeth in an encouraging smile. How proud I was when I remounted her with all the casual grace of a true Bedouin and, my rifle across my knee, began the jog up the slow-rising foothills until I was forced again to dismount and lead my patient animals foot by painful foot over the hard rock of limestone pavements scattered with pebbles. They gulleys between the pavements were full of recent drifts of soft sand and looked dangerous. The pebbles caught in my camels' toes, threatening to lame them, and I was forever stopping to check their feet, to make sure they were still unharmed. Concentrating on our slow, careful progress into the hills beneath a pulsing blue-grey sky, I did not notice when the loose sand no longer ran between rocky hillocks. Instead, there were man-made divisions – old walls worn to the same gentle golden brown of surrounding rock and sand. I realised I was leading my camels through the ruins of a good-sized city stretching as far as I could see along the eroded terraces of forgotten Zazara. A city of unguessable age, destroyed by the same forces which no doubt claimed Nineveh and Tyre. As with so many North African ruins, they might have been twenty or two thousand years old. Only an archaeologist could tell. They had been thoroughly abandoned for years. There was no vegetation, which could also mean that there was no water at the Zazara Oasis! Or was it hidden and guarded, as the powerful Senussi Bedouin protected some of their wells?

Renegade Zwayas, driven out of their traditional lands

by the ever-expanding Senussi, might even now be disputing control of the oasis. I tethered my camels as they swung restless necks back and forth, tongues curling, nostrils expanding and snuffling for the source of the water. As the afternoon shadows lengthened, I moved forward carefully, keeping to the cover of old walls until I realised I was almost at the highest point of the hill which cut off suddenly and seemed to fall sheer to a valley from where I could hear distant shouts and whistling, voices speaking a dialect I did not recognise. Behind me, my camels began to snort and grumble and, lest they give me away, I ran back to where I had left them, unhobbling them and leading them forward again. I was still careful to keep to cover wherever I found it until the sun began to drop beyond zenith. I stopped close to the brow of the hill and began crawling forward to peer carefully over the edge.

The cliff did not as I had thought fall sheer to the bottom, but was broken just below me by a great limestone spur jutting out over a shaded pool around which grew a few date palms and reeds: Zazara was not dry! From where I lay it was difficult to make out details, but obviously a camp had been made. I saw some tents and one or two figures walking rapidly to and fro. They were not Bedouin at all, but Goras, relatives of the Sudanese, whom I had already met on the caravan from al-Khufra. Tall, handsome black men, they had only a few firearms and still preferred the spear, the sword and the bow. I was surprised that the Gora could have fired with such promiscuous precision. Then, as I craned to see more, I observed, directly below, something I first took to be water and then a mirage. It actually seemed to be a vast green, white and red Italian flag draped across a wide expanse of rock, the crowned *crux blanca* flanked by the fasces of Mussolini's New Rome emblazoned onto two yards of rippling silk! As if the Italians had decided quite literally to put the Libyan Desert under their flag.

I realised the fabric was attached to ropes and if I risked raising my head and craning my neck a little further I could see that the ropes ran up to a large wicker basket, big enough to hold at least half-a-dozen people, and it was then that I understood that I was staring down upon a huge collapsed balloon. Doubtless some party of aeronauts, perhaps from the Italian garrison at Tripoli, had become stranded. I hoped that it was a military group. With the rifles and ammunition I had, together with my food, we could almost certainly kill off enough primitive Goras until they fled.

At that moment a burst of fire caused me to duck rapidly but when I looked again I saw that the only shots were coming from the balloon. Repositioning myself behind a rock I made out a narrow track leading down to the spur of limestone where the balloon basket was perched, then continuing on until it reached the water below. The Goras could not be native to this region or they would have known that there was another approach to the position. In the deep afternoon light, with arrows and spears they flung themselves up the steep rocks, only to be driven back by rapid but economical fire from the crashed balloon. Again I marvelled at the precision of the shots and, by shifting a third time, saw that in fact there was only one gun, a large old-fashioned French Gatling, a *mitrailleuse*, mounted on a brass swivel bracketed to the basket's rail. At the basket's centre was what seemed to be a small semi-dormant steam-engine. The bullets went over the heads of the determined Goras. I could see from their expressions that their worst fears were realised. Satan's agents had descended upon them. It said something for their courage and their religious faith, if not their common sense, that they were attacking rather than fleeing. I decided I could, without much difficulty and with my camels, reach the rocky spur and the stranded balloon. If the Goras could be driven away from the water, we should soon all be able to drink. It seemed the more noise and dust I made in my descent, the more I gave the impression of a large force coming to the aid of the balloonists. With luck this would make them reconsider the wisdom of their present policy. It would be no shame to them to withdraw before a superior enemy.

I returned to my camels. Using what little Italian I had learned in Otranto, when Esmé and I had come ashore after fleeing from Constantinople, I informed the balloon that help was on its way. When I removed her hobble, Uncle Tom looked at me with grateful loving eyes. I let her lead her little tribe up to the cliff and begin the difficult descent down the twisting sandy path, certain that the Italians' Gatling would deter any would-be archers. *'E da servire?'* I called, letting my Lee-Enfield off into the air and badly jarring my shoulder. I was not familiar with the rifle's legendary kick. Someone once told me that the Lee-Enfield .303 was known as the Hun's Best Friend in the trenches, yet most Tommies swear by them to this day. The smoking gun in my all-but-disabled hand, I waved friendly greeting to the ballooners. The *mitrailleuse* did not turn in my direction. This was surely a sign that I was accepted as an ally.

It was at this point that Uncle Tom went down with a look of startled disgust, legs sprawling at unlikely angles, neck straining, deeply conscious of her ruined dignity. I lost hold of her halter and, in lunging for it, fell to the ground, rolling towards the basket as my rifle went off a second time, bruising my finger and thumb. In confusion, the other camels began to buck and growl, threatening to shed their own loads. I fought to get Uncle Tom to her feet so that we might both re-order our dignity when from the basket ahead, as I settled at last in its shadow, rose a vision of womanhood so lovely that once again I questioned my own sanity. Was this all part of some complicated hallucination? Was I still out in the desert, raving my last?

She wore a helmet of pale blue silk from which escaped two exquisite red curls on either side of a lovely heart-shaped face. Her gown was fashionably short and matched her cap. Like the cap, it was stitched with scores of pink and blue pearls. I had seen costumes to rival it only in Hollywood. Her fresh complexion, touched lightly by fashion's demands, her beautiful turquoise eyes, her perfect, boyish figure, were complemented by a self-assured grace as she swung herself over the side crying, in English, 'How wonderful! Magnificent! My prayers are answered!' She ran, on low-heeled shoes which matched the rest of her outfit, towards the spot where, with curling mouth, rolling eyes and great melodramatic curses, Uncle Tom was getting to her feet. At last she was steady, to my great relief, but an expression of acute embarrassment now shadowed her sensitive features. 'Thank you!' cried the young woman. Then she turned, as if in apology. 'I'm terribly grateful. I say, would you mind taking over the Gatling and keeping an eye on the natives? They've been a nuisance ever since I crashed, but I don't want to hurt them.' She began to tug at the bales of fabric on one of our camels. 'Oh, I say! Silk! I couldn't ask for more! Silk! Silk!'

With some difficulty I clambered up the rigging and got into what was now very clearly the gondola of an ambitious scientific expedition! There were chests and instrument boxes all around the edges, while at the centre was a small spirit-fired steam-engine, capable, I was sure, of generating the heat necessary to keep the balloon inflated. The basket was oval and had a small propeller which I would guess was next to useless for powering or steering such a large balloon. Gingerly I took the handles of the Gatling in my fingers and peered over the basket's rail. Down on the other side of the water the dark-skinned Goras were standing about near their tents talking to a young man in a white turban, who would be the son of their sheikh. He was pointing back at the narrow fissure in the rock, evidently the other path into the oasis. I was glad they had lost interest in us for the moment. It gave me time to recover from my surprise that the only occupant of the balloon appeared to be a beautiful young woman whose chief problem was which material to choose for a new costume! I wondered, if I had found her out in the desert dying of thirst, she would not have called delicately for a glass of ice-cold Bollinger's '06. I was a little admiring of such sang-froid in so young a woman and I was reminded of Mrs Cornelius (whom she did not otherwise resemble). In a few minutes she returned dragging a bale of cloth, part of our bogus trading goods. 'It's just right.' She still used English. 'I'm awfully sorry. I'm being frightfully rude.' She began to speak in a slow, childish Arabic which became charming on her lips. 'I am grateful to you, *sidhi*, for your generosity in aiding one who is neither of your tribe, nor of your religion. God has blessed me.'

Her manners were rather better than her vocabulary. I decided, for the moment, to let her continue to believe me a simple son of the desert, some noble Bedouin Valentino who had arrived to save her in the nick of time. Admittedly,

Valentino had saved his young woman from a fate worse than death whereas I, apparently, had merely broken a sartorial impasse. She put her hand to her little breast and introduced herself. 'I am Lalla von Bek and I am a flyer. I meant no ill in your land. I was shot down by a stray Arab bullet. See.' And she pointed at a hole now visible just above the bag's emblazoned crown. 'I am on official business for the Royal Italian Geological Society.'

For my own amusement I replied in English. 'My brother was doubtless aiming at the cross. I see from your instruments that you are making maps. Perhaps you are seeking gold in our land?'

She was vehement. 'Oh, no! It's oil, anyway, everyone's looking for. This is a purely scientific expedition. I say, your English is wonderful. Were you educated over there? Or America? Do I detect a trace of Yankee?'

'The wanderlust of the Bedouin is legendary, even among the Nazrini,' I said. 'But I have never seen a hot-air balloon as elaborate as this.'

'Unfortunately,' she said, 'it is rather *over*-elaborate. It's very hard to keep height, you know, without throwing everything out. I'd never have been shot down if I'd had the ship I asked for. Still, I must admit, the gun did come in useful. I'm sorry if you hurt yourself. I have a little first-aid experience. If you like . . .'

I refused manfully. It did not suit me at that point to let her see the whiteness of my skin beneath my robes.

Like Kolya, I had been burned dark by the sun and had a full beard. I flattered myself that I looked every inch a Saharan nobleman.

'Let the silk be my gift to you,' I said, observing the courtesies of desert meetings. 'I hope you will look even more beautiful in it.'

She seemed impressed by my manners but baffled – then she smiled. 'Oh, the silk! It's for the balloon. We'll cut a panel, oil it with what you have in that jar and make it airtight. I'm sure I have the other things I need. Those beggars down there got the best of my kit. It rolled out when we landed. We bounced a bit, as you can see.' Reminiscently she dusted at her dress.

416

'Though I am a bit fussy about clothes.' She became thoughtful. 'It doesn't do to lose your standards.'

'A sentiment you share with the Bedouin,' I said.

She was flattered by the compliment. 'This isn't what I normally wear, but I was beginning to feel a bit down. A change of clothes will often cheer you up. Now you've arrived so I was right to look on the bright side. It's just like a film, isn't it?'

I was not happy to be reminded, just then, of the moving-picture industry. She took my silence for dignified disagreement. 'I'm sorry, I suppose you're not allowed to watch them.' She was gracious. 'I haven't given you a chance to introduce yourself.'

'I am the Sheikh Mustafa Sakhr-al-Dru'ug,' I said, borrowing my name from an old script. 'Like you, madam, I am an explorer. It is a tradition among my people. We are natural travellers.'

Enthusiastically she endorsed my opinion, betraying, I thought, a dangerous *Arabismus* which has led more than one European woman astray. Yet it did not suit me to puncture her illusion. Something told me she would have more interest joining forces with a Desert Hawk than with a Steppe Eagle. Bedouin or Cossack, we still had more in common than we had differences and it was natural of me to assume the rôle of benign protector to a young girl stranded in the deep desert. It was my instinct, a natural chivalry.

However, when I asked after 'dear old Eton', I was astonished to learn that she was not English at all and had lived there only intermittently. 'My father was Count Richardt von Bek. My mother was Irish, Lady Maeve Lever of the Dublin Levers. I was finished in England, but I am by birth an Albanian. A second cousin, as it happens, to King Zog. I became an Italian national in 1925.'

'Evidently you are an admirer of Signor Mussolini.'

'Rather! My father always said Italy only did well under brilliant individuals. He was a Saxon, of course, and inclined to overstatement. He preferred the free-and-easy atmosphere of Albania. He was employed by the Turks. Engineers could live like princes in those days. We had a simply marvellous

417

childhood. It spoiled us, really. And then, of course, Mother died of consumption, Father was shot as a traitor and that was the end of it. Luckily they'd taught us to stand on our own feet.'

'You have brothers?'

'Only sisters. They're all married but me now. Really, I'm an engineer, but I can't tell you how hard it is to convince people that I'm as good as a man. That's why I'm here, really. A sort of publicity stunt, you'd call it. So people will take me seriously.'

'I am familiar with such stunts,' I told her. 'And have an interest in engineering matters myself.' My blood quickened at this change of luck. In the middle of the Sahara I had met a personable and pretty young woman who also happened to understand engineering. Such girls, who even today are considered odd, were thrown up by the Great War. I have nothing against them. Many have natural aptitudes in that direction, though as yet we have to see a female engineering genius. They will tell you they are above such things, preferring to sew and cook. Perhaps they really do prefer such activities. If so, it rather proves my point. I continued to treat Signorina von Bek with grave courtesy, delighted at last to meet in the desert someone who understood the difference between an internal combustion engine and a magic nut. 'Not to mention,' I added for *politesse*, 'Albania.'

From where I had hobbled them, my thirsty camels were complaining – roaring and grumbling loud enough to drown parts of our conversation.

'Sons of the eagle, indeed!' she said, indicating the collapsed fabric. She referred, I suppose, to the Albanians' name for themselves, *Skayptar*. The smaller the country, the bigger its airs. Just as it is with little men. I remember the Lett, Adolf Ved. His country's self-advertisement was only matched by its vainglory. And all they had in the way of a cultural tradition was a few borrowed folk-songs, a national hero with an unpronounceable name and a Jewish university. Yet I was grace itself, and she brightened. 'Look,' she said, 'it will soon be sundown. I must offer you *daifa*. I'll get the primus going. Natives don't like to attack, you know, at night. What would you say to some turtle soup and rusks? We could start with some *pâté de foie gras* and there's still an excellent St Emilion in the locker somewhere. The champagne, I'm afraid, exploded. The heat and the altitude, I suppose.' She led me towards the centre of the gondola where she had erected two parasols for shade above a camp table set with silverware and napkin for one. From a locker she produced a second folding chair and from a chest a set of cutlery. 'I prepared for visitors, you see. Not quite knowing where I was going to land.' She hesitated. 'Oh, I say, you're not forbidden to eat anything, are you? Apart from pork, I mean.'

I assured her I had the usual traveller's dispensations and could, with her permission, even join her in a glass of claret. She apologised for her ignorance of my people's customs. At least, I said, she had an interest in correcting her ignorance and had come to see us for herself and not depend upon the Albanian newspapers to characterise us. She was pleased by this. She said she had been told of the legendary good manners of the Bedouin. 'I share that quality,' I told her, 'with your Don and Kuban Cossacks.'

She seemed surprised by the reference, since few Bedouins are prepared to be compared to anything less than a demigod, but she took my remarks for modesty, warming to me still more. I basked in this angel's approval! What ordinary man – what man of any kind – could fail to be charmed? I must admit I had no incentive for disabusing her. It had become second nature for me to disguise myself. For all her enchanting qualities I had no reason yet to trust Signorina von Bek.

The Bedouin were respected everywhere in the desert. Even a single traveller was usually left in peace, for he was likely to have blood kin across the whole region. The fundamental point of the blood feud is that it has to remain a credible threat, for it is by this means that men are dissuaded from killing, and Chaos is kept at bay. Dog rarely attacked dog unless desperate or sublimely certain of his superior strength. That was also why, since the Goras were clearly well-fed and watered, I did not expect the conflict to last much beyond another day or two. Now they believed reinforcements had arrived, they would almost certainly choose the better part of valour.

It was with a relatively easy mind that I sat down to tea with the pretty aeronaut while, visible below amongst the palms, the Goras argued over the day's developments in high, declamatory voices. It was almost impossible to ignore the babble. I was suddenly reminded of taking a sunset supper on the balcony of Kruscheff's in Kreshchatik, with the busy life of Kiev's mainstreet going on below. I became nostalgic for my native trams, the colour and warmth of my childhood Ukraine and I would have wept in nostalgia rather than sadness, had it not been necessary to control myself, to remember I was a Bedouin and a gentleman. I still long for that Kiev. But it is a model today, like Nuremberg – an unconvincing Disney lifesize working replica of the great original. In the end, the communists destroyed both cities.

Renis le Juif et tu renieras ton passé.

I no longer worried that I might be hallucinating and lost in the desert. It was clear to me that this was either an elaborate illusion or that I had actually died. I had come, as the Bishop always puts it, to my reward. Yet, although Signorina von Bek's scent was as subtle as her physical aura, and I was ready to enter any fantasy, I was not sexually aroused. Perhaps sensuality had become an over-familiar and rather horrible language to me. I was in a state of perfect platonic bliss, revelling without lust in the essence of her femininity as much as I enjoyed the quick amiability of her mind. I remained a little withdrawn, however, and as a result we kept a certain formality which was not uncomfortable. Indeed, we became quite cheerful as we discussed the accomplishments of fascism and the likely achievements of a reinvigorated Italian state. She knew my friend Fiorello. He was now a bureaucrat, she said. She apologised for the inadequacy of the shelter. 'We had simply not anticipated needing it. It's so hard to keep the sun off one's arms and face. I freckle awfully easily. Of course, your women have the right idea. I can perfectly see the practicality of their clothes. The flies alone are bad enough. I hope I haven't shocked you, *sidhi*, with my costume. I wasn't really expecting a guest. But soon, of course, it will get chilly.' She reached for her powder-blue cardigan.

I assured her that I was at ease with the ways of the

West and she could rely upon my understanding. It was important, I told her, that mutual respect be established between human beings. The desert made brutes of some – I waved my soup-spoon at the shadowy quarrelling Gora – but it also demanded that, for survival's sake, we maintain civilised discourse and behaviour.

Signorina von Bek agreed with considerable vigour. Standards were the key to everything. I was increasingly impressed by her quick wits. This woman was a true kindred spirit! We shared a fundamental political philosophy! In everything but appearance, she was a man! Myself! A perfect pal, especially under the present circumstances. As we sipped the claret and studied the agitated congress in the sun's last rays, it seemed to me that she had adopted a certain coquettish air.

I was flattered by her interest but remained unaroused. The very thought of another's flesh next to mine was almost sickening. Only Kolya or Uncle Tom had known how to soothe me. Sensing my reserve, she of course took even more of an interest in me. She was lady enough, however, to make only the subtlest hint by word or gesture and I enjoyed a growing sense of well-being. It was a timeless moment. I have never quite experienced the same combination of sensations and circumstance. I knew then that this was reality.

We finished our third cup of *thé arabien*, the delicious scent of mint augmenting the more exotic odours, and I thought I heard again the faint sounds of singing. I strained my ears and peered into the gloom, wondering if it were only the breeze, but I was fairly sure I had caught a few notes of *Tristan und Isolde*. Even as my hostess chatted on, I cocked the other drum to discover the direction of the song, but the arguing of the Goras in the torchlight drowned everything. They were all looking towards the fissure, the oasis entrance, as if wondering whether to leave or perhaps to attack from another direction. They could see little of our ledge from their own position and could have no idea how many reinforcements I had brought.

She was speaking suddenly of Tokyo, which she had visited a year or two earlier with a League of Nations party. 'There's no doubt that intellectually the Japanese are at the head of the Mongol races. And, of course, racial purity is as important to them as it is to white people. Pure blood, as they say, will always triumph over mixed.'

Although only a year or two younger than myself, she was wiser than I. Women often attain maturity earlier. I have regretted not listening at the time more carefully to her ideas. It would have saved me a great deal of inconvenience and danger in later years. But then I was wondering if she had not provided herself with some kind of protective logic: an antidote, as it were, against her sexual attraction to me. For my own part I was almost incapable of innocent conversation. I had become responsive to nuance. I had developed the profound alertness of the hunted animal. I listened to her; I listened to the Gora; I listened to all the sounds of the desert, constantly interpreting yet, relative to earlier states, thoroughly relaxed. I had learned another migrant animal's trick and took advantage of every secure moment, every chance to rest.

Again I thought I detected a tune on the wind, an aria from *Tannhäuser*, perhaps. This time I politely signalled to her, listening carefully. I began to suspect I was haunted by no more than a painful memory.

She asked what I heard, but I shook my head. 'I was listening, I suppose, to the desert,' I said.

She was impressed by this and for a while said nothing. It was not yet nine o'clock and the Goras had still failed to reach a decision. I was considering firing a burst from the *mitrailleuse*, to encourage them, when I saw that some of the blacks were coming back into their firelit camp pushing a prisoner, a bearded, wild-eyed creature, barefooted and in the torn burnoose of a Bedouin. His arms were bound behind him and a stick had been wedged in his teeth, tied with thongs to gag him. It was a moment before I recognised Count Nicholai Feodorovitch Petroff. He would, as he had promised, be the first white man to taste the waters of the Lost Oasis!

Now I understood the complexities of the Gora debate.

They were wondering if Kolya could be of any value to us. If so, with a hostage they might be able to barter, save face and regain their dignity before moving on. All that remained was for me to put down my teacup, walk to the edge of the basket, raise a large hurricane lamp and sign a greeting to the white-turbanned chief. 'I believe,' I said in my best Arabic, 'that there has been a misunderstanding.'

Signorina von Bek joined me at the rail. 'Is that a comrade of yours, Sheikh Mustafa?'

'A servant,' I explained. 'A simple-minded fellow. He wandered off some days ago. He is the son of a Caucasian woman and has a smattering of Russian. Do you speak Russian, Signorina von Bek?'

She admitted to only a few words. This meant I could address Kolya directly.

'My dear friend, I intend to rescue you,' I called. 'But you must play your part.'

I was pleased to see Kolya nod vigorously, proving he still had some control of his sanity.

Then began the long negotiation with the tribesmen as they attempted, through shouted questions, to get some measure of Kolya's value to me. I understood they were offering this slave for sale. I was in need, I said, of a strong fellow, but this one looked rather weak. Had he been exposed to the desert? And why was he gagged?

They assured me he was muscular and fit, a veritable work-camel of a creature. True, at present he was a trifle touched by the sun, but this made no difference to his value. He would recover.

By this time negotiations were settling into a rhythm and I felt my friend's cause would best be served by my pretending a lack of interest. 'A strong dog is of no use to me if he is mad. Look – he is foaming!'

They responded with shrill denials. That was merely saliva caused by the tightness of the gag. If I was not interested, they would take him to Khufra and sell him there. I remarked that I had come from Khufra and was not aware people were buying crazed outcasts to work their fields. The slave must be possessed, I added, by a *djinn*. Why else would he be bound and gagged in that way? Better allow the poor creature to wander into the desert where God would look after him.

No, they insisted, he would work. By torchlight they removed Kolya's ropes. They took the stick from his mouth. He mumbled something incomprehensible. Then, with their spear-tips, they pushed him towards the water and watched as he drank. Next he was forced to fetch skins to the oasis and fill them, which he did with some speed, aware of the importance of playing this game to the full. He hurried back and forth through the firelight. He carried a dozen skins at a time. I began to fear that he would work so hard he would put his price beyond my means.

Signorina von Bek was admiring of my bargaining skills, although I had not as yet made any kind of offer for Kolya. We were still at the stage of agreeing whether he was worth selling or not. As the moon emerged and silver light spread to the horizon, either side had yet to name a price. At length I told them I would say in the morning if I wished to make an offer for their captive. We would all sleep on the question. Kolya did not seem too pleased by this, but I spoke briefly in Russian again, as if calling back to someone in my own party. 'Be patient, old friend. I will have your release by noon tomorrow.'

That night, after I had bedded down and watered my camels using Signorina von Bek's reserves of ballast, I wearily wrapped myself in my *jerd* and prepared myself to sleep on the ground. On the other side of the wickerwork, Signorina von Bek remained awake for some while, reading by the light of the hurricane lamp while out of the darkness came the muffled rendering of some of the more familiar passages from *Lohengrin* sung against the monotonous rhythms of a Gora drum with which, I think, they were trying to drown him out. Eventually his voice cut off suddenly and I shared the relief of silence.

In the morning I was awakened by the pretty aeronaut in her loose, hooded *djellabah* offering me a cup which, from its smell, could only hold Columbian coffee. I shook my head in surprised delight and sat up.

'I hope your poor servant survived the night.' She offered me the china sugar-basin. 'He seemed very upset. Is it a kind of Bedouin blues? His singing sounded almost Wagnerian at times. Are you familiar with the composer's work?'

I explained how the poor creature had for some time been in the employ of a Beiruti gramophone-seller and had picked up snatches of German music from the records he had heard.

424

Like certain other idiots, he had a gift for musical mimicry. He would calm down, I assured her, as soon as he was returned to us. It would be best, however, to avoid the subject of the Master of Bayreuth.

'He seems quite good-looking,' she said, 'under all the filth and sunburn. Was his mother beautiful?'

'She was a Russian aristocrat,' I told her truthfully, 'who became his father's wife.'

She nodded. 'The genes sometimes do not withstand the shock. I myself have some of that dangerous old blood. Even mixed with its own kind it can produce mental deficients. My sister for instance is quite raving. It is the same with horses, of course. Would you care for a rusk and a little *confiture*? It's all I have to offer for breakfast. The butter went off.'

I agreed to join her as soon as I had said my prayers. It did no harm to show devotion, especially to the Gora, who would expect it from me. Indeed, they would become suspicious if I ignored the morning prayer.

She was peering through a binocular when I came to the table. 'He seems better rested, your fellow.' She handed me the glasses. Kolya, a trifle less red-eyed than he had been, was staring up at us in baffled agitation. Then we watched as again he was put to work to display his stamina.

It was probably better that he was occupied. It diverted him from Wagner who, after all, had contributed to his predicament. I think he had begun to realise this and his sense of humour returned. Once he glanced over his shoulder and called in Russian, quite cheerfully, 'You see, Dimka dear – I promised you we'd find slavers here.'

The problem, as I remarked drily, stroking my Bedouin beard, was not how to find the slavers, but how to lose them. I would guess that the only reason they had attacked the balloon in the first place was because they thought it undefended. Now honour had been restored and decent intercourse begun, they would almost certainly drift back towards the Sudan or whatever god-forsaken wasteland they recognised as home.

'See!' said the only Gora who spoke much Arabic. 'He is good and strong and when he works he does not sing.'

'But where will I keep him? He cannot work all the time.'

'Work him hard, then he will be too tired to sing.'

I considered this reasonable logic for a while. 'Well,' I said, 'he seems strong enough. We could perhaps use another ammunition-carrier.' I took a step or two back, out of their view. When I returned I said that we did not all agree that we required another slave. We broke for coffee. Meanwhile Kolya staggered to and from the oasis with his waterskins.

'He is very strong,' said Signorina von Bek, munching a rather inexpertly pickled cucumber, 'it seems wrong that you should have to bargain to buy your own slave back.'

'Sadly,' I said, 'there are very few circuit judges in the desert. The law of possession carries considerable authority here.'

She took my meaning and smiled. 'It's your job to keep what's yours, eh? That's the kind of individualism the New Order is encouraging in Europe. They could learn from you.'

'Oh, I think my people have taught them much already,' I quipped, almost chiding. She responded to this with a blush. I put out my hand to touch hers, to reassure her that I meant no ill-will. At which she smiled, and I was doubly entranced, yet still in that same delicious, platonically spiritual state where my ordinary senses seemed to quiver delicately on the brink of ecstasy, yet required no physical expression.

After lunch, as Kolya lay panting in the shade of a small palm, I returned to the lip of the rocky spur, Lee-Enfield crooked in my arm, and said that I had been elected to inspect the slave. I began the courtesies of approach and they responded. Carefully I climbed down the path towards where they waited on the far side of the dark water. The heavy limestone overhang, which protected the place from the sun's rays and had allowed the pool to form, was reflected in the oasis, together with the few clumps of date palms planted here, no doubt, by the civilisation which had abandoned Zazara. Beyond the gathered Gora were their somewhat threadbare woollen tents, some skinny goats and a few tethered camels. These people looked like outlaws, irregular and amateur slavers at best. I had seen the powerful Bedouin slave-masters. They were grandly dressed and heavily armed, with tents, servants, wives and beasts of burden befitting their station. They would only have taken pity on Kolya as their code demanded, and helped him to his destination. Pride would not have allowed them to spend a minute of their time considering his sale. By deigning to bargain I was myself risking losing face, but I must also give these black rogues enough face so that to trade would suffice. They could then leave with all honour. I was certain they had not instructed scouts to come round on us and did not know how few our numbers were. Perhaps they did not want to know a truth they suspected. Ignorant, they would not feel called upon to take violent action, especially since our Gatling remained our chief argument.

I reached the level rock and approached them, pausing to lay my rifle and my knife on the ground. The Arabic-speaking princeling in his white turban stepped forward and put down his own bow and spears. We had now established an understanding which would pertain no matter how heated our argument became. I was welcomed into their camp. They led me to where Kolya, grinning and still half-mad, said to me in French, 'Damn you, Dimka, if you don't like the look of me let them sell me to someone who does!'

I shook my head at this and said to the chief, 'See, it is true. Allah's mercy on him. He is possessed. A *djinn* speaks through him. What is that monkey jabbering?'

'It is Frank. Perhaps we should take his tongue off,' proposed the chief thoughtfully, looking around for a blade. 'That would make no difference to his work.'

I agreed that this might be the short-term remedy but he might as well stay intact for the moment. Suppose the *djinn* were driven out, then the poor creature would have been maimed for nothing and so rendered less valuable. Kolya seemed relieved by what he could overhear of this.

I next explained how we travelled with little to spare, all we had were a few small measures of good-quality cloth. Perhaps they would accept a foot or two for the madman. The chief smiled appreciatively at this gambit and invited me to squat down on the ground with him. So the serious bargaining began. We made jokes, exchanged insults, acted out a range of emotions from incredulity to despair, shared several cups of bitter tea, reflected on the state of the world, agreed that faith was the only road out of our dilemma and that the Jews and also the Christians were the cause of our troubles (any other analysis tended to shift the blame to God, which was of course a blasphemy). From time to time we brought the conversation back to the issue at hand and began another enjoyable round of bargaining. Sometimes trade is all the desert-dweller has in common with others of his kind and bartering becomes as elaborate a means of social intercourse as it is of arriving at a fair price. Eventually, just after three o'clock on the second day at the Zazara Oasis, I declared that my friends would curse me for a headstrong fool but I would throw in an ornamental dagger with the bale of tartan cloth they coveted. They agreed suddenly and so my friend was returned to me. I believe the tension of the moment had sobered him. He no longer spoke of Wagner but thanked me with his old civility. 'You are a natural diplomat, Dimka dear. Do you still have all our camels?'

I assured him that I had kept our little caravan together. Although weary, he was cheerful. The water and food offered him by the Gora so that he should be a better purchase had given him the strength to take hold of his senses again. 'What happened, Dimka?' He paused for breath as we climbed back towards the ledge. 'Did the Italian army find you? Are we in need of identities?'

I assured him he was in no further danger. He stopped again to get his breath and stared down at the net and the silk which draped the surrounding rocks. 'If it isn't the army, who is it? The Italian air force?'

But I would tell him no more until I had helped him ascend, pretending to curse him and goad him, until he reached the top of the ridge and stood staring in astonishment at the basket and its charming occupant.

Signorina von Bek now wore a pale green frock with dark-blue fringes, a dark-blue cloche and matching stockings. Her shoes were the colour of her dress. 'How is the poor fellow?' she asked me over his head.

'Praising Allah for His mercy, Signorina von Bek, as are we all.'

Their business done, the Gora were already striking camp.

I guessed that they were on their way to another outlaws' rendezvous where they hoped to pick up work. But they would also speak of us.

As Kolya approached, Signorina von Bek wrinkled her nose. 'Oh, dear! He'd better have a bath, don't you think?'

I agreed with her. I would also bathe, I said. Meanwhile, she decided, as soon as the slave was rested perhaps he could bring her up some water for her own ablutions. Gladly, I said, but first I must see to my camels. Our poor patient beasts had suffered too long. Leaving the loads near the balloon's basket, Kolya and I led the eager animals at last to stretch their elegant necks over the oasis. The water was good but had a peculiar taste to it from an old palm which had fallen in at the far side and rotted. The camels sniffed the pool carefully before they drank.

'I trust you do not seriously expect me to take that girl's bathwater up to her,' murmured my friend as we stripped off and waded into the shadowy pond where we could not easily be seen from above.

I smiled at his dismay and said we would carry some up in a *fantasse* on the camel. 'Since, dear Kolya, you were not in your senses I had no choice but to fall back on the familiar excuse of congenital idiocy.'

'It is not a rôle to which I'm much suited,' he admitted, but he understood my point. 'The girl I take it is here on government business?'

'Only in a manner of speaking. Hers is the first one-woman flight for the Italian Geographical Society. I gather Mussolini's giving a lot of backing to such enterprises at the moment.' It was only at that second that the inspiration came to me that Italy was the country I should offer my talents to. I could help build the power-plants and machines needed to make that country truly the nation of the future, the New Rome in every sense. They also possessed, I understood, a thriving film industry. Perhaps my meeting with Signorina von Bek had been opportune in more ways than one.

Already Kolya was discussing the next stage of our route across the desert. Now we had found Zazara and the Thieves' Road, all we had to do was head west on it. Eventually, 'in less than a thousand miles,' we should reach Morocco.

By now, of course, I saw my future following a rather different course, but I said nothing. 'First we must help Signorina von Bek reflate her balloon.' I stretched in the water. I floated. 'And then we can be on our way. It is the least we can do, Kolya, since she, effectively, saved our bacon.'

'By crashing in the desert?' (I had sketched the story for him.)

'By trusting us,' I reminded him. 'We could be a pair of rogues for all she knows.'

He was offended at this. Surely I had seen how she had already taken note of the man beneath the rags? When he was properly dressed again, he would thank her himself for her timely arrival, though she had not, after all, *deliberately* helped us. It was merely good fortune that she happened to be there. I protested this was a parsimonious compliment to her aerial navigation, especially since Kolya's own sense of direction was unremarkable. He was being churlish. He apologised at once. His privations, his nerves, the exhausting fetching of water, had all taken their toll.

By now it was sunset and the Gora had filed out of the gorge, doubtless on their way across the desert and as glad to be free of conflict as ourselves. Leaving Kolya sleeping at the water's side, I filled the metal *fantasse* myself, loaded it onto Uncle Tom and led her back up the steep path to where the aviatrix waited. Signorina von Bek had been reading to pass the time. I had already noticed the little bundle of brightly-coloured paper-covered books and magazines she kept. They were all English and seemed to be tales of adventure. She had developed a taste for blood-and-thunder, she said, at Cheltenham. 'It was so uneventful, you know, otherwise.'

Carefully marking her place, she put the book on her table and drew from another fitted locker a collapsible canvas bathtub which she stretched carefully upon its frame. Into this, I emptied the four-gallon *fantasse*. She clapped her hands. 'I have longed desperately for this for three days!' Discreetly I returned to the oasis and saw to Uncle Tom's grooming. She grumbled and snapped the whole time but could not disguise the pleasure she took in my attention. What was more, the mechanical and familiar actions helped me gather my thoughts. Our best escape from the desert must surely be in the repaired balloon. But what if it also delivered us directly into the hands of the authorities? If we continued on the Thieves' Road it would be months, perhaps longer, before we reached civilisation. If we took the balloon and kept our disguises we had every chance of slipping away into a town before the Italians or French became over-curious. There was also a good possibility we would again be waylaid and this time murdered for our camels and goods. The Gora were doubtless not the only outlaw band in these parts. They would pass on the news. At best we must expect a fight or two. And we must consider the camels.

'My dear, your feeling for those camels is positively obscene.' Kolya had risen and walked over to one of our grazing pack animals to feel for something on the beast's hump. It was only then I noticed the recently healed scars. 'I grew concerned that you would decide to trade a couple of our camels for me!'

'I would have been ashamed if I had bid more than your value,' I replied. This badinage was usual with us. In my heart I was of course deeply relieved at my friend's survival. Save for Captain Quelch I do not think I have ever had quite such love for a man. We were Roland and Oliver, fellow adventurers, followers of the Code of Chivalry.

I owed my life to him. Nonetheless, it still seemed to me pure folly to continue with his original plan. It was even possible that we might convince the lady to drop us off at some convenient spot. 'Please remember to take it easy, Kolya, dear. You are still weak and your sanity remains, I would guess, a trifle fragile.'

He shrugged this off and casually hummed some jazz number, as if to prove to me that his mind was fully restored.

When I mentioned her name my friend was anxious to be introduced to Signorina von Bek. 'I have heard of the woman. She was Benito Mussolini's mistress. I remember her from Paris! And she flew with the Spanish Barcelona-to-Rio expedition a couple of years ago.'

I explained that, given his status, it would be both dangerous and unseemly for him to socialise with our hostess. Considering her history there was some small chance she could be an Italian government agent. At all costs we had to preserve our disguises until we knew we could trust her. He understood this but did not relish, he declared, remaining a fool for long. He would be glad when we were on our way. He remained obsessively fixed in his determination to follow the Thieves' Road.

I dined that evening with my new friend. Below us my old friend cooked himself *kus-kus* to which he added a hard-boiled egg Signorina von Bek had given him. My female *alter ego* possessed the same spontaneous generosity which had led me into so many scrapes! Yet I do not regret being this way. Better to follow a virtuous impulse, I have always said, than to think always of self-interest. 'Yer give 'em too fuckin' much, Ivan, and then yer regret it, silly bugger,' said Mrs Cornelius to me the other day and it is true. But I have few regrets of that sort. I have never quite understood what she and Signorina von Bek had in common, for they were chalk and chips, but it might have been a quality of self-possession. Certainly it was not a similarity of enthusiasms! The last time I described an engineering principle to Mrs Cornelius, she ran from the pub claiming a weak bladder and I had to borrow a pound from Miss B. to pay for the round. With Signorina von Bek, however, I had an uncanny affinity. Together we discussed enormous projects. As soon as Kolya was bedded down I told her a little about my Desert Liner. She, in turn, sketched for me her rocket-powered tube-train. She said the Italian government was about to commission an experimental prototype. Knowing Mussolini's preference for co-opting famous people to help him, she had agreed to this flight for publicity reasons rather than from genuine scientific curiosity. 'I was finding it all extremely jolly until I was shot down. It was partly my own fault for dropping too low to ask those Arabs where I was. Still, I suppose even that was providential. What larks, eh, Sheikh Mustafa!'

From dawn until ten o'clock the next morning we worked on repairing the balloon fabric, and gathering material to build a fire which would funnel up air for the initial inflation. With Kolya's reluctant help, we took the whole apparatus to the top of the hill looking out over the dead city and at Signorina von Bek's instruction arranged the fabric to funnel heated air into the balloon proper. As I watched the huge egg-shaped canopy begin to fill I could hardly contain myself.

Now the Italian flag swelled across the sky. I imagined Mussolini's thrusting New Rome, his great African empire which would at last stamp Carthage into non-existence. His firmament would be full of such ships. Architecture grand and graceful as Ancient Rome's would rise upon the ruins of an honourable past. The balloon was a vision! It was as if an angel had spoken. My manhood was returning. I knew I must make my way to Il Duce's court as soon as I could and link my destiny with his. It was not idealists like me who gave fascism a bad name. However, I would not be a Christian gentleman if I did not admit to past loyalties. The excesses of Benito Mussolini's lieutenants are best seen as the excesses, say, of the Spanish Inquisition which followed Ferdinand and Isabella into Moorish Spain. They discovered corruption, dark superstitions, decadence, voluptuous orientalism, academic abstraction and answered the Holy Call to cleanse eight centuries of evil and moral turpitude from their land. They revitalised their people and gave them back a history. Sometimes a man indulging in too many scruples fails to face the evil nature of his enemy. The Italians are a sentimental people. They need a dictator, the disciplines of fascism, to make them great, or their inherent laziness will always win. That they turned their backs on the only leader who could have made them great again is proof of my point. Now what are they? What is their wealth? A few ruins and Renaissance fountains they can hire out as props for the latest Cinerama epic! For all my powers of precognition, I saw, in this case, only a glowing future. I glimpsed perfection.

Soon the canopy was swinging overhead shimmering like a netted whale and Signorina von Bek started the little engine, firing it up until blistering steam whistled through the valves. This kept hot air in the canopy but no longer powered our abandoned propeller. Now, as the basket jerked impatiently at the ropes, the aviatrix jumped expertly to her work, adjusting ballast, checking trim and giving particular attention to the neatly fixed patch of blue silk which obscured part of the national arms and the letters *Fert*. She moved like a nymph between her engine and her ropes, cheering whenever her ship responded as she should. Excitedly she leaned out of the basket waving to Kolya, who stood open-mouthed, watching the airship come to life. All the tethering ropes were at full stretch with one or two threatening to drag loose their pegs. She called for us to remove the funnelling fabric and she cheered again. 'Hooray! Wonderful! What a godsend you fellows proved to be! Let's get the luggage aboard. I say, what are you going to do about your camels?'

Kolya began to blurt something. I spoke in Russian. 'Are you babbling in tongues again, Kolya, dear? Take her offer! We can be in Tangier within a week!'

'Or in French Equatorial,' he said gloomily. 'You can't steer a balloon, Dimka. But you can follow a road. At least I'll know which direction I shall be travelling. Leave her. She's an attractive and dangerous woman. She lives for thrills. I would have thought you'd had enough of adventures for a while. There are no clear advantages to your suggestion. With our original plan, we know exactly where we're going.'

'To Hell, Kolya! The danger's now unwarranted.'

'Is he all right?' asked Signorina von Bek in English.

'He is afraid to fly in your ship, I think,' I said in English, then in Russian, 'There's nothing for you here, Kolya.'

'Only a bastard would leave these poor camels,' he said. 'I'll stay.' It was the argument which won me. I had, myself, been deeply reluctant to desert my beautiful Uncle Tom. Yet her chances of survival on that lawless road were far better than mine. I was experiencing an agony of guilt and could hardly bear the idea of parting from Kolya. Yet survival, at such moments, demands no sentiment. Uncle Tom might find new owners in the desert, even if they proved to be the returning Gora. Her beauty guaranteed she would be well treated whoever inherited her.

'Come, Kolya,' I begged my friend the last time for conscience's sake. 'Signorina von Bek says the prevailing wind will take us west. She would prefer to go north, she says, but either way we wind up in Tripoli or Tangier.'

'Or Timbuktu,' he said significantly. 'It is you who face unwarranted danger, not I. Go, if you like. Simply leave me my camels and our few remaining goods.'

'Everything. Gladly,' I said. My mind was set upon Italy. I was filled with the urgency of idealism, a sense that my true vocation was returning. Oh, Esmé! You saw me fly. My faith in the power of rational science was coming back. I was filled with the Holy Spirit. My whole body quickened. My senses returned, thanks to Allah's wisdom. I had walked dead into the desert and out of the desert I arose, to live again. My body began to sing at last.

'You have your passport?' Kolya seemed ill-tempered suddenly. I was a little put out by his brusqueness. It was I, after all, who had been rejected!

'Indeed, I have. I will fetch my kit from Uncle Tom.'

'You have plenty of water?' He drew a breath of desert air as if to renew himself. He hummed a strain from *Tristan und Isolde*.

'Plenty.'

Kolya insisted on coming with me as I parted from Uncle Tom. He helped me lead my lovely creature back up the steep path to the top of the hill where Signorina von Bek waited in the balloon. A strong breeze now stirred her hair and her chiffon scarf was blown upward to frame her head.

'You are a fool,' Kolya muttered. 'I do not fear to fly in that thing – although it's folly – but I would fear to go with her. She is dangerous, believe me. Return to the desert and its freedoms. You have never known a woman like her, Dimka. She feeds off power. She plays with power and is fated to an early death, as are all her kind. And she'll take at least one poor devil with her. She's volatile, like nitro.'

'This is nothing but jealousy, Kolya. I beg you reconsider your own decision. Do not sink, in your own anxiety, to besmirching a lady's honour. Signorina von Bek is clearly a gentlewoman. She also has a fine mind. A man's mind. But she could never come between us, Kolya. We are brothers. I merely express concern for your well-being. Can our few trade goods sustain you all that way?'

My friend responded with a brave shrug. He took Uncle Tom's halter from my hand. 'The camels are my chief asset. I have to sell them before I can do anything else. Uncle Tom I will try to keep, I swear.'

'If necessary, you should get the best price for Uncle Tom,' I assured him. 'As soon as you reach the next large oasis.'

'I will find you in Tangier,' he promised, 'and give you your share. After all, you helped get us this far.'

'Perhaps.' I gripped his shoulder. 'Meanwhile you should be more sparing, old friend, in your use of drugs. You'll have none left by the time you get to a city.'

'Oh, I'll not run out.' We had reached the balloon and he reverted to mumbling mode, handing my valise and other luggage into the basket as I climbed in to help Signorina von Bek stow the bags into the lockers.

I reached over the side and, defying Bedouin custom, shook Kolya's hand, then drew him towards me to kiss him. 'Farewell, good friend,' I said in Arabic. 'May Allah continue to protect thee and bring thee safe to thy destination.'

'Your slave really isn't coming?' Signorina von Bek seemed disappointed.

'I have given him his freedom,' I said. 'He chose to take the camels and travel the lonely road of the Darb al-Haramiya. God goes with him. At least the camels will be well kept. He has a knack with the beasts. They are of great value to him. You see, Signorina von Bek, he is like me, a man of the desert. *Unlike* his master, however, he cannot imagine being happy in any other world. So it is. We are made as we are made. It is God's will and God will protect him.'

There was nothing else I could add. My friend had chosen his path and it was no longer right for me to question his decision.

I believe there were tears in my eyes, however, when I waved goodbye to him. He released our last tethering ropes and we rose rapidly, crying 'godspeed' and 'farewell'. I watched him with pounding heart as he turned, beginning the trudge down to what remained of his fortune. Poor Kolya! I had hesitated to tell him that I had transferred some of our load to my own bags, for safety's sake, long before I had arrived at the oasis. I had three pounds of cocaine, a pound of heroin and four pounds of hashish, all removed from their hiding-place in the pack camel's humps. This had depleted the cargo quite considerably, since Kolya had already consumed a large part of his share between Khufra and Zazara. On the other hand I had certainly saved him from himself and there was now far less danger of his being robbed for the remaining drugs.

I hold no brief for 'dope-dealing' and would never willingly be involved with it, but I had come unwillingly to the trade so it seemed fair to me I should take some profit from it. There would be no difference, in the end, to its use.

Signorina von Bek was leaning away from me, studying the outer canopy, relieved to see that the repair was holding. Her lips parted in a wonderful smile as she took stock of the horizon widening as we rose, with no sensation of thrust, high into the wide blue Saharan sky. 'You are clearly a man,' she said, 'who cuts his own road through this life.'

I appreciated her recognition of my individuality but I remained cautious, determined not to flunk my chosen part. I could not afford to be discovered. 'With Allah's guidance,' I said. 'And as Allah wills.' I looked down at the oasis. I could still make out my friend, a perfect homunculus, scrambling towards the tiny pool, his miniature animals.

'Oh, see!' Signorina von Bek pointed with excitement towards the east. 'There they are! How jolly! Those are the Arabs who shot me down! Thank goodness we're on our way. Will your slave be all right?'

I looked across the dunes of the great Sand Sea. Riding with lordly languor towards Zazara, their elaborately-worked long guns cradled casually in their arms, their cruel eyes only visible from within their veils, came the same Tuareg party we had seen weeks ago near al-Jawf. It was inevitable they would discover Kolya before he could get clear. For a moment I looked towards the Gatling, thinking I might scare them off, but they were hardly in range and I had no idea how the basket would behave in concert with the force of a powerful machine-gun.

They had sighted us now. They raised their rifles to their shoulders, their legs curled tightly around their stuffed leather saddles as they took aim. But their salvo either fell short or missed us and while they reloaded we had gained more than enough height and distance to be safe from their primitive firepower.

Unfortunately for Kolya, however, a few hours of freedom were all God would allow him for the moment. He was about to become a host ge again.

'What was your man's name?' she asked me, busying herself with her lines.

'Yussef,' I said.

She came to stand beside me at the rail. 'And you are Mustafa. I do not think we need to be formal any longer.'

Signorina von Bek put her hand firmly into mine. 'You must call me Rosie,' she insisted. 'I'm so relieved to have the protection of a genuine Bedouin prince. As a matter of fact you do look rather like Rudolf Valentino. Though more refined.'

The Tuareg and Zazara and all our troubles were behind us. As our balloon sailed gracefully into the bloody light of the setting sun I embraced my Rose.

TWENTY-THREE

THE ESCAPE of sexual fantasy was no longer open to me. Instead I found more cerebral diversions. *E si risuelgo da quel sogno di sangue, con ispavento, con rimorso, e insieme con una specie di gioia* . . . Those stripes were white and the bars were black. Ripe stars teased my lips. *Yusawit! Yuh'attit! Yuh'attit! Yukhallim. Yehudim. Yukhallim. Ana'atsha'an. Bitte, ein Glas Wasser.* They refused to understand me. I never became *ein Musselman. Dawsat. Walwala.* I heard him. It was not me. I heard him betray us. *Yermeloff. Yehudim! Yehudim! Gassala. Meyne pas. Meine peitsche. Meyn streifener. Meine Herzenslust* . . .

Sometimes, in the desert, I had prayed for Faith. How I had envied my fellow-worshippers. Yet how many of them were also praying merely for social reasons?

I flew. I lived. The world below was washed by a golden tide. Atlantis emerged from the vibrant dust. My stripes were silver. They were ebony. They could not hold me in their cattle-truck. I refused to be identified. He was no *Volksgenosse* of mine. I said so. My eyes had never known such beauty; my soul had never experienced such tranquil security. We drifted on that desert wind; days and nights of wonder. And she brought me back to the Land of Life and restored my future.

'You are familiar with Manzoni!' she declared. I did not admit it was only in the Russian translation. . . . *di non aver fatto altro che immaginare* . . . Be nice, he said, be nice. Be sweet, he said, be sweet. *Oh, Dios! Oh, Jesus! Que me occurre? Sperato di diventare famoso. Qualcosa non va?* 'I believe,' she said, 'that you have given me a privileged insight into the Arab mind.' Gracefully, I accepted her compliment.

In the mornings and the evenings we sailed high above the pink and ochre Sand Sea, free from concern, but at noon, when we drifted to our lowest point, we had to be alert. The temperature could rise to 140°. More than ever, the landscape below us might have been that of the Red Planet. I imagined gigantic guns buried beneath the sand, ready to hurl their capsules to the sweet air of Earth: the deadly air of Earth. Here, in the desert, all death was honourable, all life was celebrated. Eroded mountain ranges and seas of constantly agitated sand, soft as silk, deadly as cyanide, fell away below us, mile upon mile, glittering lakes of salt, rivers of obsidian. The dreaming desert awaited a miracle that would restore it, tree by tree, animal by animal, river upon river, field upon field, city upon city, to its gorgeous past. Yet, I wondered, what hybrid might arise? How long had these wastes been nourished with Carthage's blood? *A quei tempi c'eramo oceani di luce e citta nei cieli e selvagge bestie volanti di bronzo . . . Por que lo nice? Du bist mein Simplicissimus,* she said. But that was much later. Now as we drifted over those timeless landscapes beneath unchanging skies, I became her master and her teacher, her most intimate friend; yet had no desire to penetrate her. We lay entwined while a hard wind drummed against the great canopy and set the ropes and basket to a bass thrumming. An extraordinary noise, it filled the desert like the heartbeat of Arabia. We had no sense of danger as we continued to drift towards the west, towards Algeria and Spanish Morocco. If we did not come down on the mainland, she said, we might have to put down in the Canaries, which were also Spanish. We would be welcomed by the Spaniards. 'I have several friends in the colonial service. But the Riffians are all over the place since Abd el-Krim capitulated. Some of the outlaw gangs have a thorough hatred of Europeans. Even you, Sheikh Mustafa, would be unable to protect me.'

I reminded her that I had seen her handling the *mitrailleuse* and did not think she would require much protection! This remark was not received as flattery. Rosie von Bek helped me solve no mysteries of womankind. Rather she presented me with fresh ones.

I came to my senses beneath the bright stare of heaven, in the arms of the one Kolya had called the destroyer and whom I called Rosa. My rose. *War'di War'di, ana nafsi. Sarira siri'ya. D'ruba D'ruba.* She wondered at my stripes, my whiteness, and I made some mention of prison and the Turkish heel. 'You have not always known power, *sidhi*?' She was sympathetic.

'A truly faithful man accepts the will of Allah. I am glad to say I have walked the path of humility.'

She murmured that humility did not seem to be my most obvious trait. I smiled at this as I toyed with my full, black beard. 'You must know our saying – the doe shall always kneel to the stag. Such things are also determined.'

Through her desire I found my manhood again. I found my power. I was restored. She gave herself up to her imagination, free from any restraint, certain she should have no witness save the vultures, the eagles and myself, whom she called her Hawk – *al Sakhr*. But her escape was denied me; my pleasure came purely from the thrill of my recaptured sense of power, of self. She gave me back my world of dreams, my cities and my soul. This is the gift that Woman offers Man. Only a churlish oaf refuses her. Here is a true union of flesh and spirit, such as St Paul spoke of. And yet I was for her a figure from romance; she saw nothing of the real Maxim Arturovitch Pyatnitski, of Ace Peters, conqueror of Hollywood. Instead she saw in her image of me an altar on which she might sacrifice her selfhood, to be reborn, the Eternal Feminine. I was, in that sense, immaterial.

Often, when she spoke of her childhood and youth in Albania, Italy and Spain (where she attended convent schools), it was as if she mused aloud, content that while I failed to understand some of her words, I would never fully grasp her meaning. In this she was right, for she spoke sometimes in Albanian, sometimes Italian and frequently in English. I was only fluent in English, although I had picked up some Italian during my stay in Rome with Esmé, before we went to Paris. She spoke fondly of a certain Bon-bon. After a time I came to realise that Bon-bon was the present Dictator of Italy. Clearly she still had affection for him, but equally clearly there had been some kind of falling-out. The threat of a public scandal and pressure from close family members had interfered to destroy their idyll. She also believed he had taken an interest in an American heiress, 'one of the Macraineys', and was incapable of sustaining a passion for more than one mistress at a time. 'But then his feelings about women are very clear.' Turning to me she asked, 'You have read the novel, *The Cardinal's Mistress*?'

I admitted that I had not. I had little time for sensation tales, I said.

'It is by Mussolini himself,' she said. 'I read it before I ever met him. He already displayed in that work everything Italy needed to restore herself to her old pre-eminence. He is a romantic with a strong sense of discipline.'

Save for Fiorelli, I hesitated to speak of friends in Rome. Several had been early converts to the Fascist cause. But I would have to explain too much. I had become fascinated with the character she and I between us had created for me, to our mutual benefit. Kara ben Nesi was my model, I suppose, the great German scholar-adventurer of Karl May's *Durch die Wüste*. I had read these as a child, in Kiev, in about 1912. May was one of the few novelists my teacher, Herr Lustgarten, approved. He was properly *philosophisch*, he said.

> Lasst hoch die Fahne des Propheten wehn;
> versammelt euch zum heil'gen Derwischtanze!
> Zu Narren soll man nur in Maske gehn;
> die wahre Klugheit lebt vom Mummenschanze.

The irony only became clear years later. The British claim everything for themselves. They claim universal myths as their personal experience. Is it any wonder Europe became impatient with them? One can accept so much self-proclaimed piety.

To my astonishment, Rosie von Bek had no experience of the benefits and enjoyments of cocaine and I had the privilege of introducing her to this wonderful fruit of nature. She was astonished – Simply flabbergasted! – as she put it, by the way the

442

drug amplified her imagination while it sharpened her senses. Now the subtlety of our intimacies became deeply intricate; we created arabesques of sensation and emotion, of peculiar and intellectual invention, almost abstract. While I gasped in Goethe's German, she breathed the earth of Florentine Italy, of barbarous peaks moulding the fierce beliefs and desires of Albanian brigand chieftains, warmed me with the flame of limitless passion, driven to greater spiritual and sometimes physical risks by the coolness of my own responses. At least I did not fear flesh any longer. In our different ways we both experienced the same extraordinary spiritual union. We were a single, all-destroying creature – heat and cold, male and female, good and evil. New *Homo sapiens*, androgynous, omnipotent, eternal.

It was an impossible union and yet a natural one. Bismarck had known the beauty of such equilibrium, the balancing of masculine against feminine. Adolf Hitler, representing proud masculinity, and Benito Mussolini, representing the spiritual, feminine side of the fascist discipline. Left alone, I think they would have made perfection: German practicality married to Italian flair. Had they not been set, one upon the other, by petty rivalries the great dream would have flourished. There were certain personality problems between the two charismatic leaders, I will admit. But this is true of all brilliant marriages. They were on the move – too busy to make virtues of their differences. I think, perhaps, it was the same with me and Rosie von Bek. We were almost too strong for one another. In nature, such forces, such grand and noble opposites, sometimes need only a whisker's touch to send both spinning helplessly from their orbits. While we remained aloft, without responsibilities or fears, we had our perfect universe. But eventually, the dreamer must look to the commonplace for his sustenance. If he resists his conscience's demands he resists experience; he resists reality. He loses his grip. I was determined that this would never happen to me. Of course, I blame the Jews. It is in their interests to involve the world in abstractions.

Yet that blissful episode remains forever exquisite.

Many women have loved me. I have made love to many more. But there are only three women who are to me what

443

my organs and my flesh are to me. What my own heart is to me. The first is Esmé, the innocent, wondering Esmé, my sweet sister, my little girl; the second is Mrs Cornelius, whom I loved for her sanity and her deep relish for ordinary life; the third is Rosie von Bek.

The light fell through the bars of the cattle-truck and made a pattern of black and white against the walls which stank of disinfectant. I am not the only human being alive today who cannot smell disinfectant without immediately fearing for his mortal existence.

Others flinch at the aeroplane's whine or the car's backfire. For me it is a public toilet at five in the morning. These stripes pursued me. Even in the basket they fell through ropes and guidelines to form bars across the yellow weave and trace Zion's stars upon the Moorish carpets she had heaped there; a lattice of portent, it began to seem to me. Sometimes during the long, drifting days, I sat and read her Sexton Blake stories. These taught me about the politics of the Middle East as well as English domestic life. They introduced me to imperial complexities and gave me a quiet respect for those citizens of the Empire who shouldered their moral burdens. Here were the new Knights of the Round Table bringing enlightenment and Christian ethics to the dark places of the world. Rosie also had some old Italian film magazines, one of which showed myself and Gloria Cornish in *Ace Among Aces* and, in the same issue, advertised *The Lost Buckaroo*, but of course it was not then in my interest to point the films out. Sometimes I put down my *Case of the Roumanian Envoy* and merely stared at the patterns made by the sun through a net of lines and basket-work. Sometimes she and I would discuss their meaning. She insisted that I introduce her to the more doubtful pleasures of hashish and morphine. Happily, she did not respond well to the morphine and indulged only occasionally in the hashish, usually with tobacco after a meal. It was extraordinary to lean against the gondola's brass rail with the sky and the desert at my back, to watch that beautiful woman, softly naked, cooking a delicious Albanian snack over the muttering engine, careless of any danger. I had never known a woman like her. Neither Esmé nor Mrs Cornelius were as careless of their comfort.

444

I can close my eyes and smell the desert now. There is no comparison for that smell; almost sweet, almost alive. The heat of the African beast, the patient monster. I can smell her perfumed sweat, rose and cunt and garlic on her mouth, and I can smell my own cool manhood. I regained my skills and they were now informed with a subtler knowledge. I handled her as a musician his instrument, to celebrate its beauty and its sensual potentiality. Here I became again what I had always been but which I had been made to forget at Bi'r Tefawi. I was Ace Peters, star of the screen; Maxim Pyatnitski, inventor of the Dynamite Automobile, the Flying Wing, the TeleVision. And I was *al Sakhr*, the Hawk of the Sahara. I was whatever I would wish to be or had ever desired to be. My vision and my future were restored. I saw again my cities, gold and silver, white and ebony, thrusting into the blue pallor of a Saharan evening. I saw an orderly future, where justice and equality were the common expectation. I saw escape from the grey ruins of my Russian homeland, from the squalor of the Constantinople alleys, from the wretched poverty of an Alabama shanty-town or a Cairene slum. I described some of my ideas to Rose and she responded with enthusiasm. I must certainly come back with her to Italy. Her absolute faith was invested in Il Duce. He was a man of the people, a great-hearted poet-politician like his friend D'Annunzio, who had put his own army at the Leader's disposal. He was also a sensitive, moved only by a hatred of poverty and misery. But he was finally a great realist. He understood that the Italians would never improve on their own initiative. They needed strong, but humane, leadership. She told me of an Italy encouraging the arts and sciences. 'Il Duce calls us all to the service of his noble social experiment – everyone! The greatest writers, engineers, scientists and painters of our day are shoulder to shoulder in modern Rome.' This was very like the opinion of the only clear-sighted American I ever met. When I knew him he was a journalist, then got a reputation as a poet. I understood nothing of that world. His championing of his fellow-poets was enough to put him in prison. I myself enjoyed the horrors of the Isle of Man. It does no good to speak for fairness and proper credit in this world.

I would, I said to her, very much like to journey some

day to that new Renaissance court. She said she was sure I would be more than welcome. Only the best were attracted to Mussolini, recognising in him the same self-confidence, talents and audacity which had made them great in their chosen work. I imagined this marvellous court on a larger scale than Imperial Rome, with tall, airy white marble columns and gleaming floors, like pools, stretching into shadow. There we should all meet, intellectuals, artists, scientists and adventurers from every corner of the world, representing the nations and religions of the Earth, to exchange knowledge and ideas, to discuss in fluent discourse the means by which we should truly civilise the world.

That the experiment came to nothing, I said to the older Cornelius boy, was not the fault of the visionaries who began it. It was the fault of the blind reactionaries who conspired to stop it. There are few people in modern Italy who would not rather go back to the days of Il Duce, when they could be proud of their heritage, certain of their cause. The same could be said for Hitler, but the stories are not completely parallel. I am the first to agree: in some respects the Führer went too far. But were the French completely free from blame? What does 'fascist' mean, anyway? It means nothing but 'law' and 'discipline'. Are chaos and licence, such as we have today, to be preferred? A Rolling Stone gathers no responsibility, I told him. It would be wonderful if we could all caper about in Hyde Park and howl like some Sudanese zealot and be given a million pounds for it! He could not reply.

Not merely stupefied by a spoon-feeding State, I said, but inarticulate as well. Rhetoric, I discovered, is no longer on the Holland Park syllabus. There is scarcely a school in London that retains it! We are losing the realities and the meaning of the past. Without them we shall never create the future we desire. Why must they always simplify? I told them – I embrace complexity. It is my meat and drink. But they had nothing for me. Shortly afterwards I opened my shop.

'The desert,' I told her, 'teaches us the arts of compromise. Without them, we could not survive.'

'But you would not compromise on principle, *al Sakhr*?'

'The desert makes a principle of compromise.' I smiled.

'What can you control there, in the end? The rainfall? The wind?'

She was silent for a few moments after that, standing against the wickerwork, one hand on a rope, the other on the basket's rail, wearing only her shoes to give her enough height to peer down over the flatness of what looked, from there, like a vast slab of concrete scattered with rubble. I saw it suddenly as the foundation of a gigantic temple and in that vision the scale of Atlantis was revealed to me! Only when I looked upon the monumental buildings of the new dictators would this vision be recreated! They knew the spiritual value of such architecture. This is what they shared with the cathedral-builders. What is wrong with offering hard-working people a little glimpse of perfection?

My aviatrix had lost her calendar and had only her maps and compasses. She knew that it was probably still July and it was certainly 1927. As to our distance travelled, we should soon come upon some good-sized settlement where we would, with proper caution, regain our bearings.

Some evenings, in the twilight, we would dance the Argentinian *tango* to the tune from the portable gramophone.

We had both grown a little weary and complained of a certain clamminess, doubtless caused by the steam. We longed for cool water, to bathe in and to drink. The heat was into the 120s. I spoke of the *hamman* and its luxuries; the baths the Moor gave to the Turk. There were certain establishments in Oman, I said, where men and women were encouraged to bathe together. This excited her and it seemed churlish to disappoint her imagination. I described the sensual delights of the steam baths, the nature of their attendants and their pleasures. It gave me a uniquely delicious *frisson* which had nothing in it of lust. The sensation grew stronger in me as she discovered fresh levels of sexual ecstasy and experiment. Only when we had begun to suffer the effects of the heat and of remaining aloft for so long did I think to ask her if they had put a time-limit on her expedition. I still barely understood the scientific purpose of her flight.

'My dear sheikh, it becomes whatever I wish it to be. The balloon is a relatively small expense. All I have to do to justify the voyage to the Italian government is make a few notes, a few marks on the map and take a reel or two of film until I have enough for a lecture tour! Another first for Italy! A jolly cheap one, too.' She had already had some success, she said, with a one-woman *dhow* voyage from Aden to Bombay. She had signed a contract with a Milan publisher who wanted her book about it. 'It's a peculiar way of making a living, but it enables me to travel with some security and to be almost guaranteed an adventure! The publicity I receive ensures my safety. It's only bad luck that brought me down at Zazara. Anywhere else would have had a newspaper and a wire.'

Thought of that near-disaster brought a frown to her wonderful eyes which deepened as she cocked her head to listen. She sucked her index finger and raised it into the air. She rose suddenly, plucking her compass from its box and checking our position. I grew a little concerned. 'What's wrong, Miss von Bek?' I wrapped my *jerd* about me and got to my feet. The basket shuddered. There was something unfamiliar about our movement.

'The wind's changing,' she said. 'We're beginning to turn south.' Hurriedly she got out her maps and spread them on the carpet. 'This could be awkward.'

I saw immediately what she meant. If we were flying between Ghat (which lay some 600 miles inland from Tripoli) and Touat (some 600 miles from Casablanca) and the wind had indeed shifted south then Kolya's bitter prediction might be about to come true. In fact we would be fortunate to land in Timbuktu, the forbidden city on the far side of the Sahara.

I had grown used to seeing the sun always setting directly ahead of us, of sailing always into the last of the day's light, but now I saw the sun swelling orange above the horizon off to our right. Below raced a succession of slatey drumlins, too puny to be called hills, while ahead lay the waterless dunes of the deep Southern Sahara.

I became poignantly aware of Kolya's wisdom and knew a wave of utter self-contempt. 'Orl roads lead ter Rome, Ivan,' says Mrs Cornelius, 'so yer might as well pick a comfy one.' Unfortunately it seemed to me then that I had chosen the riskiest road of all.

That night we attempted to read the map by torchlight, from time to time peering over the side at the dunes or at the magnificent stars as we tried desperately to determine our position. The stars were displayed as sharply as an astrologer's chart with every pin-point an identifiable individual, every configuration perfectly defined, but neither of us could navigate by them. We were hoping to see a good-sized settlement where we could land and risk someone taking another potshot at us. Such problems beset the first balloonists in Europe, who whenever they landed were set upon by local peasants. We at least had the advantage of our Gatling and a couple of loaded Webleys as well as my Lee-Enfield. I felt a pang when I thought of my friend. He had been a fool not to come with us, yet, just as he was suffering the consequences of his decision, I would soon no doubt be suffering the consequences of mine. At Rosie von Bek's persistent prompting, and with the help of some sustaining *sneg*, there was nothing to do but return to our habitual pursuits, praying that God was sufficiently well-disposed towards us not to let us perish in that blazing waste.

I had taken to telling her strange tales of the desert. She demanded the most complicated details, forcing me to draw more than I should have liked on my Egyptian experiences. Yet, by turning those horrors into a form of fiction, I managed further to restore myself. The knowledge I had gained at B'ir Tefawi could, by some odd alchemy, be put to my advantage. Her own motives were purely sensual, yet she enjoyed a fantasy which she might never have dared bring to reality if we had not drifted unremarked above the surface of the earth. Yet over the next two days the raw truth of our predicament grew harder to avoid. Rosie von Bek's manner became increasingly nervous as she darted from side to side of the basket, checking the balloon's functions, making certain that the engine was working. Unable to be of assistance, I continued, when not at her disposal, to absorb myself in the adventures of Sexton Blake, Detective. She chose to see my fascination as part of the stoic nature of the Bedouin, but since there was no action I could take *The Union Jack* soothed my mind, helping me ignore the unpleasant likelihood of our deaths in the desert.

I was surprised that she saw no parallels between my anodyne and her own addiction to my verbal confections. It was not surprising that I should seek the consolations of Zenith the Albino or The Master Mummer after my surfeit of sensuality and terror, just as she had doubtless meanwhile satisfied her appetite for the adventures of the famous detective, his plucky assistant Tinker and their bloodhound Pedro pitted against a thousand deadly villains. Upholding the high standards of a benign imperialism, wherever his cases led him, even Blake could not live by idealism and romance alone, though I should make it clear there was not a trace of smut in those stories.

My refusal to let anxiety take control of me was, it seemed, soon justified. I was about to begin Chapter Five of *The Clue of the Cracked Footprint*, featuring the international adventurer Dr Huxton Rymer at large in the Orient, when my companion raised a cheer like a schoolgirl at a hockey match. 'The wind, my Sheikh! *Al rih!* It's turning! We're saved! Hurrah!'

Carefully, I replaced my *Union Jack* magazine in its locker and went to stand beside her. The wind had indeed changed, but had become erratic. The balloon was buffeted violently, then struck again and again. I noted the colour of the sky, the agitated sand below us. We were on the edge of some kind of storm. There came thunder from below the horizon and the sun turned a sickly yellow. The sand ran like mud. From where we looked, it might have been a flood. Rosie moved closer to me, her eyes agitated, her manner uncertain. 'Is this something we should fear, my Hawk?'

'We are always in the hands of Allah, sweet child.' I had no notion of the cause of this phenomenon. For a while the basket began to swing like a pendulum, as if far above us somewhere was the face of an enormous clock. Then I realised we were not moving at all. We appeared to be frozen at the centre of a small whirlwind. Even as we watched, a spiral of sand rose around us and the breath was dragged from our bodies. The temperature dropped radically. We were both shivering. It was as if we were in the power of some fierce desert *djinn* furious at our invasion of his land. We found ourselves at the very Heart of Chaos.

Then, suddenly, it was as if we were being propelled through the muzzle of Verne's gigantic cannon which fired the explorers from Earth to the Moon! Now the balloon was travelling rapidly upward, the warm air of our canopy acting, in the falling barometer, to draw us out of the storm like dew to the sun. We were all at once drifting in the safety of the upper atmosphere where, we discovered from our hastily consulted compass, we were travelling north. It was my turn to exclaim with pleasure! To the north lay Tangier, Algiers or Tunis! And north of these, on busy sea-routes, were the ports of Italy! We had been miraculously saved, as Rosie remarked, by nothing more than balloonist's luck. So little was known in those days. The mapping of currents and pressures, examination of lighter-than-air crafts' behaviour was scarcely a science then. Though we were the first to experience that desert phenomenon, we were by no means the last!

Meanwhile, it took us some time before we could accept that we were thoroughly secure from the elements. The wind was once again our friend, the sun no longer an implacable enemy.

The entire bizarre episode, from the moment I had put down my *Union Jack* in response to Rosie von Bek's cries, had filled four minutes, yet it would be several hours before our nerves were calmed and our spirits restored. Still I gasp at the good fortune that took us towards the coast, to escape forever that anguish of isolation.

Below us the dunes disappeared, to be replaced by red drifts which in turn became orange *sarira*, the baked rock, sand and pebbles which made up the greater part of the Sahara. But now, here and there, we began to see glimpses of water, the occasional pool or tiny stream. Here too was cultivation; a few poor fields, some animals, huts, or the heavy felt tents of Berber nomads. We viewed these signs of humanity with much the same mixture of excitement and relief a European feels upon entering the suburbs of a new city. Gradually more and more signs of life greeted us. The balloon raced over a terracotta landscape towards far-off mountains. It became easy to make out the faces of those we passed, to note the details of their cottages and shrines. So delighted were we at our change of fortune that it was some time before we realised we were losing height faster than was safe and that we could not possibly regain enough lift to take us over the peaks. The air in our canopy had grown cool while the sun rose to zenith overhead. Hastily, we let loose our water ballast and some of the sandbags we had brought from Zazara. Rosie von Bek restarted the engine for a few seconds, only to discover that she had used the last of the methylated spirits. She could make no more steam.

Our descent became relatively gentle as we desperately tried everything possible to keep the balloon aloft, to continue on towards the Mediterranean coast. Eventually we realised we should have to land, but were unsure whether to aim for the relatively unpopulated semi-desert or head for one of the towns closer to the mountains where we would not necessarily be welcomed.

'I am beginning to understand,' declared my Rose, 'how the arms of Italy, displaying a prominent cross, are not the most diplomatic for these parts.'

I suggested we try to find some relatively isolated spot in which to control our own landfall. We would note the next large township and then bring the balloon down in the desert a half-mile or so away.

Accordingly, Rosie von Bek operated her valves and lines with pretty expertise, gradually slowing the balloon's momentum while casually whistling some old Cheltenhamian air. She wore black and pink satin pyjamas over which she had thrown a light *gelabea*. With her dishevelled hair, her wonderful violet eyes staring from that golden skin, she was a goddess of the air. We had reached a place where a wide *wadi* curved between groves of date palms and opened onto a small lake on the shores of which were built a tumble of houses, seemingly piled one on top of another like so many brick-red children's blocks, their walls contrasting sharply with the rich greens of the palms, the pale, clear water. This oasis town was quite different in appearance to the ramshackle collection of huts and houses which made up their Egyptian equivalents. I was impressed by the decoration on so many of the mud walls. There were brightly painted patterns, geometrical decorative script, and always the name of God. More surprising were the primitive representations of animals and people. These Berbers practised only a few of the eastern Arabs' cultural habits. Even from here we saw that all the women went unveiled.

I was craning my neck to make out further details of the town when from behind me came a massive gasp. Signorina von Bek had pulled the ripcord! With a great blossoming of silk our bag was losing its emblazoned outer skin. We fell towards the baked, rusty earth. On our left were mountains and on my right desert. But below us was a huge oasis, with rivers connecting pool to pool, small settlements, even, perhaps, I dared hope, some outpost of white imperialism! As we descended I remarked on the picturesque nature of the scenery. This far better resembled my imagination's Arabia than the mixture of hovels, religious monuments and ugly European façades which, with the addition of a few miserable palms on dusty boulevards, the Arab so frequently calls 'civilisation'. Here was the landscape which had inspired E. Mayne Hull and G. H. Teed, which gave us *Beau Geste* and *The Desert Song*! And, riding towards us across this romantic tundra, as we came down easily in a shelf of soft red sand, was a party of uniformed horsemen on prancing Arabs who could easily have called themselves the Red Shadow's men. With their red and gold tunics, blue trousers, dark red cloaks and brilliantly decorated saddles and bridles, they might have been the chorus of some fashionable operetta. I began to wonder again whether nature imitated art or if I were not still somewhere in the Western Desert, dreaming this dream to avoid the truth of death. Yet I had never seen such handsome native riders.

Signorina von Bek was scrambling to her feet and cocking the *mitrailleuse*. She at least had not forgotten that the Red Shadow's men were Riffians.

As I climbed up over the basket's rim I raised my Lee-Enfield high into the air, using the universal peace sign of the Sahara. Lowering myself to the sand I knelt and placed my rifle carefully on the ground before me. Then, with my hand over my heart, I stood up.

The dark-skinned riders reined in a few yards from us, controlling their half-wild stallions with economic flicks of wrists and ankles, arguing loudly amongst themselves. Each man had a scabbarded carbine on his saddle and the scabbard bore some sort of arms stamped in gold. These were no ordinary tribesmen. In careful Arabic I told them we came in peace.

We had been abducted by Italian soldiers but with Allah's blessing had managed to escape from the brutal Nazarin. Turning to Rosie von Bek I translated what I had said into Italian. She took my cue. 'Those foul swine!' She gestured melodramatically. 'They took away my clothes!' She picked up a *jerd* and wrapped her pyjama'd body in it. A chiffon scarf improved her modesty. Her sun-darkened skin would not attract their attention, now that her face was veiled.

The dandified riders made no response but continued to grin and talk amongst themselves, frequently pointing at us and either laughing heartily at some speculative joke or making a fierce declaration, probably concerning our origin. If I knew the desert, I guessed that at least half the party was arguing passionately for our supernatural nativity.

'Brothers,' I began. 'By the grace of Allah we have fallen among co-religionists! We are safe at last, my wife!' And I sent a rather theatrical prayer to Heaven.

But I was ignored. They looked back in the direction from which they had ridden. Another group of horsemen approached, sending pale pink dust into the chalky blue evening. They came over an horizon on which stood a single palm, a ruined *kasbah*, hooded riders controlling their steeds with that absolute unconscious authority characterising the true desert aristocrat. These were no passing nomads! What if we had strayed into some Berber province forbidden to all strangers? I knew the punishment received by those Europeans who had attempted to invade Timbuktu or Mecca. Our fate remained uncertain. Our lives depended, I decided, on whether or not they accepted us as Bedouin. There was often little love between the two peoples, but we here could expect at least three days' *daifa* before they decided to murder us. In that time, no doubt, we should be able to improve our position. With this in mind I drew myself up to display all my Arab dignity.

As the horsemen cantered nearer I realised that some

454

wore only a light riding *ras* over what appeared to be European dress. There were five of these followed by outriders in the same costume as our first group. They rode superb Arabs. The foremost, in khaki jodhpurs and jacket, wore a green turban. The big man just behind him wore a similar outfit save for the distinctive French *képi*; on his left rode a man whose cloak flowed back to reveal bright British scarlet; he was protected from the sun by a white solar topee. Behind them came a taller, very lean European in military khaki whose wide-brimmed hat shaded his face; the remaining heavier figure also hid his face within a hood. By the look of the party we must surely have landed in Spanish or French territory, some military or diplomatic concordance. It was in my interest to discover immediately if I was in relatively friendly territory – perhaps Spanish Morocco.

The horsemen now slowed to a trot and eventually came to a spectacular stop only a short distance from us. The leader, in the hooded cloak, was a plump, dapper individual whose antecedents clearly included most of the major African races. He had large, intelligent eyes, a poor skin and a scrawny but well-tended beard. His clothing, a mixture of Oriental and Western, was of perfect cut and evident quality. It had been fashioned, I was sure, not far from the Tour Eiffel. The European officer was equally elegant.

Behind him the two others were obscured in the horses and dust, but doubtless they were as well groomed. *'Hola muy amigos!'* I had remembered rather too late that my only available passport identified me a Spanish citizen. *'Habla el Español, señors.'* And prayed profoundly that they did not, after all, have any more Spanish than did I. The native turned and spoke in French to his nearest companion, who replied in cultured Parisian.

Pretending not to understand what was being said, I bared my head. Happily my hair had grown long enough to give me the general appearance of a Bedouin. For their part they were merely determining what language to use to me. Since Turkish seemed to be the Frenchman's choice and Spanish the natives', I decided to be audacious and try English, having always preferred to keep a language or two in reserve. 'I hope we are not

455

inconveniencing you gentlemen,' I began. 'We are somewhat off our course, I fear.' I was about to introduce myself when the huge Frenchman threw back his hood, removed his *képi* and, grinning widely, wiped his forehead with a silk handkerchief. It was Lieutenant Fromental, my acquaintance from Casablanca.

'I know that voice! I thought I recognised you, monsieur. What a wonderful coincidence! We all believed you back in Hollywood, sir!' He changed from English to French. 'Your Highness –' a formal gesture – 'may I introduce to you the man I have spoken of many times. Mr Max "Ace" Peters, the cinema star. Mr Peters, you are in the presence of His Highness, the Pasha of Marrakech, El Hadj T'hami el Glaoui.'

An impasse. There was nothing I could do but bow.

'You are very welcome here, monsieur,' said the Pasha. At that time I took his odd grin for reluctant hospitality. His frown became expectant. For a second I had forgotten my companion. I turned to introduce her. 'Mademoiselle von Bek . . .'

Oblivious of the others, she stared at me in horror. '*Peters?*' Her eyes spoke of betrayal, but her voice was a knife. '*Peters?* You're not a Bedouin sheikh?'

'Only by choice,' I murmured. 'Please keep this confidence. I am Peters of the English Secret Service. I had no option but to deceive you. I also have something of a career in the cinema. What luck to run into friends! Let me do the talking!'

In an instant my terrors had flown away. I thought surely she must share my delight in this happy turn of events, but instead she interrupted me in a strangled voice and, letting the veil fall away from her frozen face, made her own introduction. 'Rose von Bek, of the Royal Italian Geographical Expedition.' She spoke in her formal Arabic. 'I am so sorry to disturb your peace, Your Highness, and I appreciate your tolerance in permitting me to land in your beautiful realm. Both your courtesy and hospitality are famous throughout the world. I have long wished for the privilege of an audience. I trust you will not consider this unorthodox means of finding you too audacious. I have, of course, letters of introduction from various sponsors including our great Duce, Signor Mussolini, my master.'

El Glaoui seemed to frown at the name of Mussolini but

456

graciously recovered himself. 'I am flattered and enchanted,' murmured the Berber prince in husky, thrilling accents. 'Mr Beters I feel is an old friend, but you, mademoiselle . . . are a legendary jewel. Such beauty!'

I was admiring of Rose's quick wit and would have praised her had it not been clear that she was for some reason disgusted by me at that moment. And then, looking into her eyes, I understood. She had believed that she revealed her deepest desires to an inscrutable Oriental but instead she had shared her longings with a knowing European!

Lieutenant Fromental was delighted. His great broad face was beaming as he strode up to me and flung a comradely arm about me, all but crushing me. 'My dear friend, this is a most marvellous piece of good fortune.'

'Do you ride, Mr Peters?' The red-coated Englishman with the old-fashioned grey walrus moustache and flinty eyes, the most evidently military of all the company, was clearly testing me.

'Ride!' Lieutenant Fromental laughed aloud. 'Why, Mr Peters is an expert horseman!' He winked at me, sharing a droll secret. 'Since we last met, sir, I have had the pleasure of viewing *The Lost Buckaroo*. Even finer than *The Buckaroo's Code*, if I may say so. Once your films are seen in France your genius will be given its due credit. The French still honour great artists.' He became a little embarrassed. 'Well, sir, that was what I first recognised when I saw you. Those eyes! They are unmistakable! And the voice, when I heard it, from Casablanca! I am honoured, sir!' He opened his tunic and took out a piece of carefully folded newsprint – a publicity photograph of me raising my masked face to be kissed by Daphne LaCosse as she leans from the rails of a loco's moving caboose. I, of course, am kneeling on my saddle! It was from *The Fighting Buckaroo*, one of the last films of any substance I made for Lesser. 'I'm ashamed to say I've also been carrying about with me for weeks a letter I wrote to you. This is the most absurd coincidence! I thought of wiring you at Shepheard's. Then I decided you would have returned to the United States by now. I was racking my brains to remember the name of your film company when, by magic, you materialised before me!'

'We saw you descending, sir,' the redcoat told me. 'We thought the Italians were invading! The Pasha loathes the Eye-ties. You're lucky those chaps didn't shoot on sight!'

Fromental had stumped through the sand to where a restless stallion was offered by one of the Pasha's guards for my use. The man would ride double, no doubt, with a comrade. Another pony was similarly prepared for Rose but in this case the Pasha took a personal interest in its suitability.

'Anyway, here you are!' Fromental went on cheerfully. 'Large as life. And you'll be delighted by my news, Mr Peters. We have discovered your missing nigger.'

'In Morocco?' Having had rather a swift succession of surprises and reversals I was a little uncomprehending.

'No, no! Here! In the Tafi'lalet. Today. With us.' He gestured boisterously towards his companions. At last as the dust settled slowly around us, I gave my attention to the fifth hooded rider whose teeth glittered through the haze like the beam of an approaching loco. 'Good evening, colonel.'

It was none other than my faithful Mix!

I had turned up, he said, just as he thought his last run of luck was about to go dry. He dismounted and, his face filling with honest pleasure, shook me warmly by the hand. 'I can't tell you how glad I am you dropped by, colonel! Don't let us split up again. At least until we're back home!'

I must admit I was touched almost to tears by this demonstration of my dusky Sancho Panza's devoted loyalty.

TWENTY-FOUR

THE ILLUSION ONE CREATES in the cinema is not always easy to live up to in reality. Fame brings responsibility as well as power. The Pasha and his guests were returning from an antelope hunt. On our ride to the Glaoui *kasbah* at Tin'rheras, while an honoured visitor from the Hollywood heavens, I regretted that discretion demand I say nothing of stuntmen to the worshipping Lieutenant Fromental. Instead, I explained an uneasy seat as residual symptoms of my old friend, malaria.

The lieutenant showed brotherly concern at this news. He thought a Czech physician was soon to be a guest of the Pasha (who made the most of his Western acquaintances during his frequent visits to Paris). Perhaps the eminent Doctor N. could be persuaded to do something for me?

Grateful as I was, I said, for this suggestion, I merely had to ride out the disease. I was sure that in a few days (when I secretly planned to be entrained for Casablanca or Tangier) I would be as right as rain. Clapping me on the back the young Frenchman assured me we would be at the *kasbah* by the following evening. Meanwhile, if my health improved, I was welcome to join him for a gallop over the tundra while it was still possible. 'After Tafi'lalet, once we get into the Atlas,' Fromental indicated the ochre foothills of a substantial mountain range now filling the northern horizon, 'we'll have to pick our way along those damned tracks, and rock shelves which pass for tracks, above a succession of abysses. We'll be lucky to ride at all.'

Not for the first time since I had left California the prospect of an abyss or two was far preferable to my present predicament. It remains my belief (call it a betrayal of my Cossack blood) that the horse was merely a rough-and-ready stopgap we used while we were inventing the internal combustion engine. By some strange quirk, my native blood called not for the stallion's forceful gallop, but the camel's rolling plod.

The true power-holder in Morocco, thanks to his own consummate sense of strategy, El Glaoui was an animated little man in whom Arab, Negro and Berber, the three major races of this region, had married to produce a thoroughly nondescript pudgy little face which, save for his rather scrubby beard, might have been found on any bank clerk from Bangkok to Threadneedle Street. The vivacity which lit his eyes engaged one's immediate attention, however, and sometimes his whole face seemed to shine like the sun – not always with joy, but with shame or contempt or fury, perhaps, at some cosmic injustice. His self-esteem endowed him with a kind of beauty. He understood that he was what most men aspire to and what most women desire. He had proven his judgement in politics and in battle. He had conquered the South and accomplished the great pilgrimage to Mecca, thus definitively demonstrating his courage and his piety. Now he displayed his cultural sophistication, his scholarly curiosity in all that the world had to offer.

El Glaoui was by no means the first Moslem princeling to aspire to the mantle of Haroun al-Raschid or even Saladin, but for a while he alone most nearly achieved the reality. I would say he did this through his quick intelligence, personal charm and ruthless practicality. Savage as he was to his enemies, he could also be generous to those he defeated. He had the gentle but elaborate manners of the Berber nobility, a sense of quiet irony which pleased women, and a clever, self-deprecating manner which immediately made you his admirer. It was as well for Europe that the enchanting T'hami el Glaoui, Thane of this remoter Cawdor, had no greater ambition than to rule, through his French allies, one small part of the Maghrib! He was a Napoleon! An Alexander! And those who now slight him or tell me that he was nothing, that he never existed save as a Frenchman's shadow, have swallowed the official opinion of the victorious but rather less charismatic Sultan, who now calls himself a king. The truth is only ever what the dominant power declares it to be.

This is what they did to Makhno and Mosley. (Not that I admired them, as men, for anything but their audacity.) We turn these bold outlaws into goblins, driven by a will to Evil, even when we have previously used them for our own gain. Next we belittle and forget their achievements. It was the Pasha of Marrakech, not the Sultan of Morocco, nor the Bey of Algiers, who was a welcome and familiar guest in all the drawing-rooms and, indeed, the boudoirs, of the West End. Winston Churchill called him a fellow-spirit. Charles Boyer became his friend, Noël Coward wrote his famous submarine film in Marrakech and based one of the characters on El Glaoui, who was far more popular than King Farouk or the Aga Khan. He was considerably more cultured. I am the first to insist that I bear him no grudge. (We would both be victims of the same miserable Iago. But, as usual, I was not given the opportunity to explain my situation. People have no humanity, these days. Even the interrogators lack the patience of the old Tsarist professionals.)

In his domain, especially in one gorgeous room, the Pasha allowed the pace of life to remain civilised while ensuring that his guests had every modern comfort, including the latest in gramophone records and three-reeler movies, mostly French. He had a magnificent pianola and all the up-to-date rolls. I heard this from Lieutenant Fromental as we rode through a Moorish paradise, through groves of dark-green date palms whose long shadows fell across little lagoons and streams, against a flawless deep blue sky beneath which red dust blew across wind-eroded terracotta hills topped by the crenellated towers of a dozen petty chieftains, all of them vassals to our host, all of them subject to his will on pain of death. There was a wonderful silence to the place. Here was the reason for the Pasha's self-confidence, this demonstration of his immense security.

I envied him such feudal power. Yet even then I knew the cost of such power. To possess it one must also fight, second by second, to keep it. Amongst desert tribespeople, just as in modern business, there are always young contenders waiting for that one sign of weakness. Their moral behaviour is separated from the battle rituals of the stag only in the extent of the unthinking damage it does to the surrounding world. Yet still El Glaoui was a Renaissance prince. Had it not been for the French betraying him, he would have founded a dynasty as famous and as colourful as the Borgia. He, too, would have given his people prince and pope in one person.

He had formed the impression that we were American movie people in a borrowed balloon who had accidentally landed in his domain. He took it that we had come from Algeria. It suited neither of us to disillusion him, especially since it explained a movie camera he might, with his suspicion of Italian ambitions, have chosen to see as proof of our spying. Rose had offered some tale which he had accepted. He welcomed us to his court as artists and insisted we become his personal guests while in Marrakech.

His court already consisted of politicians, poets, actors and personalities from around the world. Our hunting party included Mr A. E. G. Weeks, the Sapper, late of the Royal Engineers, who was here with a tender for a set of new defences to quell any potential power bid from the Sahara Berbers, many of whom still refused to accept El Glaoui as their liege lord, and Count Otto Schmaltz, a serving officer of the Free Corps German Army in Exile, paying a courtesy visit from Constantinople to the Pasha. He was a Captain and a Count of the old, easy-going South German school, with only a veneer of his Prussian military education. He had studied at Heidelberg, he told me later that day, and had some good scars to prove it. El Glaoui, who had been riding in attentive silence nearby, remarked easily how ritual scarification was now only practised amongst the more primitive of his nomad tribes. When did the Germans over there hope to stamp the custom out? Which set the ruddy young Count to roaring, his face a fresh-quartered melon, and swearing what a good fellow the Pasha was, even as his host signalled adieu and rode on to join Miss von Bek, who he had been relieved to find was not Italian. She had refused to speak to me since we began our journey towards the mountains. At first I believed she was letting the little Moor pursue her in order to make me jealous, then I began to guess that she was determined, since I had proven nothing more than a clever imitation, to acquire for herself an authentic Arabian prince. At which point I lost emotional interest in her. My wounds were too fresh. I knew only one means of escaping the pain I had experienced at Esmé's betrayal. I reconciled myself to relying wholly upon my own resources until I had a chance at least to see Mr Mix alone.

Mr Mix, I now knew, had used his experience and acquaintance with me to find employment with the potentate. He had become El Glaoui's personal film director and official cameraman to the Court. He was always busy with his camera – the very latest Pathé – which he had lashed in a kind of cradle to his body, enabling him to turn the crank even as we moved. It seemed a shame to me that Mix's film was only intended for the Pasha's private viewing. Those reels would have been the most popular travelogues in the world, confirming every Western notion of Arabian opulence and decadent extravagance harnessed to omnipotent power against backgrounds of almost unbelievable romance as we reached the palm groves, streams and pools of the Tafi'lalet oasis. The little thatched villages, the timeworn castles and hills, the brightly-dressed women and simple dignified men, recalled some wonderful novel of Scott, Kipling or F. Marion Crawford, where nobility of soul and selfless courage were recognised, where at any moment Karl May's Kara ben Nemsi might come galloping on his white camel across the packed sand or Alan Quatermain rise from behind a rock to welcome us. We might be greeted by a chivalrous Saracen from Bohemian romance, some mediaeval French gentleman, honoured by the Moor as a hero. I have seen it in film after film. This is what made *Lawrence of Arabia* such a laughing-stock in nomad circles, I hear, and Mrs Fezi in Talbot Road merely laughs when I mention it. 'It is all a joke,' she says in Arabic. She enjoys speaking to someone who understands her. Even the Egyptians, she says, pretend to be baffled sometimes. She refuses to be shamed, she says, by those Jew-loving bastards, though she grants piously that we should all be tolerant and help one another, even benighted Christians like myself. Because I like her I repeat the prayer with her. It is a comfort to us both. I do not regret my time in the desert. It is not how one worships God but how one obeys Him, I say. But she will not speak the Lord's Prayer I wrote out for her. I do not blame her. She is a peasant, while I am heir to the blood of kings.

Anyway, I say, where would we be without the Jews in the first place? Whereupon she refuses to listen. She becomes tactful in the way that Russians do when you mention Stalin. Perhaps, after all, Stalin was not only a Georgian warlord but also an Oriental god? Perhaps, after all, Jesus was our first true prophet, in which case I am wasting my time with what I call my counter-missionary work. If these people wish to come to the West to make for themselves an Eastern slum, perhaps I should not try to improve their lot. But are they happy? In their own world, at least, they are not despised for their appearance or their beliefs. We are invaded at every turn by the Middle Ages. There is a War of Time violently taking place all around us and we pretend it is not there. We would rather talk about the quality of the fish and chips. Who are these nomads of the time-streams, bursting over the borders, flooding out of non-existent countries into the glaring realities of Paris and London and Amsterdam? Our values are the very antithesis of their own. It occurs to me that all the crimes committed against the ignorant and the innocent down the years have come home to roost in the nations of the rich. Their spirits are the ghosts haunting the treasury of our inheritance. We cannot enjoy our wealth and not be possessed by them all. War has an infinite price. We are never free of its victims. Generation upon generation is tainted by war. Generation upon generation pays the worst price of all – to watch paradise slowly slipping from its grasp. I remember Munich. I still do not believe the Führer was insincere.

I am of that generation which argues 'there are no victors in war' and I believe we have proven that contention. Yet T'hami el Glaoui would have thought me mad had I made such a statement as he rode with all the glory of his complicated retinue, its wagons and pack-animals and flags and soldiery, towards the granite seat of his family's original power. 'A great laird,' proclaimed Mr Weeks, whose mother had been a Mackenzie, 'and a gentleman through and through.'

We camped that night in a village of our own creation rather than suffer the cramped hospitality of the dignitaries who displayed the offerings of the local people, mostly lambs and goats, as *daifa* in the traditional rituals of welcome. Before our eyes they set to slaughtering an entire herd for our pleasure which was then roasted on spits over pits in the sand. Later, we feasted, as entertainers were brought in to sing those impossibly melancholy Berber love-songs having the substance and effect of the music they now call Cowboy and Western and which springs from similar peasant roots. These celebrations of cosmic self-pity were followed by a troupe of drummers, whose monotony would rival any modern *Top of the Pops* jungle dancing. Bad taste is truly universal. I sat on one side in the company of Lieutenant Fromental, Mr Weeks and Count Schmaltz while Rose von Bek was decidedly on her own with the Pasha. Both were oblivious to the music and I envied them this. The other local *kai'ds* and their retainers seemed as discomfited by the entertainment as the rest of us. Only Mr Mix gave every appearance of relishing the whole thing, filming them and us from every angle, his massive cart of batteries powering the floodlights necessary to capture anything but a flickering shadow (as it was he had to ask them to repeat their performances against that impossible background the next morning while the rest of us were packing to leave). Still I had failed to get the negro to one side. I almost wondered if he avoided me until it occurred to me that filming must be a genuine vocation for the intelligent *africain*.

Since he wished to return home to America, Mr Mix doubtless hoped to direct films for the race market. There was a thriving business in such films, which were sold throughout the African and Oriental world. I contented myself, knowing that sooner or later my old comrade would let me into his confidence.

I was still not entirely at ease with Rose von Bek's behaviour. It seemed to me that the essential man, not the name he uses, is all that is ever important. But perhaps she had thought me more powerful than I was, while T'hami el Glaoui was certainly everything a potentate should be, even if he lacked my looks and peculiar skills. I suspected that our relative power was something she had weighed up with all the speed of the practised adventuress. Grateful that I had invested little real idealism in her, merely friendship, I made the best of things, taking comfort in the company of those boisterous, manly comrades, their jokes and private conversations. It was no surprise, after the feasting and *folklorique* were done, that Rose von Bek did not tip-toe from the Pasha's tent to her own until a little before dawn. I buried all memory of pleasure. It had become second nature to me. The stiff upper lip is not the Englishman's prerogative. The next day, as we entered the last phase of the journey to his *kasbah*, the Pasha made a point of calling out for me to join him at the head of the party. Observed by genuflecting peasants, we rode along an avenue of palms. Rose was nowhere in sight, confined, I was told, to one of the wagons, suffering from the privations of our balloon journey. The balloon itself followed in another of the supply wagons. 'I gather you are something of an engineer as well as a film star, Mr Beters.' Like most Arabic speakers he had trouble with the letter 'p', but he was charming. His gentle courtesy won me over at once.

'I am lucky enough to hold a degree or two in the sciences,' I confirmed. 'My colleague Lalla von Bek has been betraying my secrets, I fear.'

He appreciated my use of the Arabic title. 'Lalla von Bek explained the extraordinary nature of your meeting. In disguise, you came out of the desert like a Bedouin legend, Mr Beters, and rescued a fair maiden! Be careful, they will be brinting your adventures in the benny dreadfuls.' He then launched into some second-hand anecdote he had overheard on the Quai d'Orsay concerning Buffalo Bill's embarrassment

466

at the fictions perpetrated in his name. 'Did you ever see a Wild West Show, Mr Beters?'

I admitted that I had only known Cody's nephew, but I had rubbed shoulders with some fairly rough types 'out West'. 'Believe me, Your Highness, there are worse villains in real life than we ever dare show on the screen.'

'I *can* believe it, Mr Beters. However, until I again have the bleasure of watching your wonderful film escabades, I must make do with the reality of your combany. What is your sbecial field?'

I quickly explained that I was by profession an inventor. I had to my credit a string of recent experimental machines, from airships to the latest dynamite car. In the pipeline were plans for great ships to carry tourists to the desert where they would learn something of the dignity of the nomad life. This of course would increase the region's wealth. It was this latter idea that intrigued him. I described further details of my Desert Liner. From there we got on to aeroplanes, for which he was a great enthusiast. 'Do you know anything about building aeroblanes, m'sieu?'

'I am the first Russian to fly,' I informed him. 'I flew a one-man craft over Kiev long before such things were thought possible. It was for my originality in this area that I was awarded my special medal from St Petersburg.'

'Ah, Betersburg. Your real name, I take it? And yet you gave ub such an exciting career to be an actor?' He found this a trifle puzzling.

I scarcely knew where to begin his enlightenment. 'I am not,' I said, 'like so many modern Westerners, desperate to slot myself into one narrow groove and roll along it for the rest of my life. I take opportunities where they arise. It is how I have always survived. The medium of the cinema intrigues me. For a while it suited me, I suppose, to make that medium my own. Now my chief pursuits are more intellectual. I possess at present a catalogue of aircraft which I have, over the years, designed. To make it a reality the catalogue only requires an enlightened backer. But, sadly, there are few such visionaries in these troubled times.'

'I flew in 1913,' said the Pasha with some pride. 'It was

467

interesting, though not terrifying. Some of my beoble did not enjoy the exberience, but I made them take it. Ha, ha! Could you berhabs build a small air fleet, m'sieu, if funds were at your disbosal?'

Taken aback, I nodded, silently. I could think of nothing to say. But this response seemed to satisfy him. He told me that we would discuss the idea further, when we got to Tafouelt.

The rest of the morning, as the tracks became steeper and we were sometimes forced to go in single file, I spent in some euphoria. Had Leonardo at last found his Prince? Perhaps this was where I was destined to begin my march back to respectability, to recover all my honours? In time I would be able to travel to Paris and make it evident that I was not some second-rate share-floater but an honest inventor. T'hami had the ear of the most powerful politicians in France. In Marrakech, I thought, I might redeem myself entirely and then, my reputation restored, make my way to Italy where, I was now convinced, I would discover my ultimate destiny. I said nothing of Italy to El Glaoui, whose dislike of that country was an obsession. So optimistic had I become, so full of plans for my improving future, that I hardly noticed as we climbed to the brow of a low hill and was astonished at the sight of the great oasis of Tafi'lalet. This was a vast valley – or series of shallow valleys – some twelve miles long and nine miles wide, where crops of red rock jutted from fertile grazing lands, from fields of wheat and barley, from every shade of green. Green blazed brighter than the valley's lakes and rivers. Green was the Holy Colour. We paused to honour it.

At length we continued on up a winding trail which took us suddenly to the gates of a large crenellated castle, built of pink *piste*, with a drawbridge and portcullis and all the trappings of a working mediaeval fortress. Tafi'lalet was one of the Glaoui family's chief forts, belonging, Fromental whispered, to T'hami's nephew, whom everyone called The Vulture. Though T'hami was head of the family, Si Hammon held the real power in this region of the High Atlas, controlling half the wealth of Southern Morocco, and T'hami, despising his relative, embarrassed by him, had every reason to keep his peace with him.

Into this gloomy fortress we now filed on weary, still-stumbling horses. When I looked back through the archway I saw a panorama of the whole Tafi'lalet valley and it was easy to understand why the great *kasbah* had been built there. It controlled the entire area and could never be secretly attacked. As the last gaudy warriors passed over it, the drawbridge was taken back up on a pully and a rope drawn by a complaining donkey. The place stank chiefly of dung while the courtyard was piled with old rags, junk and household waste which black slaves were burning slowly in mouldering heaps.

We dismounted and were led into a wide, high hall where T'hami's slaves ran forward to take our outer clothing and a majordomo led us up narrow, curving staircases to our somewhat chilly rooms. My window looked back over what the Moors called *hammada*, a pebble desert, and from here, clearly, any attack could be anticipated. My room was furnished with an ornate provincial French bed, a toilet stand in modern bamboo and a table which seemed Spanish in origin. At the glassless windows were heavy shutters and obscuring these were curtains in English chintz. A slave brought me hot water and a full change of clothing. This was far superior to my own desert finery. Soon I knew again the luxury of soap and scented silks. That night our feasting differed only by virtue of being under cover, but the hall amplified the orchestra and especially the livelier wails of the plump ladies who led the choruses and the hand-clapping. The heat of the place, coupled with the smells of half-cured ancient skins, burning garbage and roasting meat, brought on a blazing headache which I cured, at last, with so much morphine that I passed out, to be taken tenderly to bed by a concerned Fromental who carried me easily in his giant's arms and assured me they were all sympathetic. They had forgotten how desperate had been my desert ordeal.

In the morning, when we left the brooding kasbah and began the long descent into that wonderful valley, Lieutenant Fromental shook his head, wondering what fool would ever want to leave this paradise. 'I am thinking a man could retire here,' he said. 'Perhaps farm a little.'

'I understood you were planning to follow the great route

to Timbuktu when you retired,' Otto Schmaltz reminded him as he rode to join us on the path.

'That too, perhaps.' Fromental frowned. He had little time for the young German. The Frenchman's father and brother had both been killed at Ypres.

We descended for a while in silence until the trail widened and became easier. We no longer had to concentrate. Soon the trail grew into a mud road leading between date palms and olive trees. I had never, even in Egypt, seen such natural richness. Here, as before, the Berber villagers came from their work and their houses to cheer and sing as we passed by. I might have been part of some boyar's entourage in Old Russia or participating in a knightly progress through 12th-century France. Quite clearly El Glaoui was making a discreet display of his power. These lands were by no means secure for the French while they remained, Fromental told me, under the Vulture's wing.

By that evening we had crossed the great valley and entered the mountains, accepting the hospitality of a local caïd who, incidentally, sold the Pasha several black slaves he had come by in, he said, a special purchase. He seemed oblivious to a disapproving (but diplomatic) Fromental or to the laws forbidding such barbarism. At no time had El Glaoui approached me to continue our conversation. He was clearly preoccupied with Rose von Bek.

On the third day of our journey, we entered the forbidding mountains of the High Atlas proper where the trails turned into steep narrow tracks curving around the sides of those ancient crags and I only became properly aware of my surroundings as I stood to rest on a wide ledge overlooking a series of broad dales running between gentle hills rising to form the sides of great, grey cliffs. I found myself gasping at what I saw! Valley upon valley, in all directions, was a jewelled infinity of wild flowers. In their vivid variety they glowed, reflecting the light of the afternoon sun. They pulsed and undulated like an ocean of rainbows.

I had never in my life been prepared for such intense beauty, coming so suddenly after the loss of the green oases, the stark crags. It was a glimpse of a different heaven, this hidden place of peace and beauty where death was nothing but a wonderful promise, where the miraculous proof of God's existence was confirmed. And so, when T'hami and his people kneeled to pray, I joined them spontaneously, from that habit of absolute worship one acquires in the desert. I praised God and I thanked Him for all His creations and especially those which were a sign of His absolute benevolence. So overcome was I that I was forced to take an untypical risk and go to steady myself with the use of my cocaine, crouching on one side of my frisky mount as I tried to control the tube which would take the reviving powder to my nose.

A little later, as we walked back to his own beast, El Glaoui said, with a certain puzzlement, that he praised Allah for he had found a brother in an expected place. He did not speak with any particular warmth. Perhaps he suspected me of attempting to ingratiate myself with Moslems. Miss von Bek, riding by as I climbed into my own unyielding saddle, flicked at pretty hair and observed that there was surely no need for me to maintain my play-acting for their sake. Unless, she added, I intended to take up a collection later. In which case she would be delighted to reward me with a *dirham* or two for my undoubted talents. She rode on before I could give her my witty reply.

It was clear, however, that she was recovering from her embarrassment and seemed ready enough to continue our friendship. For my part, I bore her no ill-will.

Soon afterwards, El Glaoui retired into the wagon he used when the roads were good and I saw nothing of him or Rose von Bek until we stopped to make camp in a valley so saturated with perfume from the wild flowers that I feared I must faint into some exotic dream from which I would not awake for years. As the sun came down upon the crest of the western hills it spread light like an old glaze across the landscape. The flowers lost none of their glowing vitality. They seemed to have existed since the beginning of time.

We were eating the substantial remains of the previous night's feast, the smell of *couscous* and fatty meat at vulgar odds with the surrounding paradise, when I remarked to Count Schmaltz that this scenery made a man understand how civilisation and aesthetics might take many forms. Who, after all, needed to create pictures here when such a magnificent picture appeared without fail every year? But Schmaltz amiably disagreed with me. 'Only if you judge civilisation by its arts, my dear fellow. I do not. I agree that art can take many forms, some of them alien to our own ideal. But institutions are another matter. Our good old-fashioned Northern European institutions of justice and equality, they are a form of madness to our host. He pretends to understand them, but it is almost impossible for him to imagine a society in which the power is shared between a wide variety of interests and classes. He perceives civilised Europe as nothing more than a subtler, more successful and perhaps more devious example of his own world.'

'Who is to say he is not right?' I asked reasonably.

But this irritated Schmaltz. His face became melon-pink again. 'Oh, do not mistake me.' He glanced around him as he wiped his fingers on a napkin. We were eating according to local custom, with our right hands only. 'I have considerable respect for El Glaoui's *Realpolitik* as he applies it. But he grows ambitious. Soon he will try to dictate terms to us. It is like the Bolsheviks. Mark my words. Let them get on with their "social experiment" by all means, but they should not try to bully us.'

I agreed with him, though unsure of his point. I asked him what moral superiority the West could claim, when it singularly failed to come to the aid of fellow Christian nations. Were we superior to the Arab in this respect? Or the Bolshevik?

He became more impatient. 'I see no reason, Herr Peters, why a nation which does not habitually torture and otherwise terrorise its citizens should accept the dictates of one which does. In common morality, my dear sir, we are demonstrably their superiors.'

'But by how fine a degree?' It was Mr Mix going by with his film camera. He had passed on before Otto could reply, so the German turned to me again. 'I still do not take readily to being treated so casually by a nigger,' he confided. 'But these Americans are all the same, they say. Do you enjoy Hollywood, Herr Peters?'

It was my second home, I said. A golden dream of the

future. He was taken aback by this. I did not know it was then fashionable in German military circles to denigrate everything American, especially if it came from Hollywood or New York, while in France the fascination with the United States was unabated. For them it was a place where all myth was made reality. I found both points of view rather conventional. Mr Weeks's tolerant bemusement at the more extravagant aspects of American society was easier to share.

These were to be the first of several ongoing conversations, all of them refreshingly original, which the four of us (Mr Mix continuously aloof, the Pasha and Miss von Bek generally absent) came to enjoy almost greedily during our various necessary stops. After my first flush of zealotry, I now confined myself to lowering my head and murmuring the prayers where I stood, in the manner of Turkish aristocrats, explaining to my new comrades that I believed it important for diplomatic reasons to acknowledge the Muslim religion here. Though they were never easy with this aspect of my life it did not affect our hearty arguments over a pipe and a discreet glass of brandy at the end of the day (the Pasha also offered hashish) while we gathered around our camp fire, relishing the smell of the wild heather and the carpets of flowers, the wind still carrying the faintest sting of the desert back to us, the flickering light and the comradely warmth, the busy sounds of the camp slowly fading into silence as we sat close to the peaks of the mountains which the Greeks had named for the Titan who held the world upon his back. Perhaps this was also a symbolic union of Christian gentlemen sworn to uphold the name of their redeemer and take upon themselves the responsibilities of their civilisation, for the duties and sacrifices of Empire were frequent topics. Mr Weeks said there was nothing to beat a good chin-wag with a bunch of brainy chaps, each an expert in his own line. It was convenient that we all spoke French, but when the Sapper seemed to be flagging we would lapse into English.

No subject was disallowed and my only regret was that our host and Miss von Bek were not there to join in, since both were first-rate minds. However, this allowed the Pasha himself to become a frequent topic. It was Count Schmaltz's opinion, for instance, that El Glaoui was consciously creating for himself a romantic legend, well aware of the additional power this gave him, especially in liberal European circles. 'Those fellows allow you any infamy so long as you represent yourself as some sort of underdog.' The Pasha received the support of the conservatives with his military actions and his absolute dedication to the French cause, but he welcomed those bohemians whom he knew to have influence in their own countries. It was second nature to a Moslem leader to play such complicated power games. 'But the whole thing is a fantasy. It is founded upon the most appalling injustice and cruelty, which we are never allowed to witness. Did you find the dungeons in the castle the other night? I did. And saw – and smelled – something of their contents. The burning garbage hides much worse. These people still dismember their living enemies in public. There are slave markets in every village. The family – and consequently the blood feud – are their only law. Yet our great German playwrights and our composers come here to be charmed by a character from the *Arabian Nights* and return to Berlin to describe the civilised wonders of the Pasha's court. There are too many people willing to believe in marvels and sentimental folly these days, my friends.'

Puffing upon his *narghila*, Lieutenant Fromental shook his head in amiable disagreement. 'Why should we not believe in marvels and miracles and happy endings, m'sieu? It is the same with God. What on earth is the point of not believing?'

'God is not an escape but a duty,' said Schmaltz, a little upset. 'I was not referring to the kinema, Herr Leutnant, but to current urgent social problems. To politics. I am sure we all find it very pleasant to enjoy Herr Peters's displays. We all, I hope, require a little bit of fun sometimes. But to apply those values to reality – surely you would not argue that the morality of *The Masked Buckaroo* should be brought to bear on modern society?'

At this point I was forced to interrupt. 'I would suggest that you view the picture-drama before you judge it, Herr Count. It was made in the same moral tradition as *Birth of a Nation*.'

He was good enough to blush and offer me a gruff apology. He did not, he added, refer to present company in any of his pronouncements. He had every respect for the professions and the moral values of others. We lived, after all, in a modern world where certain realities had to be accepted. And thus, a model German, he returned to his original point. 'The world's predicament is too dangerous for any indulgence in fantasy, certainly not of this present glorious charade which, I admit, we all are enjoying. But we do not personally,' he added, 'very often have to overhear the screams from the dungeons.'

Mr Weeks murmured that he thought if there were any irregularities of that sort the French authorities would investigate them and, if necessary, correct them. There were, after all, certain bargains one had to strike with a powerful ally. The French could not – realistically – be seen to be supporting a tyrant.

'So he makes the tyranny less visible. And we all accept his hospitality and act to help him hide his complex systems of torture, extortion and terror!' Schmaltz would have none of it. He was of that class of over-sensitive German who made trouble for the Turks during the Armenian crisis. I could only admire him, without necessarily always agreeing with him, or even liking him.

'What action would you suggest we take?' enquired Fromental mildly. 'We cannot employ an army of spies.'

'It is not the barbarism abroad I speak of, Herr Leutnant, but the sleep-walking at home. That's my main concern.' The German was friendly. 'We should all be looking to our domestic problems first, forgetting old differences and harnessing the positive energy which exists in every ordinary person.'

Fromental wanted to know if ordinary decency could be 'harnessed' and if so how.

'Through community and idealism,' replied the Count, busy with his meerschaum, 'not through communism and rhetoric. We must all pull together for the common good.'

Lieutenant Fromental did not put his scepticism into words.

That evening the Pasha invited us to his tent. 'This has become a rare privilege since he met your beautiful colleague.' Mr Weeks winked at me. He had not detected, any more than the others, that my relationship with Miss von Bek had been other than professional. They had chosen to assume simply that we were engaged upon some joint mission of the Italian and British governments. I think it suited neither of us to make any more of our story than the Berbers would. Stories become very swiftly embroidered when translated, as it were, into literary Arabic. Fromental, my only confidant, agreed. 'Those who live under tyranny, Mr Peters, make no progress. They learn only how to stay in one place. They learn a form of silence: the banal expressions of bureaucracies and armies, the conventions of the ruling élite, who fear a living, questioning, language. Thus the public language is allowed to say nothing new, though the people make new language every day. This was how Arab literature ceased to be the seminal literature of the mediaeval world, supplying the West with almost all its present story-forms and narrative devices. New Arabic is nothing more than a way of retelling the same myths in different guises. One perceives this effect in the Turkish Empire and everywhere the hammer and sickle crush and cut. There are no advantages to tyranny, save for the tyrant.'

'And his,' I counterpointed, 'is an inefficient method of keeping power, as the financiers of New York will verify!'

El Glaoui was, I must admit, the very model of a modern benevolent tyrant; urbane, expansive, generous and humorous, anxious to understand other points of view than his own, eager to embrace the twentieth century while supremely certain of the superiority of his own way of life. As we seated ourselves on the cushions of his great tent while our hands and faces were washed by his handsome negro slaves (he was rumoured to hide his Caucasians for fear of giving Europeans offence) I was immediately seduced by his hospitality and his charm. Each guest was welcomed and questioned as to his needs. His individual tastes were courteously recollected by the Pasha. Mr Weeks, beside me, murmured that he wouldn't be surprised if the old boy hadn't been educated at Eton. Lieutenant Fromental was listening carefully to Count Schmaltz addressing his host on the matter of the recent Riffian wars.

'But you flew, did you not, Lieutenant Fromental, with the French air force?' The Pasha signed to include the young man and allow him to speak for his own people.

'For a few days, Your Highness, yes. As an observer,

of course. I've never felt any wish to control one of those things!'

Rose von Bek spoke up. 'I envy you, Lieutenant.' I had hardly noticed her in the shadows. She wore a long becoming gown, heavily embroidered in the Berber style, and her head was covered by a kind of turban. Berber women frequently went unveiled and frequently only covered their faces in imitation of more sophisticated Arab customs. In the villages, I had been told, it was considered uncouth rather than irreligious to go uncovered. (The cinema, says Mrs Fezi, changed all that. Again, she blames the Egyptians. 'Now they are all film stars in the country towns,' she says. 'But we didn't wear veils, any of my family. And that was in Meknes.')

'Envy me, mademoiselle?' said my young friend in surprise.

'You flew at will over this wonderful country. We, on the other hand, scarcely glimpsed its beauty before we crashed.' (She did not see fit to explain why we had observed so little of the passing landscape!) 'I wish I could have been your pilot! What an awfully thrilling sight. The Riff massing in all their glory!'

'Actually, mademoiselle,' said Lieutenant Fromental in some embarrassment, 'we were bombing villages. With the Goliaths, you know. They are the very latest heavy bombers. The smoke and the fires tended to obscure our view of the Riff.'

'Six thousand hours of flight and three thousand missions. What was it, forty bombing flights a day!' The Pasha exclaimed all this in terms of the warmest admiration. 'I read it in *Le Temps*. Forty bombing flights a day!'

'And still Abd el-Krim and his Riffians were able to bring those planes down. Sharp-shooters lying on their backs in rows and firing in concert! Aeroplanes make no real difference to warfare, in my opinion. Only to civilians.' Mr Weeks was a confessed admirer of the rebel chief. 'How many squadrons did you have out there? Fourteen? It was folly. The British had equally disastrous experience bombing the Kurdish villages in Iraq. The aeroplane can never be an independent agent of warfare. It should no more operate on its own than should artillery. In the end it's always up to the infantry. Or,' he admitted, after due consideration, 'sometimes the cavalry.

I doubt if the French would have had a war in Syria at all if it hadn't been for their indiscriminate bombing in the first place. *The Times* said so quite clearly. Destroying villages, of course, gives the enemy *scores* of homeless recruits.'

I began to laugh at this. 'Come now, Mr Weeks. You'll be telling us next that the airship is an invention of the Devil!'

He shrugged and held up his hands, trying to smile as he dropped the subject. His hatred of every kind of flying machine was well known.

'However, the aeroblane is effective,' pronounced the Pasha suddenly, silencing us. He paused to take some stuffed sweetmeat from the tray his slave offered him, 'as Mr Weeks says. As artillery is effective. Did you know, Mr Weeks, that much of our family's bower was founded on the ownershib of one Krubb cannon?'

Mr Weeks had told me as much, but he feigned ignorance.

'A gift from God,' said the Pasha. 'With that one excellent German gun – ' a further acknowledgement of Schmaltz's somewhat tender feelings ' – we were able to bacify rebellious tribesmen, unite the whole region as one beoble and imbrove our friendshib with the French.' He smacked his lips. He dipped his fingers to be washed and dried. 'But there are certain barts of the South which even a Krubb cannon cannot reach, where we are still irritated by unregenerate outlaws and rebels who make cowardly raids into our lands and then skulk away again. We discussed this frequently with General Lyautey, that great man. In Tangier and in Baris.' El Glaoui nodded in deep self-approval. 'He told me that if I wanted an air force I should not ask the French for one. It would be imbolitic. But if I were to build my own small fleet, merely a squadron or two, no one would steb in my way.' He looked into the middle distance as if his eyes already rested on his gleaming battle-birds, ready to carry the flame of a great new Moorish civilisation, an empire which, arm-in-arm with the French Empire, would civilise the whole of Oriental Africa. I recognised a man of vision as thoroughly as he recognised me. I felt like leaping to my feet and swearing that, in a year or two, I would give him the air power that he craved. I would give him more than that. I would give him nomad cities, moving slowly across the dunes on their mighty tracks. I would give him roads burned into existence by fusing the sand with heat-beams, just as my Violet Ray had fused the stones of Kiev. At that moment, our eyes met. He smiled, a little dazed. I would give him Utopia.

I became immediately loyal to this shared vision. I was in no doubt that it would soon begin to materialise and, once my ideas were in full realisation, I would be invited to Rome.

The conversation turned to other matters and I was left with my own optimistic thoughts. Only once did I become aware of anyone's attention on me. I looked through the jumping shadows of the firelight, through the smoke and the little wisps of mist which came up from the valley. Rose von Bek was observing me from under her long lashes even as she pretended to listen to her new lover. It was as if I had whetted her curiosity for a second time. I think she was beginning to see me for the man I was, rather than the fantasy she had created. I half-closed my own eyes before I returned, steadily, her stare. The Pasha, absorbed in some weighty philosophical discussion with Count Schmaltz and Mr Weeks, paid us no attention. Only François Fromental threw me an amused glance as he settled himself deep into his cushions and drew luxuriously upon a good Havana.

Ma sha' allah! Ma teru khush ma'er-ragil da! A 'ud bi-rabb el-fulag! A 'ud billah min esh-shaitan ev-ragim!

A little later I heard my name called. 'Mr Peters! Ace!' The young Frenchman was reaching across and shaking my arm. I opened my eyes.

I realised with a shock that I had, for an instant, been travelling again in the Land of Dreams.

It was not until the next day that I had my third vision of paradise – the great palmeries of Marrakech, filling the verdant mesa surrounded by the Atlas's noble crags and, at their centre beneath the pure blue sky, the Red City, the city which only Timbuktu rivalled as a mysterious legend, crenellated walls rising above the surrounding palms and poplars; the city who had given a whole nation her name and given the word Moor to the world. *Dreaming Marrakech, as old as romance, as sweet as forbidden wine*, says Wheldrake.

I stood in awe, that evening, and wondered how any Moor could ever turn his back on such unique beauty.

El Glaoui joined me, reaching almost delicately to touch my shoulder. 'Mr Beters, I want you to helb me build the future – here in Marrakech.' It was impossible to refuse him. At that moment I forgot my dreams of Hollywood and returned, with rising spirits, to my true vocation.

My cities will be filled with gardens. Surrounded by a halo of golden light they will rise above the earth and settle upon the mountains like proud hawks. And the first of these shall be *Marrakech*.

I must admit I had expected nothing like the reception I received as we rode into Marrakech. Bit by bit a crowd formed, chattering and pointing at me, and when I cheerfully waved back a great gasp went up, then an ululation of sheer joy.

Glad to ride beside me at that moment, El Glaoui grinned. 'You must be used to this, Mr Beters, wherever you go. I feel very small fish beside you.'

I do not think he was entirely pleased as the cheering increased and I heard the name 'Bookh'aroo!' on all their lips. By some peculiar fluke I was adored in Marrakech as Valentino was adored in Minneapolis. Lieutenant Fromental was almost drunk with reflected glory. 'One day,' he proclaimed excitedly, 'they will know about you in France. You will be as famous, my dear friend, in Paris and Marseilles as you are now in Meknes and Fez!' I had no other option but to wave and salaam as, with horribly aching muscles, I tried to control my lively horse. And so we passed through the walls of Marrakech and only Rose von Bek took no notice of my fame.

TWENTY-FIVE

NARCOTICS POSSESS none of the curative properties of the white psychedelics. By these I refer not to hippy pleasure trips on LSD but to the mind-expanding and mind-focusing properties of pure cocaine. These boys and girls today know nothing of cocaine. They have never sniffed it. They have had the illusion of pleasure on lavatory cleaner and baby laxative and they presume to condescend to the man who has imbibed 'the woman-drug' with the great and famous of the twentieth century – and by this I mean no innuendo to our present rulers and their families. I speak my mind when I have to, but otherwise am well known for my discretion. I learned the virtues of silence in Egypt and Morocco. To these people 'free speech' is synonymous with 'blasphemy'.

At a Moorish court self-discipline becomes a question of survival. I learned the old, mediaeval virtues, and began to understand the meaning of Chivalry. I had travelled in Time. On such ancient understandings were the codes of the Black Hand founded, as I have reason to know. The so-called *mafia* were in their own world the old forms of Law pitted against the new, just as today the Arab is pitted against the institutions of democracy.

At Talouet, the seat of his family's original power, El Hadj T'hami Ben Mohammed Mezouari el Glaoui, Pasha of Marrakech, had already proposed his plan to me, even before we reached the capital. The great mediaeval pile had been filled, almost like Hearst's strange fantasy, with a mixture of Moorish treasure and expensive European furniture, with unselected *objets d'art*. The castle housed much of the Pasha's great collection of concubines, at least half of whom, it was said, were French. Staffed by his huge Nubians, the palace was never completely silent.

He had been irritated, he said, by an unpleasant little Frenchman of the worst class, a man called Lapin – a Communist journalist with some profession to the Law. He was in league with an old enemy of the Glaoui, a certain discredited *kai'd* called El Hakim, who had enlisted this turncoat to bring suit against the Pasha. El Hakim's supporters had even brought Lapin a newspaper in which he uttered every kind of calumny against the Pasha and his family. One of the accusations which El Glaoui found especially rankling was that none of his wealth was put back into the region. Nothing was spent on cultural projects or scientific schemes. If the Glaoui was truly enlightened, Lapin had argued, why did he not encourage scientific and social progress in his realm? In response to this the Pasha pointed to Mr Mix, employed to record the cultural and varied rule of the great Pasha and his world 'for bosterity'. He had founded a film industry in Marrakech which would ultimately be the rival of Hollywood. And now an aeronautics industry. Nothing could be more modern. Every day his city became a second Los Angeles. Suddenly, from advising on defences, Mr Mix was commissioned to draw up plans for a series of solid English public works, 'Like the lavatories,' commanded the Pasha, 'in Leicester Square.' Other guests were recruited. Count Schmaltz's advice, concerning discipline and the chains of command appropriate to a modern standing army, was also sought, though the German, like Miss von Bek, was only the Pasha's guest.

All this he had elaborated as we stood together on the roof of his *kasbah*'s tallest tower, looking across the ragged peaks of the High Atlas, listening to the rushing of the Oued Mellah, and staring out across the surrounding semi-desert towards the true Sahara we had so recently left behind. I had never seen such vividly coloured mountains as these. The rock itself was radiant with dark greens and yellows, with luminous cerise and mauve, with deep reds and blues, slabs of stone sometimes merging with the undulating meadows of wild flowers all pulsing beneath the heat of a royal-blue sky. I remember thinking how different this landscape was from everything I had yet seen, how the desert contained a world of contrasts and variation as distinct as anything in Europe. As the sun dropped down over the crags and their shadows lengthened until it seemed they must engulf the castle itself, El Glaoui had spoken of his love of this land. This, he said, not Marrakech, was his true capital; he thought of the place as home, for which he experienced the deepest sentiment. If he had his way, he told me, he would spend far more time here. I had been introduced to half-a-dozen cousins and brothers-in-law (though not the resident Vulture himself, who was tactfully absent) and could remember none of them. They were not an especially remarkable family save for the direct branch. It was then he had asked me to work for him, to build him an air fleet. I told him I would give the matter great consideration. That night two Circassian houris of the most subtle and astonishing skills were sent to me. My lusts remained unavailable to me, but I appreciated my host's thoughtfulness. At the time I believed this was something of a guilty gesture on his part, given his interest in Miss von Bek, but I would later learn that 'guilt' was not a word in any of the Pasha's vocabularies.

He had asked me my opinion of Lieutenant Fromental: I said diplomatically that he seemed a pleasant enough young man.

'He is here to spy on me,' El Glaoui had murmured with a small smile. 'He is a secret communist, I think.'

Privately I felt this an overly strong response to Fromental's Christian humanism, but I held my tongue. I had no will to self-destruction. I am, I have often said, no martyr.

Perhaps it is a little late, even for a new messiah? Sometimes I say to Barnum the Jew, you people might have the right idea. Can things get any worse? Where is this messiah you tell us hasn't arrived yet? He cannot answer. He will be waiting for his messiah when the rest of us are two feet under, but no doubt he will be standing on my shoulders.

'I blame the whole thing on the death of the family,' says Barnum. He is particularly upset because of his girl, who Mrs Cornelius warned him about when she was six.

'The death of the family,' I said, 'is probably our only hope.' But then I think I knew something about what 'family first' means. For my own part I continued to put my faith in the great political ideals we developed throughout the 19th century. Nietzsche is not entirely to be trusted on this. It is to those 19th-century values we should return, not seek some ideal anarchy. 'Who would wish to live in your Utopia?' I asked him. Your mother! Anyone else? Some families should be dispersed at birth! I met H. G. Wells in Marrakech. He still had some notion of gigantic crêches as the answer but I suggested it would be simpler to remove, as it were, the father factor. Let the father always be anonymous. This amused him. 'There are a lot of chaps I know, including me, who'd drink to that,' he said. 'Now I know what we have in common!' *Illustre Abraham; procréateur fanatique du Mythe sacrificateur.* Herbert Wells had no time any longer for practical science and his social notions were often unsound, but as an inspiration to my generation he had enormous influence. Stalin counted him a close personal friend. Only Mr Mix, I recall, never took to him. But I had grown used to the man's odd changes of mood. He had developed a chip on his shoulder, I think. Generally he refused to exchange more than a few sentences with me but occasionally would be as amiable, as solicitous, as in old times. I began to suspect he was the slave of some wretched drug.

He would frequently disappear with his camera and his ill-matched crew of Berber donkey-boys and Jewish street-arabs up into the mountains, or would go back to Talouet. In that brooding family fortress of the Clan Glaoua high above the Salt River, the chiefs still gathered in times of crisis to decide the fortunes of the tribes who remained in the Atlas and gave the Glaoua fealty, who had not, in the Berber's droll saying, exchanged their rifle for a mule.

The Berbers referred to themselves by their clans much as the Scots did and, from my own reading of *Rob Roy*, their social system and leisure pursuits were almost identical, save that the Moroccans did not at that time have an implacable industrialising ruling power bent on driving them forever into submission, to make them bend before the firm yet not unkind hand of progress. Mr Mix had become something of an enthusiast of these clansmen ('Berber' being simply a corruption of the Greek 'barbarian') and spent an inordinate amount of time with notebooks recording their dialects and folk practices. I wondered if he did not have some misguided notion that this mysterious people were his ancestors. I suggested it: he denied it. Employed as El Hadji T'hami's personal film-maker, he said, it was his business to record the glory and variety of the Pasha's realm. Having no interest in the fine distinctions of one tribe's scarifications compared to another's, I realised how these customs must give him a better sense of his own past.

I had also begun to understand that Mr Mix's discretion came chiefly from his not wishing to embarrass me in front of the other white men. This was typical of my friend's sensitivity and I let him know that I thoroughly appreciated what he was doing. When we were alone, he resumed the old, easier manner of our comradeship. Yet even here he seemed to nurse some sort of resentment. More than once he suggested that I get on the first train to Casablanca and go from there to Italy where, he said, I really belonged. They needed me there, he said. At first I took this for a warming concern for my well-being. But then I began to realise that in certain respects he was trying to get me away from Marrakech. No doubt he feared that my authority as a spokesman for Hollywood was rather greater than his own. Yet he continued about his film-making unhindered by me, while the Pasha seemed perfectly content to use him for recording special occasions and for help with the foreign press when they required interviews or newsreel footage. Effectively, Mr Mix had been elevated to the position of press attaché to the Pasha, as well as Court Recorder. I was still unsure, in those early days at Court, exactly how Mr Mix had come by his appointments while now yearning for the railroads of home. As to my own fortunes, I joked to Lieutenant Fromental, I was now both Court Engineer, Jester and Royal Plane-maker.

Marrakech is the most exquisite of all Moorish settlements. She is a timeless city, the colour of her red marigolds and green palmeries, of bloody milk and a sky as flat, as tranquil and as blue as any perfectly painted Hollywood firmament. Her days are full of the smells of beasts, mint, saffron and musk, of henna and fresh-picked oranges, of mounded carrots and leeks and a dozen different mysteriously gnarled husks, of tea and sweet sherbet and boiling *couscous*, of roasting sheep and goat-stew, of honey and coffee and the dyer's wells, of heavy tobacco smoke and the thick, tempting whiffs of *kif*, of sour milk and sweet flesh, of heated mud in the summer and sour dampness in the winter, when the clogging open drains are flushed away and even the Frenchman's sewers cannot take the sudden flood. Marrakech is one of the magic cities of the Earth, a busy, modern Maghribi metropolis, where automobiles and camels argue on equal terms for right of way through her narrow lanes. Marrakech, at any season, is superbly beautiful. In the spring she is at her finest, with great snow-capped mountains visible on every side, and her mile upon mile of palm groves making a lush deep emerald setting for a city nestling like a glowing ruby at the heart.

She is beautiful in the rain, when her trees and shrubs are dark with the weight of water and her walls begin to glisten; she is beautiful in the summer when her rich, raw colours bring a hint of the desert. She was founded in the year William the Conqueror made London his capital. Even when the harsh sandstorms rush into her streets like some relentless *harka*, and for weeks at a time it is almost impossible to move without feeling blinded and gagged by that steady tide of red dust, even then there is a wildness to her scenery, a certain nobility in the way in which her stately palms and sturdy people take their battering. Unless your imagination has died it is impossible not to love her. More than Paris, she has the ability to seduce and hold the traveller within the comfort of her massive battlements. For Marrakech is, of necessity, a walled city. It is a few years, not decades, since her ramparts stood between her people and relentless savagery. Perhaps it is true that here, not out in the desert, I found Temptation and succumbed. El Glaoui's charm and Marrakech's magic combined to divert me. Both provided the illusion of scientific progress. El Glaoui was a generous employer. I was introduced to levels of luxury I had never dreamed of. I had the honour, the position, the goodwill – everything the Pasha's power could put at my disposal. Everything I had ever desired.

'I am not myself,' he told me, 'of an ascetic disbosition. There is more than one way of fulfilling God's will. God has given me the means to exblore the nature of bleasure. And sometimes,' he offered me a man-to-man smile, 'a little bain.'

Miss von Bek expressed the intention of remaining in Marrakech indefinitely. She was my best introduction to Il Duce. I had no choice. I accepted the Pasha's offer. I decided to give up six to nine months to start the Pasha's aeronautics industry and fulfil our mutual dream. I began to dress in combinations of tropical European clothing and local splendour – a silk shirt and trousers and silk *khufta* with pointed *babouches* on my feet. This was a comfortable style which suited me very well and made a gentle irony of my more Western official titles: Aeronautics Adviser, Chairman and Chief Engineer to *La Compagnie de l'Aviation du Monde Nouvelle à Maroc*, my task being nothing less than the setting up of a native Moroccan aviation industry that would not merely supply its own forces but would sell its machines abroad.

'Here we have ideal conditions for flying and landing aeroblanes. That is the reason why Marrakech should naturally be the aviation manufacturing cabital of the Mediterranean,' El Glaoui told me with infectious confidence on the first day he welcomed me to my up-to-date offices, which might have graced any major Parisian establishment. I make little effort here to reproduce the elaborate circumlocutions and euphemisms of his French. It was, if anything, more full of embellishments and flatteries, innuendo, subtle threats and veiled boasting than his Arabic; yet this quality also added to his enchanter's power.

Often he pretended to listen but never heard. His own interests were always paramount. Yet his casual generosity and natural intelligence charmed everyone, especially when he returned to the subjects he understood best – war and religion. Even by Moorish standards he had some of the air of the legendary past, an intellectual man of action, and perhaps he deliberately cultivated his personality in the way he built his famous library, but I do not think so. Given a civilised education and less self-destructive beliefs he would be among us to this day. He was not the only friend of the French to be ruthlessly betrayed. He was even snubbed by Princess Elizabeth when he arrived at her wedding with a small pie. In some ways he was a man of extraordinary simplicity as well as grandeur. The knife with which to cut the pie was sheathed in a scabbard of jewel-encrusted gold. But no. Coconuts from Tonga she would take, buckets of bongu beans she would take. But a priceless – and witty – offering from the great Pasha of Marrakech was spurned. By this time, of course, the pro-Zionist stranglehold on Europe and America was unbreakable. El Glaoui knew the Jews had shamed him. He had trusted them too long with his affairs. But already he was exhausted. He died without friends, humiliated and shunned by his inferiors, while the streets of his noble city rang once more to the clash of tribal arms. But that was in 1956, a year which can only be compared to 1453 in significance to Christendom. It was also, as El Glaoui knew, the Death of Arab Chivalry. 1956 was the year in which Christendom tested her strength and was found wanting; in which Bolshevism tested her strength and conquered; when godless Arabs set up a secular state and the Jews bought Tunisia from the French; when the British abolished third-class accommodation in trains by calling it second-class and let New York command her to give up the sacred trust of Suez. Britain is America's puppy-dog now. She never knows who her real friends are. She had her visionaries. They foresaw a great independent Arabia; an Arabia ruled by dignified caliphs with firm but unflinching justice. They saw an Arabia where the Knights of the Round Table might form again, to demonstrate their religious ideals through deed and word. The greatest of Arabia's lords have always taken comfort in the words of Jesus, whom they recognise as a significant prophet. Their quarrel with Christians is that they refuse to see that Mahommed was the most recent and most important of God's prophets and submit themselves to His will as their souls must surely be calling out to do. What evil, what terrible secret dishonour, can be the Christian's if he cannot accept the truth of Islam? Yet we could have respected one another. We have, after all, more than one common enemy. Which is not to say I have ever advocated intercourse between the two persuasions on anything but the most superficial level. They should be allowed to remain in their enclave, their Zone of Peace, on condition they no longer shop at Harrods and British Home Stores. Let us all live and let live, I have always said. But they were not the old, gentlemanly type of Muslim, like El Glaoui or those whom Lawrence recruited; they are a coarser breed altogether, made not in the desert's tempering heat, but in the air-conditioned halls of some artificial Florida. These oil people are not trained to power's responsibilities. Wagner knew this. One of my conversations with Graf Otto and Lieutenant Fromental concerned the composer's profound Christianity and his respect for Buddhism and Islam, both of which at their best preached the ideals of Chivalry he so thoroughly celebrated in his last mighty work, *Parsifal*, with its exhortation to us all to come together in common brotherhood, to make of ourselves the very best we can. This was the old Code of Islam, too. And the old Platonic ideal. Schmaltz was a critic of French North African policy. In destroying the Islamic codes and replacing them with French, the Quai d'Orsay was actually encouraging anarchy.

'You are contemptuous of these barbaric laws and traditions. But imagine coming to 13th-century France and deciding that chivalry, old-fashioned and primitive, should be done away with. Like it or not you have destroyed their *only* ethic, since the one you offer in exchange is to them no more than an aspect of an alien rule they already resent.'

Lieutenant Fromental protested at this: 'El Glaoui is a true friend of the French.'

'Because friendship with the French is all that sustains his rule. He has made his decisions and knows he must follow them through. I am not accusing our host of lack of courage, sir! But Moorish chivalry is dying, too, believe me. Were the French to go tomorrow they would leave behind a ruined myth – a bewildered monster. They do not ask for theories of democracy. They should be offered what those theories are based on. And that, I believe, is the Christian religion or something very much like it. In exchange for their freedom you are offering these people a modern philosophy that is at least three hundred years ahead of their needs.' I think Graf Otto was expressing some of that fashionable paganism which brought Weimar to its knees, but he was of a fine old tolerant South German stock and I later found it very difficult to believe he was guilty of those crimes. He was interested in Kolya's theories about Wagner, whom he called 'the great modern genius'. 'I should like to talk to your Russian prince,' he said. I told him that it was quite likely he would. Kolya could even now be on his way to Morocco, although Fate might also have taken him into some more remote region of the Muslim world.

'Wagner is the future,' declared Count Schmaltz. 'These gleamingly finished innovations! They turn with such novel precision, like highly-finished movements in some massively complex machine. It is the sublime music for the twentieth century. Strauss and Mahler are mere flounderers, desperately presenting us with novelties and cacophony rather than substance and sublime melody.'

'The light so bright and the shade so black!' exclaimed Fromental. 'Oh, those inspired vulgarities!' And he laughed admiringly. He had a Frenchman's traditional suspicion of German seriousness.

'You are an opponent of imperialism, I take it.' His attitude towards Count Schmaltz was rather challenging. We all knew that Schmaltz had an East African family whom he planned to visit after he left Marrakech. 'Would you rather have French influence here, my dear Count, or the kind of barbarism which existed throughout this century before we arrived?'

'We were not comparing benign foreign imperialism to savage tribalism,' declared the German. 'I would agree, the first permits at least a modicum of opposition while feudalism permits none. But those are not the only choices. That is my point.'

'You think, do you old boy, the weaker Power should be permitted to determine with which strong Power it links its destiny?' Mr Weeks's favourite argument held that, given the choice, most countries outside Europe, including America, would prefer to live under the amiable protection of the Union flag. Indeed he had some notion of a *Pax Britannica* which would dominate the globe by means of gigantic airships, expanding trade, increasing the wealth of all who elected to join his great Commonwealth of Nations. He saw his country's Empire as the core of a new World Order, making justice and peace available to all. While I had every affection for his optimistic dream I could not see it becoming a reality without invoking the power of Christ, and Mr Weeks, among many other quirks of character, attested to a firm and old-fashioned atheism. Frequently other guests (who visited for a week or two and were often clearly no more than anecdote-hunters who would use their exotic experience as after-dinner topics for the next ten or twenty years) would grow vehement with what they considered Mr Weeks's socialism, but in fact he called himself a syndicalist and based his particular creed on the work of that droning naturist William Morris, who insisted on working naked in his Oxford carpentry shop in imitation of his hero Blake. Both thought they could build the New Jerusalem upon interminable verse with an artist's palette and a couple of dove-tail joints. Mr Weeks quarrelled only with the PreRaphaelite's muscular Protestantism, but excused him for it on the grounds of being born too early. I can see the madman now, with his great bottom shining over the limewashed table, those mighty genitals, which made him they said such a Tarzan to his Jane, swinging with manly insouciance above the falling shavings as he tackles another sideboard with his ever-accurate awl! I am no denigrator of Morris as a furniture-maker, nor as a decorator. More than once Mrs Cornelius had said how much she fancied his wallpaper, but it is too expensive, even from Sanderson's. G. K. Chesterton was another disciple of that hearty Victorian visionary and came to promote his views through a newspaper he founded. I saw nothing wrong with his ideas, any more than with Mr Weeks's, but they were as flawed by Catholicism as Weeks's were flawed by apostasy. These days such large men become transvestites. They are never content.

There is a considerable similarity between working for a

Moroccan Pasha and a Hollywood Mogul. Both have a tendency to keep you waiting for hours, sometimes months. Both are inclined to change their minds rather more often than they change their undershirts and always find it surprising that you should fail to anticipate their every momentary whim (which usually involved dismantling anything which has already been created). Your master also provides a rich but erratic flow of money, which makes it impossible for you to make long-term plans and puts you permanently at his disposal. He wishes you to socialise with him, to become his confidant when, at three in the morning, he has become bored with his latest sexual conquest. On other occasions you can expect him to pass you by without even recognising you. You are no more than a shadow-player in his complicated vanities. Like one of his women or boys, you are merely something to pass the time with. And yet, while you remain in his favour, you are invested by him with considerable power of your own. Much of his authority becomes yours even though to him you are no more nor less useful and worthy of affection than a good gun-dog. My latest patron was, I had to admit, somewhat more tolerant than most tyrants of human weakness, and so weary was I of my ordeal I grew very swiftly to welcome the opulence, to rest at last under the patronage of the Pasha. I came to take as natural the power and the immediate security of my position at the Pasha's court, just as I had come to take Hollywood for granted. Indeed I might have been in Hollywood when I awoke in the morning to stand on my balcony and look through tall palms, across Moorish roofs and battlements, past the towers of the muezzin to the mountains. Why should I not give up a few months of my life to this wonderful venture? I had no great reason to rush back to America. I drank sherbet. I read books. What else could I do?

A few days after I had arrived I again buttonholed Mr Mix. This time I put my hand over his lens and humorously warned him that I should do this every time I saw him unless he came to my room at *Le Transatlantique* that evening. He agreed with the quick, unthinking air of a boy not used to following his own desires. 'I'll be there. Now let me go, Max.' But he was reluctant, disturbed. He seemed fatigued, almost maniacally distracted. For the first day or two I had been given quarters in the Pasha's palace, one of several small buildings adjacent to the courtyard housing honoured guests or high-ranking officials. All were built of the same salmon-coloured *piste*, with green tiled roofs, and their windows looking only inward, like every traditionally built house in the part of Marrakech they were beginning to call 'the Medina', meaning 'Old City'. The new French administrators and merchants raised themselves fine mansions beyond the walls. Some of these, save for their distinctive colours, could have graced any provincial street from Brussels to Barcelona. Whatever its benefits, imperialism also has a knack for banality.

I was now staying as the Pasha's guest at the only reasonable hotel in Marrakech, *Le Transatlantique*, in honour, I think, of the Americans who had begun to find the new colony safe at last for a daring fling at the mysterious East. Americans will go anywhere so long as it has familiar toilet facilities. The first action of any nation wishing to attract US dollars is to order its porcelain from Thomas Crapper and Sons, the great originals. Thus Britain, too, benefits from her new master's psychology. 'Without the Americans,' says the plumber in the pub (they call him 'Flash' Gordon), 'the British toilet industry would be down the drain.' He has no other range of metaphor. 'Once the Japanese dribble in, it'll pull the plug on Staffordshire,' he predicts. His politics are crass. He once said that people like me were blocking the sewer of history. If so, it's because history can't afford to call you out, I told him. These plumbers are all the same. They are famous throughout the world. Mention frustration to a Berliner and he will speak of plumbers, mention extortionate bills and the Bombay brahmin will cry 'plumber'. In Cairo the plumber is a term applied to any bloodsucker or blackmailer while in Sydney to 'sink a plumber' means to get your own back. Muscovites, even today, cite the plumber as the example of the vulgar *nouveaux riches* now rubbing shoulders in the same apartment blocks with academics and engineers! 'And you have the nerve,' I cry to Gordon, 'to accuse me of exploitation!' The plumbing at *Le Transatlantique* near the Mammounia Gardens left something to be desired (although it was of the European rather than the Turkish type) since the water frequently had to be turned off for mysterious reasons. However, I was able to take regular showers and use Western soap and this, just then, was luxury enough. Even the most thoroughly hospitable desert peoples tend to be parsimonious around water – unless they are of that type which delights in spectacular waste. Mrs Cornelius had a cleaning job with an Arab once. Everywhere in the house there was a tap, she said, it was running full-blast. He loved the sound of it above all other music, he said, and it was costing him nothing!

Mr Mix came to see me at my suite on the top floor of *Le Transatlantique*. From my balcony it was possible to look out into the warmth of the summer night, at the natural geometry of palmeries and distant mountains beneath the diamond stars and the golden moon. My valet having gone to bed, I opened the door for Mix myself. My whole suite was furnished in that opulent Moorish style found elsewhere only in restaurants, with a profusion of slippery leather and wood saddles no self-respecting camel would allow on her back and upon which no rider could keep a seat. Mr Mix stepped in and closed the mirrored door behind him. He was wearing his big bush hat and khaki tropical kit. He removed his hat and accepted the sherbet I offered him (I had yet to redevelop my taste for alcohol and only drank it for social reasons). He asked immediately if I had any 'snow' and I said I had a little. I could spare him a sniff or two. He was grateful and became immediately human. He apologised. 'I've had to give you the ice, Max. The Pasha doesn't like his boys having conflicting loyalties. But now you're on the team I guess it's okay. I'll tell you this fast, Max, I'm in a jam and I want to get out of here. I'm in hock to the Pasha and I'm working off my debt to him.'

Now I understood immediately and was overcome with sympathy. 'Mr Mix! You are buying yourself back! So you were, after all, captured by slavers!'

He seemed embarrassed. 'Not exactly, Max.' He leaned forward in his leather settee, found purchase and steadied himself as he lowered his nose to the straw and the straw to the little ribbon of cocaine I had laid out for him.

'It's a long story,' he said. 'But after I jumped ship at

494

Casablanca I had this idea of riding the train up as far as here and then seeing what happened.'

'You were not captured by gypsies?'

'Those guys. They're bums. They tried to rob me. No, I bought a ticket and boarded a train, first class, all my stuff in the luggage wagon. A compartment to myself once I got the idea I had to slip the right number of francs to the right people. Only it went to Rabat. I awoke still looking out at the Atlantic Ocean! Then, before I could get off, it went to Fez. Well, on the train to Fez I met an Algerian entertainment promoter. He fixed it for local acts to entertain the tourists, that kind of thing, but he also ran a couple of burlesque theatres in Tangier. He was planning to open two more in Casablanca and another one in Marrakech.'

'He offered you the chance you'd always wanted to act,' I said. 'How could you refuse? What was it – some sort of coon number? Your dancing skills alone – '

He lifted a tired hand which begged me not to interrupt. 'We came to a deal. It seemed good to me since it would give me control of the Marrakech theatre. I'd begun to figure out that Africa wasn't going to be a whole lot different to America. Nobody welcomed me as a long-lost brother. They just wanted to know why I'd been fool enough to leave and how much dough I'd brought with me. Mainly it was like Valentino said when he got back to the States – "In the world, I was a hero, in Italy, I was just another wop." Here, I'm just another nigger – and in Tangier that means about what it means in Tennessee. So I'm cheated blind by my business partner who is about to get hold of my stock in the company and I decide to get the hell out of there and come to Marrakech myself where I'd heard the boss was almost a nigger and it was possible for a gentleman of colour to get along better than in the North. So I finally got there, overland, making a little money as I went. By the time I arrived three months ago I had enough to open The Ciné Palace in what used to be an old slaughterhouse off Djema al Fna'a near the Katoubia Mosque. It was all remodelled. Believe me, Max, it's the ritziest little theatre outside Casablanca. We opened in June and business boomed. I'm not kidding you, Max, we had to have big buck Berber hillmen to keep those boys out. I've seen the alternatives. Believe me, *Ace Among Aces* beats snake-charmers and the two-thousandth re-telling of *Ali Baba and the Forty Thieves*. These boys'll pay good money to see a movie. *Any* movie! It doesn't matter a damn what the moulas say, they go anyway. All I had to do was square a couple of the big religious guys and make sure we scheduled the programmes between prayers. That's five shows a day, morning till night, seven days a week, and every one packed. The same guys came back show after show. These people don't believe they've got the best out of a story unless they've heard it told a hundred times. They never got tired of the programmes!'

It had begun to dawn on me that the reason for my reception as we entered the city, indeed the alacrity with which the Pasha put his aeroplane scheme to me, all had something to do with Mr Mix's business venture. But why was my old *compañero* now forced to work off a debt to the Pasha?

'What I didn't know is that T'hami has a financial finger in almost every pie in the city. He's the managing director of the mining companies, the import and export companies, banks, newspapers, whatever's lucrative. The smaller businesses he lets his big boys squeeze, while the little ones only have to pay a rake-off to a local official. Me, I wasn't paying anyone except the guys from the mosque. I guess nobody ever thought the Palace'd catch on. Well, it didn't take T'hami long – he's quicker than Al Capone to pick up on a new angle – and one day I get an offer. He's going to buy me out, he says, and make me manager. Or, he says, he can throw me in jail as an illegal immigrant, or he can send me back to the US, or he can fine me. That's when I found out he's not just the Mayor of Marrakech but the whole damn' Justice Department, judge and jury rolled into one. My case is already tried. I owe him a hundred thousand *dirham* in fines for my illegal business and The Ciné Palace is confiscated with all its stock. Well, Max, I had fifty thousand francs in my hotel room which his gorillas found and "taxed" and I was flat broke again!'

'You did not seek the aid of the American Consul?'

'They couldn't help me,' was all he would say to that.

'And The Ciné Palace?'

'I took some screws out of the projectors and they broke down in a couple of days. I thought I was being clever. I told El Glaoui I could get it running again but I had to take it to Tangier for repair. He said he would send for a new one. It still hasn't arrived and meanwhile two local engineers had a look at the projectors which now work pretty good except that most of their lenses are missing. I can't even get to the stock. T'hami's hidden it somewhere. So here I am. I'd even sent to Casa for some English and Egyptian movies. It would have made a change from *White Aces* with the middle reels missing and *The Lost Buckaroo* with a scratch down the middle of the final chapter.'

'They seem to have a preference for Max Peters movie plays,' I said with some satisfaction. Realisation had dawned! I saw from Mr Mix's expression that it had been he who had taken the missing films when he absconded. It was *my* films, shown over and over again, the length and breadth of Morocco, their titles changed to dramatic Arabic, that had been the basis of the darkie's lucrative business! I experienced a peculiar stirring in my stomach – the strangest mixture of betrayal and gratitude. This was why we had not been captured as Italian spies. This was why El Glaoui remained so firmly under the impression that we were American moviemakers, why he so solicitously courted me and cunningly trapped the black man.

I remained silent for several moments as Max shrugged his apologies. 'It was the only way out I had, Max. I knew there were other prints. I guess I was only stealing a little of your vanity while to me it was a way of keeping alive.'

'Easier to have remained aboard,' I said at last.

'I couldn't, Max. I'd tried to wise you up. My feet was itching. I was bound to go.'

I understood this impulse, though I could hardly sympathise with it.

'And my films are now the personal property of the Pasha?'

'I guess so. Maybe we could buy them back.'

I sighed, hardly able to blame the black man for what he had done. One must not judge other races by one's own high standards. I told him I was glad the mystery was cleared up. I was, I said sadly, still pleased we had been reunited.

'Believe me, Max,' he said. 'I was glad to see you. You don't know the half of it. My luck's been worse than a bull's in a bullock truck. I need to get to Tangier!'

'But I'm not going to Tangier.' I hardly knew how to respond.

'You will, Max,' he said. 'And when you do, I'll be right there with you.'

He thanked me for the cocaine. It would help him, he said, with his official duties. He looked at his pocket watch. 'I got to fly. Don't think too badly of me, Max. We'll get your movies back.'

When he had gone I became, for some reason, increasingly cheerful. Now I knew the cause of my current success and was relieved. What was more, the record of my Hollywood career, if not complete, was at least safe. I decided that part of my price for my services would be the films he held as security against Mr Mix's absconding. Doubtless it would not be easy to get him to agree and I must bide my time, choose my moment. With this decision firmly made I gave my whole attention to the job before me. I had made all my initial plans and projections, estimates and costings (in dollars and francs) long before the Pasha sent for me. There was trouble, apparently, with the succession, and he had been involved in the enthronement of the new Sultan. I made the most of my time. My normal lusts at last fully restored, and Marrakech famous for her beautiful whores who came to stand at night around the perimeters of the Djema al Fna'a, a short stroll from my hotel, I lost myself in possessing several partners every night.

Save that Marrakech had no coast, the city somehow seemed to be an uncanny echo of Hollywood. She set up astonishing resonances in me. Just as I had felt in Hollywood, I felt now in Marrakech as if I had come home. And still I could not readily identify any real points of similarity between those two very like cities and the very unlike city of Kiev where I spent most of my childhood.

Marrakech might eventually become Carthage's film-making capital, and spread the ethic of Islam across the Earth, as we tried to distribute the ethic of Christianity. But one ethic is Death and the other is Life. Today Life falls back before Death's steady gallop. It is time, I said to Mrs Cornelius, we had a miracle. She replied cryptically that she thought I'd had enough of miracles. And she laughed so heartily she began to experience one of her coughing fits, so I never could get her to explain. 'Your lungs will get you in the hospital,' I said. 'You should smoke filters.' But she is careless of such things. And anyway I think she is sometimes as happy now as she has ever been, sitting in her old armchair in her damp basement full of mildewing magazines, sipping from her gin glass and talking to that little black-and-white cat her son dotes on. It is unfortunate she does not notice the smell. But she insists on doing her own housework. 'I've orlways bin neat but not fussy,' she says. 'There's no point gettin' upset over a bit o' catshit on the carpet, is there?' She laughs and her fat moves like the ruffles on a seaside pierrot, reminding me of her brief return to the stage in the forties, when she entertained the troops and did six straight weeks at the Kilburn Empire with the Miller Brothers – Karl, Jonny and Max – when they were still all comedians.

I think I was happiest with her during our Hollywood days and later in the 50s when she began to seek my company more frequently. I had moved to Notting Hill because it was where she lived. I was still very active and hopeful in those days, although she complained I looked too readily on the gloomy side. Then we began to go on holiday together. At first it was just the occasional trip to Brighton or Margate or Hampton Court, but as time went on she discovered she enjoyed my company and found it amusing to book a boarding-house for a week just to talk, in the evening, about our adventurous past, before the War. 'Ther Wor sorta sobered us up,' she thought. 'But ter tell yer the troof, Ivan, I get as much fun art o' a charabang to Butlins as I do art o' swiggin' champers at Biarritz.' I must admit I have not been able to share her enthusiasm, though I always did my best to get into the spirit of her fun. We went to Minehead in Somerset two years running in 1949 and 1950 and had very good weather. We went to St Ives in Cornwall in 1952 and spent a miserable day on a boat to the Scilly Isles while she regurgitated (mostly over the side) the accumulated dainties and savouries of the previous twenty-four hours. A veritable cornucopia of half-digested tarts and pies. Arriving at the Scillies we found nothing but sand-dunes and a few unremarkable houses and I had been led to believe these were the remains of the Isle d'Avilion where Arthur came to die. 'No question abart that bit, Ivan,' she assured me between gulps of ozone and dramatic bodily eruptions as she plodded helplessly back towards the boat. The Sea of Scilly might have been the Styx.

T'hami el Glaoui, respected chief of his clan and undisputed ruler of half Morocco, power-broker to the other half, sent for me after I had been his idle employee in Marrakech for almost a month. He was in his study overlooking the palace's great courtyard in which shady shrubs surrounded a splashing fountain of the most splendid mosaic. On mornings like this I could imagine myself in Byzantium, paying a call upon some Greek dignitary. Unfortunately T'hami, for all his virtues, continued to have the reality of a suburban usurer and, until he spoke at least, was inclined to disappoint expectations. Moreover, he was dwarfed by the heavy Spanish antique furniture which gave the room the appearance of a crowded museum. Part of his great library was here. He was rumoured to read only with difficulty and to have stolen most of the books.

He wished people to think him wise, true, but T'hami had actually read much of his library and understood some of it far better than I. Like a real bookman he took pleasure in the feel and smell of his volumes. Today we stood by the window looking down at a print table on which he had spread my designs. Behind us were the lovely arches, domes and tiles of the best Moorish architecture, which again reminded me of a Hollywood tycoon's offices. It is, sadly, an architecture which has been readily vulgarised by every modernist who ever designed a suburban picture-palace or a picnic park. 'I have been looking through these just now,' said El Glaoui, smiling up at me. 'They are very good, I think. I have had one or two exberts give them a glance. I hobe you don't mind.'

I murmured something about the patents being already registered.

'Well,' he said, adjusting his little silk collar, 'in sbite of young Lieutenant Fromental's view of the matter, I think

500

we can begin building some aeroblanes, Mr Beters.' He was delighted by my response and laughed aloud.

'You are a man who loves these things!'

'More than my own life, I sometimes think.'

He enjoyed this. Like most tyrants, wherever they occur, he approved of strong expressions and opinions as long as they did not conflict with his own. He became by turns avuncular, brotherly, respectful, intimate, yet always the confident authority. As I knew from Mr Mix, he had, though it would be impolitic to employ it, the power of life and death over everyone in Marrakech and her surrounds; more power than the nominal ruler in Rabat; enough power (and he desired no more, for he was by nature a cautious man) to hold the balance between the French, the rebels and the Sultan. Even while I marvelled at the Glaoui's sudden decision, he made a further suggestion. 'I think we should have one of each tybe at first. Meanwhile brint a catalogue which will describe the virtues of our machines. Use as many colours and photos as you like. As the orders arrive, we shall make the aeroblanes. That way the cabital investment comes from the customer. What do you think?'

I was merely glad that I was again going to be busy doing the thing I loved best. I would bide my time before I raised the question of the confiscated *Buckaroos*. There was no point in arguing with the Pasha, who would jovially have promised anything and then declared that it was a police matter and out of his hands. So has the East learned to use the language and cherished institutions of the West to its sublime advantage.

'We will number them, I suggest,' he continued, 'and berhabs give them names. As I see you have done in your sketches. *The Desert Wind* is one I had in mind. Or is that a little too brovincial, do you think?'

'We should select a theme,' I suggested, 'as you see I have done over here. These are the names of animals – you will recall Sopwith's famous *Camel* – and these are of oceans – *The Pacific*, *The Atlantic*, *The Indian* – or weather conditions – *Typhoon*, *Hurricane*, *Maelstrom*, *Sandstorm*.' I admitted my own preference was for birds – *The Hawk*, *The Swallow*, *The Owl* and *The Snowgoose*. My ship is called *The Silver Cloud*.

She is crewed entirely by bright-eyed Slavs. He settled for the birds. He said he had heard that I, in fact, was nicknamed 'The Hawk' in certain quarters. I admitted I had been honoured thus by the Bedouin of the Eastern Sahara.

'I, too, have been likened to a bird of brey.' He turned to the window and the music of his fountains. 'I am sometimes named "The Eagle of the Atlas" while my boor nephew Hamoun, alas, you know, is "The Vulture". So we are "of the same feather", I think?' I have made no effort to reproduce his peculiar mixture of elaborate Arabic, rather simple French and broken English. I know women found this especially charming. 'What do you say, Brofessor Beters?'

His manly clap on the back filled me with an odd sense of pride. I had no doubt that I had discovered a fellow-genius. It was always of deep regret to me that he used it in such short-sighted and unChristian ways. I was never a hypocrite. While I came to attend the mosque at least once a week and to be as dutiful in my daily worship as El Hadji T'hami himself, frequently to be found reading from the Holy Q'ran, my deepest prayers were addressed to a somewhat more progressive God. I did not, however, live a lie. My faith matured during my time in Marrakech and I had many debates with myself concerning the nature of God and His rôle for me. I learned to accept the responsibilities of my position. I was after all a great international celebrity according to the Pasha's extraordinary court. I was as often at his palace as I was at my desk. Almost every day brought a new visitor from Europe. Our work proceeded with the leisurely pace which at first frustrates the European until, one day, he discovers he has learned to prefer it and regard it as the only civilised way. I was, I now see, lured by something very like the luxuries and the flatteries of Satan.

The Pasha's advisers were all Jews. One of the youngest was a great enthusiast of my *Masked Buckaroo* films and saw me as something of a hero. He insisted, to the amusement of his fellows, on quizzing me on every detail, every mystery of young Tex Riordan's career. I did my best to answer him and was a little flattered by his attention. He was a Europeanised Jew of the more intelligent sort. He had been educated at a French school. I knew him as Monsieur Josef. These Jews were frequently seated beside me during meals and were friendly enough to me. Some understood Yiddish. They were clever, quick-talking men, who made the Pasha laugh. To these alone he would give his full attention, for they advised him on all his many interests throughout the country, whether they were agricultural, mining or manufacturing. It was through listening to his Jews that I began to understand something of his master-plan. He was not interested in challenging the Sultan by force of arms. He was instead building himself a modern commercial empire as vast and as varied as Hearst's or Hughes's. Like them, like Rothschild or Zaharoff, he had discovered the crucial importance of modern engineering to the improvement of his fortunes and would in time come to own the Moroccan press. He would develop power and influence in the democratic style. Increasingly the echoes between my masters in Hollywood and my master in Marrakech became louder and better defined, and at first I found this amusing. Thinking it might solve our mutual problems, I suggested to Mr Mix that we make some good old-fashioned picture-plays while awaiting the Pasha's pleasure, but he threw cold water on the idea. 'Already,' he said, 'I'm running out of film stock. Some was ordered from Pathé in Casa, but it's still not here. Soon I'm going to have to start faking it. Or try for some interesting double-exposures!'

So I devoted myself to my aeroplanes. I moved into a marvellous house on several levels in the new French Quarter being built on the far side of the walls, beyond the Bab Djedid, the gateway through which the Avenue Katoubia ran. The house was fully staffed with slaves from the Pasha's own palace, including several young creatures who were provided purely for my pleasure. I had my own carriage at my permanent disposal, bearing the Pasha's arms to show that in every case I had right of way. Through the healing routines of the leisurely Moorish court I began to forget my ordeal in Egypt. I thought sometimes of Kolya, that wonderful friend, and his noble stubbornness which had left him in such a difficult position. But I had faith in Kolya! Slave or free man, he would survive somewhere and I knew in my bones we would one day meet again and share a joke about our hallucinatory desert escapade.

Although continuing to avoid any public closeness to me, Miss von Bek remained the Pasha's mistress for longer than anyone could remember. His negro vizier, Hadj Idder, who was El Glaoui's closest confidant and a freed slave, was delighted. He said that his master had found a playmate. It was true, it seemed to us, that the Glaoui had, according to his habit, selected fresh sport for his evenings, but Miss von Bek always occupied a good deal of his daily life. His horses, his golf course, his cars were at her disposal. Again, typically, he remained jealous of their friendship and more than once had turned a severe eye upon a man he suspected of admiring her. She and I had become adept at disguising our brief communications, with the result that a new intensity of feeling existed between us. Only Hadj Idder suspected us. Like so many Marrakchis, he was himself a devotee of *The Masked Buckaroo* and had complimented me several times on my acting but this enthusiasm did nothing to shake his loyalty to the Pasha to whom he was as devoted as Mr Mix was to me. Hadj Idder had the manner of a Christian nun, except that he delighted not in God's work but the Pasha's. It was rumoured that they were half-brothers and lovers, and we could believe almost anything of a relationship by far the closest El Glaoui had with any creature. Hadj Idder's great African head would grin with delight at each new pleasure his master took. At these times he and Mr Mix would look very much alike. He would chuckle and yell or grow sad in appreciation of every passing humour. And yet when acting on the Pasha's part he became as dignified as any butler of a great Southern mansion in the years of Dixie's tranquillity. At these times he was a diplomat, discreet and incorruptible – perhaps the only living human being aside from myself at that court who could not somehow be bought. He was trusted for the same good reasons the World Service of the BBC is still trusted in many quarters.

I had suggested we use the crippled cinema for a factory, hoping my reels were still there, but I was presented instead with a great shed on the city's outskirts. It had been originally an experimental palmery but was abandoned due to some dispute between El Hadj T'hami's cousin, who was the managing director, and the French interest, who made some complaint about the lack of trained staff. The staff, naturally, were all relatives or clients of the ruler. I had as yet no materials with which to begin my work and spent a good deal of my day at my drawing-board, producing the very latest in catalogues. This, eventually, was sent to a printer in Tangier, whereupon there came a further long delay, during which time I was, of course, supported in luxury but received no salary. The similarities with Hollywood became clearer by the day. My hours passed in clouds of *kif* and cocaine smoke. I learned to leave my 'plane factory' in charge of a servant and repair, after a long siesta, to the Djema al Fna'a. The great public square of Marrakech is surrounded by shops and cafés and little streets leading into a maze of souks where everything, including *arak*, is readily for sale. The square is called The Congress of the Dead and there are several legends to explain its name, the most likely being that here the rotting bodies of rebels were habitually displayed. Here, preserved by Jews whose ghetto in the Maghrib was always called *mellah* (salt), the heads of the Pasha's enemies would, before French protection, stare across the square to where the leisured classes, the great merchants and worthies of Marrakech, sipped their mint tea and discussed the price of pomegranates, gravely clear about the price of dissent. Here, towards sunset, everyone would gather to gossip, to trade and to be entertained. The leaping snake-charmers and squatting story-tellers, the gypsy fortune-tellers and Berber drummers, the sword-swallowers and sinuous fire-eaters, the tumblers and grotesques would come pouring into the Square of the Dead with their yells and whoops and wild ululations, their strutting and their boasting, their capering, their tall tales, their display of skills, of lazily curling snakes and monkeys and exotic birds, of lizards on strings and locust lanterns. In the orange warmth of the dying sun, in and out of the long shadows, the braziers sent up the smell of roasting nuts and skewers of lamb, of cooking fruit and *couscous*, of those delicious little sausages and breads for which there are a thousand names, of saffron rice and thick vegetable stews, the *tajins* and the *pastillas* of pigeon and almonds which all Southerners love to eat, for Marrakech is the Paris of the Maghrib, with the finest food cooked before your eyes on the little kerosene stoves and charcoal fires of the street-traders, gathering around the edges of the Djema al Fna'a, their lamps beginning to glow warmly in the gathering dusk. Meanwhile the huge crimson orb shudders as she falls deeper and deeper through a sky turning the colour of coral and cooling steel behind the sharp teeth of the Atlas; smells of jasmine and lavender waft by as the veiled women go about their mysterious tasks, buying the food for their husband's evening meal, visiting relatives or the mosque. The tasselled carriages, pulled by brightly harnessed horses so much healthier than those of Egyptian cities, trot slowly in and out of the square between entertainers, singers, zealots and fakirs. Every Berber and Arab in the region seems to arrive at once in the square. Nobody hurries. They swarm about the vast arena while from the balconies, and from beneath the awnings of the cafés, yelling men and women communicate to each other the latest news of relatives and friends or read important pieces from the newspapers to those who cannot read anything but Classical Arabic or the few who cannot read at all. Here men trust only the Holy Q'ran and the spoken word.

I would make my way through the wailing beggars and yelling street sellers to my favourite table outside the Hotel Atlas and join my cronies, several of whom were colleagues and friends of the Pasha, employees like Mr Weeks, or miscellaneous European visitors who arrived almost daily at the invitation of the Glaoui. Some were commercial people come to see what business could be done with the potentate. This meant, of course, that few of us were ever required to pay for our own pleasure and we were often in amused receipt of envelopes containing banknotes which we pocketed, though we had no special influence. As a result however I was soon able to open an account with the Société Marseillaise de Crédit under the name of Peters; while a more discreet account was opened in the name of Miguel Juan Gallibasta (the name on the passport I still owned) upon the Bank of British West Africa, for, though I received a little direct salary from El Glaoui, I came to understand that in common with his other officials I must make personal arrangements for myself where day-to-day cash was concerned. Mr Weeks assured me that it was quite in order. 'One must adapt, Mr Peters. When in Rome, you know.' He had a marvellous manner when some Yankee sewing-machine broker, for instance, who was attempting to sell a hundred machines to the harem at special rates, wanted to know if he could help. He would invariably tell the man that he was prepared to bribe the appropriate people and would, of course, simply pocket the money. When challenged, he would make a significant gesture and would explain the lack of action away as a perfect example of Arab perfidy, for which his victim was of course fully prepared, and accepted fatalistically. The ritual might even begin again.

Slowly but surely, and often by my own efforts, I began to put together a team of boat-builders from Agadir and Mogador, local carpenters and metal-workers who had the skills and intelligence required to turn them into aeroplane-makers. They were all masters of improvisation and set to with a will creating the beautiful shapes I had visualised. My lovely designs – *art nouveau* in practical machinery – were formed with bent woods and heavy silk, coaxed into reality by loving Moorish craftsmen until the great shed came alive with a dozen gigantic, brilliant dragonflies. All this of course quickened my blood, yet to my growing frustration we had not yet received instructions for engines. I explained to the Pasha that if we were to make our own engines we would need a number of subsidiary factories. He said he did not want more factories so had decided, after much thought, to purchase complete Portuguese engines through a firm in Casablanca. However the Casablanca people soon proved to be having 'problems with customs' (obstruction from the Sultan) and so further delays resulted until, from sheer impatience, I took matters into my own hands. I had heard of a machine found by Tuareg herders out on the *jol* towards Taroudant. Clearly it had landed safely enough, for its undercarriage was only slightly damaged, but the pilot was never found. The machine was an old French Blériot monoplane and could well have been sitting in the desert since before the War. Lieutenant Fromental failed to trace it from any reports and concluded that the plane had probably belonged to a gentleman flyer who merely abandoned it when its engine, which was even then no doubt clogged, jammed up. The flyer might well have joined a camel-train to Marrakech and from there returned to his own country. Or, even more likely, some Tuaregs caught him and sold him in-country. I never discovered the truth of it, but at least I now possessed one good, if antique, engine. Once I had worked on it for a few days, glad to get back to the practical business of spanners and plugs and cylinders, it functioned perfectly. It was a heavy old Martinez Blanco, of a type which had not been thought particularly suitable even in 1912, but it was all I had, and very soon I was able to instruct my people how carefully to fit it into my own favourite machine, the slender *Sakhr el-Drugh*, my *Hawk of the Peak*. And now I had a working aeroplane! Within a week or two I would be airborne again. I could then (I secretly thought) please myself as to whether I remained with the Pasha or went on my way to Rome with Rosie von Bek. I did not intend to betray my employer, but I felt considerably happier that I now had a working machine, a means of escape. I looked forward to testing her. She had an unusually long wing-span of some fifty feet and a slender body covered in scintillating multi-coloured silk. She resembled a magnificent insect. Her body rose on thin hydraulic rods which supported an axle for her wheels. The heavy dark engine looked a little out of place, but I improved the plane's performance by adding a longer than usual propeller which it was possible to fit thanks to the taller undercarriage, but this increased the insect-like appearance. Sent by El Glaoui to film this fantastic nativity, the production of our new Moroccan air-works, Mr Mix was the first to see her. He said she looked marvellous, like something Douglas Fairbanks might have thought up. I was flattered. Fairbanks remained my film hero for many years, even after it was revealed that the perfect marriage between himself and Mary was a sham and that he was a *Hälbjuden*. I can't say I was greatly surprised. She was never suited to adult rôles. I had taken the liberty of painting the slogan 'Ace of Aces' on both sides of the plane, behind the wings, since I thought this would appeal to possible American buyers while our Arabic recognition symbols exhorted the glory of God and the Glaoui. My workers were forever amazed by every tiny development, by every fresh marvel I had them create. I think they were as proud of our first bird as I. They could foresee a time when, perhaps led by Ace Peters himself, their veiled cavalry would take to the air, to fight with the same valiant cunning they had displayed for centuries on horseback. For my part I saw, somewhat selfishly, and more prosaically, an advertisement for my own genius which was bound to be noted in Italy. I now had, through my patron's intervention, a fresh passport in my American name as well as my Spanish passport and Moroccan papers. I could travel without fear anywhere in the world. I remembered how I laughed at Shura's 'two names are better than one, Dimka, and three are better than two'. Now I realised the wisdom of the maxim! – not for reasons of criminal expansion, but for ordinary insurance in uncertain times. Perek Rachman was a friend of mine. He was much maligned. He said most people were like cattle, neither good nor evil. But they had no imagination. They are shocked by a boy who pays a penny too little for his tram ticket. To them, one's ordinary precautions for survival are absolute proof of evil. To those of us who have been forced, stateless, from a nation upon which Satan Himself squats – feeding off human blood and souls, His mad red eyes rolling back in His bestial head, His claws reaching for fresh bodies to devour – it merely displays a prudent nature. It is the same with people who claim they have never known a whore, but they talk to one at the bus-stop and think what decent, right-thinking human beings they are, as Mrs Cornelius says, 'an' never fuckin' guessin' they're suckin' cocks fer a livin'.' Judge not lest ye be judged is something we should all remember.

I began to feel secure for the first time since we had ridden out of Egypt. I felt that the true God was once again my guide.

I go every Easter to Ennismore Gardens, to the Cathedral, for the Vigil. It is the most beautiful service, the Service of the Resurrection sung in Church Slavonic, and there is no more intimate contact with God while it is taking place. I used to watch those little girls singing the *Kyrie eleison*. Such an optimistic experience. And yet they make some story up in the newspapers and suddenly I am a dirty old man. No one could feel more sentimental than I – who have been brought low by a love of children, after all, and yet still feel no bitterness towards them, they sing so sweetly. *I shall magnify Thee with everlasting love.* Such spiritual beauty! What harm could I ever bring myself to perform against that beauty, that innocence? But they say I am guilty and bind me over. It was in *The Evening Star* and nobody locally blamed me. They all said she was a little trollop. Mis Cornelius said her mother had been on the game in Talbot Road since 1958. But nobody cares how they damage the honour of an 'old Pole'. I tell them I am Ukrainian. They think it is still a province of Poland. Anyway, they call everything over there 'Russia'. I despair of the ignorance of youth.

I stopped Mr Mix one evening as he came towards me across the guest courtyard. He seemed embarrassed for a moment, as if I had caught him in some private act, such as picking his nose. He offered me the largest smile I had seen for some time and said he heard I was going to test *The Hawk of the Peak* next week. I asked if he would like to come up with me and he surprised me by saying that he might. 'I wouldn't have to fear a plane crash if you were with me, Max.' But he said he thought his first duty was to keep his feet on the ground and film the event. 'I am the Lord High Grand Recorder, you know. What?' Whenever he talked of his duties or his titles he adopted a chortling English stage accent which I never found becoming or dignified.

He assured me he would join me in my second flight, to film the city from the air. He had found a new cache of stock, abandoned two or three years ago by a French film company which had gone bust shooting *Salammbô*. Some of it might still be good. It was a matter of luck that the sprockets almost matched, he said. I applauded his work. He was creating an archive, I said, which posterity would treasure. He was filming, I thought, a vanishing world. When I discovered that this world was not vanishing at all but was in fact growing and expanding, I did not feel quite the same elegiac sweetness, the same nostalgia for a lost age. Now my nostalgia has found more immediate subjects and I live in fear that my own way of life, not theirs, will suddenly be stolen from me. Big business in its *kasbah*s, the rest of us in *souk*s and slums. It is not much to ask, to live out one's days with a little comfort, cultivating a little garden, making enough to live on, talking to neighbours, perhaps occasionally giving someone a helping hand, but no, you are not allowed even that when these people get into power. They take everything. They eat everything up. Their God is a God of Locusts. Their God is a God of Deserts. I know this. I prayed with them but I refused to become one of them. It was impossible. Unlike Christ, says Mrs Cornelius, I was never a joiner. I did not become a *Musselman* but by then I had learned the Oriental trick of instant submission, for by this means you may survive for the time it takes to escape. *Ikh hob nicht moyre! Der flits htot vets kumen. Wie lang wird es dauern? Biddema natla'ila barra! Kef biddi a'mal?*

Mr Mix left me, saying he might join me later at the Atlas. I again reflected what pleasure I took in our camaraderie, a pleasure difficult to explain, since we were so different in temperament and intellect, yet his company gave me a sense of secure warmth and I experienced a pang of loss whenever he seemed cool towards me.

Rounding the corner of the guest-wing I next came upon Miss von Bek, who darted me a curious searching look. She seemed dishevelled and yet not in any particular hurry. She stood beside a palm drawing in deep breaths beside a blue pool crossed by an ornamental gilded bridge. She asked how my aeroplane works was progressing and I told her we had our first model ready to fly. I asked her if she would come to see it. The polite question emerged quite innocently from my mouth and yet she responded with alacrity. 'Down there?' she said. 'At the sheds? Good thinking.' And she blew me a kiss as she disappeared, a sylph in dark green and gold.

My stunned shock gave way to a thrilling sense of foreboding! I realised that inadvertently I had embarked upon a liaison which, if discovered, could very well end in dreadful consequences for us both. *Ikh veys nit . . .*

I had written to my Californian bank asking them to send me a chequebook and to let me know how they could make my funds available to me. But mail between those two notoriously tardy postal departments would take months. Even Fromental's exchange of wires (using, against specific military orders, the official telegraph) met with nothing but a vague insistence upon

511

'hand-written applications'. Meanwhile, I was dependent upon my local credit (which for the famous Max Peters was considerable) and the Pasha's good graces (notoriously whimsical). I did not realise then how, in those languorous months, I had become a slave to Oriental self-indulgence, capable of giving myself up to passing temptation like any schoolboy and moved not by lust but by pride, a kind of arrogant sloth, a profound boredom. How is it possible to be taught such unmistakable lessons as Griffith taught us in masterpieces like *Intolerance* and *Birth of a Nation* and still not learn to live by them? I, who had worshipped the work and the man, who had based much of my life and philosophy on his, had begun to act like some Victorian prodigal. Yet I could not bear to leave without my confiscated movies. El Glaoui had forgotten them. The projector from Casablanca had still not arrived. I was as they say 'double bound'. But I have made mistakes in my life and been betrayed. I am the first to admit there is no deceit worse than self-deceit.

That is what the jackal tells us. Anubis, *mein Freund*.

TWENTY-SIX

I AM NOT BY NATURE a deceiver. Deception is where women excel and in their hands we men are mere students. Their witchcraft brings us low and makes us behave in dishonourable and self-destructive ways; theirs are the wiles against which St Paul and Pushkin and Malory all warn us. A Kundry is forever ready to divert our innocent Sir Parsival from his knightly path, to lead him away from Christ. Yet, still, I do not blame them. I do not hate them. I love them. I have always loved women. They are so sweet. *Des petites dents sucent la moëlle de mes os. Esmé! Comme le désespoir a du t'endurcir tandis que la fange grisâtre du bolchevisme engloutissait ta vie, ton idéalisme. Mère! Les Teutons t'ont-ils tué là où je fis voler ma première machine? Je n'ai pas voulu te perdre. Ton regard ne reflétait jamais d'amour. Mais tu étais heureuse* . . . Rose von Bek was, I suppose, a delicious Kundry to my Parsifal, though at the time I half-believed I had found a Brünnhilde to my Siegfried, especially since, in the time between our first liaison in the balloon and now (the whores and the whips forgotten) my blood had learned again to quicken. My baser senses had returned to confuse me, threatening to lead me from my destiny. Yet it seemed, as our secret became the dominant concern in my life, that she was sharing my vocation, complementing my work, this fellow *Erdgeist* in female form – everything that a man could desire. Mrs Cornelius is

513

wrong to be so contemptuous and take such a narrow view and refer to a 'torkin' mirror'. I continue to insist, in spite of what happened, that Miss von Bek was a person in her own right. Certainly I was enamoured, but this hardly discredits my experience. Mrs Cornelius insists there was never any point in telling me anything in such circumstances. 'A Frenchman, a woman in love an' a cat up a tree, there's nuffink but grief in trying ter 'elp 'em, Ivan – an' yore ther same.' But I was always open to reason. I remind her it was she who frequently displayed violent jealousy towards my friendships with other women. She cannot reply. She merely becomes incoherent and she is never at her best when she reverts to the language of her Whitechapel youth. Usually, I try to avoid such subjects. It discomfits me to see her behaving so badly.

My ship is called *el Risha* and she is light and as complex as a snowdrop. My ship is called *Jutro* and she will carry me into the future. My ship is called *Die Schwester* and she is myself. My ship is called *Das Kind* and she is everything I ever dreamed. *Meyn schif genannt* Di Heym. *Meyn shif* is called *Di Triumf. Jemand ist ertruken. Widerhallen* . . . *Yehudi? Man sacht das nicht.* My ship is called *The Hawk.* I would not call her *Yehudi. Ikh veys nit. Ikh bin dorshtik. Ikh bin hungerik. Ikh bin ayn Amerikaner. Vos iz dos? Ya salaam! Ana fi'ardak! Biddi akul* . . . *Allah akhbar* . . . *Allah akhbar* . . . We worship, I said, the same God, who is the Sum of all the good in us. We worship what is Good. Then why do we perpetuate so much Evil? Like many intellectuals of my generation, like Wagner and Sir Thomas Lipton, I studied the teachings of the other great prophets. I did not close my mind. I do not say that any way is wrong, but I am, by accident of birth or by persuasion, a believer in the great Greek verities, the spirit and the heart combined in the rituals and teachings of the Holy Russian Orthodox Church. Each choice of faith has its disciplined responsibilities, its relinquishing of certain beloved habits or ideals at the demand of the generations' established wisdom. Sometimes mere sentiment is not enough. Sometimes it is the very enemy of truth. But my Faith is not theirs. My Faith is my own. I worship as I please. I worship as custom and courtesy dictates, in the manner of my hosts. At human

514

sacrifice, of course, I would balk. But one cannot reach out to every hungry hand.

One can only pray, I said, after I had told Mrs Cornelius that Brodmann had found me again. It was the same in Marrakech. What harm had I ever done him? He had chosen Bolshevism. I had not forced him to join the Cheka. I had not made him a Jew. What did he hate me for? For being a victim? For keeping the faith he had himself renounced. Perhaps it was true that he thought he detected in me, as Mrs Persson suggested once, the evil that was actually within himself. Perhaps he had the puritanical zeal of the truly tempted, pursuing some hated innocent rather than confronting the unexamined truth of his own conscience? I reminded him in my note that Heaven redeems only the truly repentant. Mrs Cornelius is impatient with me on this. 'Wot bloody 'arm 'as 'e done yer in forty years, Ivan?'

What harm? This is amusing, I say. He has played with me, cat and mouse, ever since I left Odessa – even before! He delights in secret information, in what he witnessed at Hrihorieff's camp! He gloats. That is why he wants to keep me alive as long as possible. Do not be surprised, I tell her, if one morning my shop is not open, and suddenly the world has never heard of me. I keep a diary, but they could always find it. It was the same in *1984*. Peter Ustinov lost four stone to play that part. He was never better. 'Ten years ter go, Ivan,' says Mrs Cornelius. 'Wot price Big Bruvver nar?' I say nothing. I would rather she was happy. Is this truly *The Country of the Blind*?

This is why they call me 'Shylock', those stupid boys. Shylock was a noble Jew. Should I be insulted? I regularly went to see Wolfit, the finest of all English actors. Beside him Sir Laurence 'Olivier'-Cohen was anaemic. Wolfit's voice was like some great Russian tenor's, reverberating through the Old Vic's tawdry music-hall plush and tarnished gilt to turn all that was vulgar into unique vibrant beauty. He was the last of the Edwardian giants. His *Lear* roared and wept and challenged Fate; his *Hamlet* looked upon the gloomy evidence of human folly and spoke only of the Pit; his *Macbeth* proclaimed in dark horror and thunderous warning the fate of those who would

515

overthrow God's established order, while his *Titus* preached the deeper danger of linking one's fate to the fate of kings. Wolfit took his Shakespeare casually and with confidence; he took it with enormous, old-fashioned respect for the immediate substance of the story and his voice was the last voice of insouciant individualism in England. By the time it was stilled, the BBC had imposed upon the country Respectable Mediocrity and the Home Service and instilled its bland decencies in every middle-class child. And so, as the British shudder through a sea-change whenever they must choose to spread their scones with margarine or butter, the rest of the world writhes in the grip of Red Carthage, screaming for help, for a miracle which only the British Empire and its allies could have provided.

For this dismissal of reality they paid the price of the Second World War. What on this globe can these islanders actually turn their backs upon? Europe? China? America? Arabia? So they throw up a scrim around the whole dreaming nation and on it project from within visions of their glorious past, reminders of their contributions to the arts and the sciences, their establishment of institutions and language around the Earth. By this means they see only vaguely the cruel and painful pageant of the world beyond their screens. This sense of distance is in all their films. It is in their radio and most of their television. It is why they pretend to despise the American programmes they love so much. They became terrified of their own vulgarity, their own capacity to kill and to destroy, to be brutes. I saw it happen during the 1950s. The old, free-wheeling, careless stage-shows of the thirties, where every aspect of life was addressed, gave way to American cosmetics and Technicolor. I went to see *London Town*. It was impossible. Even Petula Clarke had lost her earlier *charisma*, though she was never Shirley Temple. The Americans have triumphed. Only the foreign culture is remembered by the young. Alice Faye, Fred Astaire and Howard Keel, certainly; but what of Sonnie Hale and Jessie Matthews, who brought a sexuality to the screen that no Hollywood process could contain? That is why Miss Matthews returned to England and went mad. Only when I heard that the poor creature had, like Clara Bow, died insane did I begin to interpret the conundrum of *Mrs Dale's Diary*.

516

None of them know what you mean, these days. This nation got its fortunes from piracy for so long she has forgotten how to make an honest living. She has instead learned to become the good little sidekick to Uncle Sam. Auntie Samantha is busy these days with her own exercises in self-hypnosis. She is learning the arts of graceful submission. And she says she has nothing in common with Arabia!

If I had continued my acting career, I should have modelled it on Wolfit. As it was, my life had taken on some of the aspects of one of those farces they so enjoy in Belgium. Our liaisons became increasingly elaborate and secretive and I began to suspect, too late, that much of Rosie von Bek's lust was fired by an insatiable thirst for danger and novelty. I began to wonder how safe our balloon trip had actually been. *Per miracolo*, we survived. *Per miracolo*, I suspect we went undetected not through any care on our own part but through the carelessness of the Pasha himself, who no doubt would not believe anyone capable of my folly. I also wondered later if he did not merely turn a blind eye to our liaison, as these people do to the bribery system they themselves encourage: until such time as it is politic to 'discover' a crime in a no longer useful employee? Whenever I see some potentate's outraged dismay reported at his 'discovery of corruption', I remind myself of my own experience. The Bolsheviks are not the only ones to learn the usefulness of making everything uncertain and nothing completely legal. It is through unpredictability and sudden changes of mood that the successful tyrant rules. But he is not always the tyrant who rules longest, unless he devotes himself to institutionalising his tyrannies and finding some way of turning them into ideals which all his people can support. This, of course, was Churchill's great skill. He and El Hadj T'hami were close friends on the golf course and elsewhere. Both were inferior painters but masters in reconciling contradictions. Now it is fashionable to be contemptuous of qualities of leadership, but in my day we looked up to great leaders. Do we steer a better course in our years of lazy democracy? You are making me laugh, I say to the Cornelius girl, who wants to burn her underwear, and it was me who pinned her nappies. She says the world is yearning for equality. It's nonsense, I say.

Look around you. Listen! This country is yearning for a tyrant. If she is to base so much of her life on Faith, I said, I could offer her a better alternative than her friend Miss Brunner. She never listens. It is as if I am speaking a foreign language.

Even the ones who say they are 're-born', these bloodless hippies who mince into my shop playing tunes, which even a Nubian would find distasteful, on flutes imported from India at enormous profit to some immigrant entrepreneur, talk of Jesus as if he were a lisping nancy-boy. Even a C. of E. Protestant could not stomach it! It is worse than blasphemy! They are embracing only the 19th-century sugar with which the missionaries coated the gospel pill. This is not enlightenment. It is comforting darkness. Such grinning followers of Christ have no will to go forward. Are they the best of our army? Is Christendom so drained of authority, so forgetful of her own vitality, so careless of the salvation even now at their disposal? Is God dead and His Son staggering in confused retreat from Satan? Can this be nothing less than the great struggle at the end of the world. Is this Armageddon? Is this *Götterdämmerung*? Is it Christendom's Last Fight? Or was the battle already lost on the day the Winter Palace was stormed? Has everything since been a last guard falling back, fighting for every inch of moral ground, as Satan, a giant of scarlet steel with sickle in one claw and hammer in the other, comes drooling poisoned venom to stand in certain triumph upon the ruins of our last retreat? And they say Wagner was not a prophet! What would they rather play? *A Hero's Life* by Richard Strauss? I did not say I apologise for the Nazis. Their failures and follies are nowadays all too clear. But in those days it seemed we had only a limited choice and those of us opposed to Bolshevism were sometimes drawn willy-nilly into alliances with strangers. I am not the only voice of truth. I remember the Bishop in the pub, three weeks ago, telling anyone who cared to hear that he would stand by his admiration of Hitler as an intellectual no matter what his followers had done. He said the same of Enoch Powell. The pub was full, as usual, of West Indians, Irish, Greeks and so on, yet not one of them turned to protest. And this was the villain we were told would live forever in the world's nightmares? He is today as harmless, as vaguely

comforting in his familiarity, as Charlie Chaplin. *Heil Hitler!*
It has become part of the schoolboy's giggling repertory. Even
the Jews do not know what a Jew is, in Notting Hill at least. No
wonder Mosley got less than a hundred and fifty votes. It was
too late for Notting Hill. He should have stood for Surbiton
or Shirley where people still value their way of life and keep
their morals as carefully as they keep their lawns.

In Shepperton the scrim rises higher and higher, displaying
fantasies of egalitarian prosperity for all where, in actuality,
grey high-rises lurk towards infinity. The Ministry of Truth
smiles upon its favourite, its most successful, advertisement.
Here are the English orators safely confined, carried unseeing
through antiseptic tubes to the BBC, the very epitome of the
Future and the Moral Authority of Empire, to address a people
whose experience they never share, to sound upon the airwaves
their self-congratulatory celebration of their national myths,
still certain that their language is universal. But is there perhaps an underground? Some *samizdat* crawling around the very
roots of their illusion – some Blake from Barnes or Staines –
even some Thornton Heath Thackeray to tease their dreaming
noses? Is there no one to sound the horn, to begin the alarm?
Will they gaze upon the walls of their cocoon and never hear
the Last Trump when it is sounded? Do they dream themselves
to everlasting death, like the ancient Egyptians whose culture
they pretend to find so alien? Can they actually prefer this to
everlasting life? I went down there for a while, to accompany
Miss B. on her visits, but in the end I had to give it up.
Those tranquil suburbs are actually full of high-walled lunatic
asylums. Any Londoner who has had the misfortune to be
branded mentally ill by some misbegotten authority knows
what I mean. They are never visible. There are always plenty
of trees. They are never in the centre of the city. They say it
is so we can have peace. It is so that they can feel themselves
secure from an audience. But of course it is a marvellous way
of discrediting us. At a stroke we are robbed of our immediate
dignity and our future authority. Well, I had no use for their
power. I was only rarely comfortable when it was invested in
me. All I longed for was the respect of my peers, for recognition of my authority as a visionary engineer. This is what was

stolen from me that I value. Nobody seems to understand me. Что с вами? Где у вас боль? The pain, I tell them, is in my soul. My poor, Russian soul. How can we pretend to understand one another's values when we cannot even speak one another's languages? And yet I refuse to despair. Even now I still see a glimmer of hope for the world. But the world must learn to recognise its vices as well as its virtues. And, as Christ teaches us, self-knowledge must come first. That is the message of the resurrection.

They put the reverberating metal in my womb. There is a dissonance always present now. It robs me of my harmony with God. These Jews? What do they envy in me so thoroughly that they must seek me out to destroy it? *Vos hot ir gezogt? Iber morgn? Iber morgn? Ikh farshtey nit.* Why not *mitogsayt*? At noon the ships will rise from their berths, never again to be bound by the mud of Earth, and those who are not on them are doomed to decadence, brutal war and the death of their very planet. At noon we shall rise into the sun, that most reassuring of God's signs, and our skins shall glow golden and silver, our eyes shall burn like brass and our teeth shall be glittering ivory; and still we shall be human, not yet of the angels, but rising inexorably to that holy state of grace. Why should they be jealous, these Arabs and these Jews? We have offered them the helping hand of Christ and they have spurned it. They have made a choice and I respect it, but let us not mourn for them in their self-established suffering!

This was frequently the subject of the sermons I attended on the Isle of Man during the years of my captivity. The minister was Presbyterian, a carrot-nosed Scot with lips, as my bunk-mate Vos put it, like an old maid's cunt and a head of hair which might have been the fires of hell gushing from his tortured skull. He knew that we had been put upon the earth with the ability to choose between right and wrong and that if we chose wrong, we had only ourselves to blame for our plight. We have enough trouble playing shepherd to the faithful, he told me one evening, let alone the faithless. He had a supply of Irish dairy products from a cousin in Dublin and had taken a liking to me. He saw me as some future apostle to the Slavs. We would sit and eat illicitly buttered goiteycakes while he described the coming of Christ to the island, Man's long history as an outpost of light in the years of darkness. Is this how God reveals Himself? As a single flash of sunlight during the boiling torment of a storm? Does He offer no other sign of hope? These were our topics as we sat around the minister's grey stone fire gorging ourselves on his Celtic plenty. I grew fond of the Presbyterian creed during those long days of my wrongful incarceration. Nazi? Such a Fifth Columnist, I told the commander. He agreed that it was stupid. The minister was a kindly man, though unsympathetic in manner, glad to convey his religious enthusiasm and so much better company than the careerist Anglican preaching tolerance and unnatural piety while the very hordes of Hell convene upon the doorstep of his vicarage. To his kind the Twilight of the Gods means nothing worse than an interruption in the cricket season, an irritating drop in the quality of the local ale. I used to think the British had courage. Now I realise all they have is an arrogant lack of imagination. This British phlegm is the Frenchman's catarrh. He coughs it up and spits it out and pays no further attention to it. The stiff upper lip is a lip that for too long kissed the cold cup of ignorance and careless cruelty. I said as much to Major Nye, when we used to meet at Victoria, just after Suez. He said he could not follow me. 'No,' I said, 'you mean you *dare* not follow me, for where I go, why, there is the road to truth!' He preferred, he said, to call me a good chap and buy me a vodka. Kind-hearted as he was, he was the exemplar of everything I warned him against, so why should I expect him to listen? He had been brought up in a world whose realities had almost entirely eroded. The new realities simply did not exist for him. He continued to think and act as he had been trained to think and act: as a chivalrous servant of a just and honest Empire. He had none of these modern doubts. It was what made his company so refreshing to me, even when we did not agree. Most people cannot understand, for instance, the burning humiliation of a person like myself whose word and experience are today deemed unworthy of the slightest attention. Major Nye respected all men and respected them most when they pulled themselves together and worked out their own problems. 'Meanwhile,' the Major assured me,

521

'they are perfectly happy to use our toilet facilities.' In this, he expressed the same attitudes as Mr Weeks, who no longer sought my company as he had during those early days. Count Schmaltz went on to East Africa. Other whites came and left. I signed many autographs for American dowagers who promised to go and see *Ace Among Aces* as soon as they got home. Increasingly Lieutenant Fromental was called away to deal with skirmishes and local uprisings with those of Abd el-Krim's last *harka* who felt their master had betrayed them and who refused to accept the treaty he had signed. They sought alliances now with the Southern Berbers, especially the blue Tuareg and the desert warriors who challenged the power of the Glaoui. They resented new law coming to their ancient trading-places. New law always, in their experience, brought higher profits for the Arabs of the cities. Fromental confided to me he could see no point in French soldiers settling ancient tribal disputes. He feared Morocco would never be free of the Lyautey policy which encouraged the conquest of an unfriendly tribe by a tribe already friendly (or which could be courted), so using the country's own resources to pacify itself. This saved the French taxpayer money, one of the paramount concerns of French Imperial Policy since the time of Napoleon. Now, however, the political changes, the rise of 'nationalists' similar to those in Egypt and elsewhere, make the Quai d'Orsay sensitive and mistrustful of native rulers. So Fromental must ride to the fringes of the protectorate and urge his soldiers on, to extend further the benefits of their protection. Fromental disapproved. This was not protection, he said, but intervention in old squabbles. He wanted the French to withdraw to the Atlas and be content.

Such moderation however was no longer in keeping with the expansionist ideas of the French to which, of course, the Italians and Spanish must then respond. It was oil. But we were not told that at that time.

Under the influence of Islam, moderation, in any European sense, tends to disappear and one's perspectives change, as they change in the desert. Rosie von Bek's lovemaking grew in intensity as it diminished in duration – our pleasure, heightened by 'the white maiden', became so tuned to the few moments we could discover together during the day or night that it became like nothing I had experienced before. I lived each twenty-three hours and forty minutes for perhaps twenty minutes of the most exquisite passion. I began to demand more and more secrets of her adventures with El Hadj T'hami, of his harems full of slaves, more than fifty per cent of them French or Spanish, and two of them English or Irish, she was not sure. She described orgies and profound singularities of feeling, of subtle and irresistible cruelties. This further heightened my sensibilities, restored my masculinity, and made me forget the cold touch of God and Her deadly pleasures, deflected the cool breath of Death upon the back of my neck, even though I had every reason to be terrified of discovery. Perhaps I, too, could only feel my power at times of crisis. But it is preposterous to link such pleasures with the humiliation performed upon me by Grishenko and witnessed by Brodmann. I never felt the flagellant's call to piety. The thought of the Pasha's punishments brought no delicious quickening of the senses to me, merely appalled dismay.

She introduced me to nothing new. She told me he had made her call him by an Arab word. I asked her to use the word. It was familiar to me. She complained that he spent much time upon the feet. They were used, she supposed, to rather more calluses, even on their youngest girls. Some nights, she said, she had gone completely numb above the knees but was in an agony of unfulfilled sensuality below. It made her, she said, feel sick. The balance was too peculiar. She had not found the pierced girls strange, she said. They were rather beautiful and proud of their ornament, even those with the locks. She described, I said to her, the commonplace diversions of any barbarian king. Did she still find them stimulating?

'In less boring company,' she replied. Her flattery was delicious. She proclaimed my superiority over the master whose power I shared, for whom I spoke. She had become convinced of my fame as an actor and I was again of infinite interest to her. Yet she did not commiserate with me over my problems with *The Hawk*. In her first test-flight I had managed to pull the plane off the makeshift runway barely high enough to miss the single-storey houses of suburban Marrakech and, clearing the majority of the trees in the adjoining palmery, tried to ease her up towards the distant peaks of the Atlas. But the stick was useless. She wheeled and came about, almost under her own volition, dragged by a heavy engine towards the cars and pavilions of the Pasha and his entourage, barely passing over the contracting heads of his drivers and his horsemen and landing nose-first in a clump of soft red earth. The propeller snapped and flew off, one piece upon the heels of the other, towards the scattering onlookers, cut guy ropes and brought the Pasha's pavilion collapsing to the ground before shearing through the windshield of his Rolls Royce and burying themselves in the upholstery of the passenger seats; my wheels snapped off their axles and spun through groves of young palms, huts and sun-frames. They came to rest in a canal which, blocked, began to overflow, the water pouring along unseasonal courses to make marshy the Pasha's camp-ground so that the Glaoui and all his favourites, trapped beneath the heavy soaking wool of the Berber tents, floundered now in mud, while the engine, detached from its struts, turned over and over, still pouring black smoke until it burst into flames about a yard from the Pasha's surviving Mercedes and blew it to pieces just as I flung myself from wreckage flooded with gasoline, and stumbled into the Pasha. We bent against the sudden heat as *The Hawk* began to blaze and he stared with some incredulity upon the ruins of his favourite cars, his flagships. I understood his dismay. I reached out a friendly hand to him, in equal comradeship, to share this misfortune, as we people of the desert do. But he was unusually cool to me. He drew away, clearing his throat loudly.

Thereafter, I was forced to address my employer through Hadj Idder or some other third party, and it was clear I was at least for a while in disfavour. I believed he was debating the justice of blaming me for the catastrophe. He must eventually remember how I had warned him of the potential consequences of using an unsuitable engine in so finely-tuned a machine as mine and I had also, he would recall as his temper subsided, taken the risk of flying the plane myself and only by a fluke not been killed. I watched the film. Mr Mix had recorded the whole event and was happy to let me watch it, although the Pasha had forbidden anyone but himself and his chosen guests access to the projector. I told him it was very useful. From it the Pasha would learn how the old engine, not my design, had created the problem. Once the new engines came through from Casablanca, then we could begin to fly in earnest. After all, *The Hawk* had proven herself an elegant machine. It was only the borrowed second-hand engine that had failed. I heard with some dismay through Rosie von Bek that El Glaoui's only ungrowled reference to me was a joke that I had been nicknamed not 'The Hawk' by the Bedouin, but 'The Parrot'. This was the Pasha at his most childish. *Yuhattit, yuqallim, yehudim*, as the poem went. It is not as simple as that. So he thought I was better at squawking than flying. For some reason this information goaded me to even more intense sexual demands, much to her glazed relish. But when she had gone, I felt wounded. I had served the Pasha loyally. He had delighted in my catalogue, with its coloured pictures. He had boasted of our factory. No visitor to Marrakech had left the city without at least one prospectus for the new aviation company. I had not shamed him with this minor set-back. It was hardly a failure, but an experiment. We had merely been impatient. I had, I admitted to myself, been unduly optimistic in my eagerness to provide myself with a means of escaping the Pasha's employ. Thus, in one of my letters to him, I explained how we would be praised by history for our efforts, how our early frustrations would be likened to the struggle of the great prophets or the problems overcome by Wilbur and Orville Wright before their Flyer ever found the skies above Kitty Hawk. I took comfort in the fact that I still had my house and servants. Even a car, albeit a rather battered Peugeot, was still at my disposal. It was clear that my employer had not yet determined how to treat me. I consoled myself that, if he let me go, I had enough cash to live in Rome for some good while without undue anxiety. Only the still unmentioned movie reels kept me here. Rosie, I knew, would go with me. I had spent my time in Marrakech profitably.

One sign of my disfavour was the withdrawing of the Jews from my table. Only my young fan, M. Josef, dared the Pasha's disapproval. Passionately he warned me to make good my losses and leave the city. This was typical greedy pessimism and caution. The aeroplane company was still a more than viable concern and I knew the Pasha to be a man of vision. He would recover from his disappointment in due course and continue the project. How could our master possibly advertise an air force and then not provide one, I asked. These are large decisions, the Jew said. Thereafter he became a little more cautious of me. Later he refused even to nod at me in the street. I realise now how the Jews were already plotting against me with my old nemesis. Mr Mix, sharing my anxieties no doubt, became more friendly, but he also showed too little faith in my abilities and instincts. He proposed we discreetly purchase tickets from the military authorities at the railway depot. We should make for Tangier and leave Morocco while we were ahead. It felt a little churlish to point out that I was scarcely ahead! I would be *ahead* when a new *Hawk* sprang into our city's perfect sky. I would be *ahead* when the world's newsreels and papers bannered my name, when Sikorski, Sopwith and Grumman were relegated to explanatory footnotes in the History of Aviation. I would be *ahead* when Il Duce welcomed me back to Rome, birthplace and capital of the New European Order, and showed me the factories he had built to manufacture my planes.

How could I have anticipated the small-mindedness of the Berber? His willingness to bend his ear to any whispered calumny? I might have made T'hami the most honoured leader in Muslim Africa, respected by every European power, by America and the Orient. His Maghrib would have formed a true and lasting bastion against Bolshevism. His legions would have flown to battle as they had ridden all those centuries before in the service of the Moorish Emirs. Yet now their eyes would be directed not upon the Peninsula Christians but upon the waiting world of their fellow Muslims: men desperate for a sense of purpose, for noble leadership. Europe would not have demanded they be Christian, merely that they be Muslim gentlemen, like Saladin in *The Talisman*. When chivalry recognises chivalry there is rarely anything but agreement.

To a degree this anxiety did heighten my sense of danger and I longed to break the bonds of my indiscretion. Yet through missing the occasional appointment, through being on the knife-point of discovery several times, we only provided further piquancy to her lusts and, consequently, I was drawn into fascinated compliance with her insatiable and unsentimental sexual adventurings.

The suburban world sees the world of the sexual voyager as one of unrelenting sweats and groans, of bodies forever pumping and wriggling, of oddly marked buttocks, of mouths agape and eyes rolled back, of miscellaneous *objets sportifs*, but they imagine the world of pornography, not our world of erotic exploration. Our world provided as much conversation and irony, as much self-knowledge, as much concerned kindness and good humour as any human intercourse, for without it our couplings would be no more than congress between beast and beast. There would be no interest in it, no *frisson*. There would be only confirmation of previous experience and no true experiment. Sex is not merely a series of techniques whereby the woman learns to please her man. There is sharing. There is love. Even in Hell.

There is the sharing of power. And this is heaven. There is the equality of forces, the mutual education of the senses. The other condition is called in Prague and elsewhere 'erotomania', when even food and security are forgotten by those caught in its grip. The madness has driven many a man and woman to their death, especially in such circumstances as ours. Loti himself recounts the tale of how he stole a woman from the Sultan's harem and how she paid, nonetheless, the ultimate price for her perfidy.

In France they recognise this disease, just as they recognise *schizophrenia* or *megalomania*, and of course it most often arises in divorce and murder cases, where it is sympathetically taken into account. This is one difference between the Q'ranic and the Napoleonic Codes especially puzzling to a cuckolded Musselman. As a believer in rationalism I continued to place faith in the Pasha's fundamental sense of fair play. I believed he awaited only the arrival of the aero-engines before sending for me.

I had already written a number of apologies and explanations to my employer via Hadj Idder. These had cost me rather more in gratuities to the vizier than I was any longer receiving from my own petitioners. I was greatly surprised, long after my vigil had begun, to find Mr Mix also offering the vizier 'message envelopes' and expressing gushing interest in his fellow negro's goodwill. Mr Mix no longer had his film camera. He had been shooting, he said, a special-interest scene over in the dungeons – a kind of artistic light and shade study, old and new Marrakech, he said. He had not meant any harm, but the Pasha's Special Guard had come upon him and grown suspicious. They had confiscated his equipment and impounded most of his films. He was now in the process, like myself, of attempting to restore himself in the Pasha's good offices. Thereafter we spent many hours together in the ante-room, yet I found him strangely unforthcoming about his own problems.

'I ain't complaining, Max, except the bastard has me in a double-bind. I can't pay off my debt without that camera! We got to catch that train, Max. You can get us out. After all, I made you famous.' He seemed more than a little alarmed when I told him I was not leaving without my films, but appeared reconciled to this profound, if unpalatable, justice, only adding darkly, 'Remember, Max. Every day you wait on him makes T'hami more aware of his power over you. Every day gets you in deeper.'

How he had come by the fine modern camera and the elegant suits he had worn upon his arrival at the Pasha's court (and still wore) he would not say. I guessed that he had won the heart of some Westernised Moroccan heiress or of some equally wealthy sheikh from whom his camera had been a parting gift. But Mix would not be drawn. He had that deceptively innocent and flattering habit of asking you always about yourself, always diverting attention from his own activities and thoughts. I think he was genuinely interested in what I had to teach him, but my efforts to learn from him, perhaps, were not equally encouraged.

Amiable as he was, any former intimacy that had existed between us was only occasionally evident. I have since known other *naïfs* with a similar uncalled-for defeatism, a lack of faith in their own outstanding abilities. Sometimes I thought no amount of encouraging back-patting, of reassurances as to the many opportunities open in the race world to a negro of his intelligence and natural breeding, would cheer him up.

About his film-making he had an honest sense of vocation. He had undoubted gifts in that direction. I tried to reassure him. I spoke once more of the lucrative market in America and this time he listened more thoughtfully. He told me he would consider my idea. We used English. All the other petitioners in the ante-rooms used French, Arabic or Berber, yet while we shared their uncertainties and enjoyed a common misery, they showed all that friendliness, and a generosity of spirit which is one of the great wonders of the Moroccan soul. I had never felt closer to these people. It is another trait, of course, they share with the British, this approval of failure as conferring some kind of moral superiority upon the failed.

Meanwhile, Rosie von Bek had begun to show signs of nervousness and her sexual demands, though quite as urgent, had a rather ritualistic quality at times. More than once she told me how T'hami would not let her leave, that he had insisted on guards going with her to Tangier, that her passport had been held by means of a bureaucratic error which the Pasha insisted he was doing everything to correct. Everything was impounded. Moreover she had begun to object to certain sexual ideas which, she had already told him, had not found any great popularity in the West since the days of Caligula. She said this admonition had stopped him temporarily until he had made her explain who Caligula had been, whereupon the Thane of Tafouelt had grinned and told her that he could see the similarity but, Allah be praised, he had no discontented Praetorians to cut short God's purpose for him. As a result, he now had some nervous homosexual in his library, translating Gibbon into French while another limp-wristed half-caste found an innovative means of making some sense of the lives of the Caesars in the local dialect. She was not entirely joking when she told me El Glaoui was looking speculatively at his favourite horse these days. 'I pity,' she said, 'his closer relatives.' She thanked God that she had had the sense to keep quiet about the Decameron. So far she had been able to dissuade him from *The Thousand and One Days of Sodom* by assuring him that de Sade had not been a real Marquis.

Again it was impressed upon me how potent, perhaps especially to absolute monarchs, is the power of myth.

TWENTY-SEVEN

TO ALIEN EYES, says Prinz Lobkowitz, colours which to us speak of comfort, security and pleasure might for them represent death and threat. Thus we look upon Mars and find it desolate while the Martian looks on Earth and finds it foul.

I do not think I was unduly incautious in the way I conducted my life while out of the Pasha's favour. Indeed, I had planned for some while to transfer accounts to Tangier and convert francs into other currencies through my British bank.

I did not want immediately to begin such movements of money, of course, until I was restored in the Pasha's confidence. Otherwise he would construe my actions as a confirmation of any guilt he imagined me to feel. As principal shareholder in so many banks, he might easily decide to confiscate my money! Too often the failures of his own engineering schemes came about as a result of bribery and corruption, of bad materials being put in place of good, of unskilled people being employed at half the wages of the skilled. I knew that if he was investigating my factory, he would soon discover that I had conducted myself honourably in every aspect. I could not, of course, speak for individual workers or indeed for my native foremen, but I saw no way in which they could deceive me. I am not, after all, easily deceived. I would have lived for a while quietly until I found a means of slipping unnoticed from the city, preferably with Miss von Bek, and getting as quickly as possible to Rome and civilisation, where we would no longer be dependent upon the whims of a local tyrant. But then came Iago into my Moorish fantasy.

I had made her tell me of the secret rooms and what went on there. She showed me some oddly-placed bruises. It was curious what he had done to her and she gave me an insight into that alien point of view. This heady intimacy with an unknowing third partner is part of the terrible attraction of infidelity. It is why some women in particular can never fully escape from its temptations, its delightful and astonishing discoveries, its revelations of human complexity and, indeed, of human perfidy. For some, infidelity is the closest thing to a vocation they know. I am not among their number, but I suspect Rose von Bek was. She became the ever-available repository of extraordinary secrets, some of which she shared, some of which she nursed to herself, rationing the distribution of her knowledge and thus increasing her sense of power. Yet she was to learn that much of what she possessed was the illusory – or at best temporary – power of the whore. She was a woman, I once said, unworthy of her own base inclinations. Together we might, so to speak, have conquered Italy. At that time I could still see that potential in our partnership. I spoke of it. After all, I said, she had the ear of the Duce.

'That was never the part of his anatomy I influenced,' she said, and she remained uncommunicative, stroking the side of her jaw with her long fingers, staring speculatively at me with her strange, violet eyes while she considered my proposal. It was time, she agreed, that she got out. She had been a fool to play the game as long as she had. She had not backed, she said, all the winners. It was the story of her life. 'But they say you're a singularly fortunate gambler, Max.'

I could not think where she would have heard this. 'I rarely gamble,' I said. 'Life, after all, is enough of a gamble.'

'That's what they say.' She was climbing now with expert swiftness back into her camisole. We had found a useful cubicle at one end of the aeroplane factory. It had been intended to house a modern toilet and bath, but the Pasha's whims had discarded Western plumbing at the last moment. Now the room contained some quilts and cushions and a few of the things we needed for our love-making. The wonderful shapes of my planes surrounded us in the semi-darkness like the creatures of an unearthly mythology, regarding us with friendly but puzzled concern. The place still stank of glue and resin and aeroplane dope, of the treated silk and the drums of petrol, the oil and the charcoal which the absent factory-workers used to prepare their food. Sometimes, when she had gone, I would light the lamps and stroll amongst my beautiful monsters, running my hand over their smooth bodies, longing for the moment when the powerful new engines nestled in their housings, ready to give violent life to the most advanced air fleet in the world! Even in America they would be startled when my birds came shimmering over their horizon! Hever would be powerless. How on Earth could his petty accusations make sense when I returned to Hollywood a hero, a leading figure in Mussolini's wonderful Round Table of latter-day knights-errant, a famous inventor and explorer?

I must admit I came to miss the comradely pleasures of the Pasha's dinners and found fresh European company only rarely now, usually in the cafés and hotel bars around the Djema al Fna'a. These people were not always of the best type, but were the kind of petty racketeers and drifters who accumulate wherever the law we revere is weak or non-existent. I had no time for them. Even in my loneliness, my yearning for civilised company, I disdained to have much to do with them.

Of my earlier acquaintances only my young fan, Monsieur Josef, found courage to break the rules sending me to Coventry. He advised me to return at once to the USA and in the meantime suggested I get in touch with the American Consul. It was atrocious, he said, that an actor of my stature should suffer such humiliation. Then he would grin and refer to some plot ploy from *Buckaroo's Gold* and suggest I doubtless already had a daring plan up my sleeve. It was his ambition, he said, to emigrate, to visit the Wild West and emulate his hero. I said, soberly, that there were probably worse things he could do. In Europe, most of his kind joined the Communist Party. He intended to plead my case with the Pasha, he said. El Glaoui must surely realise the adverse publicity he would receive from insulting me so. I thanked the young Jew. I told him I had not yet descended to asking others for help. I hope he did not take my reply as a snub.

I had made a decision to live my life according to my usual routines, continuing to pray and visit the mosque as always, usually these days at the Katoubia, whose cool interior brought a particular peace to my soul. It was the mosque most favoured at that time by the intellectuals of the city. The Katoubia, all soft old stones and faded mosaic, is the landmark of Marrakech. It can be seen from afar by any rider approaching the city. It is a monument to the city's great days as the artistic and literary capital of the Moorish world. Outside its walls the booksellers, who gave the mosque its name, set up their stalls here and there, selling all the old holy books, the Q'ran in elaborate editions printed with exquisite detail in golds, greens, reds and blues, bound in silk and the supple leather for which Morocco is famous. I had emerged from the mosque, one Sabbath, and was going through some miscellaneous scrolls, passing the time of day with the booksellers, who were all acquaintances, and glancing through half-used account books or the occasional French tome deemed respectable enough to mingle with the texts of the Faithful, for Marrakech, in the whole of Morocco, has an easy, devoted way with her religion which deems it poor taste to indulge in excessive piety. She was what was left of the brilliant glory of the Alhambra. As I reached towards a familiar copy of some orientalist effusion by a popular female novelist of the day, which held that Maghribis were the inheritors of every virtue and, interestingly, descendants of the Lost Race of Atlantis, Mr Mix appeared almost magically at my elbow, like a devil in a pantomime, and asked, without preliminary courtesies, 'Would one of those planes of yours get to Tangier if it had the right engine?'

'Easily.' I turned puzzled eyes upon the brooding urgency of his handsome African features. 'We should have to test the machine, I suppose. But the range will be greater than most available planes. Assuming we had a good-quality engine.' Had they arrived at last from Casablanca?

'Could you, say, modify a good car engine?' he wanted to know.

I told him that it depended on the engine. But I had

learned the arts of improvisation in Odessa and Constantinople. I believed I could make almost any engine do almost any job. The truth was that I had been hasty in using an unsuitably heavy engine for that particular plane. I had learned by my mistakes. 'It will take a little time, however,' I said, 'to fit and test.'

'Then you'd better start modifying as soon as you can,' said my loyal darkie, 'because I have a feeling your number's about to come up with our mutual employer.'

I drew him away from the curious booksellers, though they could not understand a word of our English, and asked him what on Earth he meant. This, he said, was no time to play the innocent. There was now a possibility we would both be cooking in the same pot come Thursday noon. 'I want the observer's seat,' he said, 'when you go up. Until then I'll stick with you. When you decide to run, I'll run too.'

Again I was touched by his devotion to me. For all his experiences, the black man had lost none of his honest willingness, his good-natured, happy-go-lucky way of looking at the world. Though many of them meant nothing to me, I delighted in his colourful expressions. I had learned not to rise to everything he said, since his habit of droll irony frequently had meaning only to himself. I promised him that he would be the first passenger when I took the bird up. This did not satisfy him entirely and he was about to say something else when he changed his mind, glanced across the little square to the doorway of the mosque, and told me he would see me later. He vanished, leaving me feeling alarmed for no good reason. I decided to wander over to Djema al Fna'a and restore my spirits with a glass of coffee at the Atlas. It was not yet noon and I did not expect to see many of my cronies, but I felt the need to calm myself. Marrakech, so like Hollywood, is equally a city of illusion. There is commonplace work abounding, of course, or the illusion could not continue, but the hallucinatory nature of the light, the shimmering brilliance of the tiles and stucco, the hidden, peaceful fountains and courtyards one comes upon unexpectedly, the friendliness and general openness of the people, all make one city the model for the other. Hollywood is our finest example of the Moorish influence upon our civilisation. Without the Alhambra there would be no Hollywood style. Without the Moor there would be a very different Western lingo, for the cowboy borrowed it from the vaquero and the vaquero from the Arab. Go down to Mexico. Go to Guadalajara – Wadi-el-Jar means the same in Arabic as it does in Mayan. The Spaniards carried Carthage to South America. The result is self-evident. Today we see only the romantic aspects of Carthage and we borrow them for our fantasies. But the reality, as I think I have shown, is very different. We live in an age of illusions. The art of illusion has become the principal industry of the 20th century. Even our wealth is shown to be illusory. It can be taken away at any moment. The Muslim is prepared for this. We Christians are horrified. We believe in progress. The Muslim believes more thoroughly than the Westerner, whom he first instructed in astronomy, that the clear message of the spheres is that we should live within the natural order. What right, says the Muslim, have we to change God's world so radically? But I believe it is our destiny to be agents of change. There is much that requires improving. Their illusion is no more or less valuable than ours. It is simply a matter of temperamental preference. I have been to the Land of Death and Anubis was my friend. I have seen clearly into the black soul of the world. I have been afraid. I returned to the Land of Life and my message was the message I had learned from the gods. We must redeem ourselves. We must grow strong. We must forge our humanity into something positive and enduring. We must march again under the banner of Christ. But first we must know ourselves. First we must take control of our own destinies. Now I understand that. Is this God's punishment upon me? To show the truth just before I die? To reveal that one fragment of truth I have sought all my life. They put metal in my stomach. That *shtetl* was no dream. I can still smell it. There was too much fear. I found it unbearable. There should not be so much fear in the world. I have missed some small point, I sometimes think; that would explain all that.

Djema al Fna'a before noon resembles nothing so much as a deserted fairground, with a few stalls open, a little desultory business going on, a couple of fortunes being told, the occasional troupe of boys practising to be acrobats. The souks which run off the square are doing some lazy trade, but mostly men stand around and talk and smoke and watch whatever attracts their attention. On this day there was a string of fine young camels crossing, on their way to the Friday market and a large red touring car entering the square from near the *Hotel Transatlantique*. It drove ostentatiously towards Brown et Richards garage, honking for *essence*. Over at the tables outside the Atlas one of El Glaoui's Jews saw me and drank his tea hurriedly. I did not approach until he had risen. At the Pasha's court, one learned not to embarrass one's fellows lest one day they embarrass us. It was a turning world, as Hadj Idder was fond of telling us.

I let the last of the pretty little camels cross my path, and glanced towards the *souk* immediately across from me. I saw Brodmann. He was unmistakable in a crumpled linen suit and stained panama. To cool himself he carried a small child's raffia fan in his hand, of the kind the Berber women sell to tourists. When he realised I had seen him he shaded his face and looked away immediately, stepping to the darkness of a spice-seller's awning. I did not know whether to confront him or ignore him. I tried to think what damage he could do me in Marrakech and decided he must wield no power here. But I was still nervous. I called a cab immediately, telling the driver to whip the horses to a trot. I was in a hurry.

From that moment on I took serious note of Mr Mix's warnings. The next day, when I went out to my factory, largely to get rid of any evidence of my liaison, I found that a car had been delivered. It was, in fact, the Pasha's damaged Rolls Royce. A small gesture of peace, perhaps? Or had Mr Mix found a way to get me my engine? The engine, I saw immediately, was completely untouched and could easily be modified for *El Nahla*, my *Bee*. (Since the disaster, I had changed the names in the catalogue to those of insects. You can imagine my surprise when I arrived in England to hear them announce they had suddenly invented a Mosquito! I keep my own counsel these days. The truth of my achievement is known to myself and to God and that is all that matters.) With no help on that first day I was able to free the engine from its housing and by the second day I had it in a cradle poised over the yellow and black body of my *Bee*. By the third day I insisted that Miss von Bek give up more time and help me ease the engine into the modified housing while I demonstrated my ingenious belt-drive to turn the propeller, delivering more than enough power for the delicate little plane which I still considered our best Schneider chance. Miss von Bek warned me that by spending as much time as she was on the engine, she was endangering herself and others. 'If I am the others,' I said, 'do not worry about me. We now have our means of escape! If necessary we shall leave by the same way we arrived in Morocco. What happened to the balloon, by the way?'

He had told her he had put it away for safety. She now believed he kept some kind of trophy museum. She was unusually agitated, even after our love-making, where earlier she frequently became icy and distant. Now when she spoke of El Glaoui's pleasures her eyes no longer filled with unguessable lusts but with tears. 'He is a Bluebeard, of sorts,' she said. 'Murder is merely one of his more radical instruments of policy. We should not have accepted his hospitality, Max.'

I was too much of a gentleman to remark how readily she had accepted all he had to offer, almost from the moment we left our basket. She had communicated some of her terror to me and I was sympathetic. Hers was not like my fear of Brodmann, awful as that was. Hers was more like my fear of the Egyptian God, hopeless and wretched, allowed to choose only between a lifetime of utter humiliation or painful death. And so, from my position of relative freedom, I was able to comfort her. I did not have to decide between her and Mr Mix. My natural chivalry put me at the service of the woman.

Somehow we still found time for our sexual liaison but I performed now from habit, not from lust.

Sexuality for her had become almost her entire channel of escape; it was a kind of madness in her. She was like one of those people in the 'difficult' ward at the New Bethlehem who perform the same few functions over and over again, perhaps locked into some moment when they felt free or safe or alive. Their catharsis, when it comes, is always hideously violent.

And, for all that, I could not break the ties of love and fascination with which she had entranced me. I felt that our destinies would be forever entwined.

It had become her compulsion, even as we worked on the engine, to tell me El Glaoui's secrets, though I had no further interest in them. Every aspect of Eastern sexual diversion was more than familiar to me and to be told of the different pleasures claimed from circumcised and uncircumcised girls, from neutered boys and so on, was distasteful to me. The Pasha preferred his women uncircumcised in the main, she said, which is why there were so many Europeans in his harem. It was no wonder, I said, that these potentates liked to keep their concubines from public view. The amount of maiming and beating involved gave me the impression that any member of the harem at any one time resembled a boxer after a particularly dirty match. Another reason to retain the veil, I suppose.

He was taking a delight, she said, in revealing more and more to her as she became increasingly ensnared but decreasingly interested in him. She remained, he told her, a guest; her involvement must always be voluntary. That was his special pleasure, she believed. 'But he has already demonstrated the fate of those who upset him,' she said. 'He has never been the same since he saw my Italian passport.' There had been some sort of execution, I gathered, in one of the cells at Tafouelt and she had been a privileged witness.

I had a clear idea of her position. It would be inhuman to take Mrs Cornelius's view. What possible motive could Miss von Bek have for blackening the Pasha? I am not the only one to have been told such tales. In France there is a whole literature of it. Mrs Cornelius passed me on a book by a woman who was El Hadj T'hami's mistress and who worked for the French Secret Service. She was not the only adventuress – or adventurer – attracted to the Pasha's strange court, to the lure of subtle intrigue, dangerous gossip and thrilling revelations. Of the children hanging in irons, she said nothing.

After 1956 the Glaoui family became professional people and businessmen and adapted almost with relief to the life of the average middle-class Westerner. We have a habit of forgiving tyrants their crimes while alive and forgetting them entirely once they are dead. Do we have so little respect for human suffering? Are we all no more than cattle grazing in some leisurely progress to the slaughterhouse? It was the same in the camps. I could have gone that way, but I applied myself pragmatically to my problem. I made the most of what was available to me. I refused to become a *Musselman*. I am an engineer. I am a citizen of the 20th century. It is not right that I should be brought low by brutes. I carry within me the great spiritual tradition of Rome and Byzantium. The musselman has neither ambition nor understanding. He rejects all analysis. I am a scientist. I examine and I originate. I take control of my destiny. God helps those that help themselves. This was the Anglo-Saxons' secret pact with their creator – not to waste His time. If His help were not immediately forthcoming they got on with the job themselves. Sometimes they had enough energy left over to offer God a hand whenever He seemed to be flagging. The Anglo-Saxon is the miracle-worker of the great Christian alliance. The Slav is its soul.

Rosie von Bek, in spite of all anxieties, continued to romanticise me, to make a melodrama of our liaisons. This, too, terrified me. 'You are truly a Hawk,' she would say to me as I lay gasping on the piled quilts. 'You are like one of Si Hammou's hunting birds. There is a strong case for your being hooded and traced for the rest of your life. You are no longer suited for freedom. You were neither bred nor trained for it. Whoever freed you made a serious mistake. But, of course, it was the Revolution, I suppose. You'd probably be renting out bicycles on the Odessa sea-front now and more or less content, if it hadn't been for the Bolsheviks.'

I told her mildly that my ambitions were somewhat larger than that.

'So many of you released into the world,' she said. 'The nineteenth century engulfed the twentieth. So many mad birds flying out of Russia to prey upon the fat and unsuspecting pigeons of the West.' She was joking, I suppose, for she smiled and laughed the whole time. It was she, I thought, who was insane, not I. She had taken a liking to my Georgian pistols, which I had carried all the way from Ukraine when I had ridden with the Cossacks. She was not the first woman who had enjoyed speculating as to their employment, especially on the Jews. I said that all she need know is that I had never fired them at a living soul. 'They are antiques,' I told her. 'They are my birthright.' I refused to use the pistols in the way she suggested.

The hashish I was eating in larger and larger quantities, to calm my nerves, had begun to affect me. I pulled the pistols from her hands and put them back in their case, back in my bag. That bag had gone with me everywhere. Filthy and patched, it was my only link with the past, the only proof of my achievements. At twenty-nine I was a successful scientist and inventor, star and designer of a score of top-quality Hollywood movies; I had fought a last-ditch action against the Reds in my nation's Civil War; I had made my mark on American politics and the world of finance. I had achieved far more than any ordinary mortal might expect yet still I was not satisfied. What was more I was increasingly tormented by the inescapable knowledge that somewhere, on the dirty, flickering bedsheets of the world's walls, in hazy black and white, I performed the rape scene over and over again. I had only a poor memory of what was on all the other Egyptian reels, but I know my face was not always masked. Do my agonised eyes still stare out at masturbating businessmen in Athens and Frankfurt and seem for them to crease in ecstasy? Is this my only immortality? Am I the illusion of truth, confirming an uncomfortable lie? Am I to be remembered by posterity as a mere fake? I try to buy these films, but they are never the right ones. After watching them I can only pray that one pumping bottom is much the same as another to the cognoscenti. It has always struck me as odd, however, that those films, no matter what they show, always stop far short of the miserable actuality. But I hear there are more realistic pictures available in America now.

Increasingly I had begun to long for California again and the life I had made for myself there. Once I had restored my fortunes and reputation in Rome, I would return in style. Meanwhile I consoled myself with the loveliness of Marrakech. I had previously thought California the most intensely vivid place in the world, with her flowering shrubs and great palms, her ocean sunsets and desert sunrises, but first Egypt and then Morocco had surpassed her in everything save civilisation. Here in this barbaric paradise I continued to feel oddly at home, as if I were indeed in the very cradle of our history. All our ancestors swept westwards from the steppe and the desert once, so perhaps that is what my blood recollected. To say that my soul was confused would be closer to the truth, yet the experience was not entirely unpleasant. What great culture had once existed here before those wild tribesmen carried their cruel religion across the deserts from Mecca to the Atlantic and thence to Europe as far as Lyons and Vienna! What had they destroyed? Did my blood recall some Paradise before Islam? Again I saw the ghosts of great cities rising out of the plains. I saw lovely terraced gardens spread across the foothills of the Atlas. I almost heard the murmur of courteous conversation from that savagely demolished past of which scarcely more than a whisper remains. Did Arabia trample the last life from Atlantis?

Only in the Jewish quarter did I feel any real discomfort. Under El Hadj T'hami, Lion of the Atlas, the Black Panther, the Jews were flourishing. Never had the *mellah* been so merry. Never did the Jews so blatantly flourish their gaudy prosperity, their new security and power, for their relatives were the Pasha's closest advisers and this put all Jews under his benign protection. There has always been a peculiar touch of philosemitism in the Moorish character, but it is unusual to find it in a Berber warrior. One might as well expect a Cossack hetman to help build a synagogue, brick by brick, with his own hands. These people respect one another as old rivals. It takes more than a change of flag to reconcile them. Not that these *mellahim* had the pathetic posture and half-starved stare of the *shtetl Hassidim*. These were good-looking Jews with broad, well-proportioned faces and beautiful deep-set eyes. The women were notoriously handsome and, when they came on the market, were always sought after by men of the world. These were the Jews one might have seen following Moses into the desert, like those who followed Charlton Heston, self-respecting and clean. Even

542

Goering distinguished between this type and the other, but in the end his arguments went unheard. They thought him too much of a sentimentalist, I suppose. I, too, am used to being ignored for that reason. It was Goering who reminded me of the joke about never trusting the well-fed Jew, he was always the one who was cheating you most successfully. Not that I ever felt short-changed by Charlton Heston. It was Cecil B. De Mille, after all, who sought to establish Hollywood as the spiritual capital of our faith. At present, of course, Zion rules there. But not in 1929, a year in which while I dreamed in Oriental luxury the Western world changed dramatically. I spent that year with most of my senses focused on my *affaire d'amour*, so it was not until months after the event that I heard of my California bank's collapse. Banks were falling like bowling-pins all over the world, from Shanghai to Stockholm, and it seemed that Western civilisation was in collapse, that the predicted Chaos was at last upon us. Here was the signal for the final clash of armies where, for a while, it seemed the forces of good were in the ascendant. But all these opportunities have been thrown away. I do not absolve Hitler and Mussolini and the rest. They also turned their backs on salvation.

With the dawning understanding of the world's disorders, I began to count myself lucky that I enjoyed the security of El Glaoui's court and that my proposed destination would be Rome, now clearly the strongest capital in Europe. Here was sure proof of everything Mussolini had warned against. From this time on, this evidence gave authority to Hitler's claims. Bolshevism and Big Business between them were discredited. The Age of the Dictators was not an aberration, it was an attempt to cure the disease. We all willed that Age into existence. But the disease at last triumphed. Now the giants stride hand in hand, brothers in financial intercourse, the triumph not of Capitalism or Communism but of Centralised Monopolism. This is exactly what Mr Weeks had warned me about when we were still on speaking terms. This was the bleak future he predicted and now I am living in it. And nobody but me seems to care.

The plane almost ready, I resumed my petition at El Glaoui's court. Hadj Idder seemed surprised to see me. He asked me how the work progressed. I thought this a good sign. I told him very well. We were nearing completion.

'It will be as new?' he enquired a little cryptically. I thought this was an Arab expression and he meant that we would go back to square one, as the Americans say. I shared his humour. 'As good as new,' I agreed. He took my letter and my money then crossed to where Mr Mix sat rather moodily on his bench and, after sharing a friendly word, accepted his envelope.

But when he had gone away, Mix shouldered through the crowd of pleading petitioners whose envelopes had not been accepted and spoke to me rapidly. 'I wasn't kidding about what I told you. Wise up, Max, you're in deep shit! Meet me here at eight tonight. Wear a disguise if you can.' He handed me a note.

I was growing as impatient with Mr Mix's cloak-and-dagger dramatics as I was with Miss von Bek's French farce. I longed for the oblivion of my own particular Oriental romance. But Brodmann had seen to it that even this small comfort was to be removed. I slipped away that evening into the *mellah*, near the Bab Barrima, just below the French Post Office and behind the Prison. The address was familiar. It belonged to one of the Pasha's own Jews, the young man who had remained my supporter, whose greatest hero was the Masked Buckaroo, Monsieur Josef. I hated visiting those whispering alleys especially at night. What could I want that they had to sell? I consoled myself. At least they did not offer me mortal danger. I was relieved to reach the Jew's house. M. Josef was one of El Glaoui's less illustrious advisers, but he affected European clothing and manners and had ambitions beyond the confines of the *mellah*, beyond Morocco itself. Because he continued an enthusiast for my films this made me trust his friendship a little. Mr Mix had known him for some while and had often visited him. I arrived dripping with sweat in a heavy winter hooded *djellabah*, the weather having turned suddenly mild, to be greeted by a less than light-hearted Monsieur Josef. He had lost a great deal of his European *savoir-faire* and wore the hunted look of the typical Ukrainian Jew. Suddenly I began to put two and two together. This development almost certainly involved Brodmann. Where had he been lying low? Here, in the *mellah*, or perhaps as a guest of the Pasha? I was drawn by Monsieur Josef through dark corridors and across silent courtyards, deeper and deeper into that alien enclave, until at last we came to a small, windowless room where Mr Mix was waiting for me, his huge body flinging the cell into heavy shadow as he rose to block the light from the lamp-shelf behind him. 'I'm glad you made it,' he said soberly. 'I don't know how you get away with it, Max, but that ain't the only thing I don't know. Listen, the Pasha's wise to all of us. He's known about you and Rosie for months but he was waiting to see how useful you'd be to him. Did you fix his car?'

'I'm not a mechanic,' I said. 'What do you mean?'

'He sent you his Rolls to repair. The one you damaged. I think he is giving you a small chance to redeem yourself. Can you do it?'

Now Hadj Idder's remark was no longer mysterious. Inadvertently I had cannibalised the car I had assured him only that morning was now as good as new. I had not even taken especially good care of the remaining bodywork. This news stunned me for a moment and I asked Mix to repeat certain information so that I could be sure I had heard him correctly. It became quickly clear that my only hope now was to demonstrate the efficiency of my plane. That alone would fully restore me to favour.

'What do you want to do?' said Mr Mix. 'Monsieur Josef says the Pasha is out for blood. We have another friend who can arrange passage on the French military train. Or we can take the bus, but my dough's on the train. You get French protection that way. From Casablanca it's a step to Tangier, a free port.'

It was on the tip of my tongue to tell him that the plane was as good as ready but then I thought better of it. It would be a disappointment to him to know I had chosen Miss von Bek over him, though I think he was man enough to accept the news soberly. He had, anyway, his own escape route worked out. The Jew would get him away. Perhaps we could all meet up in Rome and share an amusing anecdote or two about our escapades.

I agreed that the train seemed the best idea. He told me to lie as low as I could for the next day or two and he would arrange when and where to meet. There were agricultural transporters going down to the coast in a couple of days, he said, and they often had passenger accommodation. I asked him who our other friend was. He whispered that it was Fromental, just returned from the 'front'. Doubtless he would be glad to see the back of me. My going would, he knew, effectively bring an end to the Pasha's dreams of air-power. I still did not quite trust the Jew. I asked him why he was risking so much. 'Because I admire you,' was all he would say. 'Because one day I too will smell the sweet free air of the prairie.' I was never to discover his real reasons.

The railway station, Monsieur Josef reminded us, was a good distance away on the far side of town, beyond the Nkob gate. He would arrange a car for us.

I remained for as long as seemed politic and then said I had affairs to attend to and must leave. I met my driver where I had left him in the Djema al Fna'a and made him take me at once to the factory where I packed my bag of plans, my pistols and my remaining supplies of cocaine, together with a few of my prospectuses. I stowed my new American passport with the bag then secured it firmly under the pilot's seat, the remainder of my cocaine supplies and my Spanish passport in the usual places on my person. I had now taken the basic precautions. My next step must be to warn Rosie von Bek of her danger. If I could not myself enter the Maison El Glaoui, where she was now effectively incarcerated, I could send a note to her through one of the several intermediaries we had used over the months. Then I began to suspect that those servants might already be in the confidence of the Pasha, sworn to tell him our every move. There was no reason not to suspect this and it would therefore be wise to wait until the next day and hope that the Pasha was still waiting to judge my work on his car. Happily I had used only the most fanciful of phrases in my deputation to the Glaoui that morning. Thinking back, I believed I had probably reassured him. Unless he decided to come to see the work for himself, I had at least twenty-four hours' respite. Very shortly my twin soul and I would be winging our way to Tangier.

There is a white road down which I ride and the road ends at a green cliff, a blue sea, and when I reach the end of the road I lift easily into the air and fly towards Byzantium to be reunited with God. I still see her vivid violet eyes in her tawny Albanian skin. She shared my dream of flying. I had made flight what it should be – ethereal, beautiful, as it is in nature. I was not one of those who reduced it to a lumbering metal tube carting its human baggage from city to city like so many sacks of grain. What misery Big Business makes of our dreams and visions! They should not be allowed so much power. Who should the brave boys die for? Their fatherland? Their family? Their bank?

I recognised Brodmann again. *Ihteres! Ihteres!* He had followed me into the *souk* and gone ahead of me. I first saw his back as he paused to study some piece of inferior tinsmithery. He turned towards me, his hand reaching for an ornamental dagger of the kind popular with certain tribes now forbidden to carry weapons. I think he had it in mind to use the dagger, but I darted away from him, down another alley into the shadowy maze of shops and stalls, roofed with canvas and palm leaves and lengths of old cotton, through which the sun occasionally blinded you as you moved from deep shadow into sudden rays. I avoided the open sewers and the muddy earth, keeping to the cobbles of the main streets, making my way back into Djema al Fna'a to where my driver waited. He took me out to the aeroplane factory. I told him to come back for me in two hours. A little later, through the winter drizzle, Rosie arrived in a galloping *kalash* and, as it drew up, flung herself out to come running across the makeshift tarmac towards me. 'He knows everything!' She was horribly distraught. 'He knows I've come here. You can't imagine what he'll do!' She let me pay and dismiss the cab. Agitatedly she told me that he was openly contemptuous of our affair, mocking her and insulting her about it. She was determined to suffer no more from him. 'Obviously he doesn't believe we can get clear. Is the plane ready?'

Together we fitted the propeller to *El Nahla*. The little machine stood solidly on her large undercarriage, her black and yellow striped fuselage glittering when we wheeled her into the sunshine. I tightened the last nut. Rose got into the cockpit and started the engine. The Rolls Royce dashboard looked especially elegant in the plane, although we had had to make adjustments to one or two of the instruments. The engine started perfectly and the propeller turned very slowly. Then, inch by quivering inch, my *Bee* began to move forward. She strained to be free of the ground. She demanded to fly!

Delighted, Rosie switched off the engine, jumped over the side and embraced me. In my soul was a deep sense of fulfilment. I knew that I had created a superb original. I looked at the machine with new eyes and saw my future restored! Once I had demonstrated to El Glaoui that *El Nahla* could fly, I would be redeemed. He would be apologetic, he would beg me to tell him what he could do to make up for doubting me and I would name my films. He would press them upon me. Thus equipped, I would say my farewells to my business partner and set off for Rome, for fame and fortune! I cursed myself for an idiot. I should never have allowed myself to be panicked by Mr Mix. The Pasha would certainly decide to forget my indiscretions. This was the way of the Oriental court. But when I suggested to Rose von Bek that we now had only to wait to be reinstated in the Pasha's good offices, she looked at me with such blind animal panic that I was immediately forced to assure her we would leave as soon as possible. I was prepared to make any sacrifice for her, I said. Calming herself, she told me that she appreciated my friendship. There was an instant, as we held hands, of deep platonic comradeship. Around us the great Atlas mountains, cruel and beautiful as Marrakech herself, proud as the Berber clans she sheltered, challenged with their snowy crags the pale blue certainty of the sky.

The emerald palms waved in a faint wind from the south.

In the distant city, the *muezzin* began his long cry to the glory of God.

I released her hand.

'Thank you.' She was almost pathetically sincere.

I have never forgotten that moment.

'I trust you,' she said. 'I have truly found my Lohengrin.'

She hid in the cubicle when my driver returned. She would

find her own way home. I was, she reassured me, not to be concerned for her.

When I got back to my quarters I found every door wide open and the servants fled. The place had been stripped. Everything, including all my personal documents and every stick of furniture, was gone. No doubt the Pasha now knew what had happened to his car.

I rushed outside but the driver had already left. I had little choice but to begin the walk back into Marrakech. In his present mood the Pasha would not be reasoned with. My only hope was to reach the *mellah* and lie low until I could get out to the airfield the next morning. I saw the hand of Brodmann in everything. Surely he must be directing this particular scenario? I began to understand the nature of the Pasha's games with Miss von Bek and why she was so anxious to escape.

While I hurried along the darkening road towards the city gate, the avenues of palm trees became sinister enemies, threatening a dozen different dangers, and sometimes I broke into a run. When I stopped to catch my breath, I realised my whole body was shaking. Another Westerner, without experience of a tyrant's omnipotence, might not have begun to know such nervousness until much later. But my experience was already extensive. I could easily imagine what El Glaoui intended for me. I knew what torture could make me do. I remembered how I had longed for death and yet had done anything to remain alive. I was determined not to suffer such humiliation again.

There was still also the possibility that the Pasha was enjoying some complicated practical joke at my expense, teaching me a lesson, perhaps, so that I would be a more loyal servant in future. It was all I could pray for. A miracle might save me, but nothing else. As I slipped through the narrow gate into the medina and began to pad through the dark serpentine streets leading to the *mellah* I wondered if I were not foolish in seeking out the Jew. Perhaps he was already dead? But I had no other hope. I scuttled like a doomed doodle-bug on a burning log, with every chance of escape an illusion. I could barely think for the tightness in my chest, the churning of my bowels and stomach, the thumping of my unhappy heart. I

549

shall always regret not going straight to the Pasha's palace and throwing myself on his mercy. I had proof of his trust in me. I could have saved myself the agony of being admitted to the Jew's house, of being led through corridors and cloisters, across little cobbled streets, through doorways, down steps and into a dank, stinking warren of cubicles, each with a door from behind which came a dreadful, significant silence and I knew as the door closed behind me and the head of Monsieur Josef rose upon the Pasha's jocular scimitar to confront me face to face that I had allowed myself to run like a panicked dog into El Glaoui's own dungeons.

'Good evening, Mr Beters.'

The little man reached past me with the head still on the end of his sword and used it to push open a door. Mr Mix looked out at me and shrugged. 'He was on to us from the start, I guess. Just characters in his damned melodrama. He's better at this than we are.' He used English which was mere babble to the Pasha. Our captor was no more irritated by it than by the chatter of monkeys. He was incapable of the imaginative notion that we could actually be communicating!

The Pasha was chuckling as our jackets were ripped from our bodies. He looked at us with a kind of familiar affection so reminiscent of a lusting lover's that I began to tremble and knew I must soon lose control of my bowels. I began to plead with him in the name of God to listen to me, to believe that I was his true and loyal servant, that others had encouraged me to betray him. Though a prince in my own country, I had served him loyally and celebrated his glory. My halting Arabic was responded to in haughty childish French. I had dishonoured him in every possible loathsome way. I had lied to him with infinite treachery. Worse – I had posed as a Moslem, when I was in fact a dirty little Jew from Odessa. I found this last the most wounding insult of all. He had made something up from Brodmann's innuendo. I told him that these things were lies, I was already familiar with them. I knew who had told them to him and why. I mustered my dignity. I said that Brodmann had always been my enemy. He was a known fraud. A Bolshevik agent.

El Glaoui frowned and clapped his hands to silence me. He

laughed at me. 'The famous Russian film star becomes another whining dog of a Jew. Do you subbose I allow Mademoiselle Rosie to have any secrets from me? You will be tortured for a few weeks and then you will be blaced in the basket of your Italian master's balloon, which will be set on fire just as you are released into the atmosphere. You will be heroes in the Western Bress. Thus all, with God's help, shall be broberly concluded.' He spoke with the satisfaction of a theatrical producer putting the finishing touches to his plot. He almost waited for our applause. He told me to join Mr Mix in the cell. 'I have to go to Tafouelt to deal with some rebels. They are duty. But I will have you taught a few tricks while I am away.' He clapped again, this time for slaves who appeared carrying first Mr Mix's heavy Pathé camera and then the bag I had stowed under the seat of my *Bee*. These were placed at our feet. Now El Glaoui purred. 'Mademoiselle Rosie left these for you.' He did not bother to watch as we were chained to the wall, but as an afterthought he had the Jew's head placed on top of my bag where it stared at me, rather resignedly, until at last it was dragged away by the rats.

TWENTY-EIGHT

I HAVE BEEN WITNESS, this century, to the murder of Christian decency. It was surprising how quickly rats began to bother Mrs Cornelius after the Convent of the Poor Clares was pulled down across from her flat. They were attracted first to the rubble and then they sniffed the south side of the street and found her. She had never minded a few, she said, but this was a bloody plague. We both mourned the passing of the Convent. It had been a bastion of Christian wholesomeness in surroundings of pagan squalor. Its brick was mellowed by more rural days, when the meadow ran to the brook not always downwind of the tanneries. Some Georgian manor had doubtless been levelled to provide the Convent with land and no doubt that, for its contemporaries, was the beginning of the end. It is always the beginning of the end, always the best and the worst. No matter how thoroughly attacked, the city shall always triumph. It is folly, as the Nazis did, to try to resist this fundamental condition.

What are you? he said. *Some Peradur? Some Gascon* rapiero? *Nothing so romantic*, I told him. *You give me too much credit.* What else could I say? It was the same with the Jew in Arcadia. I have always admitted I was grateful. But I was no male Venus, born of the sea, as he described. In a poet these fancies are always discounted, so one does not complain. Gascon *rapiero*? Nothing so courageous, I said.

Nothing so blind. I saw Moorcock, the one they all despise and pretend to be friendly with. He is their favourite journalist and swallows their lies. He was picking about in the ruins of the Convent after the demolition people had broken down the walls and most of the buildings, their frozen bulldozers rearing over fruit trees and vegetable gardens, squatting on lawns where the nuns used to play cricket and have picnics in the summer. It was like the War. The Convent, that sturdy Victorian acknowledgement to the needs of the spirit, was one of the first buildings to rise here, in 1860, and one of the first to fall. They are going to be council flats, she says. We need more council flats, do we, and less solace for the soul? And what else to serve them? Betting shops? Burger bars? Off-licences? I have yet to see a bookshop or a flower shop flourish in the shadow of this authoritarian concrete. For years the wall bore the slogan 'Vietgrove' and something about Eichmann. We set our watches by that wall, says the Cornelius boy, doubtless enjoying some self-induced high on Ajax and powdered milk. I warned him. It is why he is getting such a nasal accent. People will take him for an American. And yet the fall of the Convent symbolised the fall of Notting Hill. Now there are Liberal MPs and magistrates and worse living in the houses on the other side of Ladbroke Grove. I saw Moorcock putting something in his pocket. It was obvious he was looking for money.

Pretending to take photographs of miscellaneous piles of burning timber and smouldering plaster, of the few trees the machines had left standing, he would stoop and rub the mud from some object, some cracked cup or empty bottle. Most of the time he threw his discoveries away, but clearly he was occasionally lucky. I recalled some old talk of a treasure, of tunnels and secret escapes, but this was a familiar chimera. I for one had learned no longer to pursue them. Noting that Moorcock went back to the ruins every evening after the demolishers had knocked off, I was one day enough ahead of him to leave four old pennies and a threepenny bit on a slab of masonry near the altar below the dramatic crucifixion whose vivid greens, reds and yellows still blazed their message to the world. I left through the wire fence they had put up along Latimer Road and returned via Kensington Park Road to Blenheim Crescent in time to see him digging around in the rubble, taking miscellaneous pictures as usual, pausing to stare almost bewilderedly about him as if he had for a moment lost his bearings. At other moments he seemed physically to be tasting the tragedy of this 20th-century destruction, this proof that Faith had again given way to Speculation. When he had at last left I hurried through the gloomy evening, over the mud and ruins to the altar. The money was gone, of course. I told Mrs Cornelius. She laughed and said he was probably looking for souvenirs. It keeps him happy, she said. 'Happy?' I said. 'Theft is supposed to keep you happy?'

They are all the same, these people.

I can remember no sense of discomfort from my incarceration in El Glaoui's prison. My mind was too keenly focused, I think, on avoiding the anxieties of what was to come. I already understood that this night was the luxury I would look upon with nostalgia and I tried to make the most of it, but it is difficult to exercise one's sensibilities in such circumstances, as the air grows staler and the silence of the prison begins to echo with little cries and groans, with whispers and prayers, which means that the jailer is momentarily absent. Some of the wetter, more mutilated sounds, said Mr Mix, were beginning to get on his nerves. He began to tell me a wild tale of how, when he had his cinema seized, the US Consul had offered him work as an agent, getting them, as he said, 'the goods on the Pasha'. In turn they loaned him a good-quality camera. But they could give him no official help. 'I guess I was right. The US Consul won't welcome me back in Casablanca. I hate to imagine what the Pasha's going to do to us.'

I knew all too well what was in store for us. I was tempted to share vicariously in the Pasha's forthcoming pleasure and tell Mr Mix what parts of his body would be altered first, but in the end my ordinary humanity stilled my tongue. There was no point in panicking the poor negro. It would only make him sweat, and the air was bad enough already. So I let him continue with his elaborate tale of spies and international intrigue. He described a vast complex of rivalries, in which Italy played an increasingly dominant part. This, said Mr

Mix, was not wholly to the United States' taste. His job was to get a detailed plan of the Pasha's strengths as well as his financial needs and sexual predilections. It was a story I could believe of some Hungarian Secret Service plot, but not of the United States Government. Once, my irritation got the better of me and I told him the whole thing sounded as if he had been reading too many dime novels. In turn this brought me to recalling my idyll with Miss von Bek over the Sahara and I began to pass my time by resurrecting those moments until I had remembered virtually the entire action and some of the dialogue of *The Tyneside Leopard Men* up to those final scenes where Blake, that exemplary Englishman, clambers from the wreckage of the glider and addresses the remains of the evil Cult as they advance towards him. 'I warn you, my dear baroness, gentlemen, I have a Smith and Wesson in my hand and I know how to use it.' If Sexton Blake were at this moment in Morocco it would not be long before I were free. But it seemed I must reconcile myself to an eternity of torment. My night was spent in humble prayer.

In the morning Hadj Idder personally brought us fruit and coffee. He seemed to feel a certain remote concern for us. He had our upper bodies released but our legs remained manacled. As we ate he read to us from the French newspaper. Mr Noël Coward and his people were staying at the *Transatlantique* and that evening were to be El Glaoui's guests before the Pasha was called away on military business in the south. 'What a pity you will miss him. Mustafa will be working on your feet about then. He is a very witty man in French and even more in English, they say.' He lost interest in the paper and stood idly looking about the cell as we ate, turning what was left of the Jew's skull with his slippered foot. 'They did this themselves,' he offered. 'They sent the head here. They did not wish the Pasha to relax his protection of the *mellah*.' He looked at us with sudden enquiry as if it were important to him to be believed. His beloved master's reputation was as ever his chief concern.

He asked us if we had eaten and drunk enough. We said that we had. 'This is a matter of state security,' he explained. 'It is unfortunate. There are forces amongst the French that are inimical to my master's desires. If there was some way of releasing you, believe me, I would do so. But you have nothing with which to bargain.' I had the impression that he had been put up to this by the Pasha, perhaps to sweeten our torment. I quelled the hope that the visit had a different purpose. 'Normally Europeans are not treated in this way, especially celebrities. But there is a certain amount of over-crowding at the moment due to the various rebellions and the Pasha's family problems.' He had grown a little apologetic. He was hesitating, as if he had some secret he wished to share. I looked up at him enquiringly.

'Si Peters,' he said, 'I have as you know admired several of your cinema adventures and especially enjoyed your cowboy rôles. I would feel privileged if I could have your autograph before the Pasha returns from Tafouelt. Perhaps on a small poster I was lucky enough to come by?'

He did not appear upset by Mr Mix's poorly suppressed sniggering and spluttered congratulations that with such fans I might never need enemies.

I told Hadj Idder I would be honoured to oblige and perhaps he in return would see that a note was sent to a friend of mine currently staying in Tangier. His name was Mr Sexton Blake.

This impressed him as I had hoped. He frowned and said that he believed something could be arranged to suit everyone's honour.

He came back a few minutes later with the show-card for *The Buckaroo's Code* and presented it to me, together with a large silver fountain pen, so that I might sign upon my own veiled face and recollect, too poignantly, my happy days in Hollywood with Esmé and Mrs Cornelius. How I wished now that I had been content and weathered Hever's blackmail until another studio recognised my talents, but it was too late. I had let that terror the *shtetl* had put into my womb determine my actions. Now I must make my intellect rule or I would almost certainly die, and my dusky comrade with me. I wrote across my face in Arabic *Hadj Idder – May God help us all – Your brother 'Ace'* – and then in English, *Happy Trails, Pardner – Yore pal, The Masked Buckaroo!* The portly African seemed genuinely touched by the sentiments and kissed me several times on both cheeks, murmuring that God must surely help the faithful, and it was then I began to understand how he would dearly love to see us go free. But if we escaped, surely even Hadj Idder would have to forfeit his life? I told myself hopelessly that I was, as the Swiss say, clutching at feathers.

Hadj Idder did not carry away his trophy, but stood in deep thought before at last saying what was on his mind. 'I think my master might bury his pride in this case,' he said, 'if you were, for instance, to undertake some small service for him.' I remained suspicious. Cat-and-mouse was T'hami's favourite game.

'A service?'

'Something to ease his present embarrassment with the French. I understand that you are friendly with Lieutenant Fromental, in spite of his opposition to the air fleet?'

I admitted I had enjoyed the young man's company from time to time.

'Yet you were aware he was a spy?' Hadj Idder looked directly at me suddenly. I was, even in my present position, sceptical of this statement, but I said nothing.

'If you were to confide in the Pasha,' Hadj Idder continued, 'perhaps a little of what this creature Fromental said to you about spying for the French. How he deliberately sabotaged our work and so on. If he were seen by the Quai d'Orsay as, let us say, failing in his duties or exceeding his power, it would be useful to our master. Or possibly he made some sexual advance? You must be aware of something you could put in a letter –'

'That's one of the lousiest things I've ever heard.' Mr Mix was outraged. 'We get free if we rat on a friend, is that it?'

'Fromental will not be harmed – just despatched to another, less sensitive, post. It is all the Pasha wants.'

'You're asking him to betray the best friend he has here!' Mr Mix's response was understandable but scarcely politic. As Hadj Idder said, Fromental would merely receive orders to return home and from there he would go to the Cameroons or perhaps Mozambique. But I now knew I must agree to nothing without first having practical guarantees. I had learned this in Egypt, from God. I told Hadj Idder that Mr Mix was right. I could not betray my friend.

The majordomo shrugged. 'It is a shame,' he said. 'You would rather betray the Pasha?'

At his tone, rather than his words, I shuddered. 'And it would have gladdened my heart to have set you free,' the negro continued, 'since I am such an admirer. It would be in my power to ensure, with Allah's grace, that you would make many more movies.'

'Sadly, the movies I have made will never again be seen here,' I hinted. 'Would that I could lift a little of your burden, Si Idder, by taking myself and my films back to America. There, it would give me much pleasure to describe the generosity and wisdom of the Lord of Marrakech.'

'But it would not reflect well upon my master when you mentioned this unfortunate incarceration.'

'Neither, dear friend, would it reflect well upon myself, should I be asked why I found myself in jail. There are certain incidents best not spoken of. After a while they become no more than dreams, and their substance can be proven or disproven as readily as the substance of dreams. But let it be said, Si Idder, that I am proud of my achievements with the Pasha and I would use them to increase my own honour. Whose interest would be served by the spreading of lies and distortions about a trusted business colleague?'

Hadj Idder took my point and was quite clearly mulling over the bargain I had proposed while Mr Mix, whose own Arabic was less sophisticated, kept asking who the hell were the two of us selling out between us.

I took this as a joke.

I knew my casual mention of the famous English detective had given Hadj Idder pause and it was equally clear that he might release me if a face-saving formula could be discovered.

I began to hope. Against all the evidence I saw a chance of salvation. I prayed that I might after all go home to Hollywood, to *Di Heym*, the new Byzantium. Her slender minarets and gentle roofs blend with the outline of cedars, poplars and cypresses in a warm mist that wanders through silver hills and is scented with jasmine and mint and bougainvillea. I walk along her palm boulevards, beside her ocean, secure and tranquil beneath a benign golden sun. And here the great spires and domes which rise above her tall trees shall be dedicated not to the cruel and drooling patriarch who shits upon the world like an ancient losing control of his bowels, but to his Son, his Successor, who is God re-born, God cleansed and whole, God not as our brooding master but as our partner in self-improvement. I speak of the Christian God, no God that Jew or Arab can claim. Their God is the God of Carthage, senile and confused, yet full of the blind brute rage which brought the Minotaur to ruin. He is a God of the bloody past. This is not a God to advise upon the subtle problems of urban living. To call upon such a God in Notting Hill would be tantamount to summoning the Devil. I speak of the God who revealed Himself through Jesus Christ. I speak of that self-regenerated God who proclaimed the Age of Peace and then watched in dismay as He saw what Man made of it. God, says the Cornelius girl, is a woman. Then you do not know God, I say. God is a Presence. God is an Idea. She says it is typical of me to reduce everything to abstractions. But God is an Abstraction, I say. What are we reducing?

Brodmann, of course, wanted me dead. I remembered his gloating expression as Grishenko's whip fell upon my buttocks. I remember the insults. I remember Brodmann's filthy eyes darting back and forth from my penis to my arse. Let him think what he likes. I am a victim of Scientific Rationalism, not Religion. My father's knife was secular. *Ni moyle . . . Ikh farshtey nit . . .* Mrs Cornelius agrees with me. She says they all do it now in England. It has no connection with religion. And in America, too. All over the West. This is poor consolation. What does it actually proclaim? What else but that Zion has overrun Christendom? Sometimes Mrs Cornelius is so anxious to see good in the world that she is blind to the obvious. At such times she knows my logic has triumphed and she refuses to continue. That is typical of women but I do not care. I have all my life been a willing victim of the fair sex. Your eyes reflect their every fantasy, said the Jew in Arcadia. He wrote down the aphorism *Byzantium endures the laughter of Carthage; Jerusalem commands the vengeance of Rome.* It means more in Yiddish, I think. He used the Greek models, chiefly, he told me. I reminded myself that Jesus was born a Jew and was spiritually a Greek. Was this why my heart sang to him? I have not known such love since. *Your dark eye mirrors my imperfect soul. I embrace your blasphemed body.*

I admitted to some embarrassment. It was so quiet that day in Arcadia and not even a tram along the sea-front to Odessa until I had almost given up. War will often bring silence as well as noise. For a while I sold new bicycles in my shop, but there was no market for them. Now, of course, all the city-gents are wanting them. They buy in the West End, but they come to me for repairs. In the West End they would tell them to throw the thing away and get another. Personally I have no special love for these consumer cycles.

What is their bourgeois wealth giving them? I ask Mrs Cornelius. Is their life sweeter? Is their life better? Do they relish it more? Not very much, it seems.

I see them, in the pub on Saturday, these new TV people and their friends, in their identical sweaters with their ill-behaved children, cackling at one another across the bars like so many mad parrots, eyeing one another's identical wives with leering uncertainty. What are they doing? Their rituals are a mystery to me. The sound they make is not a happy one. Mrs Cornelius says I am reading too much into them. 'They're dead simple, those greedy bastards.' She finds my analyses amusing. 'Bastards is bastards and orl yer 'ave ter know is 'ow ter stop 'em. Because bastards has ter be stopped. That's anovver rule.' When the worse for drink, she is inclined to over-simplify.

Brodmann wanted me dead, but for some reason Hadj Idder did not. That seemed to be the new essence of the situation. Brodmann did not care about any political consequences for the Pasha following my death. Hadj Idder thought of little else. He did not want to see his master shamed. Yet the Pasha's honour must certainly be satisfied. I could not imagine that for whatever good reasons El Glaoui's right-hand man would betray him and so I tried to pay no attention to my leaping heart. But then it occurred to me that perhaps there had been a change of policy which he had been entrusted to implement after El Glaoui left for the south.

560

Evidently Hadj Idder did not want his master embarrassed in Europe and America. Our removal I guessed was proving less simple than they had imagined. People could be making awkward enquiries. Could it be that El Glaoui wished to reverse his reckless verdict but could not do so without losing face? Perhaps the only answer to his problem would be to free us? I grew cautiously hopeful. Was Hadj Idder even now waiting for the appropriate word from me?

'He might be changing his mind,' I told Mr Mix.

He was scarcely listening. 'What about Rosie?' he wanted to know. 'Did she get clear?' He was, I thought, overly concerned about the fate of someone he hardly knew. I could not understand his anxiety, but I too was anxious for news of Rosie. Had El Hadj T'hami let me think she had betrayed me and escaped when actually she had been recaptured and merely been forced to give up my bag?

'I gather Miss von Bek is no longer a guest of the Pasha,' I coldly remarked to Hadj Idder who was rubbing at his glossy jowls as if some prison bug had crept amongst the folds and bitten him where he could no longer reach.

'Miss von Bek is believed to have died in the mountains.' The black man looked at the floor. 'Your *El Nahla* was well named. She flew a little erratically and was unhappy with heights. You both loved her, I know. I respect your grief.'

But he had not told me she was dead. He had told me she was free. I had every faith in my plane. I was delighted. I relayed this to Mr Mix.

'It means he can't be sure she won't tell someone about what's happening to us here,' he said. 'They're stuck now, Max.' He seemed rather foolishly delighted. He winked at Hadj Idder. He grinned. And slowly the vizier began to smile back. Then Hadj Idder chuckled. The quality of the tension altered. We all became peculiarly expectant. Hadj Idder said courteously, 'I was very thrilled by your exploits in *Ace of the Aces*, Si Peters. Gloria Cornish is a beauty! I envy you.'

'As a matter of fact she is my wife,' I said. 'We were married some years ago in Russia. At present she eagerly awaits my return to our Hollywood mansion. As do our children. I'm glad you enjoyed *Ace*. My uncle, President

561

Hoover, always told me it was one of his own favourites.'

Rather than surprising or alarming Hadj Idder, my remarks seemed to confirm something he had already guessed.

'What a meal the papers will make of this!' declaimed Mr Mix, attempting a chorus of his own. I told him to keep quiet. Statements about newspapers could seem like crude and impolitic threats. I told Hadj Idder that El Glaoui had been a good and generous master. It would hurt me, I told him, if shame were to attach to the Pasha's name through any action of mine. With the vizier's permission I reached into my bag and drew out the gold I had put there. Since this, I said, was no longer of any use to me would Hadj Idder please take it and use it for whatever pious work he chose.

He accepted the money with his usual grace. He said that Allah would bless me, and no doubt favour me. It is all I pray for, I said.

'And I, Si Peters. We would both avoid this embarrassment if we could. Sadly, I do not possess the means of releasing you. That power is entirely in your hands. Naturally, I respect your decision not to use it, just as I would respect your decision to use it. It is a matter of principle and we are, Allah be praised, both men of principle.'

'Indeed,' I agreed, 'and good followers of the Prophet, I hope, who would see justice done in the world.'

'Indeed.'

A further pause while Mr Mix grunted and fidgeted in his chains saying he would rather go to the electric chair in Sing Sing than hear another minute of our bullshit. He asked what the hell was going on. In the hobo vernacular I told him to button his lip while I sweet-talked our jailer.

I paused.

'I would see justice done above all,' I said at last, to Hadj Idder's visible satisfaction.

'I will have the materials brought,' he said and clapped his hands. From somewhere not far away an old servant carried a tray with ink, pens, vellum. I briefly entertained the wild thought that my denunciation of young Fromental was to be illuminated like some monkish manuscript, but all I had to do was write a little essay. I knelt upon the cushion the servant presented and, while he held the salver steady for me, began to write with the soft-nibbed quill. I ignored Mr Mix's half-animal turmoil behind me. He was cursing and rattling his leg-irons. The poor black was beginning to lose his nerve. Perhaps he thought I was selling him.

When I had finished I left the paper unsigned. 'It will be signed when my servant and I are released with my luggage and my films,' I told him. 'At the station.'

Hadj Idder was beaming with relief and bore the happy air of one who has seen a dear friend reach a sensible decision and save himself from danger.

The vizier had taken his gold and his signed portrait away and I was beginning to suspect a further trick when ten minutes later a somewhat nervous guard in a grubby *djellabah* entered bearing a large hessian sack which obviously contained the film cans. After he dumped the sack down and turned the big crude keys to unlock our leg-irons, he lit a cigarette. Then he glared at us, as if we were to blame for his predicament, and slouched off, cursing us for dirty infidels. Though the door of the cell had been left open, this was not particularly unusual. There was no way out of the prison without permission and the jailers' charges were so well disciplined that few dared crawl a further inch towards the door, let alone enter the common corridor.

An hour later, Hadj Idder reappeared. He had brought us heavy *djellabahs* to put on over our remaining rags. He then gave stern orders to the same guard whose expression changed rapidly from chagrin to terror to reconciliation. Then, with sullen resentment, the Arab led us up the steps before pausing at the door into the warren of passages which had brought us here. In French, Hadj Idder called from below. 'When my master returns he will be angry. He is obliged to punish those who tamper with his women. Therefore you would be wise, both of you, to remove yourselves from Morocco as soon as possible.'

'We have no car,' I said. 'And the plane is gone. We were supposed to have train tickets, but – '

'How you leave is of no interest to me.' He spoke casually.

'Will you not also be punished for helping us?' I asked

the plump negro. 'Perhaps you had better come too?'

Hadj Idder was amiably reassuring. He indicated our less than knowing guide. 'What the Glaoui discovers and what he does not care to discover are his concern. But you need not fear for me. Some dog shall have to be punished so that my master's honour can be satisfied. The dog will be beaten and executed and that will be the end of the matter. Assuming, of course, that you are by then on your way to another country.' He gave a sharp order to the guard, who gloomily flung the sack onto his back.

Jacob Mix wanted to know if some of the film he himself had shot could be returned to him. Hadj Idder heard this request with appreciative amusement. 'I hope you enjoy your freedom as much as I have enjoyed your comradeship,' he said to Mr Mix in what was probably intended for a compliment, but he did not reply to the request.

I had found distasteful Hadj Idder's hint that Miss von Bek had also been involved with Mr Mix. No doubt he meant me to look on my friend with suspicion, to poison my mind against him. It was impossible to imagine even the wild Rosie von Bek contemplating an *affaire* with an ordinary American darkie! I was about to confront Hadj Idder on this when the vizier stepped backwards into the shadows and was gone. The muttering Arab, who had been ordained to the rôle of scapegoat in Hadj Idder's elegant plot, led us at such a snail's pace through the maze and took so long to reach the end that I began to suspect a further trap, or that he would abandon us to some fresh threat. But at last we were in the dark, listening streets of the *mellah*, outside the house of the wretched Jew whom Brodmann had betrayed. The guard left the sack at our feet and backed away. Mr Mix hefted the sack and grinned. 'Here's *The Masked Buckaroo*, Max. He's all yours.' But when I failed to lift both the sack and the bag, he took pity on me, though his attitude remained cool, and he picked up the bag, striding ahead while I followed with the sack. I remained nervous. I could still not fully determine El Glaoui's motives for releasing us. But Brodmann would surely be furious when he discovered my escape and would try to involve the French and Spanish authorities. We were still therefore in considerable danger. As we paused in the narrow space between one street wall and another, the archway ahead of us suddenly blazed with light and we heard the sound of an engine turning over. The Arab had already dropped well behind us. Cautiously we advanced up to the archway and the broader road beyond. A modern Buick sat in the shadows with its motor running, a pale, frowning Berber face staring from the cab. 'Taxi ordered by Monsieur Josef,' said the driver a little impatiently. 'To go to the railway depot.'

'That's us,' said Mr Mix and he opened the door for me to enter the comfortable interior and sit there with my bag on my knees desperately wishing that I could void my bowels, which had now been transmuted into water. Mr Mix put the sack of films on the floor as he settled back in the seat. 'The only problem we have now is that we don't have Fromental's tickets and have no way of buying them. It's not like an ordinary railroad office here. You *have* to do everything through the military.'

The car had left the *mellah* and pushed into the busier streets of the city. It crawled along the far edge of the Djema al Fna'a. Even now, as I fled for my life, I felt drawn to the Congress of the Dead, so ironically named. Here was every kind of life being lived at its most intense. Yet we are also the dead. We are also the ghosts of the unborn. We are our own betrayed children. Every evening at sunset these people poured into the square to perform a scene Griffith himself could not have bettered, to present a thousand cameos, a thousand little morality plays, for the benefit of an audience responding with all the spontaneity that once greeted those much-disputed performances first proclaimed across the boards of The Swan and The Globe; an audience frank and tolerant as all good-hearted peasants the world over.

The car pushed through the press of beggars, tumblers, oracles and story-tellers, through snake-charmers holding their dying, disenvenomed cobras high above their heads, through musicians with flute, tambourine and lute. Occasionally the Buick was forced to stop altogether as the bodies refused to part. Against the glass appeared the grinning faces of little boys, while behind them I observed the nosy disapproval of old men, the envious contempt of youths, the intense curiosity of the veiled women, and I had the impulse to cry out to them, to speak of the world I could have given them. Then, for a moment, I wondered if my world was indeed any better than the one they knew. Perhaps it was not right to bring the twentieth century to the fourteenth. Would it not be best to leave them in peace?

But can expansive Carthage ever leave Europe in peace? She sends Turkish and Tunisian guest-workers through the whole of Northern Europe. Now Ali Baba and Sinbad are heroes as familiar in Stockholm as Lohengrin and Tannhäuser once were. But has the musselman in his turn adopted *our* chivalric epics? Do Lancelot and Parsival thrill the blood of little boys in Baghdad and Bengazi? An honest answer tells the whole story. Carthage forbids anything save her own legend. She is paramount. Carthage conquers inch by inch. Half the slogans on the Ladbroke Grove walls are in unreadable languages. The wall is all that is left to the unheard, the unenfranchised, the silenced of this world. Why has the spray-can replaced the ballot-paper? Perhaps because people are informed by a natural will to evil and chaos, but I think it more likely that they are moved by the knowledge that nowhere in the halls of power is their opinion represented. I do not blame them for losing faith in their constitutions. I do blame them, however, for turning their backs on God.

It was the same in the camps. Half of them ignored the obvious facts of their situation. It was how they had come there in the first place. And then it was too late. Only those who accepted the realities survived. There is little room for sentiment in Camp Freedom, as our old commandant used to remind us. Sentiment is what led us to our present predicament. *Ikh bin eyn Luftmeister. Der Flugzeugführer sitzt im Führersitz* . . . I shall come back to the City of the Golden Dream.

The pain starts in my stomach. It reaches my mouth. I did not become a *Musselman*. What more could they want from me? I wore their stripes. I wore their star. Even though their punishment was unjust I performed my work. It had been my fate forever to be condemned and identified not through any action of my own, but through the careless decision of a father whom I hardly knew. But that I suppose is what becomes of the child of a free-riding Cossack when left too long in the care of its mother. I do not blame my mother, I hasten to say, but it is probably true she made me a little over-sensitive. Those stripes. Brodmann gloated. Grishenko raised his quirt. So that I should not forget the sacrifice of my friend Yermeloff. Then he gave me my pistols, ebony and silver. Those bars. Nobody blamed me for what I did in Kiev. Those people tear the skins from corpses. They carve their initials in the bodies. Their only sensation of living comes when they are performing some complicated act of cruelty on another wretched soul. And this we were told was to be the century of enlightenment!

Today on the television they discuss the problem of leisure. What leisure is that? We are all clearly on the brink of a new Dark Age but they discuss the party arrangements in paradise! They say I am mentally disturbed! Is there any aspect of their lives which is actually better than the lives of their forefathers? Their fathers had hope, at least. This generation looks into the future and sees only decay and dissolution.

Cautiously I checked that the sack really did contain only my film canisters, then I glanced back through the car's window at Djema al Fna'a. As the twilight folded over the people and the yellow radiance of oil and tallow gave the scene the quality of Flemish paint, I wondered at this luscious ordinariness. It was unfortunate, I thought, there were no Arab old masters. An over-literal interpretation of the Book of Genesis is the reason for that. These people embrace rules the way most of us embrace life. The more rules they have, the more comfortable they are. I told this to that ill-tempered hysteric in the Post Office, that *Pakistanischer*. He behaves as if the Postmaster General is some Oriental tyrant who will behead anyone for the slightest use of their own initiative. Or is the man merely exercising his power?

As our car eased its way through the gateway and out onto the Route du Safi, the wide new road that led up to the darkened military train yards beyond the Villa Marjorelle, a big Mercedes tourer swung across our path, forcing the driver to stop. A pistol was waved from the passenger window and then a small man descended from the tourer and crossed to where we were stopped, our engine still running. He held a tray: on it were ink, pen and paper.

I picked up the pen and the Mercedes reversed to allow the taxi to pass. As soon as I had signed and returned the paper the Mercedes turned and was gone. It was only another five minutes to the railroad yards, but, with Mr Mix's puzzlingly cool company, it seemed longer. There was no great activity in the yards. A few lights blazed in huts on the other side of the fence and the huge black sleeping outlines of military locomotives and goods wagons were everywhere. The place lacked the urgency of a commercial yard. Our car was allowed through the gates on the driver's presentation of a pass already provided by the unfortunate Fromental. He drove towards the buildings on the other side of the tracks but I tapped him on the shoulder. We would stop here, I said. I gave him my last spare French banknote. Then Jacob Mix and I left the car and found the deeper shadows of the big trains. My bag was proving heavy and the films, loose in the sack, were awkward for Mr Mix, but we kept a firm, almost desperate, grip on my remaining belongings. They were all we had to get us to Tangier and from there to Europe. The Pasha or his vizier could change their minds at any moment and send soldiers in pursuit.

Fromental did not remain in the army, I heard. Someone told me he had made a great success running a radio business in Lyons (home of our Christian Testament) so in fact events were fortunate for him. Apparently he was shot by the Germans in 1943. When I heard this news I could not suppress a pang of sadness, remembering his bright enthusiastic face, his honest idealism. We had much in common. I have always said that the honour the Christian values highest is the honour of honest chivalry above so-called manly courage. Fromental is in honour now, no doubt a martyr. I think when we meet he will want to shake me by the hand.

Once we had got our bearings, we began to examine the trains with our expert eyes. Both of us had learned every trick of the American railroad bum, and the French authorities had never had to contend with a skilled hobo before. It was not long before we had identified the locomotive we wanted. It was already making steam and it was clear from the markings on its

568

trucks that it was bound for Casablanca. From Casablanca we could easily transfer to Tangier, the Free City where neither Moroccan nor French law prevailed. Then we could get any one of a dozen ships to take us to Genoa. From Genoa we would be within easy reach of Rome.

Mr Mix found an unlocked door and slid it smoothly back. As we climbed into the truck we admired the modern rolling-stock, so much better maintained than civilian trains and then, with the security of familiarity we settled down, upon the slats, to sleep until our educated senses detected the first movements of the train. At that point we must be on the alert, in case of examiners finding us. But these trains made few of the sounds we were used to. Every so often a huge gasp of steam would fill the night, to be followed at once by further silence.

I sent up a prayer for Rosie von Bek, hoping she had managed to pilot the *Bee* all the way to Rome. I remembered Kolya and offered up a small prayer, too, for his safety. I thought of Esmé, my sister, my daughter, and how in the end she had failed to rise to my hopes. Yet I could not entirely condemn her. For a few years her life had been filled with a wonder and luxury, elegance and quality she would never have known had I left her to live out her days as a mere Galata whore. I still celebrated her loveliness, her quality of innocence, her child-like beauty. I still loved her.

At dawn the wagon rattled forward a few metres. I braced myself. It shuddered to a stop. We heard whistles and yells. The train shunted backwards for several revolutions of her pistons and then subsided, sniffing and hissing in a petulant undertone. We heard the locomotive giving off great masculine snorts and wheezes of impatience, like an old but dignified bulldog full of panting excitement at an outing. Suddenly I knew a moment of regret for all my lost expectations, all the pointless idealism I had invested in this world. Was it not thoroughly ironic we should be on our way to seek refuge in the ancient site of Carthage herself, to Tangier?

But perhaps it is true, and you are always safer in the cage when a lion is on the loose.

Meyn strerfener. Meyne herzenslust.

Ya muh annin, ya rabb. Meyn siostra, meyn rosa. Allah yeftah 'alek.

Hallan, amshi ma'uh. A'ud bi-rabb el-falaq. Ma shey y sharr in sha. 'Awiz minni ey? 'Awiz minni ey?

'Awiz minni ey?

At last we were moving. There had been no check of our truck. As it rolled forward, sunlight shone through the slats of the roof and made bars of intense black and white on a floor still carrying recent traces of straw and excrement but now stinking of carbolic. The procession of stripes undulated over my sprawled body, like some ethereal tide, while Mr Mix's face was thrown alternatively into vivid light and sudden darkness. Through the stink of the disinfectant and the heating engine oil I smelled for the last time the warm mint-flavoured air of Marrakech as the red city faded behind us and the train began its long climb through the gorges of the Atlas. There was a reassuring and familiar rhythm to the bumping of the wheels over the rails and I was able to reach into my bag to find one of my small packets of *restorif*. I offered Mr Mix a comradely thumbnail of the cheering drug, which he refused, saying he planned to sleep. We should be all day getting to Casablanca. With luck we would arrive at night. Otherwise we should have to wait to disembark at dark. It was October 28, 1929. In a few months I would be thirty. I planned to celebrate the event in Rome.

But soon I had grown melancholy thinking of those wonderful monsters waiting for the engines that would never come. French imperial politics and the Pasha's failure to control his own emotions meant my beautiful machines must now become museum pieces. I still, however, had a number of my expensive catalogues, though, sadly, only the Arabic version, not the French. I thought of my Desert Liner and what wealth it might have created for the whole region. I would have made their desert green. Now they would have to wait, perhaps for ever. El Glaoui's loss would be Il Duce's gain. Within a couple of weeks I would be dining with my old friends at The Wasp. I told Mr Mix he would fall in love with the city. It was the crucible of our finest institutions.

Across the truck, as the train speeded up, I saw his great

amiable African face grinning through the flickering stripes of our temporary prison giving our reality the effect of an early kinema film. I remarked on this. The rattle of the bogies might almost have been the clatter of a projector. It was the strangest illusion.

I fumed at those who had conspired to ruin both our careers and condemn us to such unjust humiliation. I was not even sure, I said, if I had enough money to get a decent passage on the ship to Italy, let alone buy some reasonable clothes. Already I was smelling of cow-dung. 'I hear Rome is very fashion-conscious, these days.' We could not be expected to parade through the Holy City like evil-smelling extras from *The Desert Song*. Besides, I did not expect our *djellabahs* to last the journey.

'Look at the stitching on this garment,' I said. 'It's of the cheapest quality. Not a double seam on the whole thing. Scarcely a fair exchange for a bag of English gold!'

Slap-happy as ever, the big black suddenly began to roar with laughter. I could not understand this at all. I thought at first he had given in to the hysteria to which his race is prone, but then it seemed he was doing nothing more than trumpet his considerable relief at being free of the Pasha's torture-chamber. I told him I was proud to see he was taking his hardships so well. Not all his race were so resilient. He need not fear in Europe, I assured him. I would be there to help. If anyone insulted him in the Eternal City they must answer to me!

At this he uttered a further wild burst of mirth, declaring that knowing me made a man believe in miracles. 'Max, you are the luckiest bastard in the whole damned universe. I never heard of anybody with your kind of luck. From now until we get back to civilisation I'm going to stick to you like a fly to fresh paint.'

I was a little baffled. 'What "luck" are you talking about, Mr Mix? I think you mean "judgement", surely! If I hadn't had the presence of mind to mention the name of one of England's most powerful and least-known men we should still be languishing in the Glaoui jail, or writhing at the first tender touch of St Paul's Pincers.' I felt sick. I could almost smell our burning flesh. 'Is that "luck"?' I pulled my

Georgian pistols from my bag to make sure no harm had come to them.

He did his best to control himself. He turned his head and let his chin settle upon his chest. But it was clear he had not really understood me.

'Luck?' I was still incredulous. From what sort of skewed illusion could the *schwartze* be suffering? 'Haven't you noticed, Mr Mix, that we are once again reduced to the discomforts of a cattle car?'

Clearly the terrors of the past few days had taken their toll. The poor fellow's mind had snapped. His head flung up, his scarlet mouth gaping, he shook with feverish mirth, and as the locomotive pulled us relentlessly into the High Atlas I became miserably reconciled to the certainty that he would still be roaring even when we passed at last through the golden gates of Rome.

APPENDIX

(The following transcript is taken from material not supplied by Colonel Pyat but given by him to Miss Christine Brunner who kindly gave permission to reproduce it here.

– M.M.)

If T'hami had aided Abd el-Krim in 1925, there would have been no foreign protector still in Morocco. Instead the tribes and the political rivals and the religious rivals and the blood rivals and the trade rivals would have returned to their time-honoured custom of dog eat foolish dog, and T'hami, almost reluctantly no doubt, would have emerged at last, encrusted with the blood of a hundred thousand innocents, as Tyrant of Morocco, the first true Islamic Dictator, to shake hands with his brothers in Europe. And with T'hami as an ally, would Christendom any longer have to fear Carthage? I think T'hami would have extended his Empire eastwards, yet never losing friendship with the West, gradually building a single nation from Casablanca to Suez, which would have formed a bulwark of Islamic chivalry against the savagery of the East and of Africa. If the French had allowed him his own air force rather than taking an active part in dissuading him from this policy, for one moment in history Carthage might have chosen to become the ally of Christ rather than the right hand of the Anti-Christ. It would not, in the end, be dreaming Carthage who was responsible for our defeat, but sleeping Christendom, ever ready to pacify the common enemy who had already devoured Russia, was about to devour half Europe and the mightiest nation of the East. Fromental was right to be suspicious of Islam but wrong to suspect T'hami. Now Carthage is Bolshevism's puppy-dog just as Britain is America's. These are the years of greed, the years of warring for the sake of war, for the sake of power alone. These are the terrible years of regression, before the final battle, when brute shall belabour brute back into the mud from which so many millions of years before we emerged. Is this to be our story? Shall this unchecked power, this irresponsible power, this profoundly pagan power, rise and rise until Christ Himself is crushed? What must we do to warn them of their folly? What can we say to them that will remind them of God's will at the moment they see their little child's head split like an egg under some devil's panga? We have a duty to our religion. It brought us our wealth and our security. We have a duty to practise that religion in the name of the Son of God; a duty to live lives of maximum value to God and Man. This I have tried to do personally and I continue, in God's name, to shoulder my responsibilities, to warn the world of what they must face if they fail to take up the Christian burden, to make that Pilgrimage of the soul through the Valley of Dread and into the light of Heaven. Each pilgrimage is personal, each private as prayer, as we ready ourselves for the perfection our Redeemer has promised. But even if we follow His path there are many who would lead us astray. I will admit I was lured into temptation during the twenties and thirties, but they were confusing times and I blame no one for what happened then, least of all myself. The Jew and the Moslem will do this, if they can. It is an instinct with them, to gnaw like Satan's rats at the very roots of our Faith! ἰ Μõῦ εζμε!

You have the press, the politicians and manners of a people who have lost their self-respect – you have everything you deserve. And unless you remember how to follow your best instincts you will never again find that self-respect.

I once asked the Bishop if he thought it was possible for a

white man genuinely to love a black man like a brother and he said he thought it might prove an illusion in the end, because of the social pressures. Other church people have not been able to answer this question. Race is not everything, I think. After all, I owe my life to a Jew in Arcadia. It was not he who put a piece of metal in my womb, nor sowed that dreadful seed in me, nor libelled me, nor humiliated me, nor betrayed me. I am not anti*Semite*, I tell them, I am merely anti*sceptic*. But they never understand these plays on words. The arts of irony and innuendo are lost to those who abuse the freedoms of democracy. Mrs Cornelius thinks I am too broad-minded for my own good but that is the way I was born, I said. What can I do? *Wie lange wird es dauern?* 'I'll get my reward in Heaven,' I tell her. *Da ma yekhessanash . . .*

'And I'll be right beside yer, Ivan,' she says. I used to think her mysterious laughter, which had little to do with what she said, a sign of her senility but now I think it has something to do with anxiety. I tell her she should see a doctor. NO! This is not God! NO! She lies to me. She lies to me. They must not hurt me not hurt me so. God made me promise. I did not do those things. Those things make me sick. It is not fair. I am justice and of the Just but I denied my birthright and God cursed me with blindness. I denied my people and God cursed me with the gift of lies. I would not listen to my father and God ordained that I should believe only untruths. For it is written that God shall make such just punishment upon any of the Just that shall err from his purpose. I am the lamb and the blood is my blood. He loved me in Odessa. He put a piece of metal in my womb. I have done what is unclean and I have repented. Anubis is my friend. *Dieser letzte weiche Kuss, Esmé. Es war ein Schlag in den Unterleib. Ich kann noch immer die Stelle spüren. Ein Reitgerte hebt sich und saust herab. Sie ist von jener grausamen Flut aus Asche mitgerissen worden. Sie ist ein Gespenst. Ein kinemaqueen.*

How could we resist them?